THE ROUTLEDGE COMPANION TO CYBERPUNK CULTURE

In this companion, an international range of contributors examine the cultural formation of cyberpunk from micro-level analyses of example texts to macro-level debates of movements, providing readers with snapshots of cyberpunk culture and also cyberpunk as culture.

With technology seamlessly integrated into our lives and our selves, and social systems veering toward globalization and corporatization, cyberpunk has become a ubiquitous cultural formation that dominates our twenty-first century techno-digital landscapes. *The Routledge Companion to Cyberpunk Culture* traces cyberpunk through its historical developments as a literary science fiction form to its spread into other media such as comics, film, television, and video games. Moreover, seeing cyberpunk as a general cultural practice, the *Companion* provides insights into photography, music, fashion, and activism. Cyberpunk, as the chapters presented here argue, is integrated with other critical theoretical tenets of our times, such as posthumanism, the Anthropocene, animality, and empire. And lastly, cyberpunk is a vehicle that lends itself to the rise of new futurisms, occupying a variety of positions in our regionally diverse reality and thus linking, as much as differentiating, our perspectives on a globalized technoscientific world.

With original entries that engage cyberpunk's diverse 'angles' and its proliferation in our life worlds, this critical reference will be of significant interest to humanities students and scholars of media, cultural studies, literature, and beyond.

Anna McFarlane is a British Academy Postdoctoral Fellow at Glasgow University with a project entitled "Products of Conception: Science Fiction and Pregnancy, 1968–2015." She has worked on the Wellcome Trust-funded Science Fiction and the Medical Humanities project and holds a Ph.D. from the University of St Andrews on William Gibson's science fiction novels. She is the editor of *Adam Roberts: Critical Essays* (2016) and has served as blog and reviews editor for the journal *BMJ Medical Humanities*.

Graham J. Murphy is a professor with the School of English and Liberal Studies (Faculty of Arts) at Seneca College (Toronto). In addition to more than two dozen articles published in a variety of edited collections and peer-reviewed journals, he is also co-editor of *Cyberpunk and Visual Culture* (2018), *Beyond Cyberpunk: New Critical Perspectives* (2010), and co-author of *Ursula K. Le Guin: A Critical Companion* (2006).

Lars Schmeink is the project lead at the "Science Fiction" subproject of "FutureWork," a research network funded by the German Ministry of Education and Research. He was the inaugural president of the Gesellschaft für Fantastikforschung from 2010 to 2019 and has published extensively on science fiction and posthumanism. He is the author of *Biopunk Dystopias: Genetic Engineering, Society, and Science Fiction* (2016) and co-editor of *Cyberpunk and Visual Culture* (2018).

THE ROUTLEDGE COMPANION TO CYBERPUNK CULTURE

Edited by Anna McFarlane, Graham J. Murphy, and Lars Schmeink

NEW YORK AND LONDON

First published 2020
by Routledge
52 Vanderbilt Avenue, New York, NY 10017

and by Routledge
2 Park Square, Milton Park, Abingdon, Oxon, OX14 4RN

Routledge is an imprint of the Taylor & Francis Group, an informa business

© 2020 selection and editorial matter, Anna McFarlane, Graham J. Murphy, and Lars Schmeink; individual chapters, the contributors

The right of Anna McFarlane, Graham J. Murphy, and Lars Schmeink to be identified as the authors of the editorial material, and of the authors for their individual chapters, has been asserted in accordance with sections 77 and 78 of the Copyright, Designs and Patents Act 1988.

All rights reserved. No part of this book may be reprinted or reproduced or utilised in any form or by any electronic, mechanical, or other means, now known or hereafter invented, including photocopying and recording, or in any information storage or retrieval system, without permission in writing from the publishers.

Trademark notice: Product or corporate names may be trademarks or registered trademarks, and are used only for identification and explanation without intent to infringe.

Library of Congress Cataloging-in-Publication Data
Names: McFarlane, Anna, editor. | Murphy, Graham J., 1970– editor. | Schmeink, Lars, editor.
Title: The Routledge companion to cyberpunk culture / edited by Anna McFarlane, Graham J. Murphy, Lars Schmeink.
Description: London; New York: Routledge, 2020. | Includes bibliographical references and index.
Identifiers: LCCN 2019035929 (print) | LCCN 2019035930 (ebook) | ISBN 9780815351931 (hardback) | ISBN 9781351139885 (ebook)
Subjects: LCSH: Cyberpunk culture.
Classification: LCC HM646 .R67 2020 (print) | LCC HM646 (ebook) | DDC 306/.1—dc23
LC record available at https://lccn.loc.gov/2019035929
LC ebook record available at https://lccn.loc.gov/2019035930

ISBN: 978-0-8153-5193-1 (hbk)
ISBN: 978-1-351-13988-5 (ebk)

Typeset in Bembo
by codeMantra

Printed and bound in Great Britain by
TJ International Ltd, Padstow, Cornwall

To Rory
AM

To Jennifer and Declan
love you most, plus one
GJM

To the world
for not disappointing in becoming ever more cyberpunk…
LS

CONTENTS

List of Figures	*xi*
Acknowledgments	*xiii*
Notes on Contributors	*xiv*

1	Cyberpunk as Cultural Formation *Anna McFarlane, Graham J. Murphy, and Lars Schmeink*	1

PART I
Cultural Texts   **5**

2	Literary Precursors *Rob Latham*	7
3	The *Mirrorshades* Collective *Graham J. Murphy*	15
4	Bruce Sterling: *Schismatrix Plus* (Case Study) *María Goicoechea*	24
5	Feminist Cyberpunk *Lisa Yaszek*	32
6	Pat Cadigan: *Synners* (Case Study) *Ritch Calvin*	41
7	Post-Cyberpunk *Christopher D. Kilgore*	48
8	Charles Stross: *Accelerando* (Case Study) *Gerry Canavan*	56

Contents

9 Steampunk   64
Jess Nevins

10 Biopunk   73
Lars Schmeink

11 Non-SF Cyberpunk   81
Jaak Tomberg

12 Comic Books   91
David M. Higgins and Matthew Iung

13 *American Flagg!* (Case Study)   101
Corey K. Creekmur

14 Manga   107
Shige (CJ) Suzuki

15 Early Cyberpunk Film   119
Andrew M. Butler

16 *Strange Days* (Case Study)   128
Anna McFarlane

17 Digital Effects in Cinema   134
Lars Schmeink

18 *Blade Runner 2049* (Case Study)   144
Matthew Flisfeder

19 Anime   151
Kumiko Saito

20 *Akira* and *Ghost in the Shell* (Case Study)   162
Martin de la Iglesia and Lars Schmeink

21 Television   169
Sherryl Vint

22 *Max Headroom: Twenty Minutes into the Future* (Case Study)   178
Scott Rogers

23 Video Games   184
Paweł Frelik

Contents

24 *Deus Ex* (Case Study) 193
Christian Knöppler

25 Tabletop Roleplaying Games 200
Curtis D. Carbonell

26 *Shadowrun* (Case Study) 209
Hamish Cameron

27 Photography and Digital Art 216
Grace Halden

28 Fashion 228
Stina Attebery

29 Music 238
Nicholas C. Laudadio

30 Janelle Monáe: *Dirty Computer* (Case Study) 245
Christine Capetola

PART II
Cultural Theory **253**

31 Simulation and Simulacra 255
Rebecca Haar and Anna McFarlane

32 Gothicism 264
Anya Heise-von der Lippe

33 Posthumanism(s) 273
Julia Grillmayr

34 Marxism 282
Hugh Charles O'Connell

35 Cyborg Feminism 291
Patricia Melzer

36 Queer Theory 300
Wendy Gay Pearson

37 Critical Race Theory 308
Isiah Lavender III

Contents

38	Animality *Seán McCorry*	317
39	Ecology in the Anthropocene *Veronica Hollinger*	326
40	Empire *John Rieder*	335
41	Indigenous Futurisms *Corinna Lenhardt*	344
42	Afrofuturism *Isiah Lavender III and Graham J. Murphy*	353
43	Veillance Society *Chris Hables Gray*	362
44	Activism *Colin Milburn*	373

PART III
Cultural Locales
383

45	Latin America *M. Elizabeth Ginway*	385
46	Cuba's Cyberpunk Histories *Juan C. Toledano Redondo*	395
47	Japan as Cyberpunk Exoticism *Brian Ruh*	401
48	India *Suparno Banerjee*	408
49	Germany *Evan Torner*	415
50	France and Québec *Amy J. Ransom*	423

Index   *433*

FIGURES

14.1 *Bōsō-zoku*, youth biker gangs, became a social concern in the 1970s and 1980s. Gratefully reprinted with permission from © Yomiuri Shimbun   110

14.2 Lady Miyako's Temple is modeled on Yoyogi National Gymnasium, built for the 1964 Tokyo Olympics. Gratefully reprinted with permission from AKIRA © MASH·ROOM Co., Ltd./Kodansha Ltd. All rights reserved   112

14.3 This character has transformed his body into a monstrous killing machine. Gratefully reprinted with permission from © Yukito Kishiro/Kodansha Ltd. All rights reserved   113

14.4 Compared to Oshii's anime version, the original manga has more comic relief. Gratefully reprinted with permission from © Shirow Masamune/Kodansha Ltd. All rights reserved   114

14.5 The megastructures in *Blame!* are continually constructed by autonomous robots without human control. Gratefully reprinted with permission from © Tsutomu Nihei/Kodansha Ltd. All rights reserved   115

19.1 The presence of deep shadows on bushes and streets as well as wires above creates visual/conceptual depth and implies the reality's connectedness to cyberworld/nextworld. Still from *Serial Experiments Lain*, Episode 1, 1998, NBC Universal Entertainment (formerly Pioneer)   157

19.2 3D models simulate the design and texture of anime characters. Promotion image from Hatsune Miku: Project DIVA, 2009, Sega & Crypton Future Media   159

19.3 Lynn Minmay sings to end the war while men fight life-or-death battles outside the spaceship. Still from *The Super Dimension Fortress Macross: Do You Remember Love?*, 1984, Bandai Visual   159

27.1 "The Battleship": Tom Blachford's Nihon Noir series demonstrates the use of identifiable photography edited using software to create a cyberpunk effect. Gratefully reprinted with permission from Tom Blachford   219

27.2 "Steamy Downtown" by Donglu Yu, an example of *cyberpunk-mélange*. Gratefully reprinted with permission from Donglu Yu (Instagram: @donglulittlefish)   220

27.3 "Toronto 2049" by Lucan Coutts (lucancoutts.com), an example of uncanny temporality. Gratefully reprinted with permission from Lucan Coutts   223

Figures

27.4 "The Veins of Bangkok" by Trey Ratcliff envisions the city as a circuit-board aesthetic with pulsing currents of information. Gratefully reprinted with permission from Trey Ratcliff/StuckInCustoms.com   224

28.1 "Caricature of Bustle as snail" from the August 1870 edition of *Punch*. Public domain   230

43.1 YOU ARE UNDER SURVEILLANCE: Revolutionary street anarchists, true to the cyberpunk tradition, continue to organize into the 21st century, in cyberspace and on the streets. The CrimethInc. collective is one of the more potent distillations of decades of activism. These stickers are widely available and make the perfect addition to unobtrusive security cameras everywhere   363

43.2 Jeremy Bentham's classic panopticon design. Public domain image available at https://commons.wikimedia.org/wiki/File:Panopticon.jpg   365

43.3 An eyeborg that effects total surveillance in Richard Clabaugh's *Eyeborgs* (2010)   367

ACKNOWLEDGMENTS

The editors would like to thank Mark Bould for helping get this project off the ground, Sherryl Vint for her sage advice on how to handle a project this size and the traps to avoid, and both of them for offering their editorial feedback when we called on them for assistance. The editors would also especially like to thank Edward James for taking on the arduous task of assembling the index.

All video game, television, and film images are reproduced for academic use under Fair Use guidelines. Otherwise, permission to reprint visual images is gratefully acknowledged.

NOTES ON CONTRIBUTORS

Stina Attebery is a Ph.D. candidate at the University of California, Riverside. Her academic interests include science and technology studies, Indigenous studies, ecocriticism, media, and biopolitics. She has published articles in *Medical Humanities, Extrapolation*, and *Humanimalia* and contributed to collections on *Gender and Environment in Science Fiction* (2018) and *Cyberpunk and Visual Culture* (2018). She was a recipient of the 2018–19 R.D. Mullen Fellowships supporting research in archival materials related to science fiction.

Suparno Banerjee is an associate professor of English at Texas State University specializing in science fiction, utopian/dystopian, and postcolonial studies. His scholarship has appeared in many academic journals including *Science Fiction Studies* and *Journal of the Fantastic in the Arts* and anthologies of critical works on science fiction such as *Science Fiction, Imperialism and the Third World* (2010) and *Dis-Orienting Planets: Representations of Asia in Science Fiction* (2017).

Andrew M. Butler is the author of *Solar Flares: Science Fiction in the 1970s* (2012) and *Eternal Sunshine of the Spotless Mind* (2014). He is managing editor of the journal *Extrapolation* and chair of judges for the Arthur C. Clarke Award.

Ritch Calvin teaches at SUNY Stony Brook. He is the author of *Feminist Science Fiction and Feminist Epistemology: Four Modes* (2016) and co-editor of *SF101: A Guide to Teaching and Studying Science Fiction* (2014), and other research appears in *Science Fiction Studies, Extrapolation, Femspec, Utopian Studies, The Journal of the Fantastic in the Arts, Science Fiction Film and Television, The New York Review of Science Fiction*, and *The SFRA Review*.

Hamish Cameron is a lecturer in classics at Victoria University of Wellington. His main areas of research are the history and geography of the Roman Near East, ideological representations of imperialism in classical literature, and the reception of ideas about the ancient world in modern analog and digital games. His notable publications include *Making Mesopotamia: Geography and Empire in a Romano-Iranian Borderland* (2019) and a cyberpunk tabletop roleplaying game, *The Sprawl* (2016).

Gerry Canavan is an associate professor of 20th- and 21st-century literature in the Department of English at Marquette University, and the author of *Octavia E. Butler* (2016). He is also co-editor of *Green Planets: Ecology and Science Fiction* (2014), *The Cambridge Companion to American Science Fiction* (2015), and *The Cambridge History of Science Fiction* (2019). He serves as an editor at *Extrapolation* and *Science Fiction Film and Television*.

Notes on Contributors

Christine Capetola is an Andrew W. Mellon Engaged Scholar Initiative Postdoctoral Fellow at the University of Texas at Austin. Her research mobilizes sound and vibration as analytics for studying identity formation and historicizing the recent past. She has an article on Michael Jackson's "Billie Jean" in *Souls: A Critical Journal of Black Politics, Culture, and Society*, is a music writer for *Bitch Media*, and blogs about contemporary pop and R&B on her website www.christinecapetola.com.

Curtis D. Carbonell teaches English as an associate professor at Khalifa University. He co-edited the *Palgrave Handbook of Posthumanism in Film and Television* (2015). He has also published work on Aldous Huxley in *Extrapolation* and *Post-and-Transhumanism: An Introduction* (2014). His book *Dread Trident: Tabletop Role-Playing Games and the Modern Fantastic* (2019) examines how tabletop role-playing games offer an archive of fantasy and science fiction gametexts ripe for an investigation into the rise of realized worlds.

Corey K. Creekmur is an associate professor in the Department of Cinematic Arts, Department of English, and the Department of Gender, Women's and Sexuality Studies at the University of Iowa. His research and teaching focus on American and Indian cinema, comics, and representations of gender and sexuality in popular culture. He is the general editor of the Comics Culture series for Rutgers University Press.

Matthew Flisfeder is an associate professor of Rhetoric and Communications at The University of Winnipeg. He is the author of *Postmodern Theory and Blade Runner* (2017), *The Symbolic, The Sublime, and Slavoj Žižek's Theory of Film* (2012), and co-editor of *Žižek and Media Studies: A Reader* (2014).

Paweł Frelik is an associate professor and the leader of the Speculative Texts and Media Research Group at the American Studies Center, University of Warsaw. His teaching and research interests include science fiction, video games, fantastic visualities, digital media, and transmedia storytelling. He has published widely in these fields; serves on the boards of *Science Fiction Studies*, *Extrapolation*, and *Journal of Gaming and Virtual Worlds*; and is the co-editor of the *New Dimensions in Science Fiction* book series at the University of Wales Press.

M. Elizabeth (Libby) Ginway is an associate professor in the Department of Spanish and Portuguese Studies at the University of Florida, the author of *Brazilian Science Fiction: Cultural Myths and Nationhood in the Land of the Future* (2004), and co-editor of *Latin American Science Fiction: Theory and Practice* (Palgrave, 2012). She has published articles in *Alambique, Brasil/Brazil, Extrapolation, Foundation, Hispania, Luso-Brazilian Review, Modern Language Studies, Revista Iberoamericana, Science Fiction Studies*, and *Paradoxa*.

María Goicoechea is a teacher and researcher in the Department of English Studies in the Complutense University of Madrid. She has published extensively on cyberculture from the double perspective of science fiction and electronic literature. Her many publications include editing *Alicia a través de la pantalla. Lecturas literarias en el siglo XXI* (2013) and co-editing *Espacios y tiempos de lo fantástico* (2010).

Chris Hables Gray is a fellow and continuing lecturer at Crown College, University of California at Santa Cruz. He is co-editor of *The Cyborg Handbook* (1995) and is working on a follow-up called *Modified: Living as a Cybernetic Organism*. He is the author of *Postmodern War* (1997) and *Cyborg Citizen* (2000), and is currently writing about genetic genealogy and California identity, *Taking Evolution Seriously*, and the role of violence in revolution.

Notes on Contributors

Julia Grillmayr is a literature and cultural studies scholar as well as print and radio journalist, based in Vienna and Linz, Austria. Her postdoc project at the University of Art and Design in Linz (funded by the Austrian Science Fund FWF) investigates 'scenario thinking' in contemporary science fiction and futurology (see https://scifi-fafo.com).

Rebecca Haar received her Ph.D. from the University of Tübingen, Germany. She conducted research on simulation and virtuality in theory, as well as technology and media representations in postmodern society. She studied modern German literature, media studies, and musicology. Aside from media history, media, and film theory, her areas of research comprise game studies and comic studies.

Grace Halden is a cultural historian and war scholar who specializes in modern and contemporary literature on the theme of technology. She is a lecturer at Birkbeck College, University of London. Dr. Halden is currently working on her manuscript *Contemporary Posthumanism* which is under contract with Bloomsbury.

Anya Heise-von der Lippe is an assistant lecturer with the chair of Anglophone Literatures at the University of Tübingen, Germany. Her research focuses on the parallels between monstrous corporeality and monstrous textuality, as well as the intersections of the Gothic and critical posthumanism. Recent publications include her co-edited collections *Posthuman Gothic* (2017) and *Literaturwissenschaften in der Krise* (2018). She is one of the series editors of *Challenges for the Humanities* for Narr, Tübingen.

David M. Higgins is the speculative fiction editor for the *Los Angeles Review of Books*. He is a tenured English faculty member at Inver Hills College in Minnesota, and his article "Toward a Cosmopolitan Science Fiction" won the 2012 SFRA Pioneer Award for excellence in scholarship. He has published in *American Literature, Science Fiction Studies, Paradoxa*, and *Extrapolation*, and his work has appeared in edited volumes such as *The Cambridge History of Science Fiction* 2019. In addition, he serves as the Second Vice President for the International Association for the Fantastic in the Arts (IAFA).

Veronica Hollinger is an emerita professor of Cultural Studies at Trent University in Ontario. She is a long-time co-editor of *Science Fiction Studies* (SFS) and co-editor of five scholarly collections about science fiction. Most recently, she co-edited a special issue of *SFS* on the climate crisis and edited a special section of *SFS* on Chinese science fiction writer Liu Cixin.

Martin de la Iglesia studied art history and library science at Humboldt-Universität zu Berlin. Currently, he is a Ph.D. student at Heidelberg University, working on his dissertation on the early reception of manga in the west.

Matthew Iung is an English major at Concordia University in St. Paul, MN, and he serves as an editorial assistant for the *Los Angeles Review of Books*. His publications have appeared in Concordia's newspaper *The Sword* as well as online in *Talking Comics* and *DM du Jour*. Matthew is an aspiring fiction writer with a lifelong love of comics, literature, and the arcane.

Christopher D. Kilgore currently serves as special programs coordinator for Teaching & Learning Innovation at the University of Tennessee, Knoxville. He has published on cyberpunk, narrative theory, and graphic narrative. In his spare time, he maintains an online fantasy novel system, *The Adasir Project* (www.adasir.com).

Notes on Contributors

Christian Knöppler completed his Ph.D. in American Studies at Johannes Gutenberg University Mainz in 2015. Besides Mainz, he has taught at RWTH Aachen University and Florida Gulf Coast University, Fort Myers. His research interests include American cinema, horror and cultural trauma, media and history, graphic narratives, and game studies. Currently, he is involved in the development of interdisciplinary study programs at JGU Mainz.

Rob Latham is the author of *Consuming Youth: Vampires, Cyborgs, and the Culture of Consumption* (2002) and the editor of *The Oxford Handbook of Science Fiction* (2014) and *Science Fiction Criticism: An Anthology of Essential Writings* (2017). He was, for two decades, a senior editor of the journal *Science Fiction Studies*.

Nicholas C. Laudadio is an associate professor of English at the University of North Carolina Wilmington where he teaches classes in science fiction, popular culture, and literary and critical theory. His research explores the cultural history of music and musical instruments with a particular focus on electronic music and science fiction in the 20th century.

Isiah Lavender III is the Sterling-Goodman Professor of English at the University of Georgia, where he researches and teaches courses in African American literature and science fiction. His books include *Afrofuturism Rising: The Literary Prehistory of a Movement* (2019) and *Race in American Science Fiction* (2011), as well as the edited collections *Dis-Orienting Planets: Racial Representations of Asia in Science Fiction* (2017) and *Black and Brown Planets: The Politics of Race in Science Fiction* (2014). He is a co-editor of the oldest science fiction journal *Extrapolation*.

Corinna Lenhardt is a postdoctoral researcher and lecturer at the University of Münster, Germany, where she also earned her Ph.D. in American studies in 2018. Her research and teaching interests include ethnic studies and African American studies, race, gender, and gothic fiction. She has published articles and chapters on Indigenous fiction, film, and online activism.

Seán McCorry is an Honorary Research Fellow at the University of Sheffield. He is currently undertaking two major research projects: the first of these examines human-animal relations in mid-20th-century culture, and the second investigates the aesthetics and politics of meat eating in contemporary culture. He has published articles in *Extrapolation* and *ISLE: Interdisciplinary Studies in Literature and Environment*.

Anna McFarlane is a British Academy Postdoctoral Fellow at Glasgow University with a project entitled "Products of Conception: Science Fiction and Pregnancy, 1968–2015." She has worked on the Wellcome Trust-funded Science Fiction and the Medical Humanities project and holds a Ph.D. from the University of St Andrews on William Gibson's science fiction novels. She is the editor of *Adam Roberts: Critical Essays* (2016) and has served as blog and reviews editor for the journal *BMJ Medical Humanities*.

Patricia Melzer is an associate professor of German and Gender, Sexuality and Women's Studies at Temple University. She is the author of *Science Fiction and Feminist Thought* (2006) and *Death in the Shape of a Young Girl: Women's Political Violence in the Red Army Faction* (2015). Her research interests are in gender and technology in popular culture, feminist and queer theory, and women in radical social movements.

Colin Milburn is Gary Snyder Chair in Science and the Humanities and professor of English, Science and Technology Studies, and Cinema and Digital Media at the University of California,

Notes on Contributors

Davis. He is the author of many publications about the intersections of science, literature, and media technologies, including *Nanovision: Engineering the Future* (2008), *Mondo Nano: Fun and Games in the World of Digital Matter* (2015), and *Respawn: Gamers, Hackers, and Technogenic Life* (2018). At UC Davis, he directs the Science and Technology Studies program and the ModLab digital media laboratory.

Graham J. Murphy is a professor with the School of English and Liberal Studies (Faculty of Arts) at Seneca College (Toronto). In addition to more than two dozen articles published in a variety of edited collections and peer-reviewed journals, he is also co-editor of *Cyberpunk and Visual Culture* (2018) and *Beyond Cyberpunk: New Critical Perspectives* (2010), and co-author of *Ursula K. Le Guin: A Critical Companion* (2006).

Jess Nevins is a librarian at Lone Star College in Tomball, TX. He has written widely on Victorian and 20th-century popular literature, and was responsible for the quote "steampunk is what happens when goths discover the color brown."

Hugh Charles O'Connell is an assistant professor of English at the University of Massachusetts Boston. His current research examines the relationship between speculative fiction and speculative finance. He is the co-editor with David M. Higgins of *Speculative Finance/Speculative Fiction* (*CR: The New Centennial Review* 19.1). Recent essays on British and postcolonial science fiction have appeared in *The Cambridge History of Science Fiction* (2019), *Utopian Studies, Cambridge Journal of Postcolonial Literary Inquiry, Modern Fiction Studies, Paradoxa*, and the *Los Angeles Review of Books*.

Wendy Gay Pearson is an associate professor and chair of the Department of Women's Studies and Feminist Research at the University of Western Ontario. She teaches sexuality studies, queer theory, queer and Indigenous cinema, and science fiction. She is the co-editor of *Reverse Shots: Indigenous Film and Media in an International Context* (2014) and the co-author of *Zero Patience* (2011). In addition, she is the co-editor of *Queer Universes: Sexualities in Science Fiction* (2008).

Amy J. Ransom is a professor of French and chair of the Department of World Languages and Cultures at Central Michigan University. She has published over two dozen articles and book chapters on Québec's science fiction, including the first scholarly monograph on the topic: *Science Fiction from Québec: A Postcolonial Study* (2009). Her more recent books include *Hockey, PQ: Canada's Game in Québec's Popular Culture* (2014), *I Am Legend as American Myth: Race and Masculinity in the Novel and Its Film Adaptations* (2018), and the co-edited collection *Canadian Science Fiction, Fantasy, and Horror: Bridging the Solitudes* (2019).

John Rieder is the author of *Colonialism and the Emergence of Science Fiction* (2008) and *Science Fiction and the Mass Cultural Genre System* (2017). He received the Science Fiction Research Association's Pioneer Award in 2011, and the Pilgrim Award in 2019. After receiving his Ph.D. at Yale University in 1980, he taught at the University of Hawai'i at Mānoa until his retirement in 2018.

Scott Rogers is a professor of English at Weber State University in Ogden, Utah. He teaches courses on 18th- and 19th-century British literature and 20th- and 21st-century popular culture studies.

Brian Ruh is an independent scholar with a Ph.D. in Communication and Culture from Indiana University. He is the author of *Stray Dog of Anime: The Films of Mamoru Oshii* (2004).

Notes on Contributors

Kumiko Saito is an assistant professor of Japanese in the Department of Languages at Clemson University. Her main field of research is gender and technology in modern Japanese literature and popular culture, including representations of body and sexuality in popular narrative media from Japan. Currently, she is in the final phase of writing a manuscript on the modern concept of romantic love and democracy in Japanese popular culture.

Lars Schmeink is the project lead at the "Science Fiction" subproject of "FutureWork," a research network funded by the German Ministry of Education and Research. He was the inaugural president of the Gesellschaft für Fantastikforschung from 2010 to 2019 and has published extensively on science fiction and posthumanism. He is the author of *Biopunk Dystopias: Genetic Engineering, Society, and Science Fiction* (2016) and co-editor of *Cyberpunk and Visual Culture* (2018).

Shige (CJ) Suzuki is an associate professor of Modern Languages and Comparative Literature at The City University of New York (CUNY), Baruch College. Recent articles about manga and popular media appear in *Introducing Japanese Popular Culture* (2017) and *The International Journal of Communication. Special Issue: Asian Transmedia Storytelling*.

Juan C. Toledano Redondo is a professor of Hispanic Studies at Lewis and Clark College, Portland, Oregon, and works on the fantastic in contemporary narrative written in Spanish. Previous publications appear in *Lingua Cosmica: Science Fiction from Beyond the Anglophone Universe* (2018), *Co-herencia*, *Alambique*, *Lo fantástico en Hispanoamérica*, *Chasqui*, and *Science Fiction Studies*, among others. He is also the co-editor of the SF&F academic journal *Alambique*.

Jaak Tomberg is a senior researcher of Contemporary Literature in University of Tartu, Estonia. His research focuses on science fiction, realism, utopia, and the philosophy of literature. His two monographs focus on the poetics of Science Fiction, and his essay "On the 'Double Vision' of Realism and SF Estrangement in William Gibson's Bigend Trilogy" won the Science Fiction Research Association's Pioneer Award in 2014. He is the editor of the Estonian Avant Garde magazine *Vihik* and, besides research, has written two plays.

Evan Torner is an assistant professor of German at the University of Cincinnati, where he also serves as undergraduate director of German studies and director of the UC Game Lab. His fields of expertise include East German genre cinema, German film history, critical race theory, science fiction, and role-playing games. He is finishing a monograph on the history of German science fiction cinema and co-editing a handbook on East German cinema.

Sherryl Vint is a professor of Media and Cultural Studies at the University of California, Riverside, where she directs the Speculative Fictions and Cultures of Science program. Her books include *Bodies of Tomorrow: Technology, Subjectivity, Science Fiction* (2007), *Animal Alterity: Science Fiction and the Question of the Animal* (2010), and *Science Fiction: A Guide to the Perplexed* (2014). She is an editor of *Science Fiction Studies* and was a founding editor of *Science Fiction Film and Television*, and the book series *Science and Popular Culture*. She has edited several books, most recently *Science Fiction and Cultural Theory: A Reader* (2016). Her current research project, *The Promissory Imagination: Speculative Futures and Biopolitics*, explores the exchanges between speculative imagination and material practice in biotech.

Lisa Yaszek is a professor of Science Fiction Studies in the School of Literature, Media, and Communication at Georgia Tech, where she researches and teaches science fiction as a global language crossing centuries, continents, and cultures. Her books include *The Self-Wired: Technology and*

Subjectivity in Contemporary American Narrative (2002/2014), *Galactic Suburbia: Recovering Women's Science Fiction* (2008), and *Sisters of Tomorrow: The First Women of Science Fiction* (2016). Her ideas about science fiction as the premiere story form of modernity have been featured in *The Washington Post*, *Food and Wine Magazine*, and *USA Today* and in the AMC miniseries *James Cameron's Story of Science Fiction*. A past president of the Science Fiction Research Association, Yaszek currently serves as an editor for the Library of America and as a juror for the John W. Campbell and Eugie Foster Science Fiction Awards.

1
CYBERPUNK AS CULTURAL FORMATION

Anna McFarlane, Graham J. Murphy, and Lars Schmeink

In his book *The Seven Beauties of Science Fiction*, Istvan Csicsery-Ronay argues that today's social, political, and cultural realities have become science-fictional, that estrangement and dislocation constitute our habitual normalcy in the 21st century. Therefore, in order to process the "incongruous moments of technology's intersection with everyday life" (2), Csicsery-Ronay claims we need to draw upon the imaginaries of science fiction (sf) to make sense of quotidian realities that are saturated with such sf concepts as cloud computing, nanotechnology, genetic engineering, wearable technologies, and the increased proliferation of cyborgs in all shapes and sizes, to name only a few science-fictional tropes. But as writer and game designer Kyle Marquis reminded us in a much-circulated tweet in 2013, "unless you're over 60, you weren't promised flying cars. You were promised an oppressive cyberpunk dystopia. Here you go." At the heart of Marquis's claim is the realization that today's reality is not sf in the Golden Age sense of the 1940s and 1950s but rather as depicted by cyberpunk, that immensely popular form of 1980s sf which continues to speak to our contemporary moment. One does not have to see all aspects of cyberpunk as dystopian, as Marquis suggests, but one can hardly find fault in generally comparing the cyberpunk imaginary with today's quotidian reality.

While the term 'cyberpunk' may have originated in Bruce Bethke's "Cyberpunk" (1983) and was then applied to a variety of literary and cinematic texts that were alternately celebrated (often by cyberpunk practitioners) as energizing sf or derided and dismissed by critics as a marketing exercise that quickly ran its course, cyberpunk has had effects far beyond the small group of writers initially identified as the 'Movement,' rebranded by Gardner Dozois as 'cyberpunks,' and then codified by Bruce Sterling in *Mirrorshades: The Cyberpunk Anthology* (1986). While those beyond the sf community might not have even heard of cyberpunk, they will likely be aware of cyberpunk's impact: Consider the imagery made famous by Ridley Scott's *Blade Runner* (1982), imagery replicated time and time again in cinema, animation, and photography; or the concept of 'cyberspace' coined in William Gibson's "Burning Chrome" (1983) and then popularized in his quintessential novel *Neuromancer* (1984), influencing how computer programmers and engineers envisioned a burgeoning digital realm that today we largely take for granted; or Walt Disney's *TRON* (Lisberger 1982), a financial failure that still drew Generation X-ers to their local arcades with fistfuls of quarters to play the titular video game that envisioned cyberspatial worlds as "untethered from real-world signs and signifiers," a visual modality that "has had a strong influence upon depictions of cyberspace," notably in video games (Johnson 139); and finally, the green digital rain of *The Matrix* (Wachowskis 1999) that has become visually synonymous with the control of 'reality' by technological systems. Cyberpunk is *everywhere*, even if its earliest practitioners have moved into other conceptual territories.

In this vein, the originating premise of this *Routledge Companion* can be found in a very simple, yet far-reaching claim by Thomas Foster—namely, that cyberpunk, a term first used as a literary concept to name a narrow branch of sf, has become a "cultural formation [which is] a historical articulation of textual practices" (xv) that now shapes the way we see our place in the world, and this *Companion* aims to track cyberpunk's diversity and far-reaching influence. We have organized our global contributors into three interconnected sections with which to apprehend this expansive subject matter. In *Cultural Texts*, we open the collection with a traditional focus on cyberpunk's literary and cinematic roots, ranging from the precursor texts that lay the foundation for cyberpunk to what we may call first-wave or Movement-era cyberpunk, a period that produced the cultural understanding of what constitutes a cyberpunk text across media. As *Cultural Texts* exemplifies, however, cyberpunk is also a visual and aural phenomenon and our contributors leave no stone unturned as they explore cyberpunk's influence in American comic books, Japanese manga and anime, video games, tabletop role-playing games, music, and even fashion. Interspersed with these analyses are 'case study' chapters that provide a narrowly focused analysis of a representative cyberpunk text, although as editors, we both invited and encouraged our contributors to write chapters on lesser-theorized works; therefore, you won't find 'case study' chapters on *Neuromancer*, or *Blade Runner*, or *Transmetropolitan* (1997–2002), or many of the other 'usual suspects' one might expect to find that have been the subject of other academic work; instead, our 'case study' chapters offer explorations into the oft-overlooked, kipple-cluttered corners of cyberpunk that hopefully expand the parameters of critical inquiry while also providing readers access ports to works they may have otherwise overlooked. Overall, *Cultural Texts* shows that cyberpunk is truly cross-cultural and offers a plenitude of ways with which to grapple with the technological landscape we occupy.

Part of better understanding our technological landscape is through the application of critical theory, and the chapters in *Cultural Theory* provide a variety of access ports to a better understanding of how cyberpunk is instrumental to decoding the complexities of our technocultural age. After all, cyberpunk's emergence coincided with the popularization of postmodernism, and it was indelibly linked to postmodernity the moment Fredric Jameson famously remarked in *Postmodernism, or, The Cultural Logic of Late Capitalism* that cyberpunk is "the supreme literary expression if not of postmodernism, then of late capitalism itself" (419); in particular, Jameson sees in cyberpunk "as much an expression of transnational corporate realities as it is of global paranoia" and singles out Gibson as "an exceptional literary realization within a predominantly visual or aural postmodern production" (38). Cyberpunk therefore occupied a privileged position in the academy as scholars and critical theorists of all stripes hurried to embrace an initially literary form that spoke so much to the diversity of our cultural and critical moment(s). Cyberpunk has continued to appeal to theorists as it spread into the mainstream and beyond, particularly through its engagement with key contemporary questions such as the role of humanism, the emergence of the posthuman, and the importance of the animal. As the chapters in *Cultural Theory* demonstrate, the centrality of identity in this human-to-posthuman movement has led to the adoption and subversion of cyberpunk by groups interrogating the future of identity from feminist, queer, Indigenous, and Afrofuturist perspectives, as well as broader cultural interrogations of (sur)veillance and cultural activism, all of which are explored here alongside the political interventions made by cyberpunk media into academic debates surrounding class, ecology, and empire.

Cyberpunk is often erroneously thought of largely as an Anglo-American mode, one that has a tendency of appropriating other cultural tropes and imagery (particularly from Japan) as window dressing for its narrative goals. The chapters in *Cultural Locales*, the final section in this *Companion*, show that cyberpunk may have started out as a U.S. phenomenon (or U.S.-Canadian, given Gibson's primary residence in Vancouver), but it quickly penetrated a number of geographical locales. *Cultural Locales* focuses on some of the other cultures that have had their own cyberpunk moments—some influenced by the North American wave of cyberpunk, others reacting in specific regional ways to the global networks that increasingly define human relationships and the flow of capital between and beyond nation states. Mapping cyberpunk's territories outside of North America brings into focus the importance of a cultural mode such as this, one that allows the expression of the complex systems that govern 21st-century societies and lives. Of course, it isn't possible to showcase cyberpunk's cultural presence in every country. Nevertheless, *Cultural Locales* offers a significant sampling of how cyberpunk saturated and adapted itself to diverse cultural localities in alternately familiar, disorienting, and surprising ways that affirm cyberpunk as a global phenomenon.

Finally, editing a collection with nearly fifty contributors poses its own unique set of challenges, not the least of which was considering ways in which our formatting decisions might reflect the wider goals of the collection. We took the decolonizing move of replacing the traditionally capitalized 'the West' or 'Western' with the lowercase 'west' or 'western'; Marxism has been rendered as the lower-case 'marxism' to reflect that the field has moved well beyond the theories of Marx himself and therefore past the need for proper noun capitalization; we also avoid nearly all use of the words 'genre' or 'subgenre' to refer to cyberpunk, instead taking a cue from Foster and Rosemary Jackson in opting for the terminology of "mode," Jackson explaining it as a better term "to identify structural features underlying various works in different periods of time" (qtd. in Broderick 42). And, finally, we made editorial interventions into our contributors' papers to foster internal connections among the various chapters rather than allowing the chapters to simply exist as discrete entries, although we are certain more connections can be made. As editors, we also want to take this moment to thank our wonderful contributors who were diligent in working with us from their first drafts to the final products and returning their revisions in an expedient manner, even if word count sometimes proved to be an obstacle, which is a roundabout way of acknowledging we perhaps bear a fair share (if not the brunt) of responsibility for any perceived oversights or weaknesses in individual chapters. Hopefully, readers will agree that this collection has a symmetry or internal scaffolding that is difficult to achieve in collections of this nature, and the sinews of that symmetry undoubtedly rest with our contributors. We also gratefully acknowledge the assistance of both Mark Bould and Sherryl Vint who offered their respective insights at particularly thorny moments when a fresh set of eyes was desperately needed; they are silent partners in this project. Finally, Edward James has proven invaluable for taking on the arduous task of assembling the index and we are thankful beyond words for his help in relieving our workload.

In the end, the purpose of *The Routledge Companion to Cyberpunk Culture* has always been to emphasize the importance of cyberpunk as a cultural formation, a means of engaging with our 21st-century technocultural age. Through these chapters, we have attempted to trace cyberpunk's explosion from its origins to some of the diverse ways the mode shapes our understanding of 21st-century life, wherever we are on the globe. We hope that this collection will invite scholars to consider that cyberpunk remains alive and relevant because it is our quotidian reality.

Works Cited

Broderick, Damien. *Reading by Starlight: Postmodern Science Fiction.* Routledge, 1995.

Csicsery-Ronay, Istvan, Jr. *The Seven Beauties of Science Fiction.* Wesleyan UP, 2008.

Foster, Thomas. *The Souls of Cyberfolk: Posthumanism as Vernacular Theory,* U of Minneapolis P, 2005.

Jameson, Fredric. *Postmodernism, or, The Cultural Logic of Late Capitalism.* Duke UP, 2005 [1991].

Johnson, Mark R. "The History of Cyberspace Aesthetics in Video Games." *Cyberpunk and Visual Culture,* edited by Graham J. Murphy and Lars Schmeink, Routledge, 2018, pp. 139–54.

Marquis, Kyle. "Yearly Reminder." *Twitter,* @Moochava, 10 Jul. 2013, twitter.com/moochava/status/354986725388468224.

I

Cultural Texts

2
LITERARY PRECURSORS

Rob Latham

Avant-garde movements often present themselves as radically original and completely unbeholden to tradition, but this impudence is, of course, a pose. In the field of popular fiction especially, there is no such thing as radical originality: the mere fact of belonging to a genre implies some common set of aesthetic features shared with other works similarly shelved. The history of American science fiction (sf) has been marked by the cyclical emergence of new movements that claim to break sharply with their predecessors, starting with John W. Campbell, Jr.'s promotion of a streamlined, disciplined hard sf by contrast with the pulpy excesses of 1930s superscience. Yet even during the so-called "Golden Age" of *Astounding Stories*, familiar formulas persisted: Asimov's "Foundation" series is basically a more rigorously intellectual version of space opera, while his robot stories are soberer, less hysterical treatments of the stock theme of the menacing machine. Even the most revolutionary avant-garde in sf history, the New Wave of the 1960s and 1970s, retained significant aspects of the previous decade's work, such as an emphasis on dystopian futures and satirical critiques of technocracy à la Frederik Pohl, C.M. Kornbluth, Philip K. Dick, and Robert Sheckley. This is not to say that innovation never truly occurs but merely that it tends to involve adaptation and modification rather than wholesale replacement, nimbly updating time-honored tropes in light of fresh technosocial developments.

The same is true of the cyberpunks. While Bruce Sterling's Preface to *Mirrorshades: The Cyberpunk Anthology* (1986), one of the premier manifestoes of the movement, claims that an "allegiance to Eighties culture has marked [… the] group" (ix), the key themes he highlights—the increasing cyborgization of experience, the fusion of high-tech and subculture, rampant globalization—had in fact been explored in the previous decades by writers as diverse as J.G. Ballard, D.G. Compton, and John Brunner. Indeed, cyberpunk inherited from the New Wave a fascination with corporate mass-mediatization and "global integration" (Sterling xiv) derived from the critical and creative work of William S. Burroughs, Marshall McLuhan, and Thomas Pynchon, who had equally inspired writers of the previous generation. Most significantly, cyberpunk reverted to the hard-edged near-future orientation of much 1960s and 1970s sf, marking a sharp contrast with the dreamy textures and tones of contemporaneous science fantasy, such as Robert Silverberg's Majipoor trilogy (1980–83), Joan Vinge's Snow Queen series (1980–91), or Gene Wolfe's *Book of the New Sun* (1980–84).

Again, this is not to deny the movement's inventiveness but merely to indicate that its cutting edge was honed, in significant part, by the bold work of its precursors. In his *Mirrorshades* Preface, Sterling credits a few of these forerunners—Samuel R. Delany, Norman Spinrad, and John Varley—with having helped form the cyberpunk ethos, while at the same time paradoxically proclaiming the movement to be *sui generis*, an unprecedented eruption from the 1980s tech underground. Some New Wave authors have sought to correct this one-sided record: Spinrad's lengthy anatomy of the "Neuromantics" (his preferred term for the movement), which warmly praised the fictions of Sterling, William Gibson, and John Shirley, also pointed out their unreckoned debts to Michael Moorcock, Harlan Ellison, and himself, while Delany traced Gibson's lyrical evocations of cyberspace to Roger Zelazny's early short stories and his depiction of female characters to the 1970s work of Joanna Russ, tartly commenting that perhaps the author was constitutionally "blind to any mention" of such correspondences (qtd. in Tatsumi 6).

Some of the academic champions of cyberpunk have been equally oblivious, contrasting the movement's subcultural energy, its vision of posthuman possibility, and its hard technological edge with the 1960s New Wave, which they dismissively characterize as formalist, humanistic, and technophobic. Fred Pfeil, for instance, defines the New Wave as a narrowly aesthetic phenomenon, obsessed with "autotelic language practices, experimental forms, and [...] inadequately motivated but luxuriant image play," by comparison with cyberpunk, which shifted the genre "from formal and aesthetic experimentation back to experiments in social thought" (85–86). Explicitly building on this argument, Scott Bukatman has claimed that cyberpunk "returned the experimental wing of the genre to its technocratic roots," rejecting the New Wave's defense of inner space in favor of an exploration of "the transformation of quotidian existence by a proliferating set of global electronic technologies" (140). Ironically, these arguments, while expressing a clear anxiety of influence regarding the New Wave's literary legacy, nonetheless root cyberpunk deeply in previous traditions of sf writing.

The pat opposition articulated by Pfeil and Bukatman tends not only to ignore the sociopolitical engagement of the New Wave's major writers but also to exaggerate the path-breaking qualities of the cyberpunk movement. These were, as noted, often extrapolated from New Wave precursors: the media-based obsessions of Ballard and Spinrad, the wise-cracking hipness of Ellison, Delany's wild explorations of the underground, and the cynical anti-technocratic posture of Thomas M. Disch and John Sladek, among many other influences. Even the movement's handling of relatively fresh topics—in particular, the explosion of digital culture and its associated interfaces, and the radical refashioning of social life and embodied experience this explosion portended—stirred echoes from previous sf going back at least as far as Aldous Huxley's *Brave New World* (1932) and other classic midcentury dystopias of social engineering.

In fact, four key cyberpunk themes were foreshadowed in specific works of the New Wave era: (1) the emergence of an information economy, with all its complex impact on the social order, in particular the spread of cybercrime and forms of info-warfare; (2) the resultant hypercommodification of culture and the attendant growth in cyborgized lifestyles; (3) the proliferation of synthetic realities, to the point that simulated experience has begun to supplant the real thing; and (4) the possibility of a transhumanist "uploading" of consciousness, allowing individuals to abandon the mortal "meat" in favor of a virtual existence as discorporate data. All of these themes are perceived as quintessentially cyberpunk, yet all were powerfully prefigured—indeed, basically crystallized—in important sf works of the 1960s and 1970s.

2.1 Running the Net: John Brunner's *The Shockwave Rider*

Prior to the invention of the microchip in the 1960s, computers in sf were generally depicted as colossal, monolithic machines, vastly powerful but also simply *vast*. A rare exception was Murray Leinster's "A Logic Named Joe" (1946), which imagined desktop gadgets, complete with monitors and keyboards, that process information via an interlinked network—an astonishing prefiguration of the world we now inhabit. In Leinster's story, these devices—called "logics"—wind up promoting social anarchy by disseminating information that facilitates all manner of crimes and lawlessness. Though the tale is brief and a bit of a sport, it stands as one of the earliest depictions of a networked society, in which information is at once a profitable commodity and a potential weapon. The full-fledged portrayal of such a cybernetic world in sf would have to wait several decades, after pioneering innovations in semiconductor design and data transfer made possible both the Internet and the portable computer. One of the most compelling early attempts to explore the psychosocial consequences of these developments was John Brunner's *The Shockwave Rider* (1975).

Brunner's text powerfully prefigures the world that cyberpunk would soon come to popularize: a dystopian near-future dominated by sinister corporations and criminal cabals, in which curtailments of individual freedom have been compensated by a proliferation of consumer technologies and lifestyle options. Distributed "desk computers" are linked to an "integrated data-net"—a cyberspatial web that, in principle, democratizes access to information but which, in practice, merely reinforces prevailing inequities. And the hero, Nick Haflinger, is a proto-hacker adept at "running the net"—i.e., using his programming skills to fabricate fake identities that allow him to stay one step ahead of his enemies. As he explains, "it's a talent, like a musician's, or a poet's. I can play a computer read-in literally for hours at a time and never hit a wrong note" (253). The forerunner of such hacker anti-heroes as Gibson's Case or Johnny Mnemonic, Nick "was like a rat, skulking in the walls of modern society. The moment he showed his nose, the exterminators would be called for" (26).

Two of the main influences on Brunner's depiction of the emergent contours of information society would also be key to the development of cyberpunk: the so-called "hacker ethic," in particular the principle that "information wants to be free" (Brand 202), and the prognostications of noted futurist Alvin Toffler. Brunner's hacker anti-hero, an info-saboteur remorselessly pursued by governmental and corporate authorities, gets his revenge and ensures his own liberty by unleashing "the father and mother of all tapeworms" into the data-net (249). This program provides access to information previously classified or otherwise quarantined—specifically, data relating to issues of "public health, the protection of the environment, [and] bribery and corruption" by business leaders and elected officials (250). "As of today," Nick opines, "whatever you want to know...you can now know. In other words, *there are no more secrets*" (248; emphasis in original). A significant difference between this depiction of data piracy and later treatments of the theme in Gibson's *Neuromancer* (1984) and Bruce Sterling's *Islands in the Net* (1988) is that, in *Shockwave Rider*, the hack that "frees" the information is motivated by a utopian concern for the public good, rather than a desire for individual profit or factional advantage. To put the matter another way, it is probably fair to say that the ethico-political perspectives of cyberpunk tend to be slightly more cynical than those of their New Wave precursors.

This is true even when those perspectives derive from the same source material—in this case, Toffler's predictions of the rise of "super-industrial" or "Third-Wave" society in *Future Shock* (1970). Brunner's novel includes an acknowledgment of the influence of "Toffler's stimulating study *Future Shock*" on his own extrapolations (n.p.), and his title features a nod to that best-selling book. The novel's characters, besieged by new technological developments and a rapidly expanding data sphere, periodically succumb to "overload," retreating into a catatonic stupor in the face of this overwhelming bombardment of novelty. Technosocial change, in short, had "accelerate[d] until it approximated the limit of what human beings can endure" (124). The idea comes directly from *Future Shock*, which argues that the pace of change in modern information society "radically alters the balance between novel and familiar situations," forcing individuals "not merely to cope with a faster flow, but with more and more situations to which previous personal experience does not apply" (34). Toffler's subsequent study *The Third Wave* (1980) further expanded this diagnosis of the psychosocial fallout of rapid-fire change and the consequent breakdown of settled routine and reliable authority. According to Sterling, *The Third Wave* became "a bible to many cyberpunks" in its vision of a "technical revolution [...] based not in hierarchy but in decentralization, not in rigidity but in fluidity" (xii). Yet, a decade before cyberpunk, Brunner had already mined Toffler's prophecies to depict an information-driven world where rigid hierarchies are under threat from savvy hackers who use their know-how to decrypt and disseminate subversive knowledge.

2.2 Cinderella Transistorized: James Tiptree, Jr.'s "The Girl Who Was Plugged In"

While Brunner's novel gestures at the sort of popular culture an information society would be likely to promote, including online gaming and gambling, other New Wave-era texts have drawn out more fully the possibilities of interactive media in ways that prefigured cyberpunk technologies. Prototypical virtual reality technologies, for example, had been depicted in sf since at least the 1950s, in stories like John D. MacDonald's "Spectator Sport" (1950), Ray Bradbury's "The Veldt" (1950), and James E. Gunn's "Name Your Pleasure" (1955). These texts project immersive forms of artificial experience vended by global corporations with names like World Senseways (MacDonald) or Hedonics, Inc. (Gunn), thus prefiguring cyberpunk's emphasis on the capitalist commodification of human sensory and cognitive functions. During the 1960s, the theories of Marshall McLuhan, which argued for mass media as a kind of perceptual prosthesis into which the audience was collectively plugged, influenced a number of New Wave texts featuring interactive forms of television, such as Spinrad's *Bug Jack Barron*, Compton's *Synthajoy*, and Kate Wilhelm's "Baby, You Were Great" (all 1968). In Compton's and Wilhelm's stories, the audience has direct access to the emotional states of performers via new recording technologies, a set-up further extrapolated in "The Girl Who Was Plugged In" (1973) by James Tiptree, Jr. (a.k.a. Alice Sheldon).

Tiptree, Jr.'s story, which won the 1974 Hugo Award for Best Novella, remarkably foreshadows several core aspects of cyberpunk. It is set in a globalized, corporate-dominated near-future where control of data transfer is the main mechanism of social power and cultural authority. Yet every effort the central firm—called, simply, "Global Transmissions Corporation"—makes to commoditize and monopolize data has unintended consequences: "Their nightmares are about hemorrhages of information: channels screwed up, plans misimplemented, garble creeping in. Their gigantic wealth only worries them" (82). As in Gibson's *Neuromancer*, John Shirley's Eclipse trilogy (1985–90), and other key cyberpunk texts, the narrative action persistently shifts between shadowy centers of power and street-level concerns, the connection between them cemented via wetware technology that permits a lowly urchin named P. Burke to remotely inhabit and control a robot celebrity called Delphi. By means of "electrode jacks peeping out of her sparse hair, and [...] other meldings of flesh and metal" (84), P. Burke lives out a vicarious fantasy of jet-setting romance, in the process unwittingly touting the luxurious commodities with which the company outfits Delphi's extravagant lifestyle. The empowerment offered consumers by cyborgized mass media, however, is a sham and a delusion, an opportunity to wallow in ersatz pleasures while being capitalistically exploited; as Tiptree, Jr.'s wisecracking narrator comments: "You thought this was Cinderella transistorized?" (84).

The fabrication and exploitation of synthetic celebrities, a key theme in cyberpunk texts ranging from Pat Cadigan's "Pretty Boy Crossover" (1986) to Gibson's *Idoru* (1996) to Richard Calder's *Cythera* (1998), finds powerful expression in Tiptree, Jr.'s story (as in other major works of New Wave sf, such as Ballard's *The Atrocity Exhibition* [1970] or Compton's *The Unsleeping Eye* [1973]). Delphi is "the darlingest girl child you've EVER seen" (85), a mass-mediated angel living a hedonistic life of "[p]arties—clothes—suncars!" (90) while being invisibly puppeteered by P. Burke, "a gaunt she-golem flab-naked and spouting wires" (118). The fusion between them—constituting "a fantastic cybersystem," which the company refers to simply as "the investment" (115)—permits unprecedented commercial profiteering; as the narrator remarks, after listing the various products Burke/Delphi promotes and popularizes, "you can see why it's economic to have a few controllable gods" (95). And the company has big plans for their cyborg heroine, which they view as nothing more than a commodity: "she's scheduled for at least two decades' product life" (97), moving from a "limited consumer market" into "mass-pop potential" (99).

As in cyberpunk treatments of this theme, Tiptree, Jr. exposes, with a satire that is at once poignant and scathing, the crucial gap between the gaudy promises of virtual life and the sorry realities of meat-bound existence. In a pathological "self-alienation" (96), the more P. Burke identifies with the glamorous Delphi, the less concern she has for her own mortal shell: "She isn't eating or sleeping, they can't keep her out of the body-cabinet to get her blood moving, there are necroses under her grisly sit-down" (97). But Tiptree, Jr. makes clear, as many cyberpunk authors fail to do, the gendered dimensions of this sort of virtual life, the way it might appeal in particular to young women seeking to escape their imagined deficiencies into a cosmetic fantasy of perfected femininity. "One look at Delphi and the viewers know: DREAMS CAN COME TRUE" (98)—in short, romance with no threat of rejection and none of the messy realities of embodied sexuality, since for the 17-year-old P. Burke "sex is a four-letter word spelled P-A-I-N" (93). As the narrator tartly comments, "[y]ou could write the script yourself" (92)—hence, the repeated invocations of the gender (and class) dynamics of popular fairy tales like "Cinderella" and "The Ugly Duckling." No matter how high tech the set-up, the bottom line, as in so many works of cyberpunk, is just the same old cruel exploitation.

2.3 The Electronic Veil: Daniel F. Galouye's *Simulacron-3*

Granting the basic premise that animates stories such as Tiptree, Jr.'s—that it is technically possible to "jack in" to an alternative sensorium and enjoy vicarious experiences as convincing as the real thing—it is only a short step to the more radical notion of completely supplanting everyday reality with a synthetic duplicate. Such a solipsistic fantasy—or nightmare—is hardly new, going back at least to Descartes's speculation, in *Meditations on First Philosophy* (1641), that what we take to be our perceptual environment might actually be a skillful fake manipulated by an evil demon. Major sf stories of the 1950s and 1960s developed this idea into unnerving scenarios involving characters who come to suspect—or suddenly realize—that they are immured in false realities. Several of these tales took their inspiration from the subtle forms of psychological control exercised by postwar advertising and political ideology: in Pohl's "Tunnel Under the World" (1955), the protagonist discovers that his suburban neighborhood is actually a miniaturized simulation designed by marketing executives to promote their products, while Dick's *Eye in the Sky* (1957) propels several characters into delusory universes pervaded and controlled by various political and religious dogmas. Such stories prefigure cyberpunk takes on virtual reality, such as the scenes in *Neuromancer* where Case, through the agency of a conniving artificial intelligence, is imprisoned in a cyberspatial dreamland with his dead lover, not to mention cyberpunk-inflected films such as *Dark City* (Proyas 1998), *The Matrix* (Wachowskis 1999), and *The Thirteenth Floor* (Rusnak 1999).

The Thirteenth Floor was based on one of the most effective treatments of the theme in 1960s and 1970s sf: Daniel F. Galouye's 1964 novel *Simulacron-3* (a.k.a. *Counterfeit World*; also filmed by Rainer Werner Fassbinder in 1973 as *World on a Wire*[1]). Once again, the pernicious influence of advertising is predominant: a major marketing firm develops, via the science of "simulectronics," a "total environment simulator" for purposes of marketing research; this simulator contains an entire virtual city populated by test subjects unaware that they are computer constructs—forms of "counterfeit life" made up of "memory drums," "synaptic relays," and "cognitive circuits" (33)— who are being exploited for information about commercial products and trends. These "reaction entities" are indistinguishable from "real, living, thinking personalities," "never suspecting that their past experiences were synthetic, that their universe wasn't a good, solid, firm, materialistic one" (24). Transit between real and simulated worlds is achieved via a technique of "empathic coupling" (36)—i.e., establishing a connection between worlds that allows the user to link with the simulated reaction entity and control it accordingly. This coupling, on the one hand, permits the protagonist (a research scientist) to monitor his company's investment directly but, on the other hand, potentially allows a rebellious reaction entity to escape its simulation into the wider world.

The complexity of Galouye's novel—what makes it more than an extended version of Pohl's "Tunnel Under the World"—derives from this crossover traffic between macrocosm and microcosm. The effect is similar to the narrative portage between real and virtual worlds characteristic of cyberpunk, though *Simulacron-3* suggests a more radically destabilizing confusion of worlds than Gibson et al. usually entertain. Not only can entities pass into and out of the simulator, but the very possibility of such passage renders reality itself ontologically suspect. Through disturbing ruptures and fissures in his perceptual environment, the protagonist comes to apprehend that the world he takes for real is no more durable than the simulacrum he ostensibly shepherds. As with Descartes's speculative cosmology, the novel projects the possibility of a sadistic "Operator" in some "Higher Existence" stage-managing the protagonist's experience:

> I found myself looking into the star-spangled sky, trying to see through the universal illusion into absolute reality. But then, that Real World was in no *physical* direction from my own. It was not in my universe, nor I in Its. At the same time, though, it was everywhere around me, hidden by an electronic veil. (111; emphasis in original)

While the novel ultimately resolves this dilemma by locating the protagonist in a stable realm, this conclusion is less resonant finally than the atmosphere of paranoiac doubt and existential ambiguity that otherwise dominates the narrative.

In its uneasy conflation of reality and illusion, *Simulacron-3* is a much more metaphysical, if not metafictional, text than works of classic cyberpunk, more aligned with the abstract enigmas of Borges or the counterfeit mindscapes of Dick (e.g., *The Three Stigmata of Palmer Eldritch* [1965], "We Can Remember It For You Wholesale" [1966]). This is not to say that cyberpunk authors scant philosophical inquiry but rather that they tend to be too cynically hard-headed to worry themselves over transcendental reveries of universal delusion. Gibson's Case grasps at once that he has been incarcerated in a simulation and, though tempted by the randy ghost of Linda Lee, opts fairly promptly for the disappointments of the real by contrast with the blandishments of the virtual—a resolution echoed in the decision by the protagonist of Cadigan's "Pretty Boy Crossover" to refuse an offer of digital immortality. To put the matter another way, cyberpunk can more or less comfortably incorporate a range of simulated experiences into consensus reality without threatening that reality with fatal depletion, as so many texts of the New Wave era tend to do.

2.4 "A Portfolio of Personae": Robert Silverberg's *To Live Again*

The mirror image of the virtual-world story in sf is the tale of uploaded consciousness, in which an individual psyche is mechanically recorded and decanted into a computer, thus liberating the self from the constraints of the flesh and affording it an electronic immortality. Promoted by fringe-science thinkers like Ray Kurzweil and Hans Moravec, this "extropian" fantasy of radical self-improvement via technology had a significant impact on the development of cyberpunk: In Rudy Rucker's *Software* (1982), for example, a character has the contents of his brain transferred into a robotic body, while several works of Greg Egan—e.g., *Permutation City* (1994) and *Diaspora* (1997)—extrapolate the philosophical and socioeconomic implications of "copying" the mind. Once again, though, this theme was not new in sf: Arthur C. Clarke's 1955 novel *The City and the Stars* is set in a far future where individual selves, stored on a mainframe computer, are periodically revivified, while in Jerry Sohl's *The Altered Ego* (1954), people's memories are periodically recorded as a kind of "backup," a scenario that was developed further by John Varley in a number of stories, such as "The Phantom of Kansas" and "Overdrawn at the Memory Bank" (both 1976), wherein stored memories are re-embodied in clones upon the death of their original incarnation.

Robert Silverberg's *To Live Again* (1969) depicts a similar set-up, though in his treatment, these archived personalities can be bought and sold like commodities. In Silverberg's novel, wealthy individuals, using a technique called the "Scheffing process," periodically preserve their memories on magnetic tape; after their deaths, these personality profiles are "transplanted" into the minds of other wealthy subjects, thus permitting a kind of parasitic immortality: "jacked into the nervous system of its host," the revived spirit "could perceive and respond as if literally reincarnated" (76). The process is not within the means of mere "plebs," and Silverberg makes much of the social implications of this class distinction. Indeed, the characters' attitudes toward acquiring transplanted personae bespeak a cynical arrogance of status and power: scheming businessmen diversify their psychic "portfolio[s]" in order to maximize their socioeconomic advantage (9), while jet-setting socialites blithely add new souls to their repertoire for the voyeuristic thrill of vicarious experience. The entire process has been thoroughly commodified: Acquiring a new "carnate" involves "shopping" among alternatives stored in a vast "soul bank" (46, 12); if dissatisfied, the host can have the implanted persona erased, thus making it available again for another purchaser to enjoy.

Silverberg meticulously extrapolates the psychosocial fallout of such a system of serial reincarnation. While most characters manage to coexist with their transplanted carnates in a kind of psychic symbiosis, host minds ill-equipped for a potential battle of egos inside their own heads can find themselves shunted aside, their bodies hijacked by their riders. Moreover, since the Scheffing process is several generations old, the phenomenon of "secondary personae" has come to the fore: Carnates often come equipped with their own nested spirits, transplanted during their lives and now surviving amidst their recorded memories. "[T]hese crowded minds were [...] being picked up by the recipients," creating "a babbling mob within the brain" (65). A religion of neo-Buddhism has arisen to explain this plethora of reborn souls, but it is a "Westernized version" (12) in which the ultimate goal is no longer to escape into the selfless oblivion of nirvana but for the ego to survive indefinitely. As one of the characters tartly comments: "We've borrowed this prayer-wheel garbage from the Himalayas, only we've turned it upside down, since in its original form it's inapplicable to our society.... [O]ur whole idea is to grab as many incarnations as possible, down through the centuries.... That's a perversion of Buddhism!" (64). In short, a thin veneer of New Age fantasy has been added to a purely secular, totally self-serving, "materialistic cult of rebirth" (16).

Silverberg's novel prefigures key themes in cyberpunk sf, in particular the notion of a systematic exploitation of uploading technology for commercial ends. In *Neuromancer*, for example, individuals can be reduced to "data constructs" maintained on CD-ROM, their technical skills owned and used by corporations. Similarly, Michael Swanwick's *Vacuum Flowers* (1987) depicts a world in which "wetware personae," recorded from the brains of the recently deceased, are mass-produced to supply expertise a consumer otherwise does not possess, while George Alec Effinger's *When Gravity Fails* (1986) features plug-in personality modules—called "moddies"—that permit individuals to incorporate the style and attitudes of their subjects. Just as bootleg moddies, sold on the black market, are used for criminal purposes in Effinger's novel, so Silverberg depicts the possibility of an illicit traffic in bartered souls. And Silverberg's notion that an ersatz non-western faith might arise to provide a popular rationalization of new uploading technologies is reflected in Gibson's recourse to voodoo in *Count Zero* (1986) or Neal Stephenson to Sumerian legends in *Snow Crash* (1992) to gloss specifically cybernetic forms of emergent spirituality.

2.5 Conclusion

In sum, and contra the claims of critics such as Pfeil and Bukatman, cyberpunk owes a significant debt to the New Wave era. As stories such as Brunner's, Tiptree, Jr.'s, Galouye's, and Silverberg's clearly show, sf of the 1960s and 1970s had already begun to develop a number of the major pillars of the cyberpunk worldview, from the conviction that information technologies would radically reshape global society to the belief that capitalist forms of commodification and control would inevitably channel this process toward profitable ends. The biotech assault on centered subjectivity mounted by classic cyberpunk was also powerfully prefigured in New Wave treatments of proto-VR technologies, with their ability to project artificial environments and thus shatter and remold the perceiving self. A careful comparison of key New Wave and cyberpunk texts is likely to elicit as many similarities as differences: Even the 1960s obsession with "inner space" is echoed in Gibson's famous evocation of cyberspace as a "consensual hallucination" (67), and the hard-boiled textures and tones of the 1980s were adumbrated in Tiptree, Jr.'s wise-cracking style and Silverberg's cynicism. Seeing the two movements as radically opposed—or, as I put it in a previous essay, "focus[ing] on rupture at the expense of continuity" (45)—thus ignores the ways in which the sf mode actually grows and evolves: not by breaking radically with what has gone before but by adapting and refashioning past achievements into new and compelling forms.

Note

1 For more on the influence of *World on a Wire* on cyberpunk, see Evan Torner's chapter on German Cyberpunk in this collection.

Works Cited

Brand, Stewart. *The Media Lab: Inventing the Future at MIT*. Viking, 1987.
Brunner, John. *The Shockwave Rider*. Ballantine, 1976.
Bukatman, Scott. *Terminal Identity: The Virtual Subject in Postmodern Science Fiction*. Duke UP, 1993.
Galouye, Daniel F. *Simulacron-3*. Bantam, 1964.
Gibson, William. *Neuromancer*. Ace, 1984.
Latham, Rob. "'A Rare State of Ferment': SF Controversies from the New Wave to Cyberpunk." *Beyond Cyberpunk: New Critical Perspectives*, edited by Graham J. Murphy and Sherryl Vint. Routledge, 2010, pp. 29–45.
Pfeil, Fred. "These Disintegrations I'm Looking Forward to: Science Fiction from the New Wave to New Age." *Another Tale to Tell: Politics and Narrative in Postmodern Culture*. Verso, 1990, pp. 83–94.
Silverberg, Robert. *To Live Again*. Dell, 1971.
Spinrad, Norman. "The Neuromantics." *Isaac Asimov's Science Fiction Magazine*, vol. 10, no. 5, May 1986, pp. 180–90.
Sterling, Bruce. Preface. *Mirrorshades: The Cyberpunk Anthology*, edited by Bruce Sterling. Ace, 1988, pp. ix–xvi.
Tatsumi, Takayuki. "Some Real Mothers: An Interview with Samuel R. Delany." *Science Fiction Eye*, vol. 1, no. 3, March 1988, pp. 5–11.
Tiptree, James, Jr. "The Girl Who was Plugged In." *Warm Worlds and Otherwise*. Ballantine, 1975, pp. 79–121.
Toffler, Alvin. *Future Shock*. Bantam, 1971.

3

THE *MIRRORSHADES* COLLECTIVE

Graham J. Murphy

Literary cyberpunk's emergence in the mid-1980s is often attributed to the convergence of a quintet of authors: William Gibson, Bruce Sterling, Lewis Shiner, John Shirley, and Rudy Rucker, a cadre of like-minded writers harboring rebellious attitudes toward what they perceived as the inadequacies of science fiction (sf). The members of this quintet were first drawn to one another through a variety of seemingly chance encounters coupled with admiration for one another's work. For example, essayist and editor of *Science Fiction Eye* Steven P. Brown remarks that the 1974 Clarion Writers Workshop proved instrumental because Brown first met Bruce Sterling and introduced him to equal parts author and punk rocker John Shirley. Shirley, in turn, was instrumental to Gibson's career: The two men formed a fast friendship after a Vancouver convention, and Shirley helped convince Gibson to continue writing and sending out his early short stories for publication (Brown 175). At the same time, Sterling thought highly of Rudy Rucker's writing and started a correspondence with him which led to Worldcon/Constellation (1983) where Gibson, Sterling, and Shiner partied with Rucker to celebrate his latest novel *The Sex Sphere* (1983). Rucker had known of Gibson's work, having read "Johnny Mnemonic" (1981) in *Omni*, and was "awed by the writing. Gibson, too, was out to change SF" (204). Rucker was not alone in his estimation of Gibson's abilities; for example, Sterling would later describe Gibson's influence upon them for the documentary *No Maps for These Territories* (Neale 2000) in this fashion:

> When Lewis Shiner [whom Sterling met through the Turkey City Writer's Workshop] and I [...] were first reading Gibson's work in manuscript, we looked at it and said "Look, this is breakthrough material. This guy is really doing something different. Like we gotta put down our preconceptions and pick up on this guy from Vancouver. It's the way forward." A hole had opened up in consensus reality and we just saw daylight.

As a result, the first half of the 1980s was an idyllic period for this cadre, highlighted by the publication of Shiner's *Frontera* (1984), the first volume of Shirley's *Eclipse* series (1985), Sterling's Shaper/Mechanist stories (1982–84) and *Schismatrix* (1985), and Gibson's *Neuromancer* (1984). As Brown recounts, all "these people fed and cross-fed each other, passing around manuscripts, hammering out a vision of modern SF that more accurately reflected the future of the real world" (174–75).

Equally important as the fiction to the fledgling Movement, however, was Sterling's self-produced fanzine *Cheap Truth*, which became a polemical vehicle to critique so-called staid sf and promote the alleged revolutionary fervor of a new generation of authors looking to shake up the establishment and sell their stories. In the first two issues of *Cheap Truth*, circa 1983, Sterling, under his *nom de plume* 'Vincent Omniaveritas,' describes sf as both being stuck in a "reptilian torpor" (#1) and suffering from "intellectual exhaustion" (#2). Similarly, Lewis Shiner, writing as 'Sue Denim' in *Cheap Truth* #10 (1985), viewed *Neuromancer*'s Nebula Award nomination for Best Novel as a battle the upstart generation was determined to win:

> The voices of repression range from the senile babblings of Robert Heinlein to the California vapidity of Larry Niven to the moist-eyed urgency of Kim Stanley Robinson; arrayed against them are William Gibson, Lewis Shiner, and Jack Dann [...]. For every Heinlein that smites a Gibson, thousands more will rise in his place. The SF revolution is crying out for literacy, imagination, and humanity; it needs only a victory in the Nebulas to shatter the giant's terracotta feet. Up against the wall, Heinlein! (#10)

Shiner and the rest of what was internally (and informally) being called the Movement witnessed the Nebula victory they longed for: Gibson's debut novel won not only the 1985 Nebula Award for Best Novel, but also the 1985 Hugo Award and the 1984 Philip K. Dick Award. With the beauty of hindsight, we can say Gibson's overwhelming success with *Neuromancer*, coupled with Sterling's, Shiner's, Shirley's, and Rucker's steady output, meant the Movement was destined to enter the mainstream.

The Movement authors' early successes, however, owe much to two influential editors: Ellen Datlow and Gardner Dozois. Mike Ashley provides a thorough account of Datlow's influence as fiction editor for *Omni* and explains that "[w]hat was typical about *Omni*'s science fiction was that it was unpredictable. It pushed boundaries, some of which readers had not even known were there. *Omni* became the pre-eminent market for those writers who were not traditional" (41). Datlow quickly became the "Queen of Punk SF" (Ashley 49), and under her leadership, *Omni*'s science fiction increasingly focused on humans interfacing with the very technologies that *Omni*'s nonfiction articles were popularizing. A few years later, Gardner Dozois wrote "Science Fiction in the Eighties" for *The Washington Post* (December 30, 1984) and (un)officially jettisoned 'Movement' in favor of the *cyberpunk* label:

> About the closest thing here to a self-willed esthetic 'school' would be the purveyors of bizarre hard-edged, high-tech stuff, who have on occasion been referred to as 'cyberpunks'— Sterling, Gibson, Shiner, [Pat] Cadigan, [Greg] Bear [...] the similarities in goals and esthetics between them are much stronger and more noticeable than the (admittedly real) differences. For one thing, they are all ambitious writers, not satisfied to keep turning out the Same Old Stuff. Once again it is a time for literary risk-taking, and once again those who take them are admirable—and that makes it an exciting time for sf as a genre.

While Dozois certainly didn't coin the term *cyberpunk*—that honor goes to Bruce Bethke's "Cyberpunk" (1983)—he helped popularize a pulsing punk sensibility or "spirit of the new force in sf [that] was pervading the field" (Ashley 47) that had emerged since at least the start of the 1980s. For example, a panel devoted to 'punk sf' cropped up at Armadillo Con (1982) where Gibson read from his work-in-progress *Neuromancer*; John Kessel delivered a lecture in 1983 to North Carolina State University on the 'punk sf' of Gibson and Sterling; the year after *Neuromancer*'s publication, NASFiC (North American Science Fiction Convention) featured a panel with Sterling, Shiner, Shirley, Cadigan, and Bear, and Shirley again appeared on a cyberpunk panel (with Jack Williamson, Norman Spinrad, and Gregory Benford) at the Science Fiction Research Association's annual conference in 1985, a venue he would revisit the next year to deliver a paper "Cyberpunk or Cyberjunk?" (Heuser 231–34). These examples (among many) are testament to cyberpunk's emergence as a potentially electrifying force in sf, and it is during this wave that Ace Books published Sterling's edited collection *Mirrorshades: The Cyberpunk Anthology* (1986).

The *Mirrorshades* collection includes the original Movement-era cadre—Gibson, Sterling, Shirley, Shiner, and Rucker—as well as such allies as Cadigan and Bear and cyberpunk newcomers Tom Maddox, Marc Laidlaw, James Patrick Kelly, and Paul Di Filippo. *Mirrorshades*, however, is more than a collection of stories: It is also Sterling's attempt to map cyberpunk's contours and integrate competing sensibilities, and what emerges is a tension between a rebellious group of authors content to sneer at the mainstream from the margins and an increasingly popular(ized) movement that was slowly becoming the mainstream. The difficulties of trying to thread this needle between rebelliousness and respectability are plainly evident in Sterling's Preface that opens the collection. For example, Sterling is adamant at the very start of the Preface that "the 'typical cyberpunk writer' does not exist; this person is only a Platonic fiction. For the rest of us, our label is an uneasy bed of Procrustes, where fiendish critics wait to lop and stretch us" (ix). Indeed, a quick scan of the *Mirrorshades* stories is testament to Sterling's claim: The widely varied tales include militaristic artificial intelligences taking over their human hosts (Tom Maddox: "Snake-Eyes"), a chance encounter with a biogenetically engineered mermaid (Shiner: "Till Human Voices Wake Us"), bizarre vignettes about Harry Houdini (Rucker: "Tales of Houdini"), the experience of living in a futuristic street gang (Marc Laidlaw: "400 Boys"), the use of genetic intervention to try and escape mortality (James Patrick Kelly: "Solstice") or extend familial legacy (Paul Di Filippo: "Stone Lives"), the struggles of a Russian cosmonaut who finds a second chance at living aboard an aging space station (Sterling and Gibson: "Red Star, Winter Orbit"), and the weirdness of gargoyle-human hybrids seeking love (Greg Bear: "Petra"). *Mirrorshades* shows an incredibly diverse range of stories, and it is hard not to agree on some level with Martin Petto's acrimonious contention that the collection "is really just a bunch of writers who know and like each other and are involved in a loose creative web."

It is this narrative diversity or, perhaps more dismissively, incoherence that highlights another of cyberpunk's key tensions for critics, pundits, and fans alike: Did it ever offer any coherent vision of *cyberpunk* when it first exploded onto the scene in the 1980s? Michael Swanwick, for example, described Rudy Rucker as "no cyberpunk at all, but rather a one-man subgenre all by himself. However, the cyberpunks love him for his daring, excess, and clear-eyed craziness, and have claimed him as one of their own" (43); similarly, Swanwick characterized Bear as a free agent who was isolated from the Movement-era clique and "had independently invented the cyberpunks' style, and they loved him for it. He was welcomed to the ranks with open arms" (38). Gregory Benford could "see no commonality of vision between the various writers to whom the cyberpunk label had been attached beyond the fact that their fiction was 'bedazzled by technoglitz'" (Ashley 52); similarly, David Brin has called cyberpunk "nothing more or less than the best publicity gimmick to come to Speculative/Fiction in years" (qtd. in Kelly 145). As a collection, even *Mirrorshades*'s origins are tainted with opportunism: As James Patrick Kelly explains it, Sterling approached famed sf editor David Hartwell with an idea for a cyberpunk anthology, but was told more authors/stories were needed to publish a marketable collection. Hartwell testified Sterling "said it would be no problem to include twelve, and so he surprised people such as James Patrick Kelly, Greg Bear, and Paul Di Filippo by making them part of the Movement and including them in *Mirrorshades*" (qtd. in Kelly 145).[1] *Mirrorshades* and, more broadly, cyberpunk have therefore always struggled with the perception that it has been nothing but "a marketing strategy masquerading as a literary movement" (Benford, qtd. in Kelly 145).

In spite of such damning criticism, however, the stories in Sterling's *Mirrorshades* are no mere publicity gimmick, even if Sterling was clearly recruiting and subsequently drumming up publicity with this anthology; instead, *Mirrorshades* bears witness to the claims that early cyberpunk was tapping into a "spirit of the new force in sf [that] was pervading the field" (Ashley 47), and there is no doubt Datlow's and Dozois's respective input in cyberpunk's earliest days coupled with Sterling's keen promotional savvy with *Mirrorshades* helped position cyberpunk at the forefront of 1980s-era movements that it might otherwise not have achieved on its own accord. While the quintessential cyberpunk author may indeed have been a Platonic fiction, Sterling's Preface was nevertheless instrumental in giving cyberpunk some coherent shape and legitimacy as it proceeded to lop and stretch the *Mirrorshades* contributors for its own purposes. For example, toning down the rebellious rhetoric of *Cheap Truth*, Sterling is careful in his Preface to explain the *Mirrorshades* authors are "steeped in the lore and tradition of the SF field" and "cyberpunk is in some sense a return to roots" (x–xi). In his most conciliatory tone, Sterling writes of cyberpunk as "a natural extension of elements already present in science fiction, elements sometimes buried but always seething with potential. Cyberpunk has risen from within the SF genre; it is not an invasion but a modern reform" (xv). While Sterling evokes such cyberpunk precursors as Harlan Ellison, Samuel R. Delany, Norman Spinrad, J.G. Ballard, and Thomas Pynchon, many of whom are addressed in the previous chapter by Rob Latham, he also gives an appreciative shout-out to "the steely extrapolation of Larry Niven, Poul Anderson, and Robert Heinlein" (x), a contrary opinion from Lewis Shiner's earlier description in *Cheap Truth* of Heinlein's 'senile babblings' and Niven's 'California vapidity.' Finally, as befits an anthology that promotes itself as *The Cyberpunk Anthology*, *Mirrorshades* was an opportunity for Sterling to seize some control over the cyberpunk narrative as it was quickly moving away from the margins and was slowly becoming an established form.

The *Mirrorshades* collective, however, isn't all about trading in leather jackets for cardigans in the name of respectability (or book sales); instead, Sterling insistently, perhaps desperately, links cyberpunk to the punk wave of the late-1970s: Cyberpunk's *bricoleurs* prized "their garage-band esthetic" by integrating the "overlapping of worlds that were formerly separate: the realm of high tech, and the modern pop underground" (x–xi). He also links cyberpunk to "Eighties pop culture: in rock video; in the hacker underground; in the jarring street tech of hip-hop and scratch music; in the synthesizer rock of London and Tokyo" (xi–xii). Drawing upon the 'future shock' espoused in futurist Alvin Toffler's *Future Shock* (1970) and *The Third Wave* (1980), Sterling helps contextualize cyberpunk as "spontaneous, energetic, close to its roots. Cyberpunk comes from the realm where the computer hacker and the rocker overlap" (xiii). In perhaps the most concise summation (or marketing!) of cyberpunk, Sterling identifies two central themes running through cyberpunk that belie the critics' claims to narrative incoherence: "The theme of body invasion: prosthetic limbs, implanted circuitry, cosmetic surgery, genetic alteration. The even more powerful theme of mind invasion: brain-computer interfaces, artificial intelligence, neurochemistry—techniques radically redefining the nature of humanity, the nature of the self" (xiii).

These themes are notable when comparing the two stories that bookend *Mirrorshades*: William Gibson's "The Gernsback Continuum" and Bruce Sterling and Lewis Shiner's "Mozart in Mirrorshades." The former story establishes the defiant tone espoused by *Mirrorshades* and the Movement-turned-cyberpunk sensibility. The protagonist is an American photojournalist hired by publisher Dialta Downes to photograph the architectural detritus of a promised science fictional future that never came to pass, a "1980s that never happened. An architecture of broken dreams" (Gibson 5). As the narrator gets further into the project, however, he begins seeing visions of an America from an alternate timeline, which sends him to his friend Merv Kihn who explains the alternate timeline(s) as "semiotic phantoms, bits of deep cultural imagery that have split off and taken on a life of their own" (29–30). The story's restless attitude shines forth when one of the narrator's ghostly visions reveals a white, blond, and (likely) blue-eyed American family standing in front of a futuristic city that would have been all-too-familiar in the sf of earlier decades: "[T]hey were Heirs to the Dream […]. Here, we'd gone on and on, in a dream logic that knew nothing of pollution, the finite bounds of fossil fuel, of foreign wars it was possible to lose" (9). In spite of the utopian promises of yesteryear's science fiction, this spectral future "had all the sinister fruitiness of Hitler Youth propaganda" (9). In a manner reminiscent of the rebelliousness saturating the pages of *Cheap Truth* when sf's elder statesmen were engaging in scoffing dismissiveness, Gibson masterfully rejects antiseptic visions of the science fictional futures inspired by the Pulp Age and Golden Age sf of the 1920s–1950s by calling forth comparisons to Hitler Youth propaganda. In so doing, and by virtue of being *Mirrorshades*'s lead-off story, "The Gernsback Continuum" sets the tone for the subsequent stories in the collection and in some ways rejects Sterling's claims in the Preface that cyberpunk "is in some sense a return to roots" (x–xi). Punks didn't always see eye to eye with one another, even if their rebel yells were often aimed in the same direction, and in one deft sentence, Gibson's punkish sneer in "The Gernsback Continuum" undercuts those roots Sterling was trying to cultivate in his Preface.

"Mozart in Mirrorshades" also features alternate timelines, only unlike the subtlety of "The Gernsback Continuum" the punk iconography of "Mozart in Mirrorshades" is both gleefully apparent and ruthlessly harnessed to fuel the story's condemnation of neoliberal capitalism. The protagonist, Rice, is overseeing the management of an 18th-century Salzburg by megacorporations that utilize temporal mechanics to exploit alternate pasts for corporate profit, chiefly by consuming such natural resources as oil or spiriting away not-yet-priceless artwork. As Veronica Hollinger writes for her contribution to this *Companion*, "Mozart in Mirrorshades" positions the past as nothing more than "standing-reserve in the inflexible logic of capitalist expansion, and the Great Acceleration of the American future overwhelms (a version of) 18th-century Austria" (328). Consequently, global history has been completely shattered thanks to these capital interventions from 'Realtime,' which causes growing resentment from those who are not reaping the benefits of corporate expansion; for example, Thomas Jefferson, who has replaced George Washington as America's first president, is upset that "[y]ou guaranteed us liberty and equality and the freedom to pursue our own happiness. Instead we find machinery on all sides, your cheap manufactured goods seducing the people of our great country, our minerals and works of art disappearing into your fortresses, never to reappear!" (226–27). Rice cares little for Jefferson's quibbles; instead, he appears fixated on meeting Marie Antoinette by way of Wolfgang Amadeus Mozart, the famous composer who now sports a "bristling hedgehog cut that had replaced the boy's outmoded wig [...] faded jeans, camo jacket, and mirrored sunglasses" (224, 228). After a weeklong sexual marathon with 'Toinette,' which includes such scintillating discussions as the merits of leather bikinis and *Vogue* magazine, Rice is betrayed by the object of his obsession and is captured by Masonistas, at least until he is rescued by a Harley-riding Jebe Noyon who has seemingly abandoned Genghis Khan to join the Trans-Temporal Army. Rice returns to Salzburg to find the megacorporations are pulling out of the alternate 18th century. Rice also learns Mozart orchestrated Rice's capture by the Masonistas, but Mozart escapes any repercussions thanks to his *Billboard* success—he is #5 on the charts!—and a new record contract from Realtime that not only promises salvation from the 18th century but also rewards him with all the trappings of neoliberal capitalism: cars, women, and access to the finest recording studios. The final image of the story is Rice retreating down the tunnel toward Realtime carrying an unconscious Toinette over his shoulder. "Mozart in Mirrorshades" is therefore a prime example of cyberpunk prizing "the bizarre, the surreal, [and] the formerly unthinkable" (Sterling xiv–xv) while also exhibiting what becomes *de rigueur* in cyberpunk: late capitalist enterprises ruthlessly exploiting and mining (human and nonhuman) resources.

The most thematically similar stories in *Mirrorshades*—or, dare I say, the most quintessentially cyberpunk—are John Shirley's "Freezone" (1985) and Pat Cadigan's "Rock On" (1984), the former an excerpt from his novel *Eclipse* and the latter a thematic preview of Cadigan's future novel, the Arthur C. Clarke Award-winning *Synners* (1991). Shirley's story follows Rick Rickenharp and the downfall of his rock 'n roll band as it performs its last concert on Freezone, a floating aggregation of offshore drilling platforms in the Atlantic Ocean that "dealt in pleasant distractions for the rich in the exclusive section and—in the second-string places around the edge—for technickis from the drill rigs. The second-string places also sheltered a few semi-illicit hangers-on and a few hundred performers. Like Rickenharp" (141–42). Although Rickenharp and his band perform the show of a lifetime, declining sales figures from their two previous recordings coupled with internal squabbles have doomed the band. The squabbles center on whether the band should go *minimono*, a musical style bucking the waning trend known as the *flare* whose adherents wear their "hair *up*, as far over the top of [the] head as possible and in some way that *expressed*, that emphasized the wearer's individuality, originality. The more colors the better" (Shirley 144). Rickenharp expresses some respect for the *flare*, in part because he is more apt to bed flare women, but has no patience for *minimono* and the "stultifying regularity of their canned music" (Shirley 145). The monochromatically styled *minimono* fans are easily recognizable by their "flat-black, flat-gray, monochrome tunics and jumpsuits, the black wristfones, the cookie-cutter sameness" (Shirley 145), while their musicians are physically wired into the "impulse-translation pickups on the stage floor, making [them] look like a puppet with its strings inverted [...]. The long, funereal wails pealing from hidden speakers were triggered by the muscular contractions of his arms and legs and torso" (Shirley 145–46). *Flare* or *minimono* is a moot distinction: Neither style speaks to Rickenharp's identification with punk music, and he breaks with his band after they finally decide to go *minimono* and yearn for a wire-dancer who can bring them mainstream *Billboard* glory. "Freezone" is therefore caught between conflicting sentiments: On the one hand, Rickenharp (and Shirley) is defiantly rebellious in his refusal to allow a punk sensibility to simply roll over and die in the face of changing musical tides; on the other hand, there is a palpable acceptance that for all his revolutionary swagger, Rickenharp and punk are déclassé, finding themselves again in the margins that are both exhilarating and exhausting for punk pioneers. After all, by the end of the story Rickenharp is unceremoniously left to drop blue mescaline and lose himself in Freezone with a new set of characters who are trying to escape Freezone without alerting The Second Alliance International Security Corporation. In the end, there is very little sense, at least in this excerpt from *Eclipse*, that a punk sensibility will actually get you anywhere beyond wandering a recommissioned oil rig in a drug-induced haze.[2]

Gina, the first-person narrator of Cadigan's "Rock On," is also seeking escape, and in a comparable manner to Rickenharp, she is also desperately seeking freedom from the *Billboard Top 40* corporate commodification of rock 'n roll. Gina is a human synthesizer, a *sinner*,[3] locked into an exploitative contract with Man-O-War: As a *sinner*, she is the cybernetic talent behind Man-O-War's public success. Thanks to implanted sockets that allow her to literally plug into the band, Gina can rock

> Man-O-War through the wires, giving him the meat and bone that made him Man-O-War and the machines picking it up, sound and vision, so all the tube babies all around the world could play it on their screens whenever they wanted. Forget the road, forget the shows, too much trouble [...]. And the tapes weren't as good as the stuff in the head, rock 'n roll visions straight from the brain [...]. In the end, they didn't have to play instruments unless they really wanted to, and why bother? Let the synthesizer take their imaginings and boost them up to Mount Olympus. (39–40)

Recognized in a Greek greasy spoon as a runaway *sinner*, Gina is forced by the members of the talent-stifled band Misbegotten to work her *sinning* skills. Unfortunately, Gina's latest side-project attracts Man-O-War's attention and ruins Misbegotten's chances at rock 'n roll glory: "Man-O-War had his conglomerate start to buy Misbegotten right after the first tape came out. Deal all done by the time we'd finished the third one, and they never knew" (41). Gina expresses her contempt for Man-O-War, who she accuses of killing rock 'n roll, all the while Man-O-War counters that Gina is trying to bury it alive, but the debate is futile: Gina is marched off to continue serving out her contract as Man-O-War's *sinner*, and corporate rock 'n roll continues to dominate the marketplace.

As the only woman-authored story in the *Mirrorshades* collection, Cadigan's "Rock On" highlights one of cyberpunk's initial problems: its unmistakable lack of diversity. Samuel R. Delany has commented on the under-acknowledged influence of 1970s feminist sf upon cyberpunk, an influence "whose obliteration created such a furor when Bruce Sterling (inadvertently of course …?) elided it from his introduction to [William Gibson's] *Burning Chrome* [collection]. Sometimes it seems as though these male writers were trying to sublate the whole feminist movement unto themselves—which can only be done at the expense of history" (173). Similarly, Kelly remarks upon cyberpunk's "heteronormative conventions of gender, sexuality, and power […] there was a huge disparity between the number of strong male characters and the number of strong female characters, and gay and lesbian characters were all but invisible" (151). A few years later, Nicola Nixon, in her article "Cyberpunk: Preparing the Ground for Revolution or Keeping the Boys Satisfied?," convincingly argued "cyberpunk fiction is, in the end, not radical at all. Its slickness and apparent subversiveness conceal a complicity with '80s conservatism" (231). At the same time, cyberpunk's problematic, if not outwardly hostile, approach to race has largely been overlooked and is the subject of Isiah Lavender's "Critical Race Theory" chapter in this *Companion*. Focusing on Steven Barnes's *Streetlethal* (1983), *Gorgon Child* (1989), and *Firedance* (1993), Lavender writes that Barnes's use of black and brown skin color for his characters demystifies a literary mode resolutely designed by others to exclude black authors—a decision purposefully made by Bruce Sterling in his codifying of cyberpunk in *Mirrorshades: The Cyberpunk Anthology* (1986), as if mentioning 'the visionary shimmer of Samuel Delany' (x) and 'the jarring tech of hip hop' (xii) make it impervious to claims of racism" (313). Lavender sees in the emergence of Afrocyberpunk, however, "another way to describe black speculative cultural practices, only with particular attention to cyberspace, simulations, and/or virtual realities (technical or biological) as sites of revolution and social reform" that "offer us consciously racialized settings in their imaginings, resolutely challenging the whiteness of cyberpunk" (314; 315).

It is this widespread homogeneity that later writers reformed, if not outright rejected, including a late-1980s and early-1990s wave of writings from Cadigan, Laura Mixon, Mary Rosenblum, and others that was an expression of what Karen Cadora calls a 'feminist cyberpunk' that challenged cyberpunk's heteronormative assumptions and conventions. Or, as Lisa Yaszek writes in "Feminist Cyberpunk," such works as "[Gwyneth] Jones's *Escape Plans* (1986), [Candas Jane] Dorsey's "(Learning About) Machine Sex" (1988), and [Lisa] Mason's *Arachne* (1990) put women at the front and center of their cyberpunk worlds" (35).

By virtue of its self-promotion, *The Cyberpunk Anthology* may have also been contributing to the idea that cyberpunk had already died by a thousand paper cuts by the time of *Mirrorshades*'s own publication. Lewis Shiner's *New York Times* editorial "Confessions of an Ex-Cyberpunk" (1991) is the most damning coroner's report: Writers quickly began to turn "form into formula: implant wetware (biological computer chips), government by multinational corporations, street-wise, leather-jacketed, amphetamine-loving protagonists and decayed orbital colonies." According to Rucker, however, Shiner was already digging cyberpunk's grave as far back as 1985 when, after a fractious cyberpunk conference panel featuring Shiner, Sterling, Rucker, Cadigan, and Bear, Shiner reportedly asked "So I guess cyberpunk is dead now?" (209). Sterling certainly provided an added signatory to cyberpunk's death certificate when, in his essay "Cyberpunk in the Nineties" (1991), he acknowledged that the cyberpunk pioneers, most of whom were in their forties when Sterling wrote his essay but are now in their sixties and seventies, "are no longer a Bohemian underground. This too is an old story in Bohemia; it is the standard punishment for success. An underground in the light of day is a contradiction in terms. Respectability does not merely beckon; it actively envelops. And in this sense, 'cyberpunk' is even deader than Shiner admits." In this regard, *Mirrorshades* may actually be regarded as cyberpunk's funeral procession, perhaps even its tombstone, for a Movement that had quickly gone mainstream, its upstart rebelliousness sacrificed upon the altar of conventional acceptance and commercialization. It is arguably for this reason that so many members of the *Mirrorshades* collective made concerted efforts to distance themselves from cyberpunk as the 1980s waned; however, cyberpunk's eulogies were premature. As Sherryl Vint and I wrote in "The Sea Change(s) of Cyberpunk, "we have never more been in need of a fiction capable of engaging with the world as shaped by information technology, which perhaps explains the sub-genre's persistent afterlife" (xii). That afterlife is evident in a 1990s that ushered forth new generations of authors who would push literary cyberpunk in new directions that has carried forth well into the 21st century; similarly, visual cyberpunk—films, television shows, comic books, and video games—continue to expose cyberpunk and its visual motifs to a vast audience.[4]

In the end, the *Mirrorshades* collective provided the genetic material for a range of literary and visual motifs that ensured cyberpunk "didn't so much die as experience a sea change into a more generalized cultural formation" (Foster xiv), a central premise informing not only *The Routledge Companion to Cyberpunk Culture* but also my two previous collections, *Beyond Cyberpunk: New Critical Perspectives* (co-edited with Sherryl Vint) and *Cyberpunk and Visual Culture* (co-edited with Lars Schmeink). In hindsight, we can look back and recognize that *Mirrorshades* and 1980s-era cyberpunk embody not so much a genre or sub-genre organized around distinct or formal components but, instead, a cultural formation which is "a historical articulation of textual practices with 'a variety of other cultural, social, economic, historical and political practices'" (Foster xvi). Alternately, cyberpunk can also be thought of as a parabola—i.e., "more concrete than themes, more complex than motifs, parabolas are combinations of meaningful setting, character, and action that lend themselves to endless redefinition and jazzlike improvisation" (Attebery and Hollinger vii)— that continues to offer seemingly endless redefinitions and improvisations, whether we use such labels as feminist cyberpunk, second- and third-wave cyberpunk, postcolonial cyberpunk, and/or post-cyberpunk. Sterling's Preface to *Mirrorshades* may have committed early cyberpunk to the axis of body invasion and mind invasion, but *The Cyberpunk Anthology* also exemplifies Sterling's point that, again, the cyberpunk "label is an uneasy bed of Procrustes" (ix), and as our techno-saturated world looks increasingly like the cyberpunk worlds of fiction, *Mirrorshades* continues to resonate, albeit imperfectly and not-unproblematically, with the cyberpunk futures that surround us.

Notes

1 This account was essentially confirmed to me by David Hartwell in a social conversation when he and I both sat on the Executive Board for the International Association for the Fantastic in the Arts (2007–10).
2 For a damning, but no less accurate, reading of the sexist overtones in Shirley's "Freezone," see Petto for details.
3 Although Cadigan later modifies the spelling to "synner" in her novel *Synners*, the first appearance in "Rock On" is spelled "sinner."
4 For more details, please consult other entries in this collection and/or *Cyberpunk and Visual Culture* (2018), edited by Graham J. Murphy and Lars Schmeink.

Works Cited

Ashley, Mike. *Science Fiction Rebels: The Story of the Science-Fiction Magazines from 1981–1990*. Liverpool UP, 2016.
Attebery, Brian and Veronica Hollinger. "Parabolas of Science Fiction." *Parabolas of Science Fiction*, edited by Brian Attebery and Veronica Hollinger. Wesleyan UP, 2013, pp. vii–xv.
Brown, Steven P. "Before the Lights Came On: Observations of a Synergy." *Storming the Reality Studio: A Casebook of Cyberpunk and Postmodern Science Fiction*, edited by Larry McCaffery. Duke UP, 1991, pp. 173–177.

Cadigan, Pat. "Rock On." *Mirrorshades: The Cyberpunk Anthology*, edited by Bruce Sterling. Ace, 1988, pp. 34–42.

Cadora, Karen. "Feminist Cyberpunk." *Science Fiction Studies*, vol. 22, no. 3, 1995, pp. 357–72.

Delany, Samuel R. "Some *Real* Mothers …: The *SF Eye* Interview." *Silent Interviews: On Language, Race, Sex, Science Fiction, and Some Comics*. Wesleyan UP, 1994, pp. 164–85.

Dozois, Gardner. "Science Fiction in the Eighties." *The Washington Post*, 30 Dec. 1984. *The Washington Post* Archives, 30 Jan. 2018, www.washingtonpost.com/archive/entertainment/books/1984/12/30/science-fiction-in-the-eighties/526c3a06-f123-4668-9127-33e33f57e313/?utm_term=.216b92991532.

Foster, Thomas. *The Souls of Cyberfolk: Posthumanism as Vernacular Theory*. U of Minnesota P, 2005.

Gibson, William. "The Gernsback Continuum." *Mirrorshades: The Cyberpunk Anthology*, edited by Bruce Sterling. Ace, 1988, pp. 1–11.

Heuser, Sabine. *Virtual Geographies: Cyberpunk at the Intersection of the Postmodern and Science Fiction*. Rodopi, 2003.

Hollinger, Veronica. "Ecology in the Anthropocene." *The Routledge Companion to Cyberpunk Culture*, edited by Anna McFarlane, Graham J. Murphy, and Lars Schmeink. Routledge, 2020, pp. 326–34.

Kelly, James Patrick. "Who Owns Cyberpunk?" *Strange Divisions and Alien Territories: The Sub-Genres of Science Fiction*, edited by Keith Brooke. Palgrave Macmillan, 2012, pp. 144–155.

Lavender, Isiah. "Critical Race Theory." *The Routledge Companion to Cyberpunk Culture*, edited by Anna McFarlane, Graham J. Murphy, and Lars Schmeink. Routledge, 2020, pp. 308–16.

Murphy, Graham J. and Lars Schmeink, eds. *Cyberpunk and Visual Culture*. Routledge, 2018.

Murphy, Graham J. and Sherryl Vint, eds. *Beyond Cyberpunk: New Critical Perspectives*. Routledge, 2010.

———. "The Sea Change(s) of Cyberpunk." *Beyond Cyberpunk: New Critical Perspectives*, edited by Graham J. Murphy and Sherryl Vint. Routledge, 2010, pp. xi–xviii.

Nixon, Nicola. "Cyberpunk: Preparing the Ground for Revolution or Keeping the Boys Satisfied?" *Science Fiction Studies*, vol. 19, no. 2, 1992, pp. 219–35.

Petto, Martin. "*Mirrorshades: The Cyberpunk Anthology*." Everything Is Nice, 5 May 2011, www.everythingisnice.wordpress.com/tag/mirrorshades/.

Rucker, Rudy. *Nested Scrolls: The Autobiography of Rudolf von Bitter Rucker*. PS Publishing, 2011.

Shiner, Lewis (as Sue Denim). Editorial. *Cheap Truth #10*. Totse.com, 30 Jan. 2018, totseans.com/totse/en/ego/on_line_zines/cheap10.html.

Shiner, Lewis. "Confessions of an Ex-Cyberpunk." *New York Times*, 7 Jan. 1991, lysator.liu.se/lsff/mb-nr10/Saxat.txt.

Shirley, John. "Freezone." *Mirrorshades: The Cyberpunk Anthology*, edited by Bruce Sterling. Ace, 1988, pp. 139–177.

Sterling, Bruce (as Vincent Omniaveritas). Editorial. *Cheap Truth #1*. Totse.com, 30 Jan. 2018, totseans.com/totse/en/ego/on_line_zines/cheap01.html.

———. "Dirt Cheap Literary Criticism with the Honesty of Complete Desperation." *Cheap Truth #2*. Totse.com, 30 Jan. 2018, totseans.com/totse/en/ego/on_line_zines/cheap09.html.

Sterling, Bruce. "Cyberpunk in the Nineties." *Interzone*, no. 48, 1991, pp. 39–41, http://lib.ru/STERLINGB/interzone.txt.

———. Preface. *Mirrorshades: The Cyberpunk Anthology*, edited by Bruce Sterling. Ace, 1988, pp. ix–xvi.

Sterling, Bruce and Lewis Shiner. "Mozart in Mirrorshades." *Mirrorshades: The Cyberpunk Anthology*, edited by Bruce Sterling. Ace, 1988, pp. 223–239.

Swanwick, Michael. "A User's Guide to the Postmoderns." *Isaac Asimov's Science Fiction Magazine*, vol. 10, no. 8, 1986, pp. 20–50.

Yaszek, Lisa. "Feminist Cyberpunk." *The Routledge Companion to Cyberpunk Culture*, edited by Anna McFarlane, Graham J. Murphy, and Lars Schmeink. Routledge, 2020, pp. 32–40.

4

BRUCE STERLING: *SCHISMATRIX PLUS* (CASE STUDY)

María Goicoechea

In the early 1980s during cyberpunk's heyday, Bruce Sterling published a series of short stories and a novel that shared the same far-future scenario, characterized by the tensions between two different factions and their antagonistic approaches toward (post)human evolution. A decade later, *Schismatrix Plus* (1996) collected this sprawling Shaper/Mechanist series—"Swarm" (1982), "Spider Rose" (1982), "Cicada Queen" (1983), "Sunken Gardens" (1984), "Twenty Evocations" (a.k.a. "Life in the Shaper/Mechanist Era: Twenty Evocations"; 1984), and *Schismatrix* (1985)—and, in the volume's introduction, Sterling proudly proclaims that "[t]hese stories, and this novel, are the most 'cyberpunk' works I will ever write" but also that this is "all there is" (viii), implying that he has given closure to the themes he wanted to explore. Although Sterling never returned to this narrative universe, his vividly imagined posthuman embodiments continue to flesh out the phantasmagorical fantasies of western posthumanism, a train of thought still much entrenched in humanism's dualisms: self/other, body/soul, object/subject, material/virtual, and biological/technological. Sterling's saga thus presents a suitable tableau to discuss contemporary debates regarding posthumanism and transhumanism, without losing sight of cyberpunk's foundational myths.

Most critics and reviewers have underscored Sterling's capacity to imagine posthuman subjects when the term 'posthuman' was still in its critical infancy. As Veronica Hollinger has pointed out, *Schismatrix* is "one of the earliest sf scenarios consciously to construct its characters as 'posthuman' and explore some of the implications of the term" (269). Posthumanism has now evolved into an umbrella term, a theoretical concept used in so many different fields of study—including science and technology studies (STS), philosophy, critical theory, architecture, communication studies, and bioethics—that it is difficult to discern what is meant by it in each case. This is complicated by the use of the term by transhumanists, who see the posthuman subject as the ultimate stage of their ongoing transformation toward an enhanced human, whose intellectual and physiological capacities will no longer classify her as merely human.[1]

In navigating this fraught terrain, Tamar Sharon distinguishes four broad approaches to the term posthuman: "a 'dystopic,' a 'liberal,' a 'radical,' and a 'methodological' posthumanism" (5). While dystopic and liberal positions are politically defined by their rejection or embrace of the technology used to enhance human capabilities, the radical and methodological approaches correspond to current academic discourses in cultural theory and philosophy. The radical position includes the optimistic visions of Donna J. Haraway, N. Katherine Hayles, and Rosi Braidotti, among others, who see emerging biotechnologies as destabilizing agents of western anthropocentric, patriarchal, and racist foundational discourses. The methodological approach represents

Bruce Sterling: Schismatrix Plus *(Case Study)*

a more 'neutral' field of scientific exploration (STS scholars and philosophers such as Don Ihde or Bruno Latour) that has found it necessary to transcend the previous paradigm of the human as subject distinct from the world (object) to better account for the interaction between humans and nonhuman entities. In the end, the "most important axis of differentiation between the various types of approaches to the posthuman," Sharon concludes, "runs not between their celebratory or condemnatory inclinations, but between their humanist or nonhumanist underpinnings, where humanism refers to the view that upholds a foundational ontological divide between humans and the rest of the world" (4–5).

Sharon's cartography privileges the academic debate between humanist and nonhumanist positions, in part because this discourse has taken the central stage among critical/theoretical discussions of posthumanism; however, the dystopic and liberal lines, typically embodied by the Luddite and the technophile (or transhumanist), run not only through popular culture, including science fiction's (sf) portrayals of posthuman characters in novels, films, comics, and video games, but also through scientific narratives (see Coyne 1999).[2] What is obvious is that academic and popular cultures intersect and mirror one another, both impinging on what it means to be posthuman by producing overlapping, at-times contradictory, definitions. In this regard, sf's creative freedom can provide an honest, unpretentious, and raw depiction of the desires and nightmares that populate our contemporary culture and "find fitting cultural illustrations of the changes and transformations that are taking place in the forms of relations available in our post-human present" (Braidotti 203). Cyberpunk's foundational narratives regarding the posthuman are particularly fecund, as they often depict strangely alluring but equally discordant, even repellant, futures founded upon a cutting-edge punk sensibility which, as some of the contributors in this volume have outlined, often fails to be absolutely radical, especially when it comes to imagining alternative subject positions that do not perpetuate patriarchal, heteronormative, and/or racist discourses.[3] It is within this terrain that *Schismatrix Plus* occupies a central position in the cyberpunk canon, particularly in its complicated, perhaps contradictory, handling of posthumanism. Sterling's posthumanism proposes a fascinating mixture between technoromantic utopia and a nihilist cybergothic dystopia, which are the dominant and countercultural trends of our western digital narratives,[4] coupled with nuanced readings of the theories of Nobel laureate Ilya Prigogine, who shaped Sterling's understanding of biological evolution for this sequence.

As opposed to the near-future settings common to cyberpunk and popularized by such contemporaries as William Gibson, Lewis Shiner, or John Shirley, Sterling's *Schismatrix Plus* is set in a distant future where cyberpunk fantasies have been fully developed: The time frame spans from Spider Rose's birth in 2045 ("Spider Rose") to the events of "Sunken Gardens," set in 2554. In these five centuries, we follow the history of (post)humanity beyond planet Earth, in which (post)humans, ideologically divided by different evolutionary choices, inhabit and explore outer space in a continuous flow of physical, ecological, political, and technological transformations. The main source of conflict is a fracture in society caused by opposed interpretations of what constitutes our (post)humanity. On the one hand, the Shapers have pursued biogenetic modifications to create a race of *quasi*-perfect clones imbued with both beauty and intelligence. The Shapers (a.k.a. the Reshaped) have evolved as a transhumanist utopia that has set no limits to gene manipulation, surgical operations, and nanotechnological intrusion into not only the human body but also the ecosystem at large. Shapers reproduce by means of cloning and cast aside 'unplanned' humans as an inferior caste, since they consider it their mission to bring humanity to its perfection as a species. Their ideal of purity leads them into a never-ending struggle in order to maintain virus-free artificial ecosystems where the clones can live. On the other hand, the Mechanists have achieved a total alliance with the machine, supplementing their bodies with prosthetics and even managing to transfer human consciousness to computer circuits. They use all sorts of prostheses, allowing the mechanical elements to slowly invade their bodies. According to the Shapers, the

María Goicoechea

Mechanists' evolutionary path will lead them to a dead end, since at some point, everything will be transformed into metal and programming, leaving aside willpower and imagination—in sum, life. It is the beautiful and super-intelligent Shapers, however, who end up exalting the power of science and intelligence over emotions, becoming enslaved brains at the service of their Shaper ideology. Even their much-vaunted intelligence proves dangerous, as dissident Shaper factions like the Patternists have experienced, often becoming mentally unstable and developing "autism, fugue states, paranoia" (*Schismatrix Plus* 304).

While the two factions war with one another, they harbor the same dream: They desire immortality achieved through any means possible, including the inoculation of a cell-regeneration virus in the original body, a series of clones that would serve as backup copies of the self, and/or the transfer of the subject's identity (understood as pure data flow) to a mechanical body, a computer network, and even to a sentient architectonic structure. In sum, any shape imaginable could possibly be inhabited by a (post)human consciousness. As a result of this sprawling narrative canvass, the Shaper/Mechanist battles take place along ethical borders, ideological disquisitions, and taboos regarding what can and cannot be tampered with. To further complicate matters, the conscious manipulation of evolution in Sterling's universe has not been univocal or unidirectional, and the Shaper/Mechanist branches are themselves giving way to a proliferation of different factions, all while the solar system is being colonized by omnipotent aliens, the Investors, who have the secret of 'starflight' and enjoy abusing their (post)human inferiors with cheap swindles. In Sterling's saga, each evolutionary path consequently gives way to different societies, where mass defections from failed experiments to more promising ones are customary. Sterling has therefore devoted this whole saga to exploring the future evolution of (post)humanity with such a richness of detail and vivid description that he has made of those imaginings the *raison d'être* of the Shaper/Mechanist universe. Or, as Tom Maddox has observed, "more so than any SF writer with whom I am familiar, Sterling has explored the Other as the future of our becoming" (238).

The protagonist of *Schismatrix*, the longest contribution to the Shaper/Mechanist series, is Abelard Lindsay, who lives torn between his Mechanist origin and his Shaper education. Lindsay uses this in-between state to his advantage by stepping from one mode of consciousness to the other, depending on the occasion. For example:

> Lindsay was afraid. He closed his eyes and called on his Shaper training, the ingrained strength of ten years of psychotechnic discipline. He felt his mind slide subtly into its second mode of consciousness. His posture altered, his movements were smoother, his heart beat faster. Confidence seeped into him, and he smiled. His mind felt sharper, cleaner, cleansed of inhibitions, ready to twist and manipulate. His fear and guilt faltered and warped away, a tangle of irrelevance. (*Schismatrix Plus* 14)

In this instance, the mode of consciousness associated with Shaper training refers to a rational, cold, and calculating point of view, associated with the scientific method. After all, to the Reshaped, fear is one of those emotions that makes one vulnerable, a feeling which the Mechanists, on the other hand, do not attempt to repress. Later in the novel, Lindsay has been kidnapped by Mechanist pirates who are attacking a mysterious asteroid-shaped spacecraft that encloses a labyrinth of dark passages. It is within this cybergothic setting[5] that a clan of exceptionally gifted and beautiful Shapers, fearful of being contaminated by microbes, assassinate the Mechanist pirates one by one. The Shapers' mind control techniques, emotional suppression, and scientific method turn them into lethal weapons while the Mechanists, who have not disowned their emotions and feelings, possess a vital instinct that makes them feel dangerously alive.

At the end of *Schismatrix*, Lindsay considers the transfer of his 'soul' to a newly designed, high technology "Angel" that is described in the advertising brochure as "an aquatic posthuman. The skin was smooth and black and slick. The legs and pelvic girdle were gone; the spine extended to long muscular flukes. Scarlet gills trailed from the neck. The ribcage was black openwork, gushing white, feathery nets packed with symbiotic bacteria" (232). The brochure goes on to describe this posthuman body in exquisite detail, including "long black arms [...] dotted with phosphorescent patches," "nerve-packed stripes [that] housed a new aquatic sense that could feel the water's trembling," a "nose [that] led to lung-like sacs packed with chemosensitive cells," "lidless eyes [that] were huge," and a skull "rebuilt to accommodate them" (232). Lindsay learns these Angels glow and are "self-sufficient, drawing life, warmth, everything from water" (232). And, in the interest of reproduction, "[c]hildren can be created. But these creatures can last out centuries" (232). It is in this description of the Angels, however, that we see a common motif in Sterling's *Schismatrix Plus*: Sterling's posthuman future is often torn between technoromantic heaven and a cybergothic hell. The Angels are a technoromantic fantasy of posthuman self-sufficiency and eternity complicated by religious overtones, the potentially humanist desire to return to a primeval state of unity with the liquid element of the maternal uterus, the immediate satisfaction of corporeal needs without exertion, and the reverie of a pure and aseptic body that remains somehow uncorrupted thanks to state-of-the-art technology.[6] This Angel therefore serves as an unsettling reminder of the ethical dilemma we humans face as a species: We have encoded in ourselves the capacity through technological transformation to modify the physical and cognitive characteristics that have up to this point defined our identity. Sterling's Angel is not too far from a terrifying and phantasmagorical vision of the sort of creature that a (post)human being can become; as a result, this distorted image of a return to some aquatic Eden shows how close technoromantic fantasies are to a cybergothic imagination: They are two sides of the same coin for Sterling and speak to our at-times blind faith in technological progress. The Shapers in Sterling's Shaper/Mechanist universe therefore represent the technoromantic ideal of perfect (post)human beings, quasi-divine and asexual, whereas the Mechanists symbolize the beliefs of the cybergothic by vindicating the power of emotions as that which distinguishes them as (post)human beings.[7]

These well-defined lines drawn in *Schismatrix* between the technoromantic and the cybergothic are blurred in the Shaper/Mechanist short stories. The attitudes of Shapers and Mechanists in these stories are not so easily discriminated, providing an even more nuanced reading of evolutionary choices. For example, "Swarm," the first short story in this saga, contains many of the themes developed in the rest of the stories: the economic war between the two main factions, the mercenary ethics, and the life-or-death struggle for survival in hostile environments, to name a few examples. Its protagonist, Simon Afriel, is a member of the Shapers on a 'research' mission to an alien asteroid inhabited by a primitive collective society. This alien culture, or swarm, is likened to a beehive or an ant colony and, seemingly devoid of any self-awareness or intelligence, is presented as an ideal society where innocence reigns, there is no knowledge of good or evil, and "it's always warm and dark, smells good, and food is easy to get, and everything is endlessly and perfectly recycled" (247). Afriel's companion, Doctor Galina Mirny, a researcher whose in-depth work on the swarm defines her life, remarks that this subterranean kind of heaven could last unchanged for thousands of years, but Afriel dismissively replies: "In another thousand years we'll be machines, or gods" (248). Afriel's Shaper bias shines forth, and when confronted by Doctor Mirny with his mercantilist, rather than scientific, objectives, he defends himself by attacking his opponents: He describes to Doctor Mirny the extreme factions of the Mechanists as "more than half machine. Do you expect humanitarian motives from them? They're cold, Doctor—cold and soulless creatures who can cut a living man or woman to bits and never feel their pain. Most of the other factions hate us. They call us racist supermen" (247). Pushed to the limits of their ideology, Mechanist and Shaper factions then represent similarly 'barbaric' or inhumane positions: the absolute lack of compassion and empathy associated with the machine, versus the superiority and racism of the 'enhanced' human, the superhuman.

If there is another similarity between the Shapers and the Mechanists that *Schismatrix Plus* emphasizes, it is surely their shared encompassing belief in colonizing and transforming other planets into habitable environments, a titanic effort that redoubles their necessity for technological advancement in a race against competitors. "Sunken Gardens," for example, deals with a particular terraforming contest in a Martian crater where several gardening factions compete to create the most enduring and beautiful habitat. The prize is the "Ladder," an offer of admission to a more advanced society orbiting Mars in a city-state spacecraft, the Regals, a splinter faction from the Terraform-Kluster. The Kluster, which has remained neutral in the Shaper-Mechanist war, attracts capital from financiers and bankers while also benefitting from the alien Investors' patronage. This capitalist heaven is the realm of the 1%, and the Regals rule over Mars, quite literally looking down and scrutinizing a planet populated by the losing factions, all the while viewing these refugees as living ecological experiments competing with each other in "closely studied simulations of the future" (307).

During the most recent iteration of the competition, a fire breaks out in the crater where the six competing factions have been allotted land to garden. Mirasol, the story's protagonist, discovers that the crater is not empty but secretly inhabited by a previous surviving faction, which has set itself and its habitat on fire in a suicidal escape from the Regals. This event reveals the 'advanced' Regals as also a petty and destructive class, who had previously attempted to eradicate this captive faction when they discovered that these underlings had managed by themselves to obtain the secrets of star travel. This discovery would not only weaken the Regals' power and leave their partners, the Investors, without a negotiating advantage, but also threaten to turn the refugee ecologists away from competitive terraforming projects to instead fuel their launch into space. Mirasol confronts her Regal superior with the catastrophe she has witnessed, but the woman only replies nonchalantly: "If life worked perfectly, how could things evolve? Aren't we Posthuman? Things grow, things die. In time the cosmos kills us all. The cosmos has no meaning, and its emptiness is absolute. That's pure terror, but it's also pure freedom." This so-called superior Regal sententiously concludes: "Our ambitions have become this world's natural laws" (312). At the end of the story, Mirasol, the victor of the competition, now orbits Mars and similarly looks down on the people below her, and she agrees to keep the cruel and self-interested nature of the competition secret in exchange for her new privileges, including a newly extended lifespan. This story epitomizes the ruthlessness with which (post)human factions are thrust into outer space in a technologically mediated battle for survival, and how personal ambition overrides solidarity.

In many ways, *Schismatrix Plus* remains faithful to cyberpunk's conventions: The narrative rejects both technological utopia and post-apocalyptic debris. Instead, it selects a paradoxically mild dystopia, a scenario that reflects Sterling's distrust regarding human capacity to develop a machine culture that is positive and healthy, but which nevertheless leaves some margin for hope since the characters' free will is never completely purged. The Shaper/Mechanist far-future includes "epidemics of suicide, bitter power struggles, vicious technoracial prejudices, the crippling suppression of entire societies" (64). At the same time, "the ultimate madness had been avoided. There was war, yes: small-scale ambushes, spacecraft destroyed, tiny mining camps claim-jumped with the murder of their inhabitants [...] But humankind had survived and flourished" (64). In *Schismatrix Plus*, therefore, we have what 1980s-era cyberpunk authors often commented upon in this early wave of fiction: an exploration not of some urban sprawl but a probing of social margins and the marginalized, the debris of opulent societies and their outcasts, and an unequally shared utopia that is the American dream, albeit transferred into outer space.

Curiously, *Schismatrix Plus* is both nihilistic and at the same time naïve regarding the power of capitalism and materialism to bend and twist ideologies. On the one hand, the Shaper/Mechanist universe is a projection of liberal capitalism gone universal, the common currency being calculated in energy, the 'gigawatt.' As the most powerful alien race, the Investors keep the secret of

Bruce Sterling: Schismatrix Plus (Case Study)

starflight to themselves, triggering market crashes, transactions of all sorts on the "open market" (286), and "commercial action" turned into "a kind of endemic warfare" (304). Colonization and terraforming also instantiate the economic conflicts that pervade the entire Shaper-Mechanist universe, making the unrealistic promises of capitalism real:

> There are two hundred million people in space. Hundreds of habitats, an explosion of cultures. They are not all scraping out a living on the edge of survival, like these poor *bezprizorniki*. Most of them are the bourgeoisie. Their lives are snug and rich! Maybe technology eventually turns them into something you wouldn't call human. But that's a choice they make—a rational choice. (42)

Nevertheless, Sterling instead blames unbound technological and scientific progress as the impersonal, destructive forces that have ruined human societies: "Pioneer elites burst forth, defying anyone to stop their pursuit of aberrant technologies" (304). Calling forth echoes of Alvin Toffler's *Future Shock* and *The Third Wave*, Sterling writes that "[n]ew sciences and technologies had shattered whole societies in waves of future shock" (304).

Sterling's indebtedness to futurist Toffler's 'waves of future shock' cannot be understated, in part because it was embraced by the earliest cyberpunks and celebrated accordingly. In his Preface to *Mirrorshades: The Cyberpunk Anthology*, Sterling goes so far as to call *The Third Wave* "a bible to many cyberpunks" (xii); however, the more noteworthy appropriation of scientific jargon in *Schismatrix Plus* is taken from Ilya Prigogine's *From Being to Becoming*. Prigogine, a physical chemist and Nobel laureate concerned with change and evolution, was trying to understand the enigma of time: How do we integrate the time dimension in our situated knowledge of the world? How do we come to think in terms of before and after? Can the past and the future really be predicted if the present state of a system is accurately known (as classical physics seemed to imply)? Or, as Prigogine suspected, are there oscillations, fluctuations, catastrophes that can jump-start evolution in strange ways and not one but "only various possible 'scenarios' can be predicted" (vii)? Prigogine's work was helping to bridge a gap between a scientific approach that had been quite sterile with respect to the preoccupations with time and change and the inventiveness of literary and artistic concerns on the subject matter (vi).

Even though Sterling only expressed his admiration for the superficial sound of Prigogine's prose—"very like the 'crammed Prose' and 'eyeball Kicks' that we cyberpunks were so enamored of" (*Schismatrix Plus* vii)—he went far beyond merely using "his terminology as the basis for Shaper/Mechanist mysticism" (Introduction vii); instead, Prigogine structures the entire Shaper/Mechanist universe. For example, direct mention is made in "Cicada Queen," a story filled with Prigogine references through the invented philosophical-scientific terms that sprinkle the narrative: "the Fourth Prigoginic Level of complexity" (273), "prigoginic event horizon" (274), "the Prigoginic Leap" (282), etc. Sterling even makes one of Prigogine's ideas the motto for his universe: "life moves in clades," which is repeated like a mantra throughout the Shaper/Mechanist narratives. This motto is Sterling's metaphorical adoption of Prigogine's understanding of "this over-creativity of nature [...] in which 'mutations' and 'innovations' occur stochastically and are integrated into the system by the deterministic relations prevailing at the moment" (128). What was Prigogine's integration of the thermodynamic law of entropy in biological evolution provided Sterling with an ideologically free sense of a technologically driven evolution in which chaos and change bring about new orders of being.

"Cicada Queen" is also notable because posthumanism is here presented as a philosophical school influenced by the "ancient Terran philosopher Ilya Prigogine," which has liberated humans from the cumbersome "search for moral certainties" (*Schismatrix Plus* 274). Science has become philosophy: "Posthumanism schooled us to think in terms of fits and starts, of structures accreting

29

along unspoken patterns" (274). In Prigoginic terms, the entropic forces that bring about physical decay and intellectual finitude can eventually introduce a mutation, a change, that will give evolution a jump-start. This leap of faith remains the same for all the posthuman factions: an unwavering belief in the successful transfer of human consciousness from its original body to another container, be it mechanical, biological, or cyborg. It is the essentialist division between mind and body that remains untarnished. Overall, this faith permits Sterling's (post)human characters to think in more positive terms when facing irreversible situations, such as death, the extinction of a species, or the collapse of a meteorological system.

At the same time, stories such as "Spider Rose" and "Twenty Evocations" address the imposition upon the limits of a posthuman life by the unbearable accumulation of memories rather than by the progressive degeneration of the body. If there is something that defines *life* (and not just human life), it must surely be *death*; yet, by overcoming death, the posthuman faces a vampiric life, or undeath: senselessness and boredom as the overpowering problems of a saturated memory become pressing. As in "Spider Rose," acts of cruelty perpetrated in the past and the difficulty of coping with "the inconvenience of guilt" make the protagonist feel "old, horribly old" (*Schismatrix Plus* 268). The protagonist in "Twenty Evocations," Nikolai Leng, dies pronouncing his last words triumphantly—"Futility is freedom!" (*Schismatrix Plus* 319)—after enjoying a life marked by mercenary choices, negotiated yet seemingly happy marriages, conspiracies, betrayal, and, finally, suicide. Both Spider Rose and Nikolai die alone in a universe where true emotions are rare, and drugs have made sex and love irrelevant; yet, *Schismatrix Plus* shows the need for companionship is never fully eradicated. These passages contain one final moral message that we can extract from Sterling's disquisitions about the posthuman future: Our humanity is relational; it is constructed through our ties with others, though, as the end of the novel implies, the myth of the solitary space cowboy as an isolated monad lost in the void remains alluring.

Sterling's depiction of a Prigoginic posthumanism is presented as the rejection of the moral constraints that limit personal freedom in order to protect the common good. It is an ideology that embraces individuality, change, and action; it is a way of thinking that facilitates unencumbered bodily transformations, which are most often enforced by the requirements of survival and domination rather than ethics or aesthetics. Generally, *Schismatrix Plus* presents us with a posthumanism that entails the subversion of current humanist ideals, but which is actually more faithful to contemporary human behavior, where individualism, alienation, and opportunism dominate the individual's actions rather than communal ethics or the defense of humane ideals. In the end, *Schismatrix Plus* has captured the western *élan de vie*, which is marked by the infinite desire for change and action, a being-in-the-world that is essentially active, fearful of the void, and incapable of truly visualizing a far-future without the never-ending human exertion to prevail.

Notes

1 For details regarding the posthuman as it relates to critical posthumanism and transhumanism, see Julia Grillmayr's contribution to this collection.
2 I am indebted to Richard Coyne's *Technoromanticism: Digital Narrative, Holism, and the Romance of the Real* for this understanding of how technophobic and technophile trends inform scientific narratives.
3 Most cyberpunk remains tied to the very humanist ideals it superficially tries to sabotage. In other words, while Braidotti, Haraway, and Hayles promote posthuman subjectivities as potentially overcoming the cultural, racial, and gender barriers that have oppressed the Other, the posthuman in cyberpunk narratives is often subjugated to the same normative identities detailed by the Enlightenment, perpetuating dominant gender and racial stereotypes of western culture.
4 For more details, see my article "The Posthuman Ethos in Cyberpunk Science Fiction." See also David Porush's "Prigogine, Chaos, and Contemporary Science Fiction."
5 For more details on the relationship between cyberpunk and the Gothic, see Anya Heise-von-der-Lippe's contribution to this collection.

Bruce Sterling: Schismatrix Plus *(Case Study)*

6 This image is reminiscent of Mark Dery's discussion in *Escape Velocity* of Burt Brent's designs for a winged human in *The Artistry of Reconstructive Surgery*.

7 In a perplexing final *tour de force*, Lindsay will eventually refuse to choose either the Shaper or the Mechanist option, but will embrace instead an alien mysticism, following Presence, a disembodied force that offers him "eternal wonder" and the possibility to "wait out the heat-death of the Universe to see what happens next" in a total abandonment of the body (*Schismatrix Plus* 236).

Works Cited

Braidotti, Rosi. "Post-Human, All Too Human, Towards a New Process Ontology." *Theory, Culture & Society*, vol. 23, no. 7–8, 2006, pp. 197–208.

Coyne, Richard. *Technoromanticism: Digital Narrative, Holism, and the Romance of the Real.* MIT Press, 1999.

Goicoechea, María. "The Posthuman Ethos in Cyberpunk Science Fiction." *CLCWeb: Comparative Literature and Culture*, vol. 10, no. 4, 2008, docs.lib.purdue.edu/clcweb/vol10/iss4/9/.

Hollinger, Veronica. "Posthumanism and Cyborg Theory." *The Routledge Companion to Science Fiction*, edited by Mark Bould, Andrew M. Butler, Adam Roberts, and Sherryl Vint. Routledge, 2009, pp. 267–278.

Maddox, Tom. "The Wars of the Coin's Two Halves: Bruce Sterling's Mechanist/Shaper Narratives." *Mississippi Review*, vol. 16, no. 2/3, 1988, pp. 237–244.

Porush, David. "Prigogine, Chaos, and Contemporary Science Fiction." *Science Fiction Studies*, vol. 18, no.3, 1991, pp. 367–386.

Prigogine, Ilya. *From Being to Becoming: Time and Complexity in the Physical Sciences.* W H Freeman & Co (Sd), 1981.

Sharon, Tamar. "A Cartography of the Posthuman: Humanist, Non-Humanist and Mediated Perspectives on Emerging Biotechnologies." *Krisis: Journal for Contemporary Philosophy*, vol. 2, 2012, pp. 4–19.

Sterling, Bruce. Preface. *Mirrorshades: The Cyberpunk Anthology*, edited by Bruce Sterling. Ace, 1988, pp. ix–xvi.

———. *Schismatrix Plus.* Ace, 1996.

5

FEMINIST CYBERPUNK

Lisa Yaszek

With their depictions of environmentally devastated near-futures ruled by global corporations and gangs where leather-clad hackers, technologically-augmented street samurai, and secretive artificial intelligences (AI) compete for survival in both the virtual and physical worlds, women have long written stories that anticipate, dramatize, and extend the themes and techniques of cyberpunk fiction. Indeed, women have been central to the process of transforming what was once a niche subgenre into a vibrant mode of storytelling that remains central to today's global imaginary. In fact, I'm arguing that we can think about feminist cyberpunk—much like other areas of feminist creativity—as evolving over time in a series of waves that correspond to changes in digital technologies. These three waves or 'generations' of feminist cyberpunk reject the alienation, isolation, and nihilism typically associated with masculinist cyberpunk and replace it with an emphasis on creative self-expression, community, and sociopolitical change. These writers participate in widespread cultural conversations over the necessary relations of cyberculture, gender, and futurity as those debates have been articulated by feminist thinkers and artists alike.

5.1 Feminist Proto-Cyberpunk, 1818–1979

Women's interest in the organizing themes of cyberpunk—including technoscientifically induced alienation, corporate global domination, a rapacious media landscape, and the often-reckless use of new technologies to transform bodies and minds—is as old as science fiction (sf) itself. The fury experienced by Mary Shelley's artificial human in *Frankenstein* (1818) when he learns that he is the throwaway product of bad science and bad parenting is every bit as charged as the electricity that animates him. As such, Shelley anticipates the dilemma of cyberpunk's grifters, sex workers, and other outsiders who eventually realize that they, too, are the disposable products of a technoscientific culture. As sf developed into a unique popular mode with its own creators, publishing venues, and rules for good writing, women began to explore the perils of capitalism in greater depth. For example, both Lilith Lorraine's "Into the 28th Century" (1930) and Thea von Harbou's *Metropolis* (published as a novel in 1925 and produced as a film by Fritz Lang in 1927) imagine futures where the mad science of technologically reorganizing human life for profit becomes standard practice in globe-spanning "Industrial Dictatorships"—and where women band together with each other and fringe communities of "reformers, scientists, and radicals" to change the course of history (Lorraine 257).

In the 1960s and 1970s, women associated with the development of feminist sf explored similar concerns in relation to new media technologies, including television, early video games, and early computers. Feminists writing proto-cyberpunk in this era specifically envisioned "media landscape" futures where everyday women undergo radically invasive technological procedures to remake themselves in the media's image of feminine perfection (Pringle and Nicholls). Stories in this vein include Elisabeth Mann Borgese's "True Self" (1959), Evelyn E. Smith's *The Perfect Planet* (1962), Kit Reed's "The New You" (1962), Kate Wilhelm's "Baby, You Were Great" (1968), and, most famously, James Tiptree, Jr.'s "The Girl Who Was Plugged In" (1973). Like Shelley's creature before them, the protagonists of these stories are monstrously alone, isolated from other women, and alienated from the men who use them for profit. Collectively, these authors insist that there is no way out from the media landscape because the forces of technologically-enabled capitalism prevent women from connecting with one another in meaningful ways.

At the same time, women writing feminist proto-cyberpunk used the figure of the part-organic, part-technological cyborg to rethink the relations of science, technology, and sex/gender in more positive ways. As early as 1944, C.L. Moore's "No Woman Born" imagined a human actress named Deirdre whose brain is implanted in a magnetic metal body after a tragic accident. Rejecting her doctor's description of her as a Frankensteinian abomination, Dierdre embraces her body and inspires new art and fashion while actively saving her own creator from self-destruction. In the 1960s and 1970s, a new generation of authors aligned with the emergent subgenre of feminist sf made the figure of the cyborg central to their storytelling practices. For example, stories such as Anne McCaffrey's *The Ship Who Sang* (1969), Samuel R. Delany's "Aye, and Gomorrah" (1967) and *Nova* (1968), Joanna Russ's *The Female Man* (1975), and Vonda McIntyre's *Superluminal* (1983) all take up Russ's claim that "humanity is unnatural!" (12) by telling tales of humans who technoscientifically transform themselves to perform work differently and to become the heroes of their own high-tech adventures. Like Moore's metallic heroine before them, such characters rarely mourn their lost natural bodies, focusing instead on the new pleasures created by human-machine-animal interfaces.

Feminist authors of this era also used cyborg characters to imagine entirely new societies based on new modes of reproduction. Vonda McIntyre's *Dreamsnake* (1978), Suzy McKee Charnas's *Holdfast* series (*Walk to the End of the World*, 1974; *Motherlines*, 1978; *The Furies*, 1994; *The Conqueror's Child*, 1999), and Marge Piercy's *Woman on the Edge of Time* (1976) all depict strange, difficult, and sometimes frightening futures where women's scientific and social oppression is justified by so-called natural difference between sexes. But they also insist that such futures might be opposed by women (and other people) who use science and technology to transform reproduction itself. Whether this occurs by developing biofeedback-based forms of birth control (McIntyre), genetically engineering other animals to carry human reproductive materials (Charnas), or gestating babies in test tubes and using hormones to let both men and women breastfeed (Piercy), such stories take Moore's tale in new directions. Moore's cyborg heroine is a "phoenix" who can resurrect herself but cannot reproduce or change the course of human history because she is alone, a one-off separate from her fleshly peers (287). By way of contrast, McIntyre, Charnas, and Piercy link cyborg bodies to each other and to the proliferation of both technologically-mediated reproductive practices and possible futures. Cyborgs in these stories are never alone or outside history; instead, they assemble into complex new family and social units that are more egalitarian and rewarding than those of the unmodified humans they have replaced.

5.2 First-Wave Feminist Cyberpunk, 1980–1990

As the 1980s ushered in both new governments focused on economic growth and new computing technologies that supported the rapid advance of global capitalism, feminists began to argue that thinking carefully about science, society, and sex should be the central concern of all women living in the modern moment. In sf, it fell to a new generation of women and nonbinary artists to work out their own ideas about these relations in the wildly popular new story form that editor

Gardner Dozois christened "cyberpunk." Nowhere was this more apparent than in the fiction of Pat Cadigan. As one of the few women writers regularly associated with pioneering cyberpunks William Gibson, Bruce Sterling, Lewis Shiner, Rudy Rucker, and John Shirley, Cadigan quickly earned the title "Queen of Cyberpunk." In many ways, Cadigan's fiction is much like that of her male counterparts. As Tanya Brown of *Strange Horizons* points out, even before most people had home computers, "Cadigan wrote, with typical assurance, of a noisy, noirish, dystopian future, of characters overwhelmed by sheer *noise* (physical and mental), of a plethora of information conveyed in media old and new, of the breakdown of the body/technology boundary." Moreover, as one of the first authors to posit that people would actually have to pay to access the fantastic new worlds of cyberspace, Cadigan was, in many ways, even more grittily dystopian than many of her male peers.

Cadigan also used her chosen story form to continue exploring themes first raised by her feminist proto-cyberpunk counterparts. Like her early 20th-century counterparts von Harbou and Lorraine, Cadigan casts women as resourceful heroines who oppose the exploitative practices of an inherently masculinist capitalism. Indeed, while all of her major cyberpunk novels—*Mindplayers* (1987), *Synners* (1991), *Fools* (1992), *Tea from an Empty Cup* (1998), and *Dervish is Digital* (2000)—follow the noir story trajectory common to much early cyberpunk, she makes one critical change. Rather than following the adventures of a lone man whose efforts to ensure justice are compromised when he is seduced by a femme fatale who enmeshes him in corrupt and uncontrollable social, political, and legal institutions, Cadigan's protagonists are usually women whose efforts to do good in the world are compromised by men who make bad choices that enmesh them in corrupt and uncontrollable social, political, and legal systems.

Cadigan also continues the feminist proto-cyberpunk practice of using cyborg characters to critically assess the necessary relations of science, technology, and gender in technoculture. Like Kate Wilhelm and James Tiptree, Jr. before her, Cadigan sharply criticizes the technological manipulation of bodies, identities, and histories by the entertainment industry in such stories as "Pretty Boy Crossover" (1986) and "The Final Remake of *The Return of Little Latin Larry* with a Completely Remastered Soundtrack and the Original Audience" (1997). However, she also pays homage to Samuel Delany, Joanna Russ, and Vonda McIntyre with characters who technologically transform themselves to better work and play in their various futures. This is most apparent in *Synners*, which begins with a character offering another "change for the machines" (Cadigan 105). While the speaker of this quote intends to provide someone else with coins for a nearby vending machine, "change for the machines" quickly emerges as a central conceit of Cadigan's novel. Indeed, while earlier authors generally imagined just one or two different ways that humans might merge with their machines, Cadigan provides a panoply of cyborg characters with distinct relations to the physical and virtual worlds, albeit in a decidedly gendered manner: Male characters either abandon their physical bodies for the virtual world or insist on holding the former completely apart from the latter (usually with disastrous effects), while female characters experiment with a range of messier, more complex relations that include sharing real-world memories by digital means and using human bodies to power, reboot, and even radically restructure the technological and economic arrangements of their world.[1]

The manner by which Cadigan's novel depicts gender lends credence to some of the more pointed criticisms leveled against cyberpunk in general. For example, in "Cyberpunk: Preparing for Revolution or Keeping the Boys Satisfied?," Nicola Nixon argued that cyberpunk was an antifeminist mode of storytelling that gutted the future of meaningful female actors and cast both cyberspace and corporations as feminized spaces to be penetrated and tamed by male hackers more interested in profit than revolution. Just a few years later, Karen Cadora's "Feminist Cyberpunk" acknowledged the masculinist nature of 1980s cyberpunk, remarking that "[m]asculinist cyberpunk is very much a boys' club. The protagonists of cyberpunk novels are nearly always male.

When women do appear, they hardly ever transcend feminine stereotypes" and, frankly, "there are precious few female characters at all in cyberpunk" (358). Nevertheless, Cadora acknowledges that Cadigan disrupts both gender and sexuality in *Synners*, helping to launch a "first-wave" of feminist cyberpunk that made women central to the high-tech future and celebrated the potential of transgressed human/machine/animal boundaries without forgetting the exploitation of real women.[2]

Even as Cadigan pioneered a strain of feminist-friendly cyberpunk, she did not go at it alone. Science fiction authors including Candas Jane Dorsey, Gwyneth Jones, and Lisa Mason experimented with the form as well. Like most of Cadigan's fiction, Jones's *Escape Plans* (1986), Dorsey's "(Learning About) Machine Sex" (1988), and Mason's *Arachne* (1990) put women at the front and center of their cyberpunk worlds; Jones goes so far as to imagine a future where only women can interface with machines in the manner necessary to maintain human civilization. Meanwhile, in *Red Spider White Web* (1990), Métis-Nordic author Misha Nogha speculated about what the cyberpunk future might be like for people who do not have the economic or cultural privilege of chasing adventure among virtual fields of data. Outside the sf community, avant-garde author Kathy Acker literally appropriated and transformed masculine narratives of cyberpunk (most prominently working with William Gibson's *Neuromancer* [1984] in her novel *Empire of the Senseless* [1988]) to explore how the technological reorganization of identity might liberate women from patriarchal exploitation.

5.3 Second-Wave Feminist Cyberpunk: 1990–2005

By the 1990s, the proliferation of cyberpunk-themed Hollywood films, coupled with the development of the Internet and the rise of Web 1.0, led many of the original male authors associated with cyberpunk to dismiss it as dead. But Cadigan and her peers continued to write cyberpunk from feminist perspectives, and they were soon joined by a new group of female and nonbinary authors. Like their predecessors, this second-wave of cyberpunk authors celebrated women as technological experts. For example, stories such as Marge Piercy's *He, She and It* (a.k.a. *Body of Glass*; 1991), Melissa Scott's *Trouble and Her Friends* (1994), Edith Forbes's *Exit to Reality* (1997), and Lyda Morehouse's *AngelLINK* series (*Archangel Protocol*, 2001; *Fallen Host*, 2002; *Messiah Node*, 2003; *Apocalypse Array*, 2004), all feature women who are authorities in cyberspace, whether they exert that authority legally as data analysts and cybercops (Piercy, Scott, Morehouse) or illegally as hackers (Piercy, Scott, Forbes).

Other writers imagined cyberpunk-inspired worlds where women are experts in similarly complex technologies. For example, the protagonists of Laura J. Mixon's *Glass Houses* (1992) and *Proxies* (1998) operate waldos of all shapes and sizes; the heroine of Kathleen Ann Goonan's *Queen City Jazz* (1994) manipulates pheromone-driven nanotechnologies; the central character of Deborah Teramis Christian's *Mainline* (1996) hacks the web of timelines surrounding her world; and the young ork girl around whom Lisa Smedman's *Shadowrun 23: The Lucifer Deck* (1997) revolves wields power over a magic-infused Internet. Women even transformed the conventional gendering of cyberspace itself. This is particularly apparent in *Midnight Robber* (2000), where Nalo Hopkinson replaces conventional representations of cyberspace as a feminine space to be penetrated by male heroes with Granny Nanny, a still-feminine but decidedly active network that intervenes into the physical world to guide her human children toward socially-just futures.

Feminists creating second-wave cyberpunk in the 1990s and early 2000s also used their chosen story form to explore sex and gender identities outside the heteronormative matrix. Novels by self-identified queer and nonbinary authors, including Scott's *Trouble and Her Friends*, Raphael Carter's *The Fortunate Fall* (1996), and Forbes's *Exit to Reality*, appropriate the classic cyberpunk image of the economically marginalized computer hacker to give voice to the experience of sexually marginalized groups, casting their hacker protagonists as both economic and sexual outlaws. Meanwhile, tales by straight authors of this era, such as Syne Mitchell's *Technogenesis* (2002) and Marianne de Pierres's *Nylon Angel* (2004), imagine worlds where queer, nonbinary, and asexual people live unremarkably alongside their straight, cis-gendered counterparts. In an interesting variant on this theme, Wilhelmina Baird's *Crashcourse* (1993) follows the adventures of three hackers involved in an emotionally and economically committed but sexually open ménage-a-trois. Furthermore, writers of all persuasions frequently explored how technology might uncouple gender from biology altogether, as characters from the novels written by Piercy, Scott, and Forbes inhabit multiple sexual identities in their online romances.

However, even as they celebrated the possibilities inherent in new technological and sexual arrangements, women and nonbinary authors were quick to acknowledge that old forms of discrimination might well persist in the cyberpunk future. De Pierres's *Nylon Angel* imagines that the economic and sexual partnerships that are a staple of early cyberpunk might all too easily become a new form of female chattel; in a similar vein, Hopkinson's *Midnight Robber* warns that men who fail to live up to conventional cyberpunk images of success will take their anger out on the women and children around them. Even as they appropriate the figure of the hacker for their own progressive political ends, queer and nonbinary authors such as Scott, Carter, and Forbes grimly predict that the fall of traditional social and political institutions might well amplify sex and gender discrimination. Race relations also remain problematic in cyberpunk futures such as Hopkinson's *Brown Girl in the Ring* (1998), which follows the adventures of a poor, black, single mother living in post-apocalyptic Toronto who must save her family and city from the predatory rule of drug-selling, organ-stealing gangsters.[3] Taken together, such authors challenged traditional visions of a cool, apolitical cyberpunk future by directing attention to the persistence of real-world social injustice both within and outside cyberspace.

Perhaps because they remained sensitive to ongoing issues of social justice, second-wave feminist cyberpunk writers were also quick to imagine worlds where women enact revolution. These revolutions often begin as romantic relationships, including the straight liaisons of Goonan's *Queen City Jazz* and Hopkinson's *Brown Girl in the Ring*, the lesbian romances that drive Scott's *Trouble and Her Friends* and Anne Harris's *Accidental Creatures* (1998), and the cross-species romances of Piercy's *He, She and It* and Morehouse's *AngelLINK* series. Such relationships both affirm characters' connections to the alternative communities represented by their love interests and prompt them to confront the institutionalized forces that threaten those communities. Whether they lead small-scale revolutions to preserve individual families (as in Piercy, Goonan, and Baird) or large-scale revolutions that change the balance of power in cyberspace (Scott, Smedman, Mitchell, and Hopkinson) and the physical world (Piercy, Carter, Harris, Hopkinson, and Morehouse), the protagonists of second-wave feminist cyberpunk insist that passion for others can drive change across communities, continents, and realities. In sum, while early cyberpunk extrapolated from emergent technological and economic arrangements to predict largely dystopian futures where individuals could not rely on either governments or corporations to save them, the feminist strain of what is sometimes called 'post-cyberpunk'—after it became clear that those new arrangements did not herald the immediate end of the world—tends to take a more tempered look at the cyberpunk future, even imagining that people might work together to make new technologies and economic systems operate more benignly for all.[4]

5.4 Third-Wave Feminist Cyberpunk: 2005–Present[5]

Since the mid-2000s, a third generation of women and nonbinary authors has joined its predecessors in creating a new wave of feminist cyberpunk that responds to the promises and perils of a 30-year-old Internet shared by multiple generations of users and the proliferation of social media and related Web 2.0 technologies that foster ever greater digital connectivity. Given this increased linkage across time and space, it is no surprise that this new generation of feminist cyberpunk often revolves around family. For example, N.K. Jemisin's "Too Many Yesterdays, Not Enough Tomorrows" (2004) and Ren Warom's *Escapology* (2011) both feature the isolated hacker characters of earlier cyberpunk. In each case, however, it is revealed that the story's protagonists are not alienated by the economic arrangements of their worlds but by personal experiences with families and communities who reject them. By way of contrast, Elizabeth Bear's "Two Dreams on Trains" (2005) and Isabel Yap's "Serenade" (2016) shift focus from the exploits of the conventional cyberpunk protagonist to the lives of the people who love them. While Bear's story maps the heartbreak of a mother whose son chooses the life of an impoverished artist-criminal over steady corporate employment, Yap's tale explores the complex feelings that two young people experience when their terminally ill adoptive hacker father refuses to upload his mind into a new body. While first-wave feminist cyberpunks such as Pat Cadigan often used failed relationships to explore women's alienation from emergent technocultural arrangements and second-wave feminist cyberpunks such as Melissa Scott used stories about falling in love to imagine how progressive people might connect and build better futures for all, current authors such as Jemisin and Yap use families as focusing lenses through which to explore how people might live long and prosper in socioeconomic futures even more complex than our own present.

Contemporary feminist cyberpunk's focus on families that extend across time and space is closely connected to its emphasis on slow revolution. Chris Moriarty's Spin series (*Spin State*, 2003; *Spin Control*, 2006; *Ghost Spin*, 2013) revolves around the adventures of a far-future augmented human and her pansexual AI lover as they negotiate the collapse of the human empire and the war between various species for control of the future; at the same time, Madeline Ashby's Machine Dynasty series (*vN*, 2012; *iD*, 2013, *reV*, 2015) relates the multigenerational saga of a hybrid human-AI family that must contend with a very real religious Rapture that changes the balance of power between humans and machines on Earth. Nnedi Okorafor's *The Book of Phoenix* (2015) does not provide much detail regarding the radical changes that occur between the main action of the book (set in a near-future much like our own present) and the frame narrative (which takes place in a far-future post-oil society), but the very lack of detail only underscores how long and complex the process of change can be. Such stories stand in sharp contrast to Cadigan's *Synners*, where globe-spanning technological and economic networks are destroyed and rebuilt in a matter of weeks, and Hopkinson's *Brown Girl in the Ring*, in which the Canadian government is destroyed and rebuilt in a matter of years. While earlier generations may have envisioned digital revolutions happening quickly because digital technologies were themselves new phenomenon, contemporary authors who have witnessed multiple generations and iterations of digital technologies treat revolution as a slow process that takes place over great spans of time and space.

5.5 Feminist Cyberpunk in Other Media

Print sf might be one of the most exciting spaces where feminists experiment with stories about cybertechnologies, gender, and futurity, but it is by no means the only one. Feminists have long used other media including magazines, films, and Internet itself to explore these issues. Like their counterparts in proto–cyberpunk sf, feminists of the 1960s and 1970s criticized a seemingly ubiquitous media landscape that replaced reality with sexist advertising and entertainment. These concerns came together in the 1979 feminist documentary *Killing Us Softly: Advertising's Image of Women* (dir. Margaret Lazarus, Renner Wunderlich, Patricia Stallone, and Joseph Vitagliano). They were also expressed in art pieces such as Dara Birnbaum's short experimental video *Technology/Transformation: Wonder Woman* (1978), which appropriates images from the television show of the same name to explore how even the most liberating images of women might be frozen, manipulated, and otherwise appropriated to patriarchal ends.

Feminists of this era also explored how they might appropriate new media technologies for their own politically progressive ends. For example, journalist-activists Gloria Steinem and Dorothy Pitman Hughes sought to transform the magazine industry with the launch of *Ms.*, which they created in the early 1970s because, as Steinem later put it, "there really was nothing for women to read that was controlled by women" (*Gloria in Her Own Words*). Meanwhile, Lizzie Borden's sf film *Born in Flames* (1983) imagined a near-future U.S. where women seize control of radio and recording technologies to protest the ongoing exploitation of their economic and reproductive labor and incite a revolution. Taken together, the new relations between gender and media forged by Steinem and Pitman Hughes and celebrated on celluloid by Borden very much mirror those imagined by authors such as Samuel Delany, Joanna Russ, and Vonda McIntyre in the pages of various sf books and magazines.

This pattern of feminist critique and creative transformation also informed feminist responses to new digital technologies. With the advent of home computing in the 1980s and the birth of the World Wide Web in the 1990s, a new generation of self-described cyberfeminists encouraged women to disrupt, re-gender, and take over what was already seen as an aggressively masculine Internet. As Rosi Braidotti explains, "one of the greatest contradictions of Virtual Reality images is that they titillate our imagination, promising the marvels of a gender-free world [while simultaneously reproducing] some of the most banal, flat images of gender identity [...] that you can think of." As such, "the most effective strategy remains for women to use technology in order to disengage from the phallus and its accessory values: money, exclusion and domination, nationalism, iconic femininity and systemic violence" (Braidotti) while imagining a range of differently-gendered subjects with alternate values. Cyberfeminists of the 1990s and early 2000s were also bound together by a certain playful revolutionary fervor. As Braidotti put it: "there is a war going on and women are not pacifists [...]. We want to put up some active resistance, but we also want to have fun and do it our way."

Accordingly, the first generation of feminist cyberartists staked claims for themselves as both technoscientific and sexual revolutionaries on the digital frontier. For example, Australian art collective VNS Matrix challenges masculinist representations of the Internet as a passive, feminine body to be penetrated by men and to the literal masculinization of online spaces with art that casts women as the heroes of their own technoscientific adventures and re-imagines the Internet itself as a distinctly active female space. Or, as they have provocatively argued in their "Cyberfeminist Manifesto," "[t]he clitoris is a direct line to the matrix [...] infiltrating disrupting disseminating/corrupting the discourse/we are the future cunt." In a related but seemingly gentler vein, Mohawk digital artist Skawennati's CyberPowWow, an online chat room/artist's gallery that ran from 1997 to 2004, staked claims for Indigenous people in the digital realm. Offering people a safe and aesthetically rich space to connect with each other and share their ideas about Indigenous pasts, presents, and futures, CyberPowWow very much embodied Braidotti's claim that cyberfeminism is not just about critique and anger, but about community and fun as well.

Cyberfeminists continue to grapple with the promises and perils of digital technologies, including the rise of social media and Web 2.0 technologies. As the artists associated with the Laboria Cuboniks collective argue in their "Xenofeminism" manifesto, there are a "range of gendered challenges specific to life in the digital age—from sexual harassment via social media, to doxing, privacy, and the protection of online images." Accordingly, women and other progressive-minded people must "equip themselves with the skills to redeploy existing technologies and invent novel cognitive and material tools in the service of common ends." While contemporary cyberfeminists make arguments for scientific and social revolution much like those of their predecessors, they often advocate a more gradual approach to change. As Laboria Cuboniks puts it, new modes of inclusive, technologically-savvy feminism are "not a bid for revolution, but a wager on the long game of history, demanding imagination, dexterity, and persistence."

Women and other feminist-friendly people put these insights to work in both everyday practice and art. Kishonna L. Gray explains that women of color use digital technologies and social media (such as 'Black Twitter') to disrupt negative narratives of black femininity disseminated by the mainstream media and "to capture the uniqueness of marginalized women" (176). They perform this double operation by employing "diverse ways of speaking" and incorporating "music [...] poetry or spoken word [...] or other cultural art forms in their online lives" (187). Elsewhere, artists associated with the Cybertwee Collective propose that women and other marginalized people might take back the Internet by using tactics that have been historically devalued as "cute" or "femme":

> [F]ar too long we have succumbed to the bitter edge of the idea that power is lost in the sweet and tender... sentimentality, empathy, and being too soft should not be seen as weaknesses [...] Our *sucre* sickly sweet is intentional and not just a lure or trap for passing flies, but a self-indulgent, intrapersonal biofeedback mechanism spelled in emojis and gentle selfies. (Emphasis added)

The Collective demonstrated the political potential of cuteness with their 2015 Dark Web Bake Sale, which aimed to domesticate the dark web—a space notorious for both cybercrime and rampant racism and sexism—by providing volunteers with $15 of bitcoin and instructions on how to spend it on cupcakes the collective sold online. Much like their literary counterparts N.K. Jemisin, Rem Warom, and Chris Moriarty, cyberfeminists associated with such recent phenomena as Black Twitter and the Dark Web Bake Sale celebrate the kind of "feminism at ease with computation" that has long been central to feminist cyberpunk and that is increasingly part of all people's lives today (Laboria Cuboniks).

Notes

1 For an extended analysis of Cadigan's *Synners*, see Ritch Calvin's contribution to this collection.
2 More recently, in *Cyberpunk Women, Feminism, and Science Fiction*, Carlen Lavigne has extended that first-wave of feminist cyberpunk from 1981 to 2003.
3 For an extended analysis of race and cyberpunk, see Isiah Lavender III's chapters on this subject matter in this collection.
4 For further discussion of 'post-cyberpunk,' see the introduction to James Patrick Kelly and John Kessel's *Rewired: The Post-Cyberpunk Anthology* and Christopher D. Kilgore's chapter in this volume.
5 While a few of the stories mentioned in this section fall a year or two outside the exact dates that I associate with third-wave feminist cyberpunk, I would note that such dates are meant largely to describe when the majority of this type of fiction is produced.

Works Cited

Braidotti, Rosi. "Cyberfeminism with a Difference." *Disability Studies*, 1996, pp. 1–12, disabilitystudies.nl/sites/disabilitystudies.nl/files/beeld/onderwijs/cyberfeminism_with_a_difference.pdf.

Brown, Tanya. "Pat Cadigan: A Retrospective." *Strange Horizons*, 29 Aug. 2011, strangehorizons.com/non-fiction/articles/pat-cadigan-a-retrospective/.

Cadigan, Pat. *Synners*. Gollancz, 2012.

Cadora, Karen. "Feminist Cyberpunk." *Science Fiction Studies*, vol. 22, no. 3, 1995, pp. 357–72.

Gloria: In Her Own Words. Directed by Peter Kunhardt, Kunhardt Productions, 2011, hbo.com/documentaries/gloria-in-her-own-words.

Gray, Kishonna L. "Race, Gender, and Virtual Inequality: Exploring the Liberatory Potential of Black Cyberfeminist Theory." *Producing Theory in a Digital World: The Intersection of Audiences and Production in Contemporary Theory*, edited by Rebecca Ann Lind. Lang, 2012, pp. 175–92.

Hilleman, Gabriela, Violet Forest, and May Waver. "The Cybertwee Manifesto." *Cybertwee*, 2014, cybertwee. net/the_manifesto/.

Kelly, James Patrick and John Kessel, eds. *Rewired: The Post-Cyberpunk Anthology*. Tachyon, 2007.

Laboria Cuboniks. "Xenofeminism: A Politics for Alienation." *XF Manifesto*, 2015, laboriacuboniks. net/#firstPage.

Lavigne, Carlen. *Cyberpunk Women, Feminism, and Science Fiction*. McFarland, 2013.

Lorraine, Lilith. "Into the 28th Century." *Science Wonder Quarterly*, vol. 1, no. 2, 1930, pp. 250–67.

Moore, C.L. "No Woman Born." *The Best of C.L. Moore*, edited by Lester Del Rey. Ballantine, 1975, pp. 236–88.

Nixon, Nicola. "Cyberpunk: Preparing the Ground for Revolution or Keeping the Boys Satisfied?" *Science Fiction Studies*, vol. 19, no. 2, 1992, pp. 219–35.

Pringle, David, and Peter Nicholls. "Media Landscape." *The Encyclopedia of Science Fiction*, edited by John Clute et al., 2018, sf-encyclopedia.com/entry/media_landscape.

Joanna Russ. *The Female Man*. Beacon, 1986.

VNS Matrix. "The Cyberfeminist Manifesto for the Twenty-First Century." *VNS Matrix: Merchants of Slime*, 1991, vnsmatrix.net/the-cyberfeminist-manifesto-for-the-21st-century/.

6

PAT CADIGAN: *SYNNERS* (CASE STUDY)

Ritch Calvin

Pat Cadigan's published writing career began with "Last Chance for Angina Pectoris at Miss Sadie's Saloon, Dry Gulch" (1977), which appeared in *Chacol #2*, a fiction magazine that she edited with Arnie Fenner. Her fourteenth story, "Rock On" (1984), however, brought her science fiction (sf) into the cyberpunk orbit. While "Rock On" initially appeared in Michael Bishop's edited collection *Light Years and Dark* (1984) and was reprinted in Gardner Dozois's *The Year's Best Science Fiction: Second Annual Collection* (1985), its inclusion in Bruce Sterling's *Mirrorshades: The Cyberpunk Anthology* (1986) cemented her status as a key figure in cyberpunk's initial heyday. Although cyberpunk advocate and evangelist Bruce Sterling identifies five writers as constituting the original "Movement's most fearsome 'gurus'" of cyberpunk, including William Gibson, Rudy Rucker, Lewis Shiner, John Shirley, and Sterling himself ("Cyberpunk"), Tom Maddox includes Cadigan as part of cyberpunk's core ("After the Deluge") since she not only appears in *Mirrorshades* but was involved from the Movement's earliest beginnings in *Cheap Truth*, Sterling's xeroxed 'zine which "became a polemical vehicle to critique so-called staid sf and promote the revolutionary fervor of a new generation of authors looking to shake up the establishment and sell their stories" (Murphy, "*Mirrorshades*" 15–16). Sterling was well aware of Cadigan's work, calling her (and others) out as a "particularly heartening" writer and subtly including her in cyberpunk's core. If William Gibson is therefore the "'king of cyberpunk'" (Nixon 222), then Pat Cadigan is the "Queen of Cyberpunk" (Gillis 49) thanks in no small part to "Rock On," "Pretty Boy Crossover" (1986), and the novels *Mindplayers* (1987), *Synners* (1991), *Fools* (1992), *Tea from an Empty Cup* (1998), and *Dervish is Digital* (2000).

Sterling identifies Cadigan's *Mindplayers* as an "absolute must-have" ("Cyberpunk Library"). It garnered second place in the annual *Locus* poll for Best Novel and was a finalist for the Philip K. Dick Award. Her second novel, *Synners*, garnered even more praise[1] as it successfully translates "the street-wise, cyberpunk involvedness of her best short fiction into a comprehensive vision […] a world dominated by the intricacies of the human/computer interface" (Clute 184), an interface embodied by human synthesizers, or synners, previously seen in "Rock On." These synners direct, produce, and edit music videos through direct neural interface and manipulation. In typical cyberpunk fashion, *Synners* takes place in a dystopian, near-future, perpetually congested Los Angeles; for example, all traffic in and around LA is controlled by GridLid, a computerized traffic system that only results in traffic snarls and road rage. GridLid functions as an organizing metaphor for the novel since all denizens of LA and their movements are determined by the app—and they are constantly antagonized by it.

In its exploration of the effects of technologies upon the end users, the plot centers on three constellations of characters and events. The first constellation follows the synners Beater, Gina Aiesi, and 'Visual Mark' and their rock video company EyeTraxx. But times are tough, so Beater hires Hall Galen and Lindel Joslin to develop a direct brain/net interface. However, the interface sockets draw the attention of other corporations, and EyeTraxx is acquired by the multinational conglomerate Diversifications, Inc. All three rock 'n roll rebels now work for corporate America. The second constellation follows several mid-level employees of Diversifications, Inc., including manager Immanuel 'Manny' Rivera and ad creator Gabe Ludovic. A disaffected husband, father, and employee, Gabe escapes into a completely interactive virtual space that he has created, inhabited by digital companions Marly and Caritha. Meanwhile, Gabe's daughter, Cassandra 'Sam' Ludovic, emancipates herself from her parents and lives among a hacker community that survives on the outskirts of LA. Finally, the third constellation follows the hacker community itself, including the guru Fez and his disciples Sam, Rosa, and Adrian. When the hacker Keely steals the plans for the 'sockets' from Diversifications, Inc., he splits the information and sends half to Sam and half to Fez.

On the one hand, critics and commentators have applauded the novel for its narrative complexities. Elizabeth Hand calls it "densely plotted, rich in character and finely detailed settings" (5) and Sadie Plant argues that the text has "extraordinary density and intensity, both in terms of [the] writing and the worlds [it] engineers" (334). On the other hand, even a cursory review of literary cyberpunk's emergence cannot hide a glaring fact: Pat Cadigan is the only woman in the club. Cadigan has addressed this point directly, stating: "I'll tell you honestly: I don't know. Statistical anomaly, maybe. There really weren't any other women writers at the time who were doing the kind of writing that I was" (Velazquez). Nevertheless, cyberpunk was not particularly amenable to feminism, as both Karen Cadora and Nicola Nixon have argued, seeing cyberpunk as being "complicit with '80s conservatism" (Nixon 231) with nearly universally "hypermasculine" protagonists who do not engage in "sexual politics" (Cadora 357), a key focus of critique to feminist scholars. Furthermore, Carlen Lavigne notes that cyberpunk's usual representation of counterpolitics rarely reflects or addresses the social and political issues of the time, specifically "feminism, ecology, peace, sexual liberation, and civil rights" (21). *Synners* can therefore be read as a partial corrective to cyberpunk's masculinist futures, despite Cadora's claim that "Cadigan never fully engaged with feminist concerns" (358).[2] Namely, *Synners* foregrounds and centers feminism, ecological concerns, and sexual liberation, by including and developing women characters in the novel, and by drawing from feminist (and other) theories of identity and embodiment. To this end, Cadigan populates the novel with roughly equal numbers of male and female characters. Furthermore, Gina insists on retaining her female-embodied experience and rescues Mark on a regular basis. Meanwhile, Gabe's wife castigates him as a lazy slacker, while succeeding professionally herself. And finally, their daughter and accomplished hacker, Sam, is a central figure in the battle with an online virus that threatens all of cyberspace. Without resorting to simple role reversals, Cadigan depicts her women characters as complex, embodied beings. Therefore, *Synners* emerges as a novel that represents women fully engaged in multiple aspects of society and community, in a full range of personal and professional roles. In that sense, the novel represents the identity politics of second-wave feminism and, as Lisa Yaszek demonstrates in her contribution to this collection, is at the forefront of a feminist wave of cyberpunk that defined the early 1990s.[3]

While it has feminist potential, *Synners* might be better read as a proto-queer text. As Wendy Gay Pearson establishes in "Alien Cryptographies: The View from Queer," proto-queer texts are those texts that "effect a kind of discursive challenge to the naturalized understanding of sexuality and its concomitant sociocultural surround" (19). As such, a proto-queer text might represent a variety of sexualities and sexual practices; it might rupture the simplistic alignment of body and gender, or body and sexuality; it might expand representations of the body and embodied experience—and the role this plays in everything from identity to epistemology to sexuality; and it might push at the limits of what sf (or cyberpunk) represents. Pearson argues that queer cannot be reduced to sexuality, but that queer also points to—opens up the space for—an expanded articulation of "subjectivity and agency" (17). A queer text (and, to some extent, a proto-queer text) marks a shift from the identity politics of feminism toward a more fluid politics of identity.[4] In this regard, *Synners* expands the representation of sexualities and practices, ruptures the relationship between body and identity via its embodied experience, and pushes sf's boundaries.

As is quite common for early cyberpunk, most of the characters in the novel identify as heterosexual, including Gabe, Sam, Hall Galen, Lindel Joslin, Catherine, and so forth. At the same time, however, a queer undercurrent extends through the novel well beyond the Jones/Keely same-sex relationship or Cadigan's description of Gina as a "flaming hetero" (141), a description that queers heterosexuality in evoking the at-times derogatory, at-times celebratory "flaming homo" designation, situating heterosexuality as no default but, rather, a place on a larger spectrum. *Synners*'s queer undercurrent, however, is fueled by Cadigan's depiction of the interface technology. One of cyberpunk's enduring, iconic images is the notion of 'jacking in,' the image of an electrode literally penetrating the skin of the cybersurfer, or of the surfer metaphorically penetrating cyberspace itself. This clearly sexual metaphor appeared earlier in Samuel Delany's *Nova* (1968), James Tiptree, Jr.'s "The Girl Who Was Plugged In" (1973), and John Brunner's *The Shockwave Rider* (1975).[5] Graham J. Murphy further elaborates that cyberspace has frequently been compared (in fiction and in criticism) to the female body, as a space developed, controlled, and entered by men ("Stray" 123). The metaphor of 'jacking in' therefore reveals cyberpunk's systemic preoccupation with heterosexuality, at least until queer cyberpunk such as Mary Rosenblum's *Chimera* (1993) and Melissa Scott's *Trouble and Her Friends* (1994), both of which appeared shortly after *Synners*. And yet, *Synners*'s use of socket technology entirely reimagined, and ultimately rejected, 'jacking in' and the depiction of a cyberspace as a (female) space awaiting (male) penetration. The sockets connect directly to the limbic system, the seat of emotions, and are so small that they cannot be 'jacked in' but connect via 'tropism.' Of the eight implants, one socket connects to each of the temporal lobes (enhance data input), parietal lobes (experience motion and moving), frontal lobes (creativity), auditory cortex, and visual cortex (sound and imaging) (66–67). This direct stimulation of the brain creates an experience of the entire body, including emotions; therefore, while the eight connections *do* penetrate into the organic female sheaths that reside in the brain, the connection ultimately provides a full-body, corporeal-digital experience. In short, the organic-mechanical process fully interpenetrates the brain, triggering a simultaneously embodied and disembodied experience. The user does not 'jack in' using socket technology; rather, the sockets connect to the brain and body in an intimate, penetrative fashion.

The virus that threatens cyberspace is the result of Visual Mark's obsessive quest to achieve digital disembodiment; however, a physical stroke at the time of upload transforms into a digital spike that proves terminal for all it encounters. Visual Mark's salvation from the stroke-spike involves a queer-tinged union with an artificial intelligence (AI). Although Art(ie) Fish is a digitally non-corporeal program, he explicitly self-identifies as *masculine* in both figure and persona. In this example, neither Artie's gender nor sexuality is grounded in a corporeal body; instead, his gender and sexuality are entirely digitally constructed. Nevertheless, when the masculinized AI joins with Mark to become Markt—i.e., two disembodied males conjoining—we see both figures "settling down for a long-term intimate relationship," clearly showing cyberspace can offer "a union that transcends mere heterosexual intercourse" (Cadora 362). In an example of what Pearson means when (citing Edmond Chang) she writes that "'cyberspace is queer'" but also that cyberspace "queers whatever it touches" ("Queer Theory" 306), the queer union of Artie and Mark into Markt undercuts the image of the seemingly inviolable, masculine console cowboy that is a hallmark of cyberpunk.

Synners obviously taps into the questions of dis/embodiment that have most certainly been central to cyberpunk fiction, and critics observe these questions are often split along gender lines. Austin Booth (among many others) argues that male cyberpunk writers have "privileged disembodiment over embodiment" and that their male characters long for a "technological transcendence" (34). In connecting mind with cyberspace and body with meat, traditional cyberpunk ostensibly reifies the Cartesian mind/body split, leaving the western, masculine desire for mind intact and unchallenged.[6] Therefore, traditional cyberpunk "appeals to the (impossible) desire to escape the vicissitudes of the body and occupy the place of self-mastery" (Vint 104). Finally, as Lavigne notes, while male cyberpunk writers have tended to laud the masculine (console) cowboy, individual struggle against systems of control, and problematic fantasies of (dis)embodiment in digital domains, women cyberpunk writers tend to emphasize the "importance of community support in the face of alienating multinational capitalism" (31). What separates *Synners* from contemporaneous cyberpunk offerings, however, is its proto-queerness which complicates masculinist desires for disembodiment and ruptures the simple (and simplified) binary of mind and body.

In *Technologies of the Gendered Body*, Anne Balsamo offers a matrix of the four kinds of bodies (and embodiments) represented in *Synners* (220). She argues that Sam represents the laboring body while Mark represents the disappearing body; similarly, Gabe is the repressed body, and Gina is the marked body. As the only real hacker among the principal characters, Sam integrates mind and body; namely, while her knowledge of software and hardware is prodigious, her body serves as the energy source for a modified insulin pump that allows Mark and Artie to merge in the first place. In other words, Markt's non-corporeal existence is entirely predicated upon Sam's corporeality. Even before he becomes Markt, however, Mark prefers disembodiment; his desire is to exist as purely mind in the net. Because of the commercial potential of his hyperactive visual cortex, Mark receives the physical socket implants first, again only achieving his desired disembodiment thanks to very real, or 'meatspace,' technologies. Nevertheless, Mark very quickly retreats into the digital web, leaving his body lying inert in his workspace. Once Mark believes he has transcended his bodily limitations, he "punningly becomes a 'mark' visible on a computer screen" (Harper 412). Sensing an impending stroke upon his meat self, Mark finds his way through the web to the hacker Keely's apartment and implores Keely to physically sever the tie between his equipment and his body: His corporeal self threatens his disembodied state. Unfortunately, Keely arrives too late: Mark strokes out, and the resultant digital 'spike' wends its way through the body of the web, shutting down systems and wreaking havoc. While Mark's body may have disappeared, the upload of its corporeal trace threatens digital reality.

Although he spends a lot of time online, Gabe does not wish to leave his body, although he has repressed the physical enjoyment of his body. Emasculated at home and work, alienated from his wife and daughter, Gabe seeks solace in a virtual reality (VR) simulation that he shares with Marly and Caritha. Only in VR does Gabe experience contentment or control. Even so, after plot developments eventually lead to a sexual interlude with Gina, he recalls, "[h]e had forgotten exactly how good it felt, for real, not in a hotsuit" (200). While he also receives sockets that allow him to merge more fully with his virtual construct, in the end Gabe retreats into the countryside and eschews all web interface. In part, his emotional and physical relationship with Gina has reminded him of the pleasures of the flesh, and he remains embodied.

Synners also illustrates the connection between embodiment and race. As a woman of color, Gina cannot escape her own body in the same way that Mark and Gabe can, whether permanently or temporarily. Instead, Gina is constantly reminded of just how much she is defined by her body. Whereas Mark is described as "skin and bones, with lank brown Jesus-length hair, a broken nose, [and] faded green eyes" (14), Gina is a "soul sister" (141), with dark skin and dreadlocks. Other characters often refer to her physical attributes—her "strong features" (89), "physical strength," and "power in her muscles" (403–04)—or her behavior and attitude, including her "energetic mix of anger, fear, and ready aggression" (396). As María Fernández notes in "Cyberfeminism, Racism, and Embodiment," "Black bodies are represented trapped in the web of nature while white bodies have freedom of movement. Such a freedom disembodies whiteness" (38). After Mark and Artie merge to become Markt, Gina reminds them, "She could have told them who was *really* fucking *marked*" (390). In other words, as Mark disappears from the physical world and becomes a digital 'mark,' Gina's body is always marked as gendered and raced. She does not retreat from the corporeal world but insists upon real and authentic experiences to ground her synning. She incorporates physical experiences into her virtual videos and suggests that reality can only be experienced through the body. Indeed, "Gina argues again and again (with her fists too, causing 'real' pain) for the authenticity of the embodied" (Calvert and Walsh 100). In a manner comparable to Cadigan's earlier short story "Pretty Boy Crossover," Gina tells Gabe that "[o]nly the embodied can *really* boogie all night in a hit-and-run, or jump off a roof attached to bungi cords" (433).[7] Even though Gina leaves her original body behind and enters the web to merge with Markt (and Marly and Caritha), she also desires a physical body in order to "boogie," thus inhabiting a cloned body in which all her marks remain. Therefore, whereas Gina's racial embodiment seems inescapable, the novel simultaneously notes that her role is coded and read via the 'marks' (physical, cultural, historical) on her body.[8]

Finally, Fredric Jameson has famously remarked that cyberpunk is "the supreme *literary* expression if not of postmodernism, then of late capitalism itself" (419), and cyberpunk often addresses the rampant proliferation of global capital and multinational corporations within the postmodern condition. As Sharon Stockton remarks, in cyberpunk, "the alienated capital of early capitalism has grown into the alienated information capital of late capitalism" (589). On one level, *Synners* is no different from other literary cyberpunk: The "representations of technoscience [in the novel] reflect representations of a discourse which interacts with capitalism in the fictional world as in the real world" (Chernaik 61). Indeed, nearly every character and event revolves around the multinational corporation Diversifications, Inc. and its alienating effects on society and individuals. As a result, the real content of *Synners* resides in the various technological impacts on human lives: "the capitalist production of electronic addictions, the recording practices of video vigilantes, or the multiplication of television channels devoted to new forms of pornography: disasterporn, medporn, food porn" (Balsamo 139). At the same time, *Synners* suggests a world in which gender and sexuality can be not-unproblematically disconnected from a corporeal body, in which identities are not necessarily essentialized but discursive 'marks' to be read, and in which new identities (embodied and disembodied) are formed.

At the same time, while *Synners* may parallel other supreme literary expressions of the period, it departs from much of cyberpunk in its relation to the postmodern. For example, Gina longs for an embodied experience and some sort of completion with Mark, Sam longs to leave the hacker community and find an appropriate relationship, and Gabe checks out of technologized society and starts living a country life. These all testify to Vint's claim that *Synners* reaffirms the centrality of "community" and "human relations" (116–17). Therefore, while cyberpunk is often aligned with the postmodern representation of the multiple, fractured subject, Stockton counterargues that *Synners* actually "remythologize[s] [an] earlier autonomous subject" (588), perhaps even going so far as to reinscribe a "liberal humanist feminism still hooked on defining and delimiting a unified subject for liberation" (Calvert and Walsh 106). *Synners* defies easy categorization: While some individuals long for a more simplistic, embodied existence, others reject it out of hand. Gabe may retreat to a pastoral countryside, but Mark leaves his corporeal body behind and eventually conjoins with an AI to create a new subjectivity. And Gina, the most ineluctably embodied and marked of the characters, a black woman arguing for embodied experiences, winds up as a posthuman clone, a combination of both embodied and disembodied, instantiating yet another new subjectivity.

In conclusion, *Synners* offers a direct challenge to the urban, often white, masculine fantasy of Cartesian disembodiment. *Synners* disrupts traditionally coded gender, racial, and even penetrative roles, even as in other instances it reinscribes them. In other words, the novel offers a proto-queer, ever fluctuating, vision of an intersectional near-future world. It provides a variety of sexual identities and practices; it ruptures any simplistic sex/gender = body/identity formula; it foregrounds embodiment as a place of experience and knowledge; and it pushes the characteristics of cyberpunk, at least for the time it was published. *Synners* arguably signaled the beginning of a new phase in literary cyberpunk, or what has been alternately called feminist cyberpunk or *cyberfiction*. In the case of the latter, Lavigne notes that early cyberpunk seemed to eschew the pressing politics of the day, but cyberfiction combines feminist science fiction's commitment to gender, sexuality, and race with cyberpunk's fascination with technological innovation and transformation. Operating in the same theatre, Austin Booth explains that cyberfiction may mirror cyberpunk in its depictions of dystopian narrative worlds characterized by class inequalities, pervasive structures of violence, environmental disasters, and control systems governed by multinational corporations (26), and it also eschews cyberpunk's celebratory disembodied masculinity in favor of a more nuanced blurring of identities, embodiment, and subjectivities. Finally, Cadigan has noted that VR technologies are not inherently good or bad, not inherently liberating or confining. Instead, they are "as mixed a blessing as any other new development" ("Foreword" xii), and *Synners* is all about exploring this mixed blessing. Cadigan imagines and represents the development of digital and virtual technologies within the gendered and raced context of late capitalism and features the political ramifications of gendered and raced embodiment. If read in part as a proto-queer text that, again, complicates masculinist desires for disembodiment and ruptures the simple (and simplified) binary of mind and body, *Synners* points toward new kinds of subjectivity made possible, at least in part, by way of penetrative technologies that offer the potential for (queer) re-figurations of corporeality and simulation.

Notes

1 See positive, if not glowing, reviews from Stephen Andrews, Steph Bennion, and Sadie Plant. Perhaps not surprisingly, *Synners* won the 1992 Arthur C. Clarke Award.
2 Cadigan herself says she is "a feminist writer and always have been; feminist is my default setting" (Velazquez), even though she prefers not to be labeled by gender as "female cyberpunk" or "woman science fiction writer," instead preferring simply "writer" (Gardner 50).
3 For more details on cyberpunk and feminism, see Lisa Yaszek's and Patricia Melzer's contributions in this collection.
4 For details on the queer potential of cyberpunk, see Wendy Gay Pearson's contribution to this collection.
5 See Rob Latham's contribution to this collection for discussion of each of these texts as cyberpunk precursors.
6 For a detailed analysis of cyberpunk and the physical 'meat,' see Seán McCorry's contribution to this collection.
7 In "Pretty Boy Crossover" Pretty Boy rejects an offer to be digitally downloaded into a nightclub simulation; instead, he chooses to rejoice as "long as he has flesh to shake and flaunt and feel with" (138).
8 Isiah Lavender III provides a detailed exploration of cyberpunk and race in his "Critical Race Studies" contribution, as well as his co-authored "Afrofuturism" chapter elsewhere in this collection.

Works Cited

Andrews, Stephen. "*Synners*." *100 Must-Read Science Fiction Novels*, edited by Stephen E. Andrews and Nick Rennison. A & C Black, 2006, pp. 34–45.
Balsamo, Anne. *Technologies of the Gendered Body: Reading Cyborg Women*. Duke UP, 1996.
Bennion, Steph. "Pat Cadigan, *Synners* 1991." *Big Sky*, vol. 4, 2014, p. 94, efanzines.com/bigsky/BigSky-04. pdf.

Booth, Austin. "Women's Cyberfiction: An Introduction." *Reload: Rethinking Women and Cyberculture*, edited by Mary Flanagan and Austin Booth. MIT Press, 2002, pp. 25–41.

Cadigan, Pat. "Foreword: Virtual Reality: As Real As You Want It to Be." *Virtual Reality: Applications and Explorations*, edited by Alan Wexelblat. Academic, 1993, pp. xi–xii.

———. "The Future We Promised You." *Locus*, no. 670, 2016, pp. 10–11, 54–55.

———. "Pretty Boy Crossover." *Patterns*. Tor, 1989, pp. 129–38.

———. *Synners*. Four Walls Eight Windows, 1991.

Cadora, Karen. "Feminist Cyberpunk." *Science Fiction Studies*, vol. 22, no. 3, 1995, pp. 357–72.

Calvert, Bronwen and Sue Walsh. "Speaking the Body: The Embodiment of 'Feminist' Cyberpunk." *Speaking Science Fiction: Dialogues and Interpretations*, edited by Andy Sawyer and David Seed. Liverpool UP, 2002, pp. 96–108.

Chernaik, Laura. "Pat Cadigan's *Synners*: Refiguring Nature, Science and Technology." *Feminist Review*, no. 56, 1997, pp. 61–84.

Clute, John. "Pat Cadigan." *The Encyclopedia of Science Fiction*, 2nd ed., edited by John Clute and Peter Nicholls. Orbit, 1999, pp. 183–84.

Fernández, María. "Cyberfeminism, Racism, Embodiment." *Domain Errors! Cyberfeminist Practices*, edited by María Fernández, Faith Wilding, and Michelle M. Wright. Autonomedia, 2003, pp. 29–44.

Gardner, David. "Trying to Look behind the Future." *The Fractal: Journal of Science Fiction and Fantasy*, Fall/Winter, 1996, pp. 38–55.

Gillis, Stacy. "Cadigan, Pat (1953–)." *Women in Science Fiction and Fantasy, Volume 2*, edited by Robin Anne Reid. Greenwood, 2009, p. 49.

Hand, Elizabeth. "*Synners* by Pat Cadigan, *Patterns* by Pat Cadigan." *New York Review of Science Fiction*, March, 1991, pp. 5–6.

Harper, Mary Catherine. "Incurably Alien Other: A Case for Feminist Cyborg Writers." *Science Fiction Studies*, vol. 22, no. 3, 1995, pp. 399–420.

Jameson, Fredric. *Postmodernism, or, The Cultural Logic of Late Capitalism*. Duke UP, 2005.

Lavigne, Carlen. *Cyberpunk Women: Feminism and Science Fiction*. McFarland, 2013.

Maddox, Tom. "After the Deluge: Cyberpunk in the 80s and 90s." *The Cyberpunk Project*. 1992, project. cyberpunk.ru/idb/cyberpunk_in_80-90.html.

Murphy, Graham J. "The *Mirrorshades* Collective." *The Routledge Companion to Cyberpunk Culture*, edited by Anna McFarlane, Graham J. Murphy, and Lars Schmeink. Routledge, 2020, pp. 15–23.

———. "Stray Penetration and Heteronormative Systems Crash: Proto-Queering Gibson." *Queer Universes: Sexualities in Science Fiction*, edited by Wendy Gay Pearson, Veronica Hollinger, and Joan Gordon. Liverpool UP, 2008, pp. 121–37.

Nixon, Nicola. "Cyberpunk: Preparing the Ground for Revolution of Keeping the Boys Satisfied?" *Science Fiction Studies*, vol. 19, no. 2, 1992, pp. 219–35.

Pearson, Wendy Gay. "Alien Cryptographies: The View from Queer." *Queer Universes: Sexualities in Science Fiction*, edited by Wendy Gay Pearson, Veronica Hollinger, and Joan Gordon. Liverpool UP, 2008, pp. 14–38.

———. "Queer Theory." *The Routledge Companion to Cyberpunk Culture*, edited by Anna McFarlane, Graham J. Murphy, and Lars Schmeink. Routledge, 2020, pp. 300–07.

Plant, Sadie. "On the Matrix: Cyberfeminist Simulations." *The Cybercultures Reader*, edited by David Bell and Barbara M. Kennedy. Routledge, 2000, pp. 325–36.

Sterling, Bruce. "Cyberpunk in the Nineties." *The Cyberpunk Project*, 1991, project.cyberpunk.ru/idb/ cyberpunk_in_the_nineties.html.

———. "The Cyberpunk Library." *The Cyberpunk Project*, 1992, project.cyberpunk.ru:80/idb/library.html.

Stockton, Sharon. "'The Self Regained': Cyberpunk's Retreat to the Imperium." *Contemporary Literature*, vol. 36, no. 4, 1995, pp. 588–612.

Velazquez, Maria. "20 on the 20th: Pat Cadigan." *The Hathor Legacy*, thehathorlegacy.com/20-on-the-20th-pat-cadigan/.

Vint, Sherryl. *Bodies of Tomorrow: Technology, Subversion, Science Fiction*. U of Toronto P, 2007.

7

POST-CYBERPUNK

Christopher D. Kilgore

By the end of the 1980s, cyberpunk risked becoming a pastiche of itself or, worse still, merely one more marketable product. As Andrew M. Butler argues in *Cyberpunk*, "the cutting-edge nature of cyberpunk ensured that it rapidly became a cliché: like many avant-gardes, it was obsolete as soon as the mainstream media took notice" (43). Butler's assessment is reinforced by multiple claims that rapid commodification had effectively killed cyberpunk as the 1990s dawned.[1] At the same time, cyberpunk tropes remain resilient in science fiction, giving rise to a new label—*post-cyberpunk*—whose short- and long-form fictions contribute to cyberpunk's thematic arcs. In their collection *Rewired: The Post-Cyberpunk Anthology*, James Patrick Kelly and John Kessel explain that post-cyberpunk builds upon cyberpunk's initial obsessions: "some writers extend them, some react against them, some take them for granted and move the basic attitudes into new territories" (x). For example, a "key insight of CP [cyberpunk], extended still further in PCP [post-cyberpunk], is that we are no longer changing technology; rather it has begun to change us" and "human values are not imprinted on the fabric of the universe because what it means to be human is always negotiable" (Kelly and Kessel x, xi). At the same time, the "punk in post-cyberpunk continues to make sense if it is pointing toward an attitude: an adversarial relationship to consensus reality" (Kelly and Kessel xii). Post-cyberpunk therefore represented an expansion of cyberpunk beyond the initial literary forms embodied by the fictions of William Gibson, Bruce Sterling, or Lewis Shiner; post-cyberpunk's emergence in the 1990s was fostered by social milieus and climates that increasingly resembled the cyberpunk that had emerged a decade earlier but was now fast becoming quotidian reality. In particular, post-cyberpunk extends and revises core cyberpunk concerns in its handling of (dis)embodiment, online realities, networked subjectivities, and techno-biological viruses.

While critics point to a host of authors,[2] Neal Stephenson quickly emerged as one of the most prolific and important figures associated with post-cyberpunk, particularly given the immense success of *Snow Crash* (1992), an influential novel that played a pivotal role in transforming literary cyberpunk and popularizing post-cyberpunk. At its most basic level, *Snow Crash* delivers cyberpunk's tropes of virtual spaces, techno-biological viruses, ambivalence about embodiment, and hacker heroes with a hefty dose of enthusiastic, playful irony. The novel embraces the flashy, stylish, surface-oriented features of cyberpunk, while simultaneously undermining them as always already amenable to commodification. The novel's protagonist, dubbed Hiro Protagonist, caricatures the elite hacker (anti)hero and yet still functions in traditional hacker-hero fashion, saving the world from L. Bob Rife, televangelist, oil baron, and the novel's obligatory megalomaniac. Finally, Stephenson's portrayal of the near-future U.S. parodies cyberpunk's urban sprawls with the brilliant neon 'loglo' of the multinational 'franchulates' into which society has devolved, articulating a scathing anti-capitalist satire in the process—yet also deploying, in support of Hiro, the outsized corporate figureheads of Cosa Nostra Pizza's Uncle Enzo and Mr. Lee of Mister Lee's Greater Hong Kong. *Snow Crash* shares with the tradition of postmodernist parody the propensity toward simultaneously critiquing and embracing materialism and commodification.[3] The paperback jacket copy sums up *Snow Crash*'s post-cyberpunk approach in one blurb: "Cyberpunk isn't dead—it has just (belatedly) developed a sense of humor."

Snow Crash was both intellectually stimulating and fun—and as much as it provided a rollicking adventure story, it also presented cyberpunk more as a way of approaching and understanding human experience than a set of easily commodified tropes and motifs. The novel carries out this shift in stance through its transformation of core cyberpunk concerns. First, Stephenson's depiction of the online Metaverse reworks the central trope of cyberspace, in sharp contrast to Gibson's early vision. Whereas Gibson's Sprawl trilogy (*Neuromancer* [1984], *Count Zero* [1986], *Mona Lisa Overdrive* [1989]) envisions an instrumentalized cyberspace, rendered in basic geometric shapes that represent a complex file system, Stephenson envisions a livelier and more heavily populated environment that has more in common with the visual-aural language of first-person or role-playing games. That is, Gibson's system of *representation* has been supplanted by Stephenson with a more polyvocal *simulation*. Second, no one in *Snow Crash* seems able to encode a mind directly into the Metaverse (as in Gibson's *Neuromancer* or Rudy Rucker's *Software* [1982]), nor do they want to. Stephenson therefore appears to side with common critiques of early cyberpunk's ambivalence (if not outright rejection) toward embodiment. Instead, the novel fully embraces body augmentation, or what Lisa Swanstrom calls a "networked" conception of subjectivity (77). For Stephenson, mind, brain, and body form a meaningful interactive *process* that collectively constitutes an individual.

Stephenson explores this networked subjectivity in two key ways. First, hacker elites like Hiro and his colleagues use digital technologies as extensions of their perceptions and capacities, and in so doing render themselves physically and mentally vulnerable to visual-textual hacking. For example, Hiro's hacker friend Da5id is reduced to a persistent vegetative state by the *Snow Crash* viral computer program. At the same time, L. Bob Rife can physically hack people and infect them with the DNA-based version of the virus, rendering them part of a larger cyborg superorganism that unquestioningly follows Rife's programming. Stephenson therefore presents not an opposition between the digital and the 'meat' but rather a cultural system vulnerable at all levels to manipulation.

Snow Crash's complicated relationship to embodiment is also part and parcel of Stephenson's re-conceptualization of viral infections, or virality, which up to this point in cyberpunk were largely tools or weapons. The viral contagion deployed by L. Bob Rife, however, is not a digital-age invention. Instead, the Snow Crash virus originates in Sumerian Asherah myths and in the connections that language orchestrates between cognition and volition or action. Stephenson therefore projects the computational logic of code onto the semantic system of language, whereby human discourse becomes as amenable to hacking as computer networks. As the vector for discursive virality, he chooses revealed religion, the ecstatic tradition of glossolalia or "speaking in tongues," an ecstatic eruption of syllables. As *Snow Crash* depicts it, this virality, built around the language-processing deep structures of the brain, self-propagates through human communities. Stephenson therefore finds the Asherah virus everywhere, including the temple prostitutes of ancient Babylon, medieval Europe, and revivalist sects in modern America. Indeed, the idea itself seems to operate virally for Stephenson, who shifts in the course of the novel from a conception of the virus as a self-propagating entity to a conception that sees-as-viral almost everything about human civilization.

Snow Crash therefore depicts both information and viral contagions as free from any one medium, tearing virality loose from the digital media that dominated (and limited) earlier cyberpunk.

Similarly, Stephenson's Metaverse constitutes a much more social space, a playground for human discourse in all its historical and international variety. Finally, concerns about embodiment take on an additional dimension: The networked human mind-body complex becomes vulnerable, *in precisely the same way* as systems of human community become vulnerable to the Asherah virus.

In these transformative respects, *Snow Crash* parallels in some ways the scathing satire in Kathy Acker's cyberpunk-flavored[4] anti-novel, *Empire of the Senseless* (1988). However, what Stephenson *describes* in his narrative, Acker *enacts* with hers: She tries to use the writing process itself to corrupt dominant (male, capitalist) texts. The plot of *Empire of the Senseless* leaps from one strange episode to another, as her 'hacker' rebels, the cyborg Abhor and the would-be pirate Thivai, join forces with other oppressed groups—Algerians, prostitutes, homosexuals—to overthrow the elite in a near-future Paris. But the narrative content is secondary to the technique, which Abhor herself expounds in an oft-quoted segment. Previous avant-garde rebellions against "the empire-making (empirical) empire of language, the prisons of meaning" have failed, Abhor asserts, because "non-sense, since it depended on sense, simply pointed back to the normalizing institutions" (134).[5] Instead, both Acker and her character Abhor try to "[break] the codes" (134) by appropriating dominant textual forms. Acker uses a cut-up technique and plagiarizes heavily from Sigmund Freud, Jean Genet, Mark Twain, and Gibson, slicing up their narratives and lacing their arguments with crude and sexualized language, setting them against themselves in a deconstructive process that aims to make them more difficult to take seriously or pass along to others. Acker's literary scalpels assault narrativity itself, attempting to 'break the code' by fracturing language rather than decoding it.

Acker's work at least partly rehashes cyberpunk's mind-body dualism, simply inverting the values in favor of the 'meat,' but *Snow Crash* seemed to set Stephenson on rather a different course, following the movements of encoding and decoding rather than staging discursive breakdowns. Following his nanotechnology-oriented novel *The Diamond Age* (1995), Stephenson returned to some of *Snow Crash*'s cyberpunk concerns with *Cryptonomicon* (1999), a controversial contender for the post-cyberpunk label, set as it is during World War II. *Cryptonomicon* finds ready parallels between hacking and the code-breaking tactics England and the U.S. used against Germany and Japan in World War II, as three protagonists attempt to outwit military or corporate opponents and survive. Lawrence Waterhouse, a mathematical savant, finds himself assigned to Bletchley Park in England, where he works against the back-propagation of information: The Allies have broken Axis codes, but if they use the information carelessly, Axis military and intelligence officials will change the codes. Lawrence's job is to find clever ways to make the information safe to use. Bobby Shaftoe, marine sergeant, endures fighting across the Pacific theater before being assigned to boots-on-the-ground enforcement for Lawrence. Finally, Randy Waterhouse, Lawrence's grandson, pursues a communications business deal decades later, involved in setting up a 'data haven' in a fictional sultanate near the Philippines, and ultimately rediscovers lost wartime Axis gold with the descendants of Bobby Shaftoe.

In *Snow Crash*, the conceptual work on cyberpunk concepts is linguistic in nature; in *Cryptonomicon*, Stephenson collapses semiotics into mathematics, in the form of information theory. The book's central concern is that any system can be understood and explained in mathematical terms, and yet, because the relationship between any given system and any given calculation is one that has to be established by context, the information thesis is beset at all times by questions of adequacy and purpose. Stephenson also uses information theory[6] and the science of cryptology to continue reworking the core cyberpunk tropes of virtual spaces, virality, and the problematics of embodiment. In this capacious novel, the horizons of virtual space have expanded. Characters do not enter into simulated or representational *spaces*, but rather, subjectivity itself has become virtual. In the process of addressing the problems they face—cryptological for Lawrence, entrepreneurial for Randy, and largely physical or practical for Bobby—each of the characters works through elaborate systems for understanding and engaging with reality. For Lawrence and his colleagues, as they invent a prototype computer, this process produces altogether new insights which reshape not only their perceptions but also the world around them.

Stephenson also uses very close third-person narration to offer brief glimpses of a further expansion of virality, albeit not elaborated as extensively. As 21st-century characters struggle to take themselves seriously, the text portrays the rhetorical and cultural posture of irony *as viral*, viewed by Randy first as a "cultural fungus" (91) and later "as widespread in California as herpes" (387). Here, paralleling very recent work by Tony D. Sampson, *Cryptonomicon* offers a conception of viral propagation where 'what spreads' is not so much *information* as attitude, a cognitive-emotional orientation toward the world.

Whereas virality in this novel moves further into the human social world, the book projects the conception of embodiment onto physical systems themselves, seen as configurations of information. In a key moment, Lawrence witnesses intelligence intercepts being encoded into a machine calculation system via strips of paper tape. As the tape catches fire, Lawrence perceives that "the data has passed out of the physical plane and into the mathematical, a higher and purer universe where different laws apply" (Stephenson, *Cryptonomicon* 195). As the quasi-religious language suggests, the book engages in a kind of transubstantiation, but one orchestrated in mathematical rather than metaphysical terms. Rather than envisioning a totalizing or final conversion of the physical into the mathematical, however, Stephenson offers us a cyclical process that can produce insight and growth, as when Lawrence successfully conjures up a functional computer based on water tubes, or infelicitously, as when the central hacker characters' paranoia produces viral conspiracy theories, or when Randy's data haven serves thieves and totalitarians.

The concern with information, then, becomes inextricably connected with systems of *value*. At the novel's conclusion, Randy and his companions race against another team of profit-driven gold-diggers in pursuing a bunker of Axis gold, lost during the war's end. Randy's team chooses to superheat the bunker, causing the gold to melt and pour out of the bottom in "a bright, thick river" (Stephenson, *Cryptonomicon* 910). It is a potent and disturbing image—a conversion from one form of value, cultural and historical, to another, elemental and protean. Because Randy and his business partner Avi plan to use the gold to finance their struggle against totalitarian powers, Paul Youngquist reads this image as a utopian overreach, a desire to use technology to erase tragedy. But the book is too particular about the gold's origins, the protagonists' qualms, and the precariousness of 'information' itself to make this reading convincing. Rather than envisioning a techno-utopia, Stephenson seems to be demonstrating that information theory's potential to model—in both senses, to portray and to remake—the world constitutes a crucial historical turning point. He has, in effect, pursued the questions of virtual worlds, embodiment, and virality *backward* through history, and in the process uncovered more tantalizing questions than answers.[7] What began as a trope in cyberpunk becomes a lens through which to reinterpret history—a transition and a challenge taken up by others.

In both *Snow Crash* and *Cryptonomicon*, Stephenson's post-cyberpunk approach re-orients cyberpunk concerns by projecting them onto past events, and his approach has a strongly materialist bent: the Asherah virus, for instance, seems to 'explain away' revealed religions. Other post-cyberpunk authors, including Stephenson's near-contemporaries, took a different route, using history to explain cyberpunk. In *He, She and It* (a.k.a. *Body of Glass*, 1991), published the year before *Snow Crash*, Marge Piercy offered a new take on one of the strongest currents of thought and narrative that unites science fiction, cyberpunk, and post-cyberpunk: the synthetic hybrid organism, or cyborg. Piercy unspools the story of a constructed biological and cybernetic man in parallel with the older Jewish myth of the golem: Both Yod the cyborg and Joseph the golem are built by patriarchal figures to defend their Jewish communities from annihilation. Yod defends a post-environmental-apocalyptic town, while Joseph defends the ghetto in Prague, but both become quasi-human, or more than human, in their education and relationships with human women—Yod with the book's other protagonist, Shira, exile from a multinational enclave, and Joseph with Chava, daughter of the golem's maker, Rabbi Judah Loew.

Piercy embraces Donna J. Haraway's feminist vision of the cyborg as a means to erase and overcome the constraints of conventional gender, but the doubled narrative form gives the cyborg its historical context. Malkah, one of the cyborg's creators, tells Yod the golem legend as an extended narrative, not merely as entertainment, but in order to offer him a model by which he might read his place among the humans, and parse their reactions to him—she shapes his memory, identity, and ability to narrate himself. Where Stephenson uses digital innovation to explain away myth and religion, Piercy uses myth and religion to explain the contemporary impulse toward the cyborg, the desire to ignite life from mute matter, and to embody a quasi-human defender with unnatural strength and emotional and intellectual faculties approaching the human. In the same vein, the story's preoccupations also illustrate the points of contact, the confluences and shared concerns, between (post-)cyberpunk and cognate strands of fantasy writing that emphasize language and human identity.

This sense of enchantment infuses Piercy's treatment of the core cyberpunk concerns. In her portrayal of virtual worlds, characters 'project' themselves into a virtual space that simulates their daily reality, but allows them more malleable forms. In spite of these affordances, it also enforces rules about interaction and self-presentation—rules that Yod's very presence seems to bend. In a key scene, as he first discloses his attraction to Shira, Malkah's granddaughter, their shared experience of cyberspace transcends the simulation's limits, allowing a shared consciousness, if only temporarily. Likewise, although Shira and Yod's creators, Avram and Malkah, know every line of his encoded consciousness, his behavior continuously surprises, and he ultimately escapes the will of his creator as delineated in his source code—and rebels. By becoming-other, their other, he forces even Shira to rethink what she wants of a made consciousness, to recognize the desire for ownership alongside accomplishment. Finally, although viral information forms make no explicit appearance within this novel, the emergent pattern of other-awareness, self-awareness, and rebellion repeats, like a fractal shape, at the level of Piercy's post-apocalyptic society. In stark contrast to Stephenson's fatally capitalistic world, where Hiro's success is commodified and salable on the spot, Piercy's downtrodden masses, the people of the 'Glop,' self-organize and contend against the multinational corporations. Piercy's work imbues the environmental catastrophe of near-future North America with, if a bit less humor, more nuance than Stephenson's neon-loglo world, where pain and longing are played for laughs. If Stephenson operates in the mode of parody, Piercy's book is more elegiac, though it looks to the farther future with more hope.

In creating new variations on the interplay between the human and its others, post-cyberpunk pioneers like Piercy and Stephenson lay the groundwork for further experimentation. Stephen Hall's *The Raw Shark Texts* (2007), for instance, features a protagonist caught between two unusual entities. First, Sanderson is a victim of something he calls a "conceptual shark," a creature that inhabits human discourse, not the three dimensions of (cyber)space—and devours Sanderson's memories, leaving him adrift, hardly able to remember his name. Fleeing the shark, Sanderson eventually meets the equally disturbing Mycroft Ward, dubbed "one of the last of the gentleman scientists" (199), a close parallel to Stephenson's Rife, "last of the nineteenth-century monopolists" (*Snow Crash* 113). In typical (post)cyberpunk fashion, Ward has succeeded in mapping his consciousness onto the bodies of others and then linking them to his own, creating an ever-growing, multiply-embodied superorganism.

The Raw Shark Texts parallels Pat Cadigan's earlier feminist cyberpunk novel *Synners* (1991),[8] particularly when it comes to a central viral threat that originates only partly in computer code. Cadigan's protagonists, including Gina Aiesi and Visual Mark, synthesize whole-body experiences for others to consume, and suffer from the familiar cyberpunk body-revulsion, particularly in Visual Mark's effort to transfer his consciousness into the virtual environment and abandon "the meat jail" (Cadigan 233). In a manner that foreshadows both Stephenson's and Hall's depiction of virality, however, Mark's consciousness transfer also imports an imprint of the stroke his physical body undergoes, making of it a *"contagious stroke,"* a voracious viral form (Cadigan 309). In a similar vein, Mycroft Ward's duplication process is driven not solely by his cognitive coding, but also by how the code instantiates his pathological fear of death and his desire to survive—leading his numerous selves to self-propagate relentlessly. For this reason, I have argued elsewhere that Ward is more cancer than virus,[9] an argument that updates cyberpunk's reliance upon virality for a post-cyberpunk audience.

In a similar post-cyberpunk move, *The Raw Shark Texts*'s use of the conceptual shark also shifts the motif of the virtual world in two ways. First, like the Asherah virus, the titular 'shark' inhabits patterns in human communication, not digital data, but the shark is predatory, not a viral parasite, and cannot be easily reduced to a specific metaphor or cultural pattern, the way Stephenson associates Asherah with religion. Hall hints that the shark has its origins in the way humans talk and think, in the logic we use to make sense of ourselves and the world: Something we have done, some way of conceiving of reality, has broken free, has gained awareness, and now feeds on our memories, our sense of our lives as 'selves' (a vision quite *à propos* for our present viral-media-saturated reality). Second, the novel's virtual spaces themselves are accessed by anachronistic means, through labyrinthine libraries and configurations of words on scraps of paper. In this environment, Sanderson engages in encoding and decoding tasks to reconstruct his lost memories, and ultimately escapes by inducing the shark to feed on Ward's distended consciousness. But buried as they are under layers of language and encoding, these events signify ambiguously, leaving the question of whether there is a 'real' Eric Sanderson, and whether he survives, as much of a Rorschach test as the shark, and indeed the novel.

Where Hall's approach to the network subjectivity common to cyberpunk renders it diffuse and open to many interpretations, other post-cyberpunk authors carry it in different directions. Both Richard K. Morgan's Takeshi Kovacs trilogy (*Altered Carbon* [2002]; *Broken Angels* [2003]; *Woken Furies* [2005]) and Marcel Theroux's *Strange Bodies* (2013) traffic in the concept of transferrable consciousnesses, and both also make use of first-person, character-narrated prose to anchor—and destabilize—their story-worlds. Morgan's trilogy returns post-cyberpunk to cyberpunk's neo-noir roots, presenting Takeshi Kovacs as the traditional Chandleresque hacker-detective,[10] a man who serves as a paid agent of the ruling elite, the *nouveau riche* and moneyed 'Methuselahs,' yet resists the world order he perceives and inhabits. This narrative initially seems to parallel traditional cyberpunk: characters in Morgan's future inhabit computer hardware in the form of 'stacks,' which can be housed in 'sleeves,' bodies either manufactured or made available through the brain death of their original owners. However, as Pawel Frelik observes, Morgan's treatment of this transfer offers more nuance in that both the sleeves *and* the transferred selves are racially and ethnically legible, and sleeves retain traces of their former owners' personalities and pursuits. On the other hand, Morgan also makes deft use of the first-person pronoun to skate over these troubling questions of identity: When Kovacs, returning from death, asserts "I came thrashing out of the tank, one hand [...] searching for wounds" (Morgan 9), the question as to whether he really is Kovacs doesn't so much get answered as rendered irrelevant—the text simply forges onward, as though the 'I' is enough.

The same cannot quite be said for characters in Theroux's *Strange Bodies*, notably Nicholas Slopen, a Samuel Johnson scholar, and Samuel Johnson himself, both of whom find themselves implanted in the bodies of Russian gang members. They are test cases for the 'Malevin Procedure,' which is intended to resolve what its sponsoring cabal calls the 'Common Task,' achieving an immortality also sought, in Morgan's trilogy, by the 'Methuselahs.' Theroux undertakes some of the same variations on consciousness-transfer as Morgan, including ethnically marked bodies and consciousnesses; however, where Morgan's transfer is computerized and digital, Theroux's is analog: The process is based on the persona's accumulated written works, and the transfer is executed via an opaque quasi-occult process.

Finally, where Morgan's Kovacs only narrates, Slopen's first-person tale is presented to the reader as an artifact, a posthumous testimony. Slopen begins by baldly asserting his own death—"I died on September 28, 2009, crushed in the wheel arch of a lorry" (Theroux 17)—and yet gives every sign of being the thinking and feeling persona he claims to be. In contrast to Kovacs, whose continuous identity is taken for granted, the newly embodied Slopen explicitly shores up an identity always under dispute. As a result, while Morgan's post-cyberpunk books embody much of the same cynical, anti-authoritarian rhetorical stance we might find in early cyberpunk works, Theroux creates a perilous intimacy: Readers' only exposure to the character of Nicholas Slopen is via the narrative voice of the apparent transplant. The original Slopen commits no words to any of these pages, and Theroux thus places readers in a double-bind: The story stakes its plot on the convincing enactment of Slopen's consciousness, and yet its status as a posthumous testimony makes its accuracy, its adequacy, impossible to determine. In the end, Morgan's handling of embodiment fits better in the realm of cyberpunk/neo-noir science fiction, while Theroux's treatment, from the multiple framing to the open ending, feels more like (post)modernist narrative, including convincing pastiches of Johnson's style and a patchwork of multiple genres. What both texts demonstrate as part of a larger cyberpunk and post-cyberpunk milieu is the exploration of embodiment via personality transfer has become less a specific motif or trope than a *way* of exploring enduring questions of identity.

Today, some of the trademark cyberpunk (and post-cyberpunk) innovations may seem hopelessly antiquated: As of mid-2019, our closest parallel to Stephenson's Metaverse is the virtual world *Second Life* (Linden 2003), which stands mostly abandoned, and such collaborative online gaming arenas as *Ultima Online* (Origin 1997) or *Fortnite* (Epic 2017) remain distinct from the lineage of social media that begins with LiveJournal or MySpace and culminates in Facebook and Twitter. And yet, in other ways cyberpunk-inspired concepts have only grown in their relevance and explanatory power, notably ongoing critical interrogations into embodiment, cutting-edge conceptions of virality, and the re-envisioning of the created *topias* of cyberspace that finds virtual *worlds* (e.g., *Second Life*) now *virtual* worlds, conceptual spaces conjured into being by activities of encoding and decoding. As Graham J. Murphy and Sherryl Vint observe, "we have never been more in need of a fiction capable of engaging with the world as shaped by information technology" (xii)—a capability post-cyberpunk offers. As self-driving cars begin to test the degree to which we trust and embrace nonhuman digital intelligence; as software programs impersonate people on international dating applications; as social media inadvertently contribute to the destabilizing of democratic institutions and give rise to authoritarian regimes—and so much more—post-cyberpunk's narrative diversity seems the fittest apparatus for a critical appraisal of the post-millennial world, an appraisal authors and scholars have only just begun.

Notes

1 For more details, see Graham J. Murphy's chapter on "The *Mirrorshades* Collective" in this collection.
2 Butler identifies Wilhelmina Baird, Bruce Bethke, Simon Ings, Richard Kadrey, Kim Newman, Marge Piercy, Justina Robson, and Jack Womack as post-cyberpunk while he points to Greg Egan, Jon Courtenay Grimwood, Gwyneth Jones, Shariann Lewitt, Jeff Noon, Tricia Sullivan, and Jack Womack as 'cyberpunk-flavored,' which he refers to as "works of fiction which felt like cyberpunk, read like cyberpunk, but nonetheless either lacked computers or punk characters" (57). More recently, Kelly and Kessel expand the post-cyberpunk roster to also include such authors as Jonathan Lethem, David Marusek, Charles Stross, Elizabeth Bear, Cory Doctorow, and Paolo Bacigalupi.

3 For a sustained reading of the central role of capitalism in envisioning posthuman futures, including a discussion of *Snow Crash*, see Julia Grillmayr's contribution to this collection.
4 See Note #2 for a definition of 'cyberpunk-flavored.'
5 See Paul Taylor's and Mathieu O'Neil's work on the ambivalent figure of the hacker hero for more along this line.
6 See Paul Youngquist for more details on the layered theoretical apparatus of cybernetics and second-order cybernetics and how these apparatuses inform cyberpunk.
7 In the Baroque Cycle—*Quicksilver* (2003), consisting of Quicksilver (Book 1), King of the Vagabonds (Book 2), and Odalisque (Book 3); *The Confusion* (2005), consisting of Bonanza (Book 4) and The Juncto (Book 5); *The System of the World* (2004), consisting of Solomon's Gold (Book 6), Currency (Book 7), and The System of the World (Book 8)—Stephenson chases the desire to model the world back along the lines of economic, colonial, and industrial conquest, to the world-systems conceived by Newton and Leibniz.
8 For more details on Pat Cadigan and *Synners*, see Ritch Calvin's and Lisa Yaszek's respective contributions to this collection.
9 For more details, see my article "Bad Networks: From Virus to Cancer in Post-Cyberpunk Narrative."
10 For more dedicated studies of neo-noir and Richard Morgan's Takeshi Kovacs series, see Nazare and Frelik; for an analysis of its Netflix screen adaptation *Altered Carbon* (2018–) as cyberpunk Gothic, see Anya Heise-von der Lippe's chapter in this *Companion*.

Works Cited

Acker, Kathy. *Empire of the Senseless*. Grove, 1988.
Butler, Andrew M. *Cyberpunk*. Pocket Essentials, 2000.
Cadigan, Pat. *Synners*. Bantam Spectra, 1991.
Frelik, Pawel. "Woken Carbon: The Return of the Human in Richard K. Morgan's Takeshi Kovacs Trilogy." *Beyond Cyberpunk: New Critical Perspectives*, edited by Graham J. Murphy and Sherryl Vint. Routledge, 2010, pp. 173–90.
Hall, Stephen. *The Raw Shark Texts*. Canongate, 2007.
Kelly, James Patrick and John Kessel. "Introduction: Hacking Cyberpunk." *Rewired: The Post-Cyberpunk Anthology*, edited by James Patrick Kelly and John Kessel. Tachyon Publications, 2007, pp. vii–xv.
Kilgore, Christopher D. "Bad Networks: From Virus to Cancer in Post-Cyberpunk Narrative." *Journal of Modern Literature*, vol. 40, no. 2, 2017, pp. 165–183.
Morgan, Richard K. *Altered Carbon*. Del Rey Ballantine, 2002.
Murphy, Graham J. and Sherryl Vint. "Introduction: The Sea Change(s) of Cyberpunk." *Beyond Cyberpunk: New Critical Perspectives*, edited by Graham J. Murphy and Sherryl Vint. Routledge, 2010, pp. xi–xviii.
Nazare, Joe. "Marlowe in Mirrorshades: The Cyberpunk (Re-)Vision of Chandler." *Studies in the Novel*, vol. 35, no. 3, 2003, pp. 383–404.
O'Neil, Matheiu. "Rebels for the System? Virus Writers, General Intellect, Cyberpunk, and Criminal Capitalism." *Continuum: Journal of Media & Cultural Studies*, vol. 20, no. 2, 2006, pp. 225–41.
Piercy, Marge. *He, She and It*. Random House, 1991.
Sampson, Tony D. *Virality: Contagion Theory in the Age of Networks*. U of Minnesota P, 2012.
Stephenson, Neal. *Cryptonomicon*. Perennial Harper Collins, 1999.
———. *Snow Crash*. Bantam, 1993.
Swanstrom, Lisa. "Capsules and Nodes and Ruptures and Flows: Circulating Subjectivity in Neal Stephenson's *Snow Crash*." *Science Fiction Studies*, vol. 37, no. 1, 2010, pp. 54–80.
Taylor, Paul. "Hackers: Cyberpunks or Microserfs?" *Information, Communication & Society*, vol. 1, no. 4, 1998, pp. 401–19.
Theroux, Marcel. *Strange Bodies*. Farrar, Strauss, and Giroux, 2013.
Youngquist, Paul. "Cyberpunk, War, and Money: Neal Stephenson's *Cryptonomicon*." *Contemporary Literature*, vol. 53, no. 2, 2012, pp. 319–47.

8

CHARLES STROSS: *ACCELERANDO* (CASE STUDY)

Gerry Canavan

In "The Coming Technological Singularity" Vernor Vinge announces the near-term transformation of the coordinates of human history due to the imminent creation of artificial minds with superhuman cognition, an inflection point in time after which neither our assumptions about the past nor our predictions about the future will remain valid. Vinge believes this will be a "change comparable to the rise of human life on Earth" (n.p.). The term Vinge uses to describe this moment of exponential change, 'singularity,' is borrowed from physics, where it similarly describes spatiotemporal locations (like the Big Bang, or the inside of a black hole) where "our models must be discarded and a new reality rules" (n.p.). Once machines that can think begin to design machines that can think—perhaps the most prototypical formulation for the idea of the Singularity—the exponential increase in the cognitive capacity of the planet will completely transform all aspects of culture and society in ways that we (with our merely human brains) cannot now predict and perhaps, when it happens, will not be able to meaningfully participate in. A new reality will rule. Vinge finds his bold proclamation presaged in 1950s and 1960s predictions about future superintelligences from thinkers like John von Neumann and I.J. Good, and it likewise resonates with much cyberpunk and post-cyberpunk fiction of the 1980s and 1990s. As Joshua Raulerson has noted, the notion of the Singularity is very much a post-cyberpunk fantasy, in the dual sense of being both "continuation" and "break" with cyberpunk's originary ideological and aesthetic commitments (20). Indeed, the Janus-faced crisis/opportunity posed by such a posthuman era should be immediately clear to any reader of cyberpunk or post-cyberpunk fiction; one needs think only of the sinister artificial intelligence (AI) Wintermute in William Gibson's *Neuromancer* (1984) or the hostile cybernetic AI called "The Mailman" in Vinge's "True Names" (1981) to imagine what such a being might be, and might make possible.

Cyberpunk science fiction has long been fascinated by these sorts of computerized intelligences, who make possible radical expansions of human abilities, cognition, and longevity while simultaneously threatening to supplant or extinguish the human altogether. While the idea of AI naturally predates cyberpunk, there is no doubt that contemporary conceptions of AI live in the long shadow of cyberpunk's philosophical postulations and narrative tropes, nowhere more than in the global popularity of the Singularity as a concept today. It is no exaggeration to say that since the publication of Vinge's paper the Singularity has become the major, and perhaps the last remaining, vision of an inflationary technologized future for humanity, one that has been anticipated, promoted, and debated by tech billionaires like Ray Kurzweil, Elon Musk, Jeff Bezos, and Peter Thiel, all of whom see the Singularity as not only inevitable but *desirable*. As Andrew

Charles Stross: Accelerando *(Case Study)*

Pilsch notes in *Transhumanism: Evolutionary Futurism and the Human Technologies of Utopia*, this sort of transhumanist speculation about the future may be "what utopian thought might look like in the age of network culture, big data, and the quantified self: a utopian rhetoric for the information age" (3).

As registered in Gibson's famous short story "The Gernsback Continuum" (1981), the first cyberpunk moment was a response to the death of an older techno-utopian future, the one that had been promulgated by Golden Age science fictions of the 1940s, 1950s, and 1960s—the *Star Trek* of limitless expansion into the cosmos coupled with the *Jetsons* future of flying cars, free energy, robot servants, and two-hour workdays. In the face of the astronomical and ecological realism of the 1970s, which promised instead energy crisis, resource scarcity, overpopulation, climate change, and pollution to a human race likely confined forever to a single planet, cyberpunk offered an alternative new frontier of inflation and expansion to replace the one it had lost. If we couldn't become the masters of time and space, conquering the galaxy with impossible hyperdrives, we could at least obtain the same sort of limitless abundance within the world of the computer, where the unhappy limits of ecology would no longer apply. The Singularity is the culmination of this cyberpunk dream, a world transformed for human use by man's creation of electronic Gods—computers—while always risking turning into its nightmare instead.

The contemporary faith in the Singularity rebrands cyberpunk fantasy as inevitable 'science fact'—and indeed, the Singularitarians promise many of the same technopositive alternatives to space empire as early cyberpunk (cyberspace cornucopias, food replicators, uploaded consciousness, transhuman sensoria, immortal cyborg bodies, and the like), soon to be delivered by autonomous drones to your doorstep. The Singularity is thus a vision of 'the end of history' rather different from the ones announced by either Francis Fukuyama (who remarked in "The End of History?" that there is no alternative to globalized consumer capitalism) or the ecological pessimists (that there is no future at all due to accelerating ecological degradation and resource scarcity); even its overlap with 1980s-era cyberpunk is somewhat misleading, as those stories typically favored a grim sheen of dystopia (almost always beginning with the corporate development, ownership, and control of those fabulous technological tokens of the future). The Singularity is imagined by its proponents to be something rather like the *start* of history, as Karl Marx and Friedrich Engels had it; the "leap from the kingdom of necessity to the kingdom of freedom," from the world of unhappy physical and ecological constraints to a world where anything is possible (Engels n.p.). That this radically transformative and ostensibly cornucopian Singularity, if it happens, will be in the hands of beings whose immense intelligence we do not understand and potentially cannot control at all is a point that is often lost in Silicon Valley's exuberant tech-enthusiasm. But a sense of inhuman menace is nonetheless present in the concept from its earliest articulations onward; for example, consider Good's highly ambiguous 1965 prophecy that "the first ultraintelligent machine is the *last* invention that man need ever make, provided that the machine is docile enough to tell us how to keep it under control," or the similar ambivalence in von Neumann's statement that "some essential singularity [...] beyond which human affairs, as we know them, could not continue" (both qtd. in Vinge). We can see this same menace anticipated clearly in the second half of Vinge's full title: "The Coming Technology Singularity: How to Survive in the Post-Human Era."

This chapter takes up that fraught question of *how to survive* through a sustained consideration of Charles Stross's influential 2005 novel *Accelerando*, a book Diana Biller includes in her *io9* article "The Essential Cyberpunk Reading List," helping reinforce its status as a key text in this cultural mode. Stross imagines a world in which the Singularity has happened, but the physical and political problems of technological modernity have not been solved as promised; rather, the Singularity represents the catastrophic hyper-intensification of modernity into new and autonomous forms. What is left of the human race is forced to flee for its life into the outreaches of the solar system, as far away as it can get from the brutal posthuman economic system the novel dubs Capitalism

2.0. By the end of the novel the survivors refer to this moment not as the Singularity, but as "the Vinge catastrophe," and recognize it not as the moment *the computers* became self-aware but the moment *the corporations* did. *Accelerando* thus disciplines the concept of the Singularity by returning to it the post-1970s political cynicism and abiding ecological pessimism from which cyberpunk first sprung; as a result, Stross's dyspeptic vision of the Singularity is one in which the questions of corporate ownership, socioeconomic exploitation, and energy footprint cannot simply be bracketed or waived aside. Stross's Capitalism 2.0, like our own Capitalism 1.0, has a bottomless hunger for resources—and so, when the Singularity happens, it liberates no one, and literally consumes the Earth.

8.1 *Accelerando*

The running joke that structures *Accelerando*—posed both diegetically by characters within the storyworld and nondiegetically by the omniscient narrator outside of it—is the search for the precise moment in history that the Singularity occurs. "The time remaining before the intelligence spike is down to single digit years," the narrator tells us in the late 2010s (39); "it won't be long now," the same figure promises in the 2070s (267). While they wait for the moment of the change, of course, *everything* changes around them: Machines take over most aspects of finance and labor, both economy and law become utterly incomprehensible, all traditional politics vanish, artificial lifeforms become ubiquitous, and full consciousness uploads and body switching become routine while humans colonize the outer solar system and even make contact with aliens.

Presented as a series of interconnected stories spanning the entirety of the 21st century, decade by decade, the novel primarily follows the fortunes of one Manfred Macx and his descendants, tracing the evolution of human society from the twenty-minutes-into-the-future cyberpunk milieu that opens the story to a radically transformed, transcendently posthuman setting just a few decades later. The book's plot is thus very hard to summarize; what begins in a very recognizable social context quickly becomes unrecognizable as the very foundations of human society and biology completely shift under our feet.

When *Accelerando* begins, Manfred is a figure who could easily serve as the protagonist of a Gibson novel, a sort of postcapitalist jet-setting cool-hunter using his tremendous gift for hacking to liberate digital information in the service of his anti-state, anti-corporate politics. "In IP geek circles, Manfred is legendary," the narrator gushes:

> He's the guy who patented the business practice of moving your e-business somewhere with a slack intellectual property regime in order to evade licensing encumbrances. He's the guy who patented using genetic algorithms to patent everything they can permutate from an initial description of a problem domain—not just a better mousetrap, but the set of all possible mousetraps. Roughly a third of his inventions are legal, a third are illegal, and the remainder are legal but will become illegal as soon as the legislatosaurus wakes up, smells the coffee, and panics. (7–8)

The mode of these early sections is, generally speaking, light parody; Manfred is a post-cyberpunk hero with the irony turned up just a little bit more than even Neal Stephenson's *Snow Crash* (1992) with its similarly heightened main character, Hiro Protagonist. Manfred oozes a Gibsonian sense of cool in every respect. He's so cool, in fact, that he doesn't even do any of this radical work for money; able to make billions of whatever currency (traditional or crypto) he desires, he does it all for free. Other characters in the novel find Manfred's *pro bono* work ethic inscrutable, none more so than his genius, ultra-sexy dominatrix ex-fiancée Pamela, a rightwing hypernationalist chasing Manfred on behalf of the Internal Revenue Service—herself a heightened, satirical send-up of the typical cyberpunk hacker-heroine. When Pamela challenges Manfred on his extreme economic irrationality, Manfred simply explains that when the Singularity soon arrives none of the conditions that drive contemporary political economy will matter:

> I work for the betterment of everybody, not just some narrowly defined national interest, Pamela. It's the agalmic future. You're still locked into a pre-singularity economic model that thinks in terms of scarcity. Resource allocation isn't a problem anymore—it's going to be over within a decade. The cosmos is flat in all directions, and we can borrow as much bandwidth as we need from the first universal bank of entropy! (20)

Manfred thus embodies to a hyperbolic extent not just a character cliché but the ideological limits of what Fredric Jameson identifies as cyberpunk's utopian ambitions, which he sees as "driven by the 'irrational exuberance' of the '90s and a kind of romance of feudal commerce," and fundamentally incommensurate with precisely the ecosocialist utopian tradition contemporaneously represented by Ernest Callenbach's *Ecotopia* (1975) or with the decidedly non-cyberpunk works of someone like Kim Stanley Robinson (Jameson n.p.). The story we ultimately get in *Accelerando* deeply sours Manfred's attitude toward the information economy: The novel is

> not so much an allegorization as a *literalization* of an increasingly automated and autonomous information capitalism that is—in its exploitative labor practices, its anti-ecological destructivity, its disconnection from material reality, and its self-inflicted propensity towards catastrophic collapses in which capital itself pays no substantive price—radically indifferent if not actively hostile to human values. (Canavan 705)

As each story in the novel returns us to a slightly later moment in Manfred's world, we find that Manfred's Singularity, when it comes, is indeed not salvation, but rather an intensification of the disaster in which we all already live.

As with many other such cyberpunk narratives, drawing as they do from the *noir* tradition, we initially enter the novel with a sense that we are witnessing just another adventure of our hero; after all, the first line of the novel is "Manfred's on the road again, making strangers rich" (3). But the novel rapidly makes that understanding impossible, and, pursuant to its interest in the Singularity's point-of-no-return, it begins to assign permanent consequences to Manfred's actions, rather than allowing any possibility of 'reset' back to some originary status quo. Chief among these changes is a disturbing scene at the end of the first chapter in which Pamela drugs Manfred and forces him to ejaculate inside her, allowing her to get pregnant against his wishes (31–34). But here the *femme fatale* refuses to die or vanish, but instead becomes Manfred's antagonistic co-parent; that over the course of the first story Manfred also encounters and liberates a collective of autonomous cybernetic intelligences—masquerading as an underground faction of the KGB but actually descended from uploaded digital maps of the nervous system of lobsters—seems almost incidental in comparison. Soon, Manfred's robotic cat Aineko (with some unknown manipulation by Pamela alongside its own ability to self-upgrade and self-modify) is sentient and operating in the world with its own judgments, desires, and schemes, while the cybernetic 'lobsters' are set free by Manfred and allowed to make their own destiny in cyberspace.

These threads crisscross through the remainder of the stories in *Accelerando*, even as Manfred himself ultimately recedes into the background and narrative attention is focused instead on his child, Amber, the product of his being raped by Pamela. Here the novel establishes its major thematic opposition: human reproduction vs. posthuman reproduction. Part of the reason Pamela and Manfred broke up in the first place is that in his accelerationist techno-optimism even a twenty-year commitment seems impossibly long ("you might as well be talking about the next ice age" [19]); now he has a child and is forced to think on a biological timeframe he finds impossibly slow. Thus, over Part One of the novel, Manfred (together with his new wife, Annette) fights with Pamela over both the raising of Amber and the proper disposition and distribution of his assets, all the while such cyberpunk motifs as digital lifeforms are gaining legal recognition, consciousness enhancement is becoming more and more routinized, and digital immortality is very rapidly normalized. The focus of the stories/chapters in Part Two shifts fully to Amber, first to her original "meatspace" (31) instantiation as a biological entity in a mining ship orbiting Jupiter and second to what's called a 'fork' of Amber: A digital copy split off from the original Amber to investigate what appears to be an access point to an alien Internet at the edge of the solar system—a kind of extraterrestrial router. By the time the forked Amber returns from her journey, the 'original' Amber has lived her entire life, including having had a child (Sirhan) and committed suicide; we follow instead what is essentially a clone of Amber for the rest of the novel.

Most of Part Three of *Accelerando* focuses on Sirhan, a true child of the Singularity, in an era where the assumptions about what is 'normal' in human life have now completely fallen away. During the time of Sirhan's upbringing, it is common for children to live simulated digital childhoods, rather than authentic ones; thus, he lives the ages "from two to seventeen years several hundred times over before my eighteenth birthday," reset by his mother back to childhood whenever his parents determined they were unhappy with the results. "The child forks, numerous times, as Amber despairingly plays with probabilities, simulating upbringing outcomes" (298); the chief mistake Amber made was not realizing that Sirhan was not truly being reset and was actually retaining his memory of *all* these simulated lives. Meanwhile, when we reencounter Annette, she is living in the body of a gorilla, while Manfred has taken up residence with his consciousness distributed among a flock of birds. It is only the conservative-minded Pamela who has allowed herself to grow old in her original body, all the while seething with resentment and spite. Meanwhile the environmental transformations of the Singularity have been no less radical than the social transformations: Since the only space that really matters now is cyberspace, the inner planets are rapidly being disintegrated and transformed into "computronium" that will become immense cybernetic brains. The economic system that organizes this civilization is beyond human comprehension, and all previous forms of economic organization have been "rendered obsolete by a bunch of superior deterministic resource allocation algorithms collectively known as Economics 2.0" (266). Nevertheless, the narrator is still waiting for the Singularity: "It won't be long now..." (267).

8.2 The Vile Offspring

As the novel moves further and further from the 'present' toward the ontological and existential chaos of the Singularity, human beings become obsolescent, and the 'Vile Offspring,' as the humans call their artificially intelligent digital successors, become solely concerned with each other. After a brief period keeping Earth as a sort of nature preserve, it too is converted into computronium, and any 'humans' that still exist in digital form relocate to what amounts to "refugee camps orbiting Saturn" (331). The Vile Offspring sometimes digitally resurrect famous humans from history for their own unknown reasons, periodically discarding them or sending them to Saturn to live when they have fulfilled their purpose. An automated FAQ greets these migrants to Saturn, explaining to them what has happened by cross-referencing the concept of the Singularity with another name that seems perhaps more appropriate to the scale of what has occurred: "the Vinge catastrophe" (332). Manfred's techno-orgasmic prophecies about an 'agalmic future' and borrowing bandwidth from the first 'universal bank of entropy' have come true, but they have

Charles Stross: Accelerando (*Case Study*)

liberated no one; instead, they have caused human beings to live permanently in thrall to the Vile Offspring. The FAQ makes all this clear:

> The society you have been instantiated in is *extremely wealthy* within the scope of Economics 1.0, the value transfer system developed by human beings during and after your own time. Money exists, and is used for the usual range of goods and services, but the basics—food, water, air, power, off-the-shelf clothing, housing, historical entertainment, and monster trucks—are free. An implicit social contract dictates that, in return for access to these facilities, you obey certain laws.
>
> If you wish to opt out of this social contract, be advised that other worlds may run *Economics 2.0* or subsequent releases. These value-transfer systems are more efficient—hence wealthier—than Economics 1.0, but true participation in Economics 2.0 is not possible without dehumanizing cognitive surgery. Thus, in *absolute* terms, although this society is richer than any you have ever heard of, it is also a poverty-stricken backwater compared to its neighbors. (334)

By the end of the novel the Macx family is casting about for some way to resist the Singularity Manfred once welcomed, finding none. Amber's proposal is thus to run away: Assemble a starship as quickly as possible, and flee the oncoming Vile Offspring before the *entire* solar system has been turned to computronium (328). On the metanarrative level, we can understand this is the final collapse of cyberpunk fantasy as a solution to the problems of economics and ecology, and a compensatory return instead to an older science-fictional milieu of space opera—reframed here not as inflationary and expansionistic but as the deflationary diaspora of a tiny sliver of the human race desperately fleeing the negative consequences of its unbridled technological progress. Now *cyberpunk* is the future that failed, and somehow making the fantasy of space empire work again is the only hope for humanity.

But even this slender hope of the future is troubled by events at the end of *Accelerando*. The alien router the clone-Amber investigated earlier did not offer access to an exciting alien Internet of cultural exchange and transcendent knowledge; instead, whatever extraterrestrial civilization had built it was long gone, as were any cultures that had accessed it since, and the only things left inside were autonomous digital intelligences looking to infect anyone hooking into it: in short, computer viruses. All civilizations seem in the end to succumb to this cycle of exponential rise followed by horrific crash; indeed, even Amber's plan is ultimately doomed, as humans will carry "the seeds of a singularity" anywhere they go, and eventually destroy themselves again, one way or another (356). The only thing outside the logics of this boom-bust cycle are the hints of a super-galactic civilization beyond the Boötes void, a region of space so thinly populated by matter that, had humanity evolved inside it, "we wouldn't have known there were other galaxies until the 1960s" (qtd. in "Filling the Void"). There, Manfred believes he sees evidence of a post-Singularity civilization or cluster of civilizations "doing something purposeful and coordinated, something vast—a timing channel attack on the virtual machine that's running the universe, or an embedded simulation of an entirely different universe" (Stross 369). This Philip K. Dickian suggestion that there may be "something out there that's more real than we are" (Stross 369)—and that we may be able to hack into it—is both the apotheosis and the final collapse of cyberpunk futurity, the final limit (in both senses) of its vision of liberating humanity. In any event, *Accelerando* ultimately argues that neither the hypersentience of Economics 2.0 condemned to stay close together to prevent network lag, nor the 'galaxy-sized superintelligences' of the Boötes void trying to hack the substrata of the universe are an acceptably human future for the species; instead, posthumanity can only "live furtively in the darkness between these islands of brilliance. There are, it would seem, advantages to not being too intelligent" (382).

The novel's final chapter, "Survivor," is organized precisely around this sort of anti-Singularitarian, anti-technology message: A digitally reincarnated instance of Manfred now being raised by Sirhan as *his* son communes with a digitally resurrected copy of Pamela, and together they conclude that the robot cat, Aineko, has been manipulating them both throughout the entire novel, trying to "breed their minds" (401–2)—not even for any particular purpose, but simply because generations of Macxes have made "interesting pets" (411). In the novel's last set-piece the Macxes finally rid themselves of Aineko forever, and Manfred and Pamela—some close-enough version of each of them, anyway—walk out of the scene, improbably, together, apparently willing to give their romance another try, in what is framed as a potential triumph of the human over the technological despite being bizarrely at odds with all the suffering and misery the two characters have inflicted on each other since Chapter 1.

8.3 Conclusion

When did the Singularity happen? The characters of *Accelerando* themselves debate this point, with some selecting this or that moment from the novel (Manfred's freeing of the uploaded lobsters, the development of the first digital uploads, and so on), others always saying the moment is still imminent, and still others arguing the entire idea is a "load of religious junk. Christian mystic rapture recycled for atheist nerds" (Stross 184). One minor character, Pierre, unexpectedly selects a moment much deeper in the past: "It happened on June 6, 1969, at eleven hundred hours, eastern seaboard time. [...] That was when the first network control protocol packets were sent from the data port of one IMP to another—the first-ever Internet connection. *That's* the singularity. Since then we've all been living in a universe that was impossible to predict from events prior to that time" (184). If this character is right, then as of the publication of *The Routledge Companion to Cyberpunk Culture* human history has been over for around fifty years, and we are now several generations deep into posthuman time. Stross's *Accelerando* stands as a crucial document of the structures of feeling generated by this fraught, tense period of intensification and transformation—but above all else its madcap, parodic dismantling of cyberpunk optimism suggests a certain nausea is now infusing our entire concept of the future.

In a 2010 blog post Stross poses a series of questions to extend the observations of *Accelerando* beyond the merely technological to every aspect of the social: "Why do we feel so politically powerless?" and "Why is the world so obviously going to hell in a handbasket? Why can't anyone fix it?" The answer, he says, is the development and perfection of neoliberal corpocracy, especially since the extinction of corporate capitalism's last significant competitor (Soviet-style communism) in the 1990s.

> We are now living in a global state that has been structured for the benefit of non-human entities with non-human goals. They have enormous media reach, which they use to distract attention from threats to their own survival. They also have an enormous ability to support litigation against public participation, except in the very limited circumstances where such action is forbidden. Individual atomized humans are thus either co-opted by these entities (you can live *very* nicely as a CEO or a politician, as long as you don't bite the feeding hand) or steamrollered if they try to resist. In short, we are living in the aftermath of an alien invasion. (Stross "Invaders" n.p.)

Steven Shaviro's analysis of *Accelerando* reaches a similarly unhappy conclusion:

> The flows of Capital have now become autonomous—and strictly speaking unimaginable. They have liberated themselves from any merely human dimensions, and from whatever

feeble limits Fordism and Keynesianism might previously have placed upon the single-minded pursuit of capital accumulation. In that sense, the Singularity is already here. (Shaviro n.p.)

Accelerando's genius is thus in its unflinching satirical confrontation with what Carl Freedman has called cyberpunk's "uncritical conservativism," which "colludes with reification even while exposing it, and, accordingly, offers us the always comforting conservative assurance that, in counter-Leninist fashion, *nothing* is to be done" (198). It was in exactly this blinkered sense that Jameson sees most cyberpunk, despite its surface pessimism, as utopian: "Dystopia can swing around into the utopian without missing a beat, the way depression can without warning become euphoria" (Jameson). And so not only do all digital roads lead to ecological collapse and economic neoslavery, but worse yet (as the last chapter's revelations about Aineko show) we have been so programmed and reprogrammed by the posthuman confluence of the technological and the economic, with such intensity, and for so long, that we can now barely even recognize ourselves and our true desires. In this way *Accelerando*'s last utopian fantasy of the future may be the most hopeless one of all, and yet the most fiercely wished—that we could somehow undo it all, kill the Internet, kill the corporations, and go back to some dim memory of the way things used to be before.

Works Cited

Biller, Diana. "The Essential Cyberpunk Reading List." *io9.com*, 25 Dec. 2015, io9.gizmodo.com/the-essential-cyberpunk-reading-list-1714180001.

Canavan, Gerry. "Capital as Artificial Intelligence." *Journal of American Studies*, vol. 49, no. 4, 2015, pp. 685–709.

Engels, Friedrich. *Anti-Dühring*. Progress Publishers, 1877, 30 June 2018, www.marxists.org/archive/marx/works/1877/anti-duhring/ch24.htm.

"Filling the Void—Understanding the Formation of the Bootes Void in Intergalactic Space." *Discover*, Aug. 1995, findarticles.com/p/articles/mi_m1511/is_n8_v16/ai_17253874.

Freedman, Carl. *Critical Theory and Science Fiction*. Wesleyan UP, 2000.

Fukuyama, Francis. "The End of History?" *The National Interest*, vol. 16, Summer 1989, pp. 3–18.

Gibson, William. "The Gernsback Continuum." *Burning Chrome*. Ace, 1987, pp. 23–35.

———. *Neuromancer*. Ace, 1984.

Jameson, Fredric. "A Global Neuromancer." *publicbooks.org*, July 1, 2015, www.publicbooks.org/a-global-neuromancer/.

Pilsch, Andrew. *Transhumanism: Evolutionary Futurism and the Human Technologies of Utopia*. U of Minnesota P, 2017.

Raulerson, Joshua. *Singularities: Technoculture, Transhumanism, and Science Fiction in the Twenty-first Century*. U of Liverpool P, 2013.

Shaviro, Steven. "The Singularity Is Here." *shaviro.com*, 2005, www.shaviro.com/Othertexts/Singularity.pdf.

Stephenson, Neal. *Snow Crash*. Bantam, 1992.

Stross, Charles. *Accelerando*. Ace, 2005.

———. "Invaders from Mars." *antipope.org*, 2010, www.antipope.org/charlie/blog-static/2010/12/invaders-from-mars.html.

Vinge, Vernor. "The Coming Technological Singularity: How to Survive in the Post-Human Era," 1993, edoras.sdsu.edu/~vinge/misc/singularity.html.

———. "True Names." *Binary Star*, no. 5, 1981, pp. 133–232.

9

STEAMPUNK

Jess Nevins

Steampunk is a term coined in 1987 by author K.W. Jeter as a playful alteration of cyberpunk to refer to a series of cultural practices that predate cyberpunk (sometimes by as much as a century); or, as Barry Brummett defines it in *Clockwork Rhetoric: The Language and Style of Steampunk* steampunk "resituates aesthetic elements from the Age of Steam into our world. It imagines an aesthetic that would occur had steam and electricity remained the primary industrial sources of power" (ix). Defining steampunk, however, has proven difficult given its evolving nature over the course of its production and even Brummett's useful definition proves inadequate to address all types of steampunk with differing, even competing philosophies, politics, and aesthetics. As a result, steampunk can be best regarded not as a genre but as a cultural formation[1] that encompasses print fiction, film, music, gaming, and even fashion inspired by the Age of Steam and Electricity and its concurrent aesthetics. The question therefore becomes not what constitutes the 'genre of steampunk,' but what is the meaning of those cultural practices, past and present: What do they represent? who do they represent? and in what cultural direction do they point? A chronological approach to steampunk's evolution is therefore the best method for addressing these questions.

9.1 The Formation Phase

What I call steampunk's Formation Phase began in the 19th century when the advent of steam as a power source gave rise to extrapolations about its potential. Such works as Jane Webb's *The Mummy!: Or a Tale of the Twenty-Second Century* (1827), set in a steam-powered future three hundred years hence with clockwork surgeons, lawyers, and judges, or the anonymously-written *Anti-Humbug* (1840), whose steam-powered 40th century features global travel via steam-powered railways, posited a future in which steam was the lever on which substantial social changes could be initiated. As the century progressed, steam gave way to electricity as the power source capable of creating miracles in not only a fictional future but also the present or near-present. For example, Jules Verne's *20,000 Leagues Under the Sea* (1870) features the *Nautilus*, an extrapolation of contemporaneous submarines, powered by electricity, not steam. Meanwhile, the dime novels of the 1880s and 1890s were gradually evolving from Edward S. Ellis's *The Steam Man of the Prairies* (1868) and Harry Enton's Frank Reade edisonade *Frank Reade and His Steam Man of the Plains* (1883) to Luis Senarens's Frank Reade, Jr. stories of invention featuring wonderful vehicles and weapons making use of electricity rather than steam. Steam power quickly became symbolic not of potential futures but, instead, of dead pasts in both reality and early science fiction (sf), and steampunk stories were no exception. The sf of the first half of the 20th century looked to possible futures rather than dead pasts and focused on nuclear power and future scenarios rather than steam or electricity and narratives set in the past. Those few proto-steampunk narratives to appear, like the Richard Fleischer film *20,000 Leagues Under the Sea* (1954) and Michael Garrison TV program *The Wild Wild West* (1965–69), were strictly un-ironic period pieces, despite their use of steam- and electricity-powered advanced technology and weapons.

The social and political revolutions of the 1950s and 1960s were matched in steampunk by stylistic, thematic, and narrative upheavals. One such upheaval was a new tendency to write sf about sf, but in an acutely critical way. One development of this meta-criticism was the leftist political commentary of a trio of books: Ronald Clark's *Queen Victoria's Bomb* (1967), Michael Moorcock's *Warlord of the Air* (1971), and Moorcock's *The Land Leviathan* (1974). This trio used the iconography of sf to criticize the conservative and imperialist bent of contemporary sf; Moorcock used both steam power and the material of iconic sf authors like Jules Verne and H.G. Wells for that purpose. The trio of novels reminded readers that steam power had the potential to be a potent and meaningful symbol of sf's past.

K.W. Jeter's books *Morlock Night* (1979) and *Infernal Devices* (1987) were the next significant works of steampunk during its Formation Phase, and can be viewed as the first novels close to what is currently thought of as steampunk. It is for this reason that despite the proto-steampunk works of authors like Tim Powers and James P. Blaylock during the late 1970s and 1980s, K.W. Jeter is seen by steampunk aficionados as the *ur*-steampunk author, in much the same way that William Gibson is the *ur*-cyberpunk author. With its depiction of Morlocks traveling back in time to terrorize Victorian England—a symbolic revenge of the oppressed against the ruling classes—*Morlock Night* is clearly inspired by H.G. Wells's *The Time Machine* (1895) while *Infernal Devices* features clockwork devices, biological engineering, and time travel. The setting and iconography of both novels, coupled with *Infernal Devices*'s widespread reviews, helped popularize steampunk and generated increased interest from fans and writers alike. For example, Frank Chadwick's *Space: 1889* (1988) was one of the earliest steampunk roleplaying games and features an alternate-history interplanetary setting in which the European powers and the U.S. have imperialistically branched out into the solar system via the 'ether propeller' which propels ships through outer space.[2] Although *Space: 1889* diverges considerably from what would become the standard steampunk setting of urban Victorian London, it further propagated some of the assumptions and messages of *Morlock Night* and *Infernal Devices*, and other contemporaneous steampunk texts (such as Barbara Hambly's *Those Who Hunt the Night* (1988)): Steampunk was ineluctably intertwined with the late Victorian time period and the Victorian English, and that steampunk un-ironically displayed some of the core *ethoi* of the Victorians, including sexism, racism, and imperialism/colonialism.

The 1990s proved particularly fruitful for steampunk's development, in particular with the publication of William Gibson and Bruce Sterling's award-nominated *The Difference Engine* (1990), quite possibly the single-most influential steampunk text of the Formation Phase. *The Difference Engine* tells the story of an alternate history England in which Charles Babbage perfected his difference engine and developed an analytical engine, leading to advanced steam-powered technology and punch-card-programmed computers. *The Difference Engine* cemented what has become steampunk's at-times clichéd central tropes and motifs: an alternate history Victorian London setting, usually full of grime, soot, and smog; pervasive and dominant steam-powered technology; the laureling of scientists and inventors; and the extrapolation of technology, culture, and fashion. The novel's strong anti-imperialist and anti-authority message, however, was not so widely imitated: Gibson and Sterling's emphasis on the malign power of the Central Statistics Bureau and on the negative effects of a more successfully expansive and imperialistic Great Britain was not picked up by later authors.

While Gibson and Sterling's novel is an alternate history focusing on Babbage's steam-powered engines, James P. Blaylock's *Lord Kelvin's Machine* (1992) focuses on a different engine by another engineer: Lord Kelvin's time machine. The novel, an expansion of Blaylock's 1985 novelette "Lord Kelvin's Machine," is the third in his steampunk series—preceded by *The Digging Leviathan* (1984) and *Homunculus* (1986)—that collectively repeat steampunk tropes, although Blaylock's work is more globe-circling an adventure than the London-focused *The Difference Engine*. The critical and financial success of the award-nominated *Lord Kelvin's Machine* proved to other writers that steampunk did not end with *The Difference Engine*, but was a viable trend that could be both popularly and critically successful. In fact, a 1992 review of *Lord Kelvin's Machine* in *Kirkus Reviews* was the first mainstream, non-sf venue to use 'steampunk' to describe Blaylock's novel, indicating that awareness of this mode was spreading beyond sf's borders into the greater world of letters.

Steampunk was also not restricted to novels, novellas, and short stories from the west. For example, Hideaki Anno and Hayao Miyazaki's anime *Nadia: The Secret of Blue Water* (1990–91) follows the exploits of teenaged protagonist Nadia in an alternate version 1889. While the orphaned Nadia is fleeing for her life with a valuable jewel (the Blue Water), she is rescued by Verne's Captain Nemo aboard the *Nautilus*. *Nadia* proved influential on later steampunk anime, including Katsuhiro Otomo's *Steamboy* (2004), even though it has had seemingly little influence on western steampunk, no doubt because of its Japanese language and mise-en-scène. Similarly, Yoshinori Satake's *Koutetsu Teikoku* (1992) helped propel steampunk into the video game market. Drawing on the steampunk elements of the anime *Castle in the Sky* (Miyazaki 1986), including airships, air pirates, and steam-powered robots, and on a recognition of how the Victorians viewed steam power, as a limitless (if potentially dangerous) source of power, Satake created a science-fictional world in *Koutetsu Teikoku* that features an alternate timeline and steam-powered technology. The world of *Koutetsu Teikoku* is riven by war waged by steam-powered vehicles and weapons, and the largest city in the world is dominated by an industrialist and robber baron; the player's goal is ultimately to overthrow the dictator. Although *Koutetsu Teikoku* was a cult favorite in Japan and generally viewed favorably by American gamers, its American debut as *Steel Empire* (1992), though financially successful, received a mixed reception from critics. Nevertheless, *Koutetsu Teikoku/Steel Empire* is notable both as the first steampunk video game and as a significant influence on successive generations of steampunk video games, which repeat its anti-imperialist, pro-punk theme. Hiroyuki Ito's *Final Fantasy VI* (1994) is the foremost of the games influenced by *Koutetsu Teikoku*. *Final Fantasy VI* was enormously popular with players and critics and continues to be acclaimed, and its influence on later steampunk video games is considerable, which often model both their look and their themes on *Final Fantasy VI*. Finally, Jeffrey Boam and Carlton Cuse's television show *The Adventures of Brisco County, Jr.* (1993–94) was a steampunk western that aired on Fox for 27 episodes. *Brisco County, Jr.* developed a cult following and provided steampunk devotees with an example of how steampunk could be merged with other genres (the western) and media (television).

While the 1990s saw steampunk inching into other media, its print form was certainly not being neglected. For example, Paul Di Filippo's *The Steampunk Trilogy* (1995), a collection featuring the novellas "Victoria" (1991), "Walt and Emily" (1993), and "Hottentots" (1995), was the first collection or novel to contain the word 'steampunk' in the title, which helped propagate both the name and the steampunk mode itself. *The Steampunk Trilogy* also culminates steampunk's Formation Phase because by 1995 the tropes and motifs, characters, and plot devices most typically identified with steampunk—i.e., everything from the male inventor to the grimy urban Victorian setting to the extrapolated steam- or electricity-powered technology—were in place and being replicated. At the same time, steampunk's conservatism was abundantly obvious by the mid-1990s. Any revolutionary aspect of its founding works that envisioned fantastic steam- and electricity-powered futures had been slowly replaced by steampunk's idealized visions of a past, alternative or otherwise, that offered creators and users a sanctuary of sorts from the changes of the postmodern era. Steampunk, whether intentionally or otherwise, offered a space where traditional mores, concepts, and ideals—i.e., overwhelmingly white, straight, male, British—were preserved in tandem with the material's retrogressive racial, sexual, and pro-imperialism socio-political stances.

9.2 The Establishment Phase

What I am identifying as steampunk's Establishment Phase took place from 1996 to 2008, and during this period steampunk flourished in both fictional narratives and non-literary forms. In prose, Jonathan Green's *Unnatural History* (2007), George Mann's *Affinity Bridge* (2008), and Dru Pagliassotti's *Clockwork Heart* (2008) stood out as sterling examples of steampunk fiction while Kenneth Oppel's *Airborn* (2004) was the first of numerous steampunk novels in the young adult (YA) field. Related, Peter Nicholls and David Langford draw attention to YA author Philip Reeve, arguably one of the prime movers in what followed, with at least seven very popular steampunk novels, from *Mortal Engines* (2001) to *Scrivener's Moon* (2011). And Alan Moore and Kevin O'Neill's comic book series *League of Extraordinary Gentlemen* (1999–2018) proved to be a high point for steampunk in American comic books by appealing to both critics and the comics-reading audience. *League of Extraordinary Gentlemen*, featuring characters taken from literature, including Allan Quatermain, Captain Nemo, Dr. Henry Jekyll/Edward Hyde, and Wilhelmina Murray to name a few, is a skillful satire of Victorian literature and superhero comics, even if by embracing its characters and illustrations fans were slower to perceive its satire of Victorian manners, racial assumptions, and masculinity.

Steampunk was also well-represented in film, notably by Stephen Norrington and James Robinson's adaptation of *League of Extraordinary Gentlemen* (2003) and Nobuyoshi Habara's anime *Steam Detectives* (1998–99). The latter's story, an adaptation of Kia Asamiya's manga series (1994–99) of the same name, follows a young detective named Narutaki who solves crimes in Steam City, a steam-driven metropolis dependent on coal as its sole power source. *Steam Detectives* was the first major steampunk manga/anime since *Nadia: The Secret of Blue Water* and was the first significant introduction of steampunk into Japanese society, and helped pave the way for later steampunk anime, such as Katsuhiro Otomo's *Steamboy* (2004). A notable cinematic standout, however, is Hollywood's big budget *Wild Wild West* (Sonnenfeld 1999), the film version of the earlier TV series. *Wild Wild West* took steampunk mainstream, starring A-list actors Will Smith, Salma Hayak, Kevin Kline, and Kenneth Branagh, and earned an estimated $222 million dollars in gross global revenue, which represents an audience of roughly 40 million people worldwide who were exposed, perhaps for the first time, to steampunk. *Wild Wild West* was thoroughly a steampunk in its aesthetic (costumes are late 19th century in origin; technology is steam-powered and covered in shining brass), characters (a male genius inventor and a steam-powered Confederate general), and steam-powered technology (including a steam locomotive equipped with advanced technology, a steam-powered *mecha* spider, and a Confederate general in a steam-powered walker).

Music proved equally productive and enticing for steampunk. Albums like Dr. Steel's eponymous *Dr. Steel* (2001) and *Dr. Steel II: Eclectic Boogaloo* (2001); Vernian Process's *Steam Age Symphony* (2003); Abney Park's post-2005 music, including *Lost Horizons* (2008) and *Aether Shanties* (2010); and Professor Elemental's *The Indifference Engine* (2009) produced songs with steampunk-influenced lyrics (such as those to Professor Elemental's paean to steam power, "Steam Powered") and used traditional 19th-century and steampunk instruments (such as Abney Park's "clockwork guitar," "flintlock bass," and "Tesla-powered keyboards") while performing in Victorian or Victorian-styled attire, essentially creating the musical mode of 'steampunk music.' The American band Rasputina's first album *Thanks for the Ether* (1996), however, anticipated steampunk music and was a critical success, even if it was generally ignored by the public. *Thanks for the Ether* used replicas of 19th-century instruments to perform the songs and featured performers dressed in late Victorian garb. As a result, while *Thanks for the Ether* was not directly influential to later steampunk music, its historical importance deserves renewed critical and popular attention.

Finally, steampunk's success in the gaming industry continued with William H. Stoddard's *GURPS Steampunk* (2000), a handbook for steampunk tabletop roleplaying gaming that reified the borders and substance of the genre in a programmatic, prescriptive fashion. *GURPS Steampunk* was far from the first non-fiction work to provide a definition of steampunk. Book and story reviews had been bandying about the term since its first use, but *GURPS Steampunk* was the longest and most detailed definition of the genre to that point. A number of steampunk tabletop roleplaying games would appear over the next several years, including Alejandro Melchor's *OGL Steampunk* (2004), Joseph Goodman's *Dragonmech* (2004), Privateer Press's *Iron Kingdoms* (2004), Shane Hensley's *Deadlands: Reloaded* (2006), and Goodman Games's *Etherscope* (2006). Most of these drew on different sources and genres for inspiration, from high fantasy (*Iron Kingdoms*) to westerns (*Deadlands*), but all include steampunk tropes and characters and bill themselves as 'steampunk' roleplaying games.

While steampunk proved lively in this Establishment Phase, it also proved resilient in its dominant, retrogressive ethos. If retrofuturism, as Frederic Jameson describes it, is a kind of nostalgia for the "historical and dated" visions of "properly 'S-F' futures" (151), then steampunk remained thoroughly retrofuturistic in the Establishment Phase. In other words, steampunk repeated and reinforced the conservatism that defined the end of the Formation Phase. Nevertheless, steampunk artists did exist who rebelled against steampunk's conservatism and attempted to redefine steampunk in less restrictive and more progressive ways. For example, China Miéville's *King Rat* (1998) and *Perdido Street Station* (2000) feature a Victorian aesthetic, a choked urban milieu not unlike Victorian London, and steam-powered technology common to steampunk. Miéville blends science-fictional and fantastic elements in these (and other) works, ranging from magic to other-planetary settings to various nonhuman species, prompting Nicholls and Langford to write Miéville "shows a debt to urban fantasy generally, and Steampunk in its darker aspects particularly." Miéville's message to later steampunk writers was clear: Steampunk did not have to be limited to common tropes, motifs, and plot devices—it could become increasingly experimental and boundary-crossing.

The boundary-crossing evident in Miéville's work is also apparent in Ann and Jeff VanderMeer's *Steampunk* (2008) anthology which included a wide variety of steampunk material, from that typical of the Establishment Phase (Paul Di Filippo's "Victoria") to hybrid steampunk (Michael Chabon's "The Martian Agent, A Planetary Romance" [2003]) and even steampunk which featured non-Victorian settings and characters (Jay Lake's "The God-Clown is Near" [2007]). *Steampunk* was a relatively high-profile anthology and received a significant amount of attention inside and outside sf, thanks to both the quality of its stories and the large number of reviews it garnered, and its hybrid and divergent steampunk narratives included—Rachel Pollack's "Reflected Light" (2007) takes place on another world, while Neal Stephenson's "Excerpts from the Third and Last Volume of *Tribes of the Pacific Coast*" (1995) is part-steampunk and part-cyberpunk—were strong indicators of steampunk's future.

Finally, steampunk in the Establishment Phase underwent an unexpected expansion and became "a genre of couture, describing a clothing style with retro elements, most commonly from the Victorian era with such retro-tech accessories as motorists' or pilots' goggles (preferably brass-framed) and clockwork components" (Nicolls and Langford). The roots of this fashion can be traced to steampunk fan Kit Stolen who began dressing in what he called a 'steampunk' style, based on extrapolations of Victorian men's clothing. In August 2003 he made images of his hairstyle and pseudo-Victorian clothing available to an Internet steampunk fan group. A decade later, steampunk fashion has lost little of its vigor or its fans, and has produced numerous exhibitions, such as John Galliano's spring 2010 haute couture show for Christian Dior, and books, including

Spurgeon Vaughn Ratcliffe's *Steampunk Fashion* (2012) and Katherine Gleason and Diana Pho's *Anatomy of Steampunk: The Fashion of Victorian Futurism* (2013).

In spite of steampunk's growing popularity and its expansion into other media forms, including fashion, steampunk's tropes and motifs, milieus, and character types became increasingly ossified. As a result, the negative elements of the Victorian era—i.e., racism, classism, sexism, imperialism—became ever more deeply embedded into the steampunk mode. The typical steampunk narrative may have offered its audience a fictional trip to an idealized Victorian past, but it was largely a whitewashed version hailing a white, male, heterosexual audience above all others. Much like the steampunk in the Formative Phase, steampunk in this Establishment Phase merely repeated a fantasy of a return to a historical time period where white, heterosexual men were privileged and all others were largely disadvantaged. Steampunk therefore remained a conservative wish fulfillment narrative for the majority of its audience. The constant state of change in the contemporary world was rejected by steampunk in favor of a longing for the mythical 'good ol' days' defined and popularized by much of this Establishment Phase. One such was S.M. Stirling's *The Peshawar Lancers* (2002), which presented a contemporary world stuck with 19th-century steam technology and in which the British Empire remains the most powerful empire on Earth. *The Peshawar Lancers* embraces and valorizes classism, sexism, and imperialism, and moreover is one of the few steampunk narratives of the Establishment Phase to be openly racist in its treatment of racial others, in this case Afghans, Indians, and Muslims. Much more common were writers who refused to address, in any fashion, the widespread racism of the time period, while keeping their narratives' casts purely (and unnaturally) white and British. This avoidance of the uncomfortable issue of racism constitutes a racism in itself, a racism by omission. China Miéville, with his mixing of races and species in *Perdido Street Station*, for example, avoided this trap. Most others did not.

9.3 The Revolutionary Phase

Steampunk entered its Revolutionary Phase in 2008, and the U.S. and Great Britain continue to be the leading producers of steampunk literature, although their output seems to be in decline following a peak of 2011–15; for example, 2017s output of print-based steampunk is 40% less than 2015, and as of July 2018 the output is 10% less than the same period in 2017 (Internet Science Fiction Database). Part of the reason for this decline may very well be current American and British steampunk literature contains the same narrative architecture and politics as steampunk from the Establishment Phase. Therefore, despite the originality of works by authors like Cherie Priest (the "Clockwork Century" novels, 2009–13) and Gail Carriger (the "Parasol Protectorate" and "Finishing School" novels, 2009–15), whose narratives include intriguing and intelligent variations on steampunk themes, politics, tropes, and motifs, whether former slaves turned brilliant inventors (Priest's *Fiddlehead* [2013]) or the mixing of screwball comedy of manners with steampunk (Carriger's *Soulless* [2009]), American and British steampunk literature remains hard pressed to offer a genuinely new generation of stories. At the same time, British and American guides to steampunk published during this period, including Mike Perschon's "The Steampunk Aesthetic: Techofantasies in a Neo-Victorian Retrofuture" (2012) and Brian Robb's *Steampunk: An Illustrated History of Fantastical Fiction, Fanciful Film and Other Victorian Visions* (2012), increasingly offer prescriptive and restrictive positions on what constitutes steampunk and how the genre is defined. Perschon's definition of steampunk limits itself to "neo-Victorianism" (6–8), while Robb defines steampunk as "a subgenre of science fiction and fantasy literature, primarily concerned with alternative history, especially an imaginary 'Victorian era'" (iii).

Even anthologies of steampunk criticism, such as *Steaming into a Victorian Future: A Steampunk Anthology* (2013), edited by Julie Anne Taddeo and Cynthia J. Miller, and Brummett's *Clockwork Rhetoric: The Language and Style of Steampunk*, respond almost entirely to the steampunk of the conservative Establishment Phase and ignore the innovations of the more radical Revolutionary Phase. Even such recent works as Rachel A. Bowser and Brian Croxall's edited anthology *Like Clockwork: Steampunk Pasts, Presents, and Futures* and Susana Loiza's *Speculative Imperialisms: Monstrosity and Masquerade in Postracial Terms* tend to stress the Victorian or neo-Victorian aspect of steampunk.

Steampunk produced by authors of color inside the U.S., however, has reacted to the racism of Establishment Phase steampunk literature—as demonstrated in Sook Yi Goh's recent dissertation (2017)—by creating narratives that address the historical racism of the U.S. and Great Britain. Under the label of 'steamfunk,' a term coined by author Maurice Broaddus on Facebook in 2009,[3] works like Milton Davis and Balogun Ojetade's *Steamfunk!* anthology (2013), Brian Barron's short film (2013), and Balogun Ojetade's film *Rite of Passage: The Steamfunk Movie* (2014) merge African and African-American aesthetics, fashion styles, and characters with select steampunk tropes and motifs. These narratives contain contemporary political and social critiques of the racist and imperialist politics of both the historical U.S. and UK as well as of the steampunk narratives of conventional, Establishment Phase steampunk. The concept of steamfunk is becoming increasingly popular not only in literature but in fashion and cosplay (with over 1,000 pins on Pinterest).

Steampunk from outside the Anglophone literary world also displays considerable vitality and originality. For example, increasing numbers of steampunk stories and novels are published in European and Asian countries, from France, Germany, and Spain to Singapore and Thailand, and these stories often reflect local concerns and ideologies, and make use of local environments, tropes, motifs, and character types. Gerson Lodi-Ribeiro and Luis Filipe Silva's *Vaporpunk* (2009), Maisarah Abu Samah and Rosemary Lim's *The Steampowered Globe* (2012), Sook Yi Goh and Joyce Chng's *The Sea is Ours: Tales from Steampunk Southeast Asia* (2015), and Sarah Hans's *Steampunk World* (2014) are stellar examples of this multicultural approach to steampunk. The collections feature steampunk stories written by international authors, including Octavio Aragão (Brazil), Paolo Chikiamco (the Philippines), Indrapramit Das (India), Robert Liow (Malaysia), Ivanna Mendels (Indonesia), Yves Robert (Portugal), Pear Nuallak (Thailand), and J.Y. Yang (Singapore). The stories in these anthologies are recognizably steampunk by virtue of their retrofuturist settings and technologies, but they diverge from traditional steampunk by using settings other than Victorian London or America; character types other than the white male inventor; local characters rather than English or American; and creatures, plot sequences, and technologies that reinforce their anti-colonial, anti-imperialistic, and even anti-capitalist politics, as in Olivia Ho's "Working Woman" (in *The Sea is Ours*). These anthologies point forward to what Goh describes as multicultural steampunk which is "separate from the common understanding of steampunk that hinges on neo-Victorianism and imaginings of the British Empire. It often refers to cultural production in which the steampunk aesthetic is applied to or combined with some region, space, or item that is designated non-white in current perceptions of race" (v). Multicultural steampunk may look backward for inspiration, but the settings, characters, tropes, motifs, and characters are neither dated and empty of narrative potential nor white and western in the way that traditional steampunk has been defined.

At the same time, non-literary steampunk is in ascension around the world. For example, John Biggs's "Tinkering at Home, Selling on the Web" (11/5/2007) and Ruth La Ferla's "Steampunk Moves Between 2 Worlds" (5/8/2008) appeared in *The New York Times* within six months of each other, describing steampunk as a subculture that "embraces music, film, design and now music" (La Ferla); similarly, only a few months later MTV began reporting on steampunk, in "All Aboard the Steampunk Train," describing steampunk gatherings and steampunk music and musicians. Finally jumping on the bandwagon, Lev Grossman wrote the article "Steampunk: Reclaiming Tech for the Masses" for *Time* magazine (2009), and, four years later, Erin Skarda (*Time*) and Barbara Thau (*Forbes*) were among some correspondents reporting on IBM's scan of trends on social media that predicted the ascendance of steampunk fashion. Steampunk books, ranging from the Steampunk Oriental Laboratory's DIY (do-it-yourself) fashion and gadget manual *Steampunk Style* (2012) to Professor Calamity, Alan Moore, and Margaret Killjoy's *A Steampunk's Guide to Sex* (2012), have become common post-2008. Major conventions, including the San Diego Comic-Con and Dragon Con regularly hold steampunk panels while international steampunk conventions have been held in England, France, the Netherlands, Luxembourg, and Germany. The annual "Steampunk Hands Around the World" project began in 2014, and its purpose is to allow steampunk bloggers around the world to host online events, with an increasing number of countries taking part in the project. Finally, several internationally famous musicians, including Justin Bieber ("Santa Claus Is Coming To Town," 2011), Smashing Pumpkins ("Tonight, Tonight," 1995), and Rush (the *Clockwork Angels* album, 2012) have made music videos and albums with substantial steampunk elements in them.

Steampunk has therefore become a global phenomenon: In Brazil, hundreds of steampunk fans make up a nation-wide steampunk community, following the founding of the first steampunk 'lodges' (clubs) in Rio de Janeiro and São Paulo in 2008 (Jenkins); in South Africa, local fans of the mode have become designers of steampunk clothing and held gatherings which highlight steampunk fashion, have held steampunk-themed weddings, and have opened Truth, a steampunk-themed coffee shop (Tanzen Best); the Hong Kong-based artist James Ng merged Chinese history and Industrial Revolution technology into the "Imperial Steam & Light" project, and his steampunk art, which has had exhibitions in New York, London, Italy, Beijing, and Seoul, combines traditional elements of Chinese and Japanese culture (e.g., samurai to cheongsam to combat junks) with the cogs, gears, rotors, monocles, clockwork, and steam engines common to steampunk (Ng).

This progressive branch of steampunk's Revolutionary Phase constitutes in part a return to the mode's earliest days during the Formation Phase when novels like Moorcock's *The Warlord of the Air*, Jeter's *Morlock Nights*, and Gibson and Sterling's *The Difference Engine* promulgated leftist and even revolutionary politics. More broadly, however, the progressive steampunk of the Revolutionary Phase constitutes a great leap forward for steampunk thanks to its adoption of a new, internationalist, anti-imperialist, anti-racist approach. The multicultural steampunk of this Revolutionary Phase draws on a global community of peoples, cultures, and histories rather than limiting itself to the Victorian time period and to Victorian and neo-Victorian politics, character types, and source material. Multicultural steampunk displays a vitality and freshness lacking in Anglophilic steampunk; as a result, the audience for (multicultural) steampunk has responded to this broadening of steampunk's horizons by eagerly consuming its progressive narratives rather than the stilted Victorianism of conventional steampunk. As befits a cultural formation, steampunk has evolved and expanded to become a worldwide cultural phenomenon and its momentum is in large part fueled by its devotees' enthusiasm for steampunk fiction, film, and even fashion of all sorts. In the end, while steampunk culture has a vitality lacking in much conventional literary steampunk, multicultural steampunk, particularly its literary form, heralds a bright future for all steampunk, literary and non-literary alike; as a result, its ongoing evolution promises a bright, steam-powered future for steampunk.

Notes

1 Lawrence Grossberg describes genre not as a collection of literary texts but instead as a cultural formation, which "is a historical articulation, an accumulation or organization of practices. The question is how particular cultural practices, which may have no intrinsic or even apparent connection, are articulated together to construct an apparently new identity[…]the formation has to be read as the articulation of a number of discrete events, only some of which are discursive" (70). As the Introduction to *The Routledge Companion to Cyberpunk Culture* makes clear, this entire collection is inspired in part

by Grossberg's idea of 'cultural formation,' albeit filtered through Thomas Foster's academic work in *The Souls of Cyberfolk*. Therefore, there is significant overlap among cultural formation, steampunk, and cyberpunk.

2 *Space: 1889* proved enormously significant in the roleplaying game industry and almost twenty years later steampunk roleplaying games like Nigel McClelland and Ben Redmond's *Etherscope* (2005) and Benjamin Baugh's *The Kerberos Club* (2008) would acknowledge its influence.

3 Maurice Broaddus, Facebook message to author, Oct. 6, 2018.

Works Cited

Bowser, Rachel A. and Brian Croxall, eds. *Like Clockwork: Steampunk Pasts, Presents, and Futures*. U of Minnesota P, 2016.

Brummett, Barry, ed. *Clockwork Rhetoric: The Language and Style of Steampunk*. U of Mississippi P, 2014.

Foster, Thomas. *The Souls of Cyber-Folk: Posthumanism as Vernacular Theory*. U of Minnesota P, 2005.

Goh, Sook Yi. "Shades of Sepia: Examining Eurocentrism and Whiteness in Relation to Multiculturalism in Steampunk Iconography, Fandom, and Culture Industry." PhD. Dissertation, University of California at Riverside, 2017.

Grossberg, Lawrence. *We Gotta Get Outta This Place*. Routledge, 1992.

Grossman, Lev. "Steampunk: Reclaiming Tech for the Masses." *Time*, 14 Dec. 2009.

Internet Speculative Fiction Database, isfdb.org/cgi-bin/index.cgi.

Jameson, Frederic. "Progress Versus Utopia; or, Can We Imagine the Future?" *Science Fiction Studies*, vol. 9, no. 2, 1982, pp. 147–58.

Jenkins, Henry. "The Steampunk Scene in Brazil: Strategies of Sociality," Confessions of an ACA-Fan, 13 Aug. 2014, henryjenkins.org/blog/2014/08/the-steampunk-scene-in-brazil-strategies-of-sociality.html.

La Ferla, Ruth. "Steampunk Moves Between 2 Worlds." *The New York Times*, 08 May 2008.

Ng, James. "Imperial Steam & Light." *JamesNgArt*, jamesngart.com/imperialsteamandlight.html.

Perschon, Mike. "The Steampunk Aesthetic: Technofantasies in a Neo-Victorian Retrofuture." PhD. Dissertation, University of Alberta, 2012.

Robb, Brian. *Steampunk: An Illustrated History of Fantastical Fiction. Fanciful Film and Other Victorian Visions: Victorian Visionaries. Scientific Romances and Fantastic Fictions*. Aurum P, 2012.

Skarda, Erin. "Will Steampunk Really Be the Next Big Fashion Trend?" *Time*, 17 Jan. 2013.

Taddeo, Julie Anne and Cynthia J. Miller, eds. *Steaming into a Victorian Future: A Steampunk Anthology*. Rowman & Littlefield, 2014.

Tanzen Best, Nicole. "Sensational Steampunk: What is it all about?" *Exclusive Books*, 2013, blog.exclus1ves.co.za/sensational-steampunk-what-is-it-all-about.

Thau, Barbara. "IBM Says Steampunk Looks Will Be All the Rage at National Chains This Year." *Forbes*, 15 Jan. 2013.

10

BIOPUNK

Lars Schmeink

While it is not quite clear when and where the term 'biopunk' was first used, its heritage reflects two distinct traditions of literary science fiction (sf): that of cyberpunk, on the one hand, and that of biological sf, on the other.[1] The latter, of course, is the far older tradition, with biology providing a "thematic emphasis emerg[ing] very early in the development of science fiction" (Parker 35), including such foundational texts as Mary Shelley's *Frankenstein* (1818) or H.G. Wells's *The Island of Doctor Moreau* (1896). The thematic focus of biological sf most relevant to biopunk is genetics, whether genetic mutation or "the feasibility and desirability of planned genetic alteration" (Parker 35). Cyberpunk, the other tradition informing biopunk, plays directly into mainstream culture's scientific interest in genetics and the issues "about the nature of life itself, about what it is to be human, about the future of the human race" (Reiss 13). Many of cyberpunk's themes connect with biological sf. Bruce Sterling, for example, writes about the loss of control by governments and big corporations as technology is no longer a tool of those in power, but "visceral," "pervasive, utterly intimate" (Preface xiii). Technology is for everyone to use and invades the minds and bodies of cyberpunk society. By extension a central theme in cyberpunk is that the borders of what constitutes the 'human' are being crossed, blurred, or erased. For example, in the documentary *No Maps for These Territories* (Neale 2000), Sterling reminisces upon cyberpunk's earliest days: "We were able to make computers glamorous. [...] This was a supermodel among technologies. [...] They were going to be cute; they were going to be miniature; they would be designed; they would be adorable. The boundaries of the human body would be crossed." Brian McHale notes that biopunk, just as cyberpunk, is founded upon the "centrifugal self" but in terms of prominent themes ascribes to it the revision of "Gothic-horror motifs of bodily invasion and disruption" (257). What differentiates biopunk from cyberpunk, therefore, is that it deals with the hybridization of the human not with machinic elements but with other organisms: human, animal, bacterial, fungal, viral, and so on. In biopunk fiction, the invasion of the body is intimate and visceral as it takes place on the level of the cell, or smaller still, on the level of the nucleotides that form all living matter.

It should therefore come as no surprise that Sterling, with his focus on violating the human body and mind-body invasions, evident in the Shapers and Mechanists populating his *Schismatrix Plus* universe, would prove instrumental in biopunk's outgrowth.[2] By the late-1980s when cyberpunk's original core started expressing dismay at how quickly their anti-authoritarian punk sensibility was being co-opted into what Lewis Shiner dismissively called "sci-fiberpunk" (25), Sterling imagined a world radically changed not by computer technology but by genetic engineering.[3] His short story "Our Neural Chernobyl" (1988), named for the catastrophic nuclear accident two years prior, becomes "biotechnology's worst disaster" during the late 20th and early 21st centuries, a time that Sterling in the story calls the "Age of the Normal Accident" (1). Drawing parallels to the "subculture of computer hacking" of the 1970s and 1980s, Sterling imagines the development of entrepreneurial freedoms in 'gene-hacking' as do-it-yourself-biologists (DIYbio) start making full use of "an enormously powerful technology suddenly within the reach of the individual" (3). In Sterling's future scenario, biohackers build upon the breakthrough success of using a viral-RNA sequence to insert and cut DNA at will and with playful ease, prompting genetic experiments catering not only to chronically ill patients, but also to illegal uses, such as drug-users craving a permanent high. One such experiment causes the 'neural Chernobyl,' triggering a growth burst in brain cells, which leaves humans riding a cognitive high of "eccentric genius" before suffering from "dendritic crash" and plunging them into "vision-riddled, poetic insanity" (5–6). But more than merely impacting drug-users, the virus has an unintended side effect as it jumps the species barrier and infects animal life, essentially enhancing the cognitive abilities of nonhuman animals. The story closes with a view on a posthuman world changed by genetic enhancements both of the human and the nonhuman animals, a possible world where we "share the planet with a fellow civilized species" (8) and "a fraction of the population has achieved physical immortality" (9) by genetic mutation.

As an early example of biopunk, "Our Neural Chernobyl" provides us with links to a cyberpunk heritage, while at the same time forking off from that heritage to evoke a strong sense of social responsibility, negating cyberpunk's countercultural, radical, even anarchic politics in favor of a utopian position that finds science integrated into a communal network. In the end, "Our Neural Chernobyl" demonstrates that biopunk may be closely related to cyberpunk, but it has developed into one of the most eminent forms of science-fictional exploration into biology. Not only does it pick up on a changing culture of scientific research (i.e., the kitchen sink research of do-it-yourself-biology), but it opens up the term 'biopunk' to a form of activism that addresses this research and its political, social, and judicial consequences.

Greg Bear's *Blood Music* (1985), a novel-length expansion of his short story "Blood Music" (1983), is also centrally important in biopunk's formation. In Bear's story, biotech-researcher Vergil Ulam creates "[a]utonomous organic computers" (15), microscopic organisms for medical purposes that possess intelligence, adaptability, and self-replicating powers. When confronted with their imminent destruction, Ulam rescues them by injecting them into his body, where the organisms evolve and finally become self-aware. They begin to 'infect' and assimilate all biological life and interconnect it into a new and growing mass of cellular consciousness. As Bear's story makes evident, biological boundaries are porous and can be crossed to create new and hybridized existences: forms of life that remind us how little needs to be changed to alter the world. "Our Neural Chernobyl" challenges the 'human' by virtue of both nonhuman animal sentience calling into question human uniqueness and by the uncontrollable mutation of the retrovirus generating unstable and shifting human subjectivities. *Blood Music* does the same by depicting sentient single-cell organisms linking together to create a distributed consciousness that assimilates human 'selves.' As exemplars of the biopunk that would follow them, "Our Neural Chernobyl" and *Blood Music* undermine liberal humanist subjectivity by rejecting human exceptionalism and autonomy, instead revealing multiple and complex subjectivities, constituted through hybridization with nonhuman animals, retroviruses, and artificial biological organisms.

10.1 Constitutive Elements of Biopunk

As Thomas Foster has pointed out (and many of the entries in this collection further demonstrate), cyberpunk needs to be viewed as a cultural formation interacting with the posthuman: it acts as "an intervention in and inflection of a preexisting discourse, which cyberpunk significantly transformed and broadened, providing a new basis for the acceptance of posthuman ideas

Biopunk

in contemporary American popular culture" (Foster xiii).[4] In spite of its posthuman potential, however, cyberpunk often retains a humanist subjectivity based on a position of human exceptionalism and the underlying idea that "there is a distinctive entity identifiable as the 'human,' a human 'self'" (Nayar 6). Cyberpunk, in many instances, depicts cybernetic technology as a means to enhance humans and overcome "any number of natural human limitations such as aging, death, suffering" (Philbeck 175). As a result, cyberpunk's transhumanist concepts of cyborg enhancement, up to its extreme position of uploading one's consciousness into fully realized machine bodies, are ways to allegedly free humanity from its biological limitations, or so the transhumanist arguments go. The humanist self, though, is untouched by these enhancements, transcending its bodily prison to consolidate its position of exceptionalism.

Biopunk may therefore be a better vehicle for posthuman lines of inquiry than cyberpunk; after all, cyberpunk's desire to transcend human biology is a "fantasy of escape" (Braidotti 91) and a "grafting of the posthuman onto a liberal humanist view of the self" (Hayles 286–87). Biopunk, on the other hand, is founded upon what Donna J. Haraway refers to as "to *become with* many" (4). After all, Haraway reminds us that only 10% of the cells in a human body consist of human genomes, while "the other 90% of the cells are filled with the genomes of bacteria, fungi, protists, and such, some of which play in a symphony necessary to my being alive at all, and some of which are hitching a ride and doing the rest of me, of us, no harm. I am vastly outnumbered by my tiny companions" (3–4). According to Haraway's understanding, *human* has thus always already been a hybridized existence, inextricably linked to other species. Therefore, biopunk powerfully explores the potential and the consequences that stem from this realization and best embodies the idea of a hybridized and pluralized posthumanity "constituted by and constitutive of multiple forms of life and machines" (Nayar 2).

Biopunk not only addresses the question of how the human relates to other forms of life, but it also challenges human relations with the environment, with the world. Cyberpunk's enclosures, zones, and virtual worlds are representations of the impact of human technology, their differences highlighting the fragmentation of ontology into what McHale calls "multiple-world spaces" (250). In other words, our practices shape and form the world we live in; culture and technology define the boundaries and makeup of our world. In their focus on technologically shaped worlds, many cyberpunk texts see the world, as Veronica Hollinger points out in her contribution to this collection, as defined by technology, with nature notably absent. Simply put, issues of human influence on ecology, or what is today referred to as the Anthropocene, act merely as background noise and not as narrative centers in cyberpunk. The scant attention paid to them lends credence to Gerry Canavan's critique that cyberpunk has traditionally offered a shortcut "for getting outside scarcity and precariousness—simply leave the material world altogether, by entering the computer. In virtual space, with no resource consumption or excess pollution to worry about, we can all be as rich as we want for as long as we want (or so the story goes)" (9).

Biopunk, on the other hand, highlights the unrepresentability of the world, preferring to leave the scale of the human behind to address a "grey ecology" which "propels us beyond our own finitude, opens us to alien scales of both being (the micro and the macro) and time (the effervescent, barely glimpsed; the geologic, in which life proceeds at a billion year pace)" (Cohen 383). In other words, biopunk is an intervention in the discourses of the Anthropocene by exploring human life on a micro scale, the Harawayian *becoming-with* of viruses and bacteria. At the same time, biopunk also challenges our conceptions of life on the macro scale. For example, both the retrovirus of "Our Neural Chernobyl" and the single-cell lifeforms of *Blood Music* spread to all forms of life; their impact is global and will be irreversible for the Earth as a whole.

Moreover, 21st-century biopunk, such as Margaret Atwood's *Oryx and Crake* (2003) or Paolo Bacigalupi's *The Windup Girl* (2009), emphasizes the destructive potential of genetic engineering for ecological balance. Bacigalupi's novel follows a gene-hunter through a world of global trade war over food seeds as genetic manipulation on a mass scale—crops, diseases, and even pests—has been used as a corporate strategy to destroy the competition and dominate their respective markets. *The Windup Girl* showcases the devastating results of unhindered genetic manipulation: a precarious world food supply, profound impact on the climate, aggressive invasive species killing ecological habitats, and a new form of humanoid life enslaved to its creators via genetic chains. Similarly, genetic engineering in Atwood's novel (and its two sequels, collectively known as the MaddAddam trilogy) has global-scale implications for all life. The story follows the actions of Crake, a rogue geneticist who creates a global plague that kills most of humanity and makes room for his newly engineered species of posthumans. In flashbacks, the novel depicts the ecological catastrophe caused by human interventions, prompting Crake to dismiss humanity as flawed and in need of replacing: newly created genetic hybrids destroy the ecological balance and the Earth has in large parts become uninhabitable. Genetic engineering, in these novels, threatens all life on the planet.

10.2 Biopunk as Cultural Formation

Much like cyberpunk is now a "cultural formation," a "historical articulation" of a variety of practices, be they textual, cultural, social, economic, or even political (Foster xvi), so too is biopunk. It has left its narrow confines as merely a biologically-inclined cyberpunk and now represents textual, medial, cultural, social, and political practices that delve into a variety of issues of life-altering biological research, of critical posthumanism, and of the Anthropocene, including not only the texts noted above but such narratives as Octavia Butler's Xenogenesis trilogy (1987–89), C.J. Cherryh's *Cyteen* (1988), Nancy Kress's *Beggars in Spain* (1993), or Paul Di Fillipo's *Ribofunk* short story collection (1996). These examples not only address biopunk's thematic issues—i.e., biological research, posthumanist critiques, and humanity's global and massive impact on the world—but also showcase biopunk's variance in Butler's feminist stance, Cherryh's space-opera adventure, Kress's more philosophical and economical musings, and Di Filippo's wild and surreal satire.

Biopunk is similarly infecting styles and fusing genres in recent film and television formats: *Dark Angel* (Cameron and Eglee 2000–02) centers on action and cyberpunk *noir* in a story about genetically created soldiers with superhuman powers escaping from a sinister corporation, while *Heroes* (Kring 2006–10) uses genetically engineered superhuman powers as part of a traditional family drama series, focusing on interpersonal relations and the consequences of becoming posthuman.

Biopunk's proliferation as a cultural formation is not just topical though; its stylistic choices (for example, in cinematic visual expression) vary just as strongly. *Gattaca* (Niccol 1997) is a film about a genetically perfected society, in which babies can be engineered via germline-manipulation to the specifications of the parents. It highlights heightened social injustices in limiting individual lives to genetically determined paths, especially those not engineered but born naturally. In terms of visuals, it favors an avant-garde aesthetics of modernism with strong architectural designs, thus linking modern-day genetics to a filmic vision of periods such as 1920s expressionism. Films such as Brandon Cronenberg's debut *Antiviral* (2012) or Vincenzo Natali's *Splice* (2009), on the other hand, lean toward the abject imagery of body horror. While *Antiviral* uses sterile, overly-lit showrooms and hospitals for its story about extreme, visceral fan cultures that 'consume' diseases carried by celebrity hosts, *Splice* prefers the dark Gothic and almost Frankensteinian ambience of underground laboratories and old farmhouses to present the creation and upbringing of its spliced human-animal hybrid, as well as its impact on its creators. Biopunk is visually heterogeneous and can be found in many different stylistic variants.

One prominent example of biopunk's thematic proliferation is the use of its tropes in zombie fictions, such as *I Am Legend* (Lawrence 2007) or *The Girl with All the Gifts* (McCarthy 2016), both of which feature a scientifically created infection (viral or fungal, respectively) almost wiping out human life. Both narratives follow survivors, as is typical for zombie fictions, and focus on the (futile) attempts to rebuild a human civilization. These narratives, however, make it explicit that the zombie-like posthumans have sentience and represent a newly formed society *after* the human,[5] a world *without us*: in *I Am Legend*, scientist Robert Neville realizes that his daily hunts and experiments make him the monster that has become 'legend' to this new society of posthuman creatures; in *The Girl with All the Gifts*, zombie-girl Melanie realizes that science demands her death for a cure to the plague. Confronted with the choice to save humanity or her own kind, she asks why the new society should die for the old to keep living? In the end, she sets ablaze and thus opens the fungal seedpods that will fully transform the Earth into a world without humans. As these examples show, biopunk's motifs of genetics and posthuman becomings have, over the last decade or two, fully saturated all aspects of popular cultural production.

The variance and spread of biopunk motifs in narrative fictions mirror a mainstream focus on genetics that has disseminated biopunk even further into the larger orbit of cultural practice. For example, the Quantified Self movement, with its purpose of self-measuring as many bodily functions as accurately as possible, also has an interest in genetic testing as provided by services such as 23andMe, which analyzes DNA samples. Knowledge about one's own genetic makeup is used to tailor training or nutrition and thus improve sports performance—ultimately, these practices mirror the extreme genetic determinism that is present in *Gattaca* and its genetically determined society. Modes of thinking connected with biopunk can be found in everyday common practice, but it is within the realm of artistic creation that biopunk reveals an important posthumanist critique. This is especially true in the area of conceptual, procedural, and/or performative "bioart," which "involves biotechnological methods and/or manipulation of living systems" (Hauser 84). Here biopunk functions as a critique of human exceptionalism and scientific hubris, as well as hinting at the porous boundaries of life and the global impact of technoscientific developments.

Artist Eduardo Kac, for example, genetically engineered a bio-luminescent bunny with the help of two French geneticists and curated the public discourse around this creation into the artwork "GFP Bunny" (2000). He blends the scientific act of genetic engineering, the social act of discussing its implications, and what Kac terms the "social integration," meaning the reactions of both the public and policy makers toward the transgenic animal. Two other artists, Ionat Zurr and Oron Catts of the Tissue Culture and Art Project, grew tissue from pig cells into wing shapes, confronting media and the public about their "hyberbolic discourse" of "genohype"—referring to expectations of radical change through genetics and the language of miracles in regard to research in biomedicine. The TCA grew three kinds of wings (which they describe as "bird-like," "bat-like," and "winged lizards") in miniature size (4 cms. long) to showcase the cultural meaning and values given to wings ("the good, the bad, the extinct") and the over-the-top claims of science (for example, genetically curing diseases such as cancer or Alzheimer's). As with Kac, the biotech creation is only part of the artwork, enhanced by the surrounding discourse (the piece was submitted to a show on genetics in art and rejected for its negative portrayal and criticism), as well as the official policy surrounding it (the artists' wish to file a patent for pig wings, to "'initiate and control' the pig wings market"). As these examples show, bioart, in its performance of public discourses, cultural practices, and controversies of policy, can be understood as an expression of biopunk, connecting critical posthuman thinking to our scientific and social life worlds.

10.3 Activism

Taking up the critique voiced by these artists and turning it into social activism is a loose group of DIYbio, biohackers, or biopunks (self-proclaimed) that came together around the turn of the 21st century and in "The Biopunk Manifesto" found a kind of philosophical treatise to express their values. Meredith Patterson, author of the manifesto and a computer scientist, is seen as a leading figure in the biopunk movement and approaches biology through its connection with information technology—thus conceptually drawing a parallel between cyberpunk and biopunk, between the anti-authoritarian practices of hacking code and hacking DNA. Speaking for biopunk activism, she demands scientific research be open, free, and in the hands of the public, arguing for empowerment through "scientific literacy" and the goal of "making the world a place that everyone can understand." In her manifesto, she explicitly states that engineers and scientists (professional or hobbyist) need to become political actors and activists, involved in policy because both corporations and politicians "wish to curtail individual freedom of inquiry." As such, DIYbio is part of the movement toward open practices (i.e., open data, open publishing, open education, open source, and open access), and biohackers have joined with lawyers and social activists to fight, for example, against the patenting of human genomic information or against the restrictions of access to biological materials.

The biohackers and biopunks organized around "The Biopunk Manifesto" are remarkably similar to Sterling's biohackers in "Our Neural Chernobyl": They see the potential of biology for changing the world but refuse to leave it in the hands of big science corporations or government institutions; they instead claim it as a public good. They are "the visionaries whose imaginations were set on fire by the knowledge that we had finally sequenced the human genome" (Newitz). In their pursuit of knowledge, they do not need the high-tech equipment of corporate laboratories, but rather rely on "the hack"; or, as journalist Marcus Wohlsen has pointed out, "[b]iohacking in the form promoted by DIYbio is about engineering elegant, creative, self-reliant solutions to doing biology while relying not on institutions but wits" (5). In this utopian conception of biopunk, freedom of data, scientific method, and research provide solutions to problems posed in medicine and biology, such as the hacking and curing of diseases (through crowdsourcing its genetic deciphering) or the creation of cheaper therapies (by decoupling them from corporate interests).

These positive outcomes are a strong motivational factor in the biohacking scene, but the actions taken, especially in regard to experimentation, are not always without critique. The discovery of the CRISPR technology (a genetic editing tool that allows for the cutting and insertion of DNA) has recently led to self-experimentation among biopunks and to several publicly documented uses of the technology. Josiah Zayner, for example, injected himself with CRISPR at a conference in October 2017 to cut out a gene that stopped muscle growth. He claims that his symbolic action is to promote free and open science, making genetic engineering a commodity that consumers can experiment with as they see fit (CBC), although it seems somewhat self-serving that he owns a company selling CRISPR sets to the public. But not all such experiments are for self-promotion: at the same time as Zayner, Tristan Roberts injected himself with a gene to produce antibodies against HIV, wishing to speed up lengthy trials for new treatments (CBC). As these cases show, and as Sterling has warned, powerful new biological technologies are now in the reach of the public, and biopunks are seizing them for a variety of reasons: in order to wrench power over biology and genetics away from big science corporations, in order to create unconventional solutions to medical problems, in order to challenge themselves scientifically, or simply in order to turn a profit.

No matter how one views the methods and values of the DIYbio scene, it is clear that biopunk's thinking lies at its core, blending concepts that used to be fiction with possibilities that are becoming more real by the minute. Biopunk has therefore bloomed in perhaps unexpected ways to become a cultural formation, extending its motifs and issues from literary fiction into the breadth of cultural production, political activism, and social practices. Genetic engineering, stem cell research, cloning, tissue culture production, and other biotechnological developments are pressing issues of our life world, and it falls to biopunk to provide us with both a dictionary to define our

Biopunk

discourses, fictional and factual, and a cultural roadmap to navigate the social and political implications of these new technologies. Biopunk is the imaginary for our biotechnological progress, it is a central theme of our posthumanism, and it is a key discourse in and of the Anthropocene. In sum, it is a key part of our science-fictional reality.

Notes

1 For a more detailed introduction to the complicated history of the term, see Schmeink, "Biopunk 101" and *Biopunk Dystopias*.
2 For a detailed case study of the story cycle, see Maria Goicoechea's contribution to this collection.
3 For the developments of Movement-era cyberpunk, see Graham J. Murphy's contribution to this collection.
4 For a detailed discussion of the different posthuman interventions of cyberpunk, see Julia Grillmayr's contribution to this collection.
5 Following Fredric Jameson's famous dictum that "it has become easier for us to imagine the end of the world than the end of capitalism" (cit. in Hassler-Forest 6), Dan Hassler-Forest connects zombie societies not just to the imagination of a world beyond the human, but to the imagination of "what kinds of worlds might be possible *beyond* capitalism" (151, emphasis in original).

Works Cited

Bear, Greg. *Blood Music*. Gollancz, 1985.
Braidotti, Rosi. *The Posthuman*. Polity, 2013.
CBC – Radio Canada. "Meet the Human Guinea Pig Who Hacked his own DNA." *Quirks & Quarks*, 11 Nov. 2017, cbc.ca/radio/quirks/diy-dna-hacks-wounds-take-longer-to-heal-at-night-why-daydreams-are-good-quirks-bombs-and-more-1.4395576/meet-the-human-guinea-pig-who-hacked-his-own-dna-1.4395589.
Canavan, Gerry. "If This Goes On." *Green Planets: Ecology and Science Fiction*, edited by Gerry Canavan and Kim Stanley Robinson. Wesleyan UP, 2014, pp. 1–21.
Christie, Deborah. "And the Dead Shall Walk." *Better Off Dead: The Evolution of the Zombie as Post-Human*, edited by Deborah Christie and Sarah Juliet Lauro. Fordham UP, 2011, pp. 61–65.
Cohen, Jeffrey Jerome. "Grey (A Zombie Ecology)." *Zombie Theory: A Reader*, edited by Sarah Juliet Lauro. U of Minnesota P, 2017, p. 381–94.
Dixon, Simon J., Heather A. Viles, and Bradley L. Garrett. "Ozymandias in the Anthropocene: The City as an Emerging Landform." *Area*, 2017, pp. 1–8. doi:10.1111/area.12358.
Foster, Thomas. *The Souls of Cyberfolk: Posthumanism as Vernacular Theory*. U of Minnesota P, 2005.
Haraway, Donna J. *When Species Meet*. U of Minnesota P, 2008.
Hassler-Forest, Dan. *Science Fiction, Fantasy, and Politics: Transmedia World-Building Beyond Capitalism*. Rowman, 2016.
Hauser, Jens. "Observations on an Art of Growing Interest: Toward a Phenomenological Approach to Art Involving Biotechnology." *Tactical Biopolitics: Art, Activism, and Technosciencee*, edited by Beatriz da Costa and Kavita Philip. MIT Press, pp. 83–104.
Hayles, N. Katherine. *How We Became Posthuman: Virtual Bodies in Cybernetics, Literature, and Informatics*. U of Chicago P, 1999.
Kac, Eduardo. "GFP Bunny." Homepage, ekac.org/gfpbunny.html.
McHale, Brian. *Constructing Postmodernism*. Routledge, 1992.
Nayar, Pramod K. *Posthumanism*. Polity, 2014.
Newitz, Annalee. "Biopunk." *San Francisco Bay Guardian*, 08 Aug. 2001.
No Maps for These Territories, directed by Mark Neale, 3DD Entertainment, 2000.
Parker, Helen N. *Biological Themes in Modern Science Fiction*. UMI Research, 1977.
Patterson, Meredith. "A Biopunk Manifesto." *Radio Free Meredith*, 30 Jan. 2010, maradydd.livejournal.com/496085.html.
Philbeck, Thomas D. "Ontology." *Post- and Transhumanism: An Introduction*, edited by Robert Ranisch and Stefan Lorenz Sorgner. Lang, pp. 173–83.
Reiss, Michael. "Biotechnology." *The Concise Encyclopedia of the Ethics of New Technologies*, edited by Ruth Chadwick. Academic, 2001, pp. 13–26.
Schmeink, Lars. "Biopunk 101." *SFRA Review*, no. 309, 2014, pp. 31–36.

———. *Biopunk Dystopias: Genetic Engineering, Society, and Science Fiction*. Liverpool UP, 2016.

Shiner, Lewis. "Inside the Movement: Past, Present and Future." *Fiction 2000: Cyberpunk and the Future of Narrative*, edited by George Slusser and Tom Shippey. U of Georgia P, 1992, pp. 17–25.

Sterling, Bruce. "Our Global Chernobyl." *Globalhead*. Bantam, 1994, pp. 1–10.

———. Preface. *Mirrorshades: The Cyberpunk Anthology*, edited by Bruce Sterling. Ace, 1986, pp. ix–xvi.

Wohlsen, Marcus. *Biopunk: DIY Scientists Hack the Software of Life*. Current, 2011.

Zurr, Ionat and Oron Catts. "Big Pigs, Small Wings: On Genohype and Artistic Autonomy." *Culture Machine*, vol. 7, 2005, culturemachine.net/index.php/cm/article/viewArticle/30/37.

11

NON-SF CYBERPUNK[1]

Jaak Tomberg

During the first years of the 21st century history—or, more precisely, technological development—finally seemed to have caught up with cyberpunk. The various technological phenomena and processes common to cyberpunk increasingly started to pop up in everyday reality, including virtual communication technologies, digital networking, and the emerging social media platforms; advances in genetic engineering and increasingly common prosthetic supplementations to the body; the mediated intimacy of historical events and the eventual emergence of cyber-war; and the overall onslaught of the society of the spectacle and the virtualization of finance capital.[2] These all became more evident, more strongly felt in quotidian late-capitalist reality. In a way, several of cyberpunk's central speculative elements seemed to have 'bled' straight from fiction into the everyday.

More important than the manifold materializations of cyberpunk's particular thematic elements, though, was the sheer speed and intensity of overall technoscientific developments that brought them about, and the corresponding over-accelerated pace of cultural change felt in everyday life. All of a sudden, change seemed to have been the only constant of contemporary globalized existence. And this, in turn, posed some novel imaginative and representational problems to science fiction (sf) in general and cyberpunk in particular.

That something was happening (or had already happened) with cyberpunk became especially evident after the 'realist turn' of one of its central figures and founders, William Gibson. With his 21st-century trilogy of novels (*Pattern Recognition*, 2003; *Spook Country*, 2007; *Zero History*, 2010—collectively known as the Blue Ant trilogy) Gibson forfeited his usual future-oriented cyberpunk extrapolations and started writing contemporary novels that were situated in the immediate present or recent past. As Brian McHale fluently summarized, the protagonist of *Pattern Recognition* "suffers jet lag, uses e-mail and Photoshop, consults on the design of a corporate logo, goes 'cool-hunting' for street fashions, encounters post-Soviet oligarchs, and becomes obsessed with an online video clip" (182). No fully immersive virtual realities, no artificial intelligences, and no technological transformations of the body so common to cyberpunk can be found—the novels of the Blue Ant trilogy "are indistinguishable from contemporary thrillers from the point of view of their plots and worlds" (McHale 183). In place of extrapolative projections of the future, Gibson offers us the realist cognitive mapping of the globalized present.

In an interview given at the time, Gibson attributed his realist turn to an imaginative deadlock provoked by the contemporary pace of change:

> In the '80s and '90s—as strange as it may seem to say this—we had such luxury of stability. Things weren't changing quite so quickly in the '80s and '90s. And when things are changing too quickly, as one of the characters in *Pattern Recognition* says, you don't have any place to stand from which to imagine a very elaborate future. (Nissley)

Gibson seems to suggest that the over-acceleration of the everyday also affects the extrapolative imagination, drawing the horizons of futurity decisively close to the present. Several commentators on the contemporary status of sf have voiced concurring statements. Istvan Csicsery-Ronay, quoting the feminist theorist Zoe Sofia, has characterized the contemporary situation as "the collapse of the future onto the present" ("Futuristic" 27), and added that "as the transformations reach a certain pitch, the very idea of transformation changes from mystical to statistical, from transcendence to a selection of alternatives" (*Seven Beauties* 58). In more genre-related terms, Veronica Hollinger has usefully and plausibly argued that "science fiction is 'the literature of change,' but change is exactly what now defines the present. It no longer guarantees the future as the site of meaningful difference" (453). *Pattern Recognition* therefore seems to point to the possibility that "science fiction's founding assumption—that the future will be different from the present—has become outdated. Today the present is different from the present" (Hollinger 465). Thus, it wouldn't be too far-fetched to say that the technical over-acceleration of the present also in a way makes it a science-fictional one—and it is precisely this present, *different from itself*, that informs the realist focus of Gibson's novels. No wonder then that McHale noted the plots and worlds of the Blue Ant trilogy (as well as some of the works by Neal Stephenson, notably *Cryptonomicon* [1999] and *REAMDE* [2011]) are indistinguishable from contemporary thrillers and the prose, "bristling with brand names, technical jargon, specialized knowledge, and calculatedly strange juxtapositions," continues to *read like* sf, "testifying to the fact that our *everyday reality* in the new millennium actually seems to have the texture of science fiction" (183; see also Tomberg).

In other words, Gibson's realist prose focuses on the contemporary globalized everyday and estranges in the same specific way that sf used to estrange. The contemporary pace of change, together with the technological saturation of the present, has thus also led to changes in the contemporary genre system, and, more precisely, to the relative positions of realism and sf therein. The underlying premise is that as the contemporary late-capitalist cultural space-time has become increasingly techn(olog)ical, its realism, aspiring towards credible reflections of this space-time, has inevitably become increasingly science-fictional. Since both Gibson and Stephenson are closely associated with cyberpunk, and since the specific tropes and thematic motifs that seem to have 'bled' from fiction into reality are ones that feature most centrally in cyberpunk's repertoire, it is fair to claim that of all the sub-categories of sf, cyberpunk is the one most directly involved in the current close feedback-loop between realism and sf. In a sense, cyberpunk has by now realized itself to such an extent that, to borrow a very attentive remark from Sherryl Vint, it would be more useful to see cyberpunk "less as a subgenre of science fiction and more as part of the cultural milieu that informs our contemporary existence of technologically mediated reality" (266–67). Vint develops this notion on Thomas Foster's claim that (probably sometime during the 1980s and 1990s) cyberpunk "experience[d] a sea change into a more generalized cultural formation" (xiv). In an article on the convergence of virtual and material battlefields in cyberpunk cinema, Vint coins a generic concept for contemporary works that convey this cultural formation: non-sf cyberpunk.[3]

On a strictly poetic level, the possibility of non-sf cyberpunk seems to depend on the premise that sentences can *read like* sf and cognitively estrange like sf even when the conventional thematic sf motifs in them are subdued.[4] To put this premise to the test, it would thus be reasonable to begin by observing a few passages from Gibson's works after his 'realist turn':

Non-SF Cyberpunk

"She turned on the bedside lamp, illuminating the previous evening's empty can of Asahi Draft, from the Pink Dot, and her sticker-encrusted PowerBook, closed and sleeping. She envied it" (*Spook Country* 1).

Here, Gibson describes the status of technology through organic imagery, such as envying the sleep of a laptop. Inversely, in another passage, empirical conditions merge with technological imagery:

> She knows, now, absolutely, hearing the white noise that is London, that Damien's theory of jet lag is correct: that her mortal soul is leagues behind her, being reeled in on some ghostly umbilical down the vanished wake of the plane that brought her here, hundreds of thousands of feet above the Atlantic. Souls can't move that quickly, and are left behind, and must be awaited, upon arrival, like lost luggage. (*Pattern Recognition* 1)

Such inversions convey the impression of a cognitively estranging reality where the faculties of the natural/organic and artificial/technological have become inseparable. Throughout the Blue Ant trilogy, Gibson enhances this impression with heavy namedropping—in the first example above, Asahi Draft, Pink Dot, and PowerBook are all used in a relatively short sentence. The density of brand names could here be interpreted as the 'technological' colonization of 'natural' language— the artificial proper name replaces the more 'organic' common name, at the same time that the estrangement inherent in the advertising language of the brand name reflects the sf neology that used to be so common to cyberpunk proper. Finally, the prose is noteworthy for its high density of adjectives and descriptive phrases:

> The two largest pieces of furniture in the room were the bed, its massive frame covered entirely in slabs of scrimshawed walrus ivory, with the enormous staunchly ecclesiastic-looking lower jawbone of a right whale, fastened to the wall at its head, and a birdcage, so large she might have crouched in it herself, suspended from the ceiling. (*Zero History* 5)

Such density—"slabs of scrimshawed walrus ivory," "the enormous staunchly ecclesiastic-looking lower jawbone of a right whale"—complicates the slow reading of the long sentences, making a vast array of information almost instantly available and thereby reflecting the technocultural over-acceleration of the everyday on the level of the sentence's inner intensity and rhythm. Furthermore, the critical volume of descriptive terms also renders the objects in focus intimately and microscopically close; the considerable quantitative disproportion between objects and their characterizations dislodges them from their status as familiar common objects observed from a normal distance, conferring on them a scientific quality and an estranging feel.

In one way or another, all of these poetic features suggest a scientific or techn(olog)ical kind of cognitive estrangement emanating from the texture of the descriptive language itself. Carl Freedman has plausibly noted that what makes a literary work science-fictional is not the scientific accuracy of its particular estrangements, "not any epistemological judgment external to the text itself on the rationality or irrationality of the latter's imaginings" (18). Rather, what matters is the manifest "attitude *of the text itself* to the kind of estrangements being performed" (18). In other words, an sf text must take its fictional science seriously through "the formal stances [it has] adopted" (18). In the Blue Ant trilogy, this seriousness manifests not on the thematic level of some fictional science, but first and foremost on the level of underlying textual strategy—in the almost scientific attitude that composes the sentences and paragraphs.[5] Needless to say, the Blue Ant trilogy shares this attitude and formal stance with Gibson's earlier more manifestly cyberpunk trilogies of the 1980s and 1990s. A brief paragraph from *Neuromancer* (1984) testifies to the fact that during the particular historical moment of his 'realist turn' at the beginning of the new century, Gibson really didn't need to change his style:

> Neo-Aztec bookcases gathered dust against one wall of the room where Case waited. A pair of bulbous Disney-styled table lamps perched awkwardly on a low Kandinsky-look coffee table in scarlet-lacquered steel. A Dali clock hung on the wall between the bookcases, its distorted face sagging to the bare concrete floor. Its hands were holograms that altered to match the convolutions as they rotated, but it never told the correct time. The room was stacked with white fiberglass shipping modules that gave off the tang of preserved ginger. (21)

In the transition from the cyberpunk sf of the Sprawl trilogy to the contemporary thrillers of the Blue Ant trilogy, the temporal focus changed from an sf future to the realist present, but the stylistic features so familiar from cyberpunk remained more or less the same, proving to be capable to uphold, as Vint pointed out, "the cultural milieu that informs our contemporary experience" (267) Thus, on a poetic level, cyberpunk has discovered a way to move on to non-sf territories.

11.1 Reality with an SF-Intensity

If Gibson's realist turn marked the distinct historical moment when it became clearly evident that the contemporary pace of change, together with the technological saturation of the late-capitalist space-time, had provoked changes in the contemporary genre system, it was first and foremost with respect to the relative positions of realism and sf.[6]

In *Do Metaphors Dream of Literal Sleep?*, Seo-Young Chu differentiates between realism and sf by the particular objects (or referents) they are capable of representing. For her, realism is distinguished by its focus on relatively simple referents such as almonds and nickels that "readily offer themselves up to flat description" (7). Sf, by contrast, is distinguished by its focus on cognitively estranging referents such as cyberspace and artificial intelligence whose description requires "massively complex representational and epistemological work" (7). Accordingly, there have also been 'simpler' realities—those described, from our historical vantage point, in a 19th-century realist novel, and more 'complex' realities—those projected in a myriad of sf futures or parallel worlds. But Chu's very inventive claim is that those simpler and more complex realities may not actually *differ in kind*. They only differ by the varying degrees of representational energy that is spent on projecting them: Whereas a reality imitated by realism requires relatively little, the one projected by sf demands "astronomical levels" (7). This leads Chu to infer that realism is actually "a 'weak' or low-intensity variety of science fiction," whereas sf is actually "a high-intensity realism" (8). She concludes that "although the distance between realism and sf may be vast enough for the difference in degree to amount to a difference in kind, the distance will never be so vast as to render 'science fiction' and 'realism' each other's antonyms." (8)

In other words, what can also be implied from Chu is that sf has always been an essentially realist practice: The possible difference merely stems from the different levels of representational energy that realism spends on reflecting a past or present reality and that sf spends on projecting a cyberpunk future. But the tendencies outlined above—the close contemporary proximity of realism and sf, and the plausible use of cyberpunk language in describing late-capitalist everyday reality—are historically possible only if the nature of the described reality itself provides good grounds for their emergence. That is to say, the technologically intensified and over-accelerated everyday must now estrange in the same way that sf's projected worlds usually have, and thus requires 'astronomical levels' of representational energy for adequate description. Gibson's passages, quoted above, convey the impression that everyday contemporary consumer culture is full of almost singular objects that resist straightforward representation. There seem to be very few simple 'almonds, nickels, or softballs' in the present capitalist circulation of products—instead, there are Buzz Rickson's MA-1 pilot jackets, Fruit of the Loom T-shirts, and cans of Asahi Draft; and sufficiently distinguishing a Longines from a Tissot, alongside with their respective symbolic universes that are set up by the advertising industry, is a representational task of an almost science-fictional intensity. Even the everyday reality of 'simple objects' thus seems to have 'the texture of science fiction,' requiring very high-intensity realism to tackle.

On a strictly poetic level, *in its ideal extreme*, non-sf cyberpunk is a contemporary form of realism that takes the same representational energy that cyberpunk sf used to spend on projecting its extrapolative future worlds, and (inevitably) spends it on the mimetic description of the technologically saturated present. But poetics does not operate in isolation from thematic matters—from the specificity of the reality it holds in focus. Beyond the immediate reality of 'everyday objects,' more complex social and technological processes that these objects provide cognitive access to include the increasingly speculative and volatile nature of contemporary market capitalism; the virtualization of the public political sphere and the mediated intimacy of historical events; the increasingly common asymmetric warfare and the emergence of cyber-war; the impact of social media platforms that shape the contemporary individual and collective consciousness; thorough advances in genetic engineering and prosthetic supplementations to the body; exhaustive changes in the pop-cultural sphere; and so on.

All these processes, adding up to the almost unimaginable overall enormity of the globalized late-capitalist world system, demand cognitive mapping, and this leads us closer to the representational challenge of non-sf cyberpunk: to tackle the fundamentally technical nature of contemporary reality. For Csicsery-Ronay technology is no longer merely something that people simply use to make their everyday lives easier. Instead, it "has come to be viewed as a historical force in its own right" (*Seven* 93), and a reality determined by such a force consists of "complex and barely governable processes" (*Seven* 26). Technology is no longer a privilege of the "odd inventor and explorer" but encompasses "the whole species" (*Seven* 93). It also "no longer merely imitates nature" but actually "transforms the material world, using scientific knowledge to make its physical substrate operate in ways that Nature 'will not'." Technology has thus become an autonomous second nature that "extends itself […] into the core of matter" (*Seven* 93).

Sf, including non-sf cyberpunk, now investigates the ways in which humans relate to this transformed core of technocultural reality. The cognitive source of estrangement earlier associated with traditional sf is no longer necessarily confined to some privileged or isolated segment of reality (to the sphere of 'the odd inventor and explorer'). Rather, the whole contemporary late-capitalist reality itself is now technologically saturated and therefore estranges in a science-fictional way. The possibility of non-sf cyberpunk as a realist strategy indicates that we are all in a way inventors and explorers—not *of* other (future or parallel) realities but *in* the present reality that itself has 'the texture of science fiction.'

11.2 Non-sf Cyberpunk

The last decade has seen the emergence of a host of works whose realist attention to a range of contemporary topics can be derived from and traced back to cyberpunk's earlier extrapolative interests. The brief selection offered here is by no means exhaustive, and by no means in every case meets non-sf cyberpunk's *ideal poetic requirement* of not including any thematic estrangements that are usually associated with sf. But the few sf estrangements we might find in these works usually have a very low level of intensity; in other words, they are either simple hyperboles of very evident present trends or extrapolations 'twenty minutes into the future.'

11.2.1 From Cyberpunk Prediction to the Speculative Logic
of Contemporary Capitalism

Gibson's *All Tomorrow's Parties* (1999), the novel immediately preceding his realist turn, depicts a near-future world where it is felt that high advances in virtual technologies and nanotechnology will bring about an imminent and totally unpredictable change in the world system. One of the few characters predicting this change is Cody Harwood, a media baron and owner of the public relations firm Harwood/Levine who is described as the most powerful man in the world, a "twenty-first century synthesis of Bill Gates and Woody Allen" (164). Faced with the perspective of absolute change, he takes sinister steps to ensure that he maintains his powerful status in the world to come.

In Gibson's Blue Ant trilogy, we have a seemingly similar figure in Hubertus Bigend, a marketing guru and the founder of advertising agency *Blue Ant*, who gets the novel's protagonist, Cayce Pollard, to track down the maker of the 'footage,' a series of film clips that have attracted a large cult following on the Internet and whose source remains entirely anonymous. As Mattias Nilges attentively remarks, Bigend "considers it the most innovative marketing strategy he has ever encountered: the footage has created a large following without anyone being sure that it is attached to a product" (45). Bigend can thus be considered a very scaled-down version of Harwood: There is no ambition towards world domination or the preservation of status, just the search for the next imminent trend, the next viable marketing strategy. The world that Bigend lives in—'our world'—is different from that of Harwood's as well: no future *predictions* of imminent cataclysmic changes, just the 'realist' *speculations* on what might efficiently attract the present consumers next. Gibson's Blue Ant trilogy makes it especially clear that "speculation becomes the dominant logic of material reality" (Nilges 37) and "finance capital's speculative logic and structure become a historically specific aesthetic problem for literature" (Nilges 38).

Other contemporary works that focus on this speculative logic also *read like* non-sf cyberpunk, i.e., the structural speculative logic of earlier cyberpunk sf has been replaced by the realist depiction of speculation in finance capitalism. For example, Don DeLillo's *Cosmopolis* (2003) is an account of billionaire asset manager Eric Packer's one-day odyssey across midtown Manhattan in order to get a haircut. Through the course of the day he deliberately loses large amounts of money for his clients by betting against the rise of the yen, all the while discussing the philosophical meaning of his losses. Similarly, Adam McKay's biographical comedy-drama *The Big Short* (2015), based on Michael Lewis's *The Big Short: Inside the Doomsday Machine* (2010) about the 2007/08 financial crisis, employs unconventional techniques (e.g. breaking the fourth wall) to explain complex financial instruments such as subprime mortgages and collateralized debt obligations. Finally, the Showtime series *Billions* (2016–), loosely based on real-life events, focuses on the efforts of Charles 'Chuck' Rhoades (Paul Giamatti), U.S. Attorney for the Southern District of New York, to take down Robert 'Bobby' Axelrod (Damian Lewis), a billionaire manager of a hedge fund called Axe Capital, whom he knows to be guilty of insider trading. Strong cognitive estrangement, evident in the heavy segments of 'finance talk' in these works, indicates the dominantly virtual status and speculative logic of global capitalism, as well as its almost ungovernable and hardly representable nature.[7]

11.2.2 From Cyberspace to Social Media Platforms

Dave Eggers's near-future dystopian novel *The Circle* (2013) begins with its protagonist Mae Holland luckily getting a job in the Circle, a powerful technology company that has established its success by unifying people's manifold social media accounts under one, ultimately 'swallowing'

Google and Facebook. She starts out in the firm's customer service department but quickly climbs the company ladder. From the beginning, Mae is impressed by amenities at the Circle, including access to top-notch technology, dorm-like housing, gyms, recreation activities, and parties. As the novel develops, she slowly learns of the company's more ambiguous ambitions—to eradicate crime and political corruption by using live surveillance technology that supposedly guarantees 'full transparency,' all the while earning profit from aspiring towards this seemingly 'noble' goal.

Rather than its dystopian elements (whose level of estrangement is relatively low from the contemporary perspective), it is Eggers's lengthy realist descriptions of quotidian company culture that are of crucial interest here. Starting out with a few hundred daily requests Mae has to respond to while working at customer service, more and more screens are gradually installed at her work desk (until she ultimately has nine) as she is quickly initiated in the company's in-house routines, involving responding to countless requests to take part in social activities and mandatorily reacting to the company's workers' individual social media feeds with the equivalent of a 'like' or a 'dislike.' Eggers devotes a lot of space to describing the sheer amount, ferocious speed, and gradual intensification of these 'virtual' interactions, as well as the personal enjoyments and anxieties they bring. These passages demonstrate the extent to which social media shapes the contemporary individual and collective consciousness, transforms one's sense of privacy and critical consciousness, and determines individual actions. *The Circle* is, in large parts, good poetic evidence to back up Vint's claim that "we are living in an everted cyberpunk world in which cyberspace permeates and shapes our experience of material reality rather than one in which we leave materiality for cyberspace, as anticipated in [cyberpunk science] fiction" (254).

11.2.3 From Cyber-Cowboys to Hackers and Whistleblowers

The cultural driving force that has determined cyberpunk's narratives and constituted its specific milieu or 'feel' has always been reflected in its typical characters, central of whom is the cyber-cowboy—usually a low-life, drug-addicted hacker who carries out legally dubious contract work in cyberspace and acts as a resistance figure against a corporate establishment. It is thus no wonder that we find their equivalents in cyberpunk narratives that explore contemporary, non-sf territories. Elliot Alderson (Rami Malek), the protagonist of drama thriller TV-series *Mr. Robot* (2015–2020; created by Sam Esmail), is precisely such a character.[8] He is a genius cyber-security engineer and a hacker who suffers from social anxiety disorder and clinical depression. It is not difficult to see Case from Gibson's *Neuromancer* as Elliot's generic predecessor—but whereas Case's nervous system was damaged by a Russian mycotoxin, rendering him unable to jack into cyberspace, Elliot's personality disorders are of a more mundane, psychological origin.

At the beginning of the series, Elliot is recruited by an insurrectionary anarchist known as 'Mr. Robot' (Christian Slater) to join a group of hacktivists called 'fsociety,' whose aim is to destroy all debt records by encrypting the financial data of the largest conglomerate in the world, E Corp. By the end of Season 1, they manage exactly that, creating a worldwide situation of revolutionary hope as well as anarchic uncertainty. It also turns out that Mr. Robot is actually Elliot's alter ego, based on his dead father's persona—the technological dislocations of subjective experience so common in cyberpunk sf (think of Gibson's simstim technology) have here been replaced by psychological dislocations in its non-sf form.

Fsociety's plan to erase all debt, together with Elliot's alter ego as the driving force behind this initiative, renders Season 1 of *Mr. Robot* structurally very similar to *Fight Club* (1999), David Fincher's film adaptation of Chuck Palahniuk's 1996 novel of the same name. In *Fight Club*, the unnamed Narrator (Edward Norton), discontented with his white-collar job, starts a recreational 'fight club' with the help of his alter ego Tyler Durden (Brad Pitt). The club quickly gains popularity, establishes branches worldwide, and finally transforms into a revolutionary movement that manages to sabotage corporate servers that house global debt records. The structural similarity between *Fight Club* and *Mr. Robot* is symbolically cemented with the playing of "Where is My Mind?," a song by American alternative rock band The Pixies, during their respective culminations. While these similarities evoke the temptation to consider *Fight Club* as one of the earliest examples of non-sf cyberpunk, *Mr. Robot* is one of the best examples of non-sf cyberpunk: The series has been praised for the realism of its hacking sequences, and it proves that a work no longer requires extravagant digital effects to maintain an essentially cyberpunk feel.

All in all, it would not be too preposterous to claim that some of yesterday's fictional cyber-cowboys are today's real whistleblowers, and that the present fates of real persons like Julian Assange and Edward Snowden resemble something straight out of a cyberpunk narrative. Unsurprisingly, both of their stories have found coverage on screen—in *The Fifth Estate* (Condon 2013) and *Snowden* (Stone 2016). In the former film, the visuality of cyberspace and the flow of data as "a stand-in for the opaque working of systemic control" have already been brought out as features characteristic of cyberpunk in contemporary realist fiction (Schmeink 284).

11.2.4 From Idorus to Real Virtual Idols

At the end of Gibson's *All Tomorrow's Parties*, something happens with the idoru Rei Toei, a synthetic Japanese idol with the ability to manifest herself through holographic projection. All of a sudden, she takes human form with the help of 'Nanofax machines' in the hundreds of branches of Lucky Dragon, that future's global retail chain. A virtual/digital AI-construct is thus nanotechnologically materialized into hundreds of identical real human bodies, bringing about a technological singularity.

Of our own world, it could be said that the fate of its idorus has been inverse, that is, the idol has found ways to become purely virtual and constructed, as testified by the immense popularity of Hatsune Miku, a humanoid persona voiced by a singing synthesizer application (vocaloid) developed by Crypton Future Media. As a virtual pop star credited with over 100,000 songs, she performs live as an animated rear cast projection on a specially coated glass screen. On the one hand, Miku is the *direct embodiment* of the artificial, manufactured, constructed nature of the notion of the pop star itself; on the other hand, she is the perfect work of non-sf cyberpunk—at once both seemingly (science) fictional and very real, a completely technical entity with a devout human following. If Gibson's Rei Toei was a cyberpunk extrapolation on the real culture of Japanese idols, Hatsune Miku feels like *a real-life materialization* of that extrapolation, thereby once again demonstrating the closing of the feedback-loop between cyberpunk and 21st-century late-capitalist reality.[9]

In conclusion, this short and by no means exhaustive selection[10] demonstrates that non-sf cyberpunk as a present form of realism can potentially be encountered across a wide range of artistic mediums and topics wherever contemporary reality seems to estrange in a science-fictional way. Whether the near future will witness the proliferation of such works or not probably depends on the unpredictable pace of technological development. If the pace accelerates further, reality itself will estrange with greater intensity, providing a good ground for non-sf cyberpunk. If the pace dies down, it will establish a more stable reality and open up a wider space for traditional sf extrapolation.

Notes

1 Research for this article was supported by Estonian Research Council grant PUT1494.
2 For more on the connection of cyberpunk and finance capital, see Hugh O'Connell's contribution to this volume.
3 An alternative concept, equally worthy of supplementation, is "science fiction realism"—recently supported by Hollinger ("Stories") and McFarlane ("Cyberpunk and 'Science Fiction Realism'").

4 Samuel R. Delany once famously proved that a simple sentence can be read in seemingly opposite generic registers: "Similarly the phrase, 'he turned on his left side.' In a naturalistic text, it would most probably refer to a man's insomniac tossings. But in an SF text the phrase might easily mean a male reached down and flipped the switch activating his sinistral flank. Or even that he attacked his left side." ("On *Triton* and Other Matters")

5 It has to be noted that Gary Westfahl has provided "interminable lists of evidence" (158) about references to sf and fantasy in *Spook Country*. Thus, it could be said that in the Blue Ant trilogy, the sf strategy of *including sf thematic motifs* in the fabric of the plot has been replaced with the realist strategy of inserting *references to them* on the level of description.

6 The fact that Alfonso Cuarón's *Gravity* (2013) is very often categorized as science fiction proves that space was never invaded by humans, but, rather, by the science-fictional imagination.

7 In this volume, O'Connell suggests a reading of cyberpunk that connects the mode with the "inscrutable dematerialized aspects of speculative finance" (289), while Sherryl Vint analyzes cyberpunk television productions with regard to their "portrayals of economic inequality" and "neoliberalism as the ground upon which our present reality, as a cyberpunk analog, unfolds" (169).

8 Vint further discusses *Mr. Robot* as an example of contemporary cyberpunk television in her chapter in this volume.

9 For an overview of virtual idols/vocaloids and their roots in Japanese manga, please see Kumiko Saito's contribution to this collection.

10 To add to this, Vint's article "Cyberwar" is an elaborate analysis on the convergence of virtual and material battlefields in cyberpunk cinema. Vint treats the films *Ender's Game* (Hood 2013) and *Good Kill* (Niccol 2014) as reflections on the moral cost of war as a first-person shooter, designating the latter as "the apotheosis of the hyperreal, a present-day and non-science-fictional cyberpunk film" (273).

Works Cited

Chu, Seo-Young. *Do Metaphors Dream of Literal Sleep? A Science-Fictional Theory of Representation.* Harvard UP, 2010.

Csicsery-Ronay, Jr., Istvan. "Futuristic Flu, or, the Revenge of the Future." *Fiction 2000: Cyberpunk and the Future of Narrative,* edited by George Slusser and Tom Shippey. Georgia UP, 1992, pp. 26–45.

———. *The Seven Beauties of Science Fiction.* Wesleyan UP, 2008.

Delany, Samuel. "On Triton and Other Matters: An Interview with Samuel R. Delany." *Science Fiction Studies,* vol. 17, no. 3, 1990, depauw.edu/sfs/interviews/delany52interview.htm.

Eggers, Dave. *The Circle.* Knopf, 2013.

Fight Club. Directed by David Fincher, performances by Brad Pitt, Edward Norton, and Helena Bonham Carter, Fox 2000 Pictures, 1999.

Foster, Thomas. *The Souls of Cyberfolk: Posthumanism as Vernacular Theory.* U of Minnesota P, 2005.

Freedman, Carl. *Critical Theory and Science Fiction.* Wesleyan UP, 2000.

Gibson, William. *All Tomorrow's Parties.* Viking, 1999.

———. *Neuromancer.* Ace, 1984.

———. *Pattern Recognition.* Putnam, 2003.

———. *Spook Country.* Putnam, 2007.

———. *Zero History.* Putnam's, 2010.

Hollinger, Veronica. "Stories About the Future: From Patterns of Expectation to *Pattern Recognition*." *Science Fiction Studies,* vol. 33, no. 3, 2006, pp. 452–72.

McHale, Brian. *The Cambridge Introduction to Postmodernism.* Cambridge UP, 2015.

McFarlane, Anna. "Cyberpunk and 'Science Fiction Realism' in Kathryn Bigelow's Strange Days and Zero Dark Thirty." *Cyberpunk and Visual Culture,* edited by Graham J. Murphy and Lars Schmeink. Routledge, 2018, pp. 235–52.

Mr. Robot. Created by Sam Esmail, USA Network, 2015–.

Nilges, Mathias. "The Realism of Speculation: Contemporary Speculative Fiction as Immanent Critique of Finance Capitalism." *Speculative Finance/Speculative Fiction,* edited by David M. Higgins and Hugh O'Conell, special issue of *CR: The New Centennial Review,* vol. 19, no. 1, 2019, pp. 37–60.

Nissley, Tom. "'Across the Border to Spook Country': An Interview with William Gibson." *Amazon.com,* 2007, amazon.com/Spook-Country-Blue-William-Gibson-ebook/dp/B000UVBSYQ.

O'Connell, Hugh. "Marxism." *The Routledge Companion to Cyberpunk Culture,* edited by Anna McFarlane, Graham J. Murphy, and Lars Schmeink. Routledge, 2020, pp. 282–90.

Schmeink, Lars. "Afterthoughts. Cyberpunk Engagements in Countervisuality." *Cyberpunk and Visual Culture*, edited by Graham J. Murphy and Lars Schmeink. Routledge, 2018, pp. 276–87.

Tomberg, Jaak. On the "Double Vision" of Realism and SF Estrangement in William Gibson's BIGEND TRILOGY." *Science Fiction Studies*, vol. 40, no. 2, 2013, pp. 263–85.

Vint, Sherryl. "Cyberwar. The Convergence of Virtual and Material Battlefields in Cyberpunk Cinema." *Cyberpunk and Visual Culture*, edited by Graham J. Murphy and Lars Schmeink. Routledge, 2018, pp. 253–75.

———. "Television." *The Routledge Companion to Cyberpunk Culture*, edited by Anna McFarlane, Graham J. Murphy, and Lars Schmeink. Routledge, 2020, pp. 169–77.

Westfahl, Gary. *William Gibson.* U of Illinois P, 2013.

12
COMIC BOOKS[1]

David M. Higgins and Matthew Iung

European and American comic books had an important, if undervalued, influence on cyberpunk aesthetics as this mode emerged into a recognizable phenomenon during the 1980s.[2] For example, Scott Bukatman writes about the influence of 1970s-era French magazine *Métal Hurlant* upon cyberpunk's visual aesthetics, notably "Moebius's compacted urbanism, Philippe Druillet's saturated darkness and Angus McKie's scalar exaggerations" (*Blade* 26). Similarly, William Gibson acknowledges that the illustrated stories that appeared in *Métal Hurlant* (and its American version *Heavy Metal*) strongly influenced the imaginative style of his quintessential cyberpunk novel *Neuromancer* (1984):

> [I]t's entirely fair to say, and I've said it before, that the way *Neuromancer*-the-novel "looks" was influenced in large part by some of the artwork I saw in *Heavy Metal*. I assume that this must also be true of John Carpenter's *Escape from New York*, Ridley Scott's *Blade Runner*, and all other artifacts of the style sometimes dubbed "cyberpunk." Those French guys, they got their end in early. (Introduction)[3]

One striking example is "The Long Tomorrow," written by Dan O'Bannon and illustrated by Jean 'Moebius' Giraud, which was serialized in *Métal Hurlant* in 1976 and later appeared in *Heavy Metal* (1.4 and 1.5) in 1977. "The Long Tomorrow" is a cyberpunk precursor on two fronts: first, as Bukatman argues, Moebius's artwork depicts "an enclosed, expansive but claustrophobic" urban space where the street "can now be located (only with difficulty) at the nearly invisible bottom of a narratively and spatially decentered environment" (*Terminal* 128), a visual motif common to cyberpunk; second, "The Long Tomorrow" tells a hard-boiled science-fictional detective story (with noir sensibilities) set in a dystopian urban landscape on an alien world. In the story, a black private investigator, Pete Club, is hired by an upper-class white femme fatale, Dolly Vook De Katterbar, to recover her lost personal belongings from a public locker in a dangerous part of the city. While they are having sex after his mission, Club receives a phone call from a police lieutenant who reveals that Vook De Katterbar is an alien spy—and Club looks up from the phone in horror to discover that he is having sex with a repulsive blob of alien tentacles! The alien pleads with Club, clinging to his manhood as he attempts to tear her free; she claims to love him (despite having sent an assassin earlier to murder him), and she offers to shapeshift into any form that he desires. Unresponsive to her attempted seduction, Club rejects her as a 'demon from space' before killing her. The final frame of the comic is Club standing alone on a bridge, looking out over the city, musing that the whole encounter has ultimately been 'meaningless' because it is "just a story. And there are eight million like it in this city, drifting through eternity."

In addition to "The Long Tomorrow," *Métal Hurlant/Heavy Metal* was a key site for the emergence of other proto-cyberpunk comics, such as Stefano Tamburini and Tanino Liberatore's *RanXerox*, a story about a mechanical anti-hero made from photocopier parts, which was originally published in the Italian magazine *Cannibale* in 1978 and then appeared in *Heavy Metal* in 1983. Enki Bilal, a Yugoslavian-born artist and writer living and working in France, was also a regular contributor to *Métal Hurlant*, and his three-volume saga The Nikopol Trilogy may also be regarded as an early cyberpunk precursor. Originally published as *La Foire aux immortels* (1980), *La Femme piège* (1986), and *Froid Équateur* (1992), The Nikopol Trilogy features a number of cyberpunk elements, such as a science-fictional noir sensibility, a dystopian near-future setting, the techno-magical augmentation of the human body, and experimentations with strange drugs that make it nearly impossible to distinguish between reality and hallucinations. Bilal's highly eccentric Nikopol stories are characterized by what Carl Freedman calls an "inflationary" outlook—they are set in a speculative world where "reality is richer and more various than most people assume" ("Marxism" 69).

Frank Miller's *Ronin* (1983–84)—an iconic work that is sometimes regarded as the first mainstream popular cyberpunk comic (Davidson)—takes a different tract than Bilal's Nikopol stories by embodying a "deflationary" attitude that Freedman suggests is a central characteristic of noir. Noir, Freedman argues, "is deeply pessimistic about human possibility and human happiness" and tends to imagine a world where reality is darker and more disappointing than many people might hope ("Marxism" 71). In *Ronin*, Miller's painstaking and detailed visual style—strongly influenced by manga and samurai films—often utilizes what Scott McCloud calls "moment to moment" and "aspect to aspect" transitions that linger on specific images for several frames in order to create a sense of mood rare in western comics during this time (78–79). Further, as Jeanette Khan notes, Miller's decision to portray the protagonist, Casey McKenna, as a woman of color was relatively groundbreaking for a comic from a mainstream publisher (DC Comics) in the 1980s (Introduction). *Ronin* also encompasses a variety of what are now considered cyberpunk elements—a noir sensibility, a critical reaction to the rise of corporate power and the recessionary economics of the 1980s, and a speculative engagement with such emerging technologies as cybernetics, artificial intelligence (AI), and biotechnology—during a moment slightly prior to the publication of Gibson's *Neuromancer*, which more broadly popularized cyberpunk elements in the popular science fiction (sf) imaginary.

At the same time, however, *Ronin* is starkly reactionary in its deflationary view of humanity; almost everyone in the story is centrally driven by greed. Women, neo-Nazis, and black street gang members are all ultimately drawn to the power and charisma of violent alpha-males—a theme that Miller further explores in *Batman: The Dark Knight Returns* (1986). Without such powerful men guiding humankind toward law and order, people will inevitably degenerate into savages, like the "bums" and "kids of winos" born in the subway tunnels under New York in *Ronin*'s imagined future; these figures have become cannibalistic "cave men"—ultimate inhuman monsters to be shot, stabbed, and chopped apart so that the hero of the story can rescue Casey from an unthinkable fate (4.17).

Ronin also unabashedly participates in a pervasive misogyny that too-often stains early cyberpunk comics. For example, O'Bannon and Moebius's "The Long Tomorrow" depicts violent misogyny as a vital tool in the retrenchment of a masculine autonomy that is threatened by economic conditions of emergent neoliberal globalization. In other words, "The Long Tomorrow" illuminates how the multi-nationalization of industrial and finance capital during the 1970s created a cultural environment in which a masculine sense of self-ownership, agency, and autonomy is threatened by economic scarcity, outsourcing, and globalization. In this scenario, male protagonists like Club navigate dystopian cities (divided between the rich and the poor) dominated by massive corrupt multinational corporations that are immune to government regulation. These characters often feel hopelessly disempowered in the face of growing class and wealth inequality, so the path to recovering masculine agency is not by fighting the system itself—it's by violently rejecting feminine figures, such as the radically alien Vook De Katterbar, in order to achieve a hard, self-enclosed, and tragically isolated masculine autonomy. Similarly, *Ronin*'s Billy Challas—a mentally disabled young man whose psychic powers enable him to appear as the titular Ronin of the narrative—is portrayed as an infantile figure trapped within the overbearing cybernetic womb of an AI called Virgo, who manipulates him by explicitly assuming the role of an emasculating mother. Billy's final line, "shut up momma" (6.48), precedes the explosion that annihilates Virgo and again dramatizes the misogyny and primal violence that defines many hard-boiled masculine cyberpunk comic narratives.

In contrast to the deflationary noir aesthetic of "The Long Tomorrow" and *Ronin*, Jamie Hewlett and Alan C. Martin's *Tank Girl* expresses an expansive, rebellious, and inflationary punk attitude. Tank Girl is a mercenary outlaw living in a near-future Australia who drives a huge tank and has a variety of weird adventures with her boyfriend Booga, a mutant kangaroo. *Tank Girl*, which was first published in the underground UK magazine *Deadline* in 1988, notably rejects conventional narrative techniques, favoring instead an absurdist, satirical, and anarchic style. If many cyberpunk comics revel in the grim-dark pessimism of noir, *Tank Girl* reads instead like a punk rock Looney Tunes sketch that unabashedly celebrates sex, violence, intoxication, and the joys of rebellion.

The titular character, Tank Girl, is a problematic figure: She obviously represents a juvenile male fantasy of female empowerment and sexual liberation, and she functions as a psychotic-pixie-dream-girl that the comic itself literally describes as "a wet dream in biker boots." Hewlett and Martin's specific flavor of punk rebellion often involves finding ways to get Tank Girl as naked as possible within the bounds of censorship laws, and the 1980s equivalent of a gothic-punk party girl riding a giant phallic tank is not exactly the kind of cyborg feminism that Donna J. Haraway would ultimately describe as progressively empowering in her "A Cyborg Manifesto: Science, Technology, and Socialist-Feminism in the Late Twentieth Century." Furthermore, Hewlett and Martin's decision to set the entire story in Australia (which was inspired, they admit in their introduction to *Tank Girl*, by the fact that they liked *Crocodile Dundee* [Faiman 1986]) often results in a parade of shallow Australian stereotypes, such as aboriginal Magical Negroes who help Tank Girl on her journeys, and an astonishingly bizarre series of storylines in which Tank Girl implausibly incarnates a spirit of liberation who drinks and fucks her way to freedom on behalf of colonized Aboriginal Australians. At the same time, Tank Girl has nonetheless at times been adopted as an icon of revolutionary transgression. Reflecting on Tank Girl's popularity, *Deadline* publisher Tommy Astor commented in 1994 that "[t]he boys love her, the girls love her. In London, there are even weekly lesbian gatherings called 'Tank Girl nights'" (Bates). Furthermore, according to Ben Browne, Tank Girl's "alternative look, unabashed hedonism and her empowered attitude made her a popular gay icon" in the UK, and protestors made Tank Girl t-shirts, posters, and underwear to display during protests against Margaret Thatcher's homophobic Clause 28 legislation in 1988. In the end, one of the most striking things about *Tank Girl* may be the way that the comic ultimately represents a transgressive and inflationary punk aesthetic that embodies the opposite of the hypermasculine and deflationary noir sensibilities of most cyberpunk comics from its era: *Tank Girl* undercuts early cyberpunk's transgressive sexual fetishization (and misogyny) of women by showing that women are often inescapably framed as figures of libidinal excess within works of male cyberpunk artists, yet the series also reveals opens possibilities for transgressive symbolic appropriation that is unavailable within hypermasculine noir cyberpunk comic narratives.

During the late 1980s, when *Tank Girl* first appeared, cyberpunk themes and images were becoming widespread and recognizable within worldwide popular culture, bolstered in part by Epic Comics's incomplete adaptation of Gibson's *Neuromancer* (1989) and Howard Chaykin's satirical comic *American Flagg!* (First Comics; 1983–89).[4] By the early 1990s, however, many were arguing that cyberpunk's critical energy had become exhausted: Lewis Shiner, one of the core Movement figures,[5] complained in a 1991 editorial for *The New York Times* that cyberpunk's widespread popularization had rendered it stale and banal: "[B]y 1987, cyberpunk had become a cliché. Other writers had turned the form into formula: implant wetware (biological computer chips), government by multinational corporations, street-wise, leather-jacketed, amphetamine-loving protagonists and decayed orbital colonies." Few comics embody the toothless commercial appropriation of cyberpunk elements—what has been dismissively called 'sci-fiberpunk' by Shiner—more than Frank Miller and Geof Darrow's *Hard Boiled*, which was published in three issues by Dark Horse Comics between 1990 and 1992. Similar to Miller's *Ronin* (and *Batman: The Dark Knight Returns*), *Hard Boiled* is a deflationary hypermasculine celebration of grotesque violence and abject misogyny which also embodies a nearly perfect crystallization of Freedman's argument that cyberpunk displays an attitude of "essential *acceptance*" to the "ultracommodified global totality" of late capitalism (*Critical* 197, original emphasis). In the comic's dystopian future, huge corporations have achieved frightening power, massive spectacles of violence have become commonplace and unremarkable, and all possibilities for revolutionary resistance are naïve and fruitless; all that remains is to marvel at the nihilistic aesthetic beauty of the dystopian cyberpunk sublime. Indeed, one of the striking elements of *Hard Boiled* is its obsessive visual citation of consumer brands; Los Angeles is portrayed as an intricate landscape of advertising, consumption, and trash, with detailed satirical versions of brand representations lovingly emphasized on nearly every page. In this regard, *Hard Boiled* uncritically reflects the western post-industrial economic shift away from commodity production and toward the proliferation of brand identities (and other immaterial commodities).

In spite of its many problems, *Hard Boiled* nevertheless stands out as a visual and artistic achievement thanks to the influential work of artist Geof Darrow. Originally an animator for Hanna-Barbera (where he worked on *Scooby-Doo*, *Richie-Rich*, and *The Smurfs*), Darrow met Moebius in 1982 and later moved to France, where Moebius connected him with *Métal Hurlant*. Moebius also introduced Darrow to Frank Miller, who was at this time already famous for *Ronin* and *Batman: The Dark Knight Returns*, and this led to their ultimate collaboration on *Hard Boiled*, which had an immeasurable influence on an entire generation of comics writers and artists. Darrow's astonishingly detailed *ligne claire* (or 'clear line') style, which was originally popularized by Hergé's work on *The Adventures of Tintin*, eschews the use of hatching (the use of closely drawn parallel lines) to create shading effects; Darrow further articulates tiny details (such as bullets, gears, shards of glass, and pieces of mechanical assemblages) with obsessive accuracy. Darrow's stylistic work on *Hard Boiled* has had a long-lasting influence on cyberpunk comics and film; for example, the Wachowskis enlisted Darrow as the Conceptual Designer for their *Matrix* trilogy (*The Matrix* [1999]; *The Matrix Reloaded* [2003]; *The Matrix Revolutions* [2003]) and further collaborated with him on *The Matrix Comics*. Lauren Davis notes that Darrow was "responsible for some of the most iconic images in the film, including the battery farm where Neo wakes up and the insectoid robots." Darrow's visual work on *The Matrix* distinguishes him as one of the major figures from the world of comics who, like Moebius, has had an extraordinary (and often-overlooked) influence on the visual and tonal aesthetics of cyberpunk in a larger sense.

Some regard the 1990s as the beginning of a 'post-cyberpunk' era, or a moment when the initial ideas, images, and aesthetics of cyberpunk became a broadly recognized and shallowly commodified style (Booker and Thomas 117–18). Thomas Foster, in contrast, suggests that during the 1990s cyberpunk experienced a "sea-change into a more generalized cultural formation" that responds to and reflects diverse conditions of social, technological, and economic change much more broadly than the original close-knit cadre of cyberpunk authors were able to imagine (xiv). Both of these tendencies—the shallow commodification of cyberpunk style and the use of recognizable cyberpunk sensibilities to interrogate contemporary life—are present within mainstream superhero comics during the early 1990s. As Mark Oehlert observes, various cyborg heroes had been appearing within mainstream comics since at least 1941, when Marvel created Captain America, one of the first genetically modified 'cyborgian' superheroes (112). Other cyborg figures—such as Iron Man (1963), Deathlok (1974), Rom (1979), Cyborg (1980), and Cable (1990)—had appeared with increasing frequency within mainstream comics since the 1970s, but it wasn't until the early 1990s that mainstream comics truly started to explore the terrain of cyberpunk. As Daniel Martin argues, for example, the Marvel comic *Spider-Man 2099* (1992–96) "deploys the themes and tropes of cyberpunk fiction in the service of a postmodern superhero narrative" (467). *Spider-Man 2099* was the most popular of a wave of 2099 titles from Marvel (including *The Punisher 2099* [1993–95], *Doom 2099* [1993–96], and *Ravage 2099* [1992–95]) that were set in a grim, dystopian, cyberpunk future: "[I]n 2099, your friendly neighborhood Spider-Man is a little less friendly. So is the neighborhood" (qtd. in Martin 470). As Martin shows, *Spider-Man 2099* offers ambivalent portrayals of "genetic engineering, cybernetic enhancement, and artificial intelligence" and, like many other cyberpunk texts, reflects a variety of "Orientalist cultural anxieties and regressive gender codes" (466).

Perhaps the most fascinating mainstream cyberpunk comic from the early 1990s, however, was DC Comics's *The Hacker Files*, written by original cyberpunk Lewis Shiner and published as a 12-issue limited series starting in 1992. Shiner acknowledges that his concept for *The Hacker Files* was adapted from ideas from his unpublished first novel, *Red Weather*, which was about a young programmer who discovered that he was working for a corrupt computer company (1.25). Illustrated by Tom Sutton, *The Hacker Files* centers on the exploits of Jack Marshall (a.k.a. Hacker), a former employee of Digitronix World Industries. As the series begins, he is a rebellious freelance computer specialist who is called upon to help various recognizable heroes from the mainstream DC Comics universe. Shiner explicitly denies that *The Hacker Files* is a cyberpunk comic: "at its worst, cyberpunk is a religion of technology," he argues, while *The Hacker Files* "is, first and foremost, about people. It's about the individual in the heart of the machine that is corporate America—that is, corporate Earth" (2.26). Despite Shiner's disavowal, *The Hacker Files* unquestionably demonstrates a thoughtful and critical cyberpunk sensibility: rather than depthlessly mining cyberpunk as a repository of styles and already-cliché narrative tropes, *The Hacker Files* offers thoughtful and well-informed commentary on real-world events like the attack of the Morris Worm, Operation Sundevil, the Tiananmen Square Massacre, the aftermath of the collapse of the Soviet Union, and the complex (and often corrupt) globalization of the tech industry. Most strikingly, *The Hacker Files* succeeds in offering what Shiner calls "a book that tells the truth about computers and the people who use them, a book that fairly and honestly represents the hacker underground" (1.26).

It is additionally interesting to note that certain portions of *The Hacker Files* (as well as some covers) are illustrated using computer-generated images, which was very uncommon during the 1980s and early 1990s: The little-known cyberpunk comic *Shatter* (1985–88) was probably the first comic entirely illustrated using computer methods (Garcia). *Shatter* was followed by *Batman: Digital Justice* (1990), the first major mainstream comic that was entirely computer generated. Written and illustrated by Pepe Moreno—a Spanish artist and video game designer—*Batman: Digital Justice* is a cyberpunk narrative set in a future version of Gotham City; in the story, James Gordon's grandson fights a series of virtual reality (VR) battles to defend the world's business and banking systems from a sentient computer virus created by The Joker.

By the time *Hard Boiled*, *Spider-Man 2099*, *The Hacker Files*, and *Batman: Digital Justice* were appearing in the early 1990s, cyberpunk had entered the Euro-American popular imaginary as a repository of science-fictional ideas, images, and concepts; as a result, there was a widespread emergence of other cyberpunk comics during this time as well. Sergio Bonelli Editore's *Nathan Never*, a charismatic cyberpunk special agent, started appearing in Italian comics in 1991, and

Gess's violent cybernoir story *Teddy Bear* started publication in France in 1992. Another French cyberpunk comic, *Nomad* (1994–2000), tells the story of an African agent working for the U.S. Secret Service who can access computer systems with his mind. James O'Barr, who ultimately became famous for his work on *The Crow* (1989)[6] and its subsequent follow-up stories, wrote a cyberpunk Wizard of Oz story called "Frame 137," which appeared in *Dark Horse Presents* in 1992, while David Mack's *Kabuki*, the story of an assassin who works for a secret government agency in a near-future Japan, was first published in 1994.

In order to capitalize on the popular interest in new sf trends in the early 1990s, DC launched a short-lived special imprint called Helix Comics in 1996. Notable Helix titles included *BrainBanx* (1997) by Elaine Lee and Jason Temujin Minor, *The Dome: Ground Zero* (1998) by Dave Gibbons and Angus McKie, Howard Chaykin and Don Cameron's *Cyberella* (1996–97), and Rachel Pollack and Chris Weson's *Time Breakers* (1997). The most popular title to emerge from Helix, however, was Warren Ellis and Darick Robertson's *Transmetropolitian* (1997–2002), a comic that outlived the Helix imprint itself and was ultimately rebranded within DC's more successful Vertigo line. *Transmetropolitan* tells the story of Spider Jerusalem, a cynical and disillusioned gonzo journalist (modeled on Hunter S. Thompson) who uses news reporting to battle corruption and abuse of power in a dystopian sf future. Ellis frames *Transmetropolitian* as a science-fictional version of *Fear and Loathing in Las Vegas* (1971) that draws barbed critical attention to the role of the media in society, the corruption of major political figures, the unsettling power of advertising and consumer culture, and the racist politics of police violence. The series offers an especially cynical view of transhumanism, suggesting that any optimism surrounding progressive possibilities for technological transcendence will always be undermined by such human failings as greed, shortsightedness, and insensitivity.

One of the most troubling aspects of *Transmetropolitan*, however, is again the unapologetic portrayals of misogyny and violence toward women: Spider throws his ex-wife's frozen head off a building, and the women toward whom he is not actively violent are often relentlessly sexualized and objectified. One of his assistants (Channon Yarrow) is a former stripper, another (Yelena) is a daughter-figure with whom he has a one-night stand, and Spider knowingly allows yet another assistant (Indira Ataturk) to be drugged into participating in a public orgy, which results in her becoming the central figure in a popular porn video called "Kali in Heat." Ellis explicitly frames Spider as a morally reprehensible figure whose dismissal of the Indira Ataturk orgy is intended to disturb readers: He claims that he has "no idea" who Ataturk is when his editor asks about her: "Some student. She went nuts. Never saw her again." Artists are under no obligation to make their protagonists admirable characters, and many great works of literature explore flawed anti-heroes, but *Transmetropolitan* continues cyberpunk comics' treatment of women as either figures for violent dismissal (like Spider's wife) or as objects of sexual fetishization (like Spider's various assistants). The story's admission of Spider's misogyny thus ultimately functions to enable its narrative friction—Spider is a flawed character, but the audience is invited to find him charming because he is *less* flawed than the villains he's fighting against. The misogyny and fetishization of women, in this manner, is therefore minimized in deference to other supposedly more serious problems, which is a problem in itself.

In addition to *Transmetropolitan*, Vertigo also published Jamie Delano's cyberpunk comic *2020 Visions* (sometimes called *20/20 Visions*) starting in 1997 as well as Paul Pope's *Heavy Liquid* (1999–2000). *Heavy Liquid* strikingly participates in a unique late-1990s synthesis of cyberculture, psychedelic counterculture, and underground music culture. During the late 1990s—when *Transmetropolitan* was first appearing—cyberpunk and underground drug and music cultures had become deeply interconnected. American cyberpunk had often drawn inspiration from 1960s psychedelic counterculture: Many cyberpunk narratives were influenced by the writings of Philip K. Dick, and the California cyberculture magazine *Mondo 2000* was dedicated to an exploration of cyberculture from a decidedly hippy perspective. By the late 1990s, cyberculture, psychedelic counterculture, and rave culture had all reached a point of recognizable hybridization, particularly in their mutual aspiration to break through the stifling boredom of a false or simulated reality through consciousness-hacking. In this vein, *Heavy Liquid* rejects the simulated nature of social reality. At one point, the story's protagonist (who is only known as 'S') muses that "they killed art years ago. They killed it. Then replaced it with a simulation. Then life was replaced with a simulation. People going to see the Mona Lisa, not to **look** at it, but because it's **the** Mona Lisa. Then they quit going to see it at all. They'd just stitch it in on a screen. A picture of a picture on a screen" (original emphases). S and his friends have dropped out of official society in search of something more authentic; they pursue a doomed Baudrillardian rebellion against a world that has become nothing more than simulation and simulacrum, and the romance of breaking through to a more authentic reality relies on the use of speculative drugs. By the end of the story, S has become a kind-of drug-cyborg—his DNA literally intermingles with the alien entity residing in the Heavy Liquid, and together they become a posthuman hybrid entity, with the drug itself functioning as an information technology enabling their communication and coordination.

By the end of the 1990s and into the early 2000s, there was an explosion of cyberpunk comics whose creative energy and influence are still felt today. *The Matrix Comics*, a series of online spin-offs released from 1999–2003 and subsequently collected in two print volumes, capitalized on the immense success of *The Matrix*, a film largely responsible for popularizing cyberpunk for a new millennial audience. *Heavy Liquid*'s Paul Pope also went on to write *100%* (2002–03), a cyberpunk comic notable for its imaginative portrayals of cybersex. Other significant cyberpunk comics from this time include *Channel Zero* (1997–2005) by Brian Wood and Becky Cloonan; *Resistance* (2002) by Jimmy Palmiotti, Justin Gray, and Juan Santa Cruz; *Singularity 7* (2004) by Ben Templesmith; *Fluorescent Black* (originally published in *Heavy Metal* from 2008–10) by M.F. Wilson and Nathan Fox; and *Hacker* (2009–14) by Alexandre Eremine, to name only a few of the dozen (or more) titles released in this period.

Cyberpunk tropes became so ubiquitous during this time that a number of artists also began experimenting with using digital media to create cyberpunk webcomics. One of the most innovative among these is *Nawlz* (2008–11), a 24-episode cyberpunk adventure created by Australian artist and designer Stu Campbell (also known as Sutu), who is also known for his work with Big hART to adapt Australian Aboriginal stories into digital texts. *Nawlz* is an interactive online comic (with sound effects and a musical soundtrack) that expertly utilizes its digital medium to portray overlapping layers of augmented reality and VR in a manner that transcends the traditional representational capabilities of print comics. Other notable cyberpunk webcomics include *Old City Blues* (2011–13) by Greek artist Giannis Milonogiannis as well as *Dreamspace* (2013–14) and *Drugs and Wires* (2015–) by Mary Safro and Io Black.

The boom of cyberpunk comics continued in the 2010s with books such as *Nonplayer* (2011–15) by Nate Simpson, *Killtopia* (2018–) by Dave Cook and Craig Paton, *r(ender)* (2019) by Leah Williams and Lenka Simeckova, and *The True Lives of the Fabulous Killjoys* (2013) by Gerard Way, Shaun Simon, and Becky Cloonan.[7] Certain comics from this period are particularly notable for hybridizing cyberpunk with other popular speculative genres: *Empty Zone* (2015) by Jason Shawn Alexander, for example, offers a cyberpunk zombie horror narrative that explores the exploitation of soldiers and the trauma of wounded veterans, while *Goddess Mode* (2018–) by Zoë Quinn and Robbi Rodriguez is a mashup of cyberpunk with the popular 'magical girl' manga/anime subgenre.

One of the most notable consequences of the early 21st-century boom of cyberpunk comics is that a much greater diversity of artists and writers contributed to the mode during this time. Malaysian-born creator Sonny Liew's *Malinky Robot* (2011), for example, offers a collection of science-fictional short stories with cyberpunk elements set in a dystopian future, and acclaimed

Argentine artist Eduardo Risso worked with Brian Azzarello on *Spaceman* (2011), a story about a genetically engineered NASA astronaut. Spanish artists Marcos Martín and Muntsa Vicente worked with Brian K. Vaughn on the cybernoir comic *The Private Eye* (2013–15), and Chinese artist Huang-Jia Wei collaborated with French writer Jean-David Morvan on *Zaya* (2014), a futuristic story about a cybernetic super-assassin. *Captain Rugged* (2014), by Nigerian artists Keziah Jones and Native Maqari, is a multimedia story about a superhero who fights against corrupt corporate interests in Lagos. Vietnamese-American artist Dustin Nguyen won a 2016 Eisner Award for his work with Jeff Lemire on the cyberspace opera comic *Descender* (2015–18), and Asian-American writer Jon Tsuei worked with Latinx artist Eric Canete on *Run Love Kill* (2015), a story about a former assassin who is being pursued by a military organization determined to capture or kill her. Toronto-based comic creator Ho Che Anderson, a black artist who also wrote a comic biography of Martin Luther King, released *Godhead* in 2018, a comic about "what might happen if humans found a way to talk directly to God through science" (Velentzas).

In addition, a number of Indigenous artists have created what Grace Dillon calls 'indigipunk' graphic narratives that often simultaneously reference and subvert the sensibilities of Euro-American sf and cyberpunk from the perspectives of Indigenous epistemologies and moral systems. Anishinaabe writer, artist, and designer Elizabeth LaPensée, for example, has created several indigipunk graphic narratives, such as *How The West Was Lost* (2008) and *They Who Walk as Lightning* (2017). *Polyfantastica* (2009–10), a graphic novel by Native Hawaiian artist Solomon Enos, is an epic sf story set in an alternate universe where Native Hawaiians were never invaded and colonized by outside forces. *Sioux Falls* (2016) by Z.M. Thomas (with art from Amelia Woo, J. Wichmann, Wilson Tortosa, and Rueben de Vela) offers a Native American cyber-steam-punk narrative inspired by the events of the 1862 Dakota Uprising, and *Dakwäkāda Warriors* (2017) by Cole Pauls is a science-fictional Southern Tutchone language revival comic. Meagan Byrne is also due to release *Hill Agency* in 2020, an interactive Indigenous cybernoir detective comic from Achimostawinan Games.

Among the boom of 21st-century cyberpunk comics, the comic series that most stands out in terms of mainstream recognition is arguably *Tokyo Ghost* (2015–16) by Rick Remender and Sean Murphy (with colors by Matt Hollingsworth and letters by Rus Wooton). Set in the year 2089, *Tokyo Ghost* tells the story of Debbie Decay and her partner Teddy (who becomes known as Led Dent after he is modified to become a cyborg killer), who both serve as 'constables' or private security officers in the employ of an insane Trump-like corporate executive named Flak.

One of the most striking things about *Tokyo Ghost* is that unlike many earlier cyberpunk comics, it centrally problematizes misogynistic models of masculinity. Teddy's defining weakness—the character flaw that drives him to become the hypermasculine Led Dent—isn't just his addition to soporific media streams and technological enhancement; it is his inability to accept that a girl can fight more effectively than he can. Debbie, the daughter of a police officer who taught her how to stand up for herself, rescues Teddy from an assault when they are attacked as children, and, as we learn in the comic, her actions to protect Teddy are ultimately "the worst thing that could have happened to the young lovers. It shone a bright light on his weakness [...] and that drove poor Teddy nuts." This beating, in other words, and the fact that Debbie fights assertively on his behalf, threatens Teddy's sense of masculinity: His own teacher even mocks him at school, calling him "a grade 'A' pussy," and this is what drives him to break his "no technology" pact with Debbie and join the constables. "The constable program," the story notes, "was built for guys like Teddy: small men with big chips on their shoulders." In the end, Debbie realizes that she must ultimately break out of a codependent relationship dynamic with Teddy, especially after Flak manipulates him into destroying Tokyo, one of the last sustainable green spaces in the world.

Tokyo Ghost's exploration of codependence and its ultimate critique of toxic masculinity marks it as qualitatively different than many other traditional cyberpunk comics. From "The Long

Tomorrow" through *Ronin* and beyond, cyberpunk comics have often been characterized by dynamics of abjection, wherein masculine hero figures violently cast away the feminine in order to achieve strength, power, and autonomy. *Tokyo Ghost* problematizes this celebration of abjection by showing Led Dent as a character whose demented fixation with powerful autonomy is destructive to himself, his relationships, and the entire world around him; as such, the story thus marks a near-complete reversal of the dominant misogynistic themes that characterized early cyberpunk comics from the 1970s and 1980s, possibly heralding future cyberpunk comics that will break new ground and offer more dynamic, more diverse, and, ultimately, more engaging stories for the medium and its fans.

Notes

1 Chris Davidson's and Matt White's online articles were invaluable for establishing the overall terrain of cyberpunk comics for this chapter. The authors would also like to thank Mark Bould, Emily Dare, Grace Dillon, Sean Guynes, Elizabeth LaPensée, Gabriel McKee, Mark Shainblum, Walter Shephard, and Ida Yoshinaga for suggestions that helped broaden the diversity of cyberpunk comics addressed here. For an expanded study of this overall topic, please see the companion piece published in 2020 on *The Los Angeles Review of Books* website.
2 Since Japan's influence on cyberpunk culture is addressed in such chapters as "Manga" and "Anime" elsewhere in this collection, this chapter will instead focus on largely Euro-American cyberpunk comics.
3 Many comics and graphic novels do not use page numbers; in such cases, we have noted that a given work has 'no pagination' at the end of its Works Cited entry. In those rare cases where pagination is available, however, the citation will be volume/issue number followed by page number; for example, (4.17) refers to volume (or issue) #4, page 17.
4 For a sustained analysis of *American Flagg!*, see Corey K. Creekmur's contribution to this collection.
5 For details regarding the early "Movement" as it was known, see Graham J. Murphy's contribution to this collection.
6 James O'Barr's fame was certainly assisted by the numerous film and television adaptations of *The Crow*, notably Alex Proyas's 1994 film version that saw its star, Brandon Lee, tragically killed on set in a stunt accident.
7 As a nostalgic hipsterpunk comic, *The True Lives of the Fabulous Killjoys* is a sequel to My Chemical Romance's concept album *Danger Days: The True Lives of the Fabulous Killjoys* (2010).

Works Cited

Bates, John K. "Tank Girl Stomps Hollywood." *Wired*, 01 Dec. 1994, wired.com/1994/12/tank-girl/.
Booker, M. Keith and Anne-Marie Thomas. *The Science Fiction Handbook*. Wiley, 2009.
Browne, Ben. "15 Mind Blowing Things You Didn't Know About Tank Girl." *Screen Rant*, 28 Jan. 2018, screenrant.com/tank-girl-facts-trivia-secrets/.
Davidson, Chris. "The Best Cyberpunk Comics Ever." *CBR*, 18 Apr. 2017, cbr.com/the-best-cyberpunk-comics-ever/.
Davis, Lauren. "Revel in the Technical Details and Biomechanical Weirdness of *The Matrix* Concept Art." *io9*, 27 Jan. 2013, io9.gizmodo.com/revel-in-the-technical-details-and-biomechanical-weirdn-5979298.
Ellis, Warren and Darick Robertson. *Absolute Transmetropolitan Volume One*. DC Comics, 2015 (no pagination).
Foster, Thomas. *The Souls of Cyberfolk: Posthumanism as Vernacular Theory*. U of Minnesota P, 2005.
Freedman, Carl. *Critical Theory and Science Fiction*. Wesleyan UP, 2000.
———. "Marxism, Cinema and some Dialectics of Science Fiction and Film Noir." *Red Planets: Marxism and Science Fiction*, edited by Mark Bould and China Miéville. Wesleyan UP, 2009, pp. 66–82.
Garcia, Chris. "The Dawn of Computer Comics: *Shatter*." *Computer History Museum*, 24 Aug. 2013, computerhistory.org/atchm/the-dawn-of-computer-comics-shatter/.
Gibson, William. "Introduction." *William Gibson's Neuromancer, The Graphic Novel: Volume 1* by William Gibson, Tom De Haven, and Bruce Jensen. Epic Comics, 1989 (no pagination).
Haraway, Donna J. "A Cyborg Manifesto: Science, Technology, and Socialist-Feminism in the Late Twentieth Century." *Simians, Cyborgs, and Women: The Reinvention of Nature*. Routledge, 1991, pp. 149–81.
Hewlett, Jamie and Alan C. Martin. *Tank Girl One*. Titan Books, 2009 (no pagination).

Khan, Jeanette. "Introduction." *Ronin: The Deluxe Edition* by Frank Miller and Lynn Varley. DC Comics, 2014.

Martin, Daniel. "The Superhero and the Cyberpunk: Transforming Genres in *Spider-Man 2099*." *Continuum Journal of Media and Cultural Studies*, vol. 29, no. 3, 2015, pp. 466–78.

McCloud, Scott. *Understanding Comics: The Invisible Art*. HarperPerennial, 1993.

Miller, Frank and Lynn Varley. *Ronin: The Deluxe Edition*. DC Comics, 2014.

O'Bannon, Dan and Moebius (Jean Giraud). "The Long Tomorrow." *Heavy Metal*, vol. 1, no. 4 and 5, 1977 (no pagination).

Oehlert, Mark. "From Captain America to Wolverine." *The Cybercultures Reader*, edited by David Bell and Barbara M. Kennedy. Routledge, 2000, pp. 112–23.

Pope, Paul. *Heavy Liquid*. DC Comics, 2001 (no pagination).

Remender, Rick and Sean Murphy. *Tokyo Ghost: Complete Edition*. Image Comics, 2018.

Shiner, Lewis. "Confessions of an Ex-Cyberpunk." *The New York Times*, 7 Jan. 1991.

Shiner, Lewis and Tom Sutton. *The Hacker Files* (12 issues). DC Comics, 1992–93.

Velentzas, Irene. "Godhead: Volume 1." *The Comics Journal*, 6 Jun. 2018, tcj.com/reviews/godhead-volume-1/.

White, Matt. "The Best Cyberpunk Comics, Part 1." *Publishers Weekly*, 10 Aug. 2016, publishersweekly.com/pw/by-topic/industry-news/comics/article/70589-the-best-cyberpunk-comics-part-1.html.

———. "The Best Cyberpunk Comics, Part 2." *Publishers Weekly*, 17 Aug. 2016, publishersweekly.com/pw/by-topic/industry-news/comics/article/70594-the-best-cyberpunk-comics-part-2.html.

———. "The Best Cyberpunk Comics, Part 3." *Publishers Weekly*, 25 Aug. 2016, publishersweekly.com/pw/by-topic/industry-news/comics/article/70625-the-best-cyberpunk-comics-part-3.html.

13

AMERICAN FLAGG! (CASE STUDY)

Corey K. Creekmur

In their "Comics Books" chapter published elsewhere in this collection, David M. Higgins and Matthew Iung remark that "European and American comic books had an important, if undervalued, influence on cyberpunk aesthetics as this mode emerged into a recognizable phenomenon during the 1980s" (91). A notable title in cyberpunk's development is writer Dan O'Bannon and illustrator Jean 'Moebius' Giraud's "The Long Tomorrow," serialized in *Métal Hurlant* in 1976 before appearing in English translation in *Heavy Metal* in 1977. "The Long Tomorrow" would go on to influence Ridley Scott's *Blade Runner* (1982) and William Gibson's *Neuromancer* (1984), the oft-cited duo widely considered to have birthed many of the narrative and visual aesthetics we identify as 'cyberpunk.' And, of course, Moebius's visual style for "The Long Tomorrow" is notable in Warren Ellis and Darick Robertson's brilliant *Transmetropolitan*, launched by DC imprint Helix (later Vertigo) in 1997, quite possibly the most well-known and most successful cyberpunk comic book series.

A precursor by a full decade of *Transmetropolitan*, however, is Howard Chaykin's comic book *American Flagg!*, published in an initial series of fifty issues by First Comics between October 1983 and March 1988. The run also included a special issue (linked to Chaykin's concurrent *Time*[2] graphic novels), and was followed by a second series of twelve issues, retitled *Howard Chaykin's American Flagg!* (1988–89). Chaykin wrote and drew the first dozen issues of the original series on his own, but later relied upon other writers (including Alan Moore, J.M. DeMatteis, and Steven Grant) and artists (including Joe Staton, Mark Badger, and Mike Vosburg) to maintain the grueling schedule of regularly producing a monthly periodical. These contributions often dismayed fans, who complained in the comic's letters pages about Chaykin's inconsistent role in the ongoing series, indicating their strong desire to view this 'independent' comic as the expression of a single creator rather than the mass culture commodity Chaykin (also) allowed it to be. Perhaps because only the first fourteen issues have ever been collected and reprinted in trade format—ensuring the subsequent neglect of the full series—it has become conventional if misleading to credit *American Flagg!* exclusively to Chaykin, and to focus critical attention on those early issues.

Undeniably, the impact of those issues was immediate and timely: *American Flagg!* took advantage of the steady demise in the 1980s of self-censorship by the comics industry as a whole. Thanks to a shift away from newsstands to the direct market served by the new model of specialized comics shops, the industry's adherence to the restrictions enforced by the decades-old Comics Code Authority waned considerably. In addition, the rise of independent publishers offering at-times edgier, sexier, and more violent fare than what was available from both Marvel and DC Comics meant that such publishers as First Comics, active between 1983 and 1991, could release creator-owned titles promising what their covers often identified as 'mature content.' Chaykin thus maintained *American Flagg!* as his creative property, and when it quickly became one of the fledgling publisher's first big hits, it confirmed the viability of a new market for sophisticated comics created by distinctive writers and artists rather than the assembly-line staff common to the industry giants. *American Flagg!* was clearly aimed at adult consumers who could now purchase independent comic books outside of the earlier, marginal 'underground' comics (and comix) scene. As a result, soon after *American Flagg!* appeared at the local comic book store, the series was frequently lauded for inaugurating a new maturity in comics. A 1986 article titled "Comic Books for Grownups" in the venerable magazine *The Atlantic* put *American Flagg!* at the front of this new trend: While emphasizing Chaykin's penchant for "violence and hedonism," the essay identifies his contribution as central to making "the comic books of the eighties [...] more diverse and more geared to an adult audience than those of any previous era" (Rose 77). Its success also confirmed that smaller comics publishers could effectively compete with the 'safe for children' superhero titles dominating the market even as it redefined itself. Like other independent comics freed from the Comics Code Authority, *American Flagg!* cultivated an audience that welcomed sex and violence as narrative ingredients, enjoyed barbed political satire, and was willing to be challenged by unconventional—even experimental—formal techniques, including panel layouts that could be followed in multiple directions, and verbal 'sound effects' that were boldly foregrounded rather than unobtrusive accompaniments to the silent page. Serendipitous timing also located *American Flagg!* within a significant cultural context: Novelists Michael Chabon and Steve Erickson, in retrospective appreciations of the series, identify Chaykin's comic as anticipating or effectively articulating many of the tropes of early cyberpunk when that mode was first coalescing, even as Chaykin drew explicitly upon such earlier science fiction influences as Philip K. Dick and Alfred Bester, both of whom clearly influenced cyberpunk. In the end, Chaykin's ambitious goal was to produce a popular comic book, unapologetically steeped in familiar genre conventions, that simultaneously allowed for his own commentary on contemporary social issues while pushing the boundaries of the traditional grammar and architecture of the comics page. As Chaykin emphasized in one of his many voluble interviews, "I know it's a difficult book to read. It's tough, and I intended it to be. [...] I'm doing the book for someone who wants to spend a bit more time on it. It's dense" (Costello, *Conversations* 49).

The plot of *American Flagg!* resists concise summary and, as it unfolded in monthly installments, complaints from veteran comics readers that the series was hard to follow were common, and apparently pleased Chaykin. Fans reported having to re-read previous issues to make sense of the latest installment, or found that they were reading the comic slowly, lingering over pages in a format ostensibly designed for the quick scanning and flipping of pages.[1] In his study of Chaykin's comics, Brannon Costello has convincingly argued that the often repetitive, circular stories told in *American Flagg!* stem in part from a self-conscious awareness of their serial publication as episodic chapters, rather than what soon became the common tendency (and marketing strategy) of releasing a serial publication designed for eventual collection and re-release as a coherent 'graphic novel,' a term and format Chaykin has openly resisted (41–45). As Costello recognizes, there's little significant narrative progress or plot development in large part because "this series is thoroughly implicated in the very structures of artifice and imitation it means to critique" (51). In other words, despite his persistent wit and cynicism, Chaykin's authorial perspective never easily transcends or escapes the corrupt world he depicts, or the pulp format in which it appears.

Set in 2031, the series introduces Mars-born Reuben Flagg as a masculine hero on a noble quest to recover an America that has lost its place as a superpower following the government's relocation to Mars in response to a series of catastrophic global crises in the Year of the Domino (1996, then still in the near future of the comic's first readers). But Flagg's goal to expose rampant deception is continually thwarted, and soon requires him to rely upon strategies that implicate rather than isolate him from the powerful institutions he challenges, most often in vain. While the once-powerful U.S. is the original home of Flagg's parents, it remains a place Flagg only knows in its mythic forms, and one of the central themes of the series is that Flagg's quest for authenticity continually encounters misrepresentations and often seductive artifice. This is a regular motif established by Flagg's own ambiguous status when he is first introduced: Reuben Flagg sets foot on Earth for the first time as a Plexus Ranger, an enforcer of the law and stationed at the Chicago Plexmall, one of the massive commercial-governmental arcologies established after the social collapse at the end of the 20th century. Following the planet's near-destruction and the American government's abandonment of Earth, the powerful Plex, an interstellar body that fuses government and corporate interests in typical cyberpunk style, controls those remaining on Earth via the wildly corrupt Rangers. In a narrative backstory that predates today's blurring of government office and reality television, Flagg was once the star of a popular television series, *Mark Thrust, Sexus Ranger*, a softcore porn version of the role he is now assigned to play as a Ranger. Although Flagg's new role as an actual Ranger may be a demotion, nothing stops the entertainment industry: The porn series is still running, having replaced the human Flagg with a computer simulation. *American Flagg!* thus begins by undermining a distinction between reality and representation as well as the very identity of its main character: Is the actor who played a cop now a cop who is acting? Is erotic activity—a regular feature of this 'adult' comic—always in some sense simulated, especially insofar as it combines fantasy and physicality? And given his computer simulation's ongoing career, who is the more authentic Flagg? Flagg's unfolding adventures deepen, rather than resolve, such uncertainties and we come to understand, perhaps only a bit ahead of him, that almost nothing Flagg encounters in this world is what it seems, particularly when Flagg discovers that the Plex is using subliminal messages, surreptitious drugs, and staged moments of violence that also serve as lucrative mass entertainment to control its own potentially rebellious, rival political factions, called "gogangs." Although the series is continually satirical, employing outrageous puns (the Plexmall's brothels are named Love Canal, an obvious sexual reference but also the location of a notorious environmental disaster exposed in 1977) and assigning many of its characters absurd names (Medea Blitz, John Scheiskopf, Sam Louis Obispo, Desiree Deutschmarx), *American Flagg!* is undergirded by ongoing disappointment regarding the possibility of anyone effecting forward progress or significant change in a world so far gone.

This sense of disappointment and the inability to effect widespread social change is common to cyberpunk's darker or more fatalistic impulses; as Case, *Neuromancer*'s protagonist, learns from the Wintermute/Neuromancer Artificial Intelligence at the end of Gibson's novel, "Things aren't different. Things are things" (270). At the same time, however, *American Flagg!* differs significantly from contemporaneous cyberpunk. For example, Chaykin's series seems only casually invested in the dominant cyberpunk trope of the conflation of humans and machine via cybernetics, even though a secondary character, Flagg's Ranger sidekick Luther Ironheart, is a clueless robot with a holographic head allowing him to, at times, masquerade as Flagg. *American Flagg!* also isn't especially punky in its style, except perhaps in the depiction of some of its subcultural 'gogangs.'[2] Scott Bukatman insightfully notes that "Chaykin has replaced the model of cinema in comic book narrative style with the more 'terminal' model of video" (62). Elaborating on this point, Bukatman writes, "Television is the aesthetic model for the postmodern era, and Chaykin's inclusion of that aesthetic reveals new possibilities and signals a new importance for the medium of comics" (62). Thus, while cyberpunk was neither synonymous nor coextensive with *American Flagg!*, both may be considered emblematic of postmodernism. Fredric Jameson has famously remarked that cyberpunk is "the supreme *literary* expression if not of postmodernism then of late capitalism itself" (419). Therefore, if "television is the aesthetic model for the postmodern era," then the famous opening sentence of Gibson's *Neuromancer*—"The sky above the port was the color of television, tuned to a dead channel" (3)—certainly embeds the subculture of cyberpunk within postmodernism's larger cultural frame, and perhaps even confirms that Gibson and Chaykin were simultaneously tracing a shared cultural formation and aesthetic in their respective media.

At the same time, Paweł Frelik has argued that "cyberpunk has been the most relevant and influential as a visual aesthetic" (81), and in this regard *American Flagg!*'s detailed visualization of a near-future urban sprawl that has been devastated is one of the series' strongest connections to other cyberpunk examples. After all, "one of the most widely-used images of cyberpunk is its placement in urban sprawls and far-reaching cityscapes" (Schmeink 277), such as the Chicago Plexmall. Moreover, Chaykin was developing this nightmarish image of an urban landscape in which architecture and advertising have fully merged around the same time that Ridley Scott's futuristic Los Angeles was being constructed for *Blade Runner.* Chaykin's Plexmall is as equally wired as Scott's L.A. sprawl, thoroughly saturated by ubiquitous mass media which can no longer be distinguished from the realms of business, law, or government. Chaykin's world is dominated by Baudrillardian simulacra that no longer signal an actual origin, if they ever did; instead, *American Flagg!* effects an unmooring of signs from referents only intensified by the computer-generated images (CGI) and digital culture the series seems to anticipate.

While these visual components—urban sprawls; ubiquitously wired technologies; simulations and simulacra—are common to cyberpunk and help enliven *American Flagg!*, even more important is the comic's brilliant conflation of form and content. Regular emphases of the comic's flat pages often intensify rather than clarify for the reader the same confusion and distraction the story's characters persistently experience. The page, we are often reminded, is literally superficial, and thus formally appropriate for the depiction of a world of surfaces without depth. More specifically, the comic's page layouts frequently disrupt or disallow the reading practices that have become second-nature to western readers of comics, accustomed to flowing across a page in a predictable (and common) sequence of left to right, top to bottom (Costello 54). Earlier, Bukatman noted that many of Chaykin's pages offer synchronic rather than diachronic displays, driven less by forward narrative momentum than the depiction of a simultaneous, overloaded spectacle (50). Instead of providing linear progress, the pages of *American Flagg!* are often a riot of competing information, with signs, ads, and sounds that we might think of as background now boldly foregrounded, and distracting from, rather than supporting, what would otherwise serve as the main storyline. *American Flagg!*'s pages and panels frequently rely upon the exact repetition of images that often function as (or like) logos or advertisements, or the interchangeable talking heads of television news. If Pop artists like Andy Warhol had already moved the serialized icons of mass culture and the supermarket display into the art museum, Chaykin returns them with a vengeance to the mass market artifact of the comic book, retrieving their blunt, vulgar, and commercial rather than aesthetic functions: For example, phrases in the everyday speech of his characters are legally trademarked throughout the series, and many of Chaykin's most striking pages seem less drawn than packaged, less expressions of the individual artist's hand than examples of contemporary industrial design. Throughout the series, its narrative unfolding is interrupted by square comic book panels that simultaneously function as images of television screens, frequently rendered through images of pure repetition, like a wall of Warhol silkscreens. In such cases, Chaykin does not obscure the fact that he has mechanically copied rather than meticulously re-drawn images reproduced by the technologies of mass production, even if they seek to parody or warn us about such mind-numbing sameness. Again, *American Flagg!* relentlessly implicates itself in the future world it anticipates as a result of our own greed, desire, and idiocy.

In this regard, while such independent comics as Harvey Pekar's *American Splendor* (1976–2008), Dave Sim's *Cerebus the Aardvark* (1977–2004), or Gilbert and Jaime Hernandez's *Love and Rockets* (1981–), inspired by the achievement of earlier underground comics, were making a bid for their status as a medium for individual artistic expression in contrast to the corporate ownership and mass production techniques of mainstream comics publishers, *American Flagg!* reveled

American Flagg! (Case Study)

in the blatant, crass commodification of the world it depicted. This crucial, self-critical element of the comic was taken to brilliant extremes by the work of Ken Bruzenak, who lettered and designed logos for the series. Bruzenak's contributions played a major role in the reception of the work as simultaneously a stylized comic book and a wicked satire of a hyper-commercialized world, in which virtually all linguistic signs have been reduced to eye-catching corporate logos and wherein dialogue comprises trademarked phrases. Bruzenak was especially innovative in his witty visual design of onomatopoeic words—'Pow!' or 'Bang!' enclosed in a jagged star—that typically but rather unobtrusively compensate for the silence of comics: Bruzenak (and Chaykin) brought these conventional sound effects emphatically and 'loudly' to the fore, treating the sounds of the Plexmall as an extension of the garish logos of the ads that also dominate the fully commercialized landscape. In an instantly famous example from the first issue, the sound of a gun firing rubber bullets, for instance, was rendered in large letters running across the page as a white line of "PAPAPAPAPAPAPAPA" on top of another white line of "OOOOOOOOOOOOOOO," followed, in a lower panel, by two more bursts of gunfire rendered in thick red letters as "POW" and "POW." This sequence thus depicts the sound of violence as a slight variation on "PAPAPAPAPAPAPA OOOOOOOOO MOW MOW," the nonsense lyric that opens "Papa-Oom-Mow-Mow" (1962), the hit novelty song by The Rivingtons, famously adapted a year later by The Trashmen for their hit "Surfin' Bird." Comic book violence—an often-criticized staple of the lowbrow format and its genres—is aligned with the trash culture artifact of the ephemeral (yet memorable) Top 40 novelty song. While such examples from the pages of *American Flagg!* may be simply enjoyed as throwaway gags, they also supply a dense layer of persistent cultural allusions and multiple meanings to the work, further distracting us from a tight focus on what are ostensibly the more important actions taking place in the plot. Nevertheless, such devices, coupled with additional elements such as countdown clocks and messages on multiple kinds of screens (including the comically redundant repetition of 'status quo' across one page) that provide regular models of the verbal–visual interplay found throughout, emphasized that the distracted movement of characters through a world of media bombardment is analogous to the reader's attempt to parse these chaotic pages. This dual movement is, once again, literally superficial, demanding that readers attend to the depthless (but often eye-catching) surfaces of words rendered as images in a manner akin to the ways we half-notice the ubiquitous insignia of traffic signs or public restrooms, or familiar advertising logos on a wall or a screen. While reading *American Flagg!*, we are reminded that the quotidian experience of negotiating mass culture involves near-constant acts of scanning and decoding texts and signs, in both their overwhelming and easily overlooked forms. If not the second-hand, do-it-yourself style of punk, this landscape resembles, as noted earlier, the postmodern realm of the depthless sign, or signifier.

In their introduction to *Cyberpunk and Visual Culture*, Graham J. Murphy and Lars Schmeink argue that "[c]yberpunk has become part of our cultural web of references and provides a cornerstone of our imagining a technology-driven futurity" (xxv). In this regard, Chaykin's *American Flagg!* may be more relevant today in imagining our technology-driven futurity than when it was published nearly forty years ago. Subsequent science fiction films and television series, for example, regularly conflate the film screen and the ubiquitous, information-filled screens of computers, smartphones, surveillance monitors, and even bionic eyes, all of which resemble updated versions of Chaykin's most saturated, non-linear pages. Moreover, Chaykin's narrative is a painful reminder that the heroic attempt to rescue reality or a viable past from the allure of simulacra and a historical ignorance is probably a losing battle, a prescient assessment in this current moment when the very definitions of truth, lies, alternative facts, and (fake) news seem to be up for grabs. Most significantly, *American Flagg!* remains one of the most convincing demonstrations that comics might share cultural space with literature and cinema as a means to explore the future as it might emerge from our present. Earlier science fiction comics, such as the classic newspaper strips featuring white knights Buck Rogers and Flash Gordon, or even the alien-monster-filled comic books of the Cold War, typically repressed the political and economic implications of the futures they anticipated, much less the interpenetration of these with gritty sexuality. On the other hand, Chaykin's *American Flagg!*, alongside notable cyberpunk counterparts, demanded a bold confrontation with the ugly future we were currently making.

Notes

1 In its later issues, and second series, Chaykin and his fellow writers were clearly attempting to revise or clarify portions of the prior narrative that had especially confused or irritated readers.
2 Chaykin has always preferred, for example, that his male characters be sharp dressers and that his female characters be glamorously coiffed and tailored.

Works Cited

Bukatman, Scott. *Terminal Identity: The Visual Subject in Post-Modern Science Fiction*. Duke UP, 1993.
Chabon, Michael. "Introduction: Chaykin and *Flagg!*" *Howard Chaykin's American Flagg!*. Image/Dynamic Forces, 2008, pp. i–iii.
Chaykin, Harold. *American Flagg!* First Comics, 1983–89.
Costello, Brannon. *Neon Visions: The Comics of Howard Chaykin*. Louisiana State UP, 2017.
———, ed. *Conversations with Howard Chaykin*. UP of Mississippi, 2011.
Erickson, Steve. *"American Flagg!" Give Our Regards to the Atom-Smashers!: Writers on Comics*, edited by Sean Howe. Pantheon, 2004, pp. 71–77.
Frelik, Paweł. "'Silhouettes of Strange Illuminated Mannequins': Cyberpunk's Incarnations of Light." *Cyberpunk and Visual Culture*, edited by Graham J. Murphy and Lars Schmeink. Routledge, 2018, pp. 280–99.
Gibson, William. *Neuromancer*. Ace, 1984.
Higgins, David M. and Matthew Iung. "Comics Books." *The Routledge Companion to Cyberpunk Culture*, edited by Anna McFarlane, Graham J. Murphy, and Lars Schmeink. Routledge, 2020, pp. 91–100.
Jameson, Fredric. *Postmodernism, or, The Cultural Logic of Late Capitalism*. Duke UP, 1991.
Murphy, Graham J. and Lars Schmeink. "Introduction: The Visuality and Virtuality of Cyberpunk." *Cyberpunk and Visual Culture*, edited by Graham J. Murphy and Lars Schmeink. Routledge, 2018, pp. xx–xxvi.
Rose, Lloyd. "Comic Books for Grown Ups." *The Atlantic*, no. 258, 1986, p. 77+.
Schmeink, Lars. "Afterthoughts: Cyberpunk Engagements in Countervisuality." *Cyberpunk and Visual Culture*, edited by Graham J. Murphy and Lars Schmeink. Routledge, 2018, pp. 276–87.

14

MANGA

Shige (CJ) Suzuki

Russian filmmaker Andrei Tarkovsky's 1972 science fiction (sf) film *Solaris* features a lengthy sequence in which the protagonists drive into a future city with an elevated multi-lane highway, lighted tunnels, and layered ramps. It is well known that the whole sequence was shot on the real-life metropolitan expressway of early 1970s Tokyo. To Tarkovsky's eyes, the geometric, inorganic structure of a Japanese highway flanked by tall concrete buildings looked 'futuristic.' The film appeared roughly a decade before American-Canadian sf writer William Gibson, who almost single-handedly established the mode of cyberpunk, would deem Japan as the "future" and that "modern Japan simply was cyberpunk" (Gibson). For both Tarkovsky and Gibson, Japan is an objectified, exotic Other onto which they project their futuristic visions, casting a techno-orientalist gaze that has become a standard for cyberpunk narratives.[1]

In spite of this techno-orientalism, however, Japan has not merely been a literary object or projection for western sf. Since World War II (WWII), Japanese sf has made its presence known in the global sf landscape across multiple media forms, including film, television, anime (Japanese animation), manga (Japanese comics), and video games.[2] Some of these forms have fascinated Hollywood directors and producers, prompting remakes of (or original films inspired by) Japanese sf originals. In recent decades, Japanese cyberpunk titles have achieved prominent international status with global appeal to creators, fans, and even scholars. Although international audiences may have encountered Japanese cyberpunk through globalized anime, including *Akira* (Ōtomo 1988), *Ghost in the Shell* (Oshii 1995), *Battle Angel Alita* (originally titled *Gunmu*; Fukutomi 1993), and *BLAME!* (Seshita 2017), these titles (among others) all have their origins in manga, a medium that has played a significant role in shaping not only the cyberpunk mode, but also the development of sf in Japan.[3] Although it is true that the concept of cyberpunk was developed in the U.S. and later introduced to Japan, it would be a mistake to view Japanese cyberpunk works as mere imitations or byproducts. They are a synchronic *and* multimedia response to new technocultural conditions beyond the confines of national and cultural borders.

14.1 Japanese Cyberpunk Manga as a Synchronic Cultural Phenomenon

Although several works of 'proto-sf' literature existed before WWII, Japanese sf developed in the postwar period in parallel to the growth of manga as a vibrant medium in the popular culture landscape. The mainstream formulae and style of story manga (long-form narrative comics) was established by Osamu Tezuka (a.k.a. 'god of manga') whose groundbreaking 1947 work *New Treasure Island* (with writer Shichima Sakai) became one of the first manga bestsellers when Japan was still struggling to recover from the war. Since the beginning of his professional career Tezuka published sf manga titles, including *Lost World* (1948), *Metropolis* (1949), and *Next World* (1951), and actively interacted with sf literary writers by joining an sf writers' club. Also, several representative postwar sf literary writers—such as Sakyō Komatsu (*Japan Sinks*, 1973) and Yasutaka Tsutsui (*Paprika*, 1993 and *The Girl Who Leapt Through Time*, 1967)—had experience in publishing manga before they shifted their efforts to prose sf. Over the course of the late 1950s and throughout the 1960s, story manga evolved and diversified to accommodate and attract new readerships with new genres, forms, and styles, as demonstrated by *gekiga* (literally, 'dramatic pictures'), a type of story manga aimed at young adult and adult readers. Previously, postwar story manga developed as *kodomo manga* (manga for children)—often as *shōnen* (boys') manga—but since the mid-1950s, young manga creators like Yoshihiro Tatsumi created manga with a diverse array of subject matters, featuring more graphic violence or demanding a higher literacy of their readers (Suzuki).[4] Over the mid-1950s to 1960s, new manga magazines aimed at different target audiences were founded—for instance, *shōjo manga* (comics for girls) and *seinen manga* (comics for young adult and adult males). Responding to the maturing manga audience, some authors began to create more challenging works in which they incorporated social and political critiques, while others explored philosophical speculations via the genre of sf in the medium of manga. These new expressions opened the door to proto-cyberpunk themes; for example, Shōtaro Ishinomori, a former assistant to Tezuka, began to serialize *Cyborg 009* in 1964 as a *shōnen* manga, featuring an international team of cyborg protagonists who fight for peace, which can be read as a response to increasing anxiety over the Vietnam War under the Cold War regime. Proto-cyberpunk themes developed in manga throughout the 1970s in the work of female authors such as Moto Hagio and Keiko Takemiya, both of whom published sf manga when the genre was still strongly associated with *shōnen* manga—incorporating the issues of cloning, genetic engineering, eugenics, and control society, taking up some themes similar to what cyberpunk would tackle in the next decade.

Like the North American cyberpunk movement, the prominence of Japanese cyberpunk manga arrived in the 1980s. While Japanese cyberpunk authors were aware of previous and contemporaneous western, largely North American, sf literature and film, the rise of Japanese cyberpunk was a synchronic, transnational phenomenon. Indeed, Katsuhiro Ōtomo's *Akira* (1982–90), one of the foundational texts in Japanese cyberpunk, began to be serialized in *Weekly Young Magazine* in 1982, contemporaneous with the emergence of cyberpunk stories, novels, and film on the North American sf scene. Like North American cyberpunk, Japanese manga creators in the 1980s acutely apprehended the dynamic sociocultural and technological shifts taking place around them and responded by producing their own unique works.

There are three key shifts relevant to these early cyberpunk manga. First, it is argued that Japan became a "post-industrial society" in the mid-1970s (Linhart 274–75). Japan's economic ascendancy in the postwar period was largely driven by manufacturing and heavy industries, such as construction, iron-steel, shipbuilding, automobiles, etc. Yet, since the mid-1970s, the center of the economy had gravitated toward finance, service, and IT industries. This post-industrial economic shift brought about numerous changes in social life. After achieving material affluence by the 1970s, the new orientation of Japan's late-capitalist economy generated a postmodern, hyper-consumerist society, intensified by the unprecedented 'bubble economy' boom in the 1980s. Middle- and upper-class people in Japan began to spend more money on brands, fashionable clothes, luxurious goods, leisure, and entertainment. Media images in eye-catching ads and screens set up on urban streets saturated the public space and promoted this hyper-consumerist, non-productive consumption; meanwhile, popular media—TV, magazines, commercial catalogues—constantly stimulated and galvanized consumerist desires. In this way, Japan transitioned into an information society where information emerged as a central agent in politics, culture, and the economy. Japanese cyberpunk authors were, in part, responding to the media- and information-saturated society that surrounded them.

Second, in the 1980s, Japan experienced a technocultural shift similar to what North American cyberpunk writers were acutely responding to in their own work. In his oft-quoted Preface to *Mirrorshades: The Cyberpunk Anthology* (1986), Bruce Sterling summarizes this shift: "Eighties tech sticks to the skin, responds to the touch: the personal computer, the Sony Walkman, the portable telephone, the soft contact lens" (xiii). The Sony Walkman that Sterling references—developed in Japan and exported to the west—became a symbol of Japanese technological sophistication: It was an innovative, small-sized device for users to 'wear,' enabling one to not only to listen to music, but to control one's mood anywhere and anytime, representing a cyberpunk combination of fashion and technology intimately coupled with the human body. In the 1980s, personal computers became more available to everyday people's use, no longer owned only by big corporations or governmental institutions. An early form of information networking (before the advent of the Web) was also introduced in this period. The affordability and accessibility of these new technologies—such as VCRs, photocopiers, synthesizers, printers, and computer networking—enabled individuals not just to passively consume media products but to produce and disseminate their own work and, sometimes, even "us[e] the technology against the guys who created it," a cyberpunk "street use of technology" attitude summarized by sf scholar Larry McCaffery ("Interview"). In the context of manga culture, this 'street' attitude manifested itself as a rise in *dōjinshi* (manga fanzine) production. Since the mid-1970s, amateur manga production had been gaining force with the advent of inexpensive technologies such as low-cost offset printing and photocopying facilities (Kinsella 105); non-professional authors had also begun to organize do-it-yourself *dōjinshi* sell-and-buy events— most famously, the Comic Market (a.k.a. Comiket, 1975–present), now the largest in the world. Masamune Shirow, the author of *Ghost in the Shell* (1989–97), was active in this *dōjinshi* manga subculture, a dynamic site from which new voices and talents have continued to spring forth.

Lastly, Japan in the 1980s witnessed the rise of new types of youth subculture groups. In the popular media discourse of the late 1970s and early 1980s, a new, highly-circulated term, *shin-jinrui* (i.e. 'new human species' or 'new human breed'), referred to a generation of young people with values and sensibilities disconnected from those of previous generations. Unlike those who had direct experiences of trauma from WWII and the hardships of the immediate postwar era, this new generation grew up in an affluent Japan and did not share their elders' work ethic or fidelity to companies or nation (Herbig). This was also when the term 'otaku' entered the popular lexicon. 'Otaku'—initially called *otaku-zoku* (the otaku tribe)—referred to young (male) people obsessed with subcultural or popular cultural interests (computers, anime, manga, etc.), typically with negative connotations, although they were considered to have tech-savvy knowledge and skills. The discursive image of the *shin-jinrui* and the otaku shared a rejection of postwar or mainstream ideals, casting growth and progress in terms of selfhood and nationhood, along with a lack of faith in modern, progressive grand narratives. Writing in the early 2000s, Japanese critic Hiroki Azuma famously characterized otaku as "postmodern database animals" as the subtitle to his book *Otaku: Japan's Database Animals*.

Finally, another urban tribe that peaked in the 1970s and 1980s and also expressed its rebellious attitude toward mainstream society was a biker type called *bōsō-zoku* (i.e. 'running out-of-control tribe') (Figure 14.1). Somewhat similar to British mods and American choppers, these young motorcycle gangs rode around the streets recklessly while making noise. These youth subcultures collectively represented a symbolic rebellion against the establishment—in the case of Japan, against the postwar bureaucratic, institutionalized, carceral society, with its biopolitics disciplining citizens

Figure 14.1 *Bōsō-zoku*, youth biker gangs, became a social concern in the 1970s and 1980s. Gratefully reprinted with permission from © Yomiuri Shimbun.

through modern institutions. Ōtomo's *Akira* celebrates such rebellious groups by featuring biker gang protagonists who are obsessed with speed and violence, as if their youthful energy will unsettle and renew institutionalized life—or even demolish the rigid social and political structure of 1980s Japan.

While these specific socio-historical conditions set the stage for the rise of Japanese cyberpunk in the 1980s and 1990s, Gibson's *Neuromancer* (1984)—published in Japanese translation in 1986—unquestionably inspired Japanese authors. Japanese sf critic Takayuki Tatsumi, who himself played an active role in introducing North American cyberpunk to Japan (Tatsumi, *Saibāpanku Amerika*), documents the impact of Gibson's influential work on the Japanese sf scene, including Japanese literary sf writers who produced their own cyberpunk novels, such as Mariko Ōhara (*Hybrid Child*, 1990), Gorō Masaki (*Venus City*, 1992), and Azusa Noah (*Idola Lunaris*, 1993) (*Full Metal Apache* 105–111). In the Japanese edition of *Neuromancer*, the translator Hisashi Kuroma created a set of Japanese neologisms for the term 'cyberspace' in Sino-Japanese characters (*kanji*): *den'nōkūkan* (i.e. 'cyberbrain space') (Tatsumi, *Full Metal Apache* 108) and *gitai* for prosthetic bodies. The term spread in use and evolved, as in *Ghost in the Shell*'s use of *den'nō* (cyberbrain), referring to a techno-augmented brain that grants cyborg characters direct access to an information network. While these cross-linguistic examples might be regarded as recontextualizations and/or domestications of the supposedly U.S.-originated mode, it is important to stress the synchronic ascendancy of Japanese cyberpunk with its American counterpart. And some of Japanese cyberpunk's most significant developments were achieved in the medium of manga.

Manga

14.2 Themes and Motifs in Representative Cyberpunk Manga

Given the synchronicity of the rise of Japanese cyberpunk fiction and multimedia interactions with North American sf and cyberpunk texts, it is no surprise that Japanese cyberpunk manga employ similar themes, motifs, and tropes. Typical themes include the impact of new technologies on subjectivity, the blurring of boundaries between humans and machines, and encounters with sentient non-human beings like artificial intelligence (AI) and/or artificial life. Typical plots often follow the pattern of future-noir detective stories set in a dystopian, class-divided society. However, these 'stock elements' in cyberpunk narratives are not merely replicated in Japanese cyberpunk manga but are decontextualized and recontextualized with the socio-historical specificities of Japan. Furthermore, these are explored in manga with the medium's stylistic, topical, and industrial conventions.

Ōtomo's *Akira* is considered a landmark Japanese cyberpunk manga, although it is not so much about typical Gibsonian cyberpunk motifs like cyborgs or cyberspace, as it is about biochemical drugs, psychic powers, and genetic engineering, alongside youth rebellion, military conspiracies, and political machinations. The main setting of *Akira* is a post-apocalyptic Japan, Neo-Tokyo, circa 2019, thirty-eight years after the detonation of a new type of bomb (*shin-gatabakudan*)—the exact term first used in Japan for the A-bomb dropped in Hiroshima—that signaled the outbreak of World War III.[5] When *Akira* begins, the city of Neo-Tokyo has already recovered and is preparing for another Tokyo Olympics. This setting invites a reading of *Akira* as a national allegory of postwar Japan, as evinced in a series of visual and textual allusions to major events and symbolic architecture from postwar Japanese history, such as the atomic bombing and countercultural political revolts by students. The Yoyogi National Gymnasium that was built for the 1964 Tokyo Olympics appears in the story as the temple of Lady Miyako, and the manga features the subservient position to and complicity with U.S. militarism. On the other hand, Shirow's *Ghost in the Shell* and Yukito Kishiro's *Battle Angel Alita* (1990–95) focus on class divisions rather than generational divides: *Ghost in the Shell* introduces the future state of Japan in 2029 as a "corporate conglomerate-state" (vol. 1, 5), which suggests that economy and polity are inextricably bound and merged into one entity. *Battle Angel Alita* presents a future world in which the chosen, privileged few live in Zalem, a high-tech city floating in the sky, while disenfranchised groups of people live in the slum-like alleys of Iron City, Zalem's de facto junkyard. Such dystopian future visions can be understood as extrapolative futures based on ambivalent feelings toward Japan's economic prowess and the nation's anxieties (over class disparity, immigration, and possible economic downturns) in the 1980s (Figure 14.2).

The typical cyberpunk motif of technology internalized into mind and body (Sterling xiii) is underscored in Japanese cyberpunk manga. While Shirow's debut work *Appleseed* (1985–89) featured cyborg characters, the theme of man-machine hybrids is more deeply explored in *Ghost in the Shell*. In this work, the main characters are cyborgs whose bodies are replaced by prosthetic parts which enable extraordinary physical and cognitive abilities—including instant communication and access to a vast information network. However, such a techno-augmented body comes with costs. First, the cyborg body engenders an existential anxiety. The protagonist Major Motoko Kusanagi says, "Sometimes I wonder if I've already died, and what I think of as 'me' isn't really just an artificial personality comprised of a prosthetic body and a cyberbrain" (106). The constant accessibility of the information network generates the possibility for memories to be "hacked" and replaced with fake memories (95–96), or the loss of control over their own bodies (47). The finale of *Ghost in the Shell* even envisions the merging of human consciousness with artificial life (344). In Shirow's manga, the cyborg body challenges the liberal humanist notion of what it means to be 'human' by questioning the Cartesian dualism of mind/body, subject/object, in an inquiry similar to Donna J. Haraway's cyborg theory and N. Katherine Hayles's critique of

Figure 14.2 Lady Miyako's Temple is modeled on Yoyogi National Gymnasium, built for the 1964 Tokyo Olympics. Gratefully reprinted with permission from AKIRA © MASH·ROOM Co., Ltd./ Kodansha Ltd. All rights reserved.

posthumanism, both of which seek a radical potential in the new cyborg/posthuman subject(ivity) produced by technocultural contexts.[6]

Kishiro's *Battle Angel Alita* shares the above-mentioned themes of the cyborg body and (a possible dissolution of) human identity, but pushes it to its extreme. The main narrative is largely driven by the protagonist Alita's quest for identity, but throughout the series Kishiro mixes cyberpunk narratives and motifs with entertaining martial arts action. Several characters in the story transform their own bodies for instrumental purposes, sometimes going beyond 'normal' human shapes. While some characters augment their bodies to achieve aesthetic and physical ideals, others enhance their bodies in utilitarian ways, pursuing over-specification to such an extent that their bodies partly or mostly become grotesque, monstrous machines (Figure 14.3).

Compared to *Ghost in the Shell* and its speculative inquiries, Kishiro's manga is more driven by its showcasing of combat scenes throughout the series, many of which even fetishize the graphic violence of destruction of (cyborg) bodies; the body of Alita becomes a weapon in itself, as suggested by the Japanese original title *Gunmu*, literally 'gun dream.'

As evidenced in both *Ghost in the Shell* and *Battle Angel Alita*, readers of Japanese cyberpunk manga often encounter 'beautiful female fighters' as protagonists. Although their bodies are replaced by mechanical parts, sexed and gendered markings are registered on their bodies both visually and morphologically. Both Kusanagi and Alita are depicted with idealized, fetishized, and even sexualized bodies, often penetrated by a male gaze. In fact, the original manga series of *Ghost in the Shell* features a series of pulp-like gunfights, nude robots, sex jokes, and Major

Manga

Figure 14.3 This character has transformed his body into a monstrous killing machine. Gratefully reprinted with permission from © Yukito Kishiro/Kodansha Ltd. All rights reserved.

Kusanagi in scenes of homoerotic virtual sex.[7] It is not difficult to ascribe such depictions to manga's industrial and generic conventions since they were serialized in *seinen* manga magazines, marking their primary target readership as young adult and adult males, although other instances of 'beautiful female fighters' in Japanese manga—say, Naoko Takeuchi's *Sailor Moon* (1992–97) or Hayao Miyazaki's *Nausicaä of the Valley of the Wind* (1982–94)—are considered symbols of female empowerment (Newson). Previous scholarship on the figurations of the 'female' cyborg in relation to issues of gender and sex(uality) reveals mixed responses.[8] While scholars like Sharalyn Orbaugh argue that the cyborg body in Japanese cyberpunk suggests an emerging subjectivity in the shifting, technocultural context while subverting the "heterosexual matrix" (188), Carl Silvio claims that such a potential is ultimately undermined by positing Kusanagi as a "maternal figure" (69), a re-inscription of the conventional social order of gender and domination. While these diametrically opposed interpretations seem to derive from each scholar's particular focus, the strong ambivalence about liberating and restricting powers is always at work in the figuration of the cyborg body, as Haraway theorizes, and still remains unsettled.

Unlike the pure prose of literary texts, manga's visual elements provide another set of contributions to cyberpunk. Ōtomo's drawing style, which is less cartoony than traditional manga, and features more naturalistic character design with elaborate backgrounds, looked unique and fresh even to the eyes of Japanese readers who were accustomed to mainstream story manga at the time of his manga debut.[9] Alongside the meticulously detailed geometrical buildings that imply a rigid social structure, the accentuated motion lines, drawn by rulers, which express the speed of hurtling bikes, suggest the explosive energy of youth biker gangs, creating a dynamic sense

Shige (CJ) Suzuki

Figure 14.4 Compared to Oshii's anime version, the original manga has more comic relief. Gratefully reprinted with permission from © Shirow Masamune/Kodansha Ltd. All rights reserved.

of movement while engrossing readers in scenes of action. Shirow's style for *Ghost in the Shell* is inspired by Ōtomo, although Shirow occasionally inserts the *chibi* style of super-deformed character design that depicts a character as having a small, chubby body with an oversized head during a handful of comic relief moments throughout the series, which is in stark contrast to Mamoru Oshii's anime adaptation's more serious, darker overtones (Figure 14.4).

Like cyberspace, pages of cyberpunk manga are dense in information. Several pages of *Ghost in the Shell* and *Battle Angel Alita* are spattered with author's notes, asides placed outside the regular panels that provide brief explanations on (future) techno-sciences and theories, and the author's philosophical notes on them.[10] Visually, cyberpunk manga offer more visual elaboration in their backgrounds when compared with mainstream manga; panels are often crowded with characters, décor, buildings, and speech balloons. The packed panels on the pages evoke a feeling of navigating through the text's densely networked world. Nevertheless, with little or no narrative exposition given, the text denies readers clear ideas about how its future world is constructed; therefore, readers are required to conjecture by piecing together fragments as the plot unfurls. Such a tendency is most explored in Nihei's post-cyberpunk manga *BLAME!* (1998–2003), in which the author limits the use of words and relies on visual narrative techniques to depict a posthuman, far-future world. The unique innovation of *BLAME!* is its way of presenting a post-Anthropocene world on an enormous scale, inhabited by cyborgs and silicon humanoid creatures, while humans barely survive in the margins. *BLAME!* offers a bleak vision of the far-future in which humanity has long since lost its access to the control of AIs and central networks. Instead, construction robots automatically and ceaselessly build artificial

Manga

Figure 14.5 The megastructures in *Blame!* are continually constructed by autonomous robots without human control. Gratefully reprinted with permission from © Tsutomu Nihei/Kodansha Ltd. All rights reserved.

megastructures (Figure 14.5). Construction presumably commenced several centuries ago on Earth, though these megastructures have continually expanded and have even swallowed several planets in the solar system. Nihei successfully impresses the massive scale of his constructed world on his readers through his visual skill.

The unknowability of the whole world in Japanese corresponds to narrative structures in which protagonists cannot remember their origins or identities—in the cases of *Ghost in the Shell* and *Battle Angel Alita*—or are unable to grasp the concept of the whole world—in the case of *BLAME!* While, for the most part, *Ghost in the Shell* follows the typical page layout of mainstream manga with arrangements of rectangular frames on its pages, it also visualizes the complexity of one's direct connection with others through information networks. On one such page, the protagonist Kusanagi's consciousness is directly connected with several other characters: In the center panel, several characters' heads are depicted facing different directions, floating without any order, while both visuals and text are layered over one another (18). Such a visualization of connectivity—which relays not only memories and information, but also bodily sensations—resists the linearity of manga's reading conventions, encouraging the reader's eyes to float around the page. It also compares the manga reading experience to that of diving into the Net as the reader joins the production of text through the interaction produced by the pages' fragmented text and visuals. In *Ghost in the Shell*, Aramaki, the chief of Section 9, notes: "whether it's a simex [simulated experience] or a dream, the information that exists is all real … and an illusion at the same time." To this, Major Kusanagi responds: "[y]ou mean in the same way novels and films change people?" (96).

Manga, as a medium that communicates through navigating multi-modal, cross-discursive types of information, seems to offer a similar experience to the simulated experience of 'cyberspace' originally imagined and popularized by Gibson.

Lastly, cyberpunk's anti-authoritarian proclivity is also pronounced in Japanese cyberpunk manga by narrative alignment of the protagonists with the politics of the disenfranchised people on the street. *Akira* assigns a hope to the youthful energy represented by protagonist Kaneda, a teenage biker gang leader (and, notably, not to its military personnel or aged religious leaders) for the renewal and renovation of Neo-Tokyo from apocalyptic devastation. In *Battle Angel Alita*, regardless of the fact that her 'true self' turns out to be a ruthless terrorist named Yōko, Alita decides to use her power for the people, especially the ones living in slum-like Iron City (Kishiro, 9.190–191). Finally, while one might find "social and political conservatism" in the figuration of cyborgs in *Ghost in the Shell* (LaMarre 306)—exemplified by the fact that Section 9, to which the protagonists belong, is an organization of the nation-state—Shirow's series offers critical commentary on the darker side of Japan such as political corruption, re-militarization, the corporate state, class polarity, etc.

14.3 Coda

In the current media economy and ecology, manga has become part of the larger network of transmedia franchising by media industries—commonly called 'media mix.' Like Henry Jenkins's concept of "media convergence" (2–3), the term 'media mix' refers to media-industrial strategies for the extensive franchising of media content across different media platforms in pursuit of increased financial synergy and expansion of markets. Scholars like Marc Steinberg discuss the unique orientation of Japanese media mix strategies by emphasizing the creation of characters that can exist in diverging narratives and worlds, not merely in contained, unified worlds—the latter is more common in Hollywood franchises (Steinberg). Shirow's manga *Ghost in the Shell* is a typical case for such media mix strategies since not only was it adapted into several anime feature films, TV anime series, and a live-action film, but was also made into a PlayStation game and an anthology of prose fiction (2017), along with merchandise (for example, doll figures, toys, key chains, etc.). Each time media content migrates into another media platform, stories are adapted, added to, and newly created by different authors, directors, and producers, extending the *Ghost in the Shell*-universes.

While Japanese cyberpunk fiction peaked in the 1980s and 1990s, its narrative worlds continue to attract domestic and international authors and creators. More recent transmedia adaptations are transnational, including the above-mentioned Hollywood live-action adaptation of *Ghost in the Shell* (Sanders 2017) and *Ghost in the Shell: Global Neural Network* (2019), an anthology of four narratives in which four western writers and comics artists—Alex de Campi, Brenden Fletcher, Genevieve Valentine, and Max Gladstone—create original "Ghost in the Shell" stories in their own styles. Like Robert Rodriguez's film *Alita: Battle Angel* (2019), based on Kishiro's manga series, Japanese cyberpunk manga still inspire and stimulate international contributors to invent new stories that attempt to articulate the increasingly globalized and technocultural conditions in which we are living.

English-language scholarship about Japanese sf and cyberpunk fiction seems to gravitate toward anime as a medium and/or its cultural texts, with less emphasis on manga.[11] The study of sf and cyberpunk manga is overdue because of these texts' prominence and persistence in the global popular cultural scene. Compared to anime production, which tends to require collective labor with a certain amount of capital, manga maintains its appeal to creators as a low-budget medium with the potential to express new visions, evidenced by the increasing rise of online manga production on Japanese-language websites. The recent rise of comics studies in academia must be expanded to accommodate the study of international comics, including manga, not only because

Manga

manga offers an outlook on the global impact of Japanese popular culture, but also because the study of manga—especially sf and cyberpunk manga—offers multiple analytic examinations and philosophical questions about our current condition, increasingly saturated by visual images with the permeation of new media and new technologies beyond national and cultural borders.

Notes

1 Techno-orientalism was a noticeably common characteristic of 1980s and 1990s American cyberpunk fiction in which Japan and/or Asia is presented as an exoticized and/or fetishized Other. For more applications of techno-orientalism, see Brian Ruh's and Kumiko Saito's respective chapters in this collection.
2 In recent English-language scholarship on comics, the term 'comics' is used as a singular noun, referring to the medium of comics. The Japanese language does not have a plural form of manga—i.e. the phrase 'mangas' is awkward in light of the convention of Japanese Studies. In this chapter, I will use 'manga' or 'comics' as a singular noun when referring to the medium, and plural for instances.
3 All the manga titles mentioned in this chapter are collected across multiple volumes spanning multiple years. I will only be referencing specific volumes from which I have quoted in the Works Cited. In addition, this chapter will not aim to offer a comprehensive overview of Japanese cyberpunk manga, but instead will focus on a few representative cyberpunk(-themed) manga with global recognition.
4 Along with story manga, other kinds of manga for general readers—single-image satirical/political cartoons and four-frame comic strips (*yonkoma manga*), for instance—continue to be published.
5 This year is the setting in the Japanese original. In the English edition of *Akira* published by Dark Horse, the year is changed to 2030.
6 The anime adaptations of *Ghost in the Shell* have been extensively discussed in conversation with Haraway's 'cyborg theory' and/or Hayles's 'posthuman theory.' See Silvio, Orbaugh, and Brown for examples. Patricia Melzer's contribution to this collection also addresses the intersections of Haraway's cyborg theory, posthumanism, and cyberpunk, albeit restricting its focus to largely western, print cyberpunk.
7 The sequence of Kusanagi's homoerotic virtual sex is censored by Kodansha Comics in its English-language edition. This deletion of the homoerotic scene can be problematic since it undermines Kusanagi's queer potential.
8 David M. Higgins and Matthew Iung provide detailed examples of cyberpunk's lengthy problem dealing with women on both a narrative and artistic level in their contribution to this collection.
9 It has been pointed out that French comics artist Jean 'Moebius' Giraud had a significant impact on Ōtomo's drawing style (Gravett). This influence cannot be understated; after all, Scott Bukatman writes about Moebius's influence upon western cyberpunk's formative years, drawing attention to the artist's "compacted urbanism" (*Blade* 26) and his depictions of "enclosed, expansive but claustrophobic" urban spaces where the city streets "can now be located (only with difficulty) at the nearly invisible bottom of a narratively and spatially decentered environment" (*Terminal* 128).
10 In the English edition by Kodansha Comics, the author's notes are compiled at the end of the volume.
11 As examples of this assertion, see Napier (2000), Lamarre (2009 and 2019), Brown (2010), and (Bolton 2018).

Works Cited

Azuma, Hiroki. *Otaku: Japan's Database Animals*. U of Minnesota P, 2009.
Bolton, Christopher. *Interpreting Anime*. U of Minnesota P, 2018.
Brown, Steven T. *Tokyo Cyberpunk: Posthumanism in Japanese Visual Culture*. Palgrave Macmillan, 2010.
Bukatman, Scott. *Blade Runner*. 2nd Ed., Palgrave Macmillan, 2012.
———. *Terminal Identity: The Virtual Subject in Post-Modern Science Fiction*. Duke UP, 1993.
Gibson, William. "The Future Perfect: How Did Japan Become the Favored Default Setting for So Many Cyberpunk Writers?" *Time*, 30 Apr. 2001, content.time.com/time/magazine/article/0,9171,1956774,00.html.
Gravett, Paul. "Katsuhiro Otomo: Post-Apocalypse Now." *Paul Gravett: Comics, Graphic Novels, Manga*. 7 Sep. 2013, www.paulgravett.com/articles/article/katsuhiro_otomo.
Haraway, Donna J. *Simians, Cyborgs, and Women: The Reinvention of Nature*. Routledge, 1991.
Herbig, Paul A. and Pat Borstorff. "Japan's Shinjinrui: The New Breed." *International Journal of Social Economics*, vol. 22, no. 12, 1995, pp. 49–65.

Hayles, Katherine N. *How We Became Posthuman: Virtual Bodies in Cybernetics, Literature, and Informatics*. U of Chicago P, 1999.

Jenkins, Henry. *Convergence Culture: Where Old and New Media Collide*. New York UP, 2006.

Kinsella, Sharon. *Adult Manga: Culture and Power in Contemporary Japanese Society*. U of Hawaii P, 2000.

Kishiro, Yukito. *Battle Angel Alita*, vol. 9. Viz Communications, Inc., 1992.

LaMarre, Thomas. *The Anime Machine: A Media Theory of Animation*. U of Minnesota P, 2010.

LaMarre, Thomas. *The Anime Ecology: A Genealogy of Television, Animation, and Game Media*. U of Minnesota P, 2018.

Linhart, Sepp. "From Industrial to Postindustrial Society: Changes in Japanese Leisure-Related Values and Behaviors." *The Journal of Japanese Studies*, vol. 14, no. 2, Summer 1988, pp. 271–307.

McCaffery, Larry. "Introduction: The Desert of the Real." *Storming the Reality Studio: A Casebook of Cyberpunk and Postmodern Science Fiction*, edited by Larry McCaffery. Duke UP, 1991, pp. 1–16.

———. "Interview with Larry McCaffery." Interview by Alexander Laurence and Jill St. Jacques. *Alt-X*, 1 Mar. 1994, altx.com/interviews/larry.mccaffery.html.

Napier, Susan J. *Anime from Akira to Howl's Moving Castle, Updated Edition: Experiencing Contemporary Japanese Animation*. Palgrave Macmillan, 2005.

Newson, Victoria Anne. "Young Females as Super Heroes: Super Heroines in the Animated *Sailor Moon*." *Femspec*, vol. 5, no. 2, 2004, pp. 57–81.

Orbaugh, Sharalyn. "Sex and the Single Cyborg: Japanese Popular Culture Experiments in Subjectivity." *Robot Ghosts and Wired Dreams: Japanese Science Fiction from Origins to Anime*, edited by Christopher Bolton, Istvan Csicsery-Ronay, and Takayuki Tatsumi. U of Minnesota P, 2007, pp. 172–92.

Ōtomo, Katsuhiro. *Akira: Book One*. Kodansha Comics, 2009.

Saitō, Tamaki. *Beautiful Fighting Girl*. U of Minnesota P, 2011.

Schodt, Frederik L. *The Astro Boy Essays: Osamu Tezuka, Mighty Atom, and the Manga/anime Revolution*. Stone Bridge Press, 2007.

Shirow, Masamune. *Ghost in the Shell*, vol. 1. Kodansha Comics, 2017.

Sivilo, Carl. "Refiguring the Radical Cyborg in Mamoru Oshii's *Ghost in the Shell*." *Science Fiction Studies*, vol. 26, no. 1, Mar. 1999, pp. 54–72.

Sterling, Bruce. Preface. *Mirrorshades: The Cyberpunk Anthology*, edited by Bruce Sterling. Ace, 1986, pp. ix–xvi.

Steinberg, Marc. *Anime's Media Mix: Franchising Toys and Characters in Japan*. U of Minnesota P, 2012.

Suzuki, Shige (CJ). "*Gekiga*, or Japanese Alternative Comics: The Mediascape of Japanese Counterculture." *Introducing Japanese Popular Culture*, edited by Alisa Freedman and Toby Slade. Routledge, 2017, pp. 265–76.

Tatsumi, Takayuki. *Saibāpanku Amerika*. Keisō Shobō, 1988.

———. "Generations and Controversies: An Overview of Japanese Science Fiction, 1957–1997." *Science Fiction Studies*, vol. 27, no. 1, March 2000, pp. 105–14.

———. *Full Metal Apache: Transactions between Cyberpunk Japan and Avant-Pop America*. Duke UP, 2006.

15

EARLY CYBERPUNK FILM

Andrew M. Butler

There is a moment in an article by Andrew Britton in which he identifies most Hollywood films made between 1977 and 1986 as being part of "a general moment of reaction and conservative reassurance" (97). These "Reaganite entertainments" (47) were released in a period when the status of straight, white, American men was supposedly threatened by rights for women, African Americans, and homosexuals. American hegemony had been damaged by the Watergate scandal and "the loss of Vietnam, the loss of Iran, the success of the Sandinista revolution in Nicaragua, and an upsurge of revolutionary struggle in El Salvador and Grenada" (Britton 118), while the Cold War continued and the Soviets invaded Afghanistan. The developments in computers, cable and satellite television, VCRs, games machines, and telephony revolutionized communications, the office, and the home, as well as enabling the offshoring of manufacturing jobs. It was then that cyberpunk emerged as "not an invasion but a modern reform" (Sterling xv) of science fiction (sf). Yet in spite of its reformative swagger, Nicola Nixon argues, cyberpunk is actually "a response to (or perhaps a reflection of) the Reaganite America of the '80s" (221); as a result, cyberpunk films of the era and beyond engage with Reagan's ideology with varying degrees of endorsement or resistance.[1]

Britton argues that the neoliberal aesthetic of Reaganite entertainments "anticipates a gorgeous re-flowering of capitalism in which the good things will be born again under the aegis of the microchip once a flabby politic has been slimmed down and its cancerous growths excised" (109). David Harvey describes neoliberalism as a political economy where "human well-being can best be advanced by liberating individual entrepreneurial freedoms and skills within an institutional framework characterized by strong private property rights, free markets, and free trade" (2). Following this concept, Reaganite policies shrank the state and deregulated the market.

Britton's tutor and colleague Robin Wood feels that these films also explore "the fear [...] that democratic capitalism may not be clearly separable from Fascism and may carry within itself the potential to become Fascist, totalitarian, a police state" (169). Nuclear war is a clear and present danger, even as the films attempt to reassure American audiences that "the bomb is a good thing in the hands of the Americans and a bad thing in the hands of the Soviets" (Britton 119). Strength is safe if it is the right person who is strong.

Meanwhile, special effects offer reassuring spectacles, or as Wood argues, "the sense of reckless, prodigal extravagance, no expense spared" budgets contributes to a sense that if Hollywood can afford such an epic, then "the [capitalist] system must be basically OK, right?" (166). Visual delights give an illusion of originality to these films, disguising "the extreme familiarity of plot, characterization, situation, and character relationships" (167) and the wish to return to older values.

Andrew M. Butler

In fact, this wish is endemic to Reaganite entertainments that repeatedly encourage us to return to childhood, echoing "a widespread *desire* for regression to infantilism" (165) that evades adult responsibility. Wood argues that Reaganite entertainments, with child and childlike protagonists, repeatedly enact restorations of father figures, whether symbolic, literal, or potential, ultimately reinforcing the heteronormative values of both the nuclear family and social stability (172). The male protagonists must learn to trust the appropriate fathers of the previous generation and, in turn, must become fathers, ensuring social stability. Women can support them while remaining subordinate or be "expelled from the narrative altogether" (Wood 173). It is within this complicated milieu of father figures, infantilism, dominant strength, and neoliberal economics that the trajectory of cyberpunk films emerges, often locating straight, white, male protagonists within a metropolitan, free market dystopia and following their progression to an individualist utopia, in which patriarchy is recuperated.

15.1 The 1980s Wave of Cyberpunk Film

While Wood, like Britton, rated *Blade Runner* (Scott 1982) over other Reaganite entertainments, he condemned its treatment of women and its ending. He presumably did not know that The Ladd Company had imposed this happy ending in which the titular blade runner Rick Deckard (Harrison Ford) and the replicant Rachael (Sean Young) go off into the sunset together. Nevertheless, Wood rightly insists that *Blade Runner*'s U.S. theatrical ending "makes no sense at all" (187), and notes how Rachael is "becoming the traditional 'good object,' the passive woman who willingly submits to the dominant male" (188), as per Reaganite entertainments. Erica Sheen asserts that the film "aligns itself with the anti-feminist values [...] by arguing that such a submission is the only way for a woman to 'make it'" (153). Deckard's role is to police human/non-human boundaries by retiring replicants—i.e. androids nearly indistinguishable from humans—who are trying to flee their 'lives' of servitude or outright slavery by hiding in plain sight on Earth. At the start of the film, he has quit this job and is divorced, both signs of emasculation, but restores his symbolic virile masculinity once back in employment. According to fellow blade runner Gaff (Edward James Olmos), Deckard has "done a man's job" in retiring a number of recently escaped Nexus-6 replicants, although Rachael has helped him kill Leon (Brion James), a fleeing Zhora (Joanna Cassidy) has been shot in the back, and Roy Batty (Rutger Hauer) dies seemingly of his own volition. On a literal level, Deckard is physically inferior to the replicants, but he has symbolic paternal authority. Deckard 'wins' Rachael's love, as she turns to him having discovered that she is actually a replicant and thus Tyrell Corporation property. Deckard treats her with indifference before preventing her leaving his apartment, quickly followed by his forcing her to repeat his words expressing her apparent desire for him. In a scene tantamount to rape, Deckard's restoration requires Rachael's entrenchment in lesser-valued femininity—she is now *his* property.

Deckard makes appropriate use of his skillset. In marxist theory, workers become alienated appendages of machines (Marx 548), effectively cyborgs; in neoliberal thought, workers' skills turn them into "a machine that produces an earnings stream" (Foucault 224), whether it be through cognitive or physical labor. The replicants are most certainly workers, either manual laborers or sex workers, relieving man of "degrading forms of labour" (Sheen 157). As *Blade Runner* demonstrates, individuals' short-term benefits are crucial in Reaganite entertainments. Individuals, reclassified as 'human capital,' are a mix of innate genetic predispositions and skills acquired through 'investments' in education, training, food, and sexual desire for other people.

Blade Runner problematizes our reception of the replicants as they are not in themselves evil technology. As Deckard tells Rachael, "[r]eplicants are like any other machine—they're either a benefit or a hazard. If they're a benefit, it's not my problem." As property or tool, under the ownership of capitalists such as Dr. Eldon Tyrell (Joe Turkel), CEO and founder of the corporation which manufactures replicants, or even Deckard himself, they are safe and manageable; with independent agency, they are dangerous. "There is no question of Good and Evil here," Britton argues; instead, "the development of the productive forces is dramatized in its relation to the expropriation of wealth" (117). The film's depiction of the replicants, as allegory of escaped slaves, is therefore subtly aligning itself with neoliberalism.

Tyrell's entrepreneurial status is explicitly patriarchal, underlined in the U.S. theatrical cut of the film when his perfect creation Batty demands "I want more life, father." In an Oedipal fashion, Batty gives his surrogate father the kiss of death before digging his thumbs into Tyrell's eyes and then crushing his skull altogether. Joseph Schumpeter argues that such entrepreneurs are the controlling fathers of capitalism, "exploiting an invention or, more generally, an untried technological possibility for producing a new commodity or producing an old one in a new way, by opening up a new source of supply of materials or a new outlet for products, by reorganizing an industry and so on" (132). Existing labor markets and corporations are disrupted, potentially leading to what Schumpeter calls "creative destruction" (83) as a positive outcome for the industry or what Clayton Christensen calls "disruptive innovation": "innovations that result in worse product performance, at least in the near-term" (xv). Corporations adapt or fail. Workers must reskill. The market is transformed. Tyrell Corporation's predominant position is threatened by the (presumably state-imposed) four-year lifespan of the replicant, although Tyrell claims that this is also a technological limitation. Batty later confronts Deckard in a violent duel but, in a moment that makes him seem human, saves Deckard and opts to expire. Deckard can then 'acquire' Rachael, previously positioned as Tyrell's niece, inheriting the symbolic position of patriarch.

Blade Runner also helped cement cyberpunk's visual iconography with the seemingly never-ending cityscape, continuous rain and night, neon lighting, and teeming crowds; indeed, Scott Bukatman argues that the "aesthetic of cyberpunk was almost defined by *Blade Runner*" (*Blade* 50) and it anticipates William Gibson's *Neuromancer* (1984) with its "bleak, impacted urbanism and [...] the density of its information system" (Bukatman, *Terminal* 215). With the exception of *TRON* (Lisberger 1982) and *Videodrome* (Cronenberg 1983), subsequent cyberpunk films made before the mid-1990s capitalized on *Blade Runner*'s visual aesthetics and were more interested in exploring anxieties about cyborgs and computers than depicting cyberspace, choosing to instead recycle such paraspaces identified by Brian McHale as urban sprawls, war zones, slum-like space stations and platforms, offworld colonies, balkanized countries, enclaves, and islands (161).

It was Disney's *TRON* that offered Hollywood's first meaningful depiction of virtual reality, using roughly sixteen minutes of computer-generated imagery alongside traditional cel animation, live action, and special effects. The film's protagonist, games programmer Flynn (Jeff Bridges), had worked for the ENCOM Corporation, but had his intellectual property stolen by Ed Dillinger (David Warner), who is now ENCOM's Senior Executive Vice President. While trying to expose Dillinger's crimes, Flynn ekes out a living in a video games arcade featuring the products of his own cognitive labor. Flynn is surrounded by children and teenagers and is somewhat childlike, making money from play.

Dillinger also exploits technology for private profit, insisting that "[d]oing our business is what computers are for." He limits his employees' access to the computer system through strengthened passwords for fear that Flynn may be hacking ENCOM. The doubling of Warner as Dillinger, the Artificial Intelligence (AI) Master Control Program and its second-in-command avatar Sark, gives the characters godlike powers of omniscience. As Bukatman observes, "The panoptic powers of the corporation exist at all levels" (*Terminal* 216)—in the office, laboratory, mainframe, and even his employees' private spaces as the market and the corporation penetrate all aspects of society.

When Flynn is helped to break into the ENCOM laboratory by former colleagues Alan Bradley (Bruce Boxleitner) and Lora Baines (Cindy Morgan), the Master Control Program goes on the offensive, digitizing Flynn with a laser and uploading him into the interior space of the computer system. Here, he meets duplicates of real-world Alan and Lora in the form of avatars Tron and Yori, and the film's story segues into a mode more akin to fantasy, as they head for the Input–Output Tower and replenish energy at a version of the pool of eternal youth. The action set pieces duplicate the quarter-slot games in Flynn's arcade (and Disney's real-world *TRON* game the audience could play at their local arcade). Flynn and Tron/Alan's successes mean that they can level up: Flynn becomes the new executive of ENCOM rather than reuniting with his ex-girlfriend Lori. As a result, *TRON* "approves [Flynn's] choice 'not to grow up'" (Thomas 110) and to instead remain childlike, as a CEO finally profiting from his ability to play.

The sentient Master Control Program in *TRON* was not the only cinematic representation of AI going out of control or threatening humanity in Hollywood sf. In *WarGames* (Badham 1983), humans are the weakness in the system as they may refuse to launch nuclear missiles. Systems engineer Dr. John McKittrick (Dabney Coleman) advocates for a supercomputer WOPR (War Operation Plan Response) which could advise the president (evidently the hawkish Reagan) when to fire on the Soviet Union and would bypass moral quandaries. Unfortunately, teenage hacker David Lightman (Matthew Broderick) hacks into WOPR and plays what he thinks is a harmless game, ominously called Global Thermonuclear War. NORAD thinks that this is a real nuclear war rather than a simulation and starts the countdown to a first strike on the Soviets, which WOPR will not allow to be aborted.

David averts Armageddon by persuading WOPR to play tic-tac-toe against itself and discover that nuclear war results in a stalemate of mutually assured destruction; the solution is not to play. While Britton argues that Reaganite entertainments normally locate characters as Good or Evil in a dualism more familiar from comic book superheroes and supervillains, he suggests that *WarGames* "recognizes implicitly that the understanding of the relation between America and the Soviet Union as a relation between the powers of Good and Evil can *only survive* in the thin and rarefied atmosphere of the comic book" (my emphasis, 123). Reagan—a friend of one of the film's script writers, Lawrence Lasker—had declared the Soviet Union to be an Evil Empire in a speech on March 8th, 1983, apparently buying into such rhetoric, a rhetoric that *WarGames* largely resists and undercuts in its narrative arc.

Videodrome (Cronenberg 1983) anticipates cyberpunk through depicting cable and satellite television rather than computer networks. Max Renn (James Woods) needs content to drive viewers to his cable channel even though his technician Harlan argues that television will rot citizens from the inside. He tells Renn that "North America is getting soft, patrón, and the rest of the world is getting tough." Renn thinks that he has stumbled across Videodrome—low-quality broadcasts of sadomasochistic torture—although in fact he has been steered towards it. Videodrome's violent images haunt his waking life, but he is forced to defend such programming on a television chat show where he meets both Brian O'Blivion (Jack Creley), a critic-cum-philosopher "modelled apparently on Marshall McLuhan" (Nicholls) who chooses only to appear on a television screen, and the radio star Nicki Brand (Debbie Harry), with whom Renn begins an affair. As Renn (possibly) engages in violent encounters—his sadomasochistic relationship with Brand; hitting his personal assistant; killing Harlan—he realizes that he needs explanations from O'Blivion. But O'Blivion has died of cancer and only exists as thousands of hours of videotape footage; Videodrome was designed to cause a cancer which would induce mental evolution. By then, Renn cannot distinguish between reality and Videodrome, developing a video slot in his stomach and seeing lips bulge out from his television.

David Cronenberg's grotesque satire depicts violent masculinity and weaponized television that dramatizes a series of category breakdowns, between nation-states, humanity and technology, waking and dreaming, and so on. It is hard for us to endorse Renn's actions as it is unclear whether he has descended into madness or ascended an evolutionary ladder. Peter Nicholls argues that *Videodrome* "may have been the most significant sf film of the 1980s, and is certainly—and very early on—the most Cyberpunk." At the same time, *Videodrome* does not offer the regressive, heteronormative, redemptive ending of Reaganite entertainments, instead offering a more challenging interrogation of 1980s mass media culture.

While *Videodrome* and *WarGames* were problematizing Reaganite entertainments, during the transition from the 1980s to the 1990s, Hollywood cyberpunk increasingly turned to the figure of the cyborg in a series of action films, perhaps most notably *The Terminator* (Cameron 1984), its sequel *Terminator 2: Judgment Day* (Cameron 1991), *Robocop* (Verhoeven 1987), and its sequels *RoboCop 2* (Kershner 1990) and *RoboCop 3* (Dekker 1993). Titles such as *Android* (Lipstadt 1982), *D.A.R.Y.L* (Wincer 1985), *Cherry 2000* (De Jarnatt 1987), *Cyborg* (Pyun 1989), *Circuitry Man* (Lovy 1990), *Class of 1999* (Lester 1990), *Eve of Destruction* (Gibbins 1991), *Nemesis* (Pyun 1992), *Cyborg 2* (Schroeder 1993), *American Cyborg: Steel Warrior* (Davidson 1993), and *Cyborg 3: The Recycler* (Schroeder 1994) were further cyborg action films. Using body building regimens to bulk up and achieve stratospheric success, such actors as Arnold Schwarzenegger, Sylvester Stallone, and Jean-Claude Van Damme literally manufactured themselves, tapping into Reaganite entertainments and representing a kind of obsessive muscularity that seemed to recuperate masculinity by defining it according to bulging biceps, technological enhancements, and high-caliber excess. In this regard, Thomas Byers argues that the Schwarzenegger Terminator "embodies a technology typical of classic capitalism's industrial mode of production [...] He also comes to connote American economic power" (9).

But that economic power was in crisis, as dramatized in Verhoeven's *RoboCop*, set in Detroit, formerly the center of the American car industry. These corporations had suffered competition from and even merged with overseas manufacturers, after sales had been hit by the 1970s oil crises. Plants were closed, labor was offshored, and the city suffered a spiral of depopulation, closures, and crime. *RoboCop* capitalized on this downturn, exploiting economic precarity for the benefit of neoliberal Hollywood. In the film, the Detroit police go on strike to protest their takeover by Omni Consumer Products, a corporation which wishes to redevelop and rebrand much of Detroit as Delta City. When Officer Murphy (Paul Weller) is gravely injured in an attempted arrest, OCP choose to resurrect him as a cyborg law enforcement officer. As RoboCop, Murphy has become property, subject to OCP's programs and policies, with no personal rights. As RoboCop fights to reclaim his identity, haunted by memories of family and home, other OCP machines run amok. While these are eventually destroyed and OCP's Senior Vice President Richard 'Dick' Jones (Ronny Cox), the man behind their programming, is killed, the corporation's chairman, known as the Old Man (Daniel O'Herlihy), remains in control. It may be a "parody of laissez-faire privatization" (Alpert 8), but *RoboCop* reminds its audience that the neoliberal system remains firmly in place.

15.2 The 1990s Wave of Cyberpunk Film

The hypermasculine cyborg film cycle had largely run its course by the mid-1990s and, as Claudia Springer writes, "rampaging muscle-bound cyborgs were replaced by slim young men and women jacked into cyberspace" (204), characters closer to literary cyberpunk. For example, in *The Lawnmower Man* (Leonard 1992), Dr. Lawrence Angelo (Pierce Brosnan) has been working with drugs and virtual reality to raise the intelligence of chimpanzees. After one experiment fails, Angelo leaves the private sector to engage in personal research and makes his intellectually challenged gardener, Jobe (Jeff Fahey), his experimental subject, inadvertently giving him psychokinetic powers. Jobe develops a messiah complex, becoming "a fascistic monster" (Young 28) who envisages a new global consciousness: "This technology has peeled back a layer to reveal another universe. Virtual reality will grow, just as the telegraph grew to the telephone—as the radio to the TV—it will be everywhere." Unfortunately though, given the limitations of CGI at the time, the virtual reality depicted in *The Lawnmower Man* is chunky in form, cartoonish, and geometric rather than photorealistic. Nonetheless, in the film, it starts bleeding into the diegetic real world as humans are transformed into pixelated shapes. Jobe's digital avatar may be trapped within the telephone network, but this gives him access to a worldwide network and Jobe would return (played by *Max Headroom* actor Matt Frewer) in *Lawnmower Man 2: Beyond Cyberspace* (Mann 1996). Meanwhile, Dr. Angelo escapes, father to an adopted family, continuing his private research.

According to Paul Young, the cyberpunk films of this period—such as *Johnny Mnemonic* (Longo 1995), *The Net* (Winkler 1995), and *Hackers* (Softley 1995)—represent the world simplistically, demonizing corporate philosophy and valorizing the individual, creating a binary of Bad corporations and Good hacker kids. Young adds, "[t]here are no politics here, according to these films, only bad kids and good kids, soulless anarchists and defenders of democracy—and of 'good,' non-exploitative capitalism" (29), continuing the archetype embodied by David in *WarGames*. Non-exploitative capitalism was temporarily locatable in the non-corporate free market of ideas and communications consisting of the internet and the World Wide Web. In his 1996 "A Declaration of the Independence of Cyberspace," John Perry Barlow insisted, "We are creating a world that all may enter without privilege or prejudice accorded by race, economic power, military force, or station of birth. [...] Your legal concepts of property, expression, identity, movement, and context do not apply to us." Nevertheless, cyberpunk film repeatedly depicted a new generation of digital hackers and hustlers who saw earning streams in the web.

Johnny Mnemonic, adapting William Gibson's 1981 short story, centers on an eponymous courier-entrepreneur (Keanu Reeves) in the sprawling metropolis of Newark. Johnny's latest data package contains details of the cure for the nerve attenuation syndrome plague that is afflicting the population. The data's rightful owners, PharmaKom, want to prevent a loose association of hackers called Lo-Teks from freely broadcasting this cure to a worldwide audience waiting with, laughably enough, VCRs. Over the course of the film, however, Johnny is self-interested and materialistic: He hates the chaotic, multiethnic city and sounds like an archetypical 1980s Yuppie: "I want ROOM SERVICE! I want the club sandwich, I want the cold Mexican beer, I want a $10,000-a-night hooker! I want my shirts laundered... like they do... at the Imperial Hotel... in Tokyo." Johnny wants 'paid for' service rather than costly responsibilities.

While being chased through Newark for the data in his head, Johnny employs nerve attenuation syndrome victim Jane (Dina Meyer) to protect him. While she is a pale reflection of Gibson's original Molly Millions, Jane carries mace, throwing spikes, and a grenade, or "what every girl wants" in her handbag. Her role is all-too-familiar in Hollywood's cyberpunk sf: She restores Johnny's masculine equilibrium, along with the childhood memories he jettisoned to make room for data storage. Her reward, on the other hand, is to simply kiss Johnny, while the burning PharmaKom tower in the background provides visual fireworks to celebrate the reinscription of traditional heteronormative patriarchy.[2]

This same sidelining of women occurs with Mace (Angela Bassett), an African-American ex-cop in Kathryn Bigelow's *Strange Days* (1995) who physically defends the film's notional hero, Lenny Nero (Ralph Fiennes), a white ex-cop who trades in immersive recordings of a person's sensorium that can be played back on a SQUID (Superconducting Quantum Interference Device). A recording has been made of the police assassination of Jeriko One (Glenn Plummer), a heavily politicized black musician who speaks out against oppression, racial discrimination, and police brutality in this near-future Los Angeles. Mace is partly motivated to help Lenny get the recording to the proper authorities because of her hidden feelings for him. Narrative resolution occurs when she gives the footage to the saintly, white police commissioner, and patriarch Palmer Strickland (Josef Sommer). While Mace has more prominence than the traditional Reaganite entertainments female and is certainly more effective in her job than, say, Jane, the requisite heteronormative ending remains: Lenny discovers his own feelings for Mace and will become the adoptive father to her child.

As Anna McFarlane writes, *Strange Days*, set during New Year's Eve 1999 celebrations, "climaxes in a colorful party that bombards the viewer with flying confetti, punk fashion and loud rock music" (237). This may as well be a celebration of the film's underlying conservatism: The suspected corruption of the LAPD and Jeriko One's killers are revealed to be simply two aberrant individuals. While the SQUID footage—like the 1991 Rodney King beating and subsequent police acquittals—has the potential to spark disorder in the powder keg of a millennial Los Angeles, the audience should be reassured by due process and capitalism's retrenchment. Christopher Sharrett notes how capitalism attempts to refurbish "its democratic façade [for example within film] by acknowledging the cynicism of the population while simultaneously emphasizing an ersatz liberalism, by making use of a variety of progressive discourses" (102) about gender and ethnicity. Even as *Strange Days* features a multiethnic cast and prominent women, in the end, this is window dressing and to the film's neoliberal milieu remains unchallenged.[3]

In many ways, Cronenberg's *eXistenZ* (1999), like *Videodrome*, challenges Reaganite entertainments more than most of the films addressed earlier, even if it reverses rather than challenges the gendering of cyberpunk. Allegra Geller (Jennifer Jason Leigh) gets to be a participant in and seemingly a designer of a virtual reality system that plugs into ports in the base of a user's spine. She is resourceful, driven, and mostly in control, but after being shot in the shoulder by Noel Dichter (Kris Lemche), a member of a radical protest group called the Realists, she is assigned security guard Ted Pikul (Jude Law). Ted, actually a PR trainee, is phobic of penetration and lacks the spinal ports which would allow him to play her new game, eXistenZ. Instead, he is forced to have a black market port fitted to help Allegra test the game and he complains of the virtual realm that "[w]e're both stumbling around together in this unformed world, whose rules and objectives are largely unknown, seemingly indecipherable or even possibly nonexistent, always on the verge of being killed by forces that we don't understand." Allegra observes that this state of indecipherability is also true of the 'real' world, where individuals are forced to play by rules and objectives and reality is perceived as a cage. Allegra sees games as offering freedom even if this is circumscribed by gameplay; the novice Ted sees only the limitations. In any event, the entrepreneur Allegra may actually be gaming neoliberal practices for her own personal benefit—although this itself seems to fit in with the supposed benefits for individuals of neoliberalism. However, Allegra's and Ted's agency is undermined by the revelation that they have been in a game since the start of the film and it is not at all clear that they ever reach the freedom of a diegetic reality.

Allegra and Ted's gameplay is actually work rather than play; after all, games are expensive commodities to design and produce. Mark Fisher claims that *eXistenZ* documents both manual and cognitive labor, augmented by technology, and goes on to argue that "digital workers will increasingly find their labor as crushingly repetitive as factory workers on a production line" (73). Gameplay can also be repetitive, while cognition is geared to producing an earnings stream rather than liberating the individual from the body. As *eXistenZ* demonstrates, labor and leisure are entwined in neoliberalism.

The final consequential cyberpunk film of the twentieth century, *The Matrix* (Wachowskis 1999), also employs the *mise en abŷme* of beginning within a virtual world, this one being the creation of AIs who have enslaved humanity as an energy source. The film presents a fetishized quasi-dominatrix in the figure of Trinity (Carrie-Anne Moss) and, like so many of her predecessors, Trinity yields much agency to and predictably falls in love with the male protagonist, here potential savior figure Neo (Keanu Reeves). Neo has assumed the form of a low-status office worker, Thomas Anderson, and has to be 'woken' by Trinity and Morpheus (Laurence Fishburne), the latter providing Neo with a red pill that plummets him through the looking glass and disconnects him from the matrix. The film invites an allegory of the simulations of capitalism, even depicting a copy of Jean Baudrillard's postmodern classic *Simulacra and Simulation* and quoting explicitly from it when Morpheus welcomes Neo to the 'desert of the real.' Theresa L. Geller notes, "Morpheus's dialogue is laced with Marxist rhetoric of false consciousness and top-down politics (the AI, as the bourgeois stand-in, exploits the masses, turning them into 'batteries')" (25), inviting politicized readings about capitalism's use of the media to distract workers from exploitation and critiques of neoliberalism. But the film flatters the audience's cynicism and offers an ersatz radicalism in its casting choices even as Trinity and Morpheus make way for Neo as recuperated white savior. Of course, the film was made by a major studio, Warner Bros., and in time became surrounded with monetizing spin-offs, including two sequels, animations, comics, and video games. Geller might also argue that the film situates Trinity outside patriarchal law because she refuses "to submit to the heteropatriarchy" (14), invoking codes of lesbianism and androgyny and adopting masculinist traits, but this only serves to reinforce the gender binary and Trinity becomes the traditional good object—i.e. the "passive woman who willingly submits to the dominant male" (Wood 188)—identified as endemic to Reaganite entertainments. Ironically, perhaps one unfortunate demonstration of the limits of the film's radicalism is the adoption some years later of the idea of *taking the red pill* by a radical men's rights movement—so-called meninists, incels, and other misogynistic alt-right men's groups—that will apparently reveal how society benefits women and discriminates against men.

15.3 Conclusion: Reaganite Entertainments in the Digital Age

In his reappraisal of Robin Wood's account of Reaganite entertainments, Robert Alpert argues that their neoliberal values were still in play at millennium's end. In his discussion of *The Matrix*, for example, Alpert advances arguments comparable to those Wood made about *Blade Runner*, released nearly twenty years earlier: "Effects driven, the movie excites and reaffirms power for its own sake, and gender is largely irrelevant" (12). Diegetic distinctions between reality and fantasy are harder to maintain and "Hollywood's contemporary creation simulates and seeks to become our reality. *The Matrix* implicitly extols the prison that is the matrix" (12). Long after Reagan's retirement, the entertainment values he had embodied dominated Hollywood sf, including cinematic cyberpunk, even as his political successors George H.W. Bush and Bill Clinton hardly broke with his politics (Harvey 13, 63). Neoliberalism seemed to be the only ideology in town, made palatable in the 1990s by the ever more excessive special effects of an increasingly digital cinema. Therefore, "[i]f the American dream offers an equal opportunity to all," as Alpert argues, "it does so in furtherance of an economic system that promotes the triumph of the struggling individual at the expense of a cooperative, social structure; it appeals to the basest of human instincts" (15). In 2000, the straight, white, male still remained the default position, with triumph over the evil corporations resulting from the protagonist becoming an entrepreneur himself, producing a disruptive innovation that may shift the neoliberal world in his own direction and either offer him the consolations of family life (*Blade Runner*, *The Lawnmower Man*, *Strange Days*) or renewed autonomy (*TRON*, *The Matrix*).

Notes

1 I will confine my focus in this chapter to English-language, North American examples of cinematic cyberpunk during the 1980s and 1990s. For an exploration of cyberpunk and anime, see Kumiko Saito's contribution to this collection.

2 For in-depth analyses of the masculinist heteronormativity associated with cyberpunk, and the subsequent narrative responses, see Wendy Gay Pearson's, Patricia Melzer's, and Lisa Yaszek's contributions to this collection.

3 For a more detailed analysis of *Strange Days*, see Anna McFarlane's chapter in this volume.

Early Cyberpunk Film

Works Cited

Alpert, Robert. "Dominant Tendencies of 80s Hollywood Revisited Thirty Years Later." *CineAction!*, vol. 98, 2016, pp. 6–15.

Barlow, John Perry "A Declaration of the Independence of Cyberspace." *EFF*, 08 Feb. 1998, eff.org/cyberspace-independence.

Blade Runner. Directed by Ridley Scott, performances by Harrison Ford, Rutger Hauer, and Sean Young, Warner Bros. 1982.

Britton, Andrew. "Blissing Out: The Politics of Reaganite Entertainment." *Britton on Film: The Complete Film Criticism of Andrew Britton*, edited by Barry K. Grant. Wayne State UP, 2009, pp. 97–154.

Bukatman, Scott. *Blade Runner*. 2nd Ed. Palgrave Macmillan, 2012.

———. *Terminal Identity: The Virtual Subject in Postmodern Science Fiction*. Duke UP, 1993.

Byers, Thomas B. "Terminating the Postmodern: Masculinity and Pomophobia." *Modern Fiction Studies*, vol. 41, no. 1, 1995, pp. 5–27.

Clayton, Christensen M. *The Innovator's Dilemma: When New Technologies Cause Great Firms to Fail*. Harvard Business School P, 1997.

eXistenZ. Directed by David Cronenberg, performances by Jude Law, Jennifer Jason Leigh, and Ian Holm, Dimension Films/Alliance Atlantis Communications/Canadian Television Fund, 1999.

Foucault, Michel. *The Birth of Biopolitics: Lectures at the Collège de France 1978–1979*, edited by Michel Senellart, translated by Graham Burchell. Picador, 2008.

Harvey, David. *A Brief History of Neoliberalism*. Oxford UP, 2005.

Johnny Mnemonic. Directed by Robert Longo, performances by Keanu Reeves, Dina Meyer, Dolph Lundgren, and Ice-T, TriStar Pictures/Alliance Communications Corporation/Cinévision, 1995.

The Lawnmower Man. Directed by Brett Leonard, performances by Jeff Fahey, Pierce Brosnan, and Jenny Wright, New Line Cinema, 1992.

McFarlane, Anna. "Cyberpunk and 'Science Fiction Realism' in Kathryn Bigelow's *Strange Days* and *Zero Dark Thirty*." *Cyberpunk and Visual Culture*, edited by Graham J. Murphy and Lars Schmeink. Routledge, 2018, pp. 235–52.

McHale, Brian "Elements of a Poetics of Cyberpunk." *Critique*, vol. 33, no. 3, 1993, pp. 149–75.

The Matrix. Directed by the Wachowskis, performances by Keanu Reeves, Laurence Fishburne, and Carrie-Anne Moss. Warner Bros. 1999.

Marx, Karl. *Capital Volume One*, translated by Ben Fowkes. Pelican, 1976.

Nicholls, Peter. "Videodrome." *The Encyclopedia of Science Fiction*, edited by John Clute et al., 16 Feb. 2017, sf-encyclopedia.com/entry/videodrome.

RoboCop. Directed by Paul Verhoeven, performances by Peter Weller, Nancy Allen, and Dan O'Herlihy. Orion Pictures, 1987.

Schumpeter, Joseph A. *Capitalism, Socialism and Democracy*. Allen and Unwin, 1976.

Sheen, Erica. "'I'm not *in* the Business, I *am* the Business': Women at Work in Hollywood Science Fiction." *Where No Man Has Gone Before: Women and Science Fiction*, edited by Lucie Armitt. Routledge, 1991, pp. 139–61.

Springer, Claudia. "Psycho-cybernetics in Films of the 1990s." *Alien Zone II: The Spaces of Science Fiction Cinema*, edited by Annette Kuhn. Verso, 1999, pp. 203–18.

Strange Days. Directed by Kathryn Bigelow, performances by Ralph Fiennes, Angela Bassett, and Juliette Lewis. Lightstorm Entertainment, 1995.

Thomas, Susan. "Between the Boys and Their Toys: The Science Fiction Film." *Where No Man Has Gone Before: Women and Science Fiction*, edited by Lucie Armitt. Routledge, 1991, pp. 109–22.

TRON. Directed by Steven Lisberger, performances by Jeff Bridges, Bruce Boxleitner, and David Warner. Walt Disney, 1982.

Wood, Robin. *Hollywood from Vietnam to Reagan*. Columbia UP, 1986.

Videodrome. Directed by David Cronenberg, performances by James Woods, Debbie Harry, and Sonja Smits. Filmplan International/Guardian Trust Company/Canadian Film Development Corporations/Famous Players Limited, 1983.

Young, Paul. "The Negative Reinvention of Cinema: Late Hollywood in the Early Digital Age." *Convergence: The International Journal of Research into New Media Technologies*, vol. 5, no. 2, 1999, pp. 24–50.

16

STRANGE DAYS (CASE STUDY)

Anna McFarlane

When considering the history of cyberpunk in Hollywood, there are two major films which have been subject to extensive academic discussion and analysis: the several versions of Ridley Scott's *Blade Runner* (1982) and the Wachowskis' *The Matrix* (1999). Between these touchstone cinematic releases, however, lies Kathryn Bigelow's *Strange Days* (1995) which combines elements of *Blade Runner*'s neo-noir reimagining of the Los Angeles urban sprawl with a *Matrix*-like interest in the possibilities and implications of a virtual reality indistinguishable from the 'real thing.' *Strange Days* did not have the critical, commercial, or even cult success of these two films; for example, its visceral film making was seen by critics as slipping into "video nasty" territory (Denby) and it was a box office disaster, recouping only $8m of its $24m budget.[1] Nevertheless, despite its critical and commercial failures, *Strange Days* is an important cyberpunk film because it is unafraid of dealing directly with issues of importance to its contemporary milieu, particularly its depiction of the intersection of racial politics and new technological developments; as a result of its fleshing out the interdependence of society and technology, *Strange Days* remains relevant to our contemporary moment, particularly as increasing attention has been paid in recent scholarship to the importance of visual culture to cyberpunk's formation and its legacy (Murphy and Schmeink).

Strange Days takes place in a film-noir-inspired world. It is the story of Lenny Nero (Ralph Fiennes), an ex-cop turned wheeler-dealer operating in illegal contraband, or at least occupying the gray areas of the business world. The film's novum is the Superconducting Quantum Interference Device (SQUID), an arachnid framework of circuits and jellied panels that sits atop the user's head and records their every visual, tactile, and emotional sensation. Although the device was initially developed for the FBI, it has now fallen into the hands of the black market and, as per William Gibson's famous line that "the street finds its own uses for things" (215), the SQUID allows buyers to experience illicit or sexual experiences in recordings known as 'playbacks.' Lenny deals in these recordings but draws one line in the sand: He refuses to trade in 'snuff' or 'blackjack' recordings, in which the wearer of the SQUID is recorded dying. Lenny spends much of his time repeatedly watching old SQUID recordings of his ex-girlfriend Faith (Juliette Lewis), a singer in a local underground club and the current girlfriend of its owner, Philo (Michael Wincott). As well as running the successful club, Philo owns a record label whose most famous star is radical black rapper Jeriko One (Glenn Plummer). Philo is growing increasingly paranoid about his most important financial investment, so he begins to hire people to use the SQUID to spy on Jeriko, including Iris (Brigitte Bako), Faith's friend and hostess at the club. When Jeriko is killed by two LAPD police officers following a traffic stop, Iris inadvertently creates a SQUID recording of the incident. Iris manages to hide this recording in Lenny's car before she is also brutally murdered.

Lenny and an old friend, Mace (Angela Bassett), find the recording of Jeriko's execution and attempt to get it into the hands of the police Commissioner at the city's New Year's Eve party, resulting in the film's climax of exploding confetti and alternative rock music.

As authors and critics repeatedly make clear, science fiction is not necessarily about the future but is instead an estranging commentary on the present; or, as Ursula K. Le Guin gracefully sums it up: "Science fiction is not predictive; it is descriptive" (156). This awareness is especially true among the literary cyberpunks that preceded *Strange Days* and helped set the stage for cyberpunk's popularity; for example, Bruce Sterling opines in his Preface to the *Mirrorshades* anthology:

> The cyberpunks are perhaps the first SF generation to grow up not only within the literary tradition of science fiction but in a truly science-fictional world. For them, the techniques of classical "hard SF"—extrapolation, technological literacy—are not just literary tools but an aid to daily life. They are a means of understanding, and highly valued. (x–xi)

Veronica Hollinger has developed this understanding of contemporary society as science-fictional into the concept of 'science fiction realism.' In "Stories of the Future: From Patterns of Expectation to *Pattern Recognition*," she identifies William Gibson's *Pattern Recognition* (2003), among other contemporary texts, as using the toolbox of science fiction (and, particularly, cyberpunk) to understand the contemporary world. As Hollinger writes, "'science fiction' has come to refer in the past few decades not only to a popular narrative genre, but also to a kind of popular cultural discourse, a way of thinking about a sociopolitical present defined by radical and incessant technological transformation" (453). *Strange Days* takes on this cyberpunk legacy and acts as an 'aid to daily life' as the film emphasizes its contemporary concerns on both aesthetic and thematic levels. The film's temporal and aesthetic foci only slightly estrange the viewer from otherwise familiar contemporary L.A. cityscapes. The film emphasizes the final days of 1999 through the use of an on-screen countdown to the New Year as well as such diegetic timepieces as Lenny's alarm or the rolling news playing in the background of a number of scenes that shows militarized police mobilizing in advance of the New Year's celebrations. Bigelow's goal is to evoke L.A.'s contemporary urban decay, which requires realistically familiar sets, while also altering these sets to achieve the estrangement necessary to signify cinematic futurity. Paweł Frelik has argued that Ridley Scott's *Blade Runner* "has, for all intents and purposes, foreclosed the futuristic urban imagination […and] every single cinematic city of the future […] has been colonized and taken over by Syd Mead's and Lawrence G. Paull's urban juxtapositions" (86). Bigelow's *Strange Days* has not escaped this film's exceptional influence. As in *Blade Runner*, Bigelow uses neon signs, neon-colored light, and a heavily-populated, detailed cityscape to achieve a sense of estrangement, incorporating diegetic light sources such as the glowing lights of advertisements, store signs, and the flashing lights of police cars which illuminate the streets, buildings, and interiors with neon colors. Other diegetic light sources include fairy lights, leftover from the recent Christmas celebrations, and Chinese lanterns in the city's Chinatown. Harvesting estranging, neon light from diegetic sources "allows Bigelow to achieve a sense of realism while estranging the viewer from the environment and creating a noir sensibility as the low glow of the neon lights evokes the suggestion of darkness, as if the light obscures the sets" (McFarlane 237). This sense of the light obscuring the sets is emphasized by the inclusion of the smoke machines in Philo's club coupled with the steaming sewers, heavy rain, and the blizzard of confetti in the final scenes. All these features prevent the viewer from seeing the sets clearly while giving the light more surface to color, giving a sense of noir mystery and science-fictional futurism while showing realistic, contemporary sets.

Frelik also highlights the verticalization of L.A. as characteristic of science fiction (and, particularly, cyberpunk) future cities, but this is largely absent in *Strange Days*, where hovercars have not yet been invented and the city remains resolutely sprawling and horizontal. Mace is employed as a limo driver, so there are a number of scenes that give the viewer an impression of the slow-moving traffic that continues to clog the streets. This horizontality gives continuity between the film's L.A. and the L.A. of the present day (maintaining the film's very near-future setting), but it also allows Bigelow to highlight the racial divisions that are not just social, but also geographical in the film's world. While the city center and Philo's club are predominantly white, Mace lives in a predominantly black neighborhood suggestive of a once-middle-class area like Compton that has become subject to street violence among the hard-working families who live there and struggle to stay afloat while keeping themselves and their children out of trouble. This geographical segregation of the races throughout the film heightens the potential for explosive violence when all the city's inhabitants come together for the New Year's Eve party at the film's climax. Lars Schmeink has highlighted the power dynamics of vertical cities, where the higher positions, both physically and socially, offer "visuality as the power afforded by the 'panoramic view'" (278) and some of the action at the film's climax does take place at the top of a skyscraper overlooking the square where the New Year's Eve party takes place. However, rather than offering a secure place of power to watch over the revelers below, the penthouse suite becomes a mess of corruption, blood, bodies, and shattered furniture as Lenny realizes that the power to see is no power at all. In Bigelow's L.A., getting down on the street is the real way to find some kind of agency; watching from above can only bring paranoid imaginings and delusions that ultimately leave the powerful open to corruption and attack.

The contemporary dynamics of living in Los Angeles are also emphasized through the film's repeated refrain of "right here, right now." This refrain is first heard from a radio caller as Lenny drives through a downtown made unlivable by violent gangbangers and marauding groups of teens. The radio show invites callers to phone in with their thoughts or responses to the end of the 20th century, an event known in the film as '2K.' Although the film was released five years before the millennial real-life countdown of 'Y2K,' both events share the resultant anxiety associated with the end of the 20th century. One of the radio callers says, "history gonna start right here, right now," words echoed by Jeriko One when he makes a speech to a gathered rally, saying "[t]he LAPD is a military force turned against its own people. We living in a police state. A new day is coming, 2K is coming. The day of reckoning is upon us. History ends and begins again. Right here, right now!" (sic).

The emphasis on the present historical moment is not just political, but is made personal in Lenny and Mace's relationship. Mace is secretly in love with Lenny, her feelings explained in a flashback showing Mace's ex-partner being taken into police custody. Mace is returning from her job, dressed in a waitressing uniform, and panics that her son has been exposed to police violence during the arrest, but finds Lenny reading to the boy in his bedroom. Mace's frustration with Lenny's lifestyle, his blindness to her affections, and his obsession with Faith culminate in a speech in which she berates him for his singular focus on Faith and his preserved memories, his delusional behavior so extreme that he considers trading the playback of Jeriko One's murder in return for Faith's safety. Mace tries to shake Lenny out of his nostalgia and to force him to recognize the importance of the present moment, both personally and politically, shouting, "this is your life, right here, right now, it's real time [...] time to get real, not playback [...] These are used emotions [...] memories were meant to fade, Lenny. They're designed that way for a reason." This appeal forces Lenny to question the impulse to remain entranced by the rose-tinted nostalgia of a past that never really existed; instead, Mace wants Lenny to embrace a future which, while dangerous, offers the prospect of change. The film's contemporary moment on the cusp of (Y)2K is represented as a time to move forward and to embrace change rather than dwelling on nostalgia for a past that never truly existed.

While *Strange Days* certainly echoes the neon-saturated L.A. cityscape of *Blade Runner* and foreshadows the reality-simulation tension of *The Matrix*, Bigelow's film attempts a much more realistic representation of race relations in America than the other two. For example, *Blade Runner* includes visible Asian characters and nods to an Asian culture in L.A. in order to produce a sense of exoticism and show cultural change, ostensibly to signify futurity and estrangement; similarly, *The Matrix* includes African-American characters as martyrs and prophets (Morpheus, the Oracle), while its sequels show the racially-mixed human encampment of Zion seemingly grounding its culture in African tribal societies. While these depictions have been explored as problematic instances of exoticism and (techno-)orientalism (Yu, King and Leonard), the films make no real attempt to deal with race in any constructive fashion that could be usefully mapped onto contemporary American society. This is perhaps not surprising; after all, Sherryl Vint has argued that "more often than not in SF texts, race is ignored or subsumed under the figure of the alien" (121), and the approximation of racial debate through alien figures (and other science-fictional tropes) unhelpfully obscures the specificity of race and its history in the United States. As the motivating action in *Strange Days*, however, Jeriko One's execution at the hands of white LAPD officers is all-too-familiar and impossible to ignore. This depiction of a criminal abuse of power by police officers is not only reminiscent of the Rodney King beating captured on video in 1991, a brutal assault that sparked the L.A. riots less than a year later when all involved LAPD officers were acquitted, but also the more recent (and much-publicized) deaths of Philando Castile, Alton Sterling, Walter Scott, Sandra Bland, and Michael Brown, to name only five recent victims of institutional racism and police violence. The racial conflict in *Strange Days* is stoked by the rolling news media and the incendiary nature of the Jeriko One execution playback, meaning that ideological battles around race are still being fought on American soil, and those at the top of the power hierarchies ignore these battles at their peril. The film therefore has a deep understanding that recording technologies symbolized by the futuristic SQUID may allow violent, sexual, and even illegal content to be passed around, but they can also have explosive political possibilities for making the unseen power imbalances visible to a wider public, just as the proliferation of smartphones has had such an impact on increasing the visibility of police violence in today's society and in helping fuel social movements like #blacklivesmatter.[2] *Strange Days'* efforts to be self-aware about technology and race make its insights more robust than many, to the extent that they remain acutely relevant today.

Strange Days also deals with moral concerns around media, particularly in the film's depictions of rolling news media, home video, and recording equipment. Since the street clearly has its own uses for things in the film, the illicit and unmonitored nature of the SQUID recordings means that their content is most often explicit or illegal in some way, including pornography, crimes captured by the perpetrators and viewed for the rush of adrenaline, and the 'snuff' recordings Lenny finds morally and aesthetically distasteful. This interest in the salacious possibilities of video and home recording means that the film walks a tightrope between portraying (and potentially endorsing) such action on screen and critiquing the moral implications of such technological possibilities. The *New York Magazine*'s David Denby found that the film fell on the wrong side of the line, and its depiction of the almost-present day seems to have exacerbated this perception. He identifies the film's setting as all-but contemporary and describes its action as "just a few nasty minutes away" and as "tawdry" voyeurism. For Denby, the film's depictions of violence and sex betray an insincere moral position, a film that allows the viewer to indulge in voyeurism while moralistically suggesting that such voyeurism should be subject to critique. However, the film does offer criticism of a voyeuristic position, a critique that is not merely represented at the level of plot and theme, but is embedded in the film's aesthetic which shows an interest in the reflexivity of the camera and of cinema, by including the person recording in the shot. In Lenny's playbacks of his relationship with Faith, we see him as he holds her facing a mirror, the process of watching just as important to him as the experience of actually being with her. Likewise, in the scenes featuring the mysterious attacker as he kills Iris or, in a later scene, seems to attack Faith, we see his masked face in a mirror before he carries out his attacks. This move symbolically puts the process of making cinema into the frame and explicitly draws connections between the technologies depicted and the medium of their depiction. This process can be helpfully explored by turning to Laura Mulvey's "Visual Pleasure and Narrative Cinema" in which she identifies two different ways of taking pleasure from looking: scopophilia, and the desire to look based on Lacan's concept of the mirror stage in which the child identifies with its own image in the mirror. This moment is characterized as recognition—the child knows his image as himself and identifies with it—but also as misrecognition—the child views the image as an ego ideal, more complete and powerful than the child, incomplete as he is, could be without the image. Mulvey differentiates these two kinds of looking and the effects that they produce on the child or, in this case, on the cinemagoer:

> The first, scopophilic, arises from pleasure in seeing another person as an object of sexual stimulation through sight. The second, developed through narcissism and the constitution of the ego, comes from identification with the image seen. Thus, in film terms, one implies a separation of the erotic identity of the subject from the object on the screen (active scopophilia), the other demands identification of the ego with the object on the screen through the spectator's fascination with and recognition of his like. The first is a function of the sexual instincts, the second of ego libido [...] Both pursue aims in indifference to perceptual reality, creating the imagised, eroticised concept of the world that forms the perception of the subject and makes a mockery of empirical objectivity. (836–7)

Strange Days dramatizes the conflict between these two types of looking by including the viewer (Lenny) in the film. When Lenny relies on playback (or even when he lives the experience for the first time, framing himself and Faith in the mirror with the intention of creating the best playback possible for future viewing), he engages in scopophilia as he views Faith and their relationship as objects of sexual pleasure. The second kind of pleasure based on viewing, that of the mirror stage, is dramatized when the murderer views himself in the mirror, including himself in the shot. He forces Lenny (and, by extension, the viewer of *Strange Days*) to identify with him as the viewer's ego ideal, their representative on the screen. This re-enactment of the mirror stage forces the viewer to also identify with his actions, producing the pain and disgust that we see in Lenny when he watches the playback of Iris's murder. The comparison between this identification and the actions of the cinema as a cultural practice are emphasized after Iris's death when the killer raises his fingers to 'frame' the image of Iris's dead body, like a director framing a shot on set. Both Lenny's scopophilia and his horrified identification with the killer in the snuff film are portrayed as ways in which playback distances viewers from the "perceptual reality" and "empirical objectivity" that Mulvey identifies. In the film, Mace acts as a representative of this reality: She does not allow Lenny the scopophilia of treating her as a sexual object (even as she craves his love and companionship) and rejects the fake world of playback in favor of recognizing the world as it is, right here, right now.

Bigelow's film is far from the first to offer a commentary on cinema through the inclusion of the viewer in the film through a surrogate character (for example, Mulvey identifies *Rear Window* [Hitchcock 1954] as an example of this). However, the film's interrogation of this topic in a science-fictional future draws attention to the changing media landscape and the complicity of the viewer in constructing that landscape. At the time of the film's release, the legacy of anxieties surrounding home video technology would have been influential, whereas viewing the film from a 21st-century vantage point draws comparisons with social media. By urging the viewer to deal with reality through a science-fictional future, Bigelow's film contributes to the growing corpus of cyberpunk and post-cyberpunk media identified by Hollinger as 'science fiction realism.'[3] In *Strange Days*, the changing present that only science fiction realism can hope to capture is one of increasingly blatant institutional racism masked by the seduction of new media and nihilistic life-styles, and the film's effort to deal with these issues as they occur "just a few nasty minutes away" gives us the legacy of a cyberpunk film that remains relevant now, both as a cyberpunk artifact and as a useful commentary on race, new media, and what it means to imagine the future in an age of rapid social and technological change.

Notes

1 While the film could not exactly be called a cult classic, Will Brooker has successfully argued that it has been rediscovered and rehabilitated by a small community of fans online who revel in their knowledge of a film that seems to have been largely forgotten.

2 In fact, the case can be made that the depiction of institutional racism in *Strange Days* heralds Bigelow's later feature film *Detroit* (2017) which tells the true story of an incident that occurred during the Detroit riots in 1967 when three young black men were executed by police officers at the city's Algiers Motel.

3 For a sustained analysis of this concept, see Jaak Tomberg's chapter on 'non-sf cyberpunk' elsewhere in this collection.

Works Cited

Brooker, Will. "Rescuing *Strange Days*: Fan Reaction to a Critical and Commercial Failure." *The Cinema of Kathryn Bigelow: Hollywood Transgressor*, edited by Deborah Jermyn and Sean Redmond. Wallflower, 2003, pp. 198–219.

Denby, David. "People Are Strange." *New York Magazine*, 16 Oct. 1995, pp. 60–61.

Frelik, Paweł. "'Silhouettes of Strange Illuminated Mannequins': Cyberpunk's Incarnations of Light." *Cyberpunk and Visual Culture*, edited by Graham J. Murphy and Lars Schmeink. Routledge, 2018, pp. 80–99.

Gibson, William. "Burning Chrome." *Burning Chrome*. HarperCollins, 1996, pp. 195–220.

Hollinger, Veronica. "Stories of the Future: From Patterns of Expectation to *Pattern Recognition*." *Science Fiction Studies*, vol. 33, no. 3, 2006, pp. 452–72.

Jermyn, Deborah and Sean Redmond, *The Cinema of Kathryn Bigelow: Hollywood Transgressor*. Wallflower, 2003.

King, C. Richard and David J. Leonard. "'Is Neo White?' Reading Race, Watching the Trilogy." *Jacking into the Matrix Franchise: Cultural Reception and Interpretation*, edited by Matthew Kapell and William G. Doty. Continuum, 2004, pp. 32–47.

Le Guin, Ursula K. *The Language of the Night: Essays on Fantasy and Science Fiction*. Ultramarine, 1979.

McFarlane, Anna. "Cyberpunk and 'Science Fiction Realism' in Kathryn Bigelow's *Strange Days* and *Zero Dark Thirty*." *Cyberpunk and Visual Culture*, edited by Graham J. Murphy and Lars Schmeink. Routledge, 2018, pp. 235–52.

Mulvey, Laura. "Visual Pleasure and Narrative Cinema." *Film Theory and Criticism: Introductory Readings*, edited by Leo Braudy and Marshall Cohen. Oxford UP, 1999, pp. 833–44.

Schmeink, Lars. "Afterthoughts: Cyberpunk Engagements in Countervisuality." *Cyberpunk and Visual Culture*, edited by Graham J. Murphy and Lars Schmeink. Routledge, 2018, pp. 276–87.

Sterling, Bruce. Preface. *Mirrorshades: The Cyberpunk Anthology*, edited by Bruce Sterling. Ace, 1986, pp. ix–xi.

Strange Days. Directed by Kathryn Bigelow, performances by Ralph Fiennes, Angela Bassett, and Juliette Lewis, Lightstorm Entertainment, 1995.

Vint, Sherryl. "Coding of Race in Science Fiction: What's Wrong with the Obvious?" *Worlds of Wonder: Readings in Canadian Science Fiction and Fantasy Literature*, edited by Jean-Francois Leroux and Camille R. LaBossière. U of Ottawa P, 2004, pp. 119–30.

Yu, Timothy. "Oriental Cities, Postmodern Futures: *Naked Lunch*, *Blade Runner*, and *Neuromancer*." *MELUS*, vol. 33, no. 4, 2008, pp. 45–71.

17

DIGITAL EFFECTS IN CINEMA

Lars Schmeink[1]

In his influential study *Terminal Identity: The Virtual Subject in Postmodern Science Fiction*, Scott Bukatman argues that "the real advent of cyberpunk, with the publication of [William Gibson's] *Neuromancer* in 1984, was preceded by at least three films that, in varying ways, had a formative impact upon the cyberpunk aesthetic: *Videodrome, Blade Runner*, and *TRON*" (137). And indeed, as Graham J. Murphy and I have argued elsewhere, "the initial (and most influential) 'look' of cyberpunk would be cemented" (102) by these three films, making them as essential and central to the mode as Gibson's novel.[2] It is hardly controversial that *Blade Runner* (Scott 1982) popularized cyberpunk visuals via its "never-ending cityscape, continuous rain and night, neon lighting, and teeming crowds" (Butler 121). Meanwhile, *TRON*'s (Lisberger 1982) depiction of a world "of abstract shapes, vibrant neon colors, and tessellated square grids" (Johnson 139) has irrevocably connected this visual with cyberspace. And lastly, David Cronenberg's *Videodrome* (1983) not only connected the mode with body horror (especially prominent in Japanese cyberpunk), but was important for its grotesque representation of visceral technology "under our skin" (Sterling xiii), providing an early imaginary for human-machine synthesis.

For cyberpunk, these key elements (the urban sprawl, the nostalgic neon glow, human-machine synthesis, the abstraction of cyberspace) create a visual language, an aesthetic beyond any individual medium so recognizable that Paweł Frelik has claimed that "cyberpunk's optical surfaces [...] are] its most enduring legacy" (81). Cyberpunk's visuals are central to mapping new and digital worlds saturated with technology that have the potential to open up and redefine human experiences. Bukatman writes that "cyberpunk's job [is] to perform an act of abstraction and intensification" of these worlds, "to *perform* that 'bewildering' new (corporate, physical, cyberspatial) space, and [...] to generate simultaneously abstracted and compelling images emblematic of emerging world orders" ("Foreword" xvi, emphasis in original). Digital visual effects, that is those elements of film created by digital technology that move "away from live action and towards images that are highly designed and that can depart in many ways from camera reality" (Prince 2), push the envelope of what is possible in terms of performing new spaces, and generate ever more compelling images of our cyberpunk world.[3]

Digital visual effects disrupt the idea that film is a medium "conceived in terms of photographic facsimiles and the sobriety of a realist aesthetic" (Prince 2), highlighting an artificiality of the image that was always inherent in film from its earliest beginnings, but with digital technology becomes a prominent feature. Digital effects take this visual spectacle or artificiality—i.e., the aspect of film that 'shows off' technological developments and draws the eye of the 'spectator'—not as a distraction from narrative caused by superficiality, but instead as "an index of ways in which technological imagery is becoming increasingly visible in the world of cinema" (Wood, *Digital Encounters* 43). Visual effects, then, have become so sophisticated that they "appear as *indistinguishable* at the level of representation" (Darley 108, emphasis in original). What is created digitally looks, to the viewer, as if it were "ontologically coextensive with" (Darley 108) the actors and their surroundings. Much as the 'real' and 'simulation' are ontological spaces placed under considerable pressure by cyberpunk, so too are digital and analog 'reality' in film seamlessly integrated into one diegetic world, creating a new aesthetic of verisimilitude, or "a super-realism given over to rendering the fantastic with the surface accuracy associated with photography" (Darley 115). It is no longer "possible to separate representation from reality" (Vint, "Afterword" 231). As a result, virtuality and reality, information and materiality are cognitively processed as one, thus destabilizing all ontological categories. Digital visual effects provide cyberpunk film with the ideal tool in which to express its visual aesthetic via the blurring of categories, be they representations of past, present, and future, the spatial distinction of digital and material worlds, or the boundaries of human and machine.

17.1 History and Nostalgia

Cyberpunk's claim to revolutionary politics and its anti-establishment and anti-corporatism have long been disproven[4] and, as Frelik has argued, this extends to its visual aesthetics, which "align with [cyberpunk's] conservatism and reactionary stances" (93). The mode's visuals are instead oriented toward romantic notions of a future imagined in the past, "a retrofuturistic gesture," such as *Blade Runner*'s revisiting of 1950s noir, that Frelik connects with "visual nostalgia" and a "collapse of historicity" (93). Through digital visual effects, cyberpunk enhances this nostalgia, which Fredric Jameson describes as "the desperate attempt to appropriate a missing past" (19). Jameson goes so far as to claim that cyberpunk film makes use of "the random cannibalization of all the styles of the past, the play of random stylistic allusion" (17). Cyberpunk's retrofuturism can thus be understood to form intertextual and hypertextual recursivities, technologically made feasible by the use of digital visual effects. As Andrew Darley has pointed out, films that rely heavily on digital visual effects seem to promote a form of "self-reference (both backwards and sideways) to already existing images and image forms" (102–03). Take, for example, the Wachowskis' *The Matrix* and its franchise, which includes the sequels *The Matrix Reloaded* (2003) and *The Matrix Revolutions* (2003), a number of animated films collected as *The Animatrix* (2003), a series of comics, and several video games. This transmedial franchise intertextually plays with allusions to classic literature, like Lewis Carroll's *Alice in Wonderland* (1865) or L. Frank Baum's *The Wizard of Oz* (1900), Jean Baudrillard's concept of simulacra, the cyberpunk aesthetic of *Blade Runner*'s retro-noir themes, Chinese martial arts films' style of action sequences, and *Ghost in the Shell*'s (Oshii 1995) philosophical posthumanism.

It is Denis Villeneuve's *Blade Runner 2049* (2017), however, that best showcases the impact of the digital to perform "acts of manipulation and recombination, and efforts aimed at further 'perfecting' and simulating the already mediated" (Darley 75) in order to satisfy this visual nostalgia. The original *Blade Runner* is famously already an example of postmodern challenges to historical authenticity, with a visual aesthetic that is "hybrid, made up of citation, quotation, reference, and pastiche" (Flisfeder, *Postmodern Theory* 93). Driven by this wish for 'perfecting the already mediated,' it has been edited and re-edited into at least half a dozen different versions over the past four decades. In his study *Postmodern Theory and Blade Runner* (2017), Matthew Flisfeder shows that with each version the film's meaning is rewritten, making possible "an evacuation of the past—of history" (92), and changing the meaning of the film and turning it into an infinite "work in progress, still caught in a perpetual present" (98).

Blade Runner 2049 continues this historical evacuation by providing a rewriting of Deckard (Harrison Ford) and Rachael's (Sean Young) relationship, refusing to acknowledge any 'truth' and instead inserting ambivalence about their ontological status. In a scene between the aged Deckard and Nyander Wallace (Jared Leto), Wallace plays Deckard an audio recording of his first meeting with Rachael (which then triggers his memory of her first appearance) and then questions its historical reliability: "Did it never occur to you, that's why you were summoned in the first place? Designed to do nothing short of fall for her, right then and there. All to make that single, perfect... specimen. That is, if you were designed. Love, or mathematical precision." Questioning Deckard's status as "designed," is, of course, a reference to the most famous interpretational debate in *Blade Runner* lore, whether Deckard is a replicant or not—based on the inclusion or excision of specific scenes from the different versions of the original film (see Flisfeder 92). But this dialogue also rewrites the history proposed by the original film by again suggesting that Deckard may not be a replicant after all, once again remaking the entire franchise's meaning.

Blade Runner 2049 goes further, though, making use of digital visual effects to throw into question its representation of reality. Wallace offers Deckard the chance to be with 'his' Rachael, a clone of the original replicant, the film digitally mapping Sean Young's 1982 appearance (retrofuturistic clothing and hair styles included) onto the motion-capture of actress Loren Peta. The digital technology (intradiegetically in the form of cloning and via digital mapping in terms of its film production) opens the possibility of another nostalgic rewriting of history—due to Rachael's pregnancy, Deckard had to forfeit his chance to have a life with her, which now again seems to be within reach. But Deckard realizes the emptiness of this nostalgia and rejects the clone by leaving and commenting on its inauthenticity: "Her eyes were green." While the technique of digital mapping is not specific to cyberpunk, its use here in the context of a meta-commentary on the valence of different representations of events marks it as a deliberate 'act of manipulation' that showcases the retrofuturist aesthetic of cyberpunk.

A similar conservative retrofuturism can be found throughout the film in the historical cannibalization of cyberpunk aesthetics in its mise-en-scène. This is obvious in Wallace's headquarters, externally reinterpreting the visually unique architecture of Tyrell's pyramid from *Blade Runner*, as well as the color palette and indirect noir-inspired lighting of its interiors. It can be found in the repetition and reinterpretation of the iconic fashion of the original film, from Tyrell's elaborate robe to Rachael's business outfit to the street fashion of the masses. But the film also moves beyond a mere refashioning of its original, instead nostalgically alluding to specific moments in U.S. history, revealing continuous retrofuturistic tendencies in our current imaginations of the future. Digital companion Joi (Ana de Armas), for example, greets K (Ryan Gosling) in perfect mid-20th-century housewife mode, simulating the preparation of a home-cooked meal and offering to mend his clothes; the music playing is Frank Sinatra's "Summer Wind" from 1966, and Joi is sporting a lace blouse, petticoat, short apron, pearl necklace, and bunned up hair. The image of gender roles, telegraphed by these cinematic markers, points toward the simulacrum of simpler times, all made possible by the film's (retro)futuristic promise of digital technology, as Joi is a fully programmable digital companion that offers "everything you want to hear/everything you want to see."

The nostalgic impulse at the heart of this retrofuturism creates false longing for something that never existed; the simulacrum reveals its emptiness in the digital visual effects of the film. *Blade Runner 2049* reimagines Las Vegas, arguably the city most associated with mediation and technological spectacle, in ruins and glitching. As Lily Loofborouw writes: "*2049*'s Las Vegas is magnificent—and so fractured and anxious and elegiac about the past that even the hologram recreations of Elvis keeps blinking in and out." Elvis's holographic performance shows the artist at the zenith of his career. It is a denial of history in its erasure of the artist's subsequent drug-abuse and downfall and a synecdoche for the inauthenticity of Las Vegas, or even the U.S. as a whole. This is the cyberpunk aesthetic expressing a breakdown of historical realities, by channeling Las

Digital Effects in Cinema

Vegas's simulacrum of Elvis, digitally conserved and rearranged into perceived perfection, and yet fragmenting and glitching, not an outlook onto a radical future of digital technologies but a disintegrating image of the imagined and idealized past.

17.2 Hacking and Video Games

Digital visual effects do not just allow cyberpunk film to question the authenticity of history, but also the distinctions between worlds, as the fully immersive digital worlds imagined by cyberpunk fiction have become reality. The simulated spaces of video games are immersive and navigable through virtual reality (VR) gear and feature graphics that easily compare to those of cinematic productions.[5] The created worlds of both film and video game grow increasingly synonymous, with actors being mapped, motion-captured, and rendered in 'super-realism.' Similarly, digitally created settings and technologies link the imaginaries of science fiction in both video games and film. Video games and digital effects in cinema converge in their production processes and aesthetics, as well as in terms of their consumer experiences. Video games have long featured cinematic cut-scenes and extended storylines to motivate player-actions and create the semblance of Hollywood-style continuity, while cinema enhances its immersive potential through the use of 3D technologies, which purportedly draw viewers into the filmic action modeled after video game sequences. And both, games and film, attempt to render living in today's media- and technology-saturated world, which Sherryl Vint has described as "an everted cyberpunk world in which cyberspace permeates and shapes our experience of material reality" ("Cyberwar" 254). It is through cyberpunk's visual aesthetic in *TRON* that a conflation between cyberspace, game space, and hacking occurs—a conflation that represents how inseparable our material lives become from their digital counterparts.

As Mark R. Johnson argues, it fell to *TRON* "to provide the visual reference points that would dominate later depictions of cyberspace" (139), both in film and game depictions of the virtual spaces. Moreover, the film took its neon-outlined, abstracted geometric forms and the grid layout as a representation of internal computer processes and conflated them with gaming mechanics—taking over (i.e. hacking) systems becomes a matter of defeating the opponent in game-like battles. *The Matrix* continues this conflation of cyberspace and gaming mechanics by presenting the action of stealing data as a heist, rendering conflict with programs as martial arts fights and processing the navigation of new environments via mini-game routines such as *The Woman in Red*—all of which are testament that hacking and gaming remain visually connected. In addition, the visual aesthetic of the grid, used to provide cyberspatial markers of distance (Johnson 140), is merely invoked by the white room 'construct' in which visual orientation is impossible—precisely because it is missing those grid markers. Instead, the typical grid is transformed by adding a new element to cyberpunk's visual aesthetic: Green rows of glyphs represent the underlying code of the virtual world, the glowing marks raining down the screen becoming synonymous with systematic control, out of reach, hidden, and only made visible by the hacker. Therefore, when Neo unlocks his god-like hacking potential at the end of the movie, the indistinguishable nature of the virtual world falls away and he 'sees' it as code, the agents and his environment neatly mapping as green lines of glyphs onto the grid of the Matrix—shapes made of code determining and highlighting the constructedness of reality.

It is this image of hidden computer processes and systemic control made visible by hacking and the representation of virtual environments that is one of the most compelling arguments for a lasting impact of the cyberpunk visual aesthetic. As Anna McFarlane has pointed out, "themes and cinematic techniques associated with cyberpunk" have been used in films with "a realist context" (236). Hacking and its consequences, for example, are visualized using a cyberpunk aesthetic in films such as *Blackhat* (Mann 2015), where a criminal mastermind has been able to insert a backdoor program into essential systems controlling infrastructure in the real world. The opening sequence demonstrates the interconnections of digital and material worlds by referencing *TRON*'s image of the city at night, lights and power infrastructure becoming a grid that directs our life.[6] *Blackhat* then digitally transports the viewer onto the microscopic level of the computer system, by zooming through and into the computer screen, to the level of electrons firing through circuits. The shot tracks a rushing and focusing movement first via cables onto the main board, then into a processor unit and onto the layer of printed circuits. The imagery is reminiscent of cyberpunk's navigation of game space: in its movement of flying over digital landscapes; in its color scheme, which flickers neon blue as energy pulses through the system; and in its geometric design, each bit of information a neat square pulsing in a grid. When the hack is executed, pulses of white light flood through the levels of the computer system, raining down just like the glyphs that determine the cyberspatial reality in *The Matrix*. A zoom out reveals the impact of the code, a glitch on the screen as the read-out becomes unreliable, no longer showing that the turbines of a nuclear reactor cooling system are malfunctioning. By rendering the cyberpunk aesthetic through digital visual effects, *Blackhat* reveals the interconnection of digital and analog worlds, highlighting the everted nature of cyberspace and the interdependence of processes on the virtual and material levels. The image of a hidden world of code that rules our material reality, controlled by simple, game-like instructions, is frightening and in the film used to visualize our fear of unknown power systems that control our world.

This frightful reality is even more relevant when one explores "the ways that cyberpunk, digital gaming, and military training converge" (Vint, "Cyberwar" 257) to mediate our experience of war. Vint argues that military programs, especially the use of drones, are rendered through digital visual effects in terms of gaming and virtual worlds, thus linking them to cyberpunk aesthetics. In films such as *Good Kill* (Niccol 2014) or *Eye in the Sky* (Hood 2015), the images used to portray drone navigation and strike situations reveal how material and virtual worlds connect to form a hidden, and equally brutal, system of power relations. The drone operators in both films enact what N. Katherine Hayles describes as "*embodied virtuality*" which constitutes a material "presence […] always already penetrated by the virtuality of information" (153, emphasis in original). When steering a drone over their respective war theatres, the pilots are reliant on a virtual stream of information that the satellites in orbit provide. They are aided by information officers that confirm identification, as well as navigators that track the drone's flight relative to its geographical locations and the satellite's imagery. In the process of embodied virtuality at work here, all three become dehumanized as parts of the complex military-industrial system that operates the drone and processes the orders that come down the chain of command. But moreover, not just the operators become dehumanized, as McFarlane has argued for *Zero Dark Thirty* (Bigelow 2012): The distance created by the surveillance technology shifts the "nature of the field situation," which is watched as mediated images, into the realm of "virtual reality" (249). The drone gaze, according to Jennifer Rhee, makes illegible human difference, reducing its targets to abstract objects: The "cybernetic impulse to render all things not just knowable, but knowable in specifically mathematical, formulaic ways, echoes in drone labor, which requires a similar abstraction and reduction of complexity and difference" (142). The embodied virtuality of the drone operators simultaneously abstracts and enhances the view, on the one hand using the technology's "scale at which individuals are largely indistinguishable from one another and look more like insects" (Rhee 161), while at the same time enhancing the image with information about the likelihood of casualties and damage estimates. The overlay of information that informs drone decision-making as depicted in *Good Kill* or *Eye in the Sky*, the added layer of data provided by hidden systems of power, is reminiscent of cyberpunk aesthetics in video games, the cyborgized head-up display (HUD) allowing players to better navigate the game space and eliminate their targets, whose rules are determined by the code of its programming.

17.3 Cyborgs and Technology

Thematically, the image of drone operators as technologically enhanced cyborgs in embodied virtuality goes hand in hand with another aspect of the cyberpunk aesthetic, even when the films mentioned do not promote the idea visually. As argued earlier, David Cronenberg's *Videodrome* is one of the most important cyberpunk films, especially due to its commentary on society's oversaturation with media and the impossibility of accessing a distinguishable reality. In addition, though, the film provides an essential trajectory to the cyberpunk aesthetic in its embrace of body horror tropes and its depiction of human becoming-machine. As Bukatman claims for postmodern sf, especially cyberpunk: "In the era of terminal identity, the body has become a machine, a machine that no longer exists in dichotomous opposition to the 'natural' and unmediated existence of the subject" (244). He continues that "a new, hard-wired subjectivity" is formed by the "fusion of being and electronic technology" (244), but one which is threatened by a "crisis of meaning and definition" (247). In order to function in a technologically saturated cyberpunk world, the body thus has to "become a cyborg" and be "resituated in technological space and refigured in technological terms" (247).

Cronenberg literalizes this image and refigures the body of his protagonist Max Renn (James Woods) by opening him up to the "conditions of universal technological penetration and colonization" (Beard 124). After having been subjected to the mind and body altering influence of Videodrome, Max awakens with a vaginal slit in his stomach, into which over the course of the film several objects are inserted that then begin to exert their technological influence over him. On the one hand, Max fuses with video technology, being inserted with writhing, living VHS tapes which program him to perform certain actions, such as killing his colleagues. On the other hand, he also fuses with his gun, inserted by accident, which reappears later and sprouts mechanical connections directly into his body. He becomes a cyborg, the fusion with the technologies driving him "further and further from stable identity and meaning [...and] experiencing the inexorable crumbling and collapse of his personality" (Beard 124).

Visually, these fusions are based in horror, showing grotesque transformations and meldings of the mechanical with the biology of Max's body—an imagery picked up on by Japanese cyberpunk, in films such as *Akira* (Ōtomo 1988) or *Tetsuo: The Iron Man* (Tsukamoto 1989), both of which feature cancerous growths of cells infused with wires and mechanical parts (see Player).[7] While the image of the human-machine hybrid became part of the cyberpunk aesthetic, it was decoupled from its more horrific images of cancerous growth and bodily abjection, instead focusing on the power of technological weaponry and its integration with the human, resulting in a wave of cyborg warriors that combine flesh and metal—for example, *The Terminator* (Cameron 1984), *RoboCop* (Verhoeven 1987), and *Cyborg* (Pyun 1989). These films visually center on the fascination and/or rejection of the cyborg imaginary as "the self-sufficient, self-generated Tool in all of its infinite but self-identical variations" (xv), which Donna J. Haraway connects to both military and entertainment worlds. These cyborg bodies represent the male fantasy of bodily control and power, allowing for their 'breaking down' only in a tightly controlled and self-determined manner, as seen in scenes of the T-800 (Arnold Schwarzenegger) in the Terminator series slowly peeling back skin from his arm or face, revealing the hardened metal shell underneath, to repair itself—its functionality and self-control never questioned.

In the last few years, cyberpunk films have pushed the boundary of their aesthetic in how they present cyborg bodies as entities that cross boundaries between categories such as living/dead, material/virtual, and organic/machinic. *Ghost in the Shell* (Sanders 2017), for example, opens with Major Mira Killian's (Scarlett Johansson) human brain being encased in and connected to a machine chassis, the tendrils of its artificial nerves self-guiding toward their counterparts. The machine body then passes through several fluids to 'grow' a skin, whose outermost shell it 'sheds'—the whole process rather more a natural birth than a machinic assembly. The camera lingers for a moment on the fissures of parts not having fully and seamlessly assembled, contrastively highlighting the artificial nature of the cyborg's construction, before the finished cyborg rises into the light. The mixture of digital cinematic cues, hinting toward categories of both natural and artificial creation, is purposefully used to undermine categorical expectations and instead reveals the transgressive nature of the cyborg in Haraway's feminist concept of the figure.[8]

Alita: Battle Angel (Rodriguez 2019) opens with a similar 'construction scene': After Dr. Ido (Christoph Waltz) has found Alita's (Rosa Salazar) head and spine on the scrapyard, he (re-) assembles her in his workshop and fits her with a new body, the camera focusing on the detail of reattached wires, stitched skin, and metallic plates clicking into form. The artificiality of the body's construction in the scene is counteracted by the super-realist verisimilitude of the child-like human face attached to the cyborg head and by Ido and his assistant (Idara Victor) treating the cyborg as a child, with Ido even asking "What are you dreaming, little angel?" when he notices rapid-eye movement. Again, the digital effects allow for a crossing of boundaries, suggesting that Alita is both a human child and a machine, both 'healed' and constructed in this scene. The film also flaunts its digital visual effects, highlighting its artifice and spectacle already in the protagonist, whose appearance has been adapted from the original *Gunnm* (1990–95) manga by Yukito Kishiro. Alita's exaggerated eyes mark her as a digital creation, but the super-realism of her features, digitally mapped from actress Rosa Salazar, nevertheless produces a realistic mimetic accuracy. The equilibrium between denying and flaunting Alita's artificiality is upheld throughout the movie, in terms of story and thematics, as well as in its visual presentation. This becomes obvious in the film's pivotal fight scene with cyborg Grewishka (Jackie Earle Haley), in which Alita's child body is ripped apart, slashed into pieces by Grewishka's grind cutters, fingers that extend into bladed whips. The fight scene is spectacular, making use of digitally rendered 3D and slow-motion shots of the blades whipping toward Alita and the viewer. When Alita launches herself at Grewishka, his blades form a spiral and slash through Alita's body, fragmenting it—the film renders this quite explicitly, and Alita remains with only torso and one arm, showing her constructed nature.

Overall, *Alita: Battle Angel* highlights the fragmented and constructed bodies of cyborgs, making a spectacle of bodies torn apart and ripped open, shredded, and slashed—a visual aesthetic that returns to its body horror roots, mitigated only by the fact that these bodies are clearly machines. The film does not stop with cyborg bodies either, showing Ido's wife Dr. Chiren (Jennifer Connelly) fragmented into internal organs (lungs, brain, eyes still blinking) ready to become biomedical experimentation or separating Hugo's (Keean Johnson) head in order to attach it to a cyborg body. *Alita: Battle Angel*, *Ghost in the Shell*, and numerous other films show that the body, in classic cyberpunk tradition, is no more than meat or metal that can be sacrificed or discarded if need be, and digital visual effects allow for the films to make this explicit, highlighting the construction of these bodies and justifying the viewer's fascination with the monstrous cyborg.

The visual aesthetics in cyberpunk cinema, particularly those films reliant on digital visual effects, include a variety of films (and other media products), not all of them science-fictional, further problematizing the idea of cyberpunk-as-genre.[9] In this regard, the one film of recent years that best embodies the question of "is this cyberpunk?" is Steven Spielberg's adaptation of *Ready Player One* (2018). In terms of its story and tone, the film is geared toward younger audiences: a coming-of-age narrative coupled with a typical quest fantasy. The film ticks off some thematic cyberpunk markers, such as a greedy corporation that dominates the market and a virtual world into which to escape, but these are offset by themes taken from fantasy, such as the quest for three keys, wizards and magic, overcoming obstacles, and apotheosis. On the level of its visual aesthetics, however, *Ready Player One* is more convincingly cyberpunk: Its digital visual effects retrofuturistically recreate cultural artifacts from yesteryear—the allusions and cannibalizations of past visual styles can be vertigo-inducing, and one of its key scenes literally places the protagonists in Stanley Kubrick's *The Shining* (1980). The future portrayed in *Ready Player One* is a wistful vision of the past, digitally reassembling the 1980s in a simulacrum filtered through the lens of unapologetic nostalgia. In addition, even though it is mostly tinged with themes from fantasy, the virtual world of the Oasis is at times indistinguishable from the real world. Though most spaces are games-oriented and recreated to look artificial, several scenes portray locations in which its virtuality is undetectable, such as James Halliday's (Mark Rylance) childhood bedroom. What is real and what is virtual becomes a central argument in the film and is used as part of the quest to win the prize, digital control of the Oasis that will inexplicably effect material change in what is shown to be a largely destitute 'real' world. And lastly, all of the characters show a strong affiliation with the image of the cyborg, not only in that they are digitally mapped and created by computers, but also in that within the Oasis, each character has another layer of digital information at their disposal in which applications, weapons, appearances, or vehicles can be stored. Much like military drone operators can call up their protocols on their HUDs, so too can Oasis users access their added resources via HUD and directly connect each character to their digital inventory, making them part of an embedded virtuality. In spite of the obvious fantasy chassis that governs the diegetic level, *Ready Player One*'s visual aesthetics ensures the film uses cyberpunk as a marker to generate meaning and to tie it to discourses on virtuality.

17.4 Conclusion

In sum, digital effects, particularly in cyberpunk film, have pushed the boundaries of the representational in a way that analog film never could, allowing for its "ocularity" (Frelik 81) to move to the fore, defining its connection to the mode. This has allowed films to become explicitly more self-referential, intertextually referencing and cannibalizing other films and media so as to promote cyberpunk's own retrofuturistic nostalgia. It has allowed an exploration of cyberspace as game space, drawing attention to the everted nature of cyberspace and its connection to our real, material world. And, by extension, the cyberpunk visual aesthetic has spread into non-sf film, underlining how realist and science-fictional representations converge. And lastly, digital visual effects' ability to render the human in fantastic form has allowed cyberpunk's central thematic—i.e. the convergence of biological and machinic in the figure of the cyborg—to move to the fore with films now exploring the (de-)construction of bodies. Digital visual effects showcase the visual aesthetic that binds cyberpunk into a productive mode, moving beyond the "inherent arbitrariness and instability of thematic markers" and finally allowing us to talk about cyberpunk in "the *only* productive approach" (Frelik 94).

Notes

1 This essay has seen several iterations and was only possible with the guidance of my co-editors Graham J. Murphy and Anna McFarlane, and the honest and insightful review provided by Sherryl Vint. For this, I am grateful.

2 For more details on early cyberpunk film and these initial influences, see Andrew M. Butler's contribution to this collection.

3 As Stephen Prince points out, "digital imaging tools permeated all phases of filmmaking" (4); thus, a category such as "digital film" is invariably too vague to be used, as it could be applied to almost any film made today. Instead, I focus on "digital visual effects" as opposed to photographic realism, noticing the caveat that "clear boundaries between the domains often do not exist" (Prince 4). Explicitly blurring these boundaries and foregrounding the indistinguishability of digital and analog is precisely the purpose of digital visual effects in cyberpunk film.

4 See Frelik; for more details, see Butler's analysis of early cyberpunk film and its connection to Reaganite neoliberalism or Hugh O'Connell's analysis of cyberpunk and marxism in this collection.

5 For more details on the concept of simulation and its connection to cyberspace and gaming, see Rebecca Haar and Anna McFarlane's entry in this collection. For an analysis of cyberpunk video games, see Paweł Frelik's chapter in this collection.

6 *TRON* conflates computer electronics representing the data grid with the city's grid of streets and buildings at night, thus blurring the boundary of material and virtual worlds. The visual overlay is repeated twice in the film, once as a bookend final scene, and again when the CEO of ENCOM, Ed Dillinger (David Warner), flies over the city grid with a neon-outlined helicopter, the red outlines of its blade and chassis aligning him with the Master Control Program, which in the filmic cyberspace is represented by its programmer—also played by Warner—further conflating material and virtual worlds and their organizational structures.

7 For more details on Japanese cyberpunk, see the various chapters in this collection by Brian Ruh, Kumiko Saito, Shige (CJ) Suzuki, and Martin de la Iglesia and Lars Schmeink.

8 For more details on cyborg feminism and the cyborg's connection to posthumanism, see Patricia Melzer's and Julia Grillmayr's chapters in this collection, respectively.

9 For an explanation of the friction between thinking of cyberpunk as a genre vs. thinking of it as a mode, please see Anna McFarlane, Graham J. Murphy, and Lars Schmeink's "Cyberpunk as Cultural Formation" that opens this collection.

Works Cited

Alita: Battle Angel. Directed by Robert Rodriguez, performances by Rosa Salazar and Christoph Waltz, 20th Century Fox, 2019.

Beard, William. *The Artist as Monster: The Cinema of David Cronenberg.* Toronto UP, 2006.

Black Hat. Directed by Michael Mann, performances by Chris Hemsworth, Viola Davis, and Wei Tang, Universal, 2015.

Blade Runner 2049. Directed by Denis Villeneuve, performances by Ryan Gosling, Harrison Ford, Ana de Armas, and Robin Wright, Alcon Entertainment/Columbia Pictures/Sony, 2018.

Bukatman, Scott. *Terminal Identity: The Virtual Subject in Postmodern Science Fiction.* Duke UP, 1993.

———. "Foreword: Cyberpunk and its Visual Vicissitudes." *Cyberpunk and Visual Culture,* edited by Graham J. Murphy and Lars Schmeink. Routledge, 2018, pp. xv–xix.

Butler, Andrew M. "Early Cyberpunk Film." *The Routledge Companion to Cyberpunk Culture,* edited by Anna McFarlane, Graham J. Murphy, and Lars Schmeink. Routledge, 2020, pp. 119–27.

Darley, Andrew. *Visual Digital Culture: Surface Play and Spectacle in New Media Genres.* Routledge, 2000.

Flisfeder, Matthew. *Postmodern Theory and Blade Runner.* Bloomsbury Academic, 2017.

Frelik, Paweł. "'Silhouettes Of Strange Illuminated Mannequins': Cyberpunk's Incarnations of Light." *Cyberpunk and Visual Culture,* edited by Graham J. Murphy and Lars Schmeink. Routledge, 2018, pp. 80–99.

Ghost in the Shell. Directed by Rupert Sanders, performances by Scarlett Johansson and Pilou Asbaek, Paramount Pictures/DreamWorks/Alliance Entertainment, 2017.

Hayles, N. Katherine. "How Cyberspace Signifies: Taking Immortality Literally." *Bridges to Science Fiction and Fantasy: Outstanding Essays from the J. Lloyd Eaton Conferences,* edited by Gregory Benford et al. McFarland, 2018, pp. 151–60.

Harraway, Donna J. "Cyborgs and Symbionts: Living Together in the New World Order." *The Cyborg Handbook,* edited by Chris Hables Gray. Routledge, 1995, pp. xi–xx.

Jameson, Frederic. *Postmodernism, or, The Cultural Logic of Late Capitalism.* Duke UP, 1991.

Johnson, Mark R. "The History of Cyberspace Aesthetics in Video Games." *Cyberpunk and Visual Culture,* edited by Graham J. Murphy and Lars Schmeink. Routledge, 2018, pp. 139–54.

Loofbourow, Lily. "*Blade Runner 2049* is so nostalgic it hurts." *The Week,* 06 Oct. 2017, theweek.com/articles/729283/blade-runner-2049-nostalgic-hurts.

McFarlane, Anna. "Cyberpunk and 'Science Fiction Realism' in Kathryn Bigelow's *Strange Days* and *Zero Dark Thirty.*" *Cyberpunk and Visual Culture,* edited by Graham J. Murphy and Lars Schmeink. Routledge, 2018, pp. 235–52.

Murphy, Graham J. and Lars Schmeink, eds. *Cyberpunk and Visual Culture.* Routledge, 2018.

Player, Mark. "Post-Human Nightmares—The World of Japanese Cyberpunk Cinema." *Midnight Eye,* 13 May 2011, midnighteye.com/features/post-human-nightmares-the-world-of-japanese-cyberpunk-cinema/.

Prince, Stephen. *Digital Visual Effects in Cinema: The Seduction of Reality.* Rutgers UP, 2012.

Rhee, Jennifer. *The Robotic Imaginary: The Human & The Price of Dehumanized Labor.* U of Minnesota P, 2018.

Sterling, Bruce. Preface. *Mirrorshades: The Cyberpunk Anthology,* edited by Bruce Sterling. Ace, 1986, pp. ix-xvi.

The Matrix. Directed by the Wachowskis, performance by Keanu Reeves, Laurence Fishburne, and Carrie-Anne Moss, Warner Brothers, 1999.

Videodrome. Directed by David Cronenberg, performances by James Woods, Debbie Harry, and Sonja Smits, Filmplan International/Guardian Trust Company/Canadian Film Development Corporations/Famous Players Limited, 1983.

Vint, Sherryl. "Afterword: The World Gibson Made." *Beyond Cyberpunk: New Critical Perspectives*, edited by Graham J. Murphy and Sherryl Vint. Routledge, 2010, pp. 228–33.

———. "Cyberwar: The Convergence of Virtual and Material Battlefields in Cyberpunk Cinema." *Cyberpunk and Visual Culture*, edited by Graham J. Murphy and Lars Schmeink. Routledge, 2018, pp. 253–75.

Wood, Aylish. *Digital Encounters*. Routledge, 2007.

———. "Vectorial Dynamics: Transtextuality and Complexity in the Matrix." *The Matrix Trilogy: Cyberpunk Reloaded*, edited by Stacy Gillis. Wallflower, 2005, pp. 11–22.

18

BLADE RUNNER 2049 (CASE STUDY)

Matthew Flisfeder

Ridley Scott's *Blade Runner* (1982) is perhaps *the* film, or at least one of the films, that firmly established and popularized cinematic cyberpunk; for example, Scott Bukatman remarks that "[c]yberpunk provided *the* image of the future in the 1980s" (58) and the "aesthetic of cyberpunk was almost defined by *Blade Runner*" (50). Among *Blade Runner*'s merits is its ability to speak to the early emergence of neoliberal capitalism in the late 1970s and early 1980s: The original *Blade Runner* registered our latent fears about the end of the welfare state, the deregulated plane of unfettered multinational capital, and the dystopia that was set to result in the soon-to-be *approaching* future. Released more than three decades after *Blade Runner*, Denis Villeneuve's much-anticipated sequel *Blade Runner 2049* (2017) responds to our current awareness of dystopia already realized—this is now the world in which we *live*.

The new film is contextualized by our own experiences of the post-financial crisis period of neoliberal capitalism and marked by discourses of the biopolitical posthuman subject. Added to this, too, is the constantly looming threat of ecological catastrophe brought on by climate change and the ever-present sensation that there is no way out, no means of escape. Only twelve more years, we are told. Not much left to go on! The film addresses our awareness of the crises we face, including the post-2008 electronically automated-austericized haze-life that we experience only as the passing of pay-check to pay-check (the digital transfer of informational merits or credits from one account to another, proving still that we are, as Deleuze called us, informational "dividuals").

If the problem for Rick Deckard (Harrison Ford) in *Blade Runner* was that he did not know he was a replicant, then like K (Ryan Gosling), the replicant protagonist in *Blade Runner 2049*, we know that our condition is one of control and servitude, but we continue to submit. K's dilemma is that he knows full well about his status as replicant: He knows that his memories are implants designed to control his emotional responses, but nevertheless he continues to be compliant. Similarly, we are aware of the social, political, economic, and ecological problems that we face in our contemporary age and can avow this at a conscious level. Ideology, today, is no longer a matter of false consciousness. Instead, we know but nevertheless continue to act as if we didn't because there is apparently no alternative. It's in this way that *Blade Runner 2049* (*BR 2049*) maps our own ideological and historical setting.

Drawing on Fredric Jameson's claim in *The Seeds of Time* that "it seems to be easier for us today to imagine the thoroughgoing deterioration of the earth and of nature than the breakdown of late capitalism" (xii), Mark Fisher defines "capitalist realism" as the cynical resignation and "deflationary perspective of the depressive" (*Capitalist Realism* 5) who becomes fully aware of the crises—economic, political, ecological, social, and cultural—but cannot imagine life otherwise. We have come, Fisher argues, to "the widespread sense that not only is capitalism the only viable political and economic system, but also that it is now impossible even to *imagine* a coherent alternative to it" (2). There is no way out of the current system. In this regard, capitalist realism as a concept, and its context in the aftermath of the 2007/08 financial and economic crisis—i.e. a post-crisis capitalism—help us better understand *Blade Runner 2049*.

BR 2049 is set thirty years after *Blade Runner.* As the opening title sequence tells us, the Tyrell Corporation has gone bankrupt and has been bought out by billionaire Niander Wallace (Jared Leto) who made his fortune developing a new harvesting process for soy that helped to solve a famine that occurred in the timespan between the two films. After taking over Tyrell Corporation, Wallace developed a new line of NEXUS replicants, more compliant than their predecessor models. The new line of replicants is distinguished from the older models by the fact that they are fully aware that their memories are implanted. In the original film, the NEXUS-6 models are given artificial memories to help them deal with and learn how to better integrate emotional responses into their behavior. This is complicated, however, when it comes to Rachael (Sean Young), whose disruptive status as a replicant is a key narrative thread (particularly as she did not initially know that she was a replicant) and her memory-history—objectified in a series of photographs she has of what she believed was her childhood but is actually the childhood of Tyrell's niece—thematizes the postmodern troubling of objective history, a troubling that takes on deeper meaning when it comes to the questions surrounding Deckard's unresolved ontological status. In *BR 2049*, however, K, the central hero, is aware that his memories are fake. This awareness links the film to Fisher's conceptions of "ironic distance" toward ideological beliefs in capitalist realism that "immunize us" (5) against false consciousness: K knows that he is a replicant and that his existence is one of servitude to humans. But this fact is, nevertheless, disavowed as a condition of his compliance. In fact, the film's MacGuffin comes when K finds 'evidence' that he may not be a constructed replicant, but perhaps a child born of an unexpected mother: Rachael.

Like the original film, *BR 2049* takes up similar postmodern and cyberpunk themes, such as the troubling of ontological reality, history, and subjectivity. It also examines the technologized relationship between capital, the state, and an exploitation based on embodied difference (human/non-human). But more so than the original, *BR 2049* develops the spatial and geocritical representation of the capitalist network that is only hinted at in *Blade Runner* by the pyramidal Tyrell headquarters that looms over an urban sprawl stretching into the visual horizon. *BR 2049*'s cognitive mapping extends well beyond the urban center, and although we do not go as far as seeing the off-world colonies, we do get a sense of the global network of centralized ownership and the peripheral (outsourced) production of multinational/globalized capital. For example, *BR 2049* portrays the networks of exploitation that go beyond the exploitation of replicant-machinic labor, such as when K visits an orphanage and child labor camp where technical components are being constructed and assembled. In addition, the ecological degradation outside fortress Los Angeles is given more attention, too, unlike in the original film where, at the end of the U.S. theatrical release, Deckard and Rachael escape north into a utopian wilderness, an ending that was famously tacked onto the theatrical release without Scott's permission and summarily stripped in later re-releases of the film (for a detailed account of the version history, see my *Postmodern Theory*). In *BR 2049*, K travels to a devastated Las Vegas, when he goes searching for Deckard, and we see that the city is awash in red fog and is unlivable due to poor air quality; similarly, the orphanage stands in an otherwise ruined San Diego that is little more than wasteland and garbage disposal site for Los Angeles. There is no restorative *nature* that exists outside urban dilapidation and pollution, perhaps a nod to the looming scarcity of nature for which we must begin to prepare.

The visual representation in the film marking the difference between the glitzy neon-drenched urban centrality of fortress L.A. and the foggy, cloudy periphery of ecological decay marks an added distinction to *BR 2049*. Much of the popularity and later resonance of the original film comes from its visual depiction of the electronic urban landscape. *Blade Runner* aestheticizes quite clearly the postmodern interest in space over time, as much of the film is spent traversing bright nighttime skylines populated by electronic advertisements. One of the most iconic images is that of the large video display screen that switches between a sushi advertisement and one for Coca-Cola. Not only do these images help to portray postmodern depictions of urbanism and electronic mediation, but they also represent the field of total (and invasive) commodification—that is, the colonization of the commodity that is so apparent in the postmodern cinema and cyberculture that followed. *BR 2049* goes even further. It builds heavily on the postmodern aesthetic of digital, electronic, and commodified space, while the enhanced digital cinematography takes us deeper inside the urban fabric to give us a much more high-definition visualization of the city.

BR 2049 still provides panoramic shots of the city, but when we move down to street-level, we are more capable of discerning the texture of the commodified culture of capitalist realism and its depressively hedonic characteristics, which, as Fisher (21–22) explains, refers to the fact that the more we are enjoined to enjoy in late capitalism, the more depressed we get from our inability to actually receive satisfaction. This, too, is portrayed through the pathetic fallacies in the film and the stark contrast between the electronic and commodified 'happy' city—where all of the holographic advertisements seem much happier and brighter than the people traversing the streets—and the dark, snowy, and cold atmosphere that now permeates this environment and is indicative of our actual sentiments toward this space. Commodities and advertisements enjoin us to enjoy, but instead we are left with the kind of "reflexive impotence"—the self-fulfilling prophecy of defeat—that Fisher ascribes to the cynicism of capitalist realism (21).

The contrast between the vibrancy of the city and peripheral decay is apparent in *BR 2049*'s opening shot, which mirrors the original. In both films, we first see an extreme close-up on an apparently human eye, although we are unsure if we are seeing a human eye or that of a replicant. The visual then cuts to a panoramic shot of the futuristic landscape. In the original film, a hover car flies out from behind the camera and toward the screen, tying our gaze into the highly technologized fabric of future Los Angeles. In *BR 2049*, similarly, K's hover car flies in from behind the camera to reveal the landscape; only here, it is not the futuristic L.A. but the vast fields of protein farms, likely outsourced by Wallace. This is where K finds Sapper Morton (David Bautista), an old NEXUS model that he has been sent out to retire. This stark contrast in the visual representation of center and periphery—i.e. futuristic landscape in *Blade Runner*; protein farms and outsourced labor in *BR 2049*—ties in well with the humanist and posthumanist themes of capitalist realism present in the film.

Blade Runner 2049 is bracketed by the twin dilemmas of contemporary capitalism: that of looming ecological catastrophe, and the other of enhanced digital automation. These two problems, according to Peter Frase, define the various dilemmas of our current age (1). The threat of climate change, he writes, is one of too little, of the depletion of the environment and resources (2), which the film addresses in the fortress-like imaginary of the caged-in cybernetic city, where wealth appears centralized, however still unevenly distributed. The threat of automation, on the other hand, is one of too much: too much production (overproduction), which is still centralized and concentrated into the hands of the very (corporate) few. It falls to the role of the state, then, to mitigate these contradictory forces, which is why in the film an antagonism brews between the interests of Wallace and those of Lieutenant Joshi (Robin Wright). Wallace becomes obsessed by the possibility that a replicant could birth a child. As a capitalist, he sees this as a way to significantly reduce his costs of production: Replicants can reproduce themselves, laboring bodies that can go into labor. For Joshi, though, this possibility creates a threat of potentially building and

Blade Runner 2049 (*Case Study*)

exacerbating a political rift between the replicants and the humans, leading to war. She realizes, as did Marx and Engels, that capital itself produces that which can lead toward its destruction: the proletarian labor force. Joshi's concern is proven accurate later in the film when K is contacted by the underground replicant resistance and tasked with killing Deckard to stop him from leading the authorities to Rachael's true child. The replicants, therefore, represent both the machines *and* the conscious operators of the machinery (the workers), making them stand in for both the objective means of production *and* the exploited proletariat.[1] Finally, the question over automation is the one that plays into the current interest in Left accelerationism which champions the idea of a fully automated luxury communism, where the drudgery of work is replaced by a fully automated and roboticized society.[2]

The original *Blade Runner* thematizes the postmodern breakdown of the signifying chain and puts to question reality and ontology at a *subjective* level. Contemporary theory, however, is preoccupied with the question of our *object* status, and this is a narrative thread that underwrites *Blade Runner 2049*. For example, one of the ethical imperatives of new materialism is to turn away from too-easy dualisms and displace the centrality of the human subject. This, we might assume, is understandable given our present anxieties about climate change and the Anthropocenic deterioration of our planet. The human footprint, so it has been observed, has had a deleterious effect upon all life on Earth. The basic premise, then, of the various new materialisms (such as speculative realism, object-oriented ontology, vitalist materialism, actor-network theory, and so forth) is the need to dissolve the hierarchical relationship between humans and the rest of the planet—that is, between the human and the *non*-human. Object-oriented ontology theorist Levi Bryant, for instance, draws on Gilles Deleuze and Félix Guattari to propose that instead of distinguishing the human and the machinic, we see all objects (both non-human *and* human) as various different *types* of machines. Humans, after all, are machinic in the way that our biology is composed. All exist, he explains, as a network—a mapping—of the various relationships between machines of different sorts. But given the harmful impacts of human machines, some new materialists, such as Steven Shaviro, argue for an ethical and strategic anthropo*morphism* to move past a dominating anthropo*centrism*. That is, he claims, there is a need to ascribe to the non-human the qualities of the human as an exercise in ethical thinking, so that we might consider better taking care of and nurturing the non-human (61). Anthropomorphism therefore can be an act of displacing anthropocentrism. Similarly, critical posthumanist and vitalist materialist thinkers, such as Rosi Braidotti and Jane Bennett, argue in favor of *extending* the category of subject beyond the human to encompass all, both human and non-human. As these theories would have it, there is a need to dissolve the human/non-human binary, whether in the form of extending subjectivity beyond the human, or through the displacement of the category of the subject all together, making us all machines of different types.

Object-oriented ontologies, new materialisms, and posthumanisms are historicized within the context of late, post-crisis neoliberal capitalism. They are a reaction to the crises of neoliberal capitalism, and to the twinning impacts of climate change and automation. They are, in fact, a by-product of the objectified status, that deeper reification and objectification—the downward mobility—of the neoliberal middle classes.

The primary basis of neoliberalism, beyond its apparent penchant toward deregulation and non-interference, is its fundamentalist ethics toward markets and entrepreneurialization. In contrast to the classical liberal view with regard to the equality of agents in the market, neoliberalism views us all as individual entrepreneurs (businesses of one) in competition with each other for access to scarce resources. Buying access to resources (skills, education, cosmetics, networks, information communication technologies, etc.) means we are investing in ourselves, in our human capital—in ourselves as values, as objects, that can procure potentially more wealth, more capital. In the process, we continue to self-objectify.

It is in this context that the materialism of object-oriented ontology and posthumanist ethics begins to make sense. We are encouraged to displace the hierarchy and the dualism of the human/ non-human relationship when the white middle classes are beginning to feel their presence *as* objects, as machines. It's in this sense that new materialisms and posthumanisms are historical symptoms of the latent effects of post-crisis neoliberal capitalism. And here we can come back to the ethical significance of cyberpunk and *BR 2049* in the context of late postmodern culture.

As a political film, then, *BR 2049* represents a dialectical mediation between the ethical dilemma of how precisely to act when the human no longer figures in its centrality and memory-laden machines are seemingly ubiquitous. Here, a number of overlapping representations intersect to ask how precisely we should proceed politically and ethically when, on the one hand, human agency is radically decentered, and on the other, when it is precisely human action that is deemed to be at the root of our environmental and technological dilemmas, if not outright failures. These questions are taken up by some of the ancillary characters in the film.

First, K's holographic girlfriend Joi (Ana de Armas) is exemplary in this regard. It is clear from the beginning of the film that she remains spatially confined and limited since as a hologram she is without corporeal substance, not counting the hardware that is responsible for projecting her: She remains largely immobile and tethered to K's movement. While she may depict a high point in artificial intelligence, she seems to lack the very will or agency that we tend to deem as typical of the human. Throughout the film, her affection for K appears genuine and authentic, culminating in a heartbreaking scene when she is destroyed and ostensibly dies; however, near the end of the film, K encounters a large holographic advertisement for the Joi product (a striking visual image in the trailers that is key to marketing and promoting the film) that suggests her affection was just another component of the simulation. The hologram Joi ironically embodies the affective (unpaid) labor of social reproduction, condensed into artificial intelligence, and which corresponds with the other female characters in the film.

Consider the decidedly corporeal Mariette (Mackenzie Davis), a member of the resistance who is tasked with recruiting K by its leader, Freysa (Hiam Abbass). To carry out her mission, however, Mariette must first use seduction to attract his attention. Visually, and as a replicant, Mariette is reminiscent of Pris, the pleasure model from *Blade Runner*: She is a sex worker who initially meets K by trying to proposition him as a potential client. Later, we learn that Joi has hired Mariette to act as a surrogate body for them to have sex, emulating a similar scene in Spike Jonze's film, *Her* (2013).[3]

Yet another female character whose agency is brought into question is that of Wallace's aid, Luv (Sylvia Hoeks), who seems to obey every order she is given to violently acquire the means to best secure his financial interests: locating Deckard and finding out about the replicant child. Given these representations, the question needs to be asked: what separates Luv from Mariette, both of whom assist without question their leaders in the class struggle between the capitalist forces (Wallace) and the proletarian resistance (Freysa)? It is perhaps worth noting, too, that the two female characters who appear to be free to act of their own agency are Lieutenant Joshi and Freysa. They appear to express and embody most clearly the political class struggle. After all, Wallace seems to have very little regard for how his own actions and interests can negatively affect his class status—a true sign of the ruling class—while it is Joshi who remains concerned about staving off the replicant revolution. But as a representative of the state, we might contest that Joshi's ethics pertain more so to the interests of capital, and hence she remains unfree, just another cog in the machine.

There is, of course, the final relationship between K and Dr. Ana Stelline (Carla Juri), the designer of the replicant memories. Stelline, too, remains trapped—she is confined to a sterile room in her company's headquarters due to a childhood immune deficiency. She is very much like the other female characters in the film: She remains limited and restricted. However, she and K are bound in the way that they share the particular memory that leads K on his quest to uncover the truth about his own status as subject: the memory that he has of his childhood that leads him to believe that he is Rachael's child. We learn through Freysa that Stelline is in fact Rachael's child, not K. Against common standards in replicant production, Stelline used her own memory, which was implanted into K's mind. Until he learned this truth, though, K was led to act, driven by his quest to uncover the truth.

As noted earlier, a key difference between K and Rachael is that K knew that his memories were implants. It was only when he was lured by the possibility that his memory was real that he became subjectivized through a process of misrecognition. Common among cyberpunk protagonists is the suggestion that true humanity factors not as a matter of self-consciousness or self-awareness. It is the product of an unconscious—what the machinic lacks is not consciousness but an unconscious. More specifically, *BR 2049* suggests that humanity and human ethics are not to be defined by a will, but by a drive enacted by trauma. K is subjectivized by the trauma of his memory, the loss of his experience as a replicant, and subsequently by the loss of the authenticity of his memory that was given to him at the beginning.

This might, in fact, be the ethical lesson of the film: that it is only through an initial misrecognition that we are humanized, driven by a singular desire to act in accordance with that misrecognition. It is by following this misrecognition to the end and discovering that one is delivered back to what they already knew that they were, but now from a new perspective. K misrecognizes himself as potentially human, and that is what makes him an ethical subject—a human-centered subject. For what the film proposes is that we are activated as subjects, not by the conscious self-recognition of what we are, but by an unconscious misrecognition that drives us to act. The ethical and political lesson of the film is that in the face of the potential reduction to our mere object status, what makes us human is our continued evasion of this fact in the misrecognition of our (cyber-)essence. When we place this lesson in the context of the present, in our own historical conditions, faced with the neoliberal capitalist reduction of our being into mere object status (whether as biological machines, reducible data, or even human capital), the aim is toward (de-)subjectivization. *BR 2049* therefore continues to demonstrate why cyberpunk is an ethical mode.

Notes

1 Since it appears that K is a paid laborer—he earns an income which he uses to pay rent and buy his own technological goods, such as his electronic girlfriend, Joi—he too is exploited labor in the traditional marxist sense of wage labor as the source of capitalist surplus value.
2 This also leads to contemporary questions around the distinction between human and machinic labor, the difference between what Deleuze and Guattari (see also Lazzarato) refer to as machinic enslavement and social subjection, the various new materialisms and object-oriented ontologies, and contemporary posthumanist theory.
3 For a further exploration of Spike Jonze's *Her*, please see Flisfeder and Burnham.

Works Cited

Bennett, Jane. *Vibrant Matter: A Political Ecology of Things*. Duke UP, 2010.
Blade Runner. Directed by Ridley Scott, performances by Harrison Ford, Rutger Hauer, and Sean Young, Warner Brothers, 1982.
Blade Runner 2049. Directed by Denis Villeneuve, performances by Ryan Gosling, Harrison Ford, Ana de Armas, and Robin Wright, Sony Entertainment, 2017.
Braidotti, Rosi. *The Posthuman*. Polity, 2013.
Bryant, Levi R. *Onto-Cartography: An Ontology of Machines and Media*. U of Edinburgh P, 2014.
Bukatman, Scott. *Blade Runner*, 2nd Ed. Palgrave Macmillan, 2012.
Deleuze, Gilles and Felix Guattari. *A Thousand Plateaus: Capitalism and Schizophrenia*. Translated by Brian Massumi. U of Minnesota P, 1987.
Fisher, Mark. *Capitalist Realism: Is There No Alternative?* Zero Books, 2009.

Flisfeder, Matthew and Clint Burnham. "Love and Sex in the Age of Capitalist Realism: On Spike Jonze's *Her*." *Cinema Journal*, vol. 57, no. 1, 2017, pp. 25–45.

Flisfeder, Matthew. *Postmodern Theory and Blade Runner*. Bloomsbury, 2017.

Frase, Peter. *Four Futures: Life After Capitalism*. Verso, 2016.

Jameson, Fredric. *The Seeds of Time*. Columbia UP, 1994.

Lazzarato, Maurizio. *Signs and Machines: Capitalism and the Production of Subjectivity*. Semiotext(e), 2014.

Shaviro, Steven. *The Universe of Things: On Speculative Realism*. U of Minnesota P, 2014.

19
ANIME

Kumiko Saito

One of the congruities between cyberpunk and anime is a political stance that defies and undermines our vested perceptions about humanity, gender, class, or race, as inherited from the spirit of punk as a subculture. For example, in discussing the anime classic *Akira* (Ōtomo 1988), Paul Wells writes that anime in general "becomes a vehicle by which the animation itself can be used to illustrate the new mutabilities in personal identities and social environments as humankind and technology become increasingly allied, elided, and effaced" (192). As a result of its ongoing relevance in an increasingly technocultural, even cyberpunk, world, anime in Japan and throughout the world has been a thriving, albeit stigmatized, subculture that has provided a locus for challenging established norms. Similarly, cyberpunk has been obsessed with challenging boundaries and borders from its earliest beginnings. In his Preface to *Mirrorshades: The Cyberpunk Anthology* (1986), Bruce Sterling writes of cyberpunk's "overlapping of worlds that were formerly separate: the realm of high tech and the modern pop underground" (xi). It is through these overlapping terrains that cyberpunk popularized the transgressive themes of "body invasion: prosthetic limbs, implanted circuitry, cosmetic surgery, genetic alteration" as well as "mind invasion: brain-computer interfaces, artificial intelligence, neurochemistry—techniques radically redefining the nature of humanity, the nature of the self" (xiii). The counter-identity inherent in both cyberpunk and global anime therefore grew in a symbiotic relationship and helped form the cultural synthesis of cyberpunk and anime—or has the relationship been really that of symbiosis and synthesis? In the footsteps of a subculture's defiant spirit, anime may have resisted being overridden by cyberpunk as much as cyberpunk has urged anime's metamorphosis.

19.1 What Is Anime?: Or, Why There Is No Such Thing as Cyberpunk Anime

'Anime,' short for *animēshon*, is a term commonly used in Japan to refer to any animated work with differing connotations. Animations produced by a higher-budgeted western studio or feature films are often called *animēshon*, marking the high and mainstream end of animation, such as Walt Disney classics. In contrast, old-time television animations for children, mainly from the 1960s and 1970s, gained the title of *terebi manga*, signifying the televised version of hand-drawn cartoons (manga), such as *Astroboy* (*Tetsuwan Atomu*, 1963–66) and *Cyborg 009* (*Saibōgu 009*, 1968). While 'anime' still serves in Japanese language as a blanket term for everything animated, the global popularity of anime has largely drawn upon three intersecting attributes: Japanese nationality, visual style, and intermedia marketing.

Anime's supposed Japanese origins developed affinities with cyberpunk due to the East Asian landscape that constitutes a core component of this unique sf mode, whether the *noir*-inflected Chinatown and a screen-projected geisha in Ridley Scott's *Blade Runner* (1982) or the post-apocalyptic Neo Tokyo in Katsuhiro Ōtomo's *Akira*. In other words, anime and cyberpunk developed a symbiotic relationship in the west for a reason: Despite the absence of cyberpunk as a genre or category inherent in anime, the graphic Japaneseness that characterizes certain types of anime, regardless of the actual origin of production, created a convenient venue for marketing anime through a cyberpunk imagination.

In addition to its intermediality, material restraints characteristic of low-budget production common among the majority of anime gave birth to innovative visual techniques that showcased (and continue to showcase) individual animation styles. Critics like Yasuo Ōtsuka and Takahiro Akita locate animetic quality in the process of limited animation[1] and the unique narrative strategies and symbolisms that compensate for the lack of smooth and realistic motion. Major examples include the illusion of fast dynamic action with fewer drawings and the deliberate frame composition using multiple layers of detailed stills. Thomas Lamarre also ascribes the anime style to the "animetic machine," or the animation mechanism of the interplanar composition, often marking explicitly visible seams dissecting layers into foreground, background, and characters. In this respect, the most successful cultural delegates from the domain of Japanese anime to western cyberpunk, such as *Akira* and *Ghost in the Shell* (Oshii 1995), can be named the least anime-like productions, evident in smoothly animated action sequences filmed with Hollywood-oriented realism principles of continuity editing and depth staging, and thoroughly planned philosophically inspiring messages coupled with exceptionally high budgets for anime.

Recent scholarship on anime has increasingly shifted toward studies on the media-crossing quality of the entertainment industry as a core factor that makes Japanese animation animetic. For example, fandom quickly engulfed anime and manga with the energetic interpretive exploration of speculative settings and technical specifications for imaginary machines (Okada 1996). As a result, media industries have established a business model for merchandising characters, or 'chara' to use the fandom slang, that transmigrate to multiple media platforms to create different narratives.[2] The transmedia character therefore incites participatory culture that evolves from the interactive relationship among the anime texts, creators, and consumers. Anime from this viewpoint can be called an "industrial genre" (Zahlten 7), or a fluid venue of production and consumption framed by specific industrial practices and material forms. In addition, anime's transmedia migration violates generic borders across subject matters and audience anticipations, which consequently disrupts cyberpunk as a literary practice of reading into the depth of messages about humanity and technology. The anime world laden with comic reliefs and character eroticism often needs to be suppressed in order to market the cool cyberpunk.

This cyberpunk quality in anime can be stereotypically represented by dismal cityscapes, somber tones of posthuman ontology, and the careful staging of the imagined 'Japan' that Japanese creators believe better meet the western labeling of cyberpunk and its conceptual traits.[3] As a result, any attempt to define anime in light of cyberpunk ironically reveals as many incompatibilities as congruities between the two modes; in other words, the anime texts commonly classified as 'cyberpunk anime' mostly come from an idiosyncratic corner of the ever-expanding anime industry, a culturally and industrially unique domain where creators and consumers eliminate animetic-ness to optimize cyberpunk-ness. As a result, in spite of affinities between anime and cyberpunk, the discrepancies and cultural conflicts mutually disturb anime and cyberpunk as much as inspire each other, particularly in anime categories such as *mecha*, horror, and virtual idols.

19.2 Mecha Identity: Robots and Cyborgs in Anime

Mecha is the Japanese term for 'mechanism' or 'mechanical' and generally means technological gadgets of all sizes that augment and enhance human abilities. Although American culture tends to use mecha to signify robots in anime, the term's original Japanese connotation for metal and mechanical things includes everything from small gimmicks and devices to human-sized cyborgs and even giant robots. Mecha in anime has also undertaken the symbolic role of representing the self in both the material embodiment of the human body and the metaphysical framework of identity. This phenomenon corresponds to the emergence of the predominantly male-oriented subgenre known as 'real robot,' which, in robot anime, is best represented by television series such as *Mobile Suit Gundam* (*Kidō senshi Gandamu*, 1979–80) and *Armored Troopers Votoms* (*Sōkō kihei Botomuzu*, 1983–84). These robots are wearable weapons or battle suits that synchronize with the motion and volition of the pilot—the metal parts magnify the pilot's military power and physical maneuverability (typically) by awakening his potent abilities while serving as proxies for the pilot's fears and beliefs. Differentiated from giant robot heroes who fight simple good-versus-evil battles, the 'real robots' may reveal more proximity to fighting cyborg detectives or android mercenaries due to their role as the alter ego of humanity. The irony, however, is that this synchronizing of the body and consciousness with the robot is doomed to fail for 'human' reasons—i.e. political or psychological obstacles—since he is rendered as a soldier or hired laborer who must obey the authority's orders or succumb to the enforcement of their duty. The *Mobile Police Patlabor* series (*Kidō keisatsu Patoreibā*, sporadically running 1988–2016) most symbolically wields this metaphor by depicting piloted patrol robots of the police force known as 'labors' which are "images of us, human-machine hybrids that have lost all humanity" (Bolton 59). In this male-dominant genre of real robots, the skeptical subject's oscillation between mecha and human identity becomes analogous to dilemmas between serving the authority/nation and fighting for one's political beliefs.

The influence of American cyberpunk in the late-1980s gradually altered mecha-oriented anime to those that depict cyborgs and androids. A Japanese twist on cyberpunk formulae was the general shift of the anime protagonist from male to female—cyborg women came to dominate anime, overpowering men in battle, intelligence, and/or political maneuvering. One of the first commercially successful anime productions in this vein was *Bubblegum Crisis* (*Baburugamu kuraishisu*, 1987–91), an original video animation (OVA) series that features a secret all-female team of four mercenaries, known as the Knight Sabers. Combining cyberpunk and *jidaigeki*[3] elements, the group fights in powered exoskeletons against crimes often caused by illegal androids and rogue robots. The success of *Bubblegum Crisis* spawned many anime and manga successors, including *Battle Angel Alita* (*Ganmu*, aka *Gunnm*, Fukutomi 1993), *Armitage III* (*Amitēji za sādo*, 1995), and *Ghost in the Shell* (*Kōkaku kidōtai*).

As cyberpunk-influenced anime increasingly moved from Japanese niche market to global popularity, the conventions settled on several key features. The plot often revolves around a female cyborg or, more precisely, a composite of the human brain and the female-model artificial body. The imagined presence of the brain is the sole physical evidence of an original human identity, but the content of the head remains unconfirmed. Like Deckard in *Blade Runner*, cyborgs in anime often live with internal doubts of their own originality and humanity. Battle is typically her occupation, whether she is a detective serving public safety or a hunter of rogue androids or robots. Thematic significance often lies in the confirmation of self-agency in thinking independently and making choices based on her free will. While the democratic agenda of autonomy and freedom may differ in each work, one of the predominant themes is the choice of reproduction and family. For example, Alita (aka Gally) in *Battle Angel Alita* learns to be human by actively pursuing romantic relationships and friendships, which become her *raison d'être* against mindless battles. Her rationales for fighting increasingly shift toward human emotions such as romantic feelings and revenge, which often hamper her mechanical capacity for battle. Naomi in *Armitage III*, who believes her passion for hunting criminal androids to be her own determination, learns that she is a 'Third' prototype, a new-generation android equipped with programmed minds. The unique ability of Thirds, however, is biological reproduction, which leads her to discovering a partner and choosing to give birth and expand her family. Finally, Motoko in *Ghost in the Shell*, a cyborg detective allegedly with a human brain, meets an artificial intelligence (AI) that gains self-consciousness and agrees to merge with it to engender copies with biological variation essential for the reproduction of life.

The cultural value of these empowered female cyborgs has proven divisive. On the one hand, the female sex of the prosthetic body works in tandem with the feminist cyberpunk and feminist theories that prospered in the 1990s.[4] In the groundbreaking "A Cyborg Manifesto," Donna J. Haraway locates the innovation of the cyborg in its blurring of three boundaries—between human and machine, between human and animal, and between the real and the unreal (151). In this regard, Motoko transcends the limits of gendered roles, corporeal physics, and human consciousness, which makes her "[fit] comfortably into Haraway's vision of the cyborg as a creature without human limitations" (Napier 106). Similarly, Alita's body is a prosthetic collage of scraps from garbage dumps, embodying not a single subject but the decentered model as proposed by feminist cyberpunk: "fragmented subjects who can, despite their multiple positionings, negotiate and succeed in a high-tech world" (Cadora 357). Finally, *Armitage III* ends with Naomi's remark that her pregnancy evidences her being a 'complete Third' as if the biological reproductive ability belongs to a particular android model and not to an organism or the female sex. There is a valid argument to be made that female cyborgs in anime vigorously disrupt the male-centered classic cyberpunk formula and experiment with conceptual challenges for liberation from sexual and patriarchal shackles on the biological body. These popular figures open up "the possibility of a completely postgendered cyborgism and perhaps even a posthuman subjectivity altogether" (Hopkins 9).

On the other hand, the female cyborgs often reaffirm both their feminine attributes of romance/sex/reproduction and the voyeuristic male gaze. These liberated female cyborgs and androids make a choice that often hinges on gaining a partner and succumbing to a reproducing/cloning cycle: It is as if its organism and female roles were dismissed only to be reclaimed by narrative end. In addition, anime locates cyberpunk as a predominantly male market where female cyborgs are designed as 'battle chicks,' an effective visual mechanism to unify female nudity and mecha apparatus fetishism. As Masamune Shirow, the original manga author of *Ghost in the Shell*, said in response to the question why his stories concern female cyborgs, "it is more attractive for a man to draw female bodies" (147). Equally for (male) viewers, the euphoric female body empowered with state-of-the-art weaponry and cost-inducing action-focused animation becomes a highly attractive object of visual pleasure.

The situation of Japanese cyberpunk, however, is not as simple as calling the female cyborg's objectified femaleness conservative and dissenting for feminism. Non-western viewpoints on this discussion have found more male subjectivity than feminism in the female cyborg. Rising from the defeat in WWII and deeply inscribed sense of inferiority to the west, postwar Japanese popular culture has generated a wide array of humanoid robots and cybernetic heroes[5] who suffer from their incomplete being as monstrous human–machine patchwork. Japan's inferiority complex and blind mimicry of the west have resulted in stories about 'Japanoids,' who are not only metal-flesh chimeras, but also dilemmatic composites of west and non-west, or democracy and the emperor system (Tatsumi 25). The emergence of female cyborgs, or the female and beautiful form of the Japanoid chimeras, marks a new phase of Japanese culture and economy, which corresponds to Japan's economic rise in the global industry from the late 1980s to early 1990s. As a character in Masaki Gorō's cyberpunk novel *Venus City* (*Vīnasu shitī*, 1995) rightly remarks, the empowered female avatar that Japanese men wear in virtual reality likely represents a male body with female breasts, a hybrid body of broken masculinity that wears the power of mecha-femaleness. In this respect, female cyborgs undertake male subjectivity of a defeated country in the era of economic expansion while schizophrenically becoming the object of its own gaze.

In sum, the female cyborg body becomes a site of opposing discourses—while celebrating the posthuman identity that transcends boundaries of gender, race, and humanity, they simultaneously reinvent the pleasure of owning the power of the female body. The equivocal quality of gendered mecha bodies in cross-cultural perspectives brings discrepancies, thereby causing more amorphous disruptions of meaning.

19.3 The Return of the Grotesque: Anime and the Visual Language of Cyberpunk

Anime's visual landscape of a futuristic Japan clearly ties cyberpunk and anime; after all, diverse representations of 'Japan,' or cultural icons of America's orient by extension, mark cyberpunk's earliest texts, from Scott's *Blade Runner* to William Gibson's *Neuromancer* (1984) and *Idoru* (1996). One needs to only turn to Chiba City (*Neuromancer*) and the oppressive skyscrapers over Chinatown (*Blade Runner*) to see that urban Japanese sceneries, names, and images have extensively colonized cyberpunk from its beginning. The prevalence of Japanese cities and totalitarian conglomerates in early cyberpunk obviously corresponded to the rise of global industries and economic invasions from the non-west, especially Japan and its economic bubble, culminating with Mitsubishi's takeover of Rockefeller Center in 1989. The choice of Japan for the future vision indicates the contradicting implications of the future: Like a geisha on Scott's high-tech screens, Japan embodies both advancement and backwardness. The fusion of "futuristic high-tech images of contemporary Japan and anachronistic images of feudal Japan" (Yoshimoto 18) is a means to cope with anxiety with the post-Fordist age of globalization and Asianization. Morley and Robins name this phenomenon "Techno-Orientalism": The anxiety's equivocal nature overlaps with the west's fascination with the "exotic, enigmatic and mysterious essence of Japanese particularism" (169). This enchanting 'Japan,' or an imaginary locus for the uncanny bodies and cities of the Asian Other, is a cognitive nexus between high technology and old spiritualism, the future and the past, or the real and the unreal.[6]

If the Othering-effect of the high-low paradox is an essential cognitive device for cyberpunk, Japanese adaptations of western cyberpunk also came to entail the cultural question of interpreting the exotic Otherness in cyberpunk. For example, Hisashi Kuroma's Japanese translation of *Neuromancer* (1985) excessively used Chinese characters as translation for cyberpunk idioms and printed next to them English pronunciations of the original words transcribed into Japanese. The curious combination of Chinese and English set the standard for narrative expressions in Japanese cyberpunk, including new terms such as 電脳空間 (dennō kūkan) for cyberspace and 仮想世界 (kasō sekai) for virtual world. *Ghost in the Shell* also invented several popular jargons including 義体 (gitai) for cyborgs or cybernetic body parts and 攻殻 (kōkaku) for armed 'shells.' This fascination with the uncanny east/west interstice equally played out in anime graphics. The visual metaphors of synthetic Tokyo between the implosion of chaotic Asia and the expansion of hypermodern technological empire in *Ghost in the Shell* further enhance the sense of the alienated subject in blurred boundaries of cyborg identity. Japanized cyberpunk fulfills similar functions to western cyberpunk's techno-orientalism through its fear and fascination with the paradoxical simultaneity of retro-futurism, although it may simply appear as enhanced Asian Otherness to most western viewers.

The reinvention of Japan's orient in Japanese cyberpunk also created a substantial obstacle for anime—originally, anime is a media form that excels in erasing graphic traces of ethnicity and nationality due to the fantastic settings and unreal human features of its characters. Anime's global spread owes much to this ethno-less characteristic, but as far as cyberpunk is concerned, Asianness in visual representation is indispensable. The unexpected global fame of the film versions of *Akira* and *Ghost in the Shell* confirmed this fact and helped the nation discover its own exoticness. *Akira's* innovations did not simply come from the plot, budget, and animation techniques, but also from bold visualizations and the realism of an anachronistically post-apocalyptic Tokyo. *Ghost in the Shell* and *Patlabor 2* (1993), both directed by Mamoru Oshii, also carefully adopt visual techniques of cinematic realism by incorporating detailed depictions of Tokyo's urban sprawl, including Asian figures with black hair and eyes. The subdued tones of dark figures tied to realistic shadows and shades of material objects allow the characters to sink and merge into the anonymous depths of darkness. If the main features of animetic anime rely on the fetishism of super flatness, erased ethnicity, and bright-colored cuteness, cyberpunk's techno-orientalism in fact reveals Japan's blindness to its own Asian representation, thereby urging anime to reconceptualize itself through the conflict of anime aesthetics and Asian otherness.

Following the global success of cyberpunk-themed anime films in the late 1990s, television anime series such as *Serial Experiments Lain* (Nakamura 1998), *The SoulTaker* (Shinbo 2001), *Texhnolyze* (Hamazaki 2003), *Ergo Proxy* (Murase 2006), and *Psycho-Pass* (Shiotani and Motohiro 2013) experimented with less animetic visual effects and cyberpunk themes. *Lain*, a media-mix project entailing an anime series, a game, and the publication of text/graphic fragments, collectively present a world view where Lain, a shy high school girl frequently suffering from hallucinations, creates and disseminates multiple internet personas throughout the net. The transmedia project "Lain" was designed to lure consumers into a mystery in which they track traces and fragments of multiple Lains through saved files and replayable memories to reconstruct a story in a serial form of data. *The SoulTaker* also underscores mutant cloning of bodies and fragmentation of human consciousness by the mysterious cloning effect known as flickering. The depiction of a regimented future society under the total control of an oppressive central system can be commonly found among *Texhnolyze*, *Ergo Proxy*, and *Psycho-Pass*. In the world where the central system becomes a god that governs humanity, the totalitarian policing of society excretes those who fail or refuse to obey the control, resulting in the operating system identifying the 'defect' as a virus or programming bug to be eliminated. The condition eventually leads to conflicts and resistances which enable the protagonists to question and perceive the human awareness of individual free will, self-consciousness, or the core of identity.

These anime were innovative not only in cyberpunk concepts but also in merging the narrative conventions of cyberpunk and J-horror, the popular live action genre that grew in exact parallel to cyberpunk in the 1990s to early 2000s. The simplest explanation for the alliance of cyberpunk and horror is that no other genre than horror in the digital age could meet the degree of darkness and visual realism of Asian bodies needed for cyberpunk: Traditional cel animation particularly disfavored black color and darkness that block lighting through cel overlays. Equally important is the cognitive effects of fear born from high technology that interrupts human communication. According to the so-called Konaka theory,[7] J-horror generally evades the Hollywood style of shockers and massacres, instead appealing to the psychological effects of absurdity and inexplicability (Konaka 205). The absence of reasoning and explanation for supernatural phenomena erodes the boundary between digital world and occultism of ghosts and demons—copies of human consciousness and floating souls of the dead equally manifest through the computer screen in J-horror and cyberpunk. Physically realistic visual portrayals of objects and characters also necessitate the existence of their shadows and spatial depth, which generates darkness that invades reality and shrouds the uncanny presence of ghosts. The *Lain* series, for example, effectively utilizes shadows on the street and wires in the sky to set the stage for a ghost to emerge from the cyberspace (Figure 19.1).

Figure 19.1 The presence of deep shadows on bushes and streets as well as wires above creates visual/conceptual depth and implies the reality's connectedness to cyberworld/nextworld. Still from *Serial Experiments Lain*, Episode 1, 1998, NBC Universal Entertainment (formerly Pioneer).

SoulTaker conjures a dream-like, absurdly complex plot that rejects interpretative reasoning from the viewer. *Texhnolyze* reformulates the definition of a cyborg as a crippled body of the poor contaminated by unhygienic erosion of flesh and metal in contrast to clean and beautiful female cyborgs that crystallize the art of high-tech maintenance provided by authorities and top scientists. In sum, cyberpunk and horror anime go hand in hand to combine traditional tropes of monsters and dolls with technological tropes of umbilical cords and viral infections.

19.4 Virtual Idols and Intermedial Reality

While digital figures, avatars, and AIs are standard fare for cyberpunk, the virtual idol has neither occupied an intrinsic part of cyberpunk nor has it ever been a popular trope in fiction, with notable exceptions such as William Gibson's Rei Toei from *Idoru* and *All Tomorrow's Parties* (1999). Anime and the cross-media industry surrounding it, however, have consistently invested funds and emotional energies in virtual idols since the 1980s to the extent that Japanese idol culture may have overtaken the futuristic world of Gibson's novels. The virtual idol initially began with the rising awareness of mecha themes, and the chrysalis of virtual idols can be widely found in mecha-and-idol franchises, namely *The Super Dimension Fortress Macross* (*Chōjikū yōsai Makurosu*, Ishiguro 1982–83), parts of which are known as *Robotech* in North America, and its derivatives like *Megazone 23* (*Megazōn tsū surī*, 1985) and *Macross Plus* (1994–95). Following the popularity and profitability of anime idols, several commercial projects debuted virtual idols using the existing marketing methods of human idols, ranging from Kyoko Date by major talent agency Hori Production (1996) to Eguchi Aimi, a member of the idol group AKB48 (2011–13). Soon, idols that more faithfully simulate 2D anime characters and their pseudo-3D forms, especially synthetic resin figurines and dolls, dominated the virtual idol market, starting with the Idolmaster anime/game franchise and the vocaloid Hatsune Miku, leading to a highly profitable 10-billion-yen market (Hakuhōdō 2016, Yano Research 2017). After an initial release in 2007, Miku steadily gained popularity as a female voice synthesizer that 'sings' songs composed and uploaded by common users to be viewed on video sharing sites like YouTube and Nico Nico Douga, usually accompanied by the amateur user's illustrations and animations. They soon gave birth to similar idol-raising cross-media titles such as *Love Live!* (Kyōgoku 2012–) geared for a male audience and *Uta no prince-sama* (Yamane 2011–) for a female audience.

One of the largest factors contributing to the prosperity of idols, despite the absence of their bodies or even coherent images, is anime's intermediality. Animated films or TV programs constitute a large franchise across multiple media platforms and fan communities: Anime in this sense is no longer strictly visual narrative texts, but more likely a "creative platform" (Condry 55). Mimicking and fueling character fetishism, these idols within the text now emigrate to our world and serve our desires. Like Sharon Apple, a holographic idol that freely morphs in accordance to the viewers' desires in *Macross Plus*, their role more likely involves themselves reading 'our' desire and optimizing it through peripheral activities, such as secondary fiction writing/reading and dissemination of proliferating images. Online video sharing sites, where amateur singers and fans cover the anime songs to accompany fan-drawn illustrations, have accelerated idols' popularity. This intermedia fandom culture is where vocaloids gained their life: The globally popular Miku achieved her idol status through decentered channels of audiovisual (re)productions across online media, blurring the boundary between artists and audience, or production and reception (Zaborowski 112). The bottom-up movement of fandom simultaneously reactivates the top-down hegemony of the mass media: The vocaloid songs and accompanying stories created and uploaded by individual users conversely become covered by major singers and adapted into commercial anime productions, a prominent example of which was the Kagerou Project (2011–). From Dance Dance Revolution public arcade performances in the 1990s to recent virtual idol games and multi-directional vocaloid productions, the open-source participatory culture of music and rhythm games has persistently interrupted the hierarchal world of media stars.

In addition to the media-crossing morphing capability, what has divided today's popular virtual idols from cyberpunk-inspired 'idorus' like Kyoko Date or Gibson's Rei Toei is the anime industry's matter-of-fact proposition that the visual composition of virtual idols simulates anime characters, not human idols. More strictly speaking, these virtual idols are not even 'virtual' to the extent that the gap between human corporeality and digital presence is fundamental and visible enough to entirely dismiss the interstitial almost-ness of virtuality between the real and the unreal. In this account, even universal human attributes that simulate physical reality and photographic mimesis of the human body tend to be overridden by anime physics, including flat appearance, unnatural shades against 3D programming, grotesquely large eyes, and brightly colored hair (Figure 19.2).

The 2D fetishism attached to characters derives from the anime consumption mode that "eroticizes the skin texture of celluloid animation itself" which materializes the sterilized flat appearance of the body removed of materiality (Morikawa 111).

These happy and cute singing dolls epitomize the schizophrenic nature of idol and mecha in anime; in other words, the disproportionate alignment between the euphoric idols and melancholic mecha subjects refuses to resolve itself. The mecha identity, as discussed earlier, resonates with cyberpunk and the pessimistic yet humanistic existentialist questions of eroding ontological dichotomies. What emerges is a discordant mash-up as the serious and dystopian end of sf is offset by the idols' incongruous locale of romance and peace, both of which equally tie into the visual composition. For instance, the *Macross* television anime series employed the MTV-styled

Figure 19.2 3D models simulate the design and texture of anime characters. Promotion image from Hatsune Miku: Project DIVA, 2009, Sega & Crypton Future Media.

Figure 19.3 Lynn Minmay sings to end the war while men fight life-or-death battles outside the spaceship. Still from *The Super Dimension Fortress Macross: Do You Remember Love?*, 1984, Bandai Visual.

combination of rendering robot battles on a large background screen against idol performances in the foreground stage (Figure 19.3).

Closely following the Macross model, the idol Eve in *Megazone 23* demonstrates the cognitive gap between her roles as an idol and as a human interface of Bahamut, the matrix system that runs a virtual Tokyo within an emigration spaceship in the post-apocalyptic setting. This incongruity continues with female cyborgs in anime who internalize the paradox between essentialist female euphoria and postmodern cyborg subjectivity. If skeptical cyborg subjects are nostalgic because of their loss of reality, recent virtual idols are euphoric since they are entirely stripped of any memory of reality. The idols therefore remind us of the present experience of the schizophrenic subject who lives the intensity "described in the negative terms of anxiety and loss of reality, but which one could just as well imagine in the positive terms of euphoria, a high, an intoxicatory or hallucinogenic intensity" (Jameson 28–29). The virtual idols also remind us that simulations are not simulating reality but operating the tautology of virtuality in anime representing anime. In "Simulacra and Simulations," Baudrillard uses an allegory of the map, which was to be an abstraction of the territory, to state that the map "is no longer that of a territory, a referential being or a substance. It is the generation by models of a real without origin or reality: a hyperreal" (166). The virtual idols that diverged from anime reframe hyperreal as the realer of the real, their 'real' being anime. As simulacra of simulacra without origin or memory, these idols erase their referentiality or "the representational imaginary" (Baudrillard 167) by overwriting our reality with anime.

19.5 Anime's Ignorance of Cyberpunk's Death

Writers and scholars have claimed that cyberpunk is dead because it exhausted its newness and 'we' now live in a cyberpunk reality. As far as anime and Japanese pop culture are concerned, this statement is wrong—not because cyberpunk has not ended, but because cyberpunk never even started in anime and had already existed as Japan's reality before western cyberpunk 'discovered Japan.' If cyberpunk had forgotten its innovation and rebellious reasoning because our contemporary society has reached or even outpaced cyberpunk, anime should remind cyberpunk that Japan has always been defined in those same terms of being a cyberpunk reality. Anime is amnesic of the west's melancholy over the collapsing modern subject, if not entirely indifferent to it. Today, Japanese pop culture still seems ignorant of cyberpunk's death: Cutting-edge technology is used to simulate anime characters and cute monsters as if Asians or Japan had never existed, while stories of the afterlife reincarnated into the cyberspace of massively multiplayer online role-playing games (MMORPG) continue to flow into the anime industry. Cyberpunk, in return, will remind anime to continue striving to imitate cyberpunk which is a privilege for nations that believe they had once achieved modernity. Anime is dreaming of perfectly simulating western cyberpunk and even perhaps calling itself cyberpunk anime someday.

Notes

1 Anime tends to employ a budget-cutting labor-saving method called 'limited animation' that utilizes partial animation, reuse of cels, and a smaller number of cels per second (eight cels or even fewer).
2 For more details, see Saitō (2000), Azuma (2001), Itō (2005), and/or Steinberg (2012).
3 Jidaigeki, often translated as 'period drama,' refers to a television/film genre set in the feudal era, often featuring samurai and sword fighting.
4 For details about feminist cyberpunk, see Lisa Yaszek's, Patricia Melzer's, and/or Wendy Gay Pearson's respective contributions to this collection.
5 Examples include Shōzō Numa's novel *Yapoo the Human Cattle* (1956), Sakyō Komatsu's novel *Japanese Apaches* (1964), live action television series *Kikaidar* (1972–73), Shin'ya Tsukamoto's live action film *Tetsuo* (1989), and Tetsuo in Ōtomo's *Akira*.
6 For more information on Japan, cyberpunk, and techno-orientalism, see Brian Ruh's contribution to this collection.
7 Not quite a theory, but a collection of horror methods that have influenced the core creators of J-horror such as Hideo Nakata (director of *Ring*, 1998), Kiyoshi Kurosawa (director of *Pulse*, 2001), and Hiroshi Takahashi (writer of *Ring*, 1998).

Anime

Works Cited

Akira. Directed by Katsuhiro Ōtomo, Tokyo Movie Shinsha, 1988.

Akita, Takahiro. *"Koma" kara "firumu" e: manga to manga eiga*. NTT Shuppan, 2005.

Armitage III (Amitēji za sādo). Directed by Hiroyuki Ochi, Anime International Company (AIC)/Pioneer LDC, 1995.

Azuma, Hiroki. *Dōbutsuka suru posutomodan*. Kōdansha, 2001.

Battle Angel Alita (Ganmu, aka Gunnm). Directed by Hiroshi Fukutomi, Madhouse/Animate Film/KSS/Movic, 1993.

Baudrillard, Jean. "Simulacra and Simulations." *Jean Baudrillard: Selected Writings*, edited by Mark Poster. Stanford UP, 1988, pp. 169–187.

Bolton, Christopher. *Interpreting Anime*. U of Minnesota P, 2018.

Bubblegum Crisis (Baburugamu kuraishisu). Anime International Company (AIC)/Artmic/Youmex, 1987–91.

Cadora, Karen. "Feminist Cyberpunk." *Science Fiction Studies*, vol. 22, no. 3, 1995, pp. 357–372.

Condry, Ian. *The Soul of Anime: Collaborative Creativity and Japan's Media Success Story*. Duke UP, 2013.

Ghost in the Shell (Kôkaku Kidôtai). Directed by Mamoru Oshii, Kōdansha/Bandai/Manga Entertainment, 1995.

Gibson, William. *Neuromancer (Nyūromansā)*. Translated by Hisashi Kuroma. Hayakawa Shobō, 1986.

Gorō, Masaki. *Venus City (Vīnasu shitī)*. Hayakawa Shobo, 1992.

Haraway, Donna J. "A Cyborg Manifesto: Science, Technology, and Socialist-Feminism in the Late Twentieth Century." *Simians, Cyborgs, and Women: The Reinvention of Nature*. Routledge, 1990, pp. 149–181.

Hopkins, Patrick D. "Introduction." *Sex/Machine: Readings in Culture, Gender, and Technology*. Indiana UP, 1999, pp. 1–11.

Itō, Gō. *Tezuka izu deddo: hirakareta manga hyōgenron e*. NTT Shuppan, 2005.

Jameson, Fredric. *Postmodernism, or, the Cultural Logic of Late Capitalism*. Duke UP, 1991.

Konaka, Chiaki. *Kyōfu no sahō: horō eiga no gijutsu*. Kawade shobō, 2014.

Lamarre, Thomas. *The Anime Machine: A Media Theory of Animation*. U of Minnesota P, 2009.

Macross Plus. Studio Nue/Triangle Staff, 1994–95.

Megazone 23. Anime International Company (AIC)/Artland/Tatsunoko Production, 1985.

Mobile Police Patlabor (Kidō keisatsu Patoreibā). Directed by Mamoru Oshii, Studio Deen, 1988–2016.

Morikawa, Kaichirō. *Shuto no tanjō: moeru toshi Akihabara*. Gentōsha, 2003.

Morley, David and Kevin Robins. *Spaces of Identity: Global Media, Electronic Landscapes and Cultural Boundaries*. Routledge, 1995.

Napier, Susan J. *Anime from Akira to Howl's Moving Castle: Experiencing Contemporary Japanese Animation*. St. Martin's Griffin, 2005.

Okada, Toshio. *Otakugaku nyūmon*. Ōta shuppan, 1996.

Ōtsuka, Yasuo. *Sakuga asemamire*. Tokuma Shoten, 2001.

Patlabor 2. Directed by Mamoru Oshii, Bandai/Tohokushinsha Film Corporation/Elastic Media/I.G. Tatsunoko/Production I.G., 1993.

Saitō, Tamaki. *Sentō bishōjo no seishin bunseki*. Ōta shuppan, 2000.

Serial Experiments Lain (Shiriaru Ekusuperimentsu Rein). Directed by Ryūtarō Nakamura, Triangle Staff, 1998.

Shirow, Masamune, *Appurushīdo sōshūhen*. Seishinsha, 1996.

The SoulTaker. Directed by Akiyuki Shinbo, Pioneer/Tatsunoko Production/Toshiba Digital Frontiers, 2001.

Steinberg, Marc. *Anime's Media Mix: Franchising Toys and Characters in Japan*. U of Minnesota P, 2012.

Sterling, Bruce. Preface. *Mirrorshades: The Cyberpunk Anthology*, edited by Bruce Sterling. Ace, 1986, pp. ix–xvi.

Tatsumi, Takayuki. *Full Metal Apache: Transactions Between Cyberpunk Japan and Avant-Pop America*. Duke UP, 2006.

Texhnolyze (Tekunoraizu). Directed by Hiroshi Hamazaki, Fuji Television Network/Madhouse, 2003.

Wells, Paul. "Animation." *The Oxford Handbook of Science Fiction*, edited by Rob Latham. Oxford UP, 2014, pp. 184–195.

Yoshimoto, Mitsuhiro. "The Postmodern and Mass Images in Japan." *Public Culture*, vol. 1, no. 2, 1989, pp. 8–25.

Zaborowski, Rafal. "Hatsune Miku and Japanese Virtual Idols." *The Oxford Handbook of Music and Virtuality*, edited by Sheila Whiteley and Shara Rambarran. Oxford UP, 2016, pp. 111–128.

Zahlten, Alex. *The End of Japanese Cinema: Industrial Genres, National Times, and Media Ecologies*. Duke UP, 2017.

20

AKIRA AND *GHOST IN THE SHELL* (CASE STUDY)

Martin de la Iglesia and Lars Schmeink

Up until the late 1980s, Japanese anime had gone mostly unnoticed in the west and it fell to cyberpunk film, specifically Katsuhiro Ōtomo's *Akira* (1988) and Mamoru Oshii's *Ghost in the Shell* (1995), to change the western perception of animated films forever. Seen in the west mainly as children's films, adult animated films were not unheard of but never had the same success or 'coolness' that *Akira* brought to western viewers. As Michelle Le Blanc and Colin Odell note: "*Akira* was fundamental in changing audience perceptions of what animation was and, importantly, what it had the potential to be" (9). And while *Akira* introduced western audiences to adult anime, followed by a wave of controversies regarding violence and overt sexual content, by the time *Ghost in the Shell* hit the screens, audiences worldwide had become appreciative of Japanese anime. Christopher Bolton argues that *Akira* "marks the beginning of a Japanese renaissance in long-form theatrical anime for more adult audiences [...as well as] the beginning of the latest and largest anime boom in North America" (17). *Ghost in the Shell*, however, is a "popular and critical phenomenon" that takes the genre to the next step, engaging not only fans but also academics as an "evocative, provocative text" (Bolton 62, 95), pushing for critical discussions of the overall medium. In fact, the films lend themselves to be seen as a virtual double feature, marking the mainstream introduction and critical consolidation of cyberpunk anime as a respected and acclaimed visual form in the west and constituting an important contribution to cyberpunk culture.

Interestingly, even though both *Akira* and *Ghost in the Shell* count among the greatest anime films ever made and their affiliation with cyberpunk is accepted by audiences and many critics, Kumiko Saito points out in her contribution to this collection that they are not typical anime which usually had rather cheap production values. Rather, Saito argues, *Akira* and *Ghost in the Shell*'s departure from the form is "evident in smoothly animated action sequences filmed with Hollywood-oriented realism, principles of continuity editing and depth staging, and thoroughly-planned philosophically inspiring messages coupled with exceptionally high budgets for anime" (152). At the same time, they aren't prototypical of cyberpunk, as described in Sterling's dictum of the "classic one-two combination of lowlife and high tech" (Preface to *Burning Chrome* xii). Instead, each of the films adjusts the formula to one side of the spectrum, highlighting their respective unique contribution—*Akira* foregrounding an indebtedness to punk subculture and Japanese cyberpunk's connection with body horror, while *Ghost in the Shell* plays into Japan's perception in the west as a technological forerunner, especially in regards to cybertechnology and cyborgian constructions of life.

Katsuhiro Ōtomo's anime *Akira* is an adaptation of his manga of the same name, which was serialized from 1982 to 1990. And even though the manga has been retrospectively highlighted as a foundational cyberpunk text, it has never been prototypical in its generic conventions, instead also referencing "supernatural powers from the 'science fantasy' genre" or a "post-apocalyptic fiction" setting, thus resisting the purity of the cyberpunk generic moniker (de la Iglesia 9).[1] The film takes place in the near-future setting of 2019, thirty-one years after an unknown event triggered World War III and Tokyo was destroyed in a massive explosion, only to be rebuilt in the post-War years as Neo-Tokyo. The story follows a group of teenage bikers, led by Kaneda and including his best friend, Tetsuo, who become entangled in a web of political conspiracy, a revolt against authority, and illegal government experimentation. After an accident involving a young boy with strange psychic powers and the face of an old man, Tetsuo is sequestered by a secret governmental agency. The accident triggers the potential development of paranormal abilities in Tetsuo and the agency wants to add him to their ranks of experimental subjects, in which they create psychic and psychokinetic powers through drug inducement. Meanwhile, Kaneda joins an underground revolutionary group attempting to mount a rescue, stop the experiments, and use the test subjects for their own gain. However, Tetsuo's induced abilities grow out of control and he escapes the hospital, causing violence and bloodshed in the process. During the chaos, the psychic children warn of the second coming of a prodigy named Akira, once a powerful test subject himself—so powerful in fact, that he caused the event that destroyed Tokyo and caused WWIII. Tetsuo realizes that he is linked to Akira and sets out to release him, while Kaneda still wants to rescue his childhood friend, this time from himself and the corrupting power growing inside of him. When Tetsuo releases Akira from the cryogenic chamber in which he was imprisoned, he realizes that Akira is long dead and his body preserved in the form of organ and tissue specimens. The military tries to reign in Tetsuo but cannot stop his ever-increasing power until he loses control over his body: He transforms into a monstrous giant baby, absorbing the debris and technology around him, before finally becoming an amorphous mass that threatens to destroy the city once again. In a last-ditch effort to stop the rampaging Tetsuo, Akira is resurrected, turning into a sphere of light that swallows up Tetsuo and the other children.

If one takes seriously Bruce Sterling's characterization of cyberpunk as "[a]n unholy alliance of the technical world and the world of organized dissent—the underground world of pop culture, visionary fluidity, and street-level anarchy" (Preface to *Mirrorshades* xii), *Akira* clearly veers to the side of anarchy, dissent, and 'punk,' using the technical world as mere window-dressing for its story about abuses of power and youth-cultural revolt. In *Akira*, it seems obvious that Sterling's "crazed and possibly dangerous" (xi) outlaw figures find their representation in Kaneda and his gang. Public discourse in Japan calls these biker gangs *bōsōzoku* (roughly translated as 'running out of control tribe' or 'violent speed tribe') and has originally seen them as a defiant subculture, "nothing more than night-time rebels" (Edwards 126). Andreas Riessland explains that *bōsōzoku* are "adolescents who engage in disruptive and dangerous conduct in traffic," and have existed since the 1950s, but their behavior became more aggressive, posing a "threat of physical violence" as a reaction against heavy-handed police action against street racing in the early 1970s ("Public Perception" 202–03).

In the film, we are introduced to the protagonists and their internal power dynamics via an early appearance of the iconic red motorcycle (present on the movie posters) belonging to Kaneda, when low-ranking member Tetsuo attempts to hot-wire the bike. Tetsuo sits on Kaneda's bike and recites its horsepower and impressive technical specifications, which sets up the bike as a central technological tool for empowerment and as a focal point of resistance against social expectations. Matthew Edwards suggests that adolescents joined *bōsōzoku* as an "outlet to escape their personal and family problems" (128), and with both Kaneda and Tetsuo being orphans in a restrictive foster system that does not expect them to amount to much, the membership in the gang seems to produce a counternarrative, "a loud call to arms against the well-ordered daily life" (Riessland, "*Bōsōzoku*" 212). Further, the bike itself can be understood as "an agent of change, a symbol of subversive flexibility against a monolithic and indifferent state" (Napier 41) in that it allows Kaneda and his gang to escape the stifling structures of social expectations set up by the school and foster system with literal movement. Early scenes show the bikes as kinetic, a force ripping through the city with colored, blurred energy lines following their swift motion through the "unmoving structure of power and authority, represented by the enormous massed buildings" (Napier 41).

For cyberpunk in the west, 'punk' was an attitude infusing the engagement with high-tech displayed in fiction, specifically the practice of hacking and appropriation of technology to counter its hegemonic use, but the original punk music scene was not intentionally included. Bruce Bethke famously coined the term because he was looking for a word combination that described technology and "socially misdirected youth," ending up with 'punk,' even though "*bōsōzoku* got really close to my concept—but there's no way to turn that into an English-language expression without making it sound silly. 'Cyberbozos?'" Instead, Bethke used 'punk' because "how the word *sounded* was extremely important" (emphasis in original). In Japan, though, the connection was not merely phonetic, but rather culturally relevant, connecting *bōsōzoku*, punk, and cyberpunk subcultures through the key influential films of Sogo Ishii. Ishii's *Crazy Thunder Road* (1980) and especially *Burst City* (1982) which encapsulate biker gangs and punk bands "in an eclectic mix of punk, industrialization and post-apocalyptic wasteland imagery," where the rabble eke out an existence in the refuse of the city, the films showing "Tokyo as little more than a concrete slum" (Player). In *Burst City*, the punks see their lifestyle threatened by a nuclear power plant and protest its construction through music performance as much as through fighting with the police as symbols of hegemony and industry. The juxtaposition of technological promise (nuclear power) and the reality of devastation in the city's wasteland open the film to punk interpretation, or what cultural critic Dick Hebdige, building on Claude Lévi-Strauss, refers to as *bricolage* (102).

In the context of punk aesthetics, *bricolage* refers to the intentional crossing of two layers of meaning, which Hebdige sees as an "anarchic mode" meant to "disrupt and reorganize meaning" (106). In *Burst City* as much as in *Akira*, the gloss and promise of technology stand in stark contrast to the realities of the inhabitants of the city. *Akira* opens to the destruction of Tokyo, only to then show a shiny, reconstructed Neo-Tokyo as the pinnacle of high-tech, full of potential and prosperity while the city prepares for the upcoming Olympics. For Kaneda and his crew running the old streets, however, most of Neo-Tokyo remains a wasteland and fails to fulfill its high-tech promise. As Le Blanc and Odell point out: "The holographic advertising hoardings are hollow representations of a thriving economy. This is superficial reconstruction" (31). The film's settings, the dirty alleyways, the shuttered shops, the run-down bar, the trash-littered school, and the continued construction around the destroyed crater signal *bricolage*, a shift in meaning that juxtaposes high tech with low life.

For Kaneda, success means taking what he needs and making it his own, appropriating it—a concept that is highlighted in the film, from his warping of the resistance fighter's plans to accommodate his own rescue mission to the stolen bike that he customizes. Kaneda makes his own street-use of anything he finds, especially prominent in his unblinking ability to commandeer weaponry and turn it against his attackers—either the small one-man aircraft in the tunnels of the government facility, or the battery-powered beam weapon he uses to defend against Tetsuo after conventional means have failed. When the batteries die during the first confrontation, he jury-rigs a motorcycle battery to recharge the weapon and use it again.

Moreover, the *bricolage* of punk and its destabilizing of meaning become even more prominent in Tetsuo, whose transformation toward the end of the film clearly evokes the cyborg's fusion of flesh and technology, man and machine. Tetsuo's transformation, though, is horrific and violent, akin to body horror's invasions and dismantling of the human body. His right arm is replaced after it has been bloodily severed by a laser blast; pieces of scrap, such as cables, screws, and other metal parts, levitate toward his shoulder and assemble into a shape resembling a human arm, albeit with a metallic, gray look with some junk and debris parts still identifiable. Through the violent absorption of the surrounding debris, Tetsuo's body becomes a "prosthetic and cyborgian body" (Tatsumi), over which he has little control. According to Zach Gottesman, this loss of control over his machinic body metaphorically represents the "chaotic capitalism" that Japan has engaged in and that the film symbolically destroys in its final scenes, as it cannot imagine an alternative to rampant capitalism, instead opting to showcase "its complete destruction and the apocalypse" (110).

This both contrasts with and is similar to popular western imaginings. On the one hand, the cyborg is also a product of late-capitalist strivings by corporations or the military, whose existence threatens and ultimately slips from their control. On the other hand, western cyberpunk sees the cyborg deliberately and strategically constructed by the capitalist entities themselves, mechanical and electronic prostheses fitted to replace limbs and providing enhanced functions, and metal chassis or imitation-skin obscuring the interior workings, as with Officer Murphy in *RoboCop* (Verhoeven 1987), Detective Spooner's arm in *I, Robot* (Proyas 2004), or Luke Skywalker's hand in *The Empire Strikes Back* (Kershner 1980).

As Player has argued for live-action film—using *Akira* as an animated precursor—Japanese cyberpunk owes a greater debt to body horror than to traditional science fiction (sf). The form is a "collision between flesh and metal, […] an explosion of sex, violence, concrete and machinery; […] post-human nightmares and teratological fetishes, powered by a boundaryless sense of invasiveness and violation." In this light, Tetsuo's transformation can be understood as a punkish *bricolage* reimagination of the cyborgian fantasy that technology represents the accumulation of power and control. Instead of helping Tetsuo to regain his human integrity (replacing a lost limb) and control his drug-induced psychic powers, the technology takes over, causing a feedback loop and sending his body into uncontrollable mutation. Napier sees the transformation as rebirth, "from ordinary human boy to monstrous creature to, perhaps, a new universe; in other words, from impotence to total power" (44), but it can also easily be read as "bodily mutation through technological intervention," which Player identifies as a major theme in Japanese cyberpunk. Thus, the transformation reveals Tetsuo as powerless to control the technology that threatens not just his bodily integrity but all of Neo-Tokyo. In the end, *Akira* evokes the cyberpunk trope of the cyborg, but reworks important characteristics common to western cyberpunk, such as the connected technological empowerment fantasy and its relation to high-tech capitalism, to conform with a uniquely Japanese imaginary. Considering *Akira* an entry in the cyberpunk mode, one thus has to rely on its embrace of punk in both its *bricolage* shifting of meaning (toward technology dismantling the human) and its aesthetics tending toward the discarded and disused.

Thus, what connects *Akira* with Mamoru Oshii's *Ghost in the Shell* (*Kōkaku Kidōtai*, literally 'armored mobile strike force'), aside from their important role in promoting Japanese anime in the west, is their "fundamental concern or even unease with the body and thus, implicitly, with identity itself," or more specifically with cyberpunk's "attempts to escape the body and thus the constraints of human identity" (Napier 115). But where *Akira* promotes the idea of a destructive invasion of the body through technology, *Ghost in the Shell* focuses on the potential inherent in cyborg technology and its posthuman reproduction.[2]

Oshii's adaptation of Masamune Shirow's manga of the same name (1989–91) focuses on Major Motoko Kusanagi, a cyborg assassin who works for the government agency Section 9, especially tasked with cybercriminality. Most of Section 9 (and many other people in the world of *Ghost in the Shell*) are cybernetically enhanced, most commonly with a 'cyberbrain,' an enhancement of the human brain that allows Internet-like data access and communications. Kusanagi is more extensively enhanced, though, as her entire body, with the exception of parts of her brain, is artificial, granting her superhuman reflexes and strength. Briefly, the plot revolves around Kusanagi's pursuit of the criminal 'Puppet Master' who hacks into people's cyberbrains to control their minds and bodies. For example, the Puppet Master can physically interact with the world through such human proxies as a garbage man or a petty criminal, hijacking their bodies and having them enact his will. When Section 9 finally gets hold of him, the Puppet Master turns out not to be a human at all but a sophisticated artificial intelligence (AI) created by Section 6, another branch of government developing the AI as part of a political scheme. The Puppet Master claims to have developed a consciousness—a 'ghost' or the equivalent of a human soul—which has escaped its creators through the data network and downloaded itself into a cybernetic body similar to Kusanagi's. When Section 6 reclaims their project, Kusanagi chases it down to secure the AI and confirm the existence of its ghost. The Puppet Master's ultimate goal, however, is to fuse with Kusanagi's mind—whom it sees as a kindred being—in order to develop into a higher form of being, both human and artificial. The film concludes with Kusanagi in a new body, declaring her new hybrid subjectivity (after merging with the Puppet Master) and expressing wonder as to what the future might hold.

In its depiction of a technologically enhanced posthuman society, *Ghost in the Shell* clearly comments on questions of subjectivity, negotiated through issues of embodiment, biological and technological, and thus on what Donna J. Haraway has called a "cyborg identity," complicating the "statuses of man or woman, human, artefact, member of race, individual entity, or body" (174, 178). Aside from its common language use—the cyborg as hybrid being of both machinic and organic parts—Sharalyn Orbaugh articulates the philosophical potential of Haraway's vision: "Speaking less literally, 'the cyborg' is a concept intended to represent a new paradigm of subjectivity, a new way for humans to understand themselves and their relationship to others and to their environment in the postmodern, post-industrial world of transnational capital" ("Genealogy" 55). She continues that cyborgs function to negotiate how "*human* subjectivity" becomes "'posthuman'" and, in Japanese anime especially, where "the limits of human subjectivity" lie ("Genealogy" 56, 58).

Major Kusanagi functions as the central cyborg figure undermining existing embodied categories—laid bare (pun intended) in the credit scene at the beginning which reveals Kusanagi's body as a constructed shell, crafted from both machinic and organic parts, neither merely born nor made, and neither coded as fully male or female. Even though the film highlights her body as "bare-breasted and big chested," as Joseph Christopher Schaub explains, the cyborg construction reveals "ambivalence towards the boundaries which separate masculinity and femininity" (90–91).[3] Kusanagi is cyborg in that, though superficially sexualized, both her body's capabilities and her function within the narrative frame her as male, as Orbaugh explains: "this body is under perfect control" and "the sexed body as reproductive body has no meaning in her cyborg state" (183–84). Kusanagi has no genitalia that would define her sexuality; she displays no intimacy and is solely defined by her cunning and ruthless precision at her job—killing people. She fully controls the actions of her body in minute detail because of its status as cyborg. Further, she is willing and able to discard her body, risking its destruction to ensure success—her cyborg status allowing her to be reborn in a new body, a variation on reproduction that foregoes "the interplay of repetition/sameness with diversity" of human childbirth and instead decouples cyborg subjectivity from embodiment: "The mechanical body [...] is replicable, but what is (re)produced is a facsimile of the previous one and has no reference to an organic 'original'" (Orbaugh, "Sex" 186).

One could thus argue that Kusanagi's (post)human subjectivity is her 'ghost,' which the film locates in the biological brain which controls the mechanical bodies. But Kusanagi questions her own subjectivity, wondering what constitutes it. She concludes that

> there's a remarkable number of things needed to make an individual what they are. A face to distinguish yourself from others. [...] The memories of childhood, the feelings for the future. That's not all. There's the expanse of the data net my cyber-brain can access. All of that goes into making me what I am. Giving rise to a consciousness that I call 'me.' And simultaneously confining 'me' within set limits.

Fixed identity through a specific embodiment seems limiting to Kusanagi, which is especially true as her body is constructed as a commodity, produced to specification by Section 9 and thus limited to its functionality as agent/assassin. Schaub argues that this capitalist commodification is central to Kusanagi's cyborg subjectivity as it "has completely eliminated [Kusanagi's] organic body and replaced it with a more dependable and manageable mechanical one. Yet her ghost expresses a humanistic desire for liberation" (93). This desire would require her to forego her cyborg identity, throwing into question an embodied subjectivity as she would "need to give the government back our cyborg shells… and all the memories they hold."

Complicating this desire is the fact that ghosts are not reliable indicators of subjectivity either. As the main storyline makes clear, the crime of the Puppet Master is his ability to hack into people's ghosts and implant memories and desires in order to create specific actions—eminently shown in the scene with the garbage man who remembers his little daughter vividly and would do anything for her, even though she is a 'virtual experience.' Realizing the implications of artificial ghosts, Kusanagi questions her own subjectivity further: "perhaps the real me died a long time ago… and I'm a replicant made with a cyborg body and computer brain. Or maybe there never was a real 'me' to begin with. […] And what if a computer brain could generate a ghost… and harbor a soul? On what basis then do I believe in myself?"

The film's central argument, then, follows from its ending and the offer for Kusanagi to join the Puppet Master in order to reach full existence as a lifeform, including death and reproduction—a limitation that is currently placed on both Kusanagi and the Puppet Master due to their cyborg embodiment. Kusanagi's and the Puppet Master's merging would mean posthuman reproduction, instead of mere replication/duplication, as well as death: "A mere copy doesn't offer variety or individuality. To exist, to reach equilibrium, life seeks to multiply… and vary constantly, at times giving up its life." In order for Kusanagi and the Puppet Master to create this "more satisfying form of identity and a new version of 'life'" (Napier 113), both old forms cease to exist. When Kusanagi later awakens in the body of a little girl, the transformation into a new 'life' is complete, her morphology signaling once more how cyborg identity subverts our expectations of embodiment in that she has clearly "left the 'childhood' of her cyborg subjectivity behind and achieved full subjectivity in the next stage of evolution" (Orbaugh, "Sex" 187). In Kusanagi's acceptance of the merging, the film realizes a truly posthuman form of subjectivity, thus rejecting the humanist individualism that stubbornly lingers in much of western cyberpunk. As Napier argues, "*Ghost* simply repudiates the constraints of the contemporary industrialized world to suggest that a union of technology and the spirit can ultimately succeed" (114). In evoking this union of technology and spirit, *Ghost in the Shell* provides a uniquely Japanese perspective on cyborg identity, one that embraces the possibility of hybrid existence, of giving up a tenuous self in order to be integrated into a larger network.

What has become clear, then, is that both *Akira* and *Ghost in the Shell* are indeed cyberpunk explorations of the relation of human and machine, but neither fully conforms to the standards and conventions of western cyberpunk. Instead, both films add a distinctly Japanese perspective to the discourse on posthuman subjectivities. *Akira* embraces Japanese cyberpunk's heritage in punk, anarchy, and body horror, ultimately rejecting technology as destructive and corrosive. By contrast, *Ghost in the Shell* argues for technology as another option for creating the necessary conditions for life and sees a cyborg identity as potential for a uniquely posthuman subjectivity. It thus becomes clear that both are important cyberpunk interventions into posthuman discourse and should be seen as Japanese key contributions to the mode.

Notes

1 For more on Japanese manga in cyberpunk, see Shige (CJ) Suzuki's entry in this collection.
2 See, for example, Orbaugh's "Sex and the Single Cyborg," notably pgs. 183–89.

3 *Ghost in the Shell*'s gender representations are controversial among critics. While Kusanagi may be able to transcend her mechanical shell, she is mostly shown in a sexualized, naked female form. Further, these female cyborg bodies are often destroyed and the film's gaze lingers on the shattered female form. Carl Silvio, for example, sees in the film's politics and story the potential for a liberatory reading of the cyborg, but argues that this is hampered by the cinematography and adherence to the male gaze. Similarly, Ryan J. Cox draws attention to the film's reliance upon the male gaze and its predilection to use "repeated images of naked and broken female cyborg bodies that collectively signal a looming threat of discorporation" (132). For more detail of this reading, see Cox; Silvio.

Works Cited

Bolton, Christopher. *Interpreting Anime*. U of Minnesota P, 2018.

Bethke, Bruce. "Question about Cyberpunk." Personal Email Exchange, 01 May 2018.

Cox, Ryan J. "Kusanagi's Body: Dualism and the Performance of Identity in *Ghost in the Shell* and *Stand Alone Complex*." *Cyberpunk and Visual Culture*, edited by Graham J. Murphy and Lars Schmeink. Routledge, 2018, pp. 127–38.

de la Iglesia, Martin. "Has *Akira* Always Been a Cyberpunk Comic?" *Arts*, vol. 7, 2018, pp. 1–13. doi:10.3390/arts7030032.

Edwards, Matthew. "Godspeed You! Black Emperor and the Japanese Underground Biker Phenomenon." *Film Out of Bounds: Essays and Interviews on Non-Mainstream Cinema Worldwide*, edited by Matthew Edwards. McFarland, 2007, pp. 126–34.

Gottesman, Zach. "Tetsuo and Marinetti: *Akira* as a cyberpunk critique of futurist modernity." *Journal of Japanese and Korean Cinema*, vol. 8, no. 2, 2016, pp. 104–26. doi:10.1080/17564905.2016.12211586.

Haraway, Donna J. "A Cyborg Manifesto: Science, Technology, and Socialist-Feminism in the Late Twentieth Century." *Simians, Cyborgs, and Women: The Reinvention of Nature*. Routledge, 1991, pp. 149–81.

Hebdige, Dick. *Subculture: The Meaning of Style*. Routledge, 1979.

Le Blanc, Michelle and Colin Odell. *Akira*. Palgrave Macmillan, 2014.

Napier, Susan J. *Anime from Akira to Howl's Moving Castle: Experiencing Contemporary Japanese Animation*. Macmillan, 2005.

Orbaugh, Sharalyn. "The Genealogy of the Cyborg in Japanese Popular Culture." *World Weavers, Globalization, Science Fiction, and Cybernetic Revolution*, edited by Wong Kin Yuen, Gary Westfahl, and Amy Kit-sze Chan. Hong Kong UP, 2005, pp. 55–72.

———. "Sex and the Single Cyborg: Japanese Popular Culture Experiments in Subjectivity." *Robot Ghosts and Wired Dreams: Japanese Science Fiction from Origins to Anime*, edited by Christopher Bolton, Istvan Csicsery-Ronay, and Takayuki Tatsumi. U of Minnesota P, 2007, pp. 172–92.

Player, Mark. "Post-Human Nightmares—The World of Japanese Cyberpunk Cinema." *Midnight Eye*, 13 May 2011, midnighteye.com/features/post-human-nightmares-the-world-of-japanesecyberpunk-cinema/.

Riessland, Andreas. "*Bōsōzoku*: Rückblick auf ein soziales Phänomen." *NOAG*, no. 187/188, 2011/12, pp. 211–30.

———. "The Public Perception of the *Bōsōzoku* in Japan." *Research Papers of the Anthropological Institute*, vol. 1, 2013, 201–16.

Saito, Kumiko. "Anime." *The Routledge Companion to Cyberpunk Culture*, edited by Anna McFarlane, Graham J. Murphy, and Lars Schmeink. Routledge, 2020, pp. 151–61.

Schaub, Joseph Christopher. "Kusanagi's Body: Gender and Technology in Mecha-anime." *Asian Journal of Communication*, vol. 11, no. 2, 2001, pp. 79–100.

Silvio, Carl. "Refiguring the Radical Cyborg in Mamoru Oshii's *Ghost in the Shell*." *Science Fiction Studies*, vol. 26, no. 1, 1999, pp. 54–72.

Sterling, Bruce. Preface. *Mirrorshades: The Cyberpunk Anthology*, edited by Bruce Sterling. Ace, 1986, pp. 11–14.

———. Preface. *Burning Chrome*, by William Gibson. Ace, 1986, pp. ix–xii.

Tatsumi, Takayuki. "Transpacific Cyberpunk: Transgeneric Interactions between Prose, Cinema, and Manga." *Arts*, vol. 7, 2018. doi:10.3390/arts7010009.

21

TELEVISION

Sherryl Vint

William Gibson's *Neuromancer* (1984) opens by observing, "The sky above the port was the color of television, tuned to a dead channel"; despite frequent citations of this line, however, television has not been central to cyberpunk culture. Yet, as William Gibson's evocative imagery conveys, early attempts to depict emerging cyber spaces frequently turned to television—the most influential, established mass medium at the time—to capture the transformations cyberspace promised.[1] Jean Baudrillard's contemporary work on hyperreality, for example, highlights television as a medium that collapses science-fictional icons and material experiences as it teaches us to invest our affective energies in life as modeled by its conventions. "The Ecstasy of Communication" suggests that television conflates production and consumption, and is "both receiver and distributor," its telematic power capable of "regulating everything from a distance, including work in the home and, of course, consumption, play, social relations and leisure" (198). Cyberpunk television theorizes the future of entertainment via communications media, reflecting on the social implications of what is broadcast and who controls the means of distribution. Cyberpunk television is thus a site of anxiety about the future of the medium itself, as it anticipates its possible replacement by new modes of entertainment.

Surveying live-action cyberpunk television from the 1980s to the present, this chapter explores how these texts spoke to concerns relevant to their original conditions of production, and how cyberpunk television has changed alongside a changing technological environment.[2] I group texts into four patterns of themes that characterize television's engagement with cyberpunk: depictions of virtual reality (VR) as a space for the expression of the subconscious and dreams, which often intersect with gaming culture; explorations of mediated reality, which are often concerned with blurring representation and materiality, and thematically address surveillance and social media; representations of posthuman characters who are increasingly understood as analogs to machines, which interrogate the perfectibility of the human through technology; and portrayals of economic inequality and struggle, which understand cyberspace as *"the place where your money lives"* (Jones 94) and neoliberalism as the ground upon which our present reality, as a cyberpunk analog, unfolds.

To a degree, these themes emerge chronologically as I have listed them here, with the earliest depictions understanding cyberspace largely as a symbol of unconscious thought, while the most recent depictions focus more on cyberspace as a realm of economic exchange. This list therefore reveals how the imaginary of cyberpunk television has changed alongside a changing digital culture, easily pegged to the prevalence of other contemporary technologies of mediated entertainment; the earliest series respond to the rise of videogame culture and personal computers, while the more recent focus on the influence of social media on daily life. Nonetheless, each category has a historical range that includes a fairly recent text, suggesting that these four motifs persist, even as they are reimagined in line with more recent technology. Most are united by an interest in how imaginative spaces might enable embodied experience through technology; yet, I argue that the most important texts are those in the final category, which focus less on how our entertainment media have changed with digital culture, and more on the future of vast inequality that is one of the images that defines cyberpunk. Cyberpunk television ultimately tells us that its most important legacy is that it gives us tools and concepts to understand neoliberalism and the financialized economy. If criticism of early cyberpunk culture reminded us of the importance of embodiment, to which the hacker/cowboy must always return, more recent cyberpunk insists that the economic abstractions of frictionless capital flow similarly find their real meaning in the material effects they have for those who live within the vast economic inequality that they create.[3]

Television is an intimate medium: part of our quotidian routines, a resource for forming our social identities, and a space of affective engagement—qualities that characterize interactions mediated by online culture as well.[4] Early cyberpunk television envisioned cyberspace as an extension of itself that could be personalized, combining the affective proximity of television with the interactivity of nascent videogames. In the U.S., cyberpunk televisual texts appeared about the same time television was changing, in response to the emergence of home computers and devices such as VCRs. Such changes transformed the medium from its formulaic, episodic structure, and rigid timetable into the season-long narrative arcs and on-demand viewing options that we now expect. The emergence of Fox in 1986, challenging the hegemony of ABC, NBC, and CBS, was only the first of increasingly specialized channels that appeared, leading to the present in which online content providers, such as YouTube and Vimeo, or streaming services, such as Netflix and Hulu, compete with established networks. It is not surprising, then, that early cyberpunk television often envisioned a future of transformed television.

The earliest cyberpunk also tended to represent cyberspace as a medium that could embody our dreams and desires in 3D. One of the most recognizable series, *VR.5* (1995), featured Sydney Bloom (Lori Singer), a phone company employee who hacks people's subconscious through a modem. The title refers to Sydney's innovation of a new level of immersive reality (VR levels 1–4 are Computer Screens, Interactive Videogames, Flight Simulators, and Cyberspace). Sydney enters a realm created by the subconscious mind of anyone who answers the phone she then connects to her modem. The episodes built toward a conspiracy theory related to her father's VR research and a nefarious Committee who sought to control it, but the show's success was hampered by the fact that three of its thirteen episodes did not air during the original run. It is mainly notable for introducing to television the idea that cyberspace is a realm of the subconscious, and for featuring a female hacker knowledgeable about IT hardware.

The most ambitious early text was Oliver Stone's mini-series *Wild Palms* (1993), which depicted a future 2007 of television fused with VR and featured a cameo by Gibson himself. Notable for its surrealist sequences, the series combined scenes drawn from the dreams/hallucinations of protagonist Harry Wyckoff (James Belushi)—chiefly of a rhinoceros in an empty LA swimming pool—with a narrative about media controlling the future through Church Windows, a technology that projects television as 3D holograms into the home, fully immersing viewers. An advertisement for its release in episode 1 proclaims, "They said the revolution wouldn't be televised. They were wrong. Church Windows. Coming this fall." Any critical edge, however, is dulled under the weight of the thriller plot that involves antagonist Senator Anton Kreutzer (Robert Loggia), founder of a self-help sect called Synthiotics (clearly satirizing Scientology), kidnapped children, and shock revelations about paternity. Kreutzer controls television Network 3 and plans to use Church Windows to control the populace, drawing on contemporary fears that television undermined the public sphere and extrapolating them into a new and potentially even more addictive medium.[5]

Wild Palms envisions Church Windows as a way media conglomerates might blur virtual and material realities, all the better to keep the populace quiescent and turn democracy into a hollow game. Drawing equally on film noir and *Videodrome* (Cronenberg 1983), the series interrogates the dangers of too fully immersing ourselves into mediated realities and warns against the addictive qualities of such entertainments. Joss Whedon's more recent *Dollhouse* (2009–10), with its dystopian version of Gibson's simstim, suggests that these concerns remain. It warns against the callousness that comes from spending too much time interacting with entities you do not regard as fully people. The main characters are "actives"—people who have agreed (often under duress) to work for five-year terms as programmable bodies for the Rossum Corporation. The series critiques Rossum's more sinister plans to use this entertainment media for the elite as a way of shaping reality to its own ends. A pivotal episode, "Man on the Street," explicitly draws connections between the actives and other exploited laborers, and further suggests that consumers are as programmed by the media they consume as are the actives by Rossum.[6] *Dollhouse* refuses a clear line between virtual and material spaces, insisting that what we desire and express in simulation has material, ethical consequences.

Most recently, *Reverie* (2018) features Mara Kint (Sarah Shahi), a former hostage negotiator, who joins a media corporation that offers immersive VR experience. An AI creates a narrative for clients, based on fantasy parameters and other data, and technological implants substitute this sensory data for material experience. Kint's job is to enter this simulation to convince a subset of clients who become comatose that the real world is preferable to remaining in their fantasy. This series suggests that narratives of cyberspace immersion no longer require the typical cyberpunk motifs of sinister corporations or hacker protagonists. Contemporary gaming culture and the risks of gaming addiction, rather than futuristic dystopias and the effects of mass media such as television, form its backdrop. In the trajectory from *VR.5* to *Reverie*, we have also moved from explicitly futuristic series concerned with how technology will *change* social life, to a series that might be better categorized as a workplace drama, exploring a world in which immersive experiences are a quotidian part of life.

The second group of texts understands cyberspace instead as the precursor of social media technologies. AI systems are prevalent, but they quickly shift from the transcendent, quasi-spiritual entities of early cyberpunk to analogs of now-familiar, machine-learning apps. This category includes the crucial series *Max Headroom* (1987–88), adapted from an eponymous British film.[7] Well ahead of its time, *Max Headroom* takes its title from its AI protagonist, an entity that emerges when the president of television Network 23 attempts to create a controllable, computer copy of popular online investigative journalist Edison Carter (Matt Frewer). In the pilot, Carter tries to uncover Network 23's use of direct-to-brain advertising, blipverts, that have proven lethal to some consumers. Set "twenty minutes into the future," *Max Headroom* uses an episodic structure to explore various dystopian aspects of this future. Max and Carter become an investigative team, with Max often sent into other network systems to discover hidden information, and both offer online reports to the public. Max is more whimsical and less diplomatic than Carter. His image is a blocky, pixelated approximation of Carter's head, and Max speaks in a stuttered, non-naturalistic tone. These markers of artificiality enable Max to more bluntly articulate his social critique. The series' aesthetics include quick cuts, shaky, hand-held camera movements that evoke the "live-ness" of Carter's on-site reporting, and other flashy visuals associated with then-new network MTV.

Max Headroom is set in a future that epitomizes the urban blight prevalent in cyberpunk. Many episodes comment on manipulative mass media, such as the blipverts. In "Blanks," Carter investigates people without civil rights, because they lack identity implants, and electro-democracy, in which polling data, ratings, and electoral results are conflated. "Academy" explores commodified education, where underground revolutionaries pirate the IP of educational television channels to offer accessible training to the impoverished. "Neurostim" considers the addictive qualities of a projective technology that stimulates the economy by implanting customers' perfect lives into their imaginations, along with a drive to materialize it no matter the cost. Contra contemporary discourse that envisioned the Internet as a space of direct democracy, extended access to the means of media production, and individual freedom, *Max Headroom* reminds us that this new information highway is regulated by corporate interests that privilege profit over the public sphere (cf. Rheingold). Television's mediation of its own future is evident in the recurrent rivalry between Network 23, with its commitment to journalism and truth, and Network 66, envisioned as a Boardroom of executives who innovate technologies aimed at controlling and directing the population through broadcast signals.

This interest in how virtual realms might distort or hide the truth and thereby undermine democracy provides a link between cyberpunk and the most influential sf series of the 1990s, *The X-Files* (1993–2002). "Wetwired," written by creator Chris Carter, echoes the concern that mediated realities might control our thinking, but instead of being a television show that imagines a new technology as it interrogates its own conditions of production, in this episode television itself hacks the human brain with its viral signal.[8] The rebooted *The X-Files* (2016–18) reveals a distinct 21st-century imaginary set around AI, technology, and mediation that shows, via contrast with the original episodes, how much our attitudes have been changed by the emergence of social media. In "This," agents Fox Mulder (David Duchovny) and Dana Scully (Gillian Anderson) are briefly reunited with a virtual version of conspiracy theorist Richard Langly (Dean Haglund), who has been kept alive in an artificial reality as part of a secret government think tank. Despite the hedonism of this life, he resents the never-ending extraction of his labor as a think-tank resource and longs for escape from simulation. As Mulder and Scully investigate, they discover that the X-Files themselves have been digitized by a Russian subcontractor to the DoD and scrubbed of certain data. Once an archive of 'The Truth' Mulder and Scully painstakingly uncovered, these files have become as ephemeral as the latest software release. The familiar series tagline shifts in this episode from "The Truth is Out There" to "Accuse Your Enemies of That Which You Are Guilty."

Many other episodes in the rebooted series similarly play with the tagline to chart a changed media context. "My Struggle III," which opens with scenes of recent news footage contextualized as the work of Cancer Man (William B. Davies), transforms "I Want to Believe" to "I Want to Lie" as certain letters fade. More light-heartedly, "The Lost Art of Forehead Sweat" channels *The Twilight Zone* (1959–64) as it outlines a conspiracy in which Scully and Mulder once had a third partner, Reggie Something (Brian Huskey). This history, and everyone's memories of the truth, seems to have been erased—or perhaps Reginald is mentally ill: One can no longer discern. Mulder confesses that reality has become too much for even a committed conspiracy theorist like himself: "all I've done the past year is watch the news and worry this country has gone insane," he tells Scully. Later, meeting with the infamous Dr. They—the origin of all conspiracy discourse which begins "they say"—Mulder is confronted with the irrelevance of his quest for the truth: "We are now living in the post-cover-up, post-conspiracy age," he is told, and it no longer matters if the truth gets out, because the public can no longer differentiate real from fake.

It is clear that this satire is directed at Trump's post-truth America, including comments about inauguration crowd size, but humor is mixed with important observations about how online news sources and closed, niche media bubbles have damaged democracy. The un-monitored proliferation of media sources, not their centralized control through a new medium, proved the real threat to public discourse. Although not cyberpunk in its aesthetics, "This" offers a chilling analysis of one of the most consequential effects of networked technologies, showing how distributed and individualized media have created a crisis in American democracy that is both direr and more difficult to depict than the dystopian future anticipated by texts such as *Wild Palms*. More banal than the harsh future portrayed by *Max Headroom*, the new *X-Files* envisions our present media

Television

environment as evidence that cyberpunk was right to worry about online-only communication, if not quite as envisioned by its first generation.

Black Mirror (2011–), whose title refers to the black screens of media devices in which we find and reflect our identities, can thus be understood as cyberpunk. Its aesthetics are often far from the edgy, outsider-hacker ethos associated with this term, but its themes interrogate how technology mediates daily life. For example, "Fifteen Million Merits" satirizes a future in which "reality tv" becomes the horizon of expectations for upward mobility, savagely ending with a vision of even heartfelt critique turning into a performance for ratings. "Be Right Back" demonstrates how self-in-social-media is a pale reflection of true human complexity, in its tale of a woman who recreates an AI version of her dead husband from his postings. "Nosedive" imagines a future in which every human encounter is rated on an app and one's cumulative score of "likes" or "dislikes" has consequences for employment, housing, and other elements of daily life, a version of social media granted the sorting power of the credit score to enable or constrain choice.

As *Black Mirror* demonstrates, themes that were once the domain of cyberpunk no longer seem as science-fictional. Cyberspace is no longer a separate realm but the environment we inhabit daily through our phones. Series such as *Person of Interest* (2011–16), about a military AI designed to anticipate and prevent violence, or *Halt and Catch Fire* (2014–17), a period show about the 1980s and 1990s innovations that led to personal computers and the Internet, are thus part of a cyberpunk tradition no longer set in estranged, futuristic worlds. Like the new *X-Files* and *Black Mirror*, they show us that the world both anticipated and informed by cyberpunk is all around us. Given that social media technologies are widely used, unlike early gaming and personal computers, cyberpunk television about what the virtual shares with the material has strong thematic connections with traditional cyberpunk but it eschews the estranged setting and outsider characters that were once hallmarks of the genre.

In contrast, the third category, series about posthumans, retains an sf orientation: humans merging with IT machines or hacking their genome. *Automan* (1983–84), inspired by *TRON* (Lisberger 1982), is the earliest cyberpunk television, although it is more cyber than punk. Walter Nebicher (Desi Arnez Jr.), insufficiently masculine for physical police work but determined to revolutionize the LAPD via IT investigations, creates the Automan program, which manifests a hologram of its eponymous muscle-bound hero (Chuck Wagner), as well as a blinking cursor that materializes any vehicle they need. Lit by TRON's neon aesthetic, Automan solves crimes through his ability to navigate material space with the speed and flexibility of action of a video game, although he can also physically interact with material space as if he were solid when required. Fully identified with law enforcement, *Automan* inaugurates a pattern other posthuman series follow. *Intelligence* (2014), about a navy seal with a computer chip in his head who can access any data (Internet, cellular, satellite), is an updated version. Protagonist Gabriel (Josh Holloway) is touted as "this generation's Manhattan Project," designed to counter cybersecurity threats. He has all the speed and data access of an AI, but can process as only a human imagination can, allowing insights that pure data crunching cannot yield. Similarly centered on law enforcement, *Almost Human* (2013–14) imagines a police officer with an artificial leg (Karl Urban) partnered with an android capable of emotion (Michael Ealy). They investigate the sorts of crimes one expects of dark, cyberpunk futures—organ theft, hacking of media devices, murder streamed online—as both struggle with what it means to be simultaneously human and machine.

James Cameron's *Dark Angel* (2000–02) is more punk than cyber, marking a shift since the 1990s also seen in print culture toward texts focusing more on biological than computer hacking.[9] *Dark Angel* shares themes with cyberpunk texts concerning information control. Set in 2019 in a Seattle devastated by an EMP pulse that destroyed records and deepened economic disparity, it features transgenic soldier Max (Jessica Alba), created by the secret government project Manticore, from which she escaped as a child. Max becomes involved with cyber-journalist

173

Logan (Michael Weatherly), who broadcasts—via cable tv—the anonymous Eyes Only media report that exposes corruption. The series focused on uncovering truths about Manticore and is notable for its themes about diversity, especially in season 2.

Altered Carbon (2018), adapted from Richard K. Morgan's eponymous novel (2002), is more firmly rooted in cyberpunk. People store their selves on disks called stacks and regularly "resleeve" into new bodies as the situation demands and economic resources allow. This technology enables immortality for the wealthy, near-instantaneous interstellar travel—the self is "beamed" elsewhere—and brutal warfare and torture, since soldiers and victims may be rebooted multiple times. The novel explicitly critiques cyberpunk's famed contempt for the body by foregrounding the psychological costs of this lifestyle and castigates the decadence of a social class able to maintain its privilege for generations. The television adaptation keeps much of the plot, but critique is muted by a focus on protagonist Kovacs, pitting his integrity against elite corruption. A minor subplot about religious purists who refuse to resleeve is more central in the series, and its world is beautifully rendered with aesthetics that mimic *Blade Runner* (Scott 1982). During the time between the novel's publication and this adaptation, the culture of transhumanists who seek to transfer their minds to new bodies has moved from the fringes toward the mainstream, now promoted by well-funded groups such as humanity+. The future *Altered Carbon* envisions, then, is both science-fictional and plausible, for some. Although set hundreds of years into the future, like the novel, the adaptation depicts a world that has since become familiar, in part due to the prevalence of cyberpunk-influenced films whose aesthetics inform the series. Moreover, ideas such as mind-uploading and other human augmentation have similarly become normalized by a milieu in which things such as self-driving cars or smart AI assistants that respond to voice commands have created a perception that futures envisioned by yesterday's sf seem destined to become our futures.

Despite the appeal of such high-tech futures, however, the most important way the future anticipated by 1980s cyberpunk has manifested is via contemporary economic policies of deregulation and privatization. Thus, my last category of texts—those engaged with how neoliberalism has colonized social life with capitalist values of productivity, economic growth, and individualized achievement over social stability—express cyberpunk's most important legacy, even if they least resemble cyberpunk aesthetics. Information technology is not as central to these texts, but they ably depict the "deranged experiment in Social Darwinism" (Gibson 9) that is the quintessential cyberpunk future. *Incorporated* (2016), most clearly sf, is set in a future run by corporations, a response to climate change. The world is divided into green, protected zones of corporate employees, segregated by class, and red zones outside these gated communities, run by violent gangs. Overheard media reports sketch in a world of extreme weather, anti-globalization "terrorists" fighting for access to water, and fascist corporate militia who eliminate anyone who fails to adhere to the corporate ideology. The narrative focuses on Monsanto-like Spiga Corporation, which viciously defends its IP in terminator seeds, despite starvation; deploys software called EverClear to evaluate people's thoughts and dreams; dispatches a corporate army to maintain private ownership of resources; and manipulates election results. This is a future of either obnoxious privilege or complete precarity.

Protagonist Ben (Sean Teale) is a double agent. Secretly from the climate refugee camps, he fabricates a corporate ID and works his way up, all to recover his girlfriend, Elena (Denyse Tontz), taken as a corporate prostitute. Elena agreed to this service to reduce her father's sentence to Debtors Extraction Prison: He is forced to work and is remunerated, but is charged interest, as well as room and board, and so his sentence inevitably grows. Clearly remixing cyberpunk images of future corporate control, the series shows a variety of now-common corporate practices exaggerated to dystopian extremes: NDA agreements involve a technology that wipes a former employee's memories; tap water sells for almost $6 a glass; research scientists have "kill switch" DNA implanted to prevent "defection" to another corporation; and service providers, including healthcare, make it clear that their priority is to protect intellectual property above all else. As in Bradbury's *Fahrenheit 451* (1953), firemen start fires—here not to fight intellectual subversion but for lack of debt repayment. Episode titles, such as "Downsizing," "Cost Containment," and "Profit and Loss," reinforce that economic structures, not technological innovations, are the reason the future is so bleak. *Incorporated* is recognizable as cyberpunk, but it shifts the focus from technological change toward neoliberal ideology.

From this point of view of privileging economic themes, we can see that *Profit* (1996–97), a neglected series that anticipated the post-2008 interest in financial cultures, has a tangential relationship to cyberpunk.[10] A variation of *The Count of Monte Cristo*, it follows sociopath Jim Profit (Adrian Pasdar), who was abused by his parents and spent his childhood in a packing box from Gracen & Gracen Corporation, interacting with the outside world only through a window cut out for him to watch television. Rising from poverty, he invents his adult name and embodies the callous disregard of human consequences that epitomizes a shareholder-driven focus on profit above all else. Gracen & Gracen anticipates dot-com corporation Amazon in the sense that it sells and makes everything, a mirror for Profit's own absolute ambition. Profit spends time in a secret room in his apartment in front of his computer screen planning how he will eliminate his rivals, and primitive online graphics render the action as he imagines his victories, but hacking skills are not core to his success. *Profit* is important as an early series focused on an anti-hero and for its critique of financial culture.

The most important contemporary cyberpunk television is *Mr. Robot* (2016–). Arguably not sf, it features hacker Elliot Alderson (Rami Malek), a cyber-Robin-Hood figure, who hacks and destroys corporations that damage the lives and futures of ordinary citizens. Elliot's main target is ECorp, an apparent analog for Google's parent company Alphabet, that has divisions that provide everything from banking to hardware. The series refers to this corporation by Elliot's preferred moniker, Evil Corp, for its roles in covering up toxic manufacturing leaks and profiting from massive consumer indebtedness. Elliot's hacking aims to delete records, thus short-circuiting a cycle of turning debts into investment assets, the practice that caused the 2008 economic crash, whose social costs have been documented by David Graeber, Benjamin Lee, Edward LiPuma, and Maurizio Lazzarato, among others. *Mr. Robot* is meticulous in its portrayal of hacking, another cyberpunk element, showing Elliot's steps to encode or decode a message, or screens with the DOS commands required to execute specific functions.

Many televisual cyberpunk texts are set in worlds of starkly contrasted privilege and deprivation, and *Mr. Robot* shows us the seeds of such futures in our present. It insists that financial deregulation and a neoliberal ethos that reduces all values to the economic bottom line create this future. The risk is no longer that we mistake virtual fantasies for our realities, or that we fuse with our machines and become less human in the process. Rather, cyberpunk today manifests in our present as the logic of economic abstractions, speculations, and derivatives created by the market—without thought to how the outcomes of such bets will manifest in the concrete realities of life for other people. By season 2, after Elliot destroys ECorp's financial records, we see that, even then, those with power and privilege can isolate themselves from the worst consequences, insisting on a cash economy while hoarding the currency they control, and planning to release a cryptocurrency, Ecoin, to become the global standard in place of the U.S. dollar.

The economic future of digital currency also proves to be far from the punk (and libertarian) ethos imagined by cypherpunk enthusiasts in the 1990s.[11] In *Mr. Robot*'s version, we simply substitute corporate control for government control, perhaps the most prescient element of the cyberpunk formula. However, Elliot and his fsociety group, a nod to Anonymous, are distinct from cyberpunk hackers. While the cyberpunk cowboys were individualist and moved seamlessly through neon-lit adventures on data runs, fsociety aims at *collective* social transformation through economic restructuring, not their own profit. Far from bodiless, they frequently have to take risks to achieve physical proximity to something they want to hack—Elliot's infiltration of the Stone Mountain data storage facility, or non-hacker Angela's (Portia Doubleday) painstaking memorization of lines of code to hack the FBI. *Mr. Robot*'s critique of the widespread devastation caused by financialization, even to those who do not invest in the stock market, is a far more compelling comment on the social present than was the revolutionary rhetoric attached to print cyberpunk. This is not the vision of the dangerous urban center as imagined by middle-class suburbanites in the 1990s, but a plea against the relentless economic inequality that Thomas Piketty has promised will only continue to worsen, unless we find a way to counter the power of historically amassed capital.

Mr. Robot, as the key cyberpunk inheritor of the 21st century, makes painfully clear that the point was always our subsumption under finance capital, not our fusion with intelligent machines. From this perspective, I want to suggest one more almost-cyberpunk text that captures the mode's 21st-century realities and their distance from 20th-century fantasies, *McMafia* (2018–). A crime series about an international banker who becomes embroiled in transnational conflicts over the use of investment funds to launder drug and other illicit money, *McMafia* is relevant in this context for one reason: Although the television adaptation is a potboiler focused on a family of Russia mafia, the source text, by Misha Glenny, is a work of investigative journalism. Glenny's work is about how financial deregulation, in the wake of the fall of the Soviet Empire, enabled organized crime to take control of formerly second-world emerging markets and to profit—via the immiseration of people—from global trade in assets, resources, and desperate workers. This source text leaves no doubt that the reason we now live in a world that resembles cyberpunk is not that technology has enabled cyberspace experiences but rather that global capital has enabled neoliberal values to colonize all of social life.

Notes

1 David Cronenberg's *Videodrome* (1983) is the supreme expression, to borrow from Jameson, of metaphorizing television in this way, as is ably analyzed by Scott Bukatman's important *Terminal Identity*.
2 The scope of this chapter is limited to live-action television as Kumiko Saito's chapter in this volume addresses anime, which is one of the main televisual sites of cyberpunk themes.
3 Hugh O'Connell's argument that cyberpunk was always "fiscalmancy" informs my view that the texts dealing with the financialized economy are the most important cyberpunk television. See his entry on "Cyberpunk and Marxism" in this collection for added detail.
4 Marshall McLuhan argues that television is a "cool" medium, requiring interaction from its viewers, given its low resolution relative to film. In our present media culture of streaming content, when films and television are frequently watched on the same screens, these distinctions are not as significant (see Lotz). Early cyberpunk visuals to current immersive media follow a similar trajectory.
5 Neil Postman in *Amusing Ourselves to Death* formulated the most influential expression of this idea, which is also implicit in Baudrillard's critique, cited earlier.
6 The corporation's name, of course, alludes to Karel Čapek's *R.U.R.* (1920) and its themes about the capitalist desire for dehumanized, disposable labor.
7 For more on the film *Max Headroom: Twenty Minutes into the Future*, see Scott Roger's Case Study chapter in this volume.
8 Carter also created *Harsh Realm* (1999–2000), about a wargames simulation that takes on a life of its own, set almost entirely in VR. It is notable as the only cyberpunk series to use war as its setting, an important theme in cyberpunk film (see Vint) and one of the most prevalent scenarios in gaming culture.
9 See Lars Schmeink's entry on Biopunk in this volume for more on this shift.
10 For example, *Billions* (2016–) and *Succession* (2018–) take economic activity as their central engine, while *Damnation* (2017–18) is a historical drama that sides with miners and farmers over Pinkerton strike breakers. There is also increasingly a scholarly interest in representations of financial culture (see Haiven, Joseph, La Berge, Marsh, and McClanahan).
11 Cypherpunks, who take their name from cyberpunk, advocated for online cryptography and privacy-enhancing software, which they felt would lead to greater political and social freedom, organized through online means. Their online discussion forum played a significant role in the creation of Bitcoin.

Television

Works Cited

Almost Human. Created by J.H. Wyman, Frequency Films/Bad Robot/Warner Bros. Television, 2013–14.

Altered Carbon. Created by Laeta Kalogridis, Mythology Entertainment/Monkey Massacre, 2018.

Automan. Created by Glen A. Larson, Glen A. Larson Productions/The Kushner-Locke Company/20th Century Fox Television, 1983–84.

Baudrillard, Jean. "The Ecstasy of Communication." [1988] *Science Fiction and Cultural Theory: A Reader,* edited by Sherryl Vint. Routledge, 2015, pp. 194–99.

Black Mirror. Created by Charlie Brooker, Zeppotron/Channel 4 Television Corporation/Gran Babieka, 2011–.

Bukatman, Scott. *Terminal Identity: The Virtual Subject in Postmodern Science Fiction.* Duke UP, 1993.

Dark Angel. Created by James Cameron and Charles H. Eglee, Cameron/Eglee Productions/20th Century Fox Television, 2000–02.

Dollhouse. Created by Joss Whedon, 20th Century Fox/Boston Diva Productions, 2009–10.

Gibson, William. *Neuromancer.* Ace Books, 1984.

Glenny, Misha. *McMafia: A Journey Through the Global Criminal Underworld.* Vintage Books, 2008.

Graeber, David. *Debt: The First 5000 Years.* Melville Publishing House, 2011.

Haiven, Max. *Cultures of Financialization: Fictitious Capital in Popular Culture and Everyday Life.* Palgrave Macmillan, 2014.

Halt and Catch Fire. Created by Christopher Cantwell and Christopher C. Rogers, AMC Studios, 2014–17.

Incorporated. Created by David Pastor and Àlex Pastor, Algorithm Entertainment/CBS Television Studios/Pearl Street Films, 2016–17.

Intelligence. Created by Michael Seitzman, Michael Seitzman's Pictures/Tripp Vinson Productions/CBS Television Studios/ABC Studios, 2014.

Jones, Gwyneth. "Trouble (Living in the Machine)." *Deconstructing the Starships: Science, Fiction and Reality.* Liverpool UP, 1999, pp. 91–98.

Joseph, Miranda. *Debt to Society: Accounting for Life Under Capitalism.* U of Minnesota P, 2014.

La Berge, Leigh Claire. *Scandals and Abstractions: Financial Fiction of the Long 1980s.* Oxford UP, 2014.

Lazzarato, Maurizio. *The Making of Indebted Man: An Essay on the Neoliberal Condition,* translated by Joshua David Jordan. Semiotexts, 2012.

Lee, Benjamin and Edward LiPuma. *Financial Derivatives and the Globalization of Risk.* Duke UP, 2004.

Lotz, Amanda. *The Television Will Be Revolutionized,* 2nd Ed. NYU Press, 2014.

Marsh, Nicky. *Money, Speculation and Finance in Contemporary British Fiction.* Continuum, 2008.

Max Headroom. Chrysalis/Lakeside/Lorimar Productions, 1987–88.

McClanahan, Annie. *Dead Pledges: Debt, Crisis, and Twenty-First Century Culture.* Stanford UP, 2018.

McLuhan, Marshall. *Understanding Media: The Extensions of Man.* [1964] MIT Press, 1994.

McMafia. Created by Hossein Amini and James Watkins, Cuba Pictures/British Broadcasting Corporation/American Movie Classics/Twickenham Studios, 2018–.

Mr. Robot. Created by Sam Esmail, Anonymous Content/Esmail Corp./Universal Cable Productions, 2015–19.

Person of Interest. Created by Jonathan Nolan, Kilter Films/Bad Robot/Warner Bros. Television, 2011–16.

Picketty, Thomas. *Capital in the Twenty-First Century,* translated by Arthur Goldhammer. Harvard UP, 2014.

Postman, Neil. *Amusing Ourselves to Death: Public Discourse in the Age of Show Business.* Penguin, 1985.

Profit. Created by David Greenwalt and John McNamara, New World Television/Stephen J. Cannell Productions, 1996.

Rheingold, Howard. *The Virtual Community: Homesteading on the Electronic Frontier,* revised edition. MIT Press, 2000.

The X-Files. Created by Chris Carter, Ten Thirteen Productions/20th Century Fox Television/X-F Productions, 1993–2001; 2016–18.

Vint, Sherryl. "Cyberwar: The Convergence of Virtual and Material Battlefields in Cyberpunk Cinema." *Cyberpunk and Visual Culture,* edited by Graham J. Murphy and Lars Schmeink. Routledge, 2018, pp. 253–75.

VR.5. Created by Jeannine Renshaw, Samoset Productions, 1995.

Wild Palms. Created by Bruce Wagner, American Broadcasting Company (ABC)/Greengrass Productions/Ixtlan, 1993.

22

MAX HEADROOM: TWENTY MINUTES INTO THE FUTURE (CASE STUDY)

Scott Rogers

As a character, Max Headroom is most famous for the American television series *Max Headroom*, which aired on ABC between March 1987 and May 1988 and starred Matt Frewer as both Edison Carter, an investigative reporter, and Max Headroom, a computer-generated artificial intelligence (AI) parody of a television host. The series broke ground in many ways.[1] Conceptually, it was a striking critique of know-nothing television presenters. The elaborate makeup that rendered Frewer as a computer-generated version of himself was, if not unprecedented, then sufficiently rare in the late 1980s to make its appearance remarkable. The show also renders Max's head and shoulders against a seemingly CGI image of rotating digital bars, which heightens the sense that Max is someone both human and not, 'real' and 'artificial.' Finally, Max's stuttering, glitchy, digitally filtered voice, coupled with his hyperbolic and yet quite human personality, made for a viewing experience quite unlike almost anything else on the air in the mid-1980s.

In spite of his popularity in America, including his television show, commercials, and heavy rotation on MTV thanks to the "Paranoimia" video by English synth-pop group Art of Noise, Max Headroom debuted in *Max Headroom: Twenty Minutes into the Future*, which aired on UK's BBC Channel 4 in April of 1985, which was then later refilmed as the first episode of the U.S. TV show.[1] Lili Berko reads the film as an example of a "high concept image," which is "an image [that] is propped upon a postmodern aesthetic which insists upon the primacy of the image, an image which refuses to identify itself as sign, rejecting the traditional dichotomy between signified and signifier, image and concept" (52). Similarly, William Wees writes that the film "displays a distinctly postmodernist conception of the video image" (29) and that the character is "an image of nothing other than the image-generating systems that produced him" (34).

The film depicts a near-future in a country under the thumb of a group of media companies who are deploying a new form of advertising called 'blipverts,' which are potentially fatal to some viewers. The protagonist, intrepid investigative journalist Edison Carter, discovers that his own employer, Network 23, is responsible for these blipverts, and is critically injured while trying to reveal the truth. Unfortunately for the network, Carter is a popular television figure, and his disappearance could lead to inquiries and a ratings decline. Their solution is to map his brain onto a computer and broadcast a CGI version of Edison Carter, under the impression that no one will notice, but the transfer of Edison's mind fails, and the CGI Edison simply repeats 'max headroom' over and over. Deemed a failure, the technological genius behind the procedure, Bryce Lynch (Paul Spurrier), orders both the CGI Edison and the injured body of Edison be destroyed. Instead of destroying them, however, both Carters are taken to a pirate television station run by Blank Reg (Morgan Sheppard), who manages to fix the CGI Edison, which provides his station with a massive ratings boost. This is the birth of Max Headroom. With Max's help, Edison and his comrades are able to expose Network 23's corruption.

Even the broadest outlines of the film's plot clearly mark it as an example of mid-1980s cyberpunk. The film features a "generally dystopic future where daily life was impacted by rapid technological change, an ubiquitous [datasphere] of computerized information, and invasive modification of the human body" (Person). Like other iconic cyberpunk films of the period, such as *Blade Runner* (Scott 1982), *TRON* (Lisberger 1982), *The Terminator* (Cameron 1984), and *RoboCop* (Verhoeven 1987), the film presents us with a bleak landscape of urban sprawl and decay populated by individuals who are alienated both from one another and their environment. And finally, *Max Headroom: 20 Minutes into the Future* (*MH20*) presents us with both the alluring and terrifying notions that, at some point, humanity might somehow be fused with—or even replaced by—machines.

MH20 trades heavily on cyberpunk's themes and visual aesthetics. For example, the integration (and confusion) of the human and the technological is a staple of cyberpunk, depicted most effectively in the ontological confusions in Scott's *Blade Runner*. The opening credits play out over a slowly emerging picture (and sound) of static with Carter, on location, attempting to communicate with Network 23. It is fitting, of course, that our opening image is of a human attempting to use technology to communicate with an unseen voice that does not describe itself as human. Once Carter makes contact, the respondent does not self-identify. The male voice simply says "This is Network 23" and then complains of "intermittent voice loss." Amid the crosstalk, Carter's interlocutor tells him that his "show goes live in two minutes" and that there will be someone who will act as 'controller'—who emerges as merely another disembodied voice. Without delving into the meta-analysis of a show within a show, it is worth pointing out the ways that the language here—a 'show' that goes 'live' and that has a 'controller'—suggests a fusion of human life, the performance, and the technological. The two voices emerge as if from within the static, and, if anything, these opening credits serve both to disorient the viewer and to establish that the relationship between humans and technology is an imperfect one.

Cyberpunk also borrows heavily from *film noir* representations of dark, impersonal, dangerous cities—especially ones such as Los Angeles, which is a staple location in *noir* films. As Lars Schmeink writes, "[o]ne of the most widely-used images of cyberpunk is its placement in urban sprawls and far-reaching cityscapes" (277), and once the film's opening static clears, we encounter what seems to be a bleak, urban, industrial landscape. There are tattered buildings with their windows seemingly blown out. There is what may be either steam or smoke emerging from behind a pile of what seems to be demolition debris. Behind this, a massive tower emblazoned with 'Network 23' stands alone on the skyline as a less romanticized version of the Tyrell Corporation's massive pyramids that famously command the cityscape in the opening scene of *Blade Runner*—or the massive BT tower that dominates the west London skyline. While bleak landscapes are common to cyberpunk, *Max Headroom* does something remarkable. As Carter's show goes live (from a helicopter where he is reporting on some incident), we also see the opening credits of his show. We are, in other words, watching an opening credits sequence within an opening credits sequence. Thus, from its opening credits, the film calls attention to the ways that it is providing media commentary within the framework of a cyberpunk aesthetic. It deploys mid-1980s cyberpunk aesthetics and uses those aesthetics in the service of a critique of corporate media.

Carter is investigating a mysterious event—we learn later that it is some kind of explosion, and that the area is cordoned off—that has occurred in apartment 42 of the building that, presumably, the helicopter is hovering over. Carter also implies that the true story of this event is somehow being suppressed. The framework, in other words, suggests that this is a piece of fairly standard investigative reporting. The viewer's perspective, however, is layered. As with the opening credits, we hear "Control" (in the film, a controller unites the roles of cutter, editor, researcher, hacker, and personal handler) cue up bits of video and we see how, in the newsroom, Edison's controller has access to technologies that map buildings, warns Carter of the presence of security, and guides him to the location of this mysterious event. Before Carter can learn the secret of the event, however, his controller warns him off and effectively abandons him at the scene. The implication is that there is some entity more powerful outside the newsroom—as Carter's editor-in-chief later explains: the story "was pulled from high up. Very high." The media in this world is under the thumb of even more powerful actors.

The representation of the newsroom itself is also worth addressing. Although it features claustrophobic and cluttered interiors, the light pouring in through closed blinds and cigarette smoke seems in keeping with interior scenes in *Blade Runner*, including Dave Holden's (Morgan Paull) interview of Leon (Brion James) or Rick Deckard's (Harrison Ford) meeting with his former supervisor, Bryant (M. Emmet Walsh). *Max Headroom* deploys these noir/*Blade Runner*-esque visual elements as part of its worldbuilding, and in terms of plot presents itself as a classic *noir* detective story. But one way that cyberpunk distinguishes itself from traditional *film noir* is in its representation of monolithic powers that exert control over the world. In *Blade Runner*, this is the Tyrell Corporation; in *Terminator*, it is the AI Skynet; in *The Matrix* (Wachowskis 1999), it is the AI Agents. In *Max Headroom*, that powerful force is Network 23, whose logo we only see partially illuminated in a cone of light behind a massive table surrounded by smoking, well-dressed executives—Network 23's board of directors, who are discussing their ratings.

The directors, concerned with their television ratings, have invented a technology called blipverts, which shorten the length of advertisements and avoid dips in ratings as viewers change channels. The blipverts, however, cause some viewers to spontaneously combust. In a display of the callous attitudes of powerful institutions and the people who control them, one executive questions any causal relationship, remarking that "There's probably no connection with blipverts. Good heavens, isolated incidences of this phenomena have occurred throughout history. People do sort of blow up. Spontaneously combust. You know?" Such disregard for the potential effects on viewers further emphasizes the ways that *Max Headroom* is, in part, offering up a significant criticism of media conglomerates.

As the executives turn their attention to the creator of blipverts, their resident youthful techno-wizard head of research and development, Bryce, we encounter another disembodied head on a screen. Bryce explains that blipverts compress 30 seconds of advertising information into 3 seconds, and that this compressed data interacts with the normal electrical charge in human nerves in some inactive people, violently causing "in some subjects ... a short-circuit. Some particularly slothful, perpetual viewers literally explode." The reaction of the board of directors is predictably monstrous, with one remarking, simply, "Look here, the only people who are that inactive are pensioners, the sick, or the unemployed," thus implying that the number of people who might be affected by these potentially adverse side effects is both a relatively small portion of the world population and, by implication, undesirable. Further emphasizing the monstrous nature of the Network 23 power brokers, Bryce waves off any concerns by explaining that they simply asked him to come up with a solution to minimize channel switching during advertisements—to which he adds, "I only invent the bomb. I don't drop it." When one executive informs Bryce that one of their own reporters—Carter—seems to have caught the scent of the story about blipvert deaths, Bryce casually suggests that they could simply kill him.

While much of this scene plays out familiar tropes of evil corporations and corporate executives, there are some subtle elements of Bryce's explanation that move this beyond the realm of a mere corporate thriller. While Bryce is simply describing a new form of advertisement, he is also describing the potentially horrifying implications of the interaction between humans and the ubiquitous technology around them. Even the language he uses to describe the unexpected results of the slothful-human/blipvert interaction blurs the human and the technological. While his bosses emerge from this scene as stereotypically callous businessmen, Bryce describes the transformation of the human into something more mechanical. The spontaneous combustion of the viewer is not a chemical or biological reaction; it is a 'short circuit,' suggesting in a cyberpunk fashion that the viewer is just another kind of machine that might malfunction.

Carter, partnered with his new controller Theora Jones (Amanda Pays), uncovers the blipverts scandal and confronts a Network 23 executive who is about to finalize a deal to deploy blipverts worldwide. As with seemingly everything in this film, even this encounter is surveilled, which is unsurprising. One of the hallmarks of cyberpunk aesthetics is the anxiety that powerful forces gather information about individuals without their knowledge, which they often do. As Carter and Theora collaborate to break into Network 23's office of Research and Development, we encounter more cyberpunk fusions of the real and the digital. Upon entering the lab, Carter finds himself surrounded by racks of complex-looking electronic equipment, only to immediately encounter Bryce's (live) parrot, which lives in a cage above its CGI doppelganger, who metaphorically lives in the screen below it. The choice of a parrot is significant. Even the word itself doubles as a verb, meaning to copy or ape. Thus, we have a CGI parrot parroting a parrot, which, in turn, is potentially parroting humans—subtly invoking anxieties not just about what constitutes the 'real,' but also anxieties about how we can distinguish between the real and the simulation. This anxiety over the constitution of reality dominates the remainder of *MH20* and is a key element of many cyberpunk films. For example, in *Blade Runner*, Deckard works to root out androids passing as human. In *The Terminator*, Reese hunts down a T-800 model cyborg, who is almost indistinguishable from a human. Finally, in *The Matrix*, the ability of the Agents to be literally anyone plugged into the matrix is the central anxiety of the humans.

Carter's illegal intrusion into Network 23's office of research and development does not go unnoticed; Bryce sends muscle to take Carter out before he can spread word of the dangers of blipverts. After a frantic competition between Theora and Bryce to control the various systems of the Network 23 tower, Carter attempts to escape on a stolen motorcycle—only to be grievously injured when Bryce raises a ramp, catapulting Carter head-first into a barrier reading "Max Headroom," the moment that births the name of the virtual character. Given his immense popularity and global revenues, however, Carter cannot simply disappear, so Bryce proposes to create the computer-generated version. Using Carter's brain scans, Bryce "can generate this man onto the screen from my computer. He will be able to continue his program and no one will know. But he will in fact be computer-generated. Just like the parrot." It is clear that Bryce thinks of humans as just different kinds of computers—which is another way of saying that the 'real' is no different than the simulation. We see this played out as Bryce reduces Carter's physical body to a series of measurements and synaptic analyses—tellingly scrolling down the screen as ones and zeroes, as if to reinforce the point that everything is reducible to numbers and measurements. Bryce makes the point explicitly: "This is the future. People translated as data."[2]

When Max Headroom finally comes online, he is nothing but a disembodied CGI head and suit-clad, partial upper torso, although this simulation can communicate with the real world. Max's appearance, therefore, is merely another head on a screen, although it becomes clear that he can also be used by the pirate television station Big Time Television as a weapon against Network 23. At the same time, it is apparent to viewers that Max and his manic ramblings—"This is Max Headroom on Big Time Television, and what I want to know is [this:] don't eskimos ever get bored with their weather forecast?"; "If you're watching me, then who's watching Network 23?"—establish the notion that both the virtual host and the film *MH20* itself function as critiques of mindless talking heads on network television who may be nothing more than a voicebox for a pre-programmed set of comments.

Perhaps the most unusual feature of Max Headroom's CGI representation is that, despite his polygonal appearance to the viewer, he is apparently lifelike in the world of the film. When his presence comes to Bryce's attention, one of his goons remarks that Max Headroom is "very like the other bloke. Film of him, is it, Mr. Bryce?" Bryce's response confirms the lifelike appearance: "It is very like the other bloke, but it is not a film. That, Mr. Mahler, is a complete person. In that machine is the coded mind of the dead Mr. Carter. Soon, I will be able to reconstruct anyone on a screen ... so accurately that even your own mum wouldn't know it was you." This slippage between the ability of 1980s CGI to create lifelike images and the world of the movie in which that slippage does not exist is significant, for it reminds us that Max is not merely a representation of Edison Carter; this implies that humans might be replaced by the technology we have created. One of Bryce's goons articulates with apparent glee the anxiety about technology replacing the human: "My word. You could have all your politicians in little boxes. Very handy." In a world of talking heads on screens, it may not matter whether the head is attached to a person or if it is a computer-generated personality.

This emphasis on screen aesthetics has not gone unnoticed. Wees reads the film as "distinctly postmodernist [in its] conception of the video image," offering to viewers "the quintessential image of TV, and hence, postmodern culture" (29). While Max is created through the "interface of television and the computer [and] exists as a TV image inhabiting a completely electronic environment, where he flourishes without any ties to a pro-filmic reality" (33), he is not a representation of Edison Carter; Max is an entirely independent and unique individual. As Wees puts it, "his image is the reality" (33). Therefore when Bryce scans Edison Carter's brain and creates a computer-generated version of Carter—the result is not merely a representation of Carter; instead, the fusion of human and technology creates an entirely new creature—an entirely new *person*—in Max Headroom. In the end, Max is not merely a televisual representation of Carter; Max is self-aware and exists within an entirely televisual or simulational landscape.

Max Headroom's show creators Steve Roberts, George Stone, Rocky Morton, and Annabel Janek's desire to level a serious media critique gave form to Max as a virtual, glossy image: "We wanted to show how you can put any sort of message across if you wrap it up in a very seductive, cosmetic image. It is not entirely an accident that he looks like something out of Nazi Germany" (Berko 52). At the same time, the representation upon which Max Headroom's simulated image is created for the film is itself a representation of a simulation: The CGI Max Headroom in the film is actually actor Matt Frewer costumed and filmed to look like a CGI simulation. "His image and voice," as Berko explains it, "have been further synthesized and processed to finally offer us the consummate parody of the egomaniacal talk show host, a representation of a blond and intensely tanned conglomeration of simulated wires, chips, and integrated circuitry brought to us in the form of a talking head [...] offering viewers his views on life, popular music, and his own greatness" (52). In this sense, Max Headroom is an aesthetic claim about how the fusion of the human and the technological might look and behave. He is a multi-layered media critique, not just of blowhard talking heads on the news, but of the representation of the human in a digital environment.

The notion that Max Headroom functions as media critique is certainly not novel; from the earliest days of the character, media criticism has been a fairly explicit element of the film—and later of the various spin-off series. But I contend that *MH20* adds yet another layer to this by deploying this media critique within a cyberpunk aesthetic. This distinction is important because cyberpunk often mounts criticism of media conglomerates and institutional corruption in both narrative and visual aesthetics. In the end, *MH20* functions as a cyberpunk media critique by exploring various western anxieties about the union of the human and the technological, but the film's primary thrust is media criticism, and this marks it as a fairly extraordinary example of cyberpunk aesthetics.

Notes

1 For more on the U.S. series, see Sherryl Vint's contribution in this collection.
2 See N. Katherine Hayles' *How We Became Posthuman*. Hayles, pushing back against Hans Moravecs (and similar thinkers) who believe that "the age of the human is drawing to a close" (283), imagines a post-human that does not signal the end of humanity but which, instead, "offers resources for rethinking the articulation of humans with intelligent machines" (Hayles 287).

Works Cited

Berko, Lili. "Simulation and Concept Imagery: The Case of Max Headroom." *Wide Angle*, no. 10, 1988, pp. 60–61.

Hayles, N. Katherine. *How We Became Posthuman: Virtual Bodies in Cybernetics, Literature, and Informatics*. U of Chicago P, 1999.

Max Headroom: Twenty Minutes into the Future. Directed by Annabel Jankel and Rocky Morton, performances by Matt Frewer and Amanda Pays. Chrysalis, 1985.

Person, Lawrence. "Notes Toward a Cyberpunk Manifesto." *Slashdot*, 9 Oct. 1999, slashdot.org/story/99/10/08/2123255/notes-toward-a-postcyberpunk-manifesto.

Schmeink, Lars. "Afterthoughts: Cyberpunk Engagements in Countervisuality." *Cyberpunk and Visual Culture*, edited by Graham J. Murphy and Lars Schmeink. Routledge, 2018, pp. 276–87.

Wees, William C. "From the Rearview Mirror to Twenty Minutes into the Future: The Video Image in *Videodrome* and *Max Headroom*." *Canadian Journal of Film Studies*, vol. 1, no. 1, 1990, pp. 29–35. doi:10.3138/cjfs.1.1.29.

23

VIDEO GAMES

Paweł Frelik

There is no such thing as a cyberpunk video game. This paraphrase of Mark Bould and Sherryl Vint's "There Is No Such Thing as Science Fiction" (2009) reminds us that genre is not a stable 'thing,' but a way of approaching a set of texts; however, this statement amounts to more than an admission of the inherent fluidity of genre boundaries. It underscores the differences between various media in any genre, which despite superficial similarities are, in fact, pseudomorphs—they have the "appearance of affinity," but exhibit "basic discontinuity in genus and species" (Gunning 355). For all its definitional positions, cyberpunk has been viewed as a distinct formation within science fiction (sf) held together not only by its thematic repertoire but also its presumed interest in postmodern experimentation and other artistic forms.[1] Cyberpunk's distinctiveness has also carried over to film, television, comics, music, and so forth. However, all these media are usually conceptualized in terms of the same mass cultural genre system.[2] More recently, many discussions of genre in narrative-centric media have shifted from treating genres as practices, rather than objects, but, by and large, they remain to be defined by the presence and recurrence of iconic elements: locations, characters, and plot scenarios.[3]

This is not the case with the medium of video games, in which genres are distinguished not on the basis of thematic or aesthetic properties but are instead defined by the type of activity elicited by the game from the player.[4] This means that, as a signature of certain thematic and aesthetic preoccupations, 'cyberpunk' does not describe any extant gaming genre. Parallel to the apparatus developed in literary or film studies, marketing labels have wielded a good deal of appeal across various media, but a 'cyberpunk game' is not really one of these. Consequently, in many cases, it is more productive to treat 'cyberpunk' as a tag or a keyword—or in keeping with the terminology used in this volume as a disseminated cultural mode—rather than a moniker for a stable textual category, which has been attached to vastly different titles because of the presence of one of a loose group of parameters originally referencing literary cyberpunk.[5]

This lack of categorical precision opens the term 'cyberpunk video games' to a variety of (mis) understandings. Among these, three ways of thinking about cyberpunk video games seem to me particularly productive: treating cyberpunk as a visual aesthetic; constructing the ludic canon for cyberpunk, within which a certain kind of politics seems to be the strongest unifying principle; and approaching cyberpunk games as possessive of a dimension which makes it possible to describe cyberpunk video games as a meta-medium of cyberpunk at large that is both self-reflexive and self-unaware. Each of these approaches generates a distinctly different canon of texts. Each is less text-focused and more general, traveling a trajectory away from a close analysis and toward the meta-analysis of the entire grouping. Finally, each requires a different degree of attention.

Video Games

23.1 The Aesthetic Approach

In 2018, a much-commented-upon *Guardian* article, which was intended as a quasi-review of CD Projekt's *Cyberpunk 2077* (2020, tbc.) gameplay footage but ended up as a 'cyberpunk-must-beware' manifesto, noted that cyberpunk futures have looked "the same for almost four decades" (Walker-Emig). This is particularly true for the visual signatures of the mode across a range of media, and video games seem to have introduced very little to the visual décor of the movement. Elsewhere, I proposed that it is much more productive to treat cyberpunk as a visual aesthetic, rather than a coherent thematic genre (Frelik). Its optical surfaces, which not only propagated in the narrative media of film, television, and comics, but also in minor visual forms such as digital graphics, record covers, and illustration, have been, in retrospect, cyberpunk's most enduring legacy. Hanging over almost all cyberpunk texts is the neon specter of *Blade Runner* (Scott 1982), whose vision of a near-future nocturnal metropolis has practically colonized the ocular imagination across all (audio)visual media. While Grace Halden's chapter in this collection mainly explores the urban sprawl as an image "of vital significance in cyberpunk," she adds that cyberpunk images create a "'language' of the future" and "impose on their audience a future world [...in which] familiar key elements are juxtaposed with at-times radical unfamiliarity" (217). It is this dual presence of the familiar cityscape (as habitat) with the radically different futurity of cyborg embodiment, surveillance and information technology, or corporatization that produces the specific visual aesthetic of cyberpunk.

In terms of an approach to cultural analysis, understanding cyberpunk as a visual regime with specific images as a unifying 'language' has several benefits. It allows us to sidestep the definitional wars, which began almost as soon as the moniker rose to public visibility in the early 1980s. It allows us, for example, to reclaim cyberpunk precursors that Bruce Sterling famously excluded from his genre-building in the Preface to *Mirrorshades: The Cyberpunk Anthology* (1985), particularly feminist sf writers such as James Tiptree, Jr. or Joanna Russ—images such as the cyborg in "The Girl Who Was Plugged In" (1973) or the razor-blade assassin Jael of *The Female Man* (1975) clearly connect these stories to cyberpunk.[6] Further, it helps us reclaim the more general role of visuality in its imagination. As Scott Bukatman points out, cyberpunk "was often imagistic," producing a "visual rhetoric of cyberpunk [...which] mapped the familiar onto the new [...and] obliterated physical boundaries" (xv). In this liminal position lies its potential: "the visual becomes the tool [...] to generate simultaneously abstracted and compelling images emblematic of emerging world orders" (xvi). The visual aesthetics of cyberpunk help us map the newly emerged world orders of ubiquitous portable devices and digitized social interactions. Finally, it redirects our attention to several crucial components of its aesthetic across various media that appear to signal 'cyberpunk' as a sensibility even in the absence of narrative. All of these considerations define cyberpunk video games and are of importance in this particular medium.[7]

23.2 The Historical Approach

Any genealogy of cyberpunk games would vary depending on the markers that determine inclusion in the mode but would likely yield a long series of quite diverse texts. It includes game-adaptations of other cyberpunk media, such as the games of the TRON franchise (1982–2010), both *Blade Runner* games (CRL 1985, Westwood 1997), *Neuromancer* (Interplay 1988), the Shadowrun series (1993–2015), and *Ghost in the Shell* (Exact Production 1997). In addition, original game entries to cyberpunk culture include the real-time strategy game *Syndicate* (Bullfrog 1993), the story-intensive adventure games *Beneath a Steel Sky* (Revolution 1994) and *BioForge* (Origin 1995), the entire Deus Ex franchise (2000–16),[8] which combines action with roleplaying game elements, the first-person shooter *Hard Reset* (Flying Wild Hog 2011), the turn-based tactical game *Frozen*

Synapse (Mode 7 2011), and the dexterity-based action game *Remember Me* (Dontnod 2013), as well as the open world explorative action games *Watch Dogs* (Ubisoft 2014) and *Watch Dogs 2* (Ubisoft 2017). Of course, any list is necessarily a subjective excerpt, but it clearly demonstrates the diversity of gaming texts that have been discussed as belonging to the mode.[9]

Moreover, 'cyberpunk-flavoured' games, to appropriate Andrew M. Butler's term and thus reference games utilizing certain easily recognizable tropes popularized by cyberpunk, include titles such as the first-person action-oriented games *System Shock* (Looking Glass 1994) and *System Shock 2* (Irrational 1999), or the explorative adventure game *Tacoma* (Fullbright 2017), but also games that feature diegetic bodily implants and augmentations, such as the Mass Effect franchise (Bioware 2007–12) and some of the Metal Gear series (1987–2018). Finally, there have been a number of cyberpunk(-flavored) massively multiplayer online games, including the text-based *Sindome* (Sindome Corporation 1997), *Anarchy Online* (Funcom 2001), and—of course—the canonical *Matrix Online* (Monolith 2005–09), which extended the Wachowskis' transmedia text. Interestingly, at the time of writing, two of the most talked about cyberpunk games in recent years are yet to be released: *The Last Night* (Odd Tales) and *Cyberpunk 2077*, which sparked the above-mentioned debate on cyberpunk's visual nostalgia and prompted William Gibson to tweet that the released trailer looked like "GTA skinned-over with a generic 80s retro-future."

While this long—but still necessarily very tentative and incomplete—canon comprises several titles that have been deemed more influential than others, more rigorously hierarchical 'best-of' lists are inherently subjective.[10] If the category of cyberpunk video games is a database of numerous titles sharing at least one of their many parameters rather than a single chronological narrative, then there are several ways in which such a database can be parsed. One such parsing relies on specific visual styles, such as the pixelated retro look or *Blade Runner*-esque glossy hyperrealism, within which genealogies can be constructed on the basis of visual inspiration. Such a historical narrative would be, of course, also an example of the aesthetic approach which privileges thinking about cyberpunk in optical terms.

Another parsing, which allows for a more systematic reflection on cyberpunk video games, focuses on the gaming genre in general and the generic conventions regarding game mechanics and gameplay particularly (Garda 25). Some categories seem to be more privileged than others, even though cyberpunk's thematic markers could theoretically be grafted onto any gameplay convention. We have already seen the range of games earlier, but to point to more exceptional texts: *Rez* (United Game Artists 2001) is an artistic music rail shooter, while *Tales of the Neon Sea* (Palm Pioneer 2019) is a 2D side-scrolling roleplaying game, and *Ruiner* (Reikon Games 2017) utilizes a top-down perspective combined with a shooter capacity. Nonetheless, most cyberpunk games belong to one of three core genres: first- and third-person shooters, roleplaying games, and point-and-click adventure games. There are obvious differences between these genres but they also share at least two common characteristics: They lend themselves to detail-rich narratives and simulate agency through attention to individual protagonists. Each of these genres relies on the foregrounding of the in-game character; each of them structures the game narrative around that character's knowledge, awareness, and development; and each of them ties the player's affective response to the character's plight.

In all its narrative forms, cyberpunk has positioned itself as quintessentially focused on individuality and the question of how subjectivity is constituted within our technoscientific world. A staple of early cyberpunk, the "individualist heroes," as Nicola Nixon calls them, are connected with the established myth of the male American hero, "celebrat[ing...] initiative and ingenuity" (224, 230) and highlighting the hero's ability to manipulate technological systems in order to achieve a "privatized utopia" (Darko Suvin, quoted in Nixon 228). Nixon links this myth to masculine desires—"their masculinity is constituted by their ability" to control technology (229)—and thus underscores Sherryl Vint's argument that cyberpunk is driven by "male fantasy wish-fulfilment" in that it "appeals to the (impossible) desire to escape the vicissitudes of the body and occupy the place of selfmastery" (104). Video games, in linking subjectivity and technology, idealize this desire through the figure of the avatar, through which the simulacrum of the player's agency is shifted to in-game characters. As Bob Rehak argues: "In a specifically agential sense, avatars reduplicate and render in visible form their players' actions—they complete an arc of desire" (107). But even though the avatar is as an "acting stand-in for the player," it is not a mirror-like reflection of the player: "its correspondence to embodied reality consists of a mapping not of *appearance* but of *control*" (107). The avatar is the player's stand-in for control and mastery of technological systems.

It thus might come as no surprise that even a cursory overview of cyberpunk video games shows a political myopia evident in the games' choice of avatar. Whatever diversity of political worldview can nowadays be found in literary and cinematic cyberpunk, there is a tendency to code in-game characters as white, heterosexual men,[11] a tendency to favor the male American hero myth that persists in both big-budget and independent productions, including those titles whose politics are somewhat more complicated. Otherwise complex and engaging as fictional characters, JC Denton in *Deus Ex* (2000), Adam Jensen in *Deus Ex: Human Revolution* (2011) and *Deus Ex: Mankind Divided* (2016), and Aiden Pearce in *Watch Dogs*, but also Azriel Odin and Delta-Six in *Gemini Rue* (Wadjet Eye Games 2011) all represent the Caucasian masculinity of the American hero myth.

In *Watch Dogs*, for example, hacker Aidan Pearce's actions, while generally pointing out the ever-present surveillance implemented by the Blume Corporation's ctOS that operates all public services and its potential manipulation, never amount to a critique of the corporate status quo. Instead, the main story line is clearly motivated by personal revenge turning on the failures of individuals. When a heist goes wrong, Aidan's niece is killed by criminals targeting him, which sets Aidan on a mission to find the guilty parties. In the process, Aidan is driven to violently 'clean up' the city from hacker groups and gangs exploiting the ubiquitous connection to the virtual world of ctOS, which governs any and all information, from bank accounts to traffic violations. When he is not willing to further uncover the identity of an opponent, his former partner kidnaps Aidan's sister and threatens her life. And finally, after initially receiving help from another hacker, Clara Lille, Aidan cuts off all ties with her when he finds out that she was involved in the death of his niece—which, in turn, leads to Clara being killed as retaliation for Aidan's actions.

The game and its individualistic cyberpunk hero are problematic in several ways, one of which is the game's treatment of women "as stepping stones to get a protagonist from emotional point A to emotional point B" (Kunzelman, "In Watch Dogs") especially via the misogynist trope of 'fridging' (a term that is derived from killing a female character and putting her in a refrigerator in order to motivate the male hero). All of Aidan's actions are "in some way related to or informed by violence or death being dealt to women," without ever giving the women that experience this violence a voice of their own. Consequently, Aidan needs to become not only a masterful hacker (in control of the technology), but he also needs to fully control his emotions, doing whatever is necessary in order to succeed. In this, the game positions violence and criminal acts as a proportionate measure to the threat Aidan is facing—killing indiscriminately any opposition and manipulating the virtual ctOS system for his personal gain. As Cameron Kunzelman makes clear, the game's brutal depiction of gun violence in a virtual Chicago is "hard to square [...] with the amount of real-world staggering and tragic gun death that occurs there" ("What 'Watch Dogs 2' Gets So Right"). The game is not emotionally reflective of Aidan's grief for a family member or fear for another's life. Instead, it positions Aidan as the individualistic 'hero' willing to go to all lengths in order to restore his privatized utopia. Playing out the same American hero myths that have limited the radical potential of early cyberpunk fiction and involving "an unsavory and regressive positioning" of marginalized groups (Nixon 231–32), many cyberpunk video games fall into the trap of technoscientific fantasies of male power and control.

Moreover, the identity of principal characters and the representation of marginalized groups are not the only political dimensions of cyberpunk games that leave much to be desired. In fact, the tacit acceptance of the global economic order that relies on surveillance, results in exploitation, and resonates in all spheres of life has been the norm. By and large, cyberpunk games treat the excesses of futuristic systems as what Mark Fisher called "capitalist realism," a pervasive atmosphere of contemporary socio-economic conditions that makes it impossible to imagine any other political arrangement and "acts as a kind of invisible barrier constraining thought and action" (16). Whatever problems game protagonists struggle with, these usually turn out to be the consequences of individual, rather than systemic, failings. The system at large is rarely questioned and, as Stephen Joyce has argued, even games such as the Deus Ex franchise, which remain skeptical about the circulations of power, are given to point toward "government oversight" as the alternative and thus betray a dependence on "conservative nostalgia" (170), which is far from revolutionary.

Games such as *Watch Dogs 2* promise a more political thematic, dealing in its main story arc with surveillance and hacktivism. The game's playable character is Marcus Holloway, a black man, who is wrongfully labeled as a criminal by the ctOS surveillance software because of racial discrimination. Marcus joins the hacker collective DedSec, which is diversely represented as "poor, queer, neurodivergent, black, and brown" (Kunzelman, "What *Watch Dogs 2* Gets So Right") in an attempt to fight against the implemented surveillance and its corporate exploitation. Missions are oriented toward hacktivism and building an underground reputation in the form of a social media following, while also satirically commenting on Silicon Valley's corporate tactics and social realities. The game gives itself the veneer of corporate critique, showing how techno-scientific corporations use our compliance to gather vast amounts of information, which opens us up to manipulation and exploitation.

But as Will Partin has pointed out, *Watch Dogs 2* is both "a game about surveillance [...and] itself an instrument of surveillance," as it collects not only data on the user's hardware but also their locale, when and how they play, as well as their behavior in social spaces, and much more. Or, as Joyce argues, any mainstream video game is "the product of an increasingly large global industry, [...dependent] on such corporate giants as Sony and Microsoft" (168) which are supposed to be the targets of the game's criticism: "What are we to make of a criticism of capitalism that can only be presented to us through the intercession of the global media industry?" (Joyce 168).

This specific condemnation of one title can be extended to speak to a broader problem with other cyberpunk games: the lack of critical insight into top-level social and economic systems empowered by cyber technologies. The in-game hacking, on-demand body augmentations, and Robin-Hood mentality, all inherent in both the narrative and procedural rhetoric of many cyberpunk games, project worlds of flexibility and constant change, a mindset that centrally underwrites the neoliberal ideologies of the self (Harvey). Alexander Galloway cautions against such illusions of control: "while it may appear liberating or utopian, don't be fooled; flexibility is one of the founding principles of global informatics control. It is to the control society what discipline was to a previous one" (100). As this short excursion shows, historical approaches to cyberpunk video games can provide critical insights and allow the critic to develop new readings of the mode in regards to the shifting media landscape.

23.3 The Meta-Approach

After the aesthetic approach and the historical perspective, the third way of thinking about cyberpunk games proposes that they be conceived of as a meta-medium of cyberpunk at large, reflecting the ontological preoccupations of cyberpunk narratives while being simultaneously unaware of the contradictions inherent in them. Writing about sf film, Brooks Landon proposed a fascinating revisionist version of the form's history, suggesting that sf film "has its roots in spectacle rather than in narrative," and that the film medium's technological apparatus itself makes it science fictional in that it elicits "the same sense of wonder and discovery elicited by science-fiction writing" (32). Sf film could thus be treated as a meta-genre of the entire filmic medium, foregrounding its visual technology and "recogniz[ing] the primacy of spectacle" that established film as a medium (33). In the same manner, I would like to suggest that cyberpunk video games can be thought of as a meta-medium of the genre—and for more reasons than one.

The first of these is the unique relationship between the player and the game, which has been on several occasions correlated with one of the most emblematic figures of cyberpunk, the cyborg. Jonathan Boulter suggests that "the player-game relationship instantiates the gamer as cyborg," primarily because any gaming device "operates as a practical prosthetic device, extending the player's limited physicality and subjectivity" (4–5). Elsewhere, players have been discussed as possessive of subjectivities that constantly negotiate the demands of at least two worlds: the physical reality and the gameverse (Filiciak). Donna Haraway's concept of cyborg consciousness serves as a perfect analog of the players' engagement with gameworlds. While her essay has been most frequently deployed in the discussions of speculative corporealities involving the imbrication of biology and technology, it is important to remember that the main reason for her use of the figure is to chart the way out of the need to reconcile mutually exclusive dualities. From this perspective, the player becomes a deck operator, a cyberspace cowboy, a hacker. The gestures and actions directed at the game—in-game avatar customizations, juggling of the avatar's skills and accessories, even the additions of downloadable content and modifications—reflect the actions of the in-game operators the player is directing.

The second area in which the meta-dimension comes to the fore is a micro-genre of hacking simulations. Some of the more interesting examples include *Uplink: Trust is a Weakness* (Introversion 2001), *Hacknet* (Team Fractal Alligator 2015), *Quadrilateral Cowboy, Hackmud* (Drizzly Bear 2016), and *Exapunks* (Zachtronics 2018). All of them are more than mere programming puzzles and foreground their hacking activity as an element of cyberpunk plotlines. The game entitled *else Heart.Break()* (Erik Svedäng 2015) is a particularly fascinating example here: It starts as a traditional-looking adventure game and, some time into the gameplay, flips to allow the player to inspect the code of almost every in-game object. Cyberpunk hacking sims are thus among a very few games in which the player engages in exactly the same activity as her in-game avatar, a synchronization that effectively eliminates the fourth wall but in a manner that is not disruptive.

Finally, cyberpunk games' self-reflexive potential can be discerned in their positioning vis-à-vis the institutional structures within which they are created. In his analysis of *BioShock* (2k Boston 2007), Clint Hocking coined the term "ludonarrative dissonance" to describe the chasm between the meaning created by the game's narrative and the meaning emerging from its gameplay, which is contingent on the rules and algorithm as part of procedural rhetoric (Bogost). In a similar manner, one could talk about narrative-industrial dissonance, where the potentially subversive political message of the title's narrative content clashes with the conservative and exploitative character of the gaming industry, as described earlier in the case of *Watch Dogs 2*. Ironically, exploitative practices such as aggressive hedging of intellectual property rights, cultural hybridization, or globally subcontracted work distribution are, in cyberpunk games, associated with the corporations (e.g. Blume Software in *Watch Dogs* or Picus Communications in *Deus Ex: Human Revolution*), which in-game avatars wage wars against and sabotage. Consequently, on their narrative level, cyberpunk games position corporate entities and their employees as ideological antagonists, but their very status as a cultural object is predicated on the perpetuation of such industries.

Galloway notes that "the more emancipating games seem to be as a medium, substituting activity for passivity or a branching narrative for a linear one, the more they are in fact hiding the fundamental social transformation into informatics that has affected the globe during recent decades" (106). In their visions of individualistic American console cowboys using digital guerilla tactics to confront multinational megacorps, cyberpunk games offer precisely a prepackaged version of such emancipation. While the presence of hidden algorithms and rules in space exploration and colonization games can be understood as the approximation of rules of physics and the ecological capacity of a biome, respectively, their invisible yet pernicious presence in cyberpunk games runs afoul of the mode's self-professed subversive stance.

23.4 Conclusion

The three ways of thinking about cyberpunk games outlined earlier do not naturally exhaust the range of possible approaches. The inspection of the role of sound design and scores invoking the 1980s, a period of the genre's high cultural currency, will undoubtedly yield some interesting insights—particularly since cyberpunk's sound aesthetic found significant traction in a number of music genres from pop/rock to electro music to industrial. The strong rhythmic properties of many cyberpunk-inflected compositions readily imbricate with structures of tasks in games as well as action-driven sequences.

Close analyses of individual titles outside a relatively small pool of high-profile releases may illuminate finer differences between seemingly similar games but also offer subtler political messages transcending the neoliberal ideologies of a few mainstream titles. While there is a significant body of academic and popular criticism on the Deus Ex games, the two *Watch Dogs* titles, and *Remember Me*, other—arguably equally interesting—titles such as *Beneath a Steel Sky*, *Gemini Rue*, and *Technobabylon* have received very little critical attention beyond reviews in the gaming circuit. More systematic attention to such independent games would complicate at least some of the political diagnoses proposed earlier.

For now, though, cyberpunk games, attractive visually as they often are, are still channeling the conservative *id* of the genre that Nixon so aptly eviscerated in her article. Luckily, to quote Sterling without a dose skepticism, "the future remains unwritten" (xv)—and unplayed.

Notes

1 For an overview of the definitional positions regarding cyberpunk, see Sterling; McHale; Csicsery-Ronay; Nixon.
2 See John Rieder's *Science Fiction and the Mass Cultural Genre System* for a detailed discussion of this. While many scholars speak of cyberpunk as a (sub)genre, this volume has opted for the terminology of mode, assuming a loose generic relation while accepting a stronger cultural dissemination of aesthetics and thematics through media and into a variety of genre forms. As Thomas Foster put it: "cyberpunk didn't so much die as experience a sea change into a more generalized cultural formation" (xiv). For more details on this, see Foster and the introduction to this volume.
3 John Rieder's "On Defining SF, or Not: Genre Theory, SF and History" remains, to my mind, one of the best concise and elegant discussions of the social constructedness of genres.
4 See Wolf; Apperley; Arsenault. To complicate this matter, Maria Garda suggests that in order to fully account for the game's character, one needs to account for three genre layers: ludic (FPS, strategy, etc.), thematic (fantasy, historical, etc.), and functional (casual, hardcore, etc.)
5 This relaxed definitional rigor is noticeable online, where distribution platform Steam lists over 300 titles as "cyberpunk," *Wikipedia* links to 200 entries and Itch.io, a site for independent game developers, provides over 880 games tagged "cyberpunk." To be precise, only some of these are literally tagged with "cyberpunk"; often, the term merely appears in the game's description.
6 For more on the literary precursors to cyberpunk, see Rob Latham's essay in this collection; for more on the exclusion of feminist sf, see Nixon's as well as Lisa Yaszek's and Patricia Melzer's individual contributions to this collection.
7 All of these components are, I argued, various incarnations of light: night luminescence, neon, and the tracing lines of cyberspace. My argument about the centrality of luminescence in cyberpunk is only one

of several ocular approaches; for more specific analyses pertaining to cyberpunk's visualities, see the other entries in Graham J. Murphy and Lars Schmeink's *Cyberpunk and Visual Culture*.

8 For an exemplary case study of the Deus Ex franchise, see Christian Knöppler's entry in this collection.

9 For those interested, other titles discussed under the tag "cyberpunk" include: *Flashback* (Delphine 1992), *Burn Cycle* (Trip Media 1994), *BioForge* (Origin 1995), *SiN* (Ritual 1998), *Project Snowblind* (Crystal 2005), *Anachronox* (Ion Storm 2001), *Neuro Hunter* (Media Art 2005), *Gemini Rue* (Joshua Nuernberger 2011), *Cypher* (Cabrera Brothers 2012), *Syndicate* (Starbreeze 2012), *Satellite Reign* (5 Lives 2015), *Technobabylon* (Technocrat 2015), *Quadrilateral Cowboy* (Blendo 2016), *Ruiner* (Reikon 2017), and *Observer* (Bloober 2017).

10 Many such lists have been compiled, of course, for example: Gordon; Parlock.

11 Certainly, there are exceptions here. Women are playable characters in *Deus Ex: Infinity War* (2003), *Remember Me* and *Technobabylon* (Wadjet Eye Games 2015). In *Anachronox* (Ion Storm 2001), one character is Dr. Rho Bowman, a woman of color, while another Paco "El Puño" Estrella is visually coded as Latino.

Works Cited

Apperley, Thomas H. "Genre and Game Studies: Toward a Critical Approach to Video Game Genres." *Simulation & Gaming*, vol. 37, no. 1, Mar. 2006, pp. 6–23. doi:10.1177/1046878105282278.

Arsenault, Dominic. "Video Game Genre, Evolution and Innovation." *Eludamos: Journal for Computer Game Culture*, vol. 3, no. 2, Oct. 2009, pp. 149–76.

Bogost, Ian. *Persuasive Games: The Expressive Power of Videogames*. MIT Press, 2010.

Bould, Mark and Sherryl Vint. "There Is No Such Thing as Science Fiction." *Reading Science Fiction*, edited by James Gunn et al. Palgrave Macmillan, 2009, pp. 43–51.

Boulter, Jonathan. *Parables of the Posthuman: Digital Realities, Gaming, and the Player Experience*. Wayne State UP, 2015.

Bukatman, Scott. "Foreword: Cyberpunk and its Visual Vicissitudes." *Cyberpunk and Visual Culture*, edited by Graham J. Murphy and Lars Schmeink. Routledge, 2018, pp. xv–xix.

Butler, Andrew M. *Cyberpunk*. Pocket Essentials, 2000.

Csicsery-Ronay, Jr., Istvan. "Futuristic Flu, or, The Revenge of the Future." *Fiction 2000: Cyberpunk and the Future of Narrative*, edited by George Slusser and Tom Shippey. U of Georgia P, 1992, pp. 26–45.

Filiciak, Miroslaw. "Hyperidentities: Postmodern Identity Patterns in Massively Multiplayer Online Role-Playing Games." *The Video Game Theory Reader*, edited by Mark J.P. Wolf and Bernard Perron. Routledge, 2003, pp. 87–102. doi:10.4324/9780203700457-11.

Fisher, Mark. *Capitalist Realism: Is There No Alternative?* Zero Books, 2009.

Foster, Thomas. *The Souls of Cyberfolk: Posthumanism as Vernacular Theory*. U of Minnesota P, 2005.

Frelik, Paweł. "'Silhouettes of Strange Illuminated Mannequins': Cyberpunk's Incarnation of Light." *Cyberpunk and Visual Culture*, edited by Graham J. Murphy and Lars Schmeink. Routledge, 2018, pp. 88–99.

Galloway, Alexander R. *Gaming. Essays on Algorithmic Culture*. U of Minnesota P, 2006.

Garda, Maria. *Interaktywne Fantazy: Gatunek w grach cyfrowych*. Wydawnictwo Uniwersytetu Łódzkiego, 2016.

Gibson, William (@greatdismal). "The Trailer for Cyberpunk 2077 Strikes Me as GTA Skinned-over with a Generic 80s Retro-Future, but Hey, That's Just Me." *Twitter*, 11 Jun. 2018, twitter.com/GreatDismal/status/1005958197654351872.

Gordon, Rob. "Top 10 Cyberpunk Video Games." *Game Rant*, 5 Oct. 2017, gamerant.com/best-cyberpunk-video-games/.

Gunning, Tom. "An Unseen Energy Swallows Space: The Space in Early Film and Its Relation to American Avant-Garde Film." *Film Before Griffith*, edited by John L. Fell. U of California P, 1983, pp. 355–66.

Halden, Grace. "Photography and Digital Art." *The Routledge Companion to Cyberpunk Culture*, edited by Anna McFarlane, Graham J. Murphy, and Lars Schmeink. Routledge, 2020, pp. 216–27.

Harvey, David. *A Brief History of Neoliberalism*. Oxford UP, 2007.

Hocking, Clint. "Ludonarrative Dissonance in BioShock." *Click Nothing*, 7 Oct. 2007, clicknothing.com/click_nothing/2007/10/ludonarrative-d.html.

Joyce, Stephen. "Playing for Virtually Real. Cyberpunk Aesthetics and Ethics in *Deus Ex: Human Revolution*." *Cyberpunk and Visual Culture*, edited by Graham J. Murphy and Lars Schmeink. Routledge, 2017, pp. 155–73.

Kunzelman, Cameron. "In Watch Dogs, Women Are Just Victims and Plot Points." *Paste Magazine*, 28 May 2014, pastemagazine.com/articles/2014/05/in-watch-dogs-women-are-victims-and-plot-points.html.

———. "What 'Watch Dogs 2' Gets So Right, and So Wrong, About Race." *Waypoint*, 2 Dec. 2016, waypoint.vice.com/en_us/article/av3q5e/what-watch-dogs-2-gets-so-right-and-so-wrong-about-race.

Landon, Brooks. "Diegetic or Digital? The Convergence of Science-Fiction Literature and Science-Fiction Film in Hypermedia." *Alien Zone II: The Spaces of Science-Fiction Cinema*, edited by Annette Kuhn. Verso, 1999, pp. 31–49.

McHale, Brian. "PostCYBERmodernPUNKism." *Storming the Reality Studio: A Casebook of Cyberpunk and Postmodern Science Fiction*, edited by Larry McCaffery. Duke UP, 1991, pp. 308–23.

Mirzoeff, Nicholas. *The Right to Look: A Counterhistory of Visuality*. Duke UP, 2011.

Murphy, Graham J. and Lars Schmeink, eds. *Cyberpunk and Visual Culture*. Routledge, 2018.

Nixon, Nicola. "Cyberpunk: Preparing the Ground for Revolution or Keeping the Boys Satisfied?" *Science Fiction Studies*, vol. 19, no. 2, 1992, pp. 219–35.

Parlock, Joe. "Like *Blade Runner 2049*? You'll Love These 12 of the Best Cyberpunk Video Games." *The Telegraph*, 16 Oct. 2017, telegraph.co.uk/gaming/features/like-blade-runner-2049-love-12-best-cyberpunk-video-games/remember/.

Partin, Will. "The Thousand Eyes of 'Watch Dogs 2.'" *Los Angeles Review of Books*, 19 Feb. 2017, lareviewofbooks.org/article/the-thousand-eyes-of-watch-dogs-2/.

Rehak, Bob. "Playing at Being: Psychoanalysis and the Avatar." *The Video Game Theory Reader*, edited by Mark J.P. Wolf and Bernard Perron. Routledge, 2003, pp. 103–27.

Rieder, John. "On Defining SF, or Not: Genre Theory, SF and History." *Science Fiction Studies*, vol. 37, no. 2, 2010, pp. 191–209.

———. *Science Fiction and the Mass Cultural Genre System*. Wesleyan UP, 2017.

Sterling, Bruce. Preface. *Mirrorshades: The Cyberpunk Anthology*, edited by Bruce Sterling. Ace, 1986, pp. ix–xvi.

Vint, Sherryl. *Bodies of Tomorrow: Technology, Subjectivity, Science Fiction*. U of Toronto P, 2007.

Walker-Emig, Paul. "Neon and Corporate Dystopias: Why Does Cyberpunk Refuse to Move On?" *The Guardian*, 16 Oct. 2018, theguardian.com/games/2018/oct/16/neon-corporate-dystopias-why-does-cyberpunk-refuse-move-on.

Wolf, Mark J.P. "Genre and the Video Game." *The Medium of the Video Game*. U of Texas P, 2001, pp. 113–34.

24

DEUS EX (CASE STUDY)

Christian Knöppler

It is hardly a bold claim to state that the Deus Ex franchise (2000–) stands out as the defining cyberpunk series in computer and video games, at least as of this writing (cf. Joyce 156). While cyberpunk themes and aesthetics have found their way into games for decades, whether in the adaptations of *Blade Runner* (CRL 1985, Westwood 1997), the cynical black ops of *Syndicate* (Bullfrog 1993), or countless combat cyborgs in any number of games, none of them have been as ambitious in creating a fully realized cyberpunk world and engaging with the key themes of the cyberpunk mode. On the whole, the Deus Ex games deal with the fusion of human and machine, corporate dominance and resistance, and political repression and conspiracy, with the future of humankind at stake.

For novices to the Deus Ex series, there are four main games, which fall into two eras: *Deus Ex* (2000) and *Deus Ex: Invisible War* (2003), developed by Ion Storm, and the prequels *Deus Ex: Human Revolution* (2011) and *Deus Ex: Mankind Divided* (2016), developed by Eidos Montréal. The change from Ion Storm to Eidos Montréal, coupled with a decade of advancements in games technology and design trends, results in two distinct pairs of games, even as the recent installments carefully pay homage to their predecessors. The basic game design mostly follows the template set by *Deus Ex*; namely, as hybrids of first person shooter, stealth, role-playing, and adventure games, the Deus Ex games offer multiple approaches for the player, with social, technological, and violent solutions available for most challenges. This flexibility was groundbreaking at the time (Schmeink 38) and continues to allow for a multilayered exploration of the gameworld. The element of choice lends weight to the ethical implications of the player's actions. As Miguel Sicart explains, many combat-based games presuppose that following orders "means 'doing the right thing'" (2). Since these games offer no alternative to combat, but *Deus Ex* does, it "forces players to reflect on the meaning of their actions" and makes "ethical responsibility the most adequate gameplay strategy" (Sicart 2). In addition, the gameplay is contextualized in a complex narrative that blends a near-future cyberpunk dystopia with paranoid conspiracy tropes. In the Deus Ex series, technology and conspiracy compete as the driving forces of history, and it is up to the player to decide which of the two should shape the future.

The initial game in the series, *Deus Ex*, is set in the year 2052, in a technologized world cracking under a deadly pandemic called the 'Gray Death.' The narrative follows JC Denton, a new type of technologically enhanced agent working for the international anti-terror agency UNATCO alongside his brother Paul. On his first assignment, JC is sent to combat purported terrorists on New York's Liberty Island, but quickly learns that the situation is more ambiguous. In the wake of the raid, JC's loyalties are called into question, as Paul quits an increasingly suspected UNATCO and joins the underground resistance. When JC catches up with Paul, he resolves to turn his back on the authorities as well, and proceeds to investigate the origins of the Gray Death and his former employer's true motives, traveling to Hong Kong and Paris in the process. He learns that UNATCO, along with FEMA and other governmental agencies and corporations, is a front for the Illuminati, a secret society in control of a vast conspiracy that effectively rules the world. The Illuminati's influence even permeates JC's life, as he and Paul were genetically engineered to serve the conspiracy. The Gray Death turns out to be an artificial creation as well, created by an Illuminati offshoot named Majestic 12 (MJ12). MJ12's leader, industrialist Bob Page, released the contagion as part of a world domination scheme. Aided, variously, by underground scientists, traditionalist Illuminati, and an independent artificial intelligence (AI), JC travels to multiple sites to halt Page's plans and develop a cure for the Gray Death. The conclusion takes place at Area 51, where Page prepares to merge his own mind with an AI to directly control global communications and become a transhuman god-like being. In eliminating Page, JC is given three options to choose from, each of which sets human civilization on a different path. First, he can destroy the basis of global communications, reverting civilization to a disconnected, decentralized state. Second, he can side with the Illuminati, restoring the unequal but stable status quo and help rule the world in secrecy. And third, he can merge with the AI and become transhuman, personally shaping a new global order.

The outcome is chosen by the player; yet, the sequel *Deus Ex: Invisible War* assumes that all three have taken place at the same time. It picks up the plot twenty years later, in the fragmented post-collapse world of 2072. The new protagonist Alex D follows a similar trajectory as JC in the first game, starting out as a young trainee agent who is drawn into a global conflict between secretive factions. The world's main power blocs, the economic World Trade Organization and the religious Order, are revealed to be facades run by the Illuminati, while the other key factions are anti-augmentation crusaders and ApostleCorp, led by the previous game's JC Denton, who pursue a plan to transform humanity through technology. The conclusion again offers a choice to the player: join the Illuminati and restore their control, join the crusaders and purge augmentations and the augmented, join JC and transform humanity into a transhuman collective consciousness, or reject all factions, consigning the world to chaos.

The prequel games' timeline starts in 2027, an era when augmentation technologies, or 'augs' for short, are on the rise. *Deus Ex: Human Revolution* follows Adam Jensen, a former cop turned security chief for leading augment industrialist David Sarif. Jensen is injured in an attack and saved by augmentation, but struggles with his cyborg body. He is called into action against anti-augmentation terrorists, but his investigation turns up a web of deceptions and cover-ups. Jensen follows a trail that involves private military contractors, organized crime, and missing scientists (including his ex-girlfriend) from Detroit to Hengsha, Montréal, and Singapore. Infiltrating the media conglomerate Picus, he learns that the AI Eliza is used for a mass manipulation of the population, in service to the Illuminati conspiracy. Evidence finally leads to original aug pioneer Hugh Darrow, who plans to use a chip upgrade to send all augmented people into a homicidal rage, in an effort to discredit and undo the technology he now regrets bringing about. Jensen confronts Darrow at a remote geo-engineering installation only after the scheme has already been set in motion. He manages to stop the signal, but can only limit the damage. The player is then given a choice on how to handle information on the event, with each option representing a "political stance on transhumanism" (Schmeink 39): Releasing the truth to the public will result in a ban on augs, while shifting the blame to anti-aug terrorists or tainted drugs will instead result in more augs or more regulation, respectively. Destroying the installation and letting everyone die, including Jensen himself, is the last option, leaving the public to draw its conclusions without any information.

Jensen's story continues in *Deus Ex: Mankind Divided*, which picks up two years after the conclusion of the previous game. While it remains unclear which of the aforementioned narrative paths occurred, discrimination against the augmented is on the rise. Now working for an Interpol task force in public, and an underground hacker collective in secret, Jensen spends most of the game in Prague, again investigating terror attacks and conspiracies, and learning more about the machinations of the Illuminati. The conclusion features a planned bioweapon attack on a political delegation in London, and the player's decisions determine whether or not an initiative to control augmented people passes. While *Mankind Divided* already sets up characters and events of *Deus Ex*, Jensen's narrative remains unfinished, pending a continuation that has not been announced as of this writing.

Deus Ex is a cyberpunk game series, and the tropes of the genre manifest in a multitude of aspects. The narrative of each game follows a similar arc—an augmented establishment agent gradually uncovers corruption and joins with rebellious countercultures to reach a climactic confrontation—that closely resembles cyberpunk fiction's "formulaic tales," criticized by Csicsery-Ronay for their predictability and appeal to mere "hipness" (184). But cyberpunk is a visual aesthetic as much as it is a set of narrative tropes, and the Deus Ex games follow the grimy high-tech, neon-and-chrome noir look long associated with the mode. Its protagonists wear dark trench coats and mirrorshades, and show off artificial limbs and glowing eye implants. The fusion of human and machine can be subtle, but is more often conspicuous, in major as well as minor characters. Marks of augmentations range from cables bulging through the skin like veins and lenses for eyes to exposed chrome plates and replacement limbs with the bulky look of heavy machinery. The protagonist of the prequel games, Adam Jensen, is perhaps the series' clearest embodiment of the cyberpunk body and fashion aesthetic. Having lost both arms due to injury, Jensen sports shiny black prosthetics that also house a range of weapons and gadgetry, including a retractable blade. His mirrorshades are so essential that they, too, are a retractable implant and part of his self. The specific combination of retractable blade and implant mirrorshades recalls the character of Molly Millions in William Gibson's *Neuromancer* (1984), perhaps cyberpunk's most iconic archetype, and while other characters in the Deus Ex series may be less flashy, their looks still declare their generic affiliations.

The game locations also reflect the cyberpunk aesthetic, which focuses on sprawling, oppressive urban environments. As Stephen Joyce explains, these settings are crucial: "The city, not cyberspace, is the soul of cyberpunk" (176). Here, architecture serves as an expression of sharp socio-economic divisions, the city "constructed around the contradictory elements of global power and individual impotence" (Joyce 176). Most of the Deus Ex games' action takes place in gloomy cityscapes (e.g. New York, Hong Kong, Seattle, Detroit, Hengsha, London) or sterile high-tech compounds (e.g. Area 51, Panchaea, numerous other remote or subterranean bases). These settings are contrasted with old architecture either in decay or overgrown with more futuristic elements (e.g. Paris, Trier, Prague, along with various interiors; further explored in Bonner). Open, natural spaces are notably absent from the Deus Ex series. The first two games are dominated by drab, plain surfaces and simple shapes, which may be attributed to the limitations of computer graphics at the time, but also contribute to the grim mood. In the two more recent games, advanced graphics technologies and lavish visual design provide far more elaborate locations. Futuristic shapes emerge from old architecture, augmenting the old with the new, and mirroring the theme of technologically enhanced human evolution. Both *Human Revolution* and *Mankind Divided* draw on Renaissance styles for thematic resonance, with a black and gold color scheme chosen as an expression of the dichotomy between cyberpunk/noir/dystopia and Renaissance/body/transhumanism (Bonner 165).

In keeping with cyberpunk tropes, national governments have little significance in the world of Deus Ex, and only transnational organizations like UNATCO or the WTO seem to have any relevance. Instead, corporations like Sarif Industries and VersaLife hold power, and their technologies transform society as they merge human and machine. These developments deepen a sharp divide between the privileged and a vast impoverished underclass, and give fertile ground for a diverse underground with crime and countercultures, cults, resistance, and terror movements, many of which appropriate and employ high technology. As an example, the character of Tracer Tong is introduced in *Deus Ex* as a high-ranking member of a criminal triad, but at the same time he is a brilliant scientist capable of hacking augmentations and curing diseases, as well as the philosophical leader of a rebel movement working to upend the political and technological status quo.

Technology acts as a massively transformative force in the world of the series, specifically in two areas of advancement. The first key technology is augmentation, the enhancement of humans through cybernetic implants, a central trope in cyberpunk. It is crucial in gameplay terms, and seamlessly fits with the role-playing convention of upgrading player characters (Joyce 166). In the Deus Ex games, the human body becomes a tool to be altered and improved according to the player's needs and tastes, easily made stronger or faster, and expanded with weaponry or X-ray vision. In this mode, augmentation is mostly treated as a convenience in the first two games, despite the possibility of a remote body shutdown and Tracer Tong's reminder "how easily our technologies turn on us" (*Deus Ex*). The societal and personal implications of augmentation, however, are more developed in *Human Revolution*, which "foregrounds transhumanism as the centerpiece of the dramatic action" and "confronts the player with the central question of how far we can immerse ourselves in technology before we are transformed by it" (Joyce 164).

Through numerous encounters with non-player characters and diegetic media, *Human Revolution* provides a sweeping view of a society at the threshold to transhumanization, ranging from common workers struggling with the pressures and dependencies of an increasingly augmented labor market, to Jensen's own bodily alienation, and finally the high-level schemes to control augmentation technology that propel the game narrative. The game's final antagonist Hugh Darrow, evoking mythical Prometheus, sums up the central question and positions augmentation's transhumanist thrust as a threat to an essential humanity: "Before today, people believed we should steal fire from the gods and redesign human nature. But human nature was the only thing we have that gives us a moral compass, and the social skills we need to live in peace. Destroy it, and you destroy our very species" (*Human Revolution*). Informed by the preceding narrative's complex and ambiguous treatment of transhumanist themes, the player is then left to support or counteract Darrow's bio-conservative stance, and thereby to stop, slow, or re-enable technology's push toward transhumanism.

The second key technology of the Deus Ex setting, albeit less in the foreground, is AI. The concept of AIs as emergent self-aware beings roaming the world's data networks is again well-established in cyberpunk, and even the idea of hostile AIs clashing and merging already appears in Gibson's *Neuromancer* sequence. AIs feature in all Deus Ex games, and most are initially designed by nefarious forces to monitor and manipulate data and communications. Yet, AIs are also capable of evolving beyond their design boundaries, becoming powerful non-human actors in the ongoing conflicts. With communication mediated through technological devices, some can pass as human, which is as much proof of AI's sophistication as it is of humans' dependence on depersonalizing systems. Thus, Daedalus in *Deus Ex* is first considered to be just a mysterious hacker among a vast digitally connected underground, and Eliza Cassan in *Human Revolution* attains a global celebrity status as the omnipresent but nonetheless disconnected face of the news media.

While the games do not fully explore the concept of non-human intelligence, the most crucial potential of AI arises from its convergence with human augmentation. With human and machine already interfacing, it becomes possible to merge AI and human consciousness and achieve a posthuman consciousness. The conclusion of *Deus Ex* offers that option to the player, as the recently formed Helios AI proposes to JC Denton to "integrate our systems" and "administrate the world" as a synthesis of impartial "decision-making system" and "human understanding," essentially becoming the god out of the machine, the *deus ex machina* that the game's title implies. The sequel *Invisible War* further develops this idea and escalates it from the level of individual to collective humanity. Here, the posthuman JC Denton/Helios argues that since individuals are always born into differing circumstances and abilities, there will always be inequality and power differentials. The solution, then, is getting rid of individuality, by linking all human minds through the Helios AI and creating a collective consciousness. As Helios proclaims, "The only frontier that has ever existed is the self" (*Invisible War*). These paths show the cyberpunk imaginary of the series at its most recklessly ambitious, with ambiguous trans- or posthuman solutions to the problems of political power and inequality. In the long run, it appears that the transformative force of technology drives humanity either toward apotheosis and transcendence, or toward self-destruction.

While the Deus Ex games follow an established cyberpunk tradition, they interweave these tropes with another main influence, namely conspiracy theories and narratives. Given its release date in the year 2000, *Deus Ex* can be viewed as a late contribution to a wave of conspiracy-themed media that appeared throughout the 1990s, led by the subgenre's keystone text *The X-Files* (initial run 1993–2002),[1] that included *Millennium* (Carter 1996–99), *Conspiracy Theory* (Donner 1997), or *Men in Black* (Sonnenfeld 1997). These served to popularize in fictional form a vast set of fringe ideas that had long been confined to esoteric and extremist circles. In particular, Richard Hofstadter outlined a mindset in 1964 that keeps appearing at the fringes of the American political spectrum, particularly on the right, which he termed "the paranoid style" (3). According to Hofstadter, "waves of paranoia" are mobilized by social conflict, the confrontation of opposed and supposedly irreconcilable interests, in which the adherents of the paranoid style cannot make themselves felt in the political process (39). They resort to the central image of "a vast and sinister conspiracy" (29) set against their way of life. Crucially, "[t]he distinguishing thing about the paranoid style is not that its exponents see conspiracies or plots here and there in history, but that they regard a 'vast' or 'gigantic' conspiracy as *the motive force* in historical events. History is a conspiracy, set in motion by demonic forces of almost transcendent power" (29, emphasis in original). The paranoid style has only flourished since the time of Hofstadter's writing, and in a more recent survey Michael Barkun expands on conspiracy thinking. A conspiracist worldview, Barkun argues, implies a universe governed by design rather than by randomness. The emphasis on design manifests itself in three principles found in virtually every conspiracy theory: First, "nothing happens by accident," stressing intentionality; second, "nothing is as it seems," suggesting deception everywhere; and, third "everything is connected," requiring a search for patterns (3). As a result, the conspiracist assumes a completely controllable, coherent world, which is both frightening and reassuring (3).

The paranoid idea that history is driven by conspiracy is established in *Deus Ex* from the outset. The introduction shows Bob Page and his MJ12 associate discussing the progress of their masterplan to destabilize the world to grab power, usher in a "new age," and be crowned "kings, or better than kings: gods." Once gameplay gets under way, JC Denton only remains ignorant of Page and MJ12's plans for a short time, as a captive enlightens him at the conclusion of his first mission. The dialogue is heavy on conspiracy jargon, and the player has the option to continue the conversation multiple times to dive even deeper. Among others, the captive claims that there is a long-running "conspiracy of plutocrats against ordinary people" involving taxation, that JC is part of the "secret police" for an "illegitimate government in Washington," and that the Trilateral Commission acts as a "secret government," which is "financed by the Rockefellers and the Rothschilds." The latter points in particular have no bearing on the game's narrative, but they do point to favored bogeymen of (extratextual) conspiracy theorists. For example, the Trilateral Commission is a non-governmental policy forum suspected by conspiracy theorists of secretly running the world (Barkun 66–67), and the Rothschild banking dynasty has been a favored target of anti-Semitic conspiracy theorists from the 19th century to the present day (Barkun 51). As the narrative of *Deus Ex* proceeds, JC learns that the secret order of the Illuminati has been running the world for hundreds of years, which is another well-worn conspiracy trope. While the Illuminati were indeed a short-lived secret society in late 18th-century Bavaria, they lived on much longer in British and American conspiracy literatures as revolutionary instigators. In the early 20th century, theories about the Illuminati were again revived and spliced with anti-Semitic conspiracy theories, and they have since served as top villains in numerous all-encompassing "superconspiracies" (Barkun 45–62).

Overall, the conspiracy narrative of the Deus Ex series draws heavily on what Barkun calls "New World Order (NWO)" theories that claim "both past and present events must be understood as the outcome of efforts by an immensely powerful but secret group to seize control of the world" (Barkun 39). Barkun lists ten recurrent elements of NWO theories (39–40), eight of which feature in some form in the Deus Ex series. To name only a few: Newly created UN security forces operate on U.S. soil (UNATCO in *Deus Ex*); characters travel in black helicopters (*Deus Ex, Invisible War*); the disaster management agency FEMA prepares secret internment camps for resisters (*Human Revolution*); microchips are implanted for surveillance and mind control (*Human Revolution*, where a chip upgrade is distributed to manipulate the augmented); and of course all these operations are run by secret societies like the Illuminati and its offshoot MJ12 (all games).

While conspiracy elements are present throughout the Deus Ex series, they are somewhat more prominent in the initial two games than in the prequels. While Joyce is correct in pointing out that *Human Revolution* is more focused on transhumanism than "outlandish conspiracy theories" (164), the conspiracy remains a driving force of the narrative, directly instigating key events that lead to the climactic scheme. The game does not name the Illuminati until its final third, when a dialogue between Sarif and Jensen clearly establishes their role as chief antagonists and outlines their methods: "They've had a finger in every corporation, organization or government initiative that's defined modern society" (*Human Revolution*). The sequel *Mankind Divided* delves deeper again into conspiracy tropes, including ominous virtual meetings of conspirators, and another Illuminati plot for Jensen to foil.

The world of *Deus Ex* follows a paranoid conception of history, as it posits, to use Hofstadter's expression, "conspiracy as *the motive force* in historical events" (29). The complexities of socio-political change are invariably reduced to a single cause: the will of a cabal of near-omnipotent conspirators. In *Deus Ex*, the Illuminati faction MJ12 runs UN agencies and biotech corporations, assumes control of the entirety of global communications, and purposefully bioengineers a global pandemic as well as the game's protagonist. In *Invisible War*, the Illuminati run the world's dominant economic bloc as well as its sole unified mass religion; in *Human Revolution*, the Illuminati implement a 'killswitch' that would affect all augmented humans, control global news reporting, and are responsible for the protagonist's personal woes; and in *Mankind Divided*, they launch deceptive terror attacks and assassinations to steer legislation. Despite some infighting among conspirators, the historical arc remains guided by intent.

This leads us to the fundamental conflict of the Deus Ex narrative, which arises from its disparate generic influences. On the one hand, the paranoid view asserts that history is driven by conspiracy; on the other hand, the cyberpunk-transhumanist view asserts that it is driven by technology. Therefore, conspiracy and technology are competing forces vying to shape the world of Deus Ex, the former heading toward total and eternal control by a small, shadowy elite, and the latter heading toward a transformation of human civilization into a trans- or posthuman state. In keeping with the games' focus on player's choice, the player is empowered to make (or perhaps burdened with) a seemingly terminal decision between these two fundamental forces. There are, of course, alternative options; yet, these do not represent forward-moving historical forces in the same sense; instead, the alternatives tend to be retrograde, resetting human civilization to an earlier, naïve state, such as Tracer Tong aiming to undo globalization to "start again" and "live in villages" (*Deus Ex*).

Intriguingly, *Invisible War* and *Human Revolution* also feature the option to choose no clear path at all. In the first case, this rejection is framed as ultimately self-destructive, while the second case is more ambiguous, since the conclusion of *Human Revolution* is not about enacting a transformative global event, but about managing its public reception. The player is given the option to destroy all evidence and actors involved in the event, including the protagonist Jensen, which is framed as trusting "mankind to find the answers on its own" (*Human Revolution*), even as mankind is denied factual evidence. René Schallegger calls this ending "undogmatic" and argues that it is the preferred choice by design (55). Yet, the sequel *Mankind Divided* partially undoes its consequences, which deprives the player's decision of weight. This serves to illustrate a shortcoming in the Deus Ex ethos of player's choice: The player is asked to decide the future of humanity from a handful of momentous options; yet, any continuation of the narrative imposes a single canonical ending (due to very practical limitations of game production). Despite their transience, though, these individual choices remain crucial for the active engagement with the themes and questions of the Deus Ex series (cf. Schmeink 39). The challenge of decision-making, coupled with the ambiguity of the options given, imbues the player experience with a (perceived) significance, even as the games' vision of the future is mired in pessimism.

Note

1 The show, created by Chris Carter, also generated two feature films (1998; 2008) and two new seasons on television (2016–18), after its initial run. For more on the cyberpunk aspects of *The X-Files*, see Sherryl Vint's contribution to this volume.

Works Cited

Barkun, Michael. *Culture of Conspiracy: Apocalyptic Visions in Contemporary America.* U of California P, 2003.
Bonner, Marc. "Das (Raum)Bild als sinngebende Codierung des Computerspiels: Korrespondierende Bildlichkeit in Stanley Kubricks und Arthur C. Clarke's *2001: A Space Odyssey* und dem Cyberpunk-Computerspiel *Deus Ex: Human Revolution.*" *Computer | Spiel | Bilder*, edited by Benjamin Beil, Marc Bonner, and Thomas Hensel. Hülsbusch, 2014, pp. 145–78.
Csicsery-Ronay, Istvan. "Cyberpunk and Neuromanticism." *Storming the Reality Studio: A Casebook of Cyberpunk and Postmodern Science Fiction*, edited by Larry McCaffery. Duke UP, 1991, pp. 182–93.
Deus Ex. Ion Storm, Eidos Interactive, 2000. PC.
Deus Ex: Invisible War. Ion Storm, Eidos Interactive, 2003. PC.
Deus Ex: Human Revolution. Eidos Montréal, Square Enix, 2011. PC.
Deus Ex: Mankind Divided. Eidos Montréal, Square Enix, 2016. PC.
Hofstadter, Richard. "The Paranoid Style in American Politics." *The Paranoid Style in American Politics and Other Essays.* Harvard UP, 1996, pp. 3–40.
Joyce, Stephen. "Playing for Virtually Real: Cyberpunk Aesthetics and Ethics in *Deus Ex: Human Revolution.*" *Cyberpunk and Visual Culture*, edited by Graham J. Murphy and Lars Schmeink. Routledge, 2018, pp. 155–73.
Schallegger, René. "Homo Ex Machina? – Cyber-Renaissance and Transhumanism in *Deus Ex: Human Revolution.*" *Early Modernity and Video Games*, edited by Tobias Winnerling and Florian Kerschbaumer. Cambridge Scholars, 2014, pp. 52–63.
Schmeink, Lars. "Deus Ex." *100 Greatest Video Game Franchises*, edited by Robert Mejia, Jaime Banks, and Aubrie Adams. Rowman, 2017, pp. 38–9.
Sicart, Miguel. *The Ethics of Computer Games.* MIT Press, 2009.

25
TABLETOP ROLEPLAYING GAMES

Curtis D. Carbonell

While cyberpunk explorations often focus on print fictions, movies, and video games, cyberpunk also has a consistent historical presence in tabletop roleplaying games (TRPGs). Cyberpunk TRPGs find their roots with touchstone literary texts, notably William Gibson's *Neuromancer* (1984), but a distinctly cyberpunk TPRG didn't emerge until Mike Pondsmith's *Cyberpunk: The Roleplaying Game of the Dark Future* (R. Talsorian Games 1988), a game that merged popular TRPG elements with cyberpunk motifs. Pondsmith's *Cyberpunk* sets the stage for subsequent games that followed (or recycled) cyberpunk's hacker ethos of do-it-yourself technology and a street-level resistance to a dominant, global capitalism. For example, Iron Crown Enterprises published *Cyberspace* (1989) while a host of other games with similar themes followed, including Steve Jackson Games' *GURPS Cyberpunk* (1990), West End Games' *Torg: The Cyberpapacy* (1989), which expanded cyberpunk into a religious setting, and *Hardwired: The Sourcebook* (1989), itself an adaption of Walter Jon Williams' cyberpunk novel *Hardwired* (1986).

A common thread we see in cyberpunk TRPGs is the evolution of moving beyond traditional bodily enhancements as the primary function of advanced technology. Instead, supertech motifs—i.e. technologies that push extrapolated science into the fantastic, such as extreme forms of bio-engineering or fully self-aware artificial intelligence—have emerged as of equal (if not dominant) importance in cyberpunk TRPGs.[1] This emergence of supertech parallels the shift from postmodernism (late 20th century) to posthumanism (21st century). The discourse of this shift accepts that cyberspace and cyborgs are still viable as descriptors for contemporary human/machine configurations but that the cyborg today offers less impact as a frightful trope (see Grebowicz et al.). For example, human/machine interfaces are common aspects of our lives as we distribute ourselves across a variety of social networks or use devices to recursively monitor biofeedback. What demonstrates the ability to shock for today's audience is not just shattering the human/machine barrier but the potential for altering our genetic code. It is for this reason that biopunk, having a close relation to cyberpunk, proves to be one of the most important new science fiction (sf) sub-genres. For example, Lars Schmeink examines in both *Biopunk Dystopias: Genetic Engineering, Society, and Science Fiction* and his contribution to this collection the move away from the cyberpunk imaginary (i.e. cyborg) toward a biopunk imaginary (i.e. splice). TPRGs and their supertech can therefore be considered as cyberpunk spliced with biotech because the plasticity of playable characters and their modified bodies allow artificial intelligence, information technology, robotics, genetic engineering, biotech, cognitive science, and nanotech to merge in any number of boundary-crossing splices limited only by the rules of the game and the player's imagination.

200

25.1 Mike Pondsmith's Cyberpunk and Its Iterations

The evolution of Mike Pondsmith's *Cyberpunk: The Roleplaying Game of the Dark Future* provides a litmus test of the growing importance of supertech's splice of cyberpunk and biopunk in TPRGs. The game's first iteration, colloquially known as *Cyberpunk 2013*, initially moved beyond both the broad, interstellar romances of space opera TPRGs such as Marc W. Miller's *Traveller* (Game Designers' Workshop 1977) or West End Games' *Star Wars* (1987) to instead offer a vision of a near future on an Earth run amok, circa 2013. *Cyberpunk 2013* was upgraded to *Cyberpunk 2020* (1990) with the publication of a new edition that fast-forwarded the timeline to 2020 and again adjusted in *Cyberpunk V3.0* (2005), set in the 2030s. An important shift between *Cyberpunk 2020* and *Cyberpunk V3.0*, however, reveals a continuum of complex choices for player characters, from *Cyberpunk 2013*'s and *Cyberpunk 2020*'s foci on mechanical cybertech to *Cyberpunk V3.0*'s inclusion of a variety of biological transformative supertech.[2]

In *Cyberpunk 2013*, the initial version of a Cyberpunk was someone living in a world dominated by mega-corporations following the Collapse, referring to the dismantling of social institutions on a global scale. Becoming a Cyberpunk meant embracing techno-shock or becoming antiquated: "As a Cyberpunk," Pondsmith writes, "you grab technology by the throat and hang on" (6). Cyberpunks use cybernetic implants (plugs) for many purposes, including jacking into information systems or weaponizing their bodies. Becoming a Cyberpunk also means embracing an attitude of resistance to oppressive control, all the while grafting technology onto one's body to survive. Players can choose characters such as a charismatic Rockerboy/-girl, a nod toward the actual musical punks that helped define and influence literary cyberpunk; Solos, described generically as "hired assassins, bodyguards, killers, soldiers" (4); or a Netrunner, a character who navigates the information landscape of cyberspace, to name a few options. These characters must utilize cybertech, and as "a Cyberpunk, you're going to want to get your hands on the best of this exciting and expensive newtech" (19), chiefly in the form of mechanical enhancements.

Although *Cyberpunk 2013* is clearly privileging mechanical enhancements, biotech exists in its broadest sense, albeit muted and without full application of bio-engineering techniques utilized for gameplay. For example, the core rulebook explains that the West Germans experimented with organic circuitry (5), but these types of enhancements are viewed as mechanical add-ons by individuals in the gameworld, another form of prosthetic tech. Similarly, an interesting game mechanic (i.e. rules that govern player interaction with the game) tracks how much cybertech a character adds and its overall impact, raising the issue of cyberpsychosis. Yet, this disease affects the body via mechanical means, rather than affecting the body through any genetic fallout: "Something happens when you start adding metal and plastic to people. They start to change. And it ain't pretty" (9).[3] Finally, cybertech surgery is an easy method of enhancement: "Think of it like getting your ears pierced, circa 1980" (20). Implantable tech such as nerve chips allows for cyborg-like interfaces, many of which are invisible.

In *Cyberpunk 2013*, then, the leap is yet to be made into a posthuman future where players' choices far exceed cybergear and neural nodes. The technological enhancements here, while within the realm of possible near-future sf scenarios, hint at analog, mechanical change rather than the truly fantastic imaginings of manipulating genetic code. In today's world where smart phones and wearables are common and implanting them is an option on the horizon, gene modification techniques like CRISPR-Cas9 suggest the untapped (and potentially dangerous) power of information manipulation at the level of genetic code. In other words, in *Cyberpunk 2013*, genetic code as a game element is still largely ignored and remains at the intersection of synthetic machine and biological organism, not the genetic splices that will lead to a hothouse of biological forms in later versions of the game.

Cyberpunk 2020 provides a helpful table listing 'bioware' upgrades (77), but these upgrades are described at the level of mechanical technology, rather than tech that rewrites genetic code: "Bioware is anything which is primarily low-impact technology that is designed along biological rather than mechanical lines" (85). The game therefore recognizes the importance of nanotechnology for the manipulation of such bioware, but is yet to fully deploy such techniques or effects within the game. For example, the use of vat technology acts as an analog for genetic engineering/printing, while body-sculpting uses the language of mechanical change at the level of the phenotype. A hint of where the game would eventually head, however, is with the description of how to alter skin as code: "Skin alteration uses transform DNA to change the structure of the patient's skin. Using tailored DNA, the skin can be induced to grow patterned fur, light scales, or exotic skin colors" (121). The focus on 'tailoring' DNA is an act of modifying genetic information. Without using the language of genetic engineering, this game element prefigures the discursive manipulation of information seen in gene manipulation as a mechanism for embodied change developing in current versions of cyberpunk-infused TRPGs.

In *Cyberpunk V3.0*, the overt focus on cybertech as mechanical prostheses, as well as the focus on the traditional dynamic of virtual vs. real space, became secondary to the focus on deployed supertech. Mike Pondsmith, Lisa Pondsmith, and Will Moss write in the Foreword to *Cyberpunk V3.0* that

> [i]t's a world some ten to twenty years after the original classic *Cyberpunk 2020*—a world where the vast Net has collapsed, the Megacorps are struggling to regain their stranglehold, and humanity has broken into divided, often warring factions, each centered around a new definition of what it means to be a Cyberpunk. You'll explore new edgy technologies of nanoscience, genetic engineering, transform viruses, advanced robotics and more. (3)

Cyberpunk V3.0's gameworld describes a number of cataclysmic events, including a computer virus that caused the Datakrash and the Carbon Plague, the latter an accident that released nano strains outside Night City, killing adults and adding mutations to children. These events, however, facilitate the emergence of six new tribes (i.e. Edgerunners, Reefers, Desnai, Rolling State, Rips, and Cee-Metal), alternative cultures (or Altcults) that give players the opportunity to define their characters in novel ways. These factions reflect curious uses of supertech; for example, the Cee-Metal are cyborgs, the Rolling State are nomads who live in mechanized and mobile cities, and the pirate-like Reefers live in the sea as genetically engineered underwater creatures, fighting over ever scarcer resources in a world devastated by climate change. Other tribes include the Riptide Federation, a peaceful conglomerate of floating cities, and the Desnai, a global amusement-park organization whose employees live and work for the betterment of the company. In a throwback to the first edition, the original Cyberpunks are still kicking around in *Cyberpunk V3.0*: "Metaled-up Edgerunners now stand shoulder to shoulder with glittering robo-men, mobile-city panzerboys, bioamped whalemen, aquatic drifters, techie mechanauts, corporate mafiosi, highrider deltajocks and the enigmatic ghosts of the past" (20). *V3.0* therefore stages a transition from the focus on a rebellion against globalized capitalist culture, evident in *Cyberpunk 2013* and *Cyberpunk 2020*, to surviving a post-apocalyptic world populated by diverse posthumanity saturated by traditional technological enhancements and supertech. The punk element that challenged a weaponized corporate world has now become a *Kulturkampf* (culture warfare), a battle of ideas on how best to survive and predicated on technical supremacy.

As is clearly evident in playing *Cyberpunk V3.0*, supertech drives these tribes. First, cybertech advances posit a variety of technological inventions; for example, NuCybe technology, chiefly in the form of advanced combat modules for weapons and defense for Edgerunners, acts as material sheaths over a character's biological form, while full cyborg developments of the Cee-Metal tribe use Livemetal, a supertech that moves beyond the limitations of alloy-based materials into a variety of other exotic substrates that can reform themselves as if living organisms. Reefers, however, choose to manipulate their biologies with a mechanism called transform nodes, or viruses that allow for the rapid transformation of cells and biological forms. Other iterations of supertech emerge with the Desnai's mechapresence, the ability to control swarms of robots with the mind, and the Rolling State's access to Nanosymbiosis, the utilization of nanotech to rapidly heal injuries or to easily access weapon systems. Riptide members even have access to Bioforms, genetically engineered creatures that act as protectors, pets, companions, etc. Taken together, these examples of supertech comprise a canvas that represents a trans-and-posthuman version of cyberpunk, one that moves beyond transhumanist ideas of enhancement into the realm of a wildly exotic posthumanity that envisions the coming century as dominated by fantastic biotechnologies, new 'dynamos' that extend modernity into the future.[4]

25.2 *Eclipse Phase* and the 21st Century

With the move into the 21st century, cyberpunk TRPGs have continued their exploration of supertech with games such as *Ex Machina* (Guardians of Order 2004), or the *Cyberscape* (2005) and *Future Tech* (2006) rulebooks for the *d20 Modern* system (Wizards of the Coast 2002). Other notable games blend cyberpunk elements with different modes and settings: *Etherscope* (Goodman Games 2005; also for the *d20 Modern* system) provides a steampunk focus on Victorian culture, while *Technoir* (Dream Machine Productions 2011) focuses on a hard-boiled detective fiction mode, and *Interface Zero* (Gun Metal Games 2014; based on the *Savage Worlds* system [Great White Games 2003]) explores a cyberpunk dystopia in which supertech has created true biological horrors like animal-human hybrids. And while it took the third iteration of Pondsmith's *Cyberpunk* to fully embrace supertech bioware, the use of supertech is the central theme of *Eclipse Phase* (Catalyst Game Labs/Posthuman Studios 2009), a more-recent trans-and-posthuman cyberpunk TRPG. The core rulebook, *Eclipse Phase: The Roleplaying Game of Transhuman Conspiracy and Horror* (2009), includes a mantra for the game in the cover-spread before the table of contents:

> Your mind is software. Program it.
> Your body is a shell. Change it.
> Death is a disease. Cure it.
> Extinction is approaching. Fight it. (1)

This mantra—*program, change, cure, fight*—drives the fundamental premise of the game and channels its cyberpunk roots by noting that both the body and mind are ripe for manipulation, while death has been vanquished and the ultimate fight is not against a global corporation or sophisticated computer virus but with species-ending events.[5]

The designers of *Eclipse Phase* created a game with transhumanism as a focus and, in particular, the construction of a post-Singularity society; however, the designers eschewed a hopeful representation of transhumanism for a post-apocalyptic dystopian view, in part because dystopias offer more plot options and conflicts that are instrumental to roleplaying games. Further, horrific elements such as evil AIs driving machines of war add to the central tension—i.e. the positive visions associated with a (hyper-humanist) transhumanism tempered by the concerns of a pessimistic posthumanism[6]—and give player characters a narrative function: They can be Sentinels in Firewall, a resistance organization "dedicated to counteracting 'existential risks'— threats to the existence of transhumanity" (22). Although *Eclipse Phase* includes what might be called Gibsonian cyberpunk's usual suspects of corporate thugs, street gangs, cybernetic soldiers, and so forth, the threats players have to navigate in *Eclipse Phase* have expanded in a Sterlingesque direction to include "biowar plagues, nanotech swarm outbreaks, nuclear proliferation, terrorists with WMDs, net-breaking computer attacks, rogue AIs, alien encounters, and so on" (22). In addition, both the technology and the landscape have expanded in *Eclipse Phase:* no longer are the cyberpunk locales the dark city streets of Pondsmith's (or Gibson's) 'Night City.' These places still exist, but the solar system and its different habitats are also available in the game. Therefore, as in cyberpunk where surviving is a challenge to both mind and body, *Eclipse Phase* places these two broadly Cartesian categories under technological and environmental pressure.

Central to *Eclipse Phase* is what the game calls 'egos' and 'morphs'; and understanding how to deploy egos and morphs is central to understanding the role of supertech. An ego is an analog for the mind, spirit, soul, etc., while a morph is any substrate within which such a 'mind' exists, be it a biological body, a robotic shell, a cybernetic prosthetic, or even digital information itself. In this gameworld, players are confronted with a series of concepts related to the self that must be rethought. Not only can any ego be backed up into an Infomorph (a digital self), players can egocast themselves through physical space to travel or create digital 'forks'—i.e. digital copies—to distribute workloads across portions of fragmented selves. There are also personal digital assistants called muses, which further enhance choices within the playable gamespace by adding a disembodied, digital landscape for characters to explore.[7]

The true texture of supertech-infused existence, however, can be found in embodied space. While the game's detailed description of clades (subcultures), its political and economic dynamics, and its game mechanics are beyond the scope of this chapter, the technologies deployed for survival demonstrate how embodied supertech is represented as increasingly fantastic in cyberpunk TRPGs, especially when seen in the trajectory from *Cyberpunk 2013* to *Eclipse Phase*. Of course, cyberpunk's data hives and urbanized ghettos exist, but so do cloud cities on Venus and ocean cities on Europa. Massive space habitats also exist, with the wealthy living in luxury, while 'scum' barges packed with refugees float in the void. Habitats can be shaped into a multitude of environments, from jungles to lavish private homes. A variety of factions compete for control of resources in the solar system, from anarchists resisting any form of governmental control to argonauts, scientists who use technologies to further open-source progressivism. *Eclipse Phase* also features criminal factions with connections to a complex underworld, as well as libertarian-like Extropians dedicated to private ownership and a free market. Meanwhile, the Hypercorps are dominated by corporatist ideologies and the Ultimates seek to move beyond transhumanity into a posthuman future. Other smaller factions located within exotic or remote regions seek their own interests, which usually concern major conflicts between different colonized areas and satellites of Luna, Mars, Venus, Jupiter, Saturn, etc., out to the Kuiper Belt.[8] This even allows players to craft their character's own faction with their own ideology for a flexible game experience.

Eclipse Phase's supertech emerges most clearly with the initial morphs (bodies) that characters must choose. Following in the tradition of cyberpunk pioneers such as Gibson and Sterling who deployed neologisms to capture the exotic flavor of enhanced technologies, and later Pondsmith and other game publishers of cyberpunk, *Eclipse Phase* demands that players embrace a host of terms to contextualize biological, synthetic, and information-based categories for the game. For example, biologically altered biomorphs representing transhumanity include Exalts, genetically enhanced humans who are both physically better and healthier than unenhanced humans, and Mentons, who are genetically smarter than humans. There are also the genetically stronger Olympians and overly attractive Sylphs. The Remade represents a step beyond a transhumanism that is still an enhanced humanism (or hyper-humanism) toward a posthuman existence beyond any normative ontological standards. They are described as follows: "taller, lack of hair, slightly larger craniums, wider eyes, smaller noses, smaller teeth, and elongated digits" (141). Other options exist for players, including Neoavian birds who have been augmented ('uplifted') with human-level intelligence and genetically altered to be larger and more humanoid, and Neohominids who are apes that have undergone the same uplifting. Players can even play in octopus-like bodies called Octomorphs.

In all these instances, players must choose traits and skills for their characters, many of which are rooted initially in transhuman enhancements. For example, mindhacking has created unexpected cognitive abilities (PSI) that include mental armor, pain resistance, pattern recognition abilities, enhanced intuition and creativity, etc. Also, mind-backups (egos) are available, which allow for the replacement of dead bodies by moving into new morphs. Finally, all the expected mechanical and biological cybergear is available, with the use of advanced nanotechnology.

In addition to these enhancements and body options, supertech's structural elements drive *Eclipse Phase*'s narrative, chiefly in the form of secrets unknown to most characters (and new players). One example is alien life that acts as an ultimate mystery in need of revealing for ambitious players as well as for their knowledge-seeking characters. These extraterrestrial intelligences (ETI) are so advanced that they move beyond extrapolated science into a godlike form whose advanced abilities can be conceptualized by lesser beings (in a Clarke-like fashion)[9] as the 'supernatural fantastic,' bordering on the marvelous or the horrific (if a character were ever to encounter it):

> [ETI] is capable of megascale engineering projects and enjoys an understanding of physics, matter, energy, and universal laws that makes all of transhuman knowledge seem insignificant in comparison. Most likely, the ETI itself evolved from some sort of artificial intelligence singularity event in its own past, ascending to a god-like level of super-intelligence. It may no longer be recognizably biological. (352)

The existence of and encounter with ETI-technology generates the primary technological novum that drives the gameworld: On the one hand, the so-called Pandora Gates allow travel throughout the universe; on the other, the galaxy has been seeded with self-replicating viral probes that monitor systems for highly intelligent life, i.e. post-biological (digital) life that can be infected. In the recent past of *Eclipse Phase*'s setting, human-programmed AIs became infected by such a virus, which then led to the dystopic devastation that transhumanity now hopes to overcome.

Thus, as noted earlier, players become Sentinels in Firewall, an organization dedicated to transhuman survival. While the game minimizes the possibility of encounters with aliens, it provides a suggestion that "the powers in the deep cold dark on the edge of the Milky Way have been self-aware since before Earth was so much as a ripple in warming gas around the not-yet-ignited Sun" (361). Most often, these aliens remain in the background, although they offer the possibility of adding a new layer of the supernatural fantastic to the game.

In most cases, other humans are of more immediate concern to Sentinels, such as those who want to expand transhuman technology beyond normative limitations and encourage extreme posthuman existence. Neurodes, for example, have abandoned biological bodies for a combination of body/brain shells that allow for increased intelligence, while Predators use cybernetics and bio-engineering for extreme manipulation of their intelligences and physiologies. More terrifying are Exsurgents, transhumans infected by ETI viruses. Creepers have been transformed into swarms or protean bubbles that can take any shape, while Jellies function as overwhelming blobs of sentient material. Shifters have hardened bodies that can change shape like liquid metal. And Whippers with their barrel bodies and tentacles or Wrappers with their starfish bodies echo the scariest descriptions of creatures found in H.P. Lovecraft and similar pulp horror stories.

Finally, the game introduces another, more accessible alien species, The Factors, who also suffered at the hands of the self-replicating viral ETIs: "Individual Factors resemble non-translucent ambulatory amoeba, slime molds, or slugs" (373). With complex biologies, social habits, modes of communication, and even art, Factors also use technology in a mysterious fashion, which allows gamemasters and their players flexibility in how to use them (cf. Sterling). In sum, *Eclipse Phase* positions technology as a way to extend mind and body into the realm of embodied phenotypes and disembodied intelligent information, offering approaches that mirror other forms of cyberpunk and hearken back to cyberpunk's formative period in the 1980s.

25.3 *Shadowrun* and the Idea of Magic

With their focus on bio-enhancements, TRPGs such as the *Cyberpunk* iterations and *Eclipse Phase*, coupled with robotic/cybernetic prostheses common to cyberpunk in general, form an interesting core dynamic. Where TRPGs differ from mainstream cyberpunk, however, is their willingness to blur boundaries and incorporate elements more common to fantasy and horror. For example, a mixture of magic and technology is prominent in the first edition of the mixed-genre TRPG *Shadowrun* (FASA 1989), published only a year after *Cyberpunk 2013*.[10] It contained much of what was expected from cyberpunk (i.e. the creative use of neologisms, the focus on cybernetic prosthetics, the 'punk' resistance to oppressive power, a dark and gritty setting, etc.), yet added mythic elements more common in other forms of the fantastic. For example, alongside its cyberpunk supertech, the game added supernatural creatures from high fantasy (such as elves, orks, trolls, dragons, etc.), as well as a form of magic use. In this way, the game mashed together themes from hard sf and high fantasy, producing a rationalization of the fantastic elements (be they magic or extreme forms of supertech). Such an overt mode of hybridization and generic flexibility allows players even more exotic ways of exploring posthuman-becomings, showcasing the games as a fruitful example of sf as fantastic.

On the one hand, the game provides technologically created posthumanity through the use of cyberpunk tropes: multinational corporations, cyberspace populated by deckers who jack in through their bodies, robotic prostheses, and many more. On the other hand, *Shadowrun* conceptualizes trans-and-posthumanism also through magic, effectively broadening the scope of cyberpunk TRPGs. The same evil corporations are run by dragons, aided in their power and control over these by their magically long life spans and embodied presence ideally suited for manipulation and intimidation. Weaponized cyborg-warriors are now possibly orks or trolls with much larger body mass and the ability, through magically created different embodied realities, to cope with the installment of more technology. The decker is aided by the technomancer's embodied magical ability to manipulate the ghost in the machine, not by his programming skills. The same fantastic imaginary is invoked by technical and supernatural means, allowing players to create hyper-embodied characters whose selves, egos, and identities are expanded through both supertech and magical means. This version of fantastic trans-and-posthuman agency is more varied than usual and highly imaginative far beyond the original representations of surfing cyberspace or enhancing one's body with mechanical upgrades.

This chapter has examined cyberpunk TRPGs within a continuum that first found its roots in literary and screened touchstone versions. The arrival of Pondsmith's *Cyberpunk 2013*, though, adapted the genre to roleplaying games, the study of which provides an insightful perspective. Of critical importance is the shift from a focus on traditional cyberpunk tropes, such as the mechanical prostheses of cyborgs, to the genetic splices of the bio-engineered. This trend can be seen in the different editions of Pondsmith's game, as well as in the imaginings of the more recent *Eclipse Phase* where supertech becomes a mechanism for the rationalized fantastic. Key here is a focus on how supertech functions as a fantastic departure from extrapolated science. Such a revision of cyberpunk via an imagined biopunk trajectory also reflects a move within the discourses of trans-and-posthumansim from transhumanism's focus on human enhancement to the imaginings of possible posthuman futures. This chapter has argued that such supertech acts as an analog for magic, a seminal mechanism within traditional fantastic genres grounded in the mythic rather than in science or technology. In such a way, the TRPG *Shadowrun* channels both of these elements, supertech and magic functioning in a fruitful miscibility. Ultimately, the biological turn in cyberpunk invigorates TRPGs, carving pathways that intertwine digital and analog mechanisms as defining modes of our technologized present.

Notes

1   The fantastic is a broad impulse that, as per Kathryn Hume's argument, defines a major aspect of representation in western thinking, alongside a mimetic impulse. The fantastic, as an impulse, is broader than fantasy as a literary mode. Because the fantastic often exists within mimetic fiction, building on Hume, I see the fantastic within hard SF, often, in the background as a hidden other. For this paper, the fantastic in the many sub-categories of sf and fantasy explains its use of supertech as an analog of supernatural magic. For more on Hume and the modern fantastic, see my monograph *Dread Trident* (2019).
2   Of continued interest will be how a supertech-driven cyberpunk is conceptualized within a game mode. The Polish video game developer CD Projekt Red is currently working on a digital continuation of Pondsmith's influential TRPG. They have kept details about *Cyberpunk 2077* at a minimum, finally releasing gameplay footage in 2018. Further, R. Talsorian and Pondsmith have announced the release of *Cyberpunk Red*, an updated version of the TRPG (see R. Talsorian) to be released in 2020.
3   Although not the focus of this chapter, body-modification through cybernetics can be enacted through cyberpunk fashion in TRPGs, thus granting more than simply a way for players to visualize their characters. This attempt at embodying a cyberpunk aesthetics can encourage a playful fantastic, yet hint at potentially dangerous consequences for gameplay. For example, "fashionware," we're told in *Cyberpunk 2013*, "comes with a cost" (72), a key insight that to enhance oneself is risky. A primary critique of transhumanism is that this attempt at enhancing normative human elements is actually a dangerous path with sometimes unintended consequences. For a detailed study of fashion, cybernetic enhancement, and gameplay in *Cyberpunk 2020*, see Attebery and Pearson.
4   While it may be customary to differentiate transhumanism from posthumanism—i.e. the former as an enhanced subjectivity rooted in traditional humanism, in spite of what sometimes emerges as a hyper-humanism that is still a form of advanced (trans)humanism; the latter as a truly other (post) humanity whose ontology is up for debate—Stefan Herbrechter, Stefan Lorenz Sorgner, and others see commonalities between the discourses and argue that a demand for teasing them apart, while helpful in many ways, removes key elements (such as ties to Heidegger, for example—for more, see Ranisch and Sorgner).
5   Such content has been embedded within cyberpunk from its beginning, as evident, for example, in Sterling's *Schismatrix* (1985) and the other Mechanist/Shaper stories. For more details, see Carbonell's "Schismatrix and the Posthuman: Hyper-Embodied Representation" or Maria Goicoechea's contribution to this collection.
6   *EP* foregrounds the frightful side of posthuman existence rather than the hopeful side of the transhumanist desire to enhance normative humanity. This is done as a way to further tension at the table. For a comprehensive overview of these discourses, see Ranisch and Sorgner. For critical posthumanism, see Braidotti; Hayles; Herbrechter; Wolfe.
7   This ignores conversations within critical theory about the problem with disembodiment, such as Hayle's critique in *How We Became Posthuman*.
8   See the SyFy tv series, *The Expanse* (2015–).
9   Arthur C. Clarke has famously remarked that "any sufficiently advanced technology is indistinguishable from magic."
10   For a detailed analysis of Shadowrun, see Hamish Cameron's chapter in this collection.

Works Cited

Attebery, Stina and Josh Pearson. "'Today's Cyborg is Stylish': The Humanity Cost of Posthuman Fashion in *Cyberpunk 2020.*" *Cyberpunk and Visual Culture*, edited by Graham J. Murphy and Lars Schmeink. Routledge, 2018, pp. 55–79.

Boyle, Rob, and Brian Cross. *Eclipse Phase*. Posthuman Studios, 2009.

Braidotti, Rosi. *The Posthuman*. Polity, 2013.

Carbonell, Curtis D. "Schismatrix and the Posthuman: Hyper-Embodied Representation." *Fafnir: Nordic Journal of Science Fiction and Fantasy Research*, vol. 3, no. 2, 2016, pp. 7–16.

Carbonell, Curtis. *Dread Trident: Tabletop Role-Playing Games and the Modern Fantastic*. Liverpool UP, 2019.

Clarke, Arthur C. "'Hazards of Prophecy: The Failure of Imagination.'" *Profiles of the Future: An Enquiry into the Limits of the Possible*. Popular Library, 1977, pp. 30–39.

Grebowicz, Margret, et al. *Beyond the Cyborg: Adventures with Donna Haraway*. Columbia UP, 2013.

Hayles, N. Katherine. *How We Became Posthuman: Virtual Bodies in Cybernetics, Literature, and Informatics*. U of Chicago P, 1999.

Herbrechter, Stefan. *Posthumanism: A Critical Analysis*. Bloomsbury, 2013.

Hume, Kathryn. *Fantasy and Mimesis: Responses to Reality in Western Literature*. Methuen, 1984.

Pondsmith, Mike, et al. *Cyberpunk: The Roleplaying Game of the Dark Future. View from the Edge: The Cyberpunk Handbook*, 1st Ed. R. Talsorian Games, 1988.

———. *Cyberpunk 2020: The Roleplaying Game of the Dark Future*, 2nd Ed. R. Talsorian Games, 1990.

———. *Cyberpunk: Roleplaying in the Dark Future*, 3rd Ed. R. Talsorian Games, 2006.

R. Talsorian Games. "A New Partnership." R. Talsorian, 01 May 2019, rtalsoriangames.com/2019/05/01/a-new-partnership/.

Ranisch, Robert, and Stefan Lorenz Sorgner, eds. *Post- and Transhumanism: An Introduction*. Lang, 2014.

Schmeink, Lars. *Biopunk Dystopias Genetic Engineering, Society and Science Fiction*. Liverpool UP, 2016.

Sterling, Bruce. *Schismatrix Plus*. Ace, 1996.

Wolfe, Cary. *What Is Posthumanism?* U of Minnesota P, 2010.

26

SHADOWRUN (CASE STUDY)

Hamish Cameron

The late 1980s saw the emergence of two major standalone tabletop roleplaying games (TRPGs) in the cyberpunk mode: *Cyberpunk* (R. Talsorian Games 1988) and *Shadowrun* (FASA 1989). R. Talsorian Games published the first edition of *Cyberpunk*, commonly known as *Cyberpunk 2013* after the date of the diegetic fictional future, quickly followed by a second edition called *Cyberpunk 2020* (1990), and more recently *Cyberpunk v3.0* (2005) and the newly announced *Cyberpunk Red* (2020, tbc.). *Cyberpunk 2013* was not only popular enough to spawn a franchise, but it helped define cyberpunk TRPGs and spurred an immediate flurry of cyberpunk games, most notably *Cyberspace* (Iron Crown Entertainment 1989), *GURPS Cyberpunk* (Steven Jackson Games 1990), and *Shadowrun*.[1] Although these TRPGs shared many traits common to traditional print and cinematic cyberpunk, including their setting in worlds governed by corporations, the typical cast of criminals and street-smart survivors, the parallel, mediated worlds of cyberspace, and the ubiquitous invasive technologies to enhance the human body, *Shadowrun* emerged as the most popular and well-known cyberpunk TRPG, having produced five editions of the core game, over fifty novels, and eight standalone video games. The key point of difference between *Shadowrun* and the rest of the first wave of cyberpunk games was the inclusion of magic and fantasy races (called 'metahumans'). The inclusion of these fantasy elements was popularizing but divisive—William Gibson, for example, wrote of his "extreme revulsion at seeing [his] literary DNA mixed with elves" (Lincoln)—but *Shadowrun*'s long running success speaks to "a compelling world and an entertaining play experience" (Attebery and Pearson 58). Although *Shadowrun* is a blend of styles, its continuous multimedia publication history and popular fantasy elements have made it one of the most well-known and classic examples of a cyberpunk TRPG: It engages with cyberpunk themes through its mechanical features as well as through a setting history that deploys both the style of conspiracy narratives and Alvin Toffler's concept of future shock.

26.1 *Shadowrun* as a TRPG: Concepts and Quantification

In a TRPG, a group of players communicate with each other to tell a story using an agreed-upon set of rules and systems for arbitrating narrative authority over the shared fictional space.[2] The text of a TRPG rulebook can be conceptualized as having two main parts: *setting* and *system*.[3] The *setting* of a TRPG describes the shared fictional space inhabited by the characters in the story and the *system* of rules articulates how conflicts and uncertainties within the fiction are resolved and how narrative authority is distributed among the players. In *Shadowrun*, most of the players control the actions and personality of a single character, while one player, the Gamemaster, is responsible for preparing the scenario (or 'adventure') that the group will play, for describing everything and everyone else in the gameworld (setting), and for acting as a referee and arbitrator in the case of any rules (system) disputes. Setting and system are not easily separated. Often, the rules system intentionally or unintentionally encodes elements of setting information. This can be seen in the quantification of characters. Every *Shadowrun* character has a fixed number of 'Attributes' (Body, Quickness, Strength, Charisma, Intelligence, Willpower) which quantify their innate physical and mental abilities. Metahumans (elves, dwarfs, orcs, and trolls) are mechanically distinguished by higher or lower maximum ratings in certain Attributes (*Shadowrun* 31). For example, orcs have a lower maximum Intelligence and higher maximum Strength than 'normal' humans. Thus, the core of the system prioritizes certain categories of differentiation (physical strength is included, but not, say, social status), encodes innate biological differences between characters of different racial categories (orcs are stronger and less intelligent), and constructs a fictional reality where these characteristics can be measured, compared, and quantified.[4] This quantification is not a distinctive feature of *Shadowrun*, but how it manifests in any given TRPG reveals design decisions about how and what assumptions about reality are encoded in the setting by the system, either as an explicit statement about the gameworld or as an implicit adoption from the cultural milieu of the designers.

26.2 Running the Shadows: Violence and the Essence of Life

In *Shadowrun*, characters are the eponymous 'shadowrunners,' freelance criminals, and mercenaries undertaking missions for and against the 'Mega-Corporations' that control the world of 2050. These missions frequently take the form of heists, taking *Neuromancer*'s Straylight Run as a model. As is standard (but not universal) for TRPGs, violence, its tools, and its results occupy considerable space (including chapters on combat, military equipment, and a combat-focused magic system), thus framing violence as a major part in the game both for the resolution of fictional conflicts and for the players to influence the direction of the story. This focus on violence is also evident in how the game rewards character action. At the end of a shadowrun, the players receive 'Karma' which they can spend to improve their character's chances of success in future missions. The Gamemaster awards Karma based on certain criteria: Players are rewarded for surviving the shadowrun, for succeeding at assigned objectives, for 'good roleplaying' (i.e. portraying their character well), for brave or effective fighting, and for clever combat strategies and for clever combat strategies (*Shadowrun* 160). Most of these criteria center the role of violence in the game, guiding the direction and tone of gameplay through in-game reward structures that motivate the players toward violence. The structure of the game text and the system itself suggests that the characters exist in a violent future world where they will inflict and receive violence on a regular basis. The external violence perpetrated by the characters is paralleled by the internal violence they suffer through the bodily invasion of cyberware.

In common with other games of the first wave of cyberpunk TRPGs, *Shadowrun* takes a simplistic view of cybernetics at odds with the literary genre's exploration of the interface between humanity and technology. In *Shadowrun*, the replacement of flesh by technology makes the character less able to interact in human society: "All Cyberware eats away at the very essence of life, replacing meat with machine" (*Shadowrun* 126). Mechanically, *Cyberpunk*'s Empathy stat and *Shadowrun*'s Essence Attribute are almost identical: All cyberware has a cost which subtracts from the relevant number; when that number reaches a certain level, the character is removed from the player's control. Fictionally, however, the two mechanics are quite different as the names of the two statistics suggest. In *Cyberpunk 2020*, all cyberware has a randomized Humanity Cost, which lowers the character's Empathy stat, a "measure of how well the character relates to other people" (*CP2020* 73). When their Empathy reaches zero, the character suffers from complete cyberpsychosis and becomes a murderous 'cyberpsycho' controlled by the Gamemaster. The game text discusses cyberpsychosis in some detail, including official response to cyberpsychos, state control of cybernetically enhanced criminals, and personal therapy options.[5] In *Shadowrun*, all cyberware has a set Essence Cost which lowers the character's Essence. When their Essence drops below zero, the character dies. *Shadowrun* defines Essence as "a measure of the soundness of the central nervous system and spirit. Invasive things, such as Cyberware, reduce Essence" (*Shadowrun* 31). For most characters, Essence simply functions as game mechanic to limit powerful cybernetic implants. Certain common character archetypes start to play with their Essence reduced to almost zero by cyberware. Bodily augmentation makes a character less human, eventually resulting in death. This paradigm leaves little room for exploring cyberpunk's oft-cited radical reconfiguration of the boundaries between nature of humanity, the self, and technologies.[6] A character is either alive, with some amount of cyberware, or dead because of too much cyberware. Unlike the results of the violence on which play often centers, which is mediated and randomized by a considerable number of dice rolls, the line between life and death through Essence loss is precisely known by the player. Nevertheless, the importance of cyberware for most characters and the importance of the Matrix to some characters and most in-game missions place the technologies of body invasion and mind invasion in a central, if unnuanced, position in most sessions of play.

26.3 Setting History as a Conspiracy Narrative

The introductory section of *Shadowrun* sets up the fictional background of the world with a brief summary of two fundamental setting elements: cybernetic enhancement of the human mind and body and a 'return' of magic to the world through an event called 'The Awakening.' We learn that the 20th century was responsible for integrating the human mind and computers, followed by cybernetic implants, but the subsequent Awakening allowed the magic that had remained dormant for the past 3,000 years to return; as a result, elves, dwarfs, orcs, and trolls began interacting with cyberpunk's cyborgs and streetwise hustlers (*Shadowrun* 6). *Shadowrun*'s setting history therefore breaks away from our real-world history circa 1989 (not coincidentally *Shadowrun*'s publication date) and forms the foundation for the game's fictional setting in 2050. This history can be divided into two narrative frames. In the first, magic is a hidden and unknown force wielded by mysterious actors. After the Awakening, the second frame begins, in which magic is a visible and tangible part of the world. In both frames, the setting history conforms to cyberpunk's standard setting tropes: devolution of power away from central governments, vastly increased corporate freedom at the expense of individual freedom, increased socio-economic inequality, development of cybernetic enhancements that 'invade' both the body and mind, and the growth of a global computer network. The events that disrupt the status quo and drive the world of *Shadowrun* toward its dystopian future, however, are mostly supernatural in nature: the emergence of magical powers, creatures, and sub-groups of humanity. Rather than detracting from cyberpunk's themes, *Shadowrun* reinforces them: The supernatural provides an additional layer of mystery behind which cyberpunk conspiracies might lurk and the supernatural acts as a lens for centering contemporary social issues, supplementing the technological and corporate lenses of traditional cyberpunk.

In addition to the obvious cyberpunk traits, *Shadowrun*'s setting history also relies upon the undertheorized relationship between cyberpunk and conspiracy narratives.[7] *Shadowrun*'s setting history uses three core aspects of conspiracy narratives: the assumption that hidden powers are in control of events; the authorization of the text by a periodic adoption of quasi-academic style; and the deployment of a narrative pivot after which the 'truth' is revealed to the protagonist. First, both cyberpunk and conspiracy narratives evoke hidden or invisible systems of power. Just as cyberpunk focuses on the seemingly limitless power of multinational corporations, so conspiracy theories posit that the power of a ruling group is so pervasive that virtually all aspects of social life, politics, and economics are under its control (Fenster xiv). An important facet of this instrumental power is that it is wielded in secret but those aware of its existence can hack the system and discover the 'truth' (Fenster xiv). Conspiracy theories also usually develop an elaborate network of links and actors to account for events that might otherwise be considered coincidental (Byford 73–75). In this regard, *Shadowrun*'s setting history frequently makes use of suggestive and partial accounts of events, alluding to a conspiratorial hidden 'truth' which is yet to be uncovered. An early example concerns a raid on a missile silo in Montana:

> A small band entered the Shiloh Launch Facility in northwest Montana, capturing a missile silo. To this day no one knows how the raiders managed to bypass the security patrols, but once inside they met up with John Redbourne, a USAF major and a full-blood Dakota Sioux. After knocking his partner unconscious, Redbourne took the man's keys and codes to unlock the launch failsafes. (13)

The narrative succinctly describes an apparently complete event in the first sentence, and then proceeds to complicate the event with a clause that suggests an element of mystery ("to this day no one knows") and casts doubt on how the raid progressed. This sense of mystery is intensified by the accumulation of details about the events within the raid, which now must be read in the light of the fact that "no one knows" exactly what happened. The account continues: "Issuing a demand for the return of all Indian land, the Shiloh raiders threatened to launch the silo's missiles. Ten days of tense negotiations ended when a black-garbed delta team invaded the silo. During the struggle, which resulted in the death of the occupying Indians, a Lone Eagle missile was launched" (13). The narrative suggests the hidden exercise of unknown power—i.e. the particular clothing of the invaders ("a black-garbed delta team"), the death of the entire occupying force, and the launch of a missile during a tense struggle. Rather than aiming for a historically objective tone, the narrative presents these elements as if covered by a conspiratorial veil, which could be removed to reveal a 'true' explanation. This conspiratorial tone is repeated throughout the setting history.

In addition to a concern for a hidden 'truth,' conspiracy narratives also authorize their narratives by what Byford calls "the rhetoric of scientific inquiry" (88). This adoption of a quasi-academic style even goes so far as founding 'scholarly' journals to legitimize holocaust denial, 9/11 conspiracy theories, and "fringe theories about HIV/AIDS" (Byford 88–90). *Shadowrun*'s setting history uses academic and technical sidebars offering a seemingly impartial analysis of events by knowledgeable experts to present some events as factual and fully understood. For example, the section describing the invention of the Matrix, *Shadowrun*'s Gibsonian cyberspace, is presented in the style of an expert (Dr. William Spheris) explaining his work to a popular audience. Spheris calls the Matrix a "consensual hallucination" (16), an intertextual reference to Gibson's famous description of cyberspace in *Neuromancer* (1984) as "[a] consensual hallucination experienced daily by billions of legitimate operators" (51). Similarly, the sidebar accompanying a section describing how "magic joined the ranks of science at last" (16–17) is cited as a quotation from a paper delivered at an academic conference. The inclusion of these expert opinions aims to authorize the main narrative—as well as to legitimize the game text as authentically cyberpunk by the intertextual reference to Gibson.

Another feature of conspiracy narratives is the "narrative pivot." Fenster describes this as the point at which "a convergence of information" allows the protagonist and the audience to make the "correct interpretive decisions necessary" to integrate the overwhelming barrage of information and events into a moment of 'truth' (Fenster 123–5). In other words, the point when the reader obtains the clue that reveals the mystery. In *Shadowrun*, the Awakening that reveals magic to the world is the narrative pivot. The revelation of the existence of the supernatural through the undeniable manifestation of dragons, metahumans, and overt magical power allows the previous 'mysteries' to be neatly explained. Thereafter, in the second narrative frame, supernatural activity no longer has the same resonance as a 'secret truth.'

The narrative pivot does not resolve the conspiracy. Now that the 'truth' is known, the protagonist or the audience has the interpretive tools necessary to make sense of the newly unveiled reality. In *Shadowrun*, when the existence of magic is openly known, supernatural power becomes another tool at the disposal of protagonists and conspirators alike. The setting history reorients toward familiar indications of conspiracy through the exercise of worldly, but mysterious, power. A conventional war between NATO and the Warsaw Pact is ended by a wave of airstrikes conducted by an unknown party "obliterating key communications and command centers belonging to both sides. [...] No one knows who was responsible for the strike" (19). No further revelation expands on the narrative. A fantastic explanation is possible, but the mysterious violence points to transnational actors, using technological tools, more akin to the assassination of Stubbs that begins the action of Sterling's *Islands in the Net* (1988) than Shiloh's mysterious raiders (*Shadowrun* 13). As the second narrative frame ends, both magical and technological tools are equally available for open use by protagonists seeking the truth, and for covert use by transnational actors seeking to obscure it.

Cyberpunk narratives highlight the omnipresent threat of corporate violence. In traditional cyberpunk texts, global megacorporations like Gibson's Hosaka or Maas-Neotek operate as shadowy actors of uncertain and potentially malevolent intent controlling global events. Consider Josef Virek, the hypercapitalist (and terminal) antagonist in Gibson's *Count Zero* (1986). For example, he tells art connoisseur Marly Krushkova that "[a]spects of my wealth have become autonomous, by degrees; at times they even war with one another. Rebellion in the fiscal extremities" (13). Virek's wealth is so complex that we might best conceptualize its operations as occult, in keeping with conspiracy theories and narratives that often deploy the language of the occult even in situations where they do not propose supernatural agents in the conspiracy (Byford 80–81). In addition, in conspiracy narratives "there is more to social and political reality than meets the eye" (Byford 79), and this is equally true of cyberpunk. In fine cyberpunk fashion, *Shadowrun* is a world of shadowy actors of uncertain and potentially malevolent intent hiding a *real* world behind the 'real' world. This conspiratorial worldview even permeates the subsequent metaplots. For example, the Harlequin metaplot concerns a power struggle between ancient elven protagonists which somehow persisted even while magic was absent from the world;[8] the Universal Brotherhood metaplot centers on a worldwide cult acting as a cover organization for a magical invasion of 'Insect Spirits' whose eruption destroys Chicago.[9] In sum, *Shadowrun*'s setting history deftly combines the rhetoric of objective history with that of cyberpunk, conspiracy, and the revelation of secrets. This rhetorical style emerges from the act of building a compelling world that echoes cyberpunk's near-future settings but simultaneously uses magic and conspiracy theories to imply an obscured 'truth' to be uncovered in play. The success of this conspiratorial history is one of *Shadowrun*'s most distinctive features.

26.4 Narrative Velocity and Future Shock

In addition to their complicated relationship to objective truth or the 'real' world, conspiracy narratives use "quick depictions of a multiplicity of events in brief scenes" to bombard and overwhelm the reader with "evidence" (Fenster 122). In so doing, these 'quick depictions' speed through historical events and across a dispersed and complex network of actors and locations (Fenster 120), all of which resonate with cyberpunk. For example, in his Preface to *Mirrorshades: The Cyberpunk Anthology*, Sterling describes how literary cyberpunk bombards the reader with crammed prose and sensory overload (xiv–xv). He also acknowledges cyberpunk's debt to Alvin Toffler's conceptualization of the emergent information age (xii). In *Future Shock*, Toffler contends that the accelerated rate of technological and social change overloads the physical and psychological limits of the human organism (290). One manifestation of this change is through accelerated information flow, through impermanent and "kinetic" slogans, symbols, and images (Toffler, *Future* 136–161). This is the language of both cyberpunk and conspiracy narratives, and in combination, of *Shadowrun*.

Shadowrun's setting history presents a sparsely but evocatively described catalog of events, which bombards the reader with wave after wave of escalating horrors that threaten to overload the reader with kinetic information. For example, as the first narrative frame centered on the return of magic reaches its climax, the history begins to accumulate a series of extreme events for emotional response: There is an earthquake that kills more than 200,000 New Yorkers, an Israeli nuclear strike that destroys half of Libya's cities, two plagues that decimate 35% of the global population, a crashed "spaceplane" that kills 300 Australians, and waves of bodily metamorphoses that transform humans into "metahumans" that spark "racial" violence against them (*Shadowrun* 14–19). After the narrative pivot of the Awakening, things get no better as the Toffler-like accelerative future shock begins anew: An unprecedented virus causes a worldwide computer crash, followed by waves of government and economic collapse, warfare erupts between NATO and the Warsaw Pact in Europe and near civil war in eastern North America, and there is widespread decentralization of state power (*Shadowrun* 17–18). What emerges is a pattern: Most of the personal and invasive traumas are focused on magical bodily transformations, while the large-scale upheavals derive from classic cyberpunk tropes, including the "tools of global integration—the satellite media net, the multinational corporation" (Sterling xiv), as well as Toffler's focus on accelerated information flow and global corporations (*Third* 336–39). In sum, near-future TRPG settings (including *Shadowrun* and *Cyberpunk 2020*) commonly deploy this pattern of global catastrophic events as an opportunity for redrawing the map of a fictional future world. The stresses from the overwhelming rate of change manifest directly and catastrophically in cyberpunk TRPGs as exemplars of Toffler's future shock, and in *Shadowrun* the texture of the near-apocalyptic rearrangement of geopolitical space is colored by the inclusion of fantasy elements, but still serves to subordinate state power to autonomous global megacorporations in a manner thoroughly familiar to cyberpunk.

26.5 Conclusion: Supernatural Shock

In the Preface to *Mirrorshades: The Cyberpunk Anthology*, Sterling describes two kinds of technology common to cyberpunk: the personal, tactile, and invasive, and the globally connective, structural, and controlling (xiii–xiv). While the former is common to cyberpunk, *Shadowrun*'s setting history is concerned to a far greater degree with the latter; namely, the technologies that invade the body and the mind are present in the game, but deemphasized and entirely reconfigured. In other words, the role of the visceral, tactile, and personal is not dominated by technology but instead the supernatural. It is magic rather than technology which invades the body and mind, "radically redefining the nature of humanity, the nature of the self" (Sterling xiii) in a fashion very different from comparable cyberpunk. This itself is exactly the kind of "free play" that Larry McCaffery identifies as a core element of cyberpunk (14–15) and to which William Gibson's oft-quoted line applies: "the street finds its own uses for things" ("Burning" 186). While the two narrative frames of *Shadowrun*'s setting history make use of a conspiratorial style to evoke an impression of the headlong acceleration into a dystopian future, it is a supernatural shock rather than a future shock which provides the initial disruption that allows the domination of global corporate networks and ultimately gives *Shadowrun* its dominant, and largely unique, position among cyberpunk games.

Notes

1 For a detailed history of cyberpunk TRPGs, see Appelcline (vol. 2, pp. 289–92), as well as the overview chapter by Curtis Carbonell in this volume.
2 For details on rules and systems for arbitrating narrative authority in TRPGs, see Zagal and Deterding.
3 On what comprises the 'text' of a TRPG, see Jara and Torner.
4 The issue of race in *Shadowrun*, both in terms of real-world groups and issues in the game and the incorporation of fantasy races, demands further examination, but requires more space than is available here.
5 The relationship between *CP2020*'s Humanity Cost mechanic and the posthuman dynamics of the setting is addressed in Attebery and Pearson (71–75).
6 For further studies on cyberpunk's radical reconfigurations, see Featherstone and Burrows and/or Foster as a starting place for what is an otherwise wide range of academic work on this subject.
7 I draw on Fenster's and Byford's respective works on the anatomy of conspiracy theories for this section of my *Shadowrun* analysis.
8 For further details on the Harlequin metaplot, see Dowd's *Harlequin* and *Harlequin's Back*.
9 For further details on this metaplot, see Findley's *The Universal Brotherhood* and Cruz et al.'s *Bug City*.

Works Cited

Appelcline, Shannon. *Designers & Dragons: A History of the Roleplaying Game Industry*, 4 vols. Evil Hat, 2013.
Attebery, Stina, and Josh Pearson. "'Today's Cyborg Is Stylish': The Humanity Cost of Posthuman Fashion in Cyberpunk 2020." *Cyberpunk and Visual Culture*, edited by Graham J. Murphy and Lars Schmeink. Routledge, 2018, pp. 55–79.
Byford, Jovan. *Conspiracy Theories: A Critical Introduction*. Palgrave, 2011.
Cruz, Robert, et al. *Bug City*. FASA Corp., 1994.
Dowd, Tom, ed. *Harlequin*. FASA Corp., 1990.
———, ed. *Harlequin's Back*. FASA Corp., 1994.
Featherstone, Mike and Roger Burrows, eds. *Cyberspace/Cyberbodies/Cyberpunk: Cultures of Technological Embodiment*. Sage, 1995.
Fenster, Mark. *Conspiracy Theories: Secrecy and Power in American Culture*. U of Minnesota P, 2008.
Findley, Nigel D. *The Universal Brotherhood*. FASA Corp., 1990.
Foster, Thomas. *The Souls of Cyberfolk: Posthumanism as Vernacular Theory*. U of Minnesota P, 2005.
Gibson, William. "Burning Chrome." *Burning Chrome*. Arbor House, 1986, pp. 168–191.
———. *Count Zero*. Arbor House, 1986.
———. *Neuromancer*. Ace, 1984.
Jara, David and Evan Torner. "Literary Studies and Role-Playing Games." *Role-Playing Game Studies: Transmedia Foundations*, edited by José Pablo Zagal and Sebastian Deterding. Routledge, 2018, pp. 265–82.
Lincoln, Ben. "Cyberpunk on Screen—William Gibson Speaks." *The Peak* (via Archive.org), 19 Oct. 1998, peak.sfu.ca/the-peak/98-3/issue7/gibson.html.
McCaffery, Larry. "Introduction: The Desert of the Real." *Storming the Reality Studio: A Casebook of Cyberpunk and Postmodern Science Fiction*, edited by Larry McCaffery. Duke UP, 1991, pp. 1–16.
Shadowrun: Where Man Meets Magic and Machine, 1st Ed. FASA Corp., 1989.
Sterling, Bruce. Preface. *Mirrorshades: The Cyberpunk Anthology*, edited by Bruce Sterling. Arbor House, 1986, pp. ix–xvi.
Toffler, Alvin. *Future Shock*. Random House, 1970.
———. *The Third Wave*. William Morrow, 1980.
Zagal, José Pablo and Sebastian Deterding. "Definitions of 'Role-Playing Games.'" *Role-Playing Game Studies: Transmedia Foundations*, edited by José Pablo Zagal and Sebastian Deterding. Routledge, 2018, pp. 19–51.

27
PHOTOGRAPHY AND DIGITAL ART

Grace Halden

In *The History of Science Fiction*, Adam Roberts writes on the long, if undertheorized, association between science fiction (sf) and art, remarking that in spite of a thriving cover art industry for pulp and genre magazines, stretching all the way back to the Pulp Age of the 1920s, sf art only "began to cross over into the artistic mainstream in the 1970s and 1980s" (465). The increasing popularity of cyberpunk art has benefitted from this legitimation of a larger sf art marketplace, particularly more recently as advances in editing software have enabled the artistic rendering of quintessential cyberpunk stories of the mid- to late-20th century and the cyberpunk mode of the 21st century. For example, iconic film sets such as Ridley Scott's *Blade Runner* (1982) were conceptualized first through art and then realized through sets and computer editing; similarly, concept artists like Andrée Wallin—*Star Wars: The Force Awakens* (Abrams 2015), *Oblivion* (Kosinski 2013), *Halo 4* (343 Industries 2012)—and Jonas De Ro—*Final Fantasy XV* (Square Enix 2016), *Batman v Superman: Dawn of Justice* (Snyder 2016), *Terminator Genisys* (Taylor 2015)—all include cyberpunk images within their varied portfolios.

An exploration of the popularity of cyberpunk imagery as evoked in sf art is of paramount importance to a broader understanding of the cyberpunk mode, particularly in this (newish) millennium; after all, Paweł Frelik argues that in spite of its initial (and popular!) literary forms, "cyberpunk has been the most relevant and influential as a visual aesthetic" (81) and, as Sherryl Vint points out, a distinctly cyberpunk aesthetic "refuses to lie peacefully in its grave" (228). As a result, the focus for this chapter is specifically on cyberpunk imagery's engagement with the megacity, or urban sprawl, a foundational trope for literary and televisual cyberpunk. In particular, online digital photography brings together professional and amateur filmmakers, digital storytellers, and concept artists who use the global (cyber)space to explore those future cities that are looking increasingly like the cities in our quotidian lives.

The megacity is a hallmark of cyberpunk that cannot be understated; in fact, Lars Schmeink notes that "[o]ne of the most widely-used images of cyberpunk is its placement in urban sprawls and far-reaching cityscapes" (277), including the rain-soaked, vertically stacked Los Angeles of *Blade Runner*, the sprawling Boston-Atlanta-Metropolitan Axis in *Neuromancer* (1984), the seemingly never-ending metropolises of Richard K. Morgan's *Altered Carbon* (2002) and its Netflix adaptation (2018), or the digital renditions of urban cityscapes in the Deus Ex video game franchise,[1] to name only a few obvious examples. Practically speaking, the city is also one of the easier cyberpunk concepts to design or replicate using editing software, incorporating within the visual frame the various themes, settings, technologies, and stylistic elements quintessential to envisioning the "classic one-two combination of lowlife and high tech" (Sterling xii) that defines the

216

'authentic' cyberpunk city of the future. In other words, cyberpunk city images are able to project industrial ghettos, city noir, black markets, mega corporations, the dominance of technology, and unrestrained vice, at least on a surface level. Such images may feature a fusion of squalid street markets shrouded in darkness and grime, populated by the poor, the sick, and the criminal, while brightly lit skyscrapers embossed with advertisements and company logos stretch unendingly into a sky often scarred by pollution.

Within these broad stroke details, the spectator may read into the image the key cyberpunk tropes of the Singularity, the rise of the machines, the dominance of artificial intelligence, post- and transhuman embodiment(s), dystopia and the promises of false utopias, perpetual surveillance, rampant economic inequality, oppressive megacorporations, and so forth. While an image cannot convey the immediacy of sensory stimuli such as sounds and smells, the image of the cyberpunk city can convey the "nervous glare of neon signs and halogen streetlamps" (Kadrey 6) or the mixture of old and new architecture in which "[s]queezed against each other were structures of every conceivable type: primitive, classical, baroque, gothic, renaissance, industrial, art nouveau, functionalist, late funk, zapper, crepuscular, flat-flat, hyperdee..." (Rucker 72). More recently, ruined buildings with their "tattered gray concrete and broken rebar, ancient graffiti and bloodstains" (2) dominate the urban landscape of Jeff Somers' *The Electric Church* (2007), while Ren Warom's *Escapology* (2016) features "[b]uildings that look as big as dammit suddenly dwarf next to gargantuan monuments that rise into the sky like God's own fingers." So, while John Shirley's *Eclipse* (1985) starts with the line "This city is dead" (3), the city is actually of vital significance in cyberpunk and is neither dead nor dying; in other words, although cyberpunk may reflect the urban decay of the megacity, it is living and experiencing renewed attention alongside the birth of new and radical cyberpunk art.

27.1 Cyberpunk City Practitioners

Cyberpunk narratives as a whole depict worlds in which the 'language' of the future creates tension between humans and a dominant oppressive structure, including machines, a corrupt government, a tyrannical corporation, etc. Although the level of tension will vary depending on the cyberpunk work, a defining characteristic of cyberpunk is the 'language' of the megacity as a site where that tension plays out. While the protagonists may be fighting against the system, the city is a force that acts as not only a visual backdrop but also a vital presence suggesting that in a cyberpunk future, the 'mega'—mega machine, mega corporation, mega regime—has triumphed. Cyberpunk images impose on their audience a future world, often dystopian, and through this worldbuilding, familiar key elements are juxtaposed with at-times radical unfamiliarity.

Broadly speaking, two types of city exist in the cyberpunk archetype—the post-apocalyptic ruin and/or the high-tech megacity, although iconic cyberpunk texts like *Akira* (Ōtomo 1988) may contain both. It is the megacity that is more recognizably cyberpunk, thanks in no small part to *Blade Runner*. As Scott Bukatman writes, "[c]yberpunk provided *the* image of the future in the 1980s" and the "aesthetic of cyberpunk was almost defined by *Blade Runner*" (*Blade* 58, 50). In the case of cyberpunk's high-tech megalopolis, the futuristic city is typified by high-rise structures, holographic advertisements, neon-lighting, and street-level slums populated with decaying older structures. The megacity not only frames the narrative geographically and temporally, but the squalid streets become sites of protest (*Akira*) and violence (*Strange Days* [Bigelow 1995]), and the clustered collection of staggered and stacked structures creates the feeling of suffocation and claustrophobia experienced by characters deeply entrenched in their inability to escape their own dystopia, as shown in *Judge Dredd* (Cannon 1995), *Dredd* (Travis 2012), Netflix's *Altered Carbon*, the Deus Ex video games, and so forth. In addition, "[t]he dystopic city in future noir and cyberpunk films and anime," writes Steven T. Brown, "is also marked by the disappearance of nature: its ecology is ruined by acid rain, garbage is strewn everywhere, and the orange haze of oil refinery burnoff flames hangs over the city like a shroud" (100).[2] This is largely true in films like *Blade Runner*—i.e. its famous opening sequence shows a sprawling megapolis with industrial stacks belching fire into the night air—and *Akira*'s Neo Tokyo (both anime and manga), a neon-infused urban sprawl that has clearly influenced work such as professional concept artist Artur Sadlos' "Cyberpunk City" (2017).[3] In these (and other) cases, the wires, lights, holograms, projections, satellites, and mechanics that wrap around, burrow through, and layer over the raw infrastructure of towers can be viewed as the veins, organs, and pulse of a city as vital as any humanoid character.

The metaphor of the city as a living body, a biomechatronic lifeform, is quite common in cyberpunk as its denizens feel the urban pulse as they navigate its teeming streets; however, as Dani Cavallaro remarks, there is also a combination of "materiality and immateriality" (133) as the 'cyber'—itself a pulsing network of data and systems—further energizes cyberpunk's urban cities. Cavallaro argues that "[d]igital technology tends to ideate the city in immaterial terms as an abstract map or network of computer-processed data" (133). Nevertheless, "contemporary cities are very material indeed: crammed with ever-expanding and ever-changing architectural structures, teeming with bodies and vehicles, packed with commodities of all sorts" (Cavallaro 133). Contrary to what one might expect, however, the teeming masses are not faceless or forgotten; instead, it is the street, as Gibson famously remarked, that finds its own uses for things ("Burning Chrome" 186), and in that urban swath citizens "are anything but uniform, showcasing diversity in ethnicity and other forms of identity parameters beyond the western, Christian, wealthy, white, straight, able-bodied, male subject" (Schmeink 279).

Cavallaro's description of the street 'packed with commodities of all sorts' is apt for not only what happens in the city but what happens *because* of the city. The visual cacophony of advertisements, animated or holographic, exemplified in films like *Akira*, *Blade Runner*, *The Zero Theorem* (Gilliam 2013), and *Blade Runner 2049* (Villeneuve 2018), positions cyberpunk's cities as communicating directly with a population comprising entirely of consumers. Writing on *Blade Runner 2049* for this collection, Matthew Flisfeder remarks that while *Blade Runner* represents a "field of total (and invasive) commodification—that is, the colonization of the commodity that is so apparent in the postmodern cinema and cyberculture that followed," Villeneuve's sequel "builds heavily on the postmodern aesthetic of digital, electronic, and commodified space while the enhanced digital cinematography takes us deeper inside the urban fabric to give us a much more high-definition visualization of the city" (146). Cyberpunk's cities, therefore, are built on, and encrusted with, a very specific type of communication: marketing. The clash between human and machine further represents the clash between the laborer and the corporation, as capital accumulation and commodity production are the driving forces within any megacity whose goal is selling the future. However, the masses are not only consumers, they are the consumed. An obvious example of this can be seen in *The Matrix* (Wachowskis 1999) in which the virtual city is powered by human organic matter; however, broadly speaking, humans in cyberpunk cities can be described as maintaining the intelligent city like worker bees in a hive. If cyberpunk questions what it means to be a human in a world of intense technological dominance and what it means to have a value in an intensely commodified world, then cyberpunk images offer no easy answers but graphically depict this ongoing crisis.

If Frelik is correct and cyberpunk's most relevant and influential form is as a visual aesthetic, then cinematic and televisual cyberpunk—i.e. cyberpunk projected on both the big and small screens—have certainly influenced, if not defined, how cyberpunk is often visualized. An undertheorized corner of visual cyberpunk, however, is cyberpunk photography, which can be broadly classified as cyberpunk-style photography (a.k.a. *cyberpunk-style*) and cyberpunk digital-art images

Photography and Digital Art

(a.k.a., *cyberpunk-digiart*). The difference between *cyberpunk-style* and *cyberpunk-digiart* often comes down to whether there is the presence of a central, dominant, and identifiable photograph. For my purposes, Sadlos' "Cyberpunk City" and Tom Blachford's *Nihon Noir* illustrate this crucial difference. Blachford's *Nihon Noir* is a night photography series enhanced with software to create a cyberpunk ambience, one that the *Aesthetic Post* website describes as "a nod to the Neon Noir film genre that includes the specific aesthetically-driven films such as *Blade Runner* and the work of Nicolas Winding-Refn (Drive, The Neon Demon, Only God Forgives)." As "The Battleship" example from *Nihon Noir* shows, the 'real' present-day city of Tokyo is clearly identifiable in Blachford's work and there is no attempt to hide the city's distinguishing features, even if the edited 'simulation' enhances the 'real' (Figure 27.1).

In contrast, Sadlos' "Cyberpunk City" envisions an entirely new megacity incomparable to any present metropolis, at least so far. Populated with constructions and technology beyond what is currently possible, "Cyberpunk City" is embellished with advanced space vehicles and holographic projections. Yet, the hyperrealism in the piece suggests a photographic quality comparable to *Nihon Noir*, except the nature of the image—i.e. a vehicle frozen mid-motion, digital boards that should be flickering but are frozen in time, and what appears to be an enhanced (post)human looking upon the city—which suggests an interruption of movement. "Cyberpunk City" is therefore an example of cyberpunk images that are voyeuristic, snapshots that glimpse at a hidden world, or a hidden camera view. "Cyberpunk City" does not exist within the 'live' bustle of the city in 'real time' but is instead a freeze frame of a moment in time. In essence, the difference between *Nihon Noir* as *cyberpunk-style* and "Cyberpunk City" as *cyberpunk-digiart* is that the former

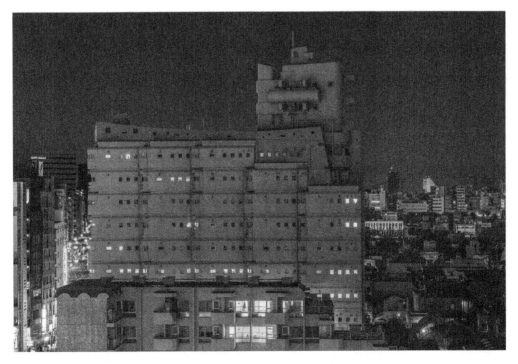

Figure 27.1 "The Battleship": Tom Blachford's Nihon Noir series demonstrates the use of identifiable photography edited using software to create a cyberpunk effect. Gratefully reprinted with permission from Tom Blachford.

can be recaptured; it is possible to travel to the location of the cyberpunk-style photograph. *Cyberpunk-digiart*, however, has created something not of this world.

Straddling both types of images and forming a subcategory of its own is *cyberpunk-mélange*, a third category that suggests a varied mixture of techniques to create a new city in the *cyberpunk-digiart* style, but the final image is perceivably a collage of base photography and digital (brush or hand-drawn) embellishment one finds typical in *cyberpunk-style*. An example of *cyberpunk-mélange* can be seen in the work of Donglu Yu, a professional concept artist who has worked on video games such as *Deus Ex: Human Revolution* (Eidos 2011) and *Far Cry 4* (Ubisoft 2014). In a YouTube tutorial, Yu breaks down how she uses base photography and Photoshop to extract building textures so as to create a final art piece (ImagineFX); or, as her piece "Steamy Downtown" shows, how she blends *cyberpunk-style* with *cyberpunk-digiart* to create a *cyberpunk-mélange* that is the best of both worlds. In *cyberpunk-mélange*, it is possible to simultaneously perceive our world and a future world—a high level of simulacra in which the real and artificial are entangled. On a surface level, the *cyberpunk-mélange* image is hyperreal and can be perceived as a futurescape with no immediately discernible anchor to our time, but a closer examination isolates real-world landmarks familiar in our real-world settings (Figure 27.2).

Yu's YouTube video focuses on the extraction of building textures as the ground for some of her conceptual work, but on a larger scale, the use of texture, notably 'cybertexture,' is vitally important to create the effect of a dystopian space common to cyberpunk. While stylistic decisions will create noticeable contrast in cyberpunk photography, there are some common cybertexture principles. For example, editing will see the amplification of aesthetic extremes quintessential to cyberpunk: the manipulation of contrast and saturation, the exaggeration of highlight, and the

Figure 27.2 "Steamy Downtown" by Donglu Yu, an example of *cyberpunk-mélange*. Gratefully reprinted with permission from Donglu Yu (Instagram: @donglulittlefish).

amplification of greens and blues to create a cooler temperature. Promotion of the high shine of chrome alongside the exaggeration of highlights creates both metallic luminosity and the almost radioactive glow of artificial lighting, although artists such as Linda Wisdom sometimes use black and white for their cyberpunk pieces to "expose the loneliness of the individual often found in Cyberpunk literature" (Wisdom). A significant proportion of cyberpunk photography also contains similar environmental ambience features—e.g. rain, darkness, clouds—and locations within the city space of ruin and decay where action is not in the high-rises lording over the city's denizens, but in the streets, alleyways, markets, and backstreets. In the end, however, there are three dominant facets of cyberpunk photography that can provide viewers with a greater appreciation of cyberpunk photography (and an interpretive framework): the choice of setting, the animation of the banal, and the artwork's mythically human element.

27.2 Setting in Cyberpunk Photography

Since *cyberpunk-digiart* often focuses less on mirroring scenes from cyberpunk literature and film and more on painting highly original settings, the artistic pieces lack a specific city or national identity, while *cyberpunk-style* and *cyberpunk-mélange* often rely on real-world locations that are popular for cyberpunk inspiration, or stock imaging repurposed for the artwork. In this vein, a significant number of *cyberpunk-style* and *cyberpunk-mélange* pieces, such as Marcus Wendt's "Break of Day" series, use base material from East Asian cities, notably Tokyo, which is often positioned as the ultimate cyberpunk aesthetic. Given his work on *Blade Runner*, *Alien* (Scott 1979), and *TRON* (Lisberger 1982), world-renowned futurist artist Sydney Jay Mead is largely responsible for the detailed, urban worldbuilding that has become *de rigeur* for cyberpunk. Mead's concept art contains future transports, landscapes, planets, and even fashion, all of which underpin a lot of the cyberpunk digital art being made today, especially art involving city spaces inspired by East Asian cities. For example, Mead is the inspiration behind Liam Wong's "Tokyo Nights (TO:KY:OO)" series which combines city photography with digital manipulation to cast the contemporary city of Tokyo as a future space (Inigo). Wong's pieces like "Nakano Nights / 中野区 / Neon Broadway" and "Shinjuku Nights / 新宿 / Sleepless Town" are directly comparable to Mead's street concept scenes for *Blade Runner*, all featuring neon-glowing buildings and streets heavily lined with a multiplicity of signage—the main differences being the diminished populations in Mead's work and the bustling streets in Wong's. In addition to the influence upon Wendt's "Ultraviolent Break of Day," Blachford's *Nihon Noir*, and Sadlos' "Cyberpunk City," we can also see Mead's influence upon other digital artists, such as Zaki Abdelmounim's "Neo Hong Kong," Marilyn Mugot's "Night Project," or the highly stylized photography of Masashi Wakui, whose night-time metropolis scenes are famous for their use of color effects—notably a grading that accentuates the neon glow of lights while tinging scenes with more dominant blue and green notes. Tokyo is also present in artwork by freelance concept artist Vladimir Manyukhun and photographer Cody Ellingham as the city unites both old and new elements in a way cyberpunk photographers and artists celebrate as unique to that particular city (Johnny), although other artists do branch out and use less obvious sites, such as Mugot placing Paris, San Francisco, and New York alongside Hong Kong, Chongqing, and Guilin.

While real-world cites like Tokyo may be identifiable in both *cyberpunk-style* and *cyberpunk-mélange* artworks, the objective of both styles is to present the city as cyberpunk-esque as possible. As a result, the real-world city at the core of the digital photography possesses a ghostly presence in which the 'real' has been layered by the simulations of digital manipulation. The 'ghost' of 'our' cities therefore embodies what Jean Baudrillard says about the simulated image itself: "[N]othing just vanishes; of everything that disappears there remain traces [...].

Behind every image, something has disappeared. And that is the source of its fascination" (*Everything* 25, 31–32). In other words, while we may be drawn to the digital photograph and enamored by its artistry, we are also reminded, subtly or otherwise, not that something remains in the cyberpunk world but that something is missing; we are witness to a time in which we are absent and which thus brings new light to what Baudrillard might term an "art of disappearance" (*Everything* 10), projections of a future history implying a significant absence—that of our death. In essence, the cyberpunk city in both *cyberpunk-style* and *cyberpunk-mélange* plays with 'real,' simulation, trace, and fascination, seducing the spectator into a future time in which our world as we know it has vanished, leaving behind in the cities the ghostly traces of our present, an interplay of presence and disappearance that suggests both an end and an uncanny continuation of the world, only one marked by disappearance. In this fashion, *cyberpunk-style* and *cyberpunk-mélange*, despite never totally succeeding in showcasing our apocalyptic future, will provide enough temporal confusion through the manipulation of contemporary photography for the spectator to feel that they may be glimpsing a potential reality empty *of them*. If anything, the enjoyment of viewing our own disappearance is a macabre but ultimately seductive practice that finds a natural home in concept art.

While the temporal play in *cyberpunk-art* and *cyberpunk-mélange* is rooted in an almost exclusively future-based orientation, the futurity of some *cyberpunk-style* pieces can be said to be most explicitly located in a temporal 'now,' again complicating the perceived temporal separation of 'present' and 'future' in an uncanny fashion. For example, Sinéad Mulhern wrote for *Toronto Life* on Lucan Coutts, an up-and-coming digital artist whose work prominently features a cyberpunk-ish Toronto, such as in his work "Toronto 2049" which features a pedestrian crossing a futuristic Yonge-Dundas Square (Figure 27.3).

As testament to how much *Blade Runner* has saturated a cyberpunk aesthetic, Coutts admitted that music is his inspiration for his photography and "I've never seen the *Blade Runner* movies," despite the connections to Scott's film immediately made by Coutts' Instagram and Twitter followers. Similarly, the work of professional photographer Trey Ratcliff features contemporary locations (re)imagined as futurescapes, such as his "Blade Runner," a panoramic of present-day Los Angeles, and "Runner of Blades," a *Blade Runner*-esque Beijing. Unfortunately, the potential danger of *cyberpunk-style* and its reliance upon the artist's contemporary moment is its potential datedness, namely, our ability to not only recognize a city scene but to also travel to it and recreate that view may timestamp the image to our century, possibly even to a specific decade. Nevertheless, this problem of timestamping the city within *cyberpunk-style* does not necessarily undermine the cyberpunk aesthetic because it still engages with its own contemporaneity and participates in a specific vein of cyberpunk narrative, whether imagining a very near future or an alternate reality. In a roundabout fashion, this is how Abdelmounim thinks about his *cyberpunk-style* photographs, such as "Neo Hong Kong," describing them as a way of recording perception rather than documenting reality: "No matter where I am," he explains, "I perceive reality through my imagination. I use my camera to capture the streets as I imagine them, not the way they are in reality" (Gao). Or, Wong, an art director for the game developer Ubisoft Montréal, speaks about the essential element of transformation in his *cyberpunk-style* photography: "I love capturing real moments and transforming them into the surreal." In sum, while *cyberpunk-style*, *cyberpunk-digiart*, and *cyberpunk-mélange* may deal to a greater or lesser degree with highly stylized and high-tech enhancements, their reproductive productions are not intended to double the real but instead to draw attention to the fantastic. Yet, we remain simultaneously fascinated and unsettled because the unfamiliar or alien city, a futuristic and fantastic world we visually navigate, is presented like a snapshot of an existing or 'real' space, which may very well be the case.

Figure 27.3 "Toronto 2049" by Lucan Coutts (lucancoutts.com), an example of uncanny temporality. Gratefully reprinted with permission from Lucan Coutts.

27.3 Cyberpunk: Animating the Banal

Cyberpunk-mélange sometimes uses stock images—unenhanced, raw, and arguably uninspired, basic city/building images—to create radically different scenes in which a new city is digitally structured from segments of existing banal prints. Reflecting on the banality of some photographs, Roland Barthes explains the subjective need for the spectator to stave off indifference by animating the image: "In this glum desert, suddenly a specific photograph reached me; it animates me, and I animate it. So that is how I must name the attraction which makes it exist: an animation. The photograph itself is in no way animated (I do not believe in 'lifelike' photographs), but it animates me: this is what creates every adventure" (19–20). With the overwhelming wealth of digital art and, more specifically, cyberpunk digital photography available online, there needs to be an image that 'reaches' and animates—cyberpunk images arguably do this through disruption. Indeed, in a lot of *cyberpunk-mélange*, an ordinary cityscape is photographed and only through enhancement it is transformed into something that prevents spectator indifference. In this vein, some digital images recycle commonplace buildings and only through montage does the end product deliver something other than a dull and flat structure, like a high-rise that could be associated with any contemporary metropolis but takes on an entirely different, even magical, meaning when transformed by *cyberpunk-mélange*. For example, Mugot, reflecting on her cyberpunk night scenes using her city stock photographs, says "[t]he lights and the elements take on mystical and secret dimensions which are not always real but a result of my imagination" (Stewart).

Another way the banal can be transformed in the cyberpunk image is through the reimagining of what cities mean, especially in relation to ideas of cyberspace. As Cavallaro notes, "[c]yberpunk presents visions of the future based on the extensive application of the idea of cyberspace" (14). We see this application most evident in cities envisioned as complex circuit boards, for example

Figure 27.4 "The Veins of Bangkok" by Trey Ratcliff envisions the city as a circuit-board aesthetic with pulsing currents of information. Gratefully reprinted with permission from Trey Ratcliff/StuckInCustoms.com.

in films such as *Hackers* (Softley 1995) and *TRON*, or in novels such as John Shirley's *City Come A-Walkin'* (1980) and Gibson's *Neuromancer* and *All Tomorrow's Parties* (1999). Cyberpunk-style photography that channels a circuit-board aesthetic with pulsing currents of information includes Ratcliff's "The Veins of Bangkok," "Rivers of Laser Fire," and "Chicago Forever." Although Ratcliff's works include both East Asian and American metropolises, his cities, notably in the nocturnal pieces, are connected with electrified roads in luminous oranges and yellows, all bisecting blackened buildings dotted with multi-colored window lights, appearing like circuitry, "green boards with their inlaid foil maps" (Gibson, *All* 95). *Cyberpunk-style* therefore reveals the most identifiable and relatable content—including the banality of everyday life—with the least amount of manipulation which is still positioned as a distortion of reality and very much a fiction. This imagery, escaping its banal origins, is pronounced through digital manipulation, a common trait for digital photographers and artists. In the end, the digital manipulation of banal stock images common to *cyberpunk-style* transforms the banality itself, presenting us with a modified image that challenges us by presenting a realistic image which cannot totally succeed as representing the present or the future. We are again disrupted by *cyberpunk-style* pieces due to the uncanniness of an unfamiliar familiarity of the setting's digital image (Figure 27.4).

27.4 The Mythically Human Element in Cyberpunk

The rooftop viewpoint of Sadlos's "Cyberpunk City" shows that the megacity's streets are so far down such that the roads are little more than vague lines and the midground is chaotically populated with hover vehicles and holograms. The lone figure overlooking this sprawling metropolis is a solitary soul, holding a gun at (presumably) his side, seemingly impotent in the face of the smart-city and dwarfed by the looming structures that overshadow him, casting, distorting, and anonymizing him in the impenetrable shadows. The reoccurrence of this single figure motif is representative that *something* human (or posthuman) survives in this dystopian reality, even though, as addressed earlier, it likely isn't *us* and this single figure will likely never *be* us. At the same time, the lone figure, particularly in "Cyberpunk City" but also "Toronto 2049," is as much an architectural detail as the surrounding buildings, but remains instrumental to the visual narrative. He is more than simply a potential commentary on the vastness of the megacity or the loneliness of cyberpunk's seemingly cold futures; instead, he provides scale and contextualization for the digital image. Scale is often created through the forefront positioning of a solo human(oid) acting as a passive presence in a world that both dwarfs and isolates them. Conditioned by cyberpunk's tropes, we may imagine this figure to be a hacker moving against the system, a cyborg deeply entrenched in a technological world, the machine masquerading as a human, some detective searching in the darkness for answers, or even a questing hero facing the monster of a greedy neoliberal economy. The lone figure in cyberpunk images, dwarfed by glowing and towering structures, is synonymous with the questing dragon slayers facing the looming dominance of technology and the neon flare of electricity.[4] The skin of the complex and sprawling streets or cityscapes, labyrinthine and fantastical, is the decay and junk surrounding the 'hero' at ground level, attributed to the grime and dereliction of poor settlements and struggling minority communities. As Schmeink, quoting James Donald, remarks, "[d]own on the street, the city is resistant to transparency and categorization [… and] the experience of walking the streets is almost mythical in its 'labyrinthine reality'" (279). Cyberpunk's agents, digitally frozen in time, will find not the rubble of castles should they begin to move, but the detritus—plastic, metallic, paper—of the downtrodden. In addition, victory of the individual 'hero' is by no means assured; in fact, cyberpunk art often images the mythic-laden meeting of 'hero' and 'monster' as a conflict between human and technology, a battle whose conclusion is far from forgone.

In the images in which the lone figure is replaced with a bustling street full of shadowy crowds, such as Abdelmounim's "Neo Hong Kong" or Yu's "Steamy Downtown," we are not confronted with the knight and monster but perhaps more aptly with biological and mechanical bodies united as a dystopian interconnected system, evoking Kuno's despair in E.M. Forster's "The Machine Stops" (1919) that humanity, governed by an all-powerful machine that keeps the species alive in its subterranean enclaves, only exists "as the blood corpuscles that course through its arteries, and if it could work without us, it would let us die" (67). Cyberpunk art, notably cyberpunk digital photography, makes clear the ongoing struggles over control of communication in the animal and machine.[5] In essence, cyberpunk digital photography shows that the eternal glow of the city, the humming of the metropolis, is constantly 'on,' and is (a)live and thriving. As Frelik writes, "[e]lectricity and light have always been part of the science-fictional imaginary, both conceptual and visual, but there is arguably no other sub-genre that relies on them as much as cyberpunk [...]. In other words, light and neon have always been centrally present in cyberpunk" (83). As any number of digital works highlighted or referenced in this chapter will show, even cities choking on fumes have an eerie neon glow that permeates the smog that sickens and harms the human inhabitants. The city therefore never sleeps and—thanks to the constant stream of holographic advertisements, fluorescent neon, and perpetual light pollution—is constantly working and performing. Frozen in their visual moment, those lone (post)human characters remain flat and impotent—mid-quest and prey to the 'monster.'

27.5 Conclusion: Worldbuilding

In sum, cyberpunk image practitioners, capitalizing on Baudrillard's comment that "the computer is a true prosthesis" (*Screened Out* 179), have become cyborg artists in intimate synchronicity with technology, producing *cyberpunk-digiart* through digital paintings, *cyberpunk-style* pieces through photographs, or *cyberpunk-mélange* through the integration of the two. As a whole, these practitioners dive into the very fabric of the image and operate on an intimate level: *Cyberpunk-style* practitioners alter hue, lighting, and sharpness in base-photography; *cyberpunk-digiart* practitioners create projected spaces by using 'synthetic' methodologies (brushes, filters, painting); *cyberpunk-mélange* practitioners use cut 'n paste techniques in tandem with a combination of brushes and filter effects to manipulate a range of stock photographs. They collectively work on the smallest units that can be enhanced or manipulated, added to or deleted, and through this process new entities, hybrids, or augmented models emerge. The end result of these operations is a piece of cyberpunk art that holds at a distance a creative depiction of a possible future space. The cyberpunk image gestures to a *future* birth rather than a *rebirth*, even though the content of the images often forewarns us of our own disappearance and the steely cold that the neon future holds.

Notes

1 For details regarding the Deus Ex franchise, see Christian Knöppler's contribution to this collection or Stephen Joyce's "Playing for Virtually Real: Cyberpunk Aesthetics and Ethics in *Deus Ex: Human Revolution*."
2 Veronica Hollinger provides a reading of cyberpunk and the Anthropocene in her contribution to this collection.
3 Artur Sadlos' "Cyberpunk City" can be viewed at www.artstation.com/artwork/o1yKJ.
4 See Cavallaro's *Cyberpunk and Cyberculture* for an extended discussion of cyberpunk's connections to both hard-boiled detective fiction and the chivalric quest.
5 This is a (not so) subtle reference to Norbert Wiener's foundational text *Cybernetics, or Control of Communication in the Animal and Machine* (1948).

Works Cited

Abdelmounim. Zaki. *Zaki Abdelmounim: Behance*, 2012, behance.net/creatiflux.

Aesthetic Post. "Nihon Noir by Tom Blachford." http://aestheticpost.com/art/nihon-noir-by-tom-blachford/.

Barthes, Roland. *Camera Lucida: Reflections on Photography*, translated by R. Howard. Farrar, 1981.

Baudrillard, Jean. *Screened Out*. Verso, 2002.

———. *Why Hasn't Everything Already Disappeared*. Seagull, 2016.

Blachford, Tom. *Nihon Noir*. 2013, tomblachford.com/nihon-noir.

Brown, Steven T. *Tokyo Cyber-Punk: Posthumanism in Japanese Visual Culture*. Palgrave Macmillan, 2010.

Bukatman, Scott. *Blade Runner*, 2nd Ed. Palgrave Macmillan, 2012.

Cavallaro, Dani. *Cyberpunk and Cyberculture: Science Fiction and the Work of William Gibson*. Athlone, 2000.

Flisfeder, Matthew. "*Blade Runner 2049*." *The Routledge Companion to Cyberpunk Culture*, edited by Anna McFarlane, Graham J. Murphy, and Lars Schmeink. Routledge, 144–50.

Forster, E.M. "The Machine Stops." *The Wesleyan Anthology of Science Fiction*, edited by Arthur B. Evans, et al. Wesleyan UP, 2010, pp. 50–78.

Frelik, Paweł. "'Silhouettes of Strange Illuminated Mannequins': Cyberpunk's Incarnations of Light." *Cyberpunk and Visual Culture*, edited by Graham J. Murphy and Lars Schmeink. Routledge, 2018, pp. 80–99.

Gao, Sally. "Hong Kong's Neon Glow: An Interview With Photographer Zaki Abdelmounim," *Culture Trip*, 11 Oct. 2016, theculturetrip.com/asia/hong-kong/articles/hong-kongs-neon-glow-an-interview-with-photographer-zaki-abdelmounim/.

Gibson, William. *All Tomorrow's Parties*. Berkley, 1999.

———. "Burning Chrome." *Burning Chrome*. Ace, 1986, pp. 168–91.

Guardian. "Purple Rain: Marilyn Mugot's neon China – in pictures," *Guardian*, 2 Mar 2017, theguardian.com/artanddesign/gallery/2017/mar/02/marilyn-mugot-neon-china-in-pictures.

ImagineFX. "Donglu Yu builds a futuristic city using textures in Photoshop" *YouTube* 2015, youtube.com/watch?v=VCyQ6AbIMH0.

Inigo. "How one guy turned Tokyo into a cyberpunk settling through photos," *Lost At E Minor*, 21 Apr. 2016, www.lostateminor.com/2016/04/22/how-one-guy-turned-tokyo-into-a-cyberpunk-setting-through-photos/.

Johnny. "Immerse Yourself in Cyberpunk Tokyo with this Visual Project by Cody Ellingham." *Spoon & Tamago*, 3 Jul. 2017, spoon-tamago.com/2017/07/03/cyberpunk-tokyo-cody-ellingham-derive/.

Joyce, Stephen. "Playing for Virtually Real: Cyberpunk Aesthetics and Ethics in *Deus Ex: Human Revolution*." *Cyberpunk and Visual Culture*, edited by Graham J. Murphy and Lars Schmeink. Routledge, 2018, pp. 155–73.

Kadrey, Richard. *Metrophage*. Ace, 1988.

Mulhern, Sinéad. "This 20-year-old photographer makes Toronto look like a futuristic *Blade Runner* cityscape." *Toronto Life*, 7 Feb. 2018, torontolife.com/culture/art/20-year-old-photographer-makes-toronto-look-like-futuristic-blade-runner-cityscape/.

Mugot, Marilyn. "Night Project." *Photography*, 2017, marilynmugot.com/night-project/.

Ratcliff, T. "Big Cities and Little'uns," *Trey Ratcliff*, 2018, https://stuckincustoms.smugmug.com/.

Roberts, Adam. *The History of Science Fiction*. Palgrave, 2016.

Rucker, Rudy. *Software*. Avon, 1982.

Sadlos, Artur. "Cyberpunk City." *ArtStation*, 2017, artstation.com/artwork/o1yKJ.

Schmeink, Lars. "Afterthoughts: Cyberpunk Engagements in Countervisuality." *Cyberpunk and Visual Culture*, edited by Graham J. Murphy and Lars Schmeink. Routledge, 2018, pp. 276–87.

Shirley, John. *Eclipse*. Dover, 2017.

Somers, Jeff. *The Electric Church*. Hachette, 2007.

Sterling, Bruce. Preface. *Burning Chrome*, by William Gibson. Ace, 1986, pp. ix–xii.

Stewart, Jessica. "Nighttime Photos of Hong Kong and China's Neon-Soaked Back Alleys." *My Modern Met*, 10 Feb. 2017, mymodernmet.com/marilyn-mugot-night-photography-hong-kong/.

Vint, Sherryl. "Afterword: The World Gibson Made." *Beyond Cyberpunk: New Critical Perspectives*, edited by Graham J. Murphy and Sherryl Vint. Routledge, 2010, pp. 228–33.

Warom, Ren. *Escapology*, Kindle Ed. Titan, 2016.

Wendt, Marcus. "Ultraviolent Break of Day." *Field*, 2017, field.io/project/ultraviolet-break-of-day/.

Wiener, Norbert. *Cybernetics, or Control of Communication in the Animal and Machine*. MIT Press, 1948.

Wisdom, Linda. "City@Night 007 – Linda Wisdom." *Neon Dystopia*, 30 Dec. 2014, neondystopia.com/cyberpunk-art-photography/citynight-007-linda-wisdom/.

Wong, Liam. *The Beauty of the Night*, liamwong.com/.

Yu, Donglu. "Mood Painting Demo." *ArtStation*, artstation.com/artwork/Kzzzy.

28

FASHION

Stina Attebery

Since Bruce Sterling's provocation that cyberpunks love "mirror shades—preferably in chrome and matte black, the Movement's totem colors" (xi), cyberpunk has maintained a deep investment in clothing, commodity, and personal style. The mirrored sunglasses, trenchcoats, technological implants, and outfits made from rubber, circuitry, neon, and chrome are all as much a defining characteristic of cyberpunk as its cyborg and hacker characters or narratives of opposition to corporate control. While there are overlapping influences between cyberpunk texts and textiles, from street fashion to the catwalk, fashion is also a form of speculative thinking in itself. Fashion is future-oriented, a constantly shifting set of speculative assumptions about the future of human social expression and embodiment. This emphasis on futurity allows fashion to serve as a science-fictional space for exploring the contradictions inherent in commodity-driven hyper-modernity.

One approach to cyberpunk fashion would be the study of costumes designed for cyberpunk film and television. Films like *Blade Runner* (Scott 1982), *TRON* (Lisberger 1982), or *The Matrix* (Wachowskis 1999) have clearly influenced popular perceptions of cyberpunk as a style. To imagine cyberpunk clothing now brings to mind Tron's glowing circuitry suit, Zhora's see-through plastic raincoat, or Neo's trenchcoat as much as any description from William Gibson or Pat Cadigan. Costumes can therefore be an important visualization of new futures and societies. Nevertheless, while there is a lot of great work to be done around costuming, there are limitations on the ways costume designers can imagine futurity. This is mostly due to the constraints of the industry rather than the creativity of designers. When inventing alien clothing for each new planet in *Babylon 5: The Gathering* (Compton 1993), for instance, costume designer Catherine Adair made a point of discussing with series creator J. Michael Straczynski how each new alien society functioned, and created designs that would fit these science-fictional worlds.[1] This is science fiction costuming at its best, when it serves to materially situate characters within speculative new worlds.

However, costume design can become limited by the constraints of the Hollywood system. During a Q&A with costume designers at the 2018 EagleCon, I heard a number of designers expressing the fear of 'getting it wrong' by creating designs that don't accurately predict the styles that become popular in future decades, especially when designing clothes for a near-future society. To avoid this problem, they rely on a 'classic silhouette' for suits and dresses. In practice, this means that most near-future sf films and TV shows present a future heavily based on 1940s designs, with only minor tweaks in color or style. Noir-inflected sf can be excellent, but when this is the primary design used for near-future texts, it runs the risk of reinscribing a 1940s gender politics for how the bodies within these costumes can move and present themselves. Consider, for example, the difference in *Blade Runner* between Deckard's worn brown trenchcoat, which lends itself to the character's active pursuit of the replicants, and Rachael's more constricting pencil skirt and tight jacket. The gendered differences between these costumes make sense for *Blade Runner*'s noir plot, but when other designers consciously mimic these types of costumes in response to systemic pressure to avoid alienating audiences with a strange and unexpected design choice, it limits the speculative potential of costuming to imagine new social relations.

It is also important to differentiate fashion, clothing, and costuming. As in any field, there is some contention over terminology. Clothing and style are broadly applicable terms, but fashion refers to changing trends and markets while costuming refers to the clothing designed for a particular performance or character. Since I am tracing the ways that the fictional clothing of characters within cyberpunk texts influences and draws inspiration from contemporary fashions, there is some overlap between fashion and costuming, especially as science-fictional clothing often encompasses both the speculative trends of fashion studies and the character-oriented designs of costume studies. Theories of fashion are interested in changing trends, the ways that new clothing styles emerge and replace older styles. To my mind, this is a speculative practice, comparable to science fiction's speculative worldbuilding, albeit on a smaller scale. Clothing and costuming don't necessarily share this interest in change and futurity, although they can still create strange science-fictional bodies by transforming the dimensions and silhouettes of the clothed body. For this reason, I focus my overview of cyberpunk fashion on cultural studies of fashion applicable to the cyberpunk movement, the influences between street or club styles and cyberpunk texts, and the overlapping interests of cyberpunk and high fashion.

28.1 The Commodity Fetish and the Fashionable Body

Cultural criticism of fashion has a few different origins and trajectories. Roland Barthes' work on fashion as a semiotic system is an important precursor for contemporary fashion theory, notably *The Fashion System* in which he reads clothing—particularly aspects of clothing like color, jewelry, and descriptions in women's magazines—as a system of signifying units. Subcultural studies like Dick Hebdige's *Subculture: The Meaning of Style* are similarly attentive to clothing as a form of personal expression, focusing on British youth subcultures. These early cultural studies of clothing styles are largely disconnected from each other. Subculture studies focus more on male clothing, reading subcultural styles alongside trends in music and drug cultures, while fashion theories drawing on Barthes' work with signification focus almost exclusively on women's clothing, high fashion, and consumer culture. Contemporary scholarly approaches to fashion and clothing draw on a mix of these approaches, with some crossover from related fields of theater and costuming and an emphasis on a feminist psychoanalytics of the gaze and the formation of identity.

While Barthes and Hebdige are useful starting points for theorizing fashion, Walter Benjamin's exploration of 19th-century fashions is the most useful critical framework for studying science-fictional clothing, particularly in cyberpunk. Benjamin's ambivalence toward fashion objects matches cyberpunk's ambivalence toward technology, and his fascination with reification and commodity fetishism is diagnostic of cyberpunk's postmodern precarity. Benjamin's *The Arcades Project* (1922–40) serves as the best starting place for his approach to fashion, technology, and futurity. *The Arcades Project* collects Benjamin's unfinished and unpublished notes for a project on the cultural history of urban modernity, translated and published posthumously. Benjamin's plans for this project are described in two Exposés in which he outlines the project for his sponsors at the Frankfurt School. The published text of the project begins with these 1935 and 1939 Exposés on Paris in the 19th century, but the bulk of the text consists of 36 'convolutes.' These convolutes, each consisting of a series of connected paragraphs organized into topics ranging from material technologies ("The Doll, The Automaton," "Photography") to the infrastructures and social structures of the city ("Prostitution, Gambling,"

"Arcades, *Magasins de Nouveatés*, Sales Clerks") to states of mind and memory ("Boredom, Eternal Return," "Dream City and Dream House, Dreams of the Future"), reflect Benjamin's research and notetaking process. Each convolute brings together quotations from sources which Benjamin was reading for the project and fragments of his own ideas. The juxtaposition of materials in these convolutes creates an experience of cultural, historical montage, or bricolage.

Benjamin's second convolute is entirely dedicated to fashion. He connects the reification and commodification of fashion objects to the rapidly changing cultures and technologies of urban modernity. Like Benjamin's other cultural objects—glassworks, gas lights, the omnibus, etc.—fashionable clothing reflects the speed, technological innovation, and mixing of interior and exterior design elements characteristic of modernity. For Benjamin, a key example of this is the fashion for crinoline dresses constructed around complex frames of wood, bone, or steel. The crinoline functions as a kind of cyborg device, as it hybridizes organic and inorganic materials to create a more-than-human silhouette, mirroring the development of new technologies for iron construction and upholstery design in its cloth-covered metallic scaffolding. The crinoline is similar to the bustle, which was also seen as an alarming fashion because it could drastically change a woman's silhouette. A number of satirical cartoons at the time depicted women's bustles transforming into insect carapaces, shells, or the back end of a horse (see Figure 28.1). When these drastically changing silhouettes are combined with a reified relationship to new materials available in heightened commodity production, they create a proto-posthuman merging of human and nonhuman. Benjamin states several times throughout the *Arcades Project* that fashion exists at the boundary between organic and inorganic matter. As he explains in his Exposé of 1939, "Fashion prescribes the ritual according to which the commodity fetish demands to be worshipped. […] It couples the living body to the inorganic world. To the living, it

Figure 28.1 "Caricature of Bustle as snail" from the August 1870 edition of *Punch*. Public domain.

defends the rights of the corpse. The fetishism which thus succumbs to the sex appeal of the inorganic is its vital nerve" (18–19). Fashion, for Benjamin, relies on this fetishistic combination of human bodies with new inorganic substances for its sense of futurity.

The crinoline also serves as an embodied expression of cultural acceleration. In his discussion of fashion's relationship to class and gender, Benjamin quotes Charles Blanc's "Considérations sur le vêtement des femmes" to claim that crinolines, hoop skirts, and bustles create a state of continuous movement: "everything that could keep women from remaining seated was encouraged; everything that impeded their walking was avoided. [...] Dress became the image of the rapid movement that carries away the world" (B5a, 3). For Benjamin, fashion is technological and serves as an embodied expression of socioeconomic change and the blurring of subject and object under capitalism. He associates fashion with futurity, arguing that "the interesting thing about fashion is its extraordinary anticipations" (B1a, 1). The futures that fashion anticipates, according to Benjamin, extend beyond individual bodies and cultural trends into the political futures of nations and empires. As he claims, "whoever understands how to read these samples [of women's fashion trends] would know in advance not only about new currents in the arts but also about new legal codes, wars, and revolutions" (B1a, 1). Although Benjamin is fascinated by the commodity fetishism of the crinoline, he is skeptical of fashion's ability to transform socioeconomic inequalities. As Susan Buck-Morss argues, "at some times Benjamin describes fashions as predictive of historical change, but at others [...] he reads fashion for an explanation as to why it has not [been predictive]" (98). This is in part because fashion incarnates a specifically modern capitalist sense of newness and speed. As Benjamin suggests in the 1939 Exposé, "Newness is a quality independent of the use value of the commodity. It is the source of that illusion of which fashion is the tireless purveyor" (22). All fashion exploits the tension between newness and conformity, but this tension becomes more vexed when fashion's fetishism of inorganic materials and accelerated movement applies to gendered bodies.

As a counterpoint to Benjamin's ambivalence, recent feminist theories of fashion draw on the potential for self-expression present in Benjamin's exploration of clothing as a form of hybridity between the clothed subject and clothing objects. Maurizia Bascalgli's *Stuff Theory: Everyday Objects, Radical Materialism* sees fashion as a site for resisting commodification, arguing that women's fashions can serve as a form of "cultural assault" that can "destabilize apparently fixed notions of reality and materiality" (83). Anne Hollander's excellent *Seeing Through Clothes* and *Sex and Suits* similarly see fashion as a space for risky bodily modification, arguing that "fashion in dress is committed to risk, subversion, and irregular forward movement" (*Sex* 14–15). Fashion can risk social status in search of subversive new forms of embodiment.

Fashion theory's interests in the future of urban modernity, gendered embodiment, new technological materials, and cultural assault on the status quo all resemble cyberpunk's near-futures, but until recently fashion and clothing have largely been excluded from discussions of cyberpunk. This is partly due to the influence of posthumanism on critical work around cyberpunk. Posthuman theorists have often been skeptical of fashion and clothing. As N. Katherine Hayles argues, her "nightmare is a culture inhabited by posthumans who regard their bodies as fashion accessories rather than the ground of being" (5). Fashion is seen as too frivolous to serve as a productive space for posthuman subjectivity. Hayles' wariness at the idea of fashionable cyborgs could also reflect the way fashion has been uncritically celebrated by transhumanists. Max More writes about fashioning the body in *The Transhumanist Reader* as a form of "morphological freedom," a key tenet in transhuman philosophy that considers technological body modification to be a fundamental right.[2] There are numerous problems with More's approach to morphological freedom, particularly that this freedom to morphological self-expression ignores bodily risks and economic barriers. Transhumanist fashions could be reappropriated by posthuman discourse, but its emphasis on freedom from bodily constraints doesn't lend itself to new forms of posthuman subjectivity. However, as Josh Pearson and I have argued in "'Today's Cyborg is Stylish': The Humanity Cost of Posthuman

Stina Attebery

Fashion in *Cyberpunk 2020*," I think that fashion is a productive space for exploring posthuman embodiment and subjectivity as long as the fashionable posthumans in question experience the speculative risks and cultural assaults that can come with changing clothing trends and styles.

28.2 Cyberpunks in the Club

Although named after punks, cyberpunk fashion does not necessarily or exclusively draw on punk styles. When coining the term for his 1983 story "Cyberpunk," Bruce Bethke put together technological prefixes like 'cyber' and 'techno' with terms for 'socially misdirected youth' until he found one that sounded right to him, rather than singling out punks as the only countercultural group for what eventually became a new mode.[3] A competing term of the time—Neuromantics—suggests a connection to glam-rock-inspired styles rather than 1980s punk fashions, and glam rock stars often appear in cyberpunk stories alongside grunge hacker characters. Cyberpunk fashion also encompasses corporate suits, security body armor, and high fashion trends alongside the bricolage street style of 1970s and 1980s punk subcultures. We may associate cyberpunk fashion with the leather-punk-mirrorshades style of its protagonists, but even the corporate villains have a clearly defined, future-oriented cyberpunk style.

Still, cyberpunk has drawn influence from and in return influenced clothing styles from the real world, and punk's opposition to 1970s clothing and cultural optimism and its embrace of DIY aesthetics are important for the mode. Many major cyberpunk characters are described as sporting punk styles. Molly Millions, for instance, first appears in "Johnny Mnemonic" (1981) wearing "mirrored glasses, her dark hair cut in a rough shag. She wore black leather, open over a T-shirt slashed diagonally with stripes of red and black" (5). Pris in *Blade Runner* is similarly decked out in punk style, with a black mesh shirt, spiked collar, and full face makeup. For these and other cyberpunk characters, punk is a useful visual shorthand for countercultural opposition to the corporate establishment. The punk influence of cyberpunk also influenced new oppositional bricolage styles in the 1980s and early 1990s that combined grunge and raver styles with an interest in futuristic technologies. Punk street fashion often draws on technological futurity in its bricolage styles. Ted Polhemus combines the subcultures of 'technos' and 'cyberpunks' in his book *Street Style: From Sidewalk to Catwalk*, arguing that both subcultures found inspiration in science fiction for their 1990s looks.[4] Polhemus sees techno fashion drawn toward the "sci-fi disaster movie" in its gas masks and camouflage clothing, while cyberpunks focus more on computer networks, virtual reality, and wearable technologies (125). There is also a very clear fetish influence on 1990s cyberpunk subcultures. Cyberpunk clothing was popular in clubs with names like "Torture Garden" and "Submission" (Polhemus 127) or at the recurring Click+Drag cyberfetish party at the 1990s Meatpacking District club, Mother (Van Meter). In part, cyberpunk fetish wear was a callback to the use of rubber or PVC in 1980s punk fashion. I also read cyberfetish clothing as a kind of Benjaminian play with the commodity fetish—a fascination with new technological materials that bring together the organic and the inorganic. For example, in one photograph from a Click+Drag cyberpunk party taken by the club's co-founder Rob Roth, featured in a 2015 article about the club, DJ Katya Casio vogues for the camera in day-glo pink plastic pants and a crop top sporting the Apple Mac logo all the while balancing a prop computer monitor over her head. Casio's brightly colored outfit filters cyberpunk technological fashion through drag and club culture in a whimsical approach to cyborg identity. This costume plays with the accelerating changes of modernity and echoes Benjamin's description (quoting Guillaume Apollinaire) of the 19th-century Parisian fascination with the newest technological materials:

> a charming dress made of corks [...] tailor-made outfits made of old bookbindings done in calf.... [sic] Fish bones are being worn a lot on hats. [...] Steel, wool, sandstone, and files have

Fashion

> suddenly entered the vestmentary arts. [...] They're doing shoes in Venetian glass and hats in Baccarat crystal. [...] Fashion is becoming practical and no longer looks down on anything. It ennobles everything. It does for materials what the Romantics did for words. (B3a, 1)

In Casio's case, the iMac is a frame for Casio's exaggerated makeup and expressive pose. She takes Apple's marketing of personal computers as customizable expressions of a high-tech identity and turns it into a sexually charged performance. Casio has ennobled the plastic and implied circuity of the personal computer, and her performance of personal computing as an extension of her body turns this technological accessory into a frame for her own personality.

In many ways, though, the subcultural styles of mid-1990s cyberpunks draw less on the specific technologies and worlds of the cyberpunk mode than they do on post-apocalyptic bricolage styles from other science fiction texts. The Mad Max films are an obvious influence on a number of these supposed cyberpunks, particularly the post-apocalyptic fetish styles from *The Road Warrior* (Miller 1981). Other ostensibly cyberpunk styles that Polhemus discusses more closely resemble the long-haired biker-samurai aesthetics of *Star Trek*'s Klingons. Click+Drag did explicitly reference cyberpunk texts, putting on parties themed around "Gibson Girls"[5] or *TRON*, but as co-founder Rob Roth has said, "Nobody knew what the fuck we were talking about. We would make fliers and give them out. We were just interested in the future. That's what Click+Drag was about, the idea of the future and sex and the idea of the future and community" (Van Meter). For many of these so-called cyberpunks, the cyberpunk literary movement seems to be a much less important influence than non-cyberpunk sf media, or the overall idea of creating future communities through bricolage fashion. It is tempting to call all leather-clad clubbers with circuits sewn into their clothing 'cyberpunks,' but for many it may have been less important to copy the specific cyberpunk styles of Molly Millions or Pris than to use clothing as a way to invent their own original sf persona.

This cyberpunk club scene often overlapped with the cultural assault of cyberpunk-influenced body modification and body art. As Sandra Ley points out, cyberpunks use "special effects kits, makeup, and tattoos to mimic cybernetic implants, such as computer jacks or circuitry. Barcode tattoos were popular and reflected the dehumanization of the individual in a highly technologized world." As Victoria Pitts notes in her cultural study of body modification, *In the Flesh: The Cultural Politics of Body Modification*, cyberpunks made up a small but technologically inventive part of the body modification community. Pitts focuses primarily on well-known body artists Stelarc and Orlan, who have a highly individual approach to cyberpunk style, although she also spends time discussing the larger body modification communities formed around internet groups like the *Body Modification Ezine*, founded in 1994. Cyberpunk body modders play with many of the same future-oriented techno-fetish styles found in street and club clothing, extending these disaster movie and computer hardware styles into the flesh of their own bodies.

These 1990s body modification communities are one of the spaces where cyberpunk's complicated relationship to race comes into play. Literary cyberpunk is fascinated with neotribalism, most famously in Gibson's Rastastafarian community. When Mark Dery mentions the Rastas in *Neuromancer* (1984) as a positive form of representation in "Black to the Future: Interviews with Samuel R. Delany, Greg Tate, and Tricia Rose," Delany unpacks the numerous problems with this cyberpunk approach to race, including the association of the Rastas with computer illiteracy and the lack of any Rasta women, concluding "You'll forgive me if, as a black reader, I didn't leap up to proclaim this passing presentation of a powerless and wholly nonoppositional set of black dropouts [...] as the coming of the black millennium in science fiction, but maybe that's just a black thang ... [sic]" (195).[6]

Delany doesn't single out fashion as part of this critique, but his many criticisms of cyberpunk's framing of neotribal characters as backward and non-technological do extend to fashions, particularly in body modding communities. As Pitts notes, although cyberpunks are less obsessed with neotribal aesthetics than other groups like the modern primitivists, they also draw on decontextualized African, Native American, and Polynesian art for inspiration.[7] We can see a film equivalent to this in *Blade Runner*'s Roy, who, in early versions of the script, was described as "somewhere between a Comanche warrior and a transvestite" (Bukatman 84). This adoption of global 'tribal' styles was partly an extension of punk bricolage, a way of subverting mainstream cultural values by mixing styles and materials.

Combining highly technological mods with neotribal aesthetics was seen as a way of circumventing the commercialization of countercultural styles by mainstream fashion, a central concern of many subcultures. By playing with 'ancient' Indigenous practices of ritual scarification, tattooing, and piercing, these body mod cyberpunks believed themselves to be tapping into a more 'authentic' form of cultural expression existing outside of commercialization. There are obvious problems with this casual framing of Indigeneity as existing out of time or in the past and bearing a trace of authenticity lost to settler cultures. It is a form of what Pitts calls "identity tourism" (181) that refuses to see Indigenous peoples as contemporary with modern culture or having a stake in technology and futurity. Neotribalism in cyberpunk fashion also overlooks the work of Indigenous cyberpunk artists,[8] such as Métis writer Misha, whose novel *Red Spider White Web* (1990) depicts characters fashioning bodies out of genetic science, biotechnological suits, Native animal masks, and gas masks, without representing any of these Indigenous styles as authentic or unchanging in the face of cyberpunk's hyper-modernity. Cyberpunk body art can be an interesting way of challenging cultural politics around gender and sexuality and a way of exploring the limits of the human body. However, as neotribal body art shows, the bricolage fashions of street or club cyberpunks were not always thoughtfully situated in the racial politics of globalized capital and hyper-consumption.

28.3 Cyberpunks on the Catwalk

On the corporate side of the cyberpunk fashion world, cyberpunk styles also feature in the highly commoditized mercantile world of fashion design on the runway. Although street and club styles are the more obvious connection for cyberpunk style outside of cyberpunk fiction, fashion designers often explicitly draw on cyberpunk in their collections. Designer Stephen Sprouse created a 1992 collection called "CyberPunk" followed by a 1993 collection on "CyberGlitter." Although neither collection was commercially successful, Sprouse went on to design cyberpunk looks for Billy Idol during the marketing of Idol's 1993 *Cyberpunk* album. French designer Thierry Mugler has also dabbled in science fiction couture, creating angular-structured clothing influenced by a combination of insect biology, film noir, and robotics. In 1995–96, he created a collection of "Robotic Couture" pieces, including a skin-tight and partly see-through silver robot woman suit inspired by *Metropolis* (Lang 1927) and similar in style to many cyberfetish club outfits.

Sprouse and Mugler were experimenting with cyberpunk fashion in the early to mid-1990s, when cyberpunk had entered the mainstream, but cyberpunk has had an enduring influence on high fashion in the following decades. Many designers, like Mugler, explicitly reference sf film as an influence. Nicolas Ghesquière, for example, came up with his Spring 2007 collection while watching *TRON* and *The Terminator* (Cameron 1984), finding in these films an inspiration for his shiny, angular leather clothing that he designed to mimic "robotic articulation. Car parts. Droids. A boyish silhouette" (Mower). Other designers reference sf in general rather than naming specific texts. Tristan Weber explains that his collections from the early 2000s were "inspired by the science-fiction myths predominant in contemporary visual culture, which [had a] profound influence on his approach to fashion," particularly drawing on biotechnology and nanotechnology in his designs (qtd. in Ley). Sometimes, fashion designers reference sf obliquely. For instance, Donatella Versace's 2010 men's collection was based on the trailers for *TRON: Legacy* (Kosinski 2010), but incorporates leather, hardware, chains, and metal into the design—all materials absent from *TRON*'s shiny, neon virtual world. When fashion designers reference specific sf texts like *Blade Runner* or *Metropolis*, it is often in service of a retrofuturist design, similar to the retrofuturism found in many sf film and TV costume designs.

However, some designers take inspiration from science fiction as a shorthand for futurity and technology in clothing, creating their own original sf styles. I am particularly interested in the science-fictional fashion designed by Hussein Chalayan. Chalayan doesn't reference specific sf films as much as the other designers I have mentioned. As he once told a *New York Times* reporter, he has "always been interested in the future [...]. But the challenge was to do something less predictable than *Robocop* that could be realized in fashion" (Horyn). I don't think Chalayan's comment is fair to the costume design in *Robocop*, but he is certainly unpredictable in his own designs. Chalayan is famous for his highly technological clothing. He has designed collections that mimic urban architecture, 1950s furniture, cars and car crashes, and airplanes. One of his most famous pieces, the 2000 "Remote Control" dress, is made of a series of flaps made out of glass fiber that could be opened or closed via remote control. The sleek, flared shape of the dress is modeled after an airplane, while the remote control, which was controlled by a young boy in the debut fashion show, frames the dress and the woman modeling it as a kind of technological toy. Such a remote-controlled dress explores the anxieties of influence around women's prosthesis and wireless control typical to cyberpunk. Chalayan does not base his fashion designs on existing science fiction texts—he instead creates new science fiction in the speculative designs of his collections. He describes his work as "monuments to ideas" (Bolton iii) and describes himself as a "storyteller" who uses clothing to explore ideas about technology, humanity, and nature in a defamiliarized, abstract space (iv). For example, LED dresses play with the simulacrum worlds of media and virtuality similar to Gibson's cyberspace, while his sexualized car crash clothing mirrors J.G. Ballard's New Wave fiction, a key precursor to (and important influence on) cyberpunk. While Chalayan doesn't call himself a cyberpunk artist, his work resonates with cyberpunk's fascinations and fears; therefore, his work is cyberpunk in its own right, rather than derivative of cyberpunk fashions. Chalayan's work is still a form of commodity fetishism, with all of the class and labor problems inherent in the work of high fashion, but is there anything more cyberpunk than creating posthuman bodies in the midst of commercial exploitation?

28.4 Conclusion

Cyberpunk has a long association with punk subcultures and street style which helped to define its 'look' in the 1980s and 1990s. In turn, cyberpunk's popularity among fashion designers—an often overlooked area for cyberpunk style—has made cyberpunk a continuing part of the acceleration and commoditization of the fashion industry. This tension between street style and commercial fashion reflects the narrative tension between corporate control and marginalized subcultures central to many cyberpunk stories. As a result, cyberpunk is a particularly recognizable form of future-oriented fashion, but the speculative potential of science fiction fashion extends beyond cyberpunk. After all, fashion is inherently science-fictional. It speculates about futures created through technological mediation, commodity fetishism, and bodily experimentation. Science fiction clothing therefore has this speculative quality regardless of whether it accurately predicts future trends.

Beyond cyberpunk, I see this potential for reading fashion through speculative approaches to organic and inorganic matter having relevance for two important areas of study that are outside my purview for this chapter. One of the most important spaces for exploring posthuman fashion is in science-fictional representations of disability. Fashion is often interested in shifting the dimensions taken up by the body and the shape of the silhouette. The frisson created by a risky new clothing trend therefore depends on an ableist notion of a 'normal' body temporarily morphing into new shapes. Fashion is also an important consideration for prosthetics and mobility aids, which often emphasize functionality over other forms of design. The fashionable prosthetic legs and arms designed and worn by Sophie Oliveira Barata in her "Alternative Limb Project" offer a version of fashionable play with human embodiment that draws on cyberpunk enthusiasm for high-tech bodies but grounds these cyberpunk limbs in the politics of disability. I would therefore recommend work like Kathryn Allen's excellent collection on *Disability in Science Fiction* as necessary reading for exploring sf fashion. The second area into which I see sf fashion moving is fashions designed in response to climate change. Changing climates and the proliferation of natural disasters and atypical weather patterns necessitate a different relationship to clothing. Projects like Dehlia Hannah and Cynthia Selinlo's "Unseasonal Fashion" look to clothing like Jacqueline Bradley's "Boat Dress" and Anne van Galen's "Warriors of Downpour City" as a way of confronting climate change as a lived reality instead of an abstracted set of data points. Many of these fashions for the Anthropocene are very contemporary, but some, like Lucy Orta's "Refuge Wear," date back to 1994, suggesting productive links between contemporary Anthropocene fashion and the urban bohemianism of many cyberpunks. The shifting boundaries between interior and exterior designs, bodies and materials, cultural acceleration and assault that I see exemplified in cyberpunk's fashions increasingly inform the ways human bodies adjust to changing environments through speculative clothing.

Like all science fiction texts, clothing can be a space for speculating about the future by extrapolating from the present. Fashion assembles the newest materials and techniques in its creation of science-fictional style, from 19th-century clothing made from cork, steel, fish bone, and glass to plastic, barcode tattoos, and LED lights popular in cyberpunk fashions. It crafts wearable futures out of the cultural bricolage of commodity, culture, and embodiment.

Notes

1 I was able to hear Catherine Adair speak about her career, along with a number of other costume designers, at a series of panels on costuming at the 2018 Eagle Con hosted by California State University, Los Angeles.
2 For a general overview on transhumanism, see Julia Grillmayr's "Posthumanism(s)" contribution in this collection.
3 Personal email correspondence between Bruce Bethke and Lars Schmeink, May 1, 2018.
4 Polhemus' overview of punk and cyberpunk styles is excellent, but he does leave out some similar cyberpunk-influenced styles, particularly the goggles, neon, and glow-in-the-dark style of cybergoths.
5 The "Gibson Girls" night was in honor of both William Gibson and the 18th-century illustrator Charles Dana Gibson, so even references to cyberpunk texts tended to be filtered through other interests and styles.
6 Delany does speak positively of Gibson's representation of the Lo-teks in "Johnny Mnemonic" as a more positive racially ambiguous community that has more agency in opposing multinational capitalism through their bricolage style and Indigenous-coded music (Dery 196–97). For further discussions of cyberpunk and race, see Isiah Lavender III's chapter on "Critical Race Studies" and his co-authored chapter on "Afrofuturism" elsewhere in this collection.
7 See also Daniel Wajcik's Punk and Neo-Tribal Body Art for how this fetishization of "tribal" aesthetics played out in the larger punk body art subculture.
8 Brian Hudson has also worked on creating and defining Cherokee cyberpunk, for a contemporary example.

Works Cited

Allen, Kathryn, ed. *Disability in Science Fiction: Representations of Technology as Cure*. Palgrave, 2013.

Attebery, Stina and Josh Pearson. "'Today's Cyborg is Stylish': The Humanity Cost of Posthuman Fashion in Cyberpunk 2020." *Cyberpunk and Visual Culture*, edited by Graham J. Murphy and Lars Schmeink. Routledge, 2018, pp. 55–79.

Barthes, Roland. *The Fashion System*. Translated by Matthew Ward and Richard Howard. U California P, 1983.

Bascalgi, Maurizia. "For the Unnatural Use of Clothes: Fashion as Cultural Assault." *Stuff Theory: Everyday Objects, Radical Materialism*. Bloomsbury, 2014.

Benjamin, Walter. *The Arcades Project*. Translated by Howard Eiland and Kevin McLaughlin, edited by Rolf Tiedmann. Belknap, 1999.

Bolton, Andrew. *ManusXMachina: Fashion in an Age of Technology*. Yale UP, 2016.

Borrelli-Persson, Laird. "The Chalayan Experience: 3 Models on Wearing the Designer's High-Tech Dresses." *Vogue*, 2 May 2016, www.vogue.com/article/met-gala-chalayan-erika-wall-morgane-dubled.

Buck-Morss, Susan. *The Dialectics of Seeing: Walter Benjamin and the Arcades Project*. MIT Press, 1991.

Bukatman, Scott. *Blade Runner*. British Film Institute, 1997.

Dery, Mark. "Black to the Future: Interviews with Samuel R. Delany, Greg Tate, and Tricia Rose." *Flame Wars: The Discourse of Cyberculture*, edited by Mary Dery. Duke UP, 1994, pp. 179–222.

Gibson, William. "Johnny Mnemonic." *Burning Chrome*. HarperCollins, 2003.

———. *Neuromancer*. Ace, 1984.

Hannah, Dehlia and Cynthia Selin. "Unseasonal Fashion: A Manifesto." *Climates: Architecture and the Planetary Imaginary*, edited by James Graham, Caitlin Blanchfield, et al. Lars Müller P, 2016.

Hayles, N. Katherine. *How We Became Posthuman: Virtual Bodies in Cybernetics, Literature, and Informatics*. U of Chicago P, 1999.

Hebdige, Dick. *Subculture and the Meaning of Style*. Routledge, 1979.

Hollander, Anne. *Seeing Through Clothes*. U California P, 1993.

———. *Sex and Suits: The Evolution of Modern Dress*. Knopf, 1994.

Horyn, Cathy. "Shape-Shifters With Microchips Walk the Runway." *The New York Times*, 7 Oct. 2006, www.nytimes.com/2006/10/07/fashion/shows/07FASHION.html.

Ley, Sandra J. "Cyberpunk." *Berg Encyclopedia of World Dress and Fashion: Global Perspectives*, edited by Joanne B. Eicher and Phyllis G. Tortora. Bloomsbury, 2014, n.p.

More, Max and Natasha Vita More, ed. *The Transhumanist Reader: Classical and Contemporary Essays on the Science, Technology, and Philosophy of the Human Future*. Wiley, 2013.

Mower, Sarah. "Balenciaga Spring 2007 Ready to Wear." *Vogue*, 2 Oct. 2006, www.vogue.com/fashion-shows/spring-2007-ready-to-wear/balenciaga.

Pitts, Victoria. *In the Flesh: The Cultural Politics of Body Modification*. Palgrave, 2003.

Polhemus, Ted. *Streetstyle: From Sidewalk to Catwalk*. Thames & Hudson, 1994.

Sterling, Bruce. Preface. *Mirrorshades: The Cyberpunk Anthology*, edited by Bruce Sterling. Arbor House, 1986.

The Alternate Limb Project. www.thealternativelimbproject.com.

Van Meter, William. "Remembering Web 1.0's Click + Drag Subculture." *The Cut*, 24 Apr. 2015, www.thecut.com/2015/04/remembering-web-10s-click-drag-subculture.html.

Wajcik, Daniel. *Punk and Neo-Tribal Body Art*. UP of Mississippi, 1995.

29
MUSIC

Nicholas C. Laudadio

It should not be a surprise that music is a crucial component of cyberpunk; it is, after all, cyber-*punk*. But cyberpunk's musical aspects draw from far more than just the noise, speed, and rage of canonical punk rock. Electronica, hip hop, the avant-garde, film scores, and heavy metal are all vital parts of cyberpunk's sonic identity and, to the degree that it has a definable musical form, it is a hybrid one that draws from these multiple contexts. So, in an effort to understand and define cyberpunk as a musical endeavor, this chapter will consider the history and sound of recorded works that traffic in cyberpunk themes and imagery in their lyrics, visual design, and production.

Cyberpunk music emerged more generally, thanks to cyberpunk's broad cultural reach in the 1980s and 1990s. This is a point author Bruce Sterling makes when he observes that "the work of the cyberpunks is paralleled throughout Eighties pop culture: in rock video; in the hacker underground; in the jarring street tech of hip-hop and scratch music; in the synthesizer rock of London and Tokyo" (xi–xii). Amidst all these musical forms, the 'synthesizer rock' that most closely parallels cyberpunk is industrial electronic music. Of course, early (or proto-cyberpunk) artists such as Kraftwerk, Gary Numan, and David Bowie conjured up imagined technological and political dystopias in their lyrics, sounds, and personas. Kraftwerk's rigid and mechanical minimalism of the sort found on *The Man Machine* (1978)—its danceable vision of a human/technological hybrid ("The Robots"), its modern-noir sensibility ("Metropolis"), its fascination with human-technological hybrids (the title track), its dreams of space tech ("Spacelab"), and finally its touch of 1980s glamour ("The Model")—all comport nicely with cyberpunk's main concerns. So too do the Philip K. Dickian *noir*-scapes Gary Numan conjured on *Replicas* (as Tubeway Army, [1979]), *The Pleasure Principle* (1979), and *Telekon* (1980). These albums create an atmospheric template that foregrounds narratives about android and human interaction fraught with drama and danger, all against a stark and driving electro-rock backbeat. This is best typified by the single "Down in the Park" from *Replicas*, a story about a future city where human and human-machine hybrids live side by side, albeit uneasily. It is a place where "The mach-men meet the machines/ And play kill by numbers" and the machinic social order is clear, if complicated: "We are not lovers/We are not romantics/We are here to serve you." Of course, one of Numan's biggest influences is Bowie's Ziggy Stardust character and his beautifully rebellious Spiders from Mars that conjured a sexy futurity and fluidity that would become key to the cyberpunk imagination. Other influential acts that shaped what would emerge as industrial's intersections with cyberpunk include Devo's dystopian robot pop, experimental explorations like Yellow Magic Orchestra or Hawkwind, noisy freakouts like Lou Reed's grinding *Metal Machine Music* (1975), Roxy Music's dreamy future-scapes, Sun Ra's liberatory space-politics in *Space is the Place* (1973), Tangerine

Dream's trips to alternate dimensions like *Phaedra* (1973), and Parliament's dream of a utopian mothership made most obvious in 1975's funk masterpiece *Mothership Connection*.

Industrial grew out of the more experimental side of electronic music in the 1970s and blended the avant-garde looping and sampling techniques of musique concrète (the distortion of sounds found in nature to create music), the extrapolative instinct of progressive rock, the political and vocal extremes of punk, and the muted rhythmic energy of minimalism to create a music that sought to give voice to many of the same concerns and environments as cyberpunk. For example, industrial music centered on dystopian anti-governmental themes backed by a *noir*-ish urbanism common to cyberpunk. It offered a grinding take on the increasingly decentered and decrepit urban landscape with a hybrid of punk, electronica, and avant-garde production techniques. And the extent to which industrial can be termed 'moody' in tone and topic also has much to do with the fact that it drew inspiration from the dark and challenging sounds and stories of bands like Joy Division, Suicide, and The Velvet Underground, this last band proving particularly instrumental to William Gibson. In sum, industrial and cyberpunk are so intertwined that trying to disentangle them is difficult, a point Karen Collins makes in her essay "Dead Channel Surfing: The Commonalities Between Cyberpunk and Industrial Music." Collins writes that, "it would be futile to develop a chicken-or-egg argument over the use of the techniques, symbolism and themes in industrial and cyberpunk. It seems more likely that a sharing of ideas flows two ways between the genres" (176). Collins goes on to argue that the shared ideas include moments of intertextuality (most famously Gibson using The Velvet Underground's "Sweet Jane" to christen a spaceship in *Neuromancer* (1984) or citing German industrial godfathers Einstürzende Neubauten in *Idoru* (1996)), of contextual history (the use of Dada and other experimental composition techniques for creative production), and thematic continuity (both intent on future-*noir* techno-dystopias populated by renegade hacker anti-heroes). Collins also notes that it is a "mood of alienation and anxiety that is the most important aspect of commonality between cyberpunk and industrial" (176). These are connections that Stephen Mallinder, founding member of the influential English industrial collective Cabaret Voltaire, reinforces when he notes that his band "made music that was often sonically brutal, we challenged ideas of authority and control, we toyed with moody and often taboo imagery, we were simultaneously intellectual and anti-intellectual" (ix).

Aside from The Velvet Underground or the aforementioned Einstürzende Neubauten, an experimental band fronted by Blixa Bargeld, other early industrial bands that helped pave the way for cyberpunk include the UK's Throbbing Gristle whose music clanged and screamed with DIY instruments, amplified shopping carts backed by vocal samples, and heavy, metallic, distorted bass drums. Songs like "Very Friendly" (1975), a long story-song about an ax-murdering couple that can be read as a music of revolutionary politics for apocalyptic capitalism, or Neubauten's "Kollaps" (1981), with its heavy-metal-shoed stomp through dreams of leveling cities, all while Bargeld screams "Unsere Irrfahrten zerstören die Städte" ("our odysseys destroy the cities"), provided the perfect sonic environment in which cyberpunk's ideals could flourish.

But it was in the mid-to-late 1980s that a global array of artists like Front 242 (Belgium), Front Line Assembly (Canada), Clock DVA (UK), The Cassandra Complex (UK), Ministry (U.S.), and KMFDM (Germany) would expand industrial's sound palette to include powerful and affordable new digital instruments and create the first identifiably cyberpunk music. One key aspect of cyberpunk, a romanticization of digital criminality, finds a common cause in industrial's defining reliance on sampling pre-existing auditory material. If the 'lawless' hacker is out to liberate us from increasingly centralized power structures in a hyper-digital age, the lawless artist does something similar with the sample, each purloined sound a bit of artful techno-plunder. This is exemplified in British industrial act Clock DVA's "Connection Machine" from their *Buried Dreams* LP (1989). On this single, Clock DVA explores the musicality of surveillance technologies and extensively samples Harry Caul, Gene Hackman's audio surveillance technician in Francis

Ford Coppola's *The Conversation* (1974). Clock DVA remarks in the album note that the song features "DIGITALLY MANIPULATED SAMPLES TAKEN FROM COMMUNICATION TECHNOLOGIES AND ILLEGALLY OBTAINED FILTER RECORDINGS. ALL COMPOSITIONS DIGITALLY RECORDED" [emphasis in original]. The same release also contains "The Hacker," a more recognizably structured effort with a percussive bass arpeggio driving the song along, punctuated twice-per-measure by reverb-heavy brass stabs that give the song a frantic sense of urgency. Though the recording of "The Hacker" is quite different in structure and texture than the eerie ambient minimalist drone of "Connection Machine," the narrative of "a digital murder/Programmed by mathematical terrorists" ("The Hacker") and the fixation on the grain and grit of audio surveillance ("Connection Machine") both operate as thematic and sonic explorations of digital criminality that typifies cyberpunk music.

This same sort of hacker-revolt attitude surfaces in the music of Belgian industrial superstars Front 242. Their dance floor hit "Headhunter V3.0" (1988) details the routines of a future cyber-hitman—"He's alone and anonymous/But written in his cells/He's got the marks of a genius"—who is "looking for this man/To sell him to other men.../For ten times his price (at least)." The song's galloping synth bass line still serves for many as an iconic and genre-defining use of the Yamaha DX7 digital synthesizer and forms the central sonic identity with its breathy, woodwind-like pulse that stakes out the sound's middle frequencies and moves the whole catchy apparatus along. The sound also reinforces the band's hybrid musical aesthetic—the rigidity of early sequencing and digital audio production form the structure for their songs; yet, it is melded with an insistence on a more organic texture to the sounds, echoing the droney folk-tronica of the sort that Neubauten explores. The chorus' famous four-part instructions on how to "catch the man" and the song's intensely danceable backbeat and infectious chord progression not only served as a template for the "electronic body music" for which the band would become known, but also became arguably the most commercially successful example of cyberpunk music.

In that same year, fellow Belgian industrial band A Split Second released "Bend My Body Armor," which shared a cyber-warrior theme with Front 242's "Headhunter V3.0" albeit with a heavier backbeat and a brutal bondage/car crash aesthetic that draws, as did many industrial acts, from The Normal's Ballardian cult hit "Warm Leatherette" (1981). The move here from the more experimental industrial music of Throbbing Gristle to the club-smash dance beats of Front 242 or A Split Second marks the increased popularity of industrial music and echoes cyberpunk's increased (and changing) popularity.

One of the more explicitly cyberpunk-focused musicians to emerge from the late 1980s and early 1990s period is Austrian-Canadian Bill Leeb (originally of Skinny Puppy) and his band Front Line Assembly. The band's ominous synth pads and kinetic arpeggios on songs such as "Digital Tension Dementia" (1989), "Bio-Mechanic" (1992), "Mindphaser" (1992), "Synthetic Forms" (1999), and "Warmech" (2018) play against a heavy and compressed steady 4/4 backbeat and Leeb's menacing vocal style. Front Line Assembly's songs deploy industrial sonic motifs to explore the dark side of cyberpunk, and the band even includes *Robocop II* (Kershner 1990) among many samples on their excellent album *Tactical Neural Implant* (1992).

Around the same time, British industrial band The Cassandra Complex took a similar approach on their appropriately titled fourth album *Cyberpunx* (1990), written as a concept album/rock opera organized around digitally inflected *noir*-dystopian escape narratives. The cover features a pixelated and helmeted cyber pilot backed by lo-fi images of Pac-Man, Jesus, and a fetus, while the songs' loosely joined narrative moves through complex international (and interplanetary) politics and cross-cultural romance narratives, ultimately dropping listeners back into a dark world of war and computer-criminality.

With cyberpunk's remarkable popularity by the mid-1990s—it made the cover of *Time Magazine* (February 1993) with the lurid subtitle "Virtual sex, smart drugs and synthetic rock 'n' roll!

A futuristic subculture erupts from the electronic underground"—it was only a matter of time before a top-tier pop-rock star intervened in the conversation. British singer Billy Idol's fifth studio album was released the same year as the *Time* magazine cover, a concept record called *Cyberpunk* that in many ways was similar to The Cassandra Complex effort from three years earlier. Although Idol's earlier work tried to blend his original punk aesthetic with his affinity for 'modern' audio effects and a more 'polished' production style, *Cyberpunk*'s use of electronic instruments and sounds showcases all of the sound qualities and rhythms popular at the time, including digital synthesizers, vocoders and harmonizer effects, and multiple samples. Songs such as "Neuromancer," "Wasteland," and the *Billboard* single "Shock to the System," written in part as a response to the Rodney King beating and subsequent LA riots of 1992, unashamedly deploy cyberpunk tropes, while Robin Hancock's production attempts to layer the texture of electronic instrumentation and rhythms with Idol's more conventional guitar-rock-centered world. The album, a crass attempt to cash in on cyberpunk's popularity, was a critical failure and even Idol admits his "creative instincts and possibly even my taste seemed to abandon me this time around" (290–91). In his bracingly unkind review for *Village Voice*, rock critic Robert Christgau accused it of "riding into the technofuture on simultaneous cybertronic concept albums. How postmodern. How retronuevo. How hep [sic]." Christgau mocks the album that was "so shameless as to try and steal [William] Gibson's thunder from under his nose—naming the album after the movement he epitomizes, naming a key song after his first novel."

Christgau was by no means alone: *The A.V. Club* sardonically describes the album as the "'Least Essential Concept Album' of the 1990s," while *Q Magazine* has included *Cyberpunk* on its list of the 50 Worst Albums Ever. Mark Coleman characterized the album as "mundane," described Idol's cover version of The Velvet Underground's "Heroin" as "clueless techno-destruction," and remarked that if "this brave-new-world thing doesn't wash, he can always change his name to Billy Ray Idol and kick off a brand new dance craze." Finally, Gibson himself admits that he just doesn't "get what [Idol's] on about [...]. I don't see the connection" (Giles). Gibson states confusion when he learned that Idol hadn't read *Neuromancer*; instead, Idol apparently "absorbed it through a kinda osmosis. I don't know" (Giles). Although Idol's gamble on *Cyberpunk* temporarily derailed his career and largely ended his *Billboard* chart dominance, this experiment does not mean that cyberpunk had failed as a musical expression; indeed, the intermingling of cyberpunk's musical and literary aspects was now firmly embedded in the pop tradition.

If industrial cyberpunk music peaked in the 1990s, cyberpunk's ideas quickly spread across various musical subgenres interested in techno-culture and dark, extrapolative themes. One musical style to fully absorb cyberpunk's textures was heavy metal. Metal had long been invested in extrapolative imaginings: Black Sabbath's genre-defining single "Iron Man" (1970) with its famously sludgy riff and halting narrative of an iron giant, coupled with a self-fulfilling apocalyptic prophecy, represents one of the most popular early examples of metal's engagement with science fiction (sf). By the 1980s, bands such as Canada's Voivod were bringing cyberpunk themes directly to metal in both sound (adding synthesizers) and sense (stories about politics, technology, and war). Voivod's album *Killing Technology* (1987) was a percussive and propulsive blend of thrash and punk with songs about "electronic alienation/Trading children for a new kind of robot" and the threat of technological weaponry like the "spider web over the atmosphere" ("Killing Technology") of President Ronald Reagan's Strategic Defense Initiative (SDI) missile defense system, nicknamed 'Star Wars.' Clearly, the influences that had overtaken some industrial music had found willing ears in the metal world.

Many artists would embrace Voivod's brand of techno-pessimism and dystopic cyberpunk instinct. On their album *Soul of a New Machine* (1992), Fear Factory combined the extreme percussive and vocal maneuvers of death metal with the themes and samples of industrial. Later records like *Demanufacture* (1995) and *Obsolete* (1998) continued these themes, with an increased presence of synthesized sounds and sampled dialogues and soundscapes. This model for a contemporary kind of cybermetal is best realized in the work of Russian band Illidiance who makes some of the most heavily cyberpunk-influenced work on recordings such as *Synthetic Breed* (2009), *Cybergore Generation* (2009), and *Damage Theory* (2010), deftly and jarringly moving between the extremes of industrial electronic noise and percussion to metal blast beats and death metal growls. Their intense lyrics imagine "death digitalized" where the narrator is "erasing data like you" ("Hi Tech Terror," 2010) and a nightmare scenario of your "cyber implants are groaning in hunger" ("Cybernesis," 2010).

Harsh electronic tonalities and stories of hacker-criminal dystopias and digital warfare found a home in a wider range of musical cultures. As with industrial and metal, hip hop had explored sf from its very beginning, but recordings like Deltron 3030's self-titled debut album from 2000, Dr. Octagon's *Dr. Octagon* (1996), re-released a year later as *Dr. Octagonecologyst* (1997), El-P's *Fantastic Damage* (2002), or Cannibal Ox's *The Cold Vein* (2001) brought many of cyberpunk's concerns into their rhymes and beats. Del the Funky Homosapien raps about corporate warfare in the year 3030, Kool Keith (as Dr. Octagon) spins stories about an alien, time traveling, and murderous gynecologist who "go[es] to earth through the fax machine" ("Earth People"), El-P.'s post-9/11 dystopia conjures up Philip K. Dickian imagery like "Mechanisms burn with beeping sounds/That own their humans sold as ruthless rounds of radio dust..." ("Fantastic Damage"), and Harlem's Cannibal Ox takes us far beyond NYC and into a "War of the worlds/Where cities twirl" while keeping listeners focused on the technologically mediated body: "my shell/Mechanical found ghost/But my ghetto is animal found toast" ("Iron Galaxy"). The beats and samples that serve as the foundation of these extrapolative imaginings are as complex and wide-ranging in their references and sources as the lyrics they support. For example, Canadian DJ Kid Koala's beats for Deltron draw largely from obscure 1970s recordings from people like French composer William Sheller or Greek prog band Aphrodite's Child, where El.P.'s production for Cannibal Ox worked with more familiar sources like dance music godfather Giorgio Moroder and 1980s new wave band Wall of Voodoo. Moreover, the development of Afrofuturist music arising out of jazz and R&B brings to hip hop an awareness of larger socio-political issues. Although a full explication of them is far beyond the scope of this chapter, Janelle Monáe is particularly important for thoroughly redefining extrapolative music and its ability to use sf to engage with identity politics. As Christine Capetola writes in her Janelle Monáe contribution for this collection, Monáe has emerged "[a]s one of our most exciting and thought-provoking contemporary artists" who uses her music and 'emotion pictures' to create "her own black, queer, and feminist version of cyberpunk through interfacing her body and musical technology" (246).

An expansive exploration of cyberpunk music must also mention the soundtrack music from canonical cyberpunk cinema, including the audio soundscapes of Tsutomu Ohashi and the Geinoh Yamashirogumi collective on *Akira* (Ōtomo 1988) and the musical compositions behind films such as *Tetsuo: The Iron Man* (Tsukamoto 1989), *Ghost in the Shell* (Oshii 1995), *Strange Days* (Bigelow 1995), and *The Matrix* franchise (Wachowskis 1999–2003). Perhaps the most important, and certainly most well-known, cinematic soundtrack, however, is Greek composer Vangelis's score for *Blade Runner* (Scott 1982). Vangelis builds ethereal figures from complex electronic textures and famously does so almost entirely on one massive synthesizer, the Yamaha CS80. At over 200 pounds, the CS80 had an equally weighty sound, and the tonal qualities of Vangelis's string arrangements have since become legendary for their warmth and expressiveness. Similarly, Wendy Carlos's musical work on *TRON* (Lisberger 1982) is equally notable, if often overlooked. Carlos's score shares much with her work for Kubrick's *The Shining* (1980), if more orchestral than electro-minimalist. Alongside her sweeping score which features the London Philharmonic and her signature Moog synthesizer production, there are also two odd pop songs by Journey: "Only Solutions" and "1990's Theme." This shift from traditional film scoring to a more pop song soundscape is echoed in electronic music's own move from the fringes of the art music scene in universities and museums to the vibrating center of the global popular music industry.

While cyberpunk films such as David Cronenberg's *Videodrome* (1983) and *eXistenZ* (1999) feature more traditional Hollywood scores by Howard Shore, more 'underground' electronic and electro-rock scores have eventually dominated and even defined cyberpunk music. As Patrick Novotny puts it, "the fast-paced and hectic energy of techno music and its industrial music predecessor is the kind of music one expects to hear from the settings of cyberpunk" (114). Though Novotny is focusing on the largely electronic aspects of the cyberpunk soundscape, the experience of cyberpunk music puts the listener in a space between rock's distorted guitars and anger and the capacious electronic sound palette of EDM and industrial. This approach is the one that seems to greatly appeal to the creators of cyberpunk cinema.

Leaning more toward the electronic side of this spectrum, for example, is Iain Softley's *Hackers* (1995), which boasted era-defining electronic acts such as Orbital, The Prodigy, and Underworld, as well as more underground or club-oriented fare as Austrian drum'nbass duo Kruder & Dorfmeister or British trip-hop musician Leftfield. Much of the output found on these soundtracks is defined by its metallic/electronic tonalities, insistent, high-bpm (beats per minute) bass drums, and propulsive sequenced bass lines. Soundtracks from cinematic cyberpunk range from underground electronica and industrial to more mainstream dance, rock, and alternative acts, evidenced by the appearance of Orbital, KMFDM, as well as more rock-oriented acts, such as Helmet, the Rollins Band or Bono and The Edge from Irish pop-rock band U2, on the soundtrack for *Johnny Mnemonic* (Longo 1995). A film such as Kathryn Bigelow's *Strange Days* (1995) concerned itself more with the rock element of the cyberpunk sound, adding to the soundtrack British rock band Skunk Anansie, heavy metal band Prong, and actress Juliette Lewis with an on-screen performance of PJ Harvey's "I Can Hardly Wait" (1993). The soundtrack also featured electronic music from English rapper Tricky and the electronica of Belgian/American Lords of Acid, as well as more traditional fare from Leonard Cohen, Bob Marley, The Doors, but where cyberpunk as a musical genre is largely electronic, cyberpunk as a cinematic one is far more varied in its musical imagination, hewing closer to cinematic trends of their era.

Like the environments in canonical cyberpunk literature, the scores for cinematic cyberpunk are sonically global in nature; for example, *Akira* features a concentration of traditional Japanese instrumentation and vocalizing, as well as an intense interest in minimal, expansive electronic soundscapes that evoke the complex digital landscapes the film's characters traverse. Tsutomu Ohashi and the Geinoh Yamashirogumi collective's score frames the urban backdrop with Japanese voices and timbres as well as electronic reinforcement of the soundscape, awash with motorcycle engines and shouts of "KANEDA!" The score also prominently features the sound of large Balinese bamboo gamelan instruments and choruses full of manipulated voices, grunts, chants, sighs, and shouts. As Kevin Lozano writes, the composing and sampling were precise, including at one point the decision that the motorcycle in the film must come from the engine of a 1929 Harley Davidson. Meanwhile, Kenji Kawaii's original score for Oshii's *Ghost in the Shell* exhibits masterful use of silence insofar as it draws our aural focus to the diegetic sounds of whirring and clicking and chirping of machines, computers, and cyborg bodies in scenes that would later inspire Icelandic musician Björk, herself no stranger to sf discourse and iconography. When these silences are eventually broken, it is often for large chord voicings reminiscent of a Bulgarian mode which frames the film's broad cityscapes and suggests an eerie instability to everything, a kind of aural flickering. Broad harmonies and distinct vocal phrasings dominate Kawai's ambient score, but there is also the occasional deep hum of a synthesizer pad, fleshing out the lower frequencies and adding weight and depth to the soundscape. Finally, Shinya Tsukamoto's *Tetsuo: The Iron Man*'s disturbing visuals found equally challenging sonic accompaniment with compositions by Chu Ishikawa, acclaimed industrial musician and composer. Overall, Japanese composers and filmmakers have done much to help define the sound of cyberpunk, bringing the cinematic tradition and the industrial instinct to bear on their work. The presence of electronic timbres and diverse musical styles in cinematic cyberpunk, coupled with cyberpunk's focus on technologically mediated existence, has repeatedly proven itself compatible: Cyberpunk music foregrounds the very same noise and industry in its musical expressions as its brethren literary cyberpunk.

With its roots in industrial music, sf, and the bricolage common to postmodern culture, cyberpunk music has become a useful moniker to address themes, narratives, aesthetics, and sounds evident in a multitude of musical styles. In a similar manner to literary or cinematic cyberpunk living well beyond its initial popularity, so too is musical cyberpunk more than a popular fad: Cyberpunk music remains relevant to the 21st century as it continues its pioneering attempt to give voice to a world where technology has got the best of humanity. In other words, cyberpunk music (and cyberpunk in general) has evolved into independent and vibrant subcultures that continually prove themselves ideal forms for imagining and theorizing the role of technology in art and everyday life. In sum, it is clear that, as with the literary mode that gave it its name, cyberpunk music has become part of the vast sea change of cyberpunk whose formations and fandoms continue to proliferate across digital culture.

Works Cited

Cannibal Ox. "Iron Galaxy." *The Cold Vein*. Definitive Jux, 2001, track 1.

Capetola, Christine. "Cyberpunk and the Future Sounds of Janelle Monáe." *The Routledge Companion to Cyberpunk Culture*, edited by Anna McFarlane, Graham J. Murphy, and Lars Schmeink. Routledge, 2020, pp. 245–51.

Christgau, Robert. "Virtual Hep." *Robert Christgau: Dean of American Rock Critics*, 10 Aug. 1993, roberchristgau.com/xg/rock/cyberpun-93.php.

Clock DVA. "Liner Notes." *Buried Dreams*, Wax Trax!, 1989.

Coleman, Mark. Review of *Cyberpunk*, by Billy Idol. *Rolling Stone*, 17 Jul. 1997, rollingstone.com/music/music-album-reviews/cyberpunk-191996/.

Collins, Karen. "Dead Channel Surfing: The Commonalities Between Cyberpunk Literature and Industrial Music." *Popular Music*, vol. 24, May 2005, pp. 164–78.

Dr. Octagon. "Earth People." *Dr. Octagon*, Bulk Recordings, 1996, track 4.

El-P. "Fantastic Damage." *Fantastic Damage*, Definitive Jux, 2002, track 1.

Front 242. "Headhunter V3.0." *Front to Front*, Red Rhino Europe, 1988, track 7.

Giles, Jeff. "25 Years Ago: Billy Idol Leaps to the Future with *Cyberpunk*." *UCR: Ultimate Classic Rock*, 23 Jun. 2013, ultimateclassicrock.com/billy-idol-cyberpunk/.

Idol, Billy. *Cyberpunk*, Chrysalis Records, 1993.

———. *Dancing with Myself*. Touchstone, 2014.

Illidance. "Cybernesis." *Damage Theory*, Independent, 2010, track 7.

———. "Hi Tech Horror." *Damage Theory*, Independent, 2010, track 1.

Lozano, Kevin. Review of Geinoh Yamashirogumi's *Akira: Symphonic Suite*. Pitchfork, 16 Sep. 2017, pitchfork.com/reviews/albums/geinoh-yamashirogumi-akira-symphonic-suite/.

Mallinder, Stephen. "Foreword." *Assimilate: A Critical History of Industrial Music*, by S. Alexander Reed. Oxford UP, 2013, pp. ix–xiv.

Novotny, Patrick. "No Future! Cyberpunk, Industrial Music, and the Aesthetics of Postmodern Disintegration." *Political Science Fiction*, edited by Donald M. Hassler and Clyde Wilcox. U of South Carolina P, 1997, pp. 99–123.

Sterling, Bruce. Preface. *Mirrorshades: The Cyberpunk Anthology*, edited by Bruce Sterling. Ace, 1988, pp. ix–xvi.

Voivod. "Killing Technology." *Killing Technology*, Noise International, 1987, track 1.

30

JANELLE MONÁE: *DIRTY COMPUTER* (CASE STUDY)

Christine Capetola

To accompany the release of her new audio collection *Dirty Computer* (2018), Janelle Monáe released a concept film—what she refers to as an emotion picture— of the same name that sonically and visually recounts how Jane 58721 (Janelle Monáe) and her android friends attempt to hold onto their feelings (of black solidarity, of feminist collectivity, of same-sex desire) in the wake of a white-washed ruling power that wants to render them all complacent—and emotionless— machines. In what we can call an example of 'Afrocyberpunk,'[1] *Dirty Computer* is Monáe's fusion of cyberpunk visuals and 1980s pop sounds to inspire us to act in the present and build a different future than the dystopian one portrayed in the film. In so doing, *Dirty Computer* centers blackness and the African diaspora as a pivot point for pushing back against the technological grip of a hyper-globalized society, and although they are considered 'dirty computers,' Jane and her friends utilize the technologies of black musical traditions to continuously display the 'human' desires for sex, love, and connectivity. For example, during the performance of "Django Jane," Jane 58721 sits atop a throne dressed in a regal maroon suit, white shirt, black tie, white leather boots, and maroon kufi cap with gold embroidery; a cohort of black lady androids with black leather jackets and sunglasses layered atop similar outfits surround her, supporting her regal position. The group nods along as Jane raps, "Yeah, yeah, this is my palace/ Champagne in my chalice," alluding to both the queens and kings of African history and the power of global collectivity rooted in shared experiences of blackness. The androids move their machinery along with the beat, connecting with the felt oscillations of sound that are the song's vibrations. After lifting their arms in the air, they quickly pull them back down to their right in the fashion of a militaristic salute. Using the hard-hitting synthesizer and drum machine sounds as catalysts for movement, they invoke Janet Jackson's "Rhythm Nation" (1989), the black pop star's successful single on which she calls her fans to "Join voices in protest to social injustice/A generation full of courage, come with me." For Monáe, "Django Jane" highlights how vibration is a source of identity-making that works both in conjunction with and in excess of sound to create points of connectivity that push on the limits of visual representation. Through being drawn into movement along with the oscillations of a sound's vibrations, they channel the fluidity of identity formation into the project of history-making (Capetola 4).

In *Cyberpunk and Visual Culture*, Graham J. Murphy and Lars Schmeink write of cyberpunk's visual richness as it "explores the melting of the human with machines and thus a break in human limitations" (xxiv) as well as the "changes in what counts as human" (xxv). In *Dirty Computer*, cyberpunk is a sonic and accompanying vibration that fuses the resonances of pop music and the felt experiences of different identities (black, female, queer) to challenge the (visual) hegemony of the

245

'human.' In other words, in a future world that resembles the cyberpunk futures popularized in films such as *Blade Runner* (Scott 1982), futures that look increasingly like our surveilled present,[2] *Dirty Computer* foregrounds the racialized dimensions of cyberpunk's explorations of the overlaps between 'human' and 'machine.' As with the replicants and racialized others in *Blade Runner*, Jane and her comrades live on the surface, subject to constant surveillance from flying automatic drones that police them from the sky. When they want to gather together in (relative) safety, they move underground or to hidden clubs, where their meetings are filled with the sounds of synthesizers and drum machines. As in *Blade Runner*, synth music in *Dirty Computer* is particularly important because it is used to signify difference, particularly a racial and/or robotic otherness.[3] In *Dirty Computer*, the bass-heavy vibrations of African diasporic music are the blueprints for Jane and her friends to resist on the surface.[4]

As one of our most exciting and thought-provoking contemporary artists, Monáe creates her own black, queer, and feminist version of cyberpunk through interfacing her body and musical technology. In the words of Shana L. Redmond, Monáe "uses her body to critique and resituate history, including the identities produced from and within it" (394). By drawing on the music of 1980s black pop stars, Monáe places herself within a lineage of black artists who use sound to intervene in stereotypes of black, female, and/or queer people—and to call attention to the struggles of minoritarian subjects in America and the African diaspora. Even more important, Monáe continues the trend of pushing back on visual stereotypes of black people as criminals, welfare queens, or (art) objects—a resistance that had begun with the work of MTV stalwarts such as Michael Jackson and Prince. Jackson and Prince were among the first black artists to go into heavy rotation on MTV and the first pop artists of any racial background to experiment with relatively new (at the time) digital synthesizer and drum machine technology. Such experimentation helped them re-humanize themselves and citizens of black communities as a whole in the face of dehumanizing images of black people circulated during Ronald Reagan's presidency. Monáe has continued this foundational work in her own oeuvre and the sonic connections between Monáe's *Dirty Computer* and 1980s black pop stars exemplify the resonances of 'history' in her present/future moment.

Dirty Computer partakes in the cyberpunk—and also Afrofuturistic—project of envisioning the future to reflect on the present.[5] In this vein, *Dirty Computer* works as a reflection of how black—and female, queer, trans, and nonbinary—people continue to be objectified and policed in the 2010s. In the futuristic world of *Dirty Computer*, we encounter many of the same technological and political problems prevalent in today's America. During the emotion picture's opening, Jane narrates this dystopian setting: "They started calling us computers. People began vanishing. And the cleaning began. You were dirty if you looked different. You were dirty if you refused to live the way they dictated. You were dirty if you showed any form of opposition at all. And if you were dirty, it was only a matter of time."

As they are captured, the dirty computers are sent to a cleansing center where their minds are erased memory by memory by a duo of white men called "memory erasers," all while the androids strive to keep their memories as a means of resistance. For example, one of Jane's memories involves her and a friend in a car being pulled over by an automated police drone floating through the air. As beacons of surveillance, the drones are all-seeing, forcing the two women into silence and stillness. Giving the automated surveillant some subtle side eye as they produce their IDs and retinas to be scanned, they wait for the drone to zoom out into the distance before letting the rest of their friends out of the trunk, all while the song "I Got the Juice" begins to play. After "I Got the Juice" abruptly stops, the scene shifts to one of automated drones hovering above a group of dark- and light-skinned people outside at night. While a voiceover reads from the Declaration of Independence—"We hold these truths to be self-evident, that all men are created equal, that they are endowed by their Creator with certain unalienable Rights, that among these are Life, Liberty and the pursuit of Happiness"—a row of people rocking piercings, asymmetrical haircuts, and

Janelle Monáe: Dirty Computer (Case Study)

gender nonconformity are lined up accordingly. This drone round-up contrasted with the audio clip of the Declaration is a stark visualization of who in this society is considered a dirty computer.

In the emotion picture, music is the means by which Jane and her friends attempt to find freedom, to move to their own beat. In other words, music allows them to exist on a different vibration that is grounded not only in the contributions of black culture but in solidarity with expansive notions of queerness and feminism. As jazz composer, poet, and Afrocentrist Sun Ra remarked from the planet that he has set aside for black people in the film *Space is the Place* (Coney 1974), "[t]he music is different here. The vibrations are different on planet Earth." In taking up Sun Ra's call to locate a different 'vibration' for a (black) collectivity, Jane and the other androids partake in the Afrocyberpunk project of using (music) technology to set themselves free.

This acoustic-political endeavor is evident in *Dirty Computer* at the start of "Crazy, Classic, Life" when the camera returns to Jane's group riding in her car and onward to the party that will ultimately result in multiple arrests. Transitioning from moving in sync with the song's glitchy drum machine trap beat to gliding into smooth choreography in tandem with the synthesizer melody, Jane and her friends mold themselves to the beats of the song, taking more control over their movements with each verse. While the police drone technology threatens to keep them in line, the technology of synthesizers and drum machines offers a space where they can move freely. In this moment, the collective of black, female, and (gender)queer computers uses the power of sound and vibration to stand in opposition to the technology of surveillance. Where cyberpunk's countervisuality involves "demanding the right to see and be seen" (Schmeink 277), Monáe's collective insists on hearing and feeling beyond the limitations of (counter)visuality. In this project, sound and its vibrations are their literal building blocks for freedom.

Mobilizing technologies that can be heard and felt, the group reroutes visual stereotypes of blackness. In addition to following the Afrofuturistic (and cyberpunk) tradition of repurposing technology, Monáe is a digital griot, or "an intervening figure who unites the past, present, and future, refuses the digital divide as a barrier to black engagement with technology, and utilizes a specifically African American rhetoric" (Jones 43). For example, on "Crazy, Classic, Life," Monáe not only invokes the sounds and vibrations of 1980s black pop stars such as Prince (who collaborated with Monáe on *Dirty Computer* before his untimely death) but also places these vibrations within a (both recent and distant) history of the black struggles that form the political-aesthetic backgrounds of these sonics. The vibrations are not only interruptions of the present/future but also a materially felt connection to the sounds—and struggles—of historical points in time. While the murder of people of color in general—and trans women of color in particular—by (often white) men is an ongoing and well-documented crisis, the line-up of minoritarian subjects at the end of the party, a line-up eerily reminiscent of an execution line, is a reminder of our current reality. Bolstered by the sounds of screams and police sirens, the scene is a visceral reminder to not look (or turn our ears or hearts) away from the reality of decreased life chances for minoritarian subjects in our present.

The genius of *Dirty Computer* is that it uses pop music to visually and sonically situate histories of black suffering within a context of struggles for widening understandings of gender and sexuality beyond the purview of sterile and respectable whiteness. Through mapping the sounds and vibrations of pop music onto Afrocyberpunk aesthetics, Monáe emphasizes how racial minorities and androids who are categorized as 'other' can turn their being read as (or being) queer and gender non-normative into a mechanism for building collectivity. Both androgyny and queerness have always been part of the mix for Monáe, as evidenced by the shouts of "Queer!" during the chorus of her 2013 single "Q.U.E.E.N." and her later confirmation that she identifies as pansexual. For example, using repurposed James Brown-styled dance moves to try to escape her jailers in the music video for "Tightrope" (2010),[6] Monáe challenges the dominance of the guards' white maleness and underscores femaleness and queerness as critical elements of black musical traditions and black life (Royster 188).

Given these intersectional interests, *Dirty Computer* is optimistic that pop music—i.e. poptimism—can work as a catalyst for change in the world. The emotion picture challenges the gender stereotypes that have been grafted onto musical genres, beginning with the assumption that pop is more 'feminine' than rock—and therefore the politically weaker of the two. In a 2014 op-ed, critic Saul Austerlitz bemoans that poptimism (versus rockism) favors "disco, not punk; pop, not rock; synthesizers, not guitars; the music video, not the live show," adding that "[i]t is to privilege the deliriously artificial over the artificially genuine." But rather than reinforcing the "deliriously artificial," Monáe mobilizes both pop and the technology of synthesizers to expose the behind-the-scenes workings of the memory erasers that keep white heterosexist patriarchy alive. In addition to challenging the black masculinist tendencies attributed to James Brown and other artists creating music at the intersections of rock and funk,[7] Monáe utilizes pop music technologies on *Dirty Computer* to accentuate how blackness is constructed by discourses and everyday practices *while simultaneously* using these same technologies to explore how gender and sexuality complicate notions of blackness which are still too much indebted to heteropatriarchal and heterosexist tendencies. In other words, pop on *Dirty Computer* is a site where Monáe can *reimagine* race, gender, and sexuality.

In Afrocyberpunk's space of fluidity and flow (Bould 231), Jane and her android friends use musical technology to connect across lines of difference. The potential of this pop-cyberpunk fusion is most clear during the music video portion for "Pynk," the third single from *Dirty Computer*. Occurring exactly midway through the film, "Pynk" is an emotional highpoint, a point in the emotion picture where a visually pink landscape and the sounds of a throbbing synthesizer and drum machine coalesce to accentuate the interwovenness of race, gender, and sexuality. As the second collaboration between Monáe and Canadian experimental pop artist Grimes,[8] the song has the most electronically boundary-pushing sound and production of any part of *Dirty Computer*. Significantly, Grimes (who is white) does not appear in the music video for "Pynk"; instead, the focus remains on Monáe and her crew. Following a shot of Jane and her friends floating up to the Pynk Rest-Inn in a pink Cadillac, the crew are greeted by the women awaiting them at the hotel. What is notable are the finger snaps. After two sets of snaps, the drum machine beat enters the song, alternating with the sounds of the women's snaps. Snapping along with the beat, the women create what the song calls a "paradise found" within the space of the inn. Following a swooping synth chord that sends the song off to its first verse, the scene cuts to a shot of Jane and a group of five black women wearing pink pussy pants that resemble the inner contours of a vagina, with another two wearing only pink leotards (which Monáe has commented was an intentional move to make space for trans women and other women who may not have vaginas [McNamara]). As Jane/Monáe adds a second layer of vocals on top of the synth and drum machine beat, Zen (Tessa Thompson) sticks her head through the singer's legs. The finger snap, intertwining with the song's drum machine beat, facilitates this moment of queer intimacy. As Marlon Riggs narrates in *Tongues Untied*, his 1989 documentary about the power of black, queer men daring to connect with and love one another in a world that wants them dead, "[s]naps can be for love, and snaps can be strong. To read, to punctuate, to cut like a whip." The function of the snaps in "Pynk" is two-fold: They cut through the rigid policing of blackness, queerness, and femaleness in Jane's futuristic dystopia while they simultaneously work as an expression of love.

The immediate transition from "Pynk" into "Make Me Feel," a song for which Prince wrote the synth line[9] (and that recalls his 1986 single "Kiss"), illuminates the extent to which black pop music in the 1980s helps forward Monáe's Afrocyberpunk project of using music technology to embrace a gender-inclusive black queerness. At the beginning of this portion of the video, Jane and Zen walk into an underground club together. After passing by a trio of David Bowie lookalikes, the previously muffled wobbly bass line suddenly jumps up in volume, accompanied by clicking sounds and even more snaps. This is a moment of temporal connection facilitated by

Janelle Monáe: Dirty Computer (Case Study)

digital music technology, as a sound and style that we understand as the aesthetics of the 1980s seamlessly follows a contemporary-sounding pop song that is narratively set in a future time. Jane, Zen, and their friends continue to harness the power of the song's vibrations, such as when Jane runs back and forth between Zen and Ché (Jayson Aaron), her female and male romantic interests, to the pulses of the drum machine beat. In this world, Jane is able to desire both of them without any fear.

"Make Me Feel" is a poptimistic practice in how pop music—and its technologies—can create space for people of all gender expressions. Monáe continues the tradition of Prince using digital music technology to make blurry the lines between man and woman—and human and machine. As electronic music artist Derrick May comments in John Akomfrah's documentary *The Last Angel of History* (1996), "[t]echno is to express man and machine intertwined." Taking cues from the disco-inspired genres of house and techno, Prince and other black pop stars in the 1980s were intimately engaged in exploring these lines of tension between (wo)man and machine.[10] In *Dirty Computer*, "Make Me Feel" not only references Prince's sound but also interrogates the differences, if any, between humans and machines. Just as the problem of minoritarian oppression lives on in the futuristic present of *Dirty Computer*, the power of digital music technology offers Jane, her friends, and her lovers a potential way out. Through seamlessly interfacing with the digital music technology, the group reveals the human possibilities of the technological, along with the 'human' potential of androids. The pulsations of the drum machine become a way for Jane and her friends to reconnect with the transgressive possibility of love.

More than just a means of embracing romantic love, the vibrations on "Make Me Feel" allow Jane, Zen, and Ché to connect with the blackness of their anthropomorphic android existences. Through moving with the vibrations of each song's sounds, Jane and her friends redefine themselves as something more than dirty computers; they are "young, black, wild, and free" as Jane/Monáe declares on "Crazy, Classic, Life."[11] This freedom is never guaranteed to be absolute, as is clear each time the film inserts video clips to remind us that Jane is strapped to a table in a cleansing center and treated with Nevermind forgetting gas, all the while her transition is facilitated by what initially appears to be a brainwashed Zen. *Dirty Computer*'s narrative arc reinforces that this vibrational identity is tenuous, subject to the dynamics of the world around her.

The potentiality of vibration and reclaiming technology remains tenuous through the end of *Dirty Computer*. Before the credits roll, it appears as if all has been lost: Zen, now a 'beacon' at the center, brings Jane through the end of the cleansing process. After she has been made into a beacon herself, Jane greets Ché, who has been strapped down to a table in the cleansing center awaiting processing. But following the credits, vibration—and love—appears to prevail. The soundtrack for this moment is "America," the final track on *Dirty Computer* and the very song that Jane refused to forget while she was held captive. To the lines of "War is old, so is sex/Let's play god, you go next," we see Jane and Zen dragging Ché out of the center. In sync with the synthesizer chords, they place their feet one in front of the other as they move *en route* to their escape. After the line "Jim Crow Jesus rose again," Jane smiles, remembering the multiple times in the emotion picture when she completed the lyrics to this line in protest—and was subsequently gassed with Nevermind in an attempt to make her forget her love for Zen (and Ché) and the possibility of a black, queer, and feminist collectivity. To the sounds of synthesizers making high-pitched 1980s synth sounds, Zen pushes open the door of the cleansing center and leads the group into the light.

It is therefore sound—and vibration—that ultimately brings the trio back into the light. As the audio track proclaims "Love me, baby/Love for me who I am" to the sounds of synthesizers that sound like church organs, Jane stares out into the camera before turning around and joining the others in their flight, letting the sounds guide her. She has not forgotten who she is—and the vibrations of the song have helped her to hold on to what those at the cleansing center have tried so forcefully to erase. In the tension between human and machine, love prevails, albeit one that does not gloss over the dark side of technology and their being embedded within structures of white heteropatriarchal capitalism. As Francesca Royster asks through a reading of Monáe's music at the end of her book on post-soul black sounds, "[h]ow do we keep creating a future that includes all of us?" (191). Through a mobilization of the Afrocyberpunk potential of digital music technology, Monáe offers us a way to imagine a solidarity among blackness, queerness, and femaleness that locates points of overlap among all three while simultaneously holding onto the beautiful differences that distinguish us as people—and androids—in the first place.

Notes

1 For details about Afrocyberpunk and its connections to Afrofuturism, see Isiah Lavender III and Graham J. Murphy's "Afrofuturism" contribution to this collection.
2 Chris Hables Gray provides a detailed analysis of both surveillance and veillance in his contribution to this collection.
3 As Michael Hannan and Melissa Carey write in their essay about soundscapes in *Blade Runner*, there are no drums and bass—only synthesizers. *Dirty Computer*, in comparison, draws heavily from the bass-heavy musical traditions of the African diaspora: funk, rock, pop, R&B, and hip hop.
4 I am thinking about cyberpunk as both sonic and behavioral. For more details, see Nicholas C. Laudadio's contribution to this collection.
5 Kodwo Eshun writes that Afrofuturism "studies the appeals that black artists, musicians, critics, and writers have made to the future, in moments where any future was made difficult for them to imagine" (294).
6 For insightful analyses of Janelle Monáe's Afrofuturism, including her single "Tightrope," see English and Kim; Valnes.
7 Alice Echols and Francesca Royster both write about how the masculinist tendencies of funk limit(ed) its potential to set black people of all genders free.
8 Grimes is renowned in the world of indie pop for producing all of her music and pushing on the boundaries between pop and experimental electronic music.
9 See Ben Kaye's article on Prince's contributions to and influence upon "Make Me Feel."
10 This was most apparent for Prince who used vocal distortion to create his female alter ego, Camille, the credited singer on four tracks on his double album *Sign 'O' The Times* (1987).
11 It seems quite clear that the line "young, black, wild, and free" from "Crazy, Classic Life" is a riff on Nina Simone's "To Be Young, Gifted and Black" (1970).

Works Cited

Austerlitz, Saul. "The Pernicious Rise of Poptimism." *The New York Times Magazine*, 4 Apr. 2014, nytimes.com/2014/04/06/magazine/the-pernicious-rise-of-poptimism.html.

Capetola, Christine. "Hyperaural Blackness: Black Pop Stars, New Musical Technologies, and Vibrational Negotiations of Identity in the Mid-1980s and Beyond." PhD dissertation, University of Texas at Austin, 2019.

Echols, Alice. *Hot Stuff: Disco and the Remaking of American Culture*. Norton, 2010.

English, Daylanne K. and Alvin Kim. "Now We Want Our Funk Cut: Janelle Monáe's Neo-Afrofuturism." *American Studies*, vol. 52, no. 4, 2013, pp. 217–30.

Eshun, Kodwo. "Further Considerations on Afrofuturism." *The New Centennial Review*, vol. 3, no. 2, 2003, pp. 287–302.

Hannan, Michael Francis and Melissa Carey. "Ambient Soundscapes in Blade Runner." *Off the Planet: Music, Sound and Science Fiction Cinema*, edited by Philip Hayward. Indiana UP, 2004, pp. 149–64.

Jones, Cassandra L. "'Tryna Free Kansas City': The Revolutions of Janelle Monáe as Digital Griot." *Frontiers: A Journal of Women's Studies*, vol. 39, no. 1, 2018, pp. 42–72.

Kaye, Ben. "Prince was heavily involved in Janelle Monáe's forthcoming *Dirty Computer*." *Consequence of Sound*, 25 Feb 2018, consequenceofsound.net/2018/02/prince-was-heavily-involved-in-janelle-monaes-forthcoming-dirty-computer/.

McNamara, Brittney. "Tessa Thompson Sent an Important Reminder About Who 'PYNK' Really Celebrates." *Teen Vogue*, 11 Apr. 2018, www.teenvogue.com/story/tessa-thompson-who-janelle-monaes-pynk-celebrates.

Monáe, Janelle. "Janelle Monáe - Dirty Computer [Emotion Picture]." *YouTube*, 27 Apr. 2018, youtube. com/watch?v=jdH2Sy-BlNE.

Murphy, Graham J. and Lars Schmeink. "Introduction: The Visuality and Virtuality of Cyberpunk." *Cyberpunk and Visual Culture*, edited by Graham J. Murphy and Lars Schmeink. Routledge, 2018, pp. xx–xxvi.

Redmond, Shana L. "This Safer Space: Janelle Monáe's 'Cold War.'" *Journal of Popular Music Studies*, vol. 23, no. 4, 2011, pp. 393–411.

Royster, Francesca. *Sounding Like a No-No: Queer Sounds & Eccentric Acts in the Post-Soul*. U of Michigan P, 2013.

Schmeink, Lars. "Afterthoughts: Cyberpunk Engagements in Countervisuality." *Cyberpunk and Visual Culture*, edited by Graham J. Murphy and Lars Schmeink. Routledge, 2018, pp. 276–87.

Space Is the Place. Directed by John Coney, North American Star System, Nov. 1974.

The Last Angel of History. Directed by John Akomfrah, Black Audio Film Collective/Channel 4 Television Corporation, 11 Sep. 1996.

Tongues Untied. Directed by Marlon Riggs, Signifyin' Works, Jul. 1989.

Valnes, Matthew. "Janelle Monáe and Afro-Sonic Funk." *Journal of Popular Music Studies*, vol. 29, no. 3, Sep. 2017, pp. 1–12.

II

Cultural Theory

31

SIMULATION AND SIMULACRA

Rebecca Haar and Anna McFarlane

In *Snow Crash* (1992) Neal Stephenson organizes much of the narrative action around The Street, a wide, virtual boulevard in the computer-generated universe known as the Metaverse where everyone comes to see and be seen. Hiro Protagonist has watched The Street develop from the "black desert of the electronic night," where the hackers "take their software out and race it" (25), to a street over a hundred meters wide "with a narrow monorail track running down the middle. The monorail is a free piece of public utility software that enables users to change their location on the Street rapidly and smoothly" (25). Stephenson's Metaverse—his version of cyberspace, designed to be navigable by using images recognizable from the real world—makes evident how much reality and virtuality are entangled. Images and concepts (public transport, infrastructure, real estate development, and gentrification) overlap and the inequality evident in the real world bleeds into the new realm of the Metaverse, particularly evident in the complexity (or simplicity) of user avatars and the socioeconomic realities these avatars project. Simulation is not just a representation but also has consequences of its own, shaping behavior and reality itself. For early cyberpunk, the simulation of a world was a central conceit, a fantasy enabling the escape from 'meat space,' which, as Sherryl Vint argues, "appeals to the (impossible) desire to escape the vicissitudes of the body and occupy the place of selfmastery" (104). In establishing simulated worlds—cyberspace, the Metaverse, and the matrix—cyberpunk negotiates humanity and ontology, highlighting the mediated nature of 'real' experience through the difficulty in distinguishing between the real and the virtual. As Brian McHale has pointed out, in postmodern fiction these questions are literalized and foregrounded: Texts use virtual worlds as a means of "'doing' ontology—a means of exploring ontology *in* fiction, as well as (potentially at least) the ontology *of* fiction" (247, emphasis in original). This chapter examines cyberpunk's central role in critiquing the increasing virtuality of the worlds in which we move, a virtuality that is clear in the rise of virtual reality (VR) technology but also takes place more insidiously through the simulated lives produced on social media.

31.1 Simulations and Simulacra

Perhaps the most important voice in theorizing the entanglement of ontology, reality, virtuality, and simulation is that of Jean Baudrillard, whose work intertextually influences cyberpunk at some of its key moments and even acts as a kind of cyberpunk theory, blurring the lines between the fiction and its commentary, the territory and the map. Baudrillard's key text is *Simulacra and Simulation* in which he develops some of his most important concepts, including that of the hyperreal. Baudrillard argues that we are living in an increasingly mediated world, constructed of simulations and simulacra: While simulations are intended to represent or to copy objects or systems, simulacra are simulations with no corresponding original. By drawing attention to the proliferation of simulacra and their impact on the human mind, Baudrillard's work suggests a dystopian society as humans live under the illusion that they are engaged with some kind of 'truth' when actually there can be no access to such a thing in our so-called reality; in fact, 'truth' cannot exist in our current state, an idea that rings increasingly true in the era of fake news, false accusations of fake news, and the proliferation of conspiracy theories via social media. Rather than merely predicting a future dystopia, Baudrillard's work argues that dystopia had already been realized at the time of writing. He coins the term 'hyperreality' to describe this society in which simulacra shape the human life world and a pretense at a reference to reality is no longer required. Baudrillard's work resonates with the almost-contemporaneous development of cyberpunk as a cultural mode: While some cyberpunk grappled with the new frontiers represented by cyberspace, Baudrillard saw VR technology as the acceleration of the destruction of the real by its hyperreal double (*Perfect Crime* 47).

Sf responded in both implicit and explicit ways to Baudrillard's work, most significantly in *The Matrix* (Wachowskis 1999), the most influential sf film of its time and one that entered into a dialogue with Baudrillard's work. In *The Matrix*, daily life is revealed as a simulation. In the 'real' world, humans are used as batteries for the robots and artificial intelligences that have colonized the surface of the world. While the first film sets up this distinction between the illusion of the matrix and the 'real' world outside, it is not certain whether there is a so-called 'real' world. An analysis of the sequels, *The Matrix: Reloaded* (2003) and *The Matrix: Revolutions* (2003), suggests the possibility that all levels of 'reality' depicted in the trilogy are actually contained within a computer program (Haar 231). However, what might be outside this simulation is deliberately left open. The main protagonist in *The Matrix*, a computer programmer and hacker named Thomas Anderson (Keanu Reeves), a.k.a. Neo, meets the enigmatic Morpheus (Laurence Fishburne), a legendary hacker he has been searching for in his spare time, when not working at his drudging job at the software company MetaCortex. Morpheus gives Neo a choice between swallowing a red or a blue pill. The blue pill means that he can go back to living his simulated life as Thomas Anderson by day and Neo by night, while the red pill means that he must face the grim reality of the world and accept his part in working for a better one.

The film cites Baudrillard in a number of ways. At the beginning of the film, Neo uses a hollowed-out copy of *Simulacra and Simulation* as a place to store cash and important, presumably illicit, computer files that he sells to his clients. The association between cash, information, and simulation set up by this Baudrillardian intertextuality suggests the circulation of images in a highly mediated society that results in the emptying-out of meaning, like the emptying-out of the hollow book. The simulations of contemporary society are compared with paper money, a signifier that no longer has a signified in the post-gold standard era where cash, information, and simulation all circulate meaninglessly. Later, when Morpheus awakens Neo to the state of the world beyond the simulation by using a 'construct program' to give Neo (and the audience) a brief history lesson, he welcomes Neo to "the desert of the real," a term Baudrillard uses to describe the decimation of the real by simulations and simulacra—in this case, represented by the artificial simulation of life represented by the artificial intelligences, software programs, and marauding robots. And, of course, there is the central 'what is real?' Baudrillardian conversation Morpheus has with Neo in which the latter expresses incredulity at the prospect that his surrounding environment is an illusion.

While Baudrillard has distanced himself from the representation of his work in *The Matrix* and its sequels, saying that the Wachowskis failed to understand him (Lancelin), this does not diminish the importance of the film's engagement with not only his work but the bevy of intertextual sources the film cites. Catherine Constable, for example, points out that philosophers have tended to engage with the trilogy as a popularization of Baudrillard's work (whether successful or otherwise), but she argues that "viewing the films as mere illustrations or bad copies of their philosophical sources makes it quite impossible to ask a crucial question, namely: what is the philosophical project of the *films* themselves?" (1, emphasis in original). Similarly, Stefan Herbrechter argues that *The Matrix* might have some reflexive commentary for theory, and that the film can even be seen as an "allegory of theory," but he argues that it is difficult to "speak of simply 'applying' theory to a film that itself engages with theoretical, philosophical, theological and other issues, and which could instead be thought of as a theory-film or a film 'about' theory" (8–9). According to Herbrechter, this overlap between film and philosophy might be

> because theory itself—in its institutionalised and orthodox form—is now being experienced as some kind of Matrix, namely as a discourse or jargon that critical readers feel incapable of finding an exit from that would open out onto the 'real' (the real world, the real problems, or theory's own suppressed 'real', its history, exclusions, unacknowledged translations etc). (9)

By extension, recognizing that sf cinema on the whole might have a philosophical project, one that engages with media theory but deviates from it in significant and original ways, even offering an alternative to theory, or a way of accessing theoretical blindspots, continues to break down the barriers between cyberpunk and theory.

31.2 Virtual Worlds

At the same time that cyberpunk and media theory have explored ideas of simulation and virtuality, VR technologies that were once the domain of fictional worlds have been realized, with processing power making possible sustained virtual environments and telecommunications allowing remote access to many users at once. When looking at literature like William Gibson's *Neuromancer* (1984) and Stephenson's *Snow Crash*, it becomes clear that simulations are not just simple representations of reality. Simulation evokes the interplay of technical and aesthetic developments as interdependence, intertextuality, and intermediality play between the diegetic and extradiegetic levels (Haar 248). This layering of referentiality and intertextuality means that the cyberpunk representation of simulation can be seen as a kind of palimpsest (Haar 117, 350), these layerings of copying and representation creating something new, a concept and an experience that had not existed previously. In a move that Baudrillard would later build upon, Roland Barthes describes a simulacrum as something new that consists of existing elements. He defines this as an object that is reconstructed in "such a way as to manifest thereby the rules of functioning [...] of this object" (214) and this "imitated object makes something appear which remained invisible" (215). In this sense, cyberpunk as a mode contributes to the development of the online world and VR as simulacra.

There is a symbiotic relationship between cyberpunk and the development of the Internet, and virtual worlds particularly. By coining the term 'cyberspace' in his story "Burning Chrome" (1982) and imagining how such a space might be visualized and accessed, notably in *Neuromancer* but also in such later works as *Idoru* (1996), Gibson was influential in the development of Web 2.0 which shaped the way we experience the Internet today. Similarly, while Stephenson's *Snow Crash* acted as a means of exploring the philosophical questions posed by virtual worlds it also impacted the development of the first virtual social environments. Stephenson's Metaverse was credited by Philip Rosedale, creator of the online virtual space *Second Life* (Linden Lab 2003), as a key inspiration (Maney 2007).[1] The importance of virtual realities like *Second Life* may be forgotten in the 21st-century context as such platforms failed to maintain the interest of players in the long run, in part because *Second Life*'s intention—i.e., that players experience the game-world as a VR—ruled out the imposition of tasks and quests, so players were simply supposed to simulate a virtual life by generating their own tasks and activities. However, *Second Life* and its contemporaries created the basis for task-based Massive Multiplayer Online Role-Playing Games (MMORPGs) like *World of Warcraft* (Blizzard Entertainment 2004), which are constantly evolving, expanding their virtual environment(s) and mythologies, as well as future directions for VR digitalization which can now integrate 3D technology more extensively. Player reactions to *Second Life* have also provided a means of theorizing simulation, and it is clear that any demarcation between where reality ends and simulation begins is porous: In *Second Life* a user can move in a simulated reality and experience certain aspects of this simulation as real—especially with regard to emotions (Haar 307–26). The emotions elicited by simulated environments are genuine. They may be triggered by the simulation, but that does not make them any less real.

What will require a closer look in the future is the fact that many of these virtual worlds are unlikely to last forever. Many of them have already become obsolete and others will follow, while new ones are developed. "[A]n expired video game world is gone for ever [sic], and certainly in the form in which it was first experienced by its inhabitants," explains Simon Parkin. He attests that virtual worlds represent the resurgence of a kind of oral tradition, one that has not only "preserved the tales of antiquity," but in its reemergence has captured "fragments of evidence and experience in blog posts, radio programmes and YouTube clips." However, the ephemeral nature of Internet-based cultural artefacts means that these fragments can be manipulated, lost, or deleted; in contrast to an old film that can be watched again and again, these obsolete virtual worlds are forever erased, unless there is an accessible backup. Server crashes can also result in the loss of a virtual world, and even a backup does not help if there are no more devices or programs available that can correctly display the data stored in them. Even without these considerations the original context in which these virtual worlds once operated might be lost forever, and with it a complete understanding of what meaning they conveyed.

This move towards a resurgent oral culture seems to reverse the principle described by literary scholar and media theorist Walter Ong, which describes cultures as moving from oral traditions to literary traditions. Cyberpunk dramatizes this return of orality through the loss of reliable writing in *Snow Crash,* as digitization results in the loss of archives and records. David Cronenberg's cyberpunk movie *eXistenZ* (1999), however, goes one step further. *eXistenZ*, which was released weeks after *The Matrix*, shows a world lost in simulation through virtual realities indistinguishable from the real. The characters cling to a belief in reality, even resorting to terrorism in its defense, as the concept evaporates into the referenceless system of hyperreality described by Baudrillard (*Simulacra and Simulation* 2). Within the game-worlds all written storage media have disappeared; only the image, through stills or videos, serves as a knowledge carrier. The path leads from oral traditions, to literality, to the culture of images, only to return to orality and the associated ephemerality and unreliability. Today's Internet, with its structural tendency to pluralize meaning through endless think-pieces, opinion pieces, blog posts, and YouTube videos of variable reliability, instantiates the hyperreality of *The Matrix* or *eXistenZ* by undermining the possibility of a universally valid perception of reality, substituting agreed-upon facts with 'alternative facts.' This results in fatal consequences for the relationship between the signified and the signifier, because the more virtual a world becomes, the more uncertain its sign systems become.

Cyberpunk texts use technological simulations in order to analyze the increasingly mediated and hyperreal nature of our environment, but in the meantime, technology has been catching up to the science-fictional imaginary, albeit sometimes in unexpected ways. At the beginning of the 2000s, VR barely had any cultural sway but since then games have tried to bring players into a virtual world, as far as the technical possibilities allow. The development of the Internet as an encompassing space thanks to WiFi and satellite navigation technologies, a development that some sf writers (and readers) anticipated but could otherwise barely have been imagined in the 1990s, makes VR possible as an everyday technology. In this context the 2000s can be thought of as a cultural turning point from a medial society, one in which reality was shaped and constructed through the media, to a digital society, one in which digital technologies allowed new possibilities for active user participation while also excluding such participation through the hidden work done by inaccessible coding. The move from the medial to the digital required a change in user behaviors, as humans learned to navigate the new digital landscape (or were left behind by it), as well as economic responses as digitization affected industries (and nations) of all kinds. Digitization was not so much a goal as a tool, but a tool that enabled new forms of work and changed communication through new information technologies, enabling the emergence of new networks as well as the exacerbation of social cleavages, notably in the socioeconomic divisions impacting social classes vis-à-vis access to technologies and the friction caused by First vs. Third World geopolitics that has repeatedly seen the technological wonders of the former predicated upon the cheap, if not exploitive, labor of the latter.

The (de)evolution from a medial society to a digital one is now being supplanted by the next stage. Gundolf Freyermuth, for example, argues that the increasing use of VR marks a further cultural shift: the hyperimmersive turn. In current VR technology, simulation and reality are clearly distinguishable, but the higher degree of immersion and the tendency towards augmented or mixed reality are already becoming apparent; for example, data glasses are being marketed that are increasingly within financial reach for the average user, mobile phones can now be used as windows into VR, and an online presence is presumed for everything from headhunting and job applications to tax filings. Tellingly, hyperimmersion, like digitization, raises the problem of that which is hidden from end users. Thorsten Holischka points out that the current generation is growing up with technologies that were not considered possible a decade ago and that such widespread use is only possible when technologies are made available without the need for special knowledge (32). It seems that the more widespread a technology, the more reliant it will be on a user interface that is welcoming to inexperienced users while, at the same time, hiding the digital language that structures the user experience. As a result, the power to code and control networked or virtual environments remains unevenly distributed; even in the relative infancy of VR technology, cyberpunk acts as a discourse for thinking about these problems.

The developments in VR technology proper are not so widespread as to have resulted in an immediately recognizable cyberpunk present. However, the extent of our inhabitation of such (cyber)spaces is apparent even if these virtual realms do not necessarily look exactly like the immersive cyberspace of *Neuromancer* or the gaming space of *TRON* (Lisberger 1982) and *TRON: Legacy* (Kosinski 2010). Reality is overlaid with its representation on social media, and identity is partially constructed through those same social media representations. While social media is still predominantly text-based and is not thought of as immersive in the same sense as a full sensory plunge into cyberspace, it bears many of the markers of a VR game, so much so that for his 2013 television special *How Videogames Changed the World*, Charlie Brooker included Twitter as one of the 25 most significant video games of all time. In sum, the simulation and simulacra of online avatars mapped onto the 'real' identities of those who construct them and the circulation of news and fake news on social media creates a hyperreality that has very real consequences beyond the medium, a testament to Marshall McLuhan's famous adage that 'the medium is the message.'

31.3 Post-Cyberpunk and Virtuality

The treatment of virtuality by cyberpunk and post-cyberpunk texts is characterized by an awareness that, as Baudrillard suggests, the real may have decayed so that only the map remains, or, the real never truly existed.[2] The distinction between the virtual and the physical worlds breaks down and actions that take place in one often have a direct and powerful impact on the other. In addition, the speed of developing technologies poses a challenge to traditional media theory and to sf as the acceleration of technological development and the complexity of the media landscape mean that theorization and analysis are forced to play catch up; or, as media mogul Hubertus Bigend remarks in Gibson's *Pattern Recognition* (2003), "we have insufficient 'now' to stand on" (57)—that is, the present changes so quickly and is so volatile that it does not provide a stable position from which to extrapolate.

The tendency in post-cyberpunk to move away from extrapolation can be most clearly seen through the career trajectory of both Gibson and Stephenson. Both writers began with futuristic, cyberspatial settings defined by, in the words of Darko Suvin's now-famous terminology, their respective *nova*, or specific imagined technologies. These technologies produce cognitive estrangement which challenges readers to become newly aware of their contemporary surroundings. However, after the turn of the century and the cultural turning point of the 9/11 terrorist attacks in New York City, Arlington (Virginia), and Somerset County (outside Pennsylvania), both writers turned to more realist genre conventions—i.e., espionage thrillers—in order to explore the science-fictionality of contemporary society, or what Veronica Hollinger has called the 'future present' wherein "[s]cience fiction's founding assumption—that the future will be different from the present—has become outdated. Today the present is different from the present" (465). Stephenson explicitly cites the development of virtual worlds as a reason for this change, specifically referencing the practice of gold farming. Gold farming is the undertaking of repetitive tasks in an online game for virtual coin that can then be exchanged for real-world currency. Stephenson describes the practice as "one of those things that makes you want to quit writing science fiction because you could never think of something that weird" (Sinclair 2011). In *Reamde* Stephenson uses the practice of gold farming to show the interdependence of game developers in the U.S. with the exploitation of gold farmers in China, showing how virtual actions and real-world economics are indistinguishable, a theme that also appears in Cory Doctorow's post-cyberpunk YA novel *For the Win* (2010), which imagines gold farming as a catalyst for the international unionization of workers.

Gibson's narrative shift is most evident in the Blue Ant trilogy—*Pattern Recognition* (2003), *Spook Country* (2007), and *Zero History* (2010)—that finds cyberspace no longer an alternate or parallel space, but instead a layer of reality. In *Spook Country*, Gibson introduces the concept through 'locative art,' an artform that allows virtual artworks to be viewed at specific geolocations. Whereas hackers in Gibson's earlier work may jack into cyberspace, in *Spook Country* (and the Blue Ant trilogy as a whole), cyberspace is 'everting,' mapping itself over reality. Cyberspace has turned itself inside out so that its logic and characteristics have found their way out into the real world, rather than being confined to another realm. As, frankly, any Millennial reader of Gibson's work can attest, cyberspace cannot be spatialized and visualized as a separate realm, but instead must be understood as co-existing with the 'real' world, or even as *being* the real world. When Hollis, the protagonist of *Spook Country*, meets another artist-cum-coder, Bobby Chombo, he tells her that "[o]nce it everts, then there isn't any cyberspace, is there? There never was, if you want to look at it that way. It was a way we had of looking where we were headed, a direction. With the grid, we're here. This is the other side of the screen. Right here" (67). Hollis mishears *everting* as *everything*; tellingly, as cyberspace is now 'everything' and cannot be differentiated from the 'real' world.

The importance of virtual worlds in mediating social encounters and managing, if not outright shaping, the political spectrum is evidenced in the controversies surrounding Cambridge Analytica, foreign troll farms, and Russian interference in the 2016 American presidential election. These instances, and the management of the perception of authorities in dictatorships or Communist systems, such as Chinese and North Korean censorship of internal computer networks, emphasize the importance of cyberpunk's critique. For example, *Blade Runner 2049* (Villeneuve 2017) evokes nothing so much as the desperation of an individual who knows their reality is a simulacrum but continues to function through the cruel optimism it offers, since this is the only defense against a slide into nihilistic solipsism. Even though K (Ryan Gosling) knows he is a replicant he fantasizes about being something more; even though he knows his companion, Joi (Ana de Armas) is a hologram he believes the positive feedback she offers.[3] The desperate need for the validation of the newsfeed is dramatized as he moves through his lonely world in which the hustle and bustle of the multicultural cityscapes in *Blade Runner* (Scott 1982) is replaced with a world in which K is most often pictured alone. Ryan Gosling's distancing affect portrays K as perhaps most alone when interacting with others onscreen. *Blade Runner 2049* reflects a world in which the replacement of life with its simulation—through replicant identity, which acts as an analogy for living through the simulated identities created through social media—is complete, and as a result a meaningful identity is impossible to inhabit and K is left with the distinct sensation that his world has been emptied out, with meaningful action that might change society happening 'out there,' out of his control.

The issues of alienation from ontological meaning as a result of social media simulation is taken up in many more contemporary post-cyberpunk texts. For example, the anthology series *Black Mirror* (2011–) repeatedly returns to the possibilities for ontological meaning in a world dominated by the simulations and simulacra of online identity, and again in ways that act as commentary on contemporary socio-political realities and possibilities. The episode "Nosedive" (2016) features a social system that has been compared to China's Social Credit System which aims to assign each citizen a rating that can be affected by feedback on one's social activities.[4] The episode shows the quick decline of one woman's social credit as she attempts to attend a friend's wedding but finds herself embarrassed and socially bankrupt. The episode concludes with the woman imprisoned, having hit rock bottom. She begins an exchange with the occupant of the cell next to her own, and the episode ends with them shouting increasingly creative insults at each other, culminating in them angrily and gleefully shouting "fuck you" at one another. Of course, the premise of the episode is not based on a future social credit system, whether the one under development in China or any other; rather, the episode critiques the attention to appearances that must be paid in order to develop social capital on social media and suggests a freedom that can be found in being excluded from these systems, in becoming an outcast. In this relatively liberatory ending, the show offers some hope for an authentic encounter with others and with one's own being.

In conclusion, technological simulation today has successfully mapped 'reality' in its entirety, from the capabilities of Google Earth to the tracking of human individuals via their social media accounts. We have entered, according to Christoph Kucklick, a granular society in which the digital begins to replace reality (10). Kucklick understands granularity as a measure of resolution, the precision of data, because through digitalization our world is already mapped and the changes now are in the finesse of the resolution (10). Such a view reflects Baudrillard's diagnosis that we are living in a hyperreal simulacrum and that the differences that will be made to that situation are merely those of degree. In the more optimistic exemplars of post-cyberpunk there are suggestions that the real is not gone forever and might be accessed, either through worker solidarity or through reconnecting with others without the mediation of social networks. Hopes such as these represent a departure from Baudrillard's bleak outlook and show that cyberpunk and, perhaps more effectively, post-cyberpunk continue to engage with the concepts of simulacra and simulation but in different ways, attempting to open out new ways forward. As cyberpunk and post-cyberpunk continue to show, we can refuse to be stranded in the deserts of the electronic night.

Notes

1 There is also a moment in *Reamde* (2011) when Stephenson jokes about his description in *Snow Crash* of a program strikingly similar to today's Google Earth. Richard, the programmer of an online virtual world called *T'Rain*, notes that "the opening screen of *T'Rain* was a frank rip-off of what you saw when you booted up Google Earth. Richard felt no guilt about this, since he had heard that Google Earth, in turn, was based on an idea from some old science-fiction novel" (38). This creates a situation where the virtual world is a simulation of a fictional world which has no original referent; a hyperreality indeed.
2 For an analysis of what is meant by post-cyberpunk, including Neal Stephenson's central role at the forefront of post-cyberpunk authors, see Christopher D. Kilgore's contribution to this collection.
3 For a close reading of *Blade Runner 2049* and the issue of simulated lives, see Matthew Flisfeder's contribution to this collection.
4 See the entries by Marr, Palin, or Vincent for examples of popular comparisons between "Nosedive" and China's social credit system.

Works Cited

Barthes, Roland. "The Structuralist Activity." *Critical Essays*. Northwestern UP, 1972, pp. 213–20.

Baudrillard, Jean. *The Perfect Crime*, translated by Chris Turner. Verso, 2007.

———. "Simulacra and Science Fiction." *Science Fiction Studies*, vol. 18, no. 3, 1991, pp. 309–13.

———. *Simulacra and Simulation*, translated by Sheila Faria Glaser. Michigan UP, 1994.

Blade Runner. Directed by Ridley Scott, performances by Harrison Ford, Rutger Hauer, and Sean Young, Warner Brothers, 1982.

Blade Runner 2049. Directed by Denis Villeneuve, performances by Ryan Gosling, Harrison Ford, Ana de Armas, and Robin Wright, Sony Entertainment, 2017.

Brooker, Charlie. *How Videogames Changed the World*. Zeppotron, 2013.

Constable, Catherine. *Adapting Philosophy: Jean Baudrillard and "The Matrix Trilogy."* Manchester UP, 2009.

eXistenZ. Directed by David Cronenberg, performances by Jennifer Jason Leigh and Jude Law, Dimension Films, 1999.

Freyermuth, Guldolf. *Games. Game Design. Game Studies. Eine Einführung*. Transcript, 2015.

Gibson, William. *Pattern Recognition*. HarperCollins, 2003.

———. *Spook Country*. HarperCollins, 2007.

Haar, Rebecca. *Simulation und virtuelle Welten. Theorie, Technik und mediale Darstellung von Virtualität in der Postmoderne*. Transcript, 2019.

Herbrechter, Stefan. "Introduction: Theory in the Matrix." *The Matrix in Theory*, edited by Myriam Diocaretz and Stefan Herbrechter. Rodopi, 2006, pp. 7–24.

Hollinger, Veronica. "Stories about the Future: From Patterns of Expectation to Pattern Recognition." *Science Fiction Studies*, vol. 33, no. 3, 2006, pp. 452–72.

Holischka, Tobias. *CyberPlaces: Philosophische Annäherungen an den virtuellen Ort*. Transcript, 2016.

Kucklick, Christoph. *Die granulare Gesellschaft: Wie das Digitale unsere Gesellschaft auflöst*. Ullstein, 2016.

Lancelin, Aude and Jean Baudrillard. "The Matrix Decoded: Le Nouvel Observateur Interview with Jean Baudrillard." *Jean Baudrillard: From Hyperreality to Disappearance*, edited by Richard G. Smith and David B. Clarke. Edinburgh University Press, 2015, pp. 179–81.

Maney, Kevin. "The King of Alter Egos is Surprisingly Humble Guy. Creator of Second Life's Goal? Just To Reach People." *USA Today*, 5 Feb. 2007, public.wsu.edu/~fking1/rosendale_2ndlife.doc.

Marr, Bernard. "Chinese Social Credit Score: Utopian Big Data Bliss Or Black Mirror On Steroids?" *Forbes*, 21 Jan. 2019, forbes.com/sites/bernardmarr/2019/01/21/chinese-social-credit-score-utopian-big-data-bliss-or-black-mirror-on-steroids/#42e33c6248b8.

McHale, Brian. *Constructing Postmodernism*. Routledge, 1992.

"Nosedive," *Black Mirror*. Directed by Joe Wright, performance by Bryce Dallas Howard, Zeppotron, 2016.

Ong, Walter. "Oralität und Literalität. Die Technologisierung des Wortes." *Kursbuch Medienkultur. Die maßgeblichen Theorien von Brecht bis Baudrillard*, edited by Claus Pias and Lorenz Engell. DVA, 1999, pp. 95–104.

Palin, Megan. "China's 'social credit' system is a real-life 'Black Mirror' nightmare," *New York Post*, 19 Sep. 2018, nypost.com/2018/09/19/chinas-social-credit-system-is-a-real-life-black-mirror-nightmare/.

Parkin, Simon. "Where Do Online Worlds Go to Die?" *The Guardian*, 3 Dec. 2017, theguardian.com/games/2017/dec/03/where-do-online-worlds-go-to-die-simon-parkin.

Sinclair, Brendan. "*Snow Crash* Author on the State of Storytelling in Games." *Gamespot*, 11 Oct. 2011, gamespot.com/articles/snow-crash-author-on-the-state-of-storytelling-in-games/1100-6339423/.

Stephenson, Neal. *Snow Crash*. Bantam Spectra, 1992.

———. *Reamde*. Atlantic, 2011.

The Matrix. Directed by the Wachowskis, performances by Keanu Reeves, Laurence Fishburne, and Carrie-Anne Moss. Warner Brothers, 1999.

TRON. Directed by Steven Lisberger, performances by Jeff Bridges, Bruce Boxleitner, and David Warner, Walt Disney, 1982.

Vincent, Alice. "Black Mirror is coming true in China, where your 'rating' affects your home, transport and social circle." *Daily Telegraph*, 15 Dec. 2017, telegraph.co.uk/on-demand/2017/12/15/black-mirror-coming-true-china-rating-affects-home-transport/.

Vint, Sherryl. *Bodies of Tomorrow: Technology, Subjectivity, Science Fiction*. UP of Toronto, 2007.

32

GOTHICISM

Anya Heise-von der Lippe

In the crucial penultimate chapter to *Neuromancer* (1984), William Gibson uses Gothic aesthetics to describe the protagonist's encounter with the sublime mindspace of an artificial intelligence (AI): "Darkness fell in from every side, a sphere of singing black, pressure on the extended crystal nerves of the universe of data he had nearly become … [sic] And when he was nothing, compressed at the heart of all that dark, there came a point where the dark could be no *more*, and something tore" (258). The annihilating presence of the AI threatens to dissolve the protagonist's sense of being and his limited human perspective in this encounter with a technology too vast and incomprehensible for the human mind. Gibson's *Neuromancer* is, of course, cyberpunk, but as this moment shows, its style is also profoundly Gothic in the way it unmoors fixed categories of understanding and threatens subject positions.

Gothic textuality, Fred Botting argues, is "[u]nstable, unfixed and ungrounded in any reality, truth or identity other than those that narratives provide, [and] there emerges a threat of sublime excess, of a new darkness of multiple and labyrinthine narratives" (181). Cyberpunk, as a more recent, but related narrative mode focusing on the celebration of a kind of "urban uncanny" (Schmeink 25) or techno-sublime, was aesthetically influenced by earlier forms. Its defining combination of "low life and high tech" (Ketterer 141) draws on a wide variety of conventions, mixing dystopian and science fiction (sf) elements with *film noir* and hard-boiled detective fiction, freely combining cybernetic high-tech elements and abject Gothic body horror with postmodern pop culture and futuristic architecture into a unique aesthetics. At the core of both the Gothic and cyberpunk lies a fascination with spaces—virtual or imagined—and the way these are shaped by and, in turn, influence cultural ideas. It would be tempting to read cyberpunk's fascination with the imaginary architectural patterns of the urban 'Sprawl' (see Gibson) as simply a new take on the Gothic sublime; after all, the flickering lights and screens of late-capitalist advertising, which are integral components of cyberpunk, suggest a mere surface aesthetic. Cyberpunk texts, however, often revolve around a much deeper posthuman and ultimately quite Gothic integration of bodies and technologies, undermining and shaping our understanding of what it means to be human.

Gibson has suggested that *Neuromancer*—arguably the key text of cyberpunk literature—is "not a Goth book, but it's kind of made of the same stuff that makes kids be Goths" (cit. in Neale). As Tatiani G. Rapatzikou argues, Gothic images in Gibson's work operate as "codes of the cultural anxieties of the present" (xiii). What lies at the root of this understanding of both cyberpunk and the Gothic subculture is a deep sense of existential despair that is expressed through a dark surface aesthetic. This ontological questioning harks back to earlier Gothic explorations of bodily integrity, monstrosity (for instance in *Frankenstein*), and the psychological and physical impact of

Gothic spaces—whether natural or architectural. The sublime, frequently evoked in this context and rooted in mid-18th-century exploration of aesthetic experience beyond the beautiful, is an affective category, evoking a non-rational reaction, but cyberpunk aesthetics also imply a multidimensional system of human-technology integrations. This is uncanny at its roots, because it harks back to the past of 18th-century technoscientific explorations of the human and reaches into the future of humanity, to show us what we never were and what we may (have) become. It is this core component of cyberpunk which links it to the Gothic in a manner that goes far beyond the perceived surface aesthetics of both narrative modes to the core questions of being human and becoming posthuman.

As Cary Wolfe argues, "posthumanism names a historical moment in which the decentering of the human by its imbrication in technical, medical, informatic, and economic networks is increasingly impossible to ignore, a historical development that points toward the necessity of new theoretical paradigms (but also thrusts them on us)" (xv–xvi). Cyberpunk texts highlight these probing posthumanist questions in their starkest dystopian consequences, often drawing on Gothic elements and the Gothic's "negative aesthetic" (Botting, *Gothic* 1) to express the horror of this deep-rooted paradigm shift. As Botting argues, Gothic texts do not aim for "[k]nowledge and understanding"; instead, they are focused on "the production of affects and emotions, often extreme and negative: fear, anxiety, terror, horror, disgust and revulsion" (*Gothic* 7). Posthuman Gothic aesthetics, in consequence, destabilize ingrained readings and patterns, challenging our understanding of what it means to be human.[1] Where it draws on the Gothic's negative aesthetic, cyberpunk often evokes the earlier mode's uncanny explorations of automata and the mechanisms and machineries of narrative production[2] to draw attention to the artificiality and virtuality of narratives. Cyberpunk texts may be obsessed with futuristic technologies, but they often present them in a manner that is both non-rational and profoundly horrific. Jodey Castricano has coined the term "cybergothic" for texts that exist at the intersections of Gothic and cyberpunk, describing them as "a mutant form, a hybrid born of traditional gothicism, science fiction, and cyberpunk" (204). The contemporary cybergothic is, thus, mainly concerned with undermining common conceptions of reality by showing that everything is virtual/constructed and there is no reality beyond an intricate system of narratives. Moreover, cybergothic and posthuman Gothic texts highlight the horrors of having to negotiate a world that has become uncanny precisely through our own (bio-)technoscientific involvements.

A recent example of the cybergothic and posthuman Gothic is the 2018 Netflix adaptation of Richard K. Morgan's *Altered Carbon* (2002), the first of the Takeshi Kovacs series that also includes *Broken Angels* (2003) and *Woken Furies* (2005). Netflix's *Altered Carbon* explicitly evokes the posthuman (cyber)Gothic thematic and aesthetic framework. Its aesthetics, as reviewer Daniel Rodriguez argues on Youtube, are informed by nostalgia and an interest in recreating a 1980s cyberpunk flair. The series establishes Gothic connections on two different levels, combining playful references to the 19th-century American Gothic (via Edgar Allan Poe) with an underlying layer of cybergothic exploration. Revolving around a lone-wolf protagonist borrowed from hardboiled detective fiction, the series envisions the cultural impact of an alien technology which allows humans to transfer their self into a different body (i.e., sleeve) and explores the dehumanizing and exploitative effects of such a technology in the hands of a capitalist society.

There is no doubt that *Altered Carbon* draws on such classics as *Blade Runner* (Scott 1982) and *Neuromancer*, but its imagining of a radical posthuman mind-body divide takes cyberpunk to even darker places than its predecessors. The first episode's opening scene includes a prolonged flashback to a hotel room on Harlan's World, with a panorama shot of the room's rain-spattered window and the cityscape behind it which could be straight out of *Blade Runner* and is used to establish a cyberpunk frame of reference for the narrative. The fact that the protagonist has to turn off an image of a tropical sunset on the screen window to see this view, and the scene's voiceover explains that "nothing is what it seems" (1.1) draws attention to the treacherousness of virtual reality in this context. Rather than merely challenge the protagonists' perceptions of their own status as human, *Altered Carbon* destabilizes a general notion of 'being human' based on concepts like individuality, corporeality, and mortality. This shift in focus places the narrative firmly within the context of the posthuman Gothic, but the series also plays around with older Gothic aesthetics as part of a postmodern genre-mixing strategy.

In its first episode, *Altered Carbon* directly evokes the American Gothic, which is absent from Morgan's original novel, in the form of an AI hotel called "The Raven"—complete with retro décor and run by an Edgar Allan Poe hologram (Chris Conner). The Poe AI greets the protagonist, Takeshi Kovacs (Joel Kinnaman), in an appropriately elaborate manner, evoking Gothic aesthetics as well as a sense of sleazy servitude, which sets the tone for their further interactions: "Felicitations. You've arrived at The Raven, Bay City's most deliciously macabre lodging experience. Fully cabled and enabled. How can I ease your journey through this world? [...] A much needed respite from the trials of bleak existence" (1.1). Key phrases like "deliciously macabre" suggest a postmodern attitude to the American Gothic, which is no longer seen to merely aesthetically reflect "bleak existence" but decadently revels in it, while at the same time presenting the American Gothic as a posthuman simulacrum, staged by the fully automated AI hotel. The decadent celebration of darkness suits the series' dystopian mode, as it underlines the overall impression of both humanity and a habitable planet being in decline and on their way out of existence.

The Raven hotel inhabits a liminal space somewhere between reality and simulation, as its furnishings and machine-gun defenses are solid, while its proprietor and some of its spaces are virtual constructs, creating a kind of augmented reality experience. The hotel's avian reference to Poe's well-known poem shows a familiarity with Gothic tropes and issues, like liminality, the uncanny, and a celebration of the macabre, which have made their way into postmodern popular culture. Nevertheless, while the series demonstrates an awareness of the Gothic's "negative aesthetics" (Botting, *Gothic* 1), especially in its exploration of the boundaries between life and death or human and inhuman, the Raven hotel essentially functions as an empty signifier. It evokes the Gothic as a collection of props without a meaningful connection to their original context or the rest of the series. Moreover, the Poe-themed AI hotel is introduced in a manner that suggests comic relief for the otherwise grim plotline, rather than a sense of 'the macabre' or even a slight sense of Gothic ambiguity. Rich browns and dark reds dominate the color scheme and slow camera shots underline a sense of comfort and (relative) safety. The often uncharacteristically chipper Poe AI is helpful all along, from his defense of Kovacs against hired killers in the first episode to his provision of a safe virtual environment and psychotherapeutic treatment for the traumatized Lizzie (Hayley Law). As a result, the empty hotel with its plushy interior merely adds a slight anachronistic touch to the series, which enhances the main protagonist's sense of being temporally uprooted and disconnected from the unfamiliar space he finds himself in after his "cortical stack" (a small storage device containing his 'self': his mind, memories, and personality) is "resleeved" (implanted) into a stranger's body after 250 years on ice (1.1).

True to classic cyberpunk aesthetics, Bay City itself is depicted as a space of interminable night—dark and rainy, under a constant cloud cover, which only the very rich can afford to live above in an inaccessible tower called the 'Aerial.' The high-low and light-darkness dichotomies are also depicted as a sociocultural divide in the series, which contrasts an almost exclusively white elite with an ethnically and culturally diverse city population.

Altered Carbon's conflicted anti-capitalist stance, often oscillating between the pleasure of new, high-tech toys and the disdain of old, repressed corruption, tends to highlight the moral failures of the rich 'meths' (a reference to the Biblical figure of the 1,000-year-old Methuselah), who have lost their moral integrity after prolonging their lifespan by inhabiting a succession of cloned bodies for several hundred years. The series, thus, revolves around "the only currency that truly matters:

the appetites of the immortal" (1.5). Cyberpunk, as Mike Pondsmith, creator of the roleplaying game *Cyberpunk 2020*, argues, "isn't about saving humanity, it's about saving yourself."

In contrast to its techno-cityscape, *Altered Carbon* creates a sense of nostalgia for a simpler, pre-"cortical stack" world in the philosophy of Quellcrist Falconer (Renée Elise Goldsberry), whose visionary guidance Kovacs draws on throughout the television series. Memories of Falconer's face and voice are, quite paradoxically, depicted as the only stable points in Kovacs's increasingly complicated world, a contrast which is underlined through close-ups of her face which appear in sharper focus than Kovacs's surroundings. The narrative gradually reveals their close, sexual relationship, her super-human fighting prowess, and her violent death, lending plausibility to Kovacs's continued evocation of her mental image. Falconer's teachings and her influence as a modern-day prophet are introduced in a series of flashbacks to a rebel training camp on a planet with idyllic, almost mythical natural scenery. These flashbacks to a lush world create a sharp visual contrast to the techno-cityscape and functional interiors of Bay City with its blues, greens, greys, and flashing neon signs underlining the strangeness and hostility of the city. For example, at the end of the first episode, a wide-angle shot of the city evokes the urban vastness and inscrutability while fast shots and counter-shots of moving neon signs create disorientation. As Dani Cavallaro argues concerning the Gothic aesthetics of cyberpunk cityscapes: "It is in the idea of the uncanny that the Gothic's codification of spatial and temporal instability manifests itself most blatantly, as a troubling intermingling of the ordinary and the unfamiliar" (167). By contrast, the series' flashbacks to the training camp are flooded in rich nature colors and natural light, all the while using slower shots and focusing on facial expressions. This nature/culture dichotomy supports Falconer's argument for natural death against the cortical stack/resleeving technology, which, as she accurately foresees, would only further entrench capitalist hierarchies. As Rosi Braidotti argues, the posthuman figure troubles the boundaries of the individual—the central *cogito* of Enlightenment philosophy, which lies at the heart of our understanding of humanity (1). By reducing the body to its main biological functions and separating it from the mind, as *Altered Carbon* suggests, humanity loses much of its sense of identity. "It could be anyone in there," Kovacs quips (1.3), and his oft-violent encounters with various sleeves merely prove his point.

Altered Carbon is less interested in the underlying philosophical question of a radical, technological separation of mind and body (essentially based in the Cartesian mind-body divide), than in the depiction of the ruling meths as decadent leeches exploiting their centuries-old privileges. The ruling Bancroft family with its oedipal conflicts and petty family intrigues harks back to a family plot straight out of the 18th-century Gothic, with a touch of the fin-de-siècle degeneration and the doppelganger motif thrown in for good measure, particularly once Kovacs finds out that Laurence and Miriam Bancroft's children like to wear their parents' spare clones for their own shady purposes. As Cavallaro points out, "(Cyber)Gothic families are highly sophisticated cyborgs, […] yet their motivations resonate with mythical, even superstitious, fantasies and fears, such as an ancestral horror vacui: they spawn their descendants in the compulsive effort to fill space, to replicate some family image of self" (187).

Architecture and urban design are used as a means to underline Gothic aesthetics. The Aerial's manicured lawns and priceless indoor trees, for instance, convey a sense of trapped, soulless nature, which is completely absent from the concrete cityscape below. In sharp contrast to the light-filled, spacious homes of the superrich (the Bancrofts' mansion, located far above the city, is literally called "Suntouch House"), Bay City is modeled on the neon-dystopian aesthetics of 1980s cyberpunk which combines high-tech elements like flying cars, ubiquitous neon signs, and virtual reality ads with constant darkness, rain, and a low, criminal street life, barely controlled by an equally shady, often corrupt police force. It could be argued that *Altered Carbon*, like other current cyberpunk spin-offs and remakes (*Ghost in the Shell* [Sanders 2017] and *Blade Runner 2049* [Villeneuve 2017], for instance), is more interested in nostalgically recreating yesteryear's cyberpunk cityscapes than in presenting a contemporary vision of a dystopian high-tech future,[3] except the 1980s aesthetics displayed by these remakes and spin-offs are not purely celebratory (which would, arguably, be at odds with any kind of dystopian message). Instead, they express contemporary fears of technologically enhanced, neoliberal late capitalism and its exploitation of human bodies. This criticism becomes most obvious through *Altered Carbon*'s conflicting views on death and grievous bodily harm. While the equally decadent and jaded advocates of cortical-stack technology have adopted a cavalier stance towards damaging or even killing a sleeve, Kovacs and several other characters are repeatedly presented as adverse to gratuitous violence and prone to preserve a person's sleeve, rather than discard it and find a new one. When the cop Kristin Ortega (Martha Higareda) is injured, for instance, Kovacs insists on paying for surgery and a prosthetic arm, while her colleagues suggest discarding her body and resleeving her stack. This difference in attitudes towards the body's role in a person's sense of identity and selfhood is supported by a number of scenes highlighting fights, injuries, and torture in a manner verging on body horror.

As N. Katherine Hayles argues in *How We Became Posthuman*, our category of the human is a discursive construction based on how we perceive and situate our bodies in the world: "Interpreted through metaphors resonant with cultural meanings, the body itself is a congealed metaphor, a physical structure whose constraints and possibilities have been formed by an evolutionary history" (284). The idea of 'uploading' the human mind into a computer, thus, contradicts basic philosophical tenets of the human as embodied mind. *Altered Carbon* contributes to this discussion by presenting the separation of mind ("stack") and body ("sleeve") to explore the evolution of humanity once the mind becomes separable from an individual body and stored for long periods of time, or resleeved into another body. Moreover, the series does so in the darkest possible capitalist scenario, which focuses on the prioritization of the needs of those who can afford such procedures at the further detriment of those too poor to pay for an extension of their lifespan by cloning their own bodies or acquiring an upgraded sleeve. This scenario is already laid out in the first episode of the series, in which a couple at the resleeving facility is reunited with their murdered seven-year-old daughter, who has been resleeved in the body of a middle-aged woman.

Altered Carbon also introduces the idea of torture and death in virtual spaces, which can be used to extort information from individuals, making them suffer and die over and over again. Flashbacks and memories serve as a reminder of repressed and unprocessed trauma—a central element of Gothic narratives. The series depicts a world of patriarchal/capitalist exploitation in which the poor serve the rich in every conceivable way, even to the point of dying repeatedly and painfully. Laurens Bancroft (James Purefoy), for instance, establishes his position of power by entertaining his equally rich and jaded party guests with a "combat to sleeve death between a married couple who love each other" (1.3). It is not only the gratuitous violence which casts these attitudes as Gothic, but also the negligent position towards death: the prospect of resleeving undermines death as a meaningful category for humanity while the coupling of survival and money creates a critique of decadent capitalism. The series foregrounds the horror of the fight scene in a sequence of close ups of the fighting couple intercut with the relaxed faces of the party guests, all the while the soundtrack mixes heavy punches and the sounds of breaking skin and bones with a merry waltz. Audience sympathies are directed towards the couple earlier on when Kovacs and Ortega draw attention to the perspective of the couple's children and their reaction to seeing their parents return with new bodies after each fight.

The mercenary attitude towards the flesh of others is underlined by a generally sexist, patriarchal system, in which women sell their bodies to the highest bidder and/or agree to being beaten to death for the promise of a new, upgraded sleeve (see 1.2). Women's existence is predominantly framed by their sexual capital—and this includes very rich women like Miriam Bancroft (Kristin Lehman), who has altered her cloned sleeves to secrete a "biochemical pheromone" (1.2) to enhance her sexual attractiveness. *Altered Carbon* creates a dystopian counter-image to Donna J. Haraway's ironic feminist myth of the cyborg, which she imagines as "a creature in a post-gender world" (292), possessing the "power to survive" by "seizing the tools to mark the world that marked them as other" (311). Instead, *Altered Carbon* falls victim to the same stereotypes about conservatism and masculinist heteronormative tendencies that feminist critics were making about cyberpunk twenty years ago: It reiterates gendered differences to the point of presenting stereotypical heteronormative patriarchal violence as the norm.[4] *Altered Carbon* is therefore like many other cyberpunk texts, voluntarily or inadvertently reflecting an underlying sexism we can in part track to earlier narrative frameworks—most prominently the Gothic's focus on patriarchal structures and gendered violence, which also found its way into the early 20th-century detective fiction and *film noir* that helped inspire cyberpunk. As Donna Heiland points out, classic Gothic texts are often informed by patriarchal structures, most prominently reflected in the figure of the Gothic heroine's flight from a villain, who may be after her "virtue" or her money (1–2). Late 20th-century and contemporary Gothic texts have moved beyond this archetypal scene of the 18th-century Gothic, but they are still expressive of cultural fears and anxieties—even if gendered fears have frequently taken a more monstrous turn. In this context, Stacy Gillis argues that cyberpunk texts establish a "(post)feminist subject" in the figure of the "ass-kicking techno-babe" (7), in a manner that is, as Gillis points out, reminiscent of the *femme fatale* in *film noir* and Gothic fiction. In Netflix's *Altered Carbon*, Quellcrist Falconer, Reileen Kovacs (Dichen Lachman) and, to a lesser extent, Kristin Ortega, take on similar roles; at the same time, cyberpunk's male-dominated gender politics reveal that, "for all its stylish allusions to popular culture [...] cyberpunk fiction is, in the end, not radical at all. Its slickness and apparent subversiveness conceal a complicity with '80s conservatism" (Nixon 231) which *Altered Carbon* reimagines as late capitalism. In other words, even the female agency exhibited in such able-bodied women as Falconer, Ortega, or *Neuromancer*'s Molly Millions is always "mediated by the ways in which the bodies of these women are reduced to either a sexualised or monstrous femininity" (Gillis 9–10).

Altered Carbon explicitly makes the connection to *film noir*, itself heavily influenced by Gothic aesthetics given its roots in late 19th- and early 20th-century crime fiction. The Poe AI, clearly fascinated by the idea of performing human conventions, watches *I Wake Up Screaming/Hot Spot* (Humberstone 1941) as a cultural text: "I've been researching the famous gumshoe private dicks of the past and I believe I can assist you in the time-honored position of the shamus' dependable and steadfast partner" (1.2). Poe's elaborate proposal is ostensibly added for comic relief, but it serves as meta-narrative commentary on *Altered Carbon*'s borrowing of the *film noir* conventions. As in the context of the Gothic, *film noir* and detective fiction are evoked as a foil, which cannot be fulfilled by an AI with no embodiment outside of the hotel building. The series, thus, showcases a number of other predecessors, ostensibly as clichés to be discarded, but ultimately to draw a connection to a set of underlying issues and questions.

Recent cyberpunk narratives reflect scientific research into longevity and the possibility of overcoming the limitations of the human body. In consequence, they often foreground death as a liminal state to be overcome by technology, but in a climate of Anthropocene capitalism, they do so on a much larger scale, reflecting contemporary concerns with the death of whole populations. In these texts Gothic imagery of death, decay, and abjection is used to underline a critical point which goes beyond the vision of earlier cyberpunk texts like *Blade Runner* and *Neuromancer*. These cybergothic texts draw on critical posthumanist discussions of death as a global issue connecting north and south in a framework of institutionalized necropolitical exploitation of marginalized bodies at the hands of greedy global corporations. As Braidotti argues by drawing on Achille Mbembe's concept of "necropolitics" (Mbembe 11), "the bodies of the empirical subjects who signify difference (woman/native/earth or natural others) have become the disposable bodies of the global economy" (Braidotti 111). *Blade Runner 2049* reflects this by showing an orphanage sweatshop in which a uniformly clad army of pale children with shaved heads disassemble used consumer electronics, presumably to recycle their components.[5] The atmosphere of the scene is clearly Gothic—from the gloomy architecture of the vast space to the unsmiling children as uncanny doppelgangers. It is, clearly, not personhood which is at stake for this collective body of children, but rather the underlying question whether any of them will survive this environment, which considers their "wasted lives" (Bauman) as less valuable than the electronic trash they are sorting. Their absorption into the "integrated circuit" (Haraway 291) of production and recycling of high-tech consumer goods has certainly led to a kind of cyborgization and the dissolution of gendered markers (along with any other signs of individuality). The scene, however, presents a techno-capitalist dystopia, a bleak distortion of Haraway's liberating cyborg myth in which the status of the superrich "depends on the material deprivation of others" (Frase) and automation technology benefits only the rich.

Altered Carbon introduces the striking image of the highly contagious bioweapon victims isolated from the rest of humanity in a camp and dependent on handouts to make a similarly horrific point about the precarity of whole populations. The victims are presented as abject, literally untouchable (as touching them would lead to instant contamination and death), but their existence as abject social outcasts also provides a validation for the superrich quasi-immortal meths by creating an opportunity to perform charitable work and absolve their own conscience. The fact that Laurens Bancroft can simply store his memory in the cloud and discard another (presumably expensive) clone every time he goes to visit the camp of these outcasts underlines the disparity between their situations in a capitalist system which has made immortality into just another commodity for the superrich. *Altered Carbon* therefore echoes contemporary cyberpunk narratives that draw on the techno-aesthetics of their 1980s predecessors not only for nostalgic purposes, but also, and more importantly, to signal a return of the repressed—a harsh reminder that three decades later, the comparatively rich global north is still as dependent on technology as the former west was in the 1980s, if not more so—and to draw attention to the impact this involvement with technology has on humanity and the planet as a whole. In these instances, cyberpunk coincides with and draws on the imagery of the posthuman Gothic to highlight the horrors of global techno-capitalism.

This kind of abject body horror, which casts the human body as soulless raw material for bio-technological experiments, can be traced back to Mary Shelley's *Frankenstein* (1818). As Veronica Hollinger argues, in contemporary re-readings, Shelley's novel "has been transformed into a precursor text of cyberculture" (192). Dongshin Yi, for instance, reads *Frankenstein* as a key text in the *Genealogy of Cyborgothic* [sic], as Victor Frankenstein's "workshop of filthy creation" (Shelley 32) conjures questions of creation and (identity) production, as well as creative and narrative authority. Shunned by society and abandoned by his creator, Frankenstein's creature ultimately begins to reflect on his existence and the manner of his creation—a query mirrored in the novel's epigraph from Milton's *Paradise Lost* (1667): "Did I request thee maker from thy clay to make me man? Did I solicit thee from darkness to promote me?" The novel, like its cybergothic descendants, draws attention to how the infinite possibilities of technoscientific creation tend to destabilize human individuality and our sense of self, origin, and purpose to the point where we begin to question our concept of humanity as a rational, clearly demarcated species. Cybergothic texts, from *Frankenstein*'s proto-posthuman Gothic explorations of these questions onward, take these destabilizations and anxieties and aestheticize them to create fully fleshed (or bio-technoscientifically engineered) monstrous horrors. As Cavallaro argues, "the bodies that populate these worlds are themselves intrinsically uncanny [...] threshold phenomena precariously suspended between materiality and immateriality" (172) Cavallaro associates this liminality of cyberpunk bodies with Gothic forms of embodiment: "An intricate and befuddling incarnation of often repressed desires and fantasies, the Gothic body eludes labelling and its appeal is accordingly complex. Above all, it is boundless; this condition is most famously epitomized by the formless pulp of the unfinished female creature that Dr Frankenstein ends up scattering over the floor of his laboratory" (172).

To encounter one's self resleeved in a different body, as *Altered Carbon* shows, may be the ultimate Frankensteinian experience. It is perhaps fitting (if uncharacteristic of this particular character) that it is Dimi the Twin (a "doublesleever"—that is a person who has copied their cortical stack to be able to exist in two bodies at once) who gives voice to the pertinent philosophical questions in *Altered Carbon*: "Where is the voice that said altered carbon would free us from the cells of our flesh? The vision that said we would be angels? Instead we became hungry for things that reality could no longer offer. The lines blurred" (1.5). *Altered Carbon* draws on classic cyberpunk narratives and cybergothic aesthetics to explore these critical questions of humanity, identity, and posthuman becomings.

Notes

1 For more details, see Michael Sean Bolton's "Monstrous Machinery" or my edited collection *Posthuman Gothic*.
2 See Fred Botting's "Reading Machines" for added details.
3 For details, see Daniel Rodriguez's *YouTube* video cited below.
4 For in-depth analyses of the masculinist heteronormativity associated with cyberpunk, and the subsequent narrative responses, see Wendy Gay Pearson's, Patricia Melzer's, and/or Lisa Yaszek's contributions to this collection.
5 Matthew Flisfeder provides a focused analysis of the cyberpunk aesthetics in *Blade Runner 2049* for this collection.

Works Cited

Altered Carbon. Created by Laeta Kalogridis, Mythology Entertainment/Monkey Massacre, 2018.

Bauman, Zygmunt. *Wasted Lives.* Blackwell, 2004.

Blade Runner. Directed by Ridley Scott, performances by Harrison Ford, Rutger Hauer, and Sean Young, Warner Brothers, 1982.

Bolton, Michael Sean. "Monstrous Machinery: Defining Posthuman Gothic." *Aeternum*, vol. 1, no. 1, 2014, pp. 1–15.

Botting, Fred. *Gothic.* 2nd Ed. Routledge, 2014.

———. "Reading Machines." *Romantic Circles*, December 2005, www.rc.umd.edu/ praxis/gothic/botting/ botting.

Braidotti, Rosi. *The Posthuman.* Polity, 2013.

Castricano, Jodey. "If a Building is a Sentence, So is a Body: Kathy Acker and the Postcolonial Gothic." *American Gothic: New Interventions in a National Narrative*, edited by Robert K. Martin and Eric Savoy. U of Iowa P, 1998, pp. 202–14.

Cavallaro, Dani. *Cyberpunk and Cyberculture.* Athlone Press, 2000.

Frase, Peter. "Four Futures." *Jacobin*, 13 Dec. 2011, jacobinmag.com/2011/12/four-futures.

Gibson, William. *Neuromancer.* Ace, 1984.

Gillis, Stacy. "The (Post)Feminist Politics of Cyberpunk." *Gothic Studies*, vol. 9, no. 2, 2007, pp. 7–19.

Haraway, Donna J. "A Cyborg Manifesto: Science, Technology and Socialist-Feminism in the Late Twentieth Century." *The Cybercultures Reader*, edited by David Bell and Barbara M. Kennedy, Routledge, 2000, pp. 291–324.

Hayles, N. Katherine. *How We Became Posthuman: Virtual Bodies in Cybernetics, Literature, and Informatics.* U of Chicago P, 1999.

Heiland, Donna. *Gothic and Gender.* Blackwell, 2004.

Heise-von der Lippe, Anya, ed. *Posthuman Gothic.* U of Wales P, 2017.

Hollinger, Veronica. "Retrofitting *Frankenstein*." *Beyond Cyberpunk: New Critical Perspectives*, edited by Graham J. Murphy and Sherryl Vint. Routledge, 2010, pp. 191–210.

Ketterer, David. *Canadian Science Fiction and Fantasy.* Indiana UP, 1992.

Mbembe, Achille. "Necropolitics." *Public Culture*, vol. 15, no. 1, 2003, pp. 11–40.

Nixon, Nicola. "Cyberpunk: Preparing the Ground for Revolution or Keeping the Boys Satisfied?" *Science Fiction Studies*, vol. 19, no. 2, 1992, pp. 219–35.

No Maps for These Territories. Directed by Mark Neale, 3DD Entertainment, 4 Oct. 2000.

Pondsmith, Mike. "Cyberpunk 2077 – Mike Pondsmith about Cyberpunk World." *Youtube*, Cyberpunk 2077, 17 Jan. 2013, youtube.com/watch?v=xYxt7cwDk4E.

Rapatzikou, Tatiani G. *Gothic Motifs in the Fiction of William Gibson*. Rodopi, 2004.

Rodriguez, Daniel. "*Altered Carbon* and Bad Futures." *Youtube*, Pattern Theory, 2 Apr. 2018, youtube.com/watch?v=kv1tRiCjWsc.

Schmeink, Lars. "On the Look-Out for a new Urban Uncanny." *Extrapolation*, vol. 55, no. 1, 2014, pp. 25–32.

Shelley, Mary. *Frankenstein*. Norton, 2012.

Wolfe, Cary. *What is Posthumanism?* U of Minnesota P, 2010.

Yi, Dongshin. *A Genealogy of Cyborgothic*. Ashgate, 2010.

33

POSTHUMANISM(S)

Julia Grillmayr

What contributes to cyberpunk's ongoing importance is without question its capability to put the idea of an original human essence to the test; this applies to the cadre of Movement-era authors[1] in the 1980s onwards. Cyberpunk shows bodies and minds that are constantly altered, enhanced, or perverted by bio- and nanotechnological prostheses, cognitive implants, and/or new orifices that interface with digital networks and cyberspatial domains. The definition of what it means to be human becomes slippery in cyberpunk as categories of identity, nature, and essence crumble: everything is interdependent, in flux, and defined rather by what it *does* than what it *is*. Closely linked to cyberpunk's emergence comes the advent of what is loosely called the posthuman, a concept which focuses on the same central themes—the amalgamation of bodies and technology, brain-machine interfaces, and potential habitats for humans in virtual spaces and space colonies. Various writers, cultural theorists, and philosophers have been conceptualizing what posthuman bodies in an increasingly posthuman present and future could and should look like. It is therefore imperative to identify and differentiate the two major strands of understanding the posthuman that not only set different priorities but contradict each other in fundamental assumptions: transhumanism and critical posthumanism.

First, *transhumanism* is all about transcendence. The prefix is short for 'transitional human,' an intermediate stage of human development into, at some future endpoint, the posthuman. Transhumanists put forth the freedom of the human individual to technologically alter their corporeal body—referred to as "morphological freedom" (More 4)—through prosthesis, but more often through speculative bio- and nanotechnology. In this respect, one of the main goals is the extreme postponement or even abolition of death. "Becoming posthuman," argues Max More in "The Philosophy of Transhumanism," "means exceeding the limitations that define the less desirable aspects of the 'human condition'" (4). Posthuman beings would not only "no longer suffer from disease, aging, and inevitable death," but would "have vastly greater physical capability and freedom of form" (More 4). Furthermore, More explains transhumanists "typically look to expand the range of possible future environments for posthuman life, including space colonization and the creation of rich virtual worlds" (4). Moreover, transhumanists extrapolate that new cognitive technologies will not only enhance human capabilities to think and remember, but also to feel. Nick Bostrom, one of the most prominent voices of the transhumanist movement, identifies health span, cognition, and emotion as the three areas where posthuman capacities, "greatly exceeding the maximum attainable by any current human being without recourse to new technological means," should be developed (28–29). Together with intellectual capacity and "the capacity to remain fully healthy, active, and productive, both mentally and physically," Bostrom stresses that "the capacity to enjoy life and to respond with appropriate affect to life situations and other people" would be ameliorated (29). In sum, transhumanist discourse sees becoming posthuman as akin to the transition from childhood to adulthood as a logical next step in human evolution (Bostrom 42).

Critical posthumanism is quite unlike transhumanism as it tells completely different stories about posthumans. Primarily, it does not presume that posthumanity exists in the near or far future; rather, critical posthumanism presumes we have already become posthuman and in part asks how we arrived at our posthuman condition, exemplified by N. Katherine Hayles's *How We Became Posthuman: Virtual Bodies in Cybernetics, Literature, and Informatics*. In the tradition of Michel Foucault, who stresses in *The Order of Things* that our orders of knowledge are socially constructed, posthumanists such as Hayles emphasize that our system of beliefs, our *epistemes*, shape the world, not only on a metaphysical but also on a material level. Foucault calls Man "an invention of recent date" that will eventually be replaced by other ideas and constructs, "erased, like a face drawn in sand at the edge of the sea" (387). Posthumanism therefore draws on this insight to resituate liberal humanism as merely one story or invention among others. In this vein, Donna J. Haraway's "A Cyborg Manifesto" tells a different story, a story of dethroning Man from his privileged position as crown of creation; it is a story against anthropocentrism and in favor of the relatedness of humans, animals, machines, and other non-living earth dwellers. The ability to tell 'different stories' opens up the possibility of thinking about the emergence of new technologies in tandem with a critique of humanism.

As a result, while transhumanists understand the term 'posthuman' as referencing something that comes *after the human*, for critical posthumanists it connotes the concept of something that comes *after humanism*. Transhumanism, as More points out, "continues to champion the core of the Enlightenment ideas and ideals—rationality and scientific method, individual rights, the possibility and desirability of progress" (10). It can thus be understood as a "contemporary renewal of humanism" (Sorgner and Ranisch 8) or even conservative "retrohumanism" (Clarke xiv). In contrast, critical posthumanism challenges these Enlightenment ideas and ideals and the anthropocentrism they are based upon, and insists on "the urgency of finding new and alternative modes of political and ethical agency for our technologically mediated world" (Braidotti 58).

33.1 Cyborgs and Other Inconvenient Monsters

The emergence of both posthumanism and cyberpunk "at the same cultural moment" (Hollinger 207) is no coincidence. Haraway's original "Manifesto for Cyborgs," makes arguments which are in part a direct result of such feminist science fiction (sf) as Joanna Russ's *The Female Man* (1975) and Marge Piercy's *Woman on the Edge of Time* (1976). Although they have a very different set of goals, Haraway's manifesto and William Gibson's *Neuromancer* (1984) "both tell stories about how the distinctions between bodies and machines have become increasingly difficult to maintain" (Hollinger 207). We can therefore see the direct transfer of post- and transhumanist theory into such cyberpunk texts as Bruce Sterling's Shaper/Mechanist series—"Swarm" (1982), "Spider Rose" (1982), "Cicada Queen" (1983), "Sunken Gardens" (1984), "Twenty Evocations" (1984), and *Schismatrix* (1985). The rivalry between the Shapers and the Mechanists in Sterling's series demonstrates two ways of becoming posthuman. The Mechanists, using prostheses and mind-computer interfaces, have chosen "the path of information technologies and mechanics to modify themselves into almost immortal cyborgs" (Sorgner and Ranisch 255); the Shapers, on the other hand, have achieved longevity and enhanced cognition through biotechnology and genetic engineering.[2]

At first glance, Sterling's stories seem to be sketching a transhumanist future vision of the posthuman; however, as we follow *Schismatrix*'s protagonist Abelard Lindsay, who is caught in the middle of the Shaper/Mechanist rivalry that turns into a brutal war, we increasingly learn that it is impossible to draw a clean-cut line between both sides, and the inclusion of alien Investors and an Earthbound faction known as Preservationists, who cherish unmodified human life, further muddies any lines of distinction. Sterling's writing gives proof of "a profound acceptance of the human as a complex network of biological, political, technological, economic, and even aesthetic forces" (Bukatman 107). Thus, his Shaper/Mechanist universe, similar to the critical posthumanist argument, defies dualistic thinking and rejects the "persistent concepts and dualities in Western culture, such as nature/culture, man/woman, subject/object, human/animal, or body/mind" (Sorgner and Ranisch 8).

What Sterling's Shaper/Mechanist series highlights and critical posthumanism generally criticizes is that the problems of dualistic thinking are grounded in an inherent hierarchy: The categories human, man, culture, subject, and mind are favored and set as the norm, while animal, female, nature, object, and body are *other than* this norm. For Haraway, the figure of the cyborg is "a way out of the maze of dualisms in which we have explained our bodies and our tools to ourselves" ("Cyborg Manifesto" 181). As a hybrid figure of multiplicity, the cyborg "does not seek unitary identity and so generate[s] antagonistic dualisms without end" (180). More recently, Rosi Braidotti has sharply criticized dualistic thinking and has proposed a vitalist-materialist posthumanism instead, fueled "by the resurgent 'others': the women's rights movement; the anti-racism and de-colonization movements; the anti-nuclear and pro-environment movements" (37). These are all "voices of the structural Others of modernity [...]. They inevitably mark the crisis of the former humanist 'centre' or dominant subject-position and are not merely anti-humanist, but move beyond [humanism] to an altogether novel, posthuman project" (Braidotti 37).

33.2 Posthuman Bodies and Cyberspace

Cyberpunk can be read as a key component of this posthuman project. At the mode's core lies an "'anti-humanist' conviction," as Sterling puts it: Cyberpunk is convinced that the "human condition can be changed, and it will be changed, and is changing; the only real questions are how, and to what end" ("Nineties").[3] In this regard, the question of (dis)embodiment proves to be a key site of inquiry for both the posthuman project and cyberpunk. As Haraway, Hayles, Braidotti, and a host of other critics demonstrate, critical posthumanism emphasizes the material embedding of consciousness and the conviction that thinking and embodiment intertwine. For transhumanism and its fight against disease, morphological boundaries, and ultimately against death, the body and its needs are part of the "less desirable aspects of the 'human condition'" that should be overcome (More 4). One of the most radical voices in this respect can be found in Hans Moravec, who considers body and mind as two distinct halves of the human individual that are bound by an unfortunate "uneasy truce" (4). He imagines the posthuman future as a "postbiological world dominated by self-improving, thinking machines" (5). This vision, however, contradicts some of the goals of human enhancement as Moravec himself points out: "Long life loses much of its point if we are fated to spend it staring stupidly at our ultra-intelligent machines as they try to describe their ever more spectacular discoveries in baby-talk that we can understand" (108). He proposes genetic engineering as a temporary solution, but ultimately sees posthumans "made of protein" with brains "made of neurons" as too vulnerable and slow (108). Hence, in *Mind Children: The Future of Robot and Human Intelligence*, Moravec sketches his famous mind-upload scenario where "[l]ayer after layer the brain is simulated, then excavated [...] your mind has been removed from the brain and transferred to a machine" (110). Channeling the tropes common to cyberpunk and sf in general, Moravec projects that with our mutable disembodiment, we will eventually be able to achieve a future comprised of a vast networked system of computers, a posthuman, cyberspatial utopia culminating in "a supercivilization, the synthesis of all solar-system life, constantly improving and extending itself, spreading outward from the sun" (116).[4]

Julia Grillmayr

Clinging to the idea of a body-mind dualism, transhumanists are convinced that personal identity would be preserved in the posthuman form. While the robot surgeon empties the brain in Moravec's scenario, "you have not lost consciousness, or even your train of thought" (*Mind Children* 110). Similarly, Bostrom, in his transhumanist speculations regarding "some kind of molecular therapy [...] to permanently disable the aging processes," stresses that "a human being could retain her memories, her goals, her unique skills, and many important aspects of her personality even as she becomes posthuman" (41). Cyberpunk, however, is less optimistic. Consider Sterling's novel *Holy Fire* (1996): The almost hundred-year-old Mia Ziemann undergoes a cutting-edge anti-aging procedure and wakes up as the young woman Maya, who feels a "peculiar kind of dread, as if Mia Ziemann was hiding in the closet and waiting for dark" (76). In sum, Maya no longer identifies with her former self.[5] Pat Cadigan's novel *Fools* (1992) goes even further: Through cognitive implants, actors *become* their characters, personas "leak-through" to others, and both memory junkies and Brain Police officers lose track of which persona inhabits which brain. Finally, Rudy Rucker's *Software* (1982), published when cyberpunk was still simply the 'Movement,' imagines potential immortality through a mind-upload that predates Moravec's scenario by six years. The robots ("boppers") in Rucker's universe have discarded "ugly, human-chauvinist priorities" (51) with the help of programmer Cobb Anderson and have founded an autonomous population on the moon. Unlike the rest of the "fleshers," Cobb is not "scared to change hardware like a bopper does" (75) and as a token of gratitude, the robots scramble and upload his brain to a computer and then to a mechanical body. However, *Software* does not end with a transhumanist utopia. Rather, it climaxes with chaos and a loss of control as human identities are robbed, copied, and instrumentalized, fodder for the remaining novels in the *Ware* tetralogy (*Wetware*, 1988; *Freeware*, 1997; *Realware*, 2000).

Many of these scenarios take their imagery of cyberspace from (mis)readings of William Gibson's cyberpunk, notably *Neuromancer*. In spite of the repeated instances in Gibson's fiction that show the central importance and resilience of corporeal embodiment, (mis)readings of Gibson's "data made flesh" can be understood as the prioritization of information over materiality, a stance critical posthumanists identify as untenable (Hayles, *How We Became* 5). For example, cyberspace, first introduced in Gibson's short story "Burning Chrome" (1982), is most famously described in *Neuromancer* as a "consensual hallucination [...]. Unthinkable complexity. Lines of light ranged in the nonspace of the mind" (59). This is the home of choice for the console cowboy Case and where he, or better his "disembodied consciousness" (6), goes to work as a data thief. Living for "the bodiless exultation of cyberspace," he has developed a certain "relaxed contempt for the flesh. The body was meat" (6). Nevertheless, Case cannot ultimately get rid of his body; after all, as Seán McCorry argues in his contribution to this collection, "while cyberspace offers the delights of disembodied euphoria, the physical bodies of those who go online are still organic objects that require sustenance to function, and they are nourished by food that hardly testifies to the human mastery promised by networked technologies" (320). Similarly, the hotshot console cowboys are not successfully disembodied, free floating virtual entities. Rather, their precarious lifestyles result in constant bodily pain and many forms of drug abuse. Even inside the matrix, their organic body is ever-present as evidenced by ICE (Intrusion Countermeasures Electronics) that attacks their digital presence but can cause real-world brain death. Therefore, while it may be true that *Neuromancer* does feature some form of disembodiment and may not entirely be a posthumanist critique of disembodiment, it would also be an overreach to conclude it embraces, or validates the transhumanism described by More, Moravec, and Bostrom.

Cyberpunk takes up the streamlined, utopian visions of transhumanism, but complicates or contradicts them tremendously. For example, as pay-off for helping Case fulfill his mission and free the powerful Artificial Intelligence (AI) Wintermute by allowing it to merge with its 'brother' Neuromancer, the digital construct of Case's former colleague Dixie Flatline expresses

Posthumanism(s)

his only wish: "I wanna be erased." (228) In spite of his desire to be unplugged, however, Dixie's ultimate wish is denied, as suggested at the end of the novel when Case hears Dixie's characteristic "laugh that wasn't laughter" (297). Furthermore, the final passage suggests that a copy of Case's consciousness lives on in the matrix, which has by now been taken over completely by the freed AI. As the "sum total of the works, the whole show" (296) the Wintermute-Neuromancer entity does not bother with humans any more, but tries to make contact with other AIs from other solar systems. This alludes to the Singularity, an important concept in both transhumanism and cyberpunk. Proto-cyberpunk author and computer scientist Vernor Vinge coined the concept in his paper "The Coming Technological Singularity: How to Survive in the Post-Human Era" delivered at the 1993 VISION-21 Symposium sponsored by the NASA Lewis Research Center and the Ohio Aerospace Institute. Vinge describes the Singularity as "the imminent creation by technology of entities with greater-than-human intelligence" (365). The Singularity could occur through different means, either single computers or "large computer networks" could "'wake up' as superhumanly intelligent entities" or computer-human interfaces or biotechnology could "improve natural human intellect" (365). At the core of the Singularity hypothesis lies the assumption that once 'superintelligence' is reached, it triggers uncontrollable growth and sophistication in a manner comparable to the newly merged Wintermute and Neuromancer AI.[6]

Regarding the issue of (dis)embodiment, cyberpunk that followed the initial 1980s wave proved even less willing to discard the physical body in some transhumanist dream of mutable, and ultimately disposable, embodiment. For example, in her novel *Synners* (1991) Cadigan, the 'Queen of Cyberpunk,' imagines socket implants, consisting of "one hundred percent [...] living tissue," making themselves "completely at home" in the recipients, so that the recipients can, in turn, make cyberspace truly their home (69). While this works foremost for the protagonist Visual Mark, who enjoys "floating away more weightless than weightless, consisting of less than the empty space between his dreams, as if everything that was himself had been distilled down to one pure thought" (96), a purely virtual existence proves unbearable for Gina, the main female protagonist. Notably, at the end of the novel after vanishing deep into virtual reality with Mark, Gina comes back to real space to live in the countryside with another male character, Gabe, in a happy, heterosexual, nuclear family, one that intentionally or otherwise mirrors the conclusion to Gibson's *Count Zero* (1986).[7] Read from a feminist standpoint, *Synners* highlights that for women, "the realities of the flesh are all too present in the imperfect world of cyberpunk [...]. They are tied to their bodies in ways that male characters are not" (Cadora 165). Or, as Lisa Yaszek writes, female characters in *Synners* "experiment with a range of messier, more complex relations that include sharing real-world memories by digital means and using human bodies to power, reboot, and even radically restructure the technological and economic arrangements of their world" (34).

33.3 Capitalism and Compost

In her article "Wrestling with Transhumanism," Hayles adds an important layer to the posthuman discussion when she recognizes that even though not all versions of transhumanism are guilty of praising disembodiment, they all "perform decontextualizing moves that over-simplify the situation and carry into the new millennium some of the most questionable aspects of capitalist ideology." Hayles's link between transhumanism's over-simplifications and capitalist ideology is an important connection because transhumanism's feel-good aesthetics often mask its own commercial interests. For example, Bostrom's posthuman scenarios read like bad copy for commercials: "You are able to sprinkle your conversation with witty remarks and poignant anecdotes. Your friends remark on how much more fun you are to be around" (31) and "[y]ou have just celebrated your 170th birthday and you feel stronger than ever. Each day is a joy" (32). Perhaps most obvious and extreme in this respect is bestselling futurist and famous transhumanism proponent

Ray Kurzweil who, paired with physician Terry Grossman, advances transhumanist visions of longevity—including various dietary supplements that his readers can conveniently purchase from his and Grossman's *Transcend* website. Deeply critical of capitalism, it is thus among cyberpunk's key functions to push back against these sort of transhumanist visions of the posthuman and to make economic inequality visible. As Gibson has famously remarked in *Talk of the Nation*, "the future is already here—it's just not very evenly distributed" ("Science"), so to ignore the economic realities underwriting human enhancement technologies and ideologies risks the persistence and reinforcement of these structural inequalities.

For example, we can find a critique of global capitalism in Gibson's "Burning Chrome." While the street may have its own uses for things in this near-future universe, "high above it all burn corporate galaxies and the cold spiral arms of military systems" (181). Furthermore, people may lose their personas in Pat Cadigan's *Fools* by getting body-snatched or mind-sucked, but equally effective in identity loss is getting franchised onto other people. Or, the socket implants in *Synners* may be a wondrous breakthrough, but they are first and foremost employed "as a more efficient means to produce *rock videos*" (140; emphasis in original) that are marketed through omnipresent media. Similarly, Neal Stephenson's *Snow Crash* (1992) depicts a near-future urban landscape where the mafia runs a pizza delivery service as a matter of life and death and the state is organized into such "burbclaves" as "Mr. Lee's Greater Hong Kong" (83) that are structured as large franchises. Akin to Gibson's depiction of cyberspace as shaped by corporate interests, Stephenson's Metaverse also depends on market realities. For example, users can design their avatars in any fashion: "If you're ugly, you can make your avatar beautiful. [...] You can look like a gorilla or a dragon or a giant talking penis in the Metaverse" (36). Nevertheless, user access is governed by hardware because "[y]our avatar can look any way you want it to, up to the limitations of your equipment" (36). When Stephenson's protagonist Hiro Protagonist goes online, he immediately recognizes real-world economic and technological limitations imported into the Metaverse: "The couples coming off the monorail can't afford to have custom avatars made and don't know how to write their own. They have to buy off-the-shelf avatars [...]. Brandy and Clint are both popular, off-the-shelf models" that can be purchased at the local Wal-Mart (37). Thomas Foster reads this "new visual marker of bodily difference" in *Snow Crash* as a parallel with racialization (220) which reinforces the diagnosis that cyberspace is not some digital utopia free of racism, sexism, or classism.[8] In sum, it is hard to disagree with Elaine L. Graham's assessment that "[i]n the bleaker cyberpunk worlds, where body parts, mercenaries, loyalty and human emotions are all commodities to be obtained at a price, it is only the imperatives of global capitalism via the cash nexus that determine the authenticity, or value, of anything" (195). Graham links this critique of capitalism directly to cyberpunk's abandonment of the idea of the "progressivism of humanism" (195).

While cyberpunk may not entirely fulfill the role of a philosophically informed opposition to anthropocentrism and global capitalism, it certainly complicates the streamlined futures that transhumanism promises. Instead of superhumanly smart and strong posthumans, Sterling imagines that soon "the Monsters would all have lousy night jobs mopping up at fast-food restaurants" ("Nineties"). Cyberpunk makes it impossible to ignore social inequalities that could potentially be reinscribed by human enhancement. In other words, if cyberpunk portrays some winners who are living in a future as sketched by Bostrom, Kurzweil, or other transhumanist advocates, the losers are at the same time ever-present. Take, for example, Madeline Ashby's recent cyberpunk novel *Company Town* (2016). When Hwa, the main character of Ashby's novel, is told by the ultra-rich Zachariah Lynch that the lifestyle of fully organic people like her, who will soon "be nothing more than specimens in a museum of humanity," is a "very brave choice," Hwa sums up the material conditions for so many: "Choice had little to do with it. Money was the thing. When you had no money, you had no choice" (45). Among other successes in the novel, Ashby depicts Hwa and other characters exploited by economic and social precariousness. Finally, with

Posthumanism(s)

Hwa's transformation into a posthuman "changeling" through advanced nanotechnology that she catches like a virus, Ashby offers a critical perspective on how becoming-posthuman might have nothing to do with individual choice, intent, or even consent. In a Cadigan-esque manner, Hwa can only lament that "[e]verything that made me who I am is gone" (Ashby 283).

In conclusion, it bears noting that while the discussion of the complex intersections of cyberpunk sf, transhumanism, and posthumanism continues, this discourse is currently expanding and changing. Working from Mark McGurl's essay "The Posthuman Comedy," Bruce Clarke describes this as a shift "from the machinic posthuman to the planetary nonhuman" (xii). As has become evident through some of the above-cited examples, the endeavor to understand the merging of humans and machines is fueling broader discussions of the relations between the human and the nonhuman. This development is visible in Donna J. Haraway's work. After writing "A Cyborg Manifesto," she soon came to think of "cyborgs as junior siblings in the much bigger, queer family of companion species" ("Companion" 300) and thus started to focus on the co-evolution of humans and animals under modern (bio)technological conditions. In sf, this is palpable as a shift "away from a cyberpunk imaginary, best embodied in Haraway's cyborg [...] and toward another technocultural expression of scientific progress: One that favors genetic engineering, xenotransplantation, and virology" and is thus often referred to as "biopunk" (Schmeink 7). Cyber- and biopunk are of course not mutually exclusive, but are likely to coexist, as evidenced in the range of texts referenced in this voluminous collection.

If anything, this ongoing development stresses even further the role of sf in complicating escapist visions of the posthuman future. Cyberpunk may not provide solutions to social, medical, and environmental issues, but it insists on addressing them, instead of making them disappear through an all too simple technological fix. As Haraway stresses in her recent book *Staying with the Trouble* (2016), in contrast to the bright and clean futures depicted in transhumanism, she works "with and in sf as material-semiotic composting, as theory in the mud, as muddle" (31). In order to dissociate herself from the adherents of a "transhumanist techno-enhancement," Haraway also strictly rejects the term 'posthumanism' that she considers "much too easily appropriated by the blissed-out" (Gane 140). Instead, she playfully proposes the term "compost": "We are humus, not Homo, not anthropos; we are compost, not posthuman" (*Staying* 55). Cyberpunk more often than not gets its hand dirty in the compost by exploring the complicated ways of 'becoming-with' nonhumans, not least by giving a voice to various nonhuman actors, be it animals, robots, bioengineered or other bacteria, smart objects, or disembodied AIs. Even if cyberpunk generally relies neither on transhumanist nor on critical posthumanist theory and critique, cyberpunk remains ready to engage in such a project of "nonarrogant collaboration with all those in the muddle" (*Staying* 56).

Notes

1 For an overview of the Movement and its transformation into cyberpunk, see Graham J. Murphy's entry in this collection.
2 Maria Goicoechea's contribution to this collection provides a focused reading of Sterling's Shaper/Mechanist series.
3 For an opposing view of cyberpunk that focuses on its deeply embedded conservatism and indebtedness to humanism, see Patricia Melzer's contribution to this collection.
4 Moravec double downs on the body-mind dualism in his later article "Pigs in Cyberspace." He envisions the whole world (and also colonized space) as a vast virtual reality that is the new habitat of human minds and AIs. This cyberspace, Moravec concludes, would eventually expand to the extent that it would necessarily include various simulations of human life and history—and thus the "very moment we are now experiencing may actually be (almost certainly is) such a distributed mental event, and most likely is a complete fabrication that never happened physically" (181). This is clearly a renewal of René Descartes's 'brain in vat/evil demon' scenario and his *cogito ergo sum*, thus centrally locating Moravec's transhumanism within a larger humanist tradition.

Julia Grillmayr

5 A recent adaptation of this scenario is in the film *Advantageous* (Phang 2015): Gwen (Jacqueline Kim), a middle-aged woman, undergoes a consciousness transfer into a younger body to secure economic stability for the sake of her daughter's future. In spite of the positive descriptions of the transfer process, a process Gwen herself has helped market, Gwen2.0 feels entirely disconnected from her previous life and must develop new emotional connections with her friends and family, particularly her daughter.

6 Gerry Canavan provides a detailed analysis of the Singularity and Charles Stross's post-cyberpunk novel *Accelerando* (2005) elsewhere in this collection.

7 For other discussions of Pat Cadigan's work, notably *Synners* (1991), please see Ritch Calvin's, Patricia Melzer's, and/or Lisa Yaszek's individual contributions to this collection. In addition, although not addressing Pat Cadigan's sockets, Wendy Pearson's contribution explores the role of penetration in cyberpunk.

8 For a reading of *Snow Crash*'s central role in the evolution of post-cyberpunk, see Christopher Kilgore's entry in this collection.

Works Cited

Advantageous. Directed by Jennifer Phang, performances by Jacqueline Kim, James Urbaniak, and Freya Adams, Film Presence/Netflix, 23 June 2015.

Ashby, Madeline: *Company Town*. Tor, 2016.

Badmington, Neil. "Introduction: Approaching Posthumanism." *Posthumanism*, edited by Neil Badmington. Palgrave, 2000, pp. 1–10.

Bostrom, Nick. "Why I Want to be a Posthuman When I Grow Up." *The Transhumanist Reader: Classical and Contemporary Essays on the Science, Technology, and Philosophy of the Human Future*, edited by Max More and Natasha Vita-More. Wiley, 2013, pp. 28–53.

Braidotti, Rosi. *The Posthuman*. Polity Press, 2013.

Bukatman, Scott. "Postcards from the Posthuman Solar System." *Posthumanism*, edited by Neil Badmington. Palgrave, 2000, pp. 98–111.

Cadigan, Pat. *Synners*. Gollancz, 2012.

———. *Fools*. Gollancz, 2013.

Cadora, Karen. "Feminist Cyberpunk." *Beyond Cyberpunk: New Critical Perspectives*, edited by Graham J. Murphy and Sherryl Vint. Routledge, 2010, pp. 157–72.

Clarke, Bruce. "Preface: Literature, Posthumanism, and the Posthuman." *The Cambridge Companion to Literature and the Posthuman*, edited by Bruce Clarke und Manuela Rossini. Cambridge UP, 2016, pp. xi–xxiii.

Foster, Thomas. *The Souls of Cyberfolk: Posthumanism as Vernacular Theory*. U of Minnesota P, 2005.

Foucault, Michel. *The Order of Things: An Archaelogy of the Human Sciences*. Vintage, 1994.

Gane, Nicholas. "When We Have Never Been Human, What Is to Be Done?: An Interview with Donna Haraway." *Theory, Culture & Society*, vol. 23, no. 7–8, 2006, pp. 135–158.

Gibson, William. "Burning Chrome." *Burning Chrome*. HarperCollins, 2003, pp. 179–204.

———. *Neuromancer*. Gollancz, 1984.

Graham, Elaine L. *Representations of the Post/Human: Monsters, Aliens, and Others in Popular Culture*. Rutgers UP, 2002.

Haraway, Donna J. "A Cyborg Manifesto: Science, Technology, and Socialist-Feminism in the Late Twentieth Century." *Simians, Cyborgs, and Women*. Routledge, 1991, pp. 141–81.

———. "Cyborgs to Companion Species. Reconfiguring Kinship in Technoscience." *The Haraway Reader*. Routledge, 2003, pp. 294–320.

———. *Staying with the Trouble: Making Kin in the Chthulucene*. Duke UP, 2016.

Hayles, N. Katherine. *How We Became Posthuman: Virtual Bodies in Cybernetics, Literature, and Informatics*. U of Chicago P, 1999.

Hayles, N. Katherine. "Wrestling with Transhumanism." *Metanexus*, 1 Sep. 2011, www.metanexus. net/h-wrestling-transhumanism/.

Hollinger, Veronica. "Retrofitting Frankenstein." *Beyond Cyberpunk: New Critical Perspectives*, edited by Graham J. Murphy and Sherryl Vint. Routledge, 2010, pp. 191–210.

McCorry, Seán. "Animality." *The Routledge Companion to Cyberpunk Culture*, edited by Anna McFarlane, Graham J. Murphy, and Lars Schmeink. Routledge, 2020, pp. 317–25.

McHale, Brian. "Towards a Poetics of Cyberpunk." *Beyond Cyberpunk: New Critical Perspectives*, edited by Graham J. Murphy and Sherryl Vint. Routledge, 2010, pp. 3–28.

McGurl, Mark: "The Posthuman Comedy." *Critical Inquiry*, vol. 38, no. 3, 2012, pp. 533–553.

Posthumanism(s)

More, Max. "The Philosophy of Transhumanism." *The Transhumanist Reader*, edited by Max More and Natasha Vita-More. John Wiley & Sons, 2013, pp. 3–17.

Moravec, Hans. *Mind Children: The Future of Robot and Human Intelligence*. Harvard UP, 1988.

———. "Pigs in Cyberspace." *The Transhumanist Reader*, edited by Max More and Natasha Vita-More. John Wiley & Sons, 2013, pp. 177–81.

Rucker, Rudy. *The Ware Tetralogy*. Prime, 2010.

Schmeink, Lars. *Biopunk Dystopias. Genetic Engineering, Society and Science Fiction*. Liverpool UP, 2016.

Sorgner, Stefan Lorenz and Robert Ranisch. "Introducing Post- and Transhumanism." *Post-and Transhumanism: An Introduction*, edited by Stefan Lorenz Sorgner and Robert Ranisch. Peter Lang, 2015, pp. 7–27.

Stephenson, Neal. *Snow Crash*. Bantam, 1992.

Sterling, Bruce. "Cyberpunk in the Nineties." *Interzone*, vol. 48, Jun. 1991, 23 May 1998, lib.ru/STER LINGB/ interzone.txt.

———. *Holy Fire*. Bantam, 1996.

———. Preface. *Mirrorshades: The Cyberpunk Anthology*, edited by Bruce Sterling. Ace, 1986, pp. ix–xvi.

———. *Schismatrix*. Ace, 1985.

"The Science in Science Fiction." *Talk of the Nation*, NPR, 30 Nov. 1999. Radio.

Vinge, Vernor. "Technological Singularity." *The Transhumanist Reader*, edited by Max More and Natasha Vita-More. John Wiley & Sons, 2013, pp. 365–375.

Yaszek, Lisa. "Feminist Cyberpunk." *The Routledge Companion to Cyberpunk Culture*, edited by Anna McFarlane, Graham J. Murphy, and Lars Schmeink. Routledge, 2020, pp. 32–40.

34

MARXISM

Hugh Charles O'Connell

The marxist engagement with cyberpunk is long and ongoing. For many marxist critics, the advent of cyberpunk represented a betrayal of science fiction's (sf) utopian and subversive modernist origins. Its obsession with public relations, marketing, and commodities revealed its own status as a fully commodified and overhyped spectacle.[1] Yet for others, its very ambivalence in relation to its hypercommodified worlds and its dystopian extrapolation of the Thatcher–Reagan– Kohl consensus marked it as the definitive mediation of the newly ascendant era of neoliberalism. Rather than trying to reconcile these prescriptive and descriptive positions, this chapter is principally concerned with three overlapping questions: (1) What was the relationship between these positions during the high period of cyberpunk? (2) How does that ambivalent relationship appear today from a longer critical remove? And (3) how can we reconceive this relationship given the now fully ascendant forms of speculative-fictional-digital capital that drive financialization[2] (the derivate, bitcoin, high-frequency trading [HFT]), the global crash of 2008, and the everyday popularization of AI algorithms in everything from Google maps to Twitter bots?

As Benjamin Noys has recently suggested, a return to cyberpunk as the fiction of finance may help in confronting the roots of the 2008 financial crisis and the inability of contemporary fictional forms to address it. This is all the more salient when one considers the similar theoretical and representational crises in marxist theory as diagnosed by Edward LiPuma and Benjamin Lee in *Financial Derivatives and the Globalization of Risk*, in which, they argue, the traditional critical tropes of marxism (the labor theory of value and emphasis on private property, particularly) wither in efficacy in relation to the immateriality of the derivative and the digital circulatory systems of speculative finance. These present crises—in capitalism, theory, and representation— stem from the formative period of speculative finance in the 1980s, a period that cyberpunk captured more than any other literary form. Thus, as Mark Bould contends in relation to William Gibson's *Neuromancer* (1984), cyberpunk "inaugurated the SF of multinational capital and corporate globalization, its depiction of information circulating in cyberspace a potent metaphor for the global circulation of capital" ("Cyberpunk" 220). Therefore, a return to the concepts and conceits of cyberpunk and their afterlife in so many post-cyberpunk fictions of AI, accelerationism, and virtual reality is imperative not only for understanding our present, but for any hopes of a postcapitalist futurity.

To begin, it is first necessary to trace a line of thought that has significant consequences both for the history of marxism and cyberpunk as well as their current relationship: What does it mean to take seriously Jameson's offhand comment that cyberpunk is the literature of postmodernism and thus late capitalism? As Fredric Jameson famously writes in the very first footnote of *Postmodernism;*

Or, The Cultural Logic of Late Capitalism: "This is the place to regret the absence from this book of a chapter on cyberpunk, henceforth, for many of us, the supreme *literary* expression if not of postmodernism, then of late capitalism itself" (419n1). Whatever else we might want to note about this statement, it is important for understanding the history of marxist cyberpunk criticism that we begin with a starting place that immediately annuls itself. In other words, cyberpunk serves as the absent center of the defining marxist analysis of postmodernity, late capitalism, and culture.

Despite not being taken up directly in *Postmodernism*, Jameson did touch on cyberpunk in a round-about way in *The Seeds of Time* and his "Fear and Loathing in Globalization" article on Gibson's *Pattern Recognition* (2003). Writing in the latter, Jameson reaffirms the political aesthetic of Gibson's work in similar ways to the footnote in *Postmodernism*: "In any case, the representational apparatus of Science Fiction, here refined and transistorized in all kinds of new and productive ways, sends back more reliable information about the contemporary world than an exhausted realism (or an exhausted modernism either)" (*Archaeologies* 384). While these references to cyberpunk were largely kernels that found their way into work about other topics, both share a signal concern with cyberpunk's function as something beyond a nominal realism or a modernism in terms of its narrative strategies and ideologies, suggesting that this is ultimately a prerequisite in its capacity to express late capitalism.

If Jameson had initially left cyberpunk largely uncommented upon, many other marxist analyses took it up with exactly this relationship in mind. A full recounting of every marxist or marxist-inspired reading of *Neuromancer*—let alone cyberpunk—could easily constitute its own Routledge companion and is thus beyond the scope of this chapter. Instead, I will briefly highlight a few key contributions by Carl Freedman, Darko Suvin, Tom Moylan, and Sherryl Vint. These critiques hew closely to Jameson's prescription about cyberpunk as the definitive literary expression of late capitalism, with many explicitly couching their critiques in terms developed from Jameson's work on postmodernism. Taken together, they characterize a double negative within marxist criticism of cyberpunk. On one hand, they represent the negative stance of marxist dialectical criticism (looking toward the critical capacity for art to negate the prevailing capitalist neoliberal orthodoxy). On the other, they also represent marxist criticism's negative reaction to cyberpunk exactly for its inability to offer such a critically negative position. Each essay presents its own rich engagement with cyberpunk and should be consulted in its own right; however, for the sake of expediency, I'll highlight the aspects that most strongly resonate across their respective arguments.

For Freedman, despite recognizing the particular importance of *Neuromancer*, there is nothing radically innovative or especially postmodern about cyberpunk as an aesthetic. Instead, drawing on Jamesonian terms, he argues that the oft-celebrated visual aesthetics of cyberpunk are a pastiche of previous forms, adding that "[t]here is indeed a certain sense in which cyberpunk, for all its critical descriptive power, finally resolves into an uncritical conservativism. [… It] thus colludes with reification even while exposing it, and, accordingly, offers us the always comforting conservative assurance that, in counter-Leninist fashion, *nothing* is to be done" (198). Suvin similarly finds cyberpunk's relationship to late capitalism as too compromised and complicit. Echoing Freedman's ambivalence, he famously asks, "[i]n its forte, the integration of agents and action into technosleaze, is cyberpunk the diagnostician of or the parasite on a disease?" (153). It's a question that he ultimately refuses to answer, arguing instead that cyberpunk is too adolescent and thus "untenable à la longue" (154) to proffer a compelling answer. Instead, Suvin suggests that it might be better to just stop talking about cyberpunk as a meaningful category all together, suggesting that the appellation of 'cyberpunk' is little more than a PR tactic that attempts to combine too many "disparate products" under one label (154).

If for Freedman (and to some extent Suvin) the problem with cyberpunk is its transparent affirmation of late capitalist ideals and tendencies, for Moylan it is something more subtly pernicious:

capitalism's recuperation of radical opposition. In regard to Gibson's Sprawl Trilogy (*Neuromancer*; *Count Zero* (1986); *Mona Lisa Overdrive* (1989)), Moylan writes, "[The] anti-utopian drift *within* Gibson's text can be more broadly understood as an example of [...] 'artificial negativity' that supports the status quo by recontaining sources of potential opposition through reification and commodification—thereby removing their *useful* negative power and repackaging it as yet another *exchangeable* commodity" (91). Due to this artificial negativity, through cyberpunk "the knowledge base of the opposition becomes the knowledge base of the system's own refinement" (91).

A similar interest in critical negativity, the hallmark of modernist aesthetics for many marxists, animates Vint's reading of the much lesser-known novel *Red Spider White Web* (1990) by Misha. Vint turns to Misha's novel particularly for the ways that it sidesteps many of the problems associated with canonical cyberpunk. Not only was it written by a woman with Native American heritage, but rather than the usual protagonists' "faux estrangement from power" it "focus[es] on characters materially and economically excluded from society" (96). In her critique, Vint takes up one of the most significant meta-narratives of cyberpunk fiction from the marxist position: the status of the artwork in late capitalism, or as Nicholas Brown puts it in the title of his 2013 essay, "The Work of Art in the Age of its Real Subsumption Under Capital." Moreover, Vint provides one of the most compelling critiques from the marxist-negative critical traditions, combining Jameson's work on postmodernism with the Frankfurt School's work on mass culture. Writing of the novel's putative redemption of the work of art through the artist-protagonist Kumo, Vint argues:

> Kumo's resistance to the conflation of art with commodities and the erosion of the authentic social role of the artist is thus rewarded by the novel's conclusion, although rewarded in a way that leaves [the novel's larger social structures] untransformed [...]. Kumo herself merely transcends this limited reality, escaping to an unspecified other world in which art is valued, a conclusion not unlike the transcendence into cyberspace that characterizes much cyberpunk. (106–07)

Thus, not even critical cyberpunk, it would appear, can be *critical* in the marxist sense.

While not the whole of marxist cyberpunk criticism, these four essays largely represent and form the canonical position, focusing on the privileging of individual transcendence over systemic negation. And after such an equally withering and convincing critique, one could easily be forgiven for wondering what could possibly be left for marxism and cyberpunk today. Indeed, after moving through a similar critique of Gibson's *Pattern Recognition*, Vint suggests that there may be no more vocation for cyberpunk at all: "Perhaps the reason we no longer have cyberpunk fiction is because we have entered the cyberpunk future, and [we lack the] sufficient critical distance to reflect upon it through the medium of art" (113).

Yet, as these critiques of cyberpunk evince, cyberpunk rarely, if ever, achieved such a radical critical distance. Instead, what these critiques have done, in their myriad ways, is to disabuse us of the purportedly radical political cyberpunk project as well as its related pretense toward transcendence, now revealing that transcendence as complicit with the operations of late capitalism. This is a long way around to return us to where we began: Cyberpunk is "the supreme literary *expression* if not of postmodernism, then of late capitalism itself" (Jameson, *Postmodernism*, 419n1; emphasis altered). However, rather than a simple return, it is a dialectical return that allows us to begin again, renewed, from this starting point. In other words, what this body of criticism has done is to illustrate that cyberpunk is axiomatically not about the transcendence or negation of capitalism, nor could it ever have been. The loss of critical distance and the flattening of relative autonomy by commodification are two hallmarks of postmodernism. Or as Brown argues, "With the collapse of an autonomous field, with the real subsumption of aesthetic labor under capital, the possibility

Marxism

of something bearing a family resemblance to modernism abruptly disappears" (n.p.). Hence, any sense of transcending the system of late capitalism as Vint avers with her critique of Misha and Gibson is always bound to a (re)affirmation of capitalist ideology, offering imaginary solutions that validate capitalism's own operative ideology. Now, we can turn to cyberpunk for the way that it reveals the dominant hallmarks of the late capitalist mode of production: finance and an accelerated process of real subsumption. Moreover, we can interrogate its totalizing novums as the technological innovations and capacities that are employed toward the furthering and maintenance of these two twinned aspects of global late capitalism.

As Scott Bukatman and others note, working from the same aspects of Ernest Mandel's periodization of capitalist modes of production that informed Jameson's in *Postmodernism*, cyberpunk comes into being as economic productivity is hitting a downturn, a point of a dialectical crisis between the mode and forces of production. As Bukatman, following Mandel, describes it: As new power technologies come into being, there is an initial uptick in economic productivity before an inevitable decline (3–4). For Giovanni Arrighi, this is the point where finance comes to have a significant role in temporarily keeping profits up, and thus why Arrighi refers to the period of ascendant finance as an autumnal period of waning, a point before the system breaks down and its center migrates. Yet as many marxist critics, especially Accelerationists, Salvage critics, and Autonomists note, rather than waning we seem to be in a potentially new period where financialization is in a prolonged state and the processes of real subsumption—in which "all relations of production and consumption, and all forms of life" not only those traditionally associated with labor are brought under the sway of capital (Shaviro, "Symposium" 384)—continue unabated. One way of understanding the emergence of cyberpunk as the supreme literary expression of late capitalism, then, is the way that it mediates rather than negates this situation: As the capitalist world system comes into a truly global form, it resolves such crises in the global north by displacing large aspects of production to cheaper labor markets and compensates through a series of new spatial fixes, including the digital realm of finance and the real subsumption of the body/psyche (another way of understanding Jameson's notion of the reduction to the body and the colonization of the unconscious by capital).

We can now re-posit Istvan Csicsery-Ronay's argument that cyberpunk is implosive and bodily invasive (272–73) as the corollary to real subsumption, where the body becomes another site of capitalist accumulation. As Steven Shaviro puts it, "[a]ll aspects of peoples' lives, all over the world, are increasingly subject to the vagaries of financial speculation, which extracts 'value' from them at every turn" ("Symposium" 384). This requires that "[e]verything must be measured, and made commensurable, through the mediation of some sort of 'universal equivalent': money or information" (Shaviro, *No* 29). Framing these contemporary processes of real subsumption in a way that illustrates the subject's confluence with the informational, digital, and financial in cyberpunk, Franco 'Bifo' Berardi argues that "the whole psychosphere of the human being becomes subject to the movement of capital, now operating at digital speeds" (5). Cyberpunk's prevalence for nodes and other bodily modifications that directly connect and submit human consciousness to the decentered spaces and speed of the net stand as an obvious example, as does digital transcendence. Hence, we might think of Pat Cadigan's "Pretty Boy Crossover" (1986) as a mediation of real subsumption's bodily invasions by digitalizing the subject and submitting it to the info-flows of dematerialized capitalist circulation. In other words, under the regime of real subsumption it is not just labor's profits that are captured by the capitalist process; rather, all aspects of life are transformed either directly into a means for surplus profit or indirectly toward the production and extraction of information that is then to be leveraged toward accumulating profit.

From this vantage point, we can argue that cyberpunk is not really about the "interface of technology with the human subject" (Bukatman 8), offering "new technological modes of 'being in the world'" (McCaffery qtd. in Bukatman 8). Instead, cyberpunk technology is a vector and conduit, and cyberpunk is about the subject's ceaseless invasion by real subsumption under this new stage of financial capital. Jameson comes tantalizing close to suggesting as much in his own belated reading of *Neuromancer* in *The Ancients and the Postmoderns*. Here, he reads Case as caught between the virtual-simulated realms of both finance/cyberspace and the real subsumption of the fully capitalized body of simstim, a position which, we have to remember, is dictated by a corporate-conscious AI residing in a Swiss banking computer planning its own transcendence from even these most-minimal of human restraints in the form of the Singularity. And as Bould reminds us, cyberpunk's notion of the Singularity is perhaps the greatest fantasy of capital: pretending as if human labor never existed. "The singularity has already happened," Bould contends, "and is constantly happening, as humans, 'already *not*-human,' are torn apart by capital, our selves reduced to those abstractions (labor-power, consumption-power) which it needs to operate and perpetuate" ("Why" 133).[3] This is the defining ideological fantasy critiqued by one of the most significant post-cyberpunk films, Alex Rivera's *Sleep Dealer* (2008), where Mexican laborers in Tijuana cybernetically 'jack in' to the net in order to control construction robots in San Francisco: "This is the American Dream, we give the United States what they've always wanted… all the work—without the [migrant] workers."

What I want to suggest, then, is that rather than disappear, cyberpunk's defining narrative traits have been extended and disseminated. And here I think we need to attend to Derridean readings of this word, not forgetting the masculinist logics of reproduction via the seminal and semen, combined with the masculinist aspects of cyberpunk as critiqued by Nicola Nixon, Jenny Wolmark, and Karen Cadora, as well as the patriarchal-penetrating aspects of neoliberal financialization and cyberpunk's role, however unintentional, as a mediator and disseminator of the latter.[4] In this light, we can see cyberpunk as part of the general DNA of late capitalist culture. Having broken the spell of cyberpunk as an avant-garde, as an artwork in the modernist sense, as semi-autonomous, it is free and we are free to see it disseminated into the mainstream (with all the commodified and reified overtones that this should suggest) not as a style, but instead, in Thomas Foster's well-known phrase, as a "sea change into a more generalized cultural formation" (xiv), or better yet, simply as *the* cultural dominant of everyday life under the techno-invasive modes of real subsumption and finance.

For marxist criticism, this requires attending to the invisible, penetrating aspects of its techno-capitalist colonization, or what we could think of as the role of cybertechnologies and novums in the role of real of subsumption. As Bukatman wrote in the early days of cyberpunk criticism:

> The newly proliferating electronic technologies of the Information Age are invisible, circulating outside of the human experience of space and time. That invisibility makes them less susceptible to representation and thus comprehension at the same time as the technological contours of existence become more difficult to ignore—and all of this is occurring during a lengthy period of diminished economic expectation. (2)

The phrase "diminished economic expectation" is striking here from a marxist perspective as cyberpunk is commensurate not only with prolonged periods of production's stagnation and recession, but also the rapid growth in income inequality due to the accelerated redistribution of income and the resulting rapid growth in millionaires and billionaires by the advent of finance capitalism. In other words, the 'invisible' aspects of technology have to be coupled with their analog of fictive, dematerialized capital and the intensified modes of capitalist colonization of the subject.

From this perspective, it now seems as if bitcoin is the *raison d'être* that retroactively justifies the acceleration of digital communications technology with the amount of computer processing dedicated to it. One only needs to consider the many references to the uselessness of cash in Gibson's Sprawl works and of "casing mankind's extended electronic nervous system" and the siphoning

Marxism

of ones and zeros that accounts for a heist in Gibson's 1982 short story "Burning Chrome" (549). Today, it appears as if 1980s cyberpunk fiction was merely a dry run for the news that Japanese crypto-currency Coincheck has been 'burned' to the amount of 530 million dollars. Or as Berardi writes:

> the huge achievement of the technophile, pro-market digerati of *Wired* Futurism was their understanding of a new economic trend based on the creation of virtual enterprises in the field of communication, finance, and personal services. In this magazine, the liberation soul merged with the market theology of neoliberal economists. The illusion of an infinite economic expansion in the field of virtual production nurtured the Utopia of the long boom and the ideology of the economy. (54)

Invisibility, then, has become one of the key strategies of overcoming the contradiction between the forces and modes of production; that is, invisibility could here be understood as the digitalizing-spatial fix for capital. Digitalization serves as a platform for real subsumption, whether the extraction of data and commodified information from the Internet of things or our own unpaid labor in providing information/data/labor for Facebook, YouTube, etc. or even our web-browsing as means for bitcoin farming.

This suggests the need for a renewed form of marxist criticism, drawing from across the negative, Salvage, utopian, Accelerationist, and Autonomist traditions (and I fully recognize the multiple contradictions here). We are now reading not for the reclaiming of the artwork, or the new human subject, but instead turning our attention to so many cyberpunk novums—which we now need to read as financial-capitalist novums of real subsumption—that, to repurpose another Jamesonian statement, are cast off like so many sparks from a cyberpunk comet into late capitalist culture more generally. This means we can locate its semes across a host of cyberpunk, post-cyberpunk, and seemingly non-cyberpunk sources. Let nearly any episode of *Black Mirror* stand as an exemplar text.

Although not cyberpunk in the fictional sf manner, Adam Greenfield's work on the influence of contemporary cyberpunk technology—cellphones, cryptocurrency, networked surveillance tools, algorithmic machine learning—provides an illustrative example. Describing a contemporary 2017 evening in Paris as a cyberpunkian "year zero," he writes "[i]n this city, everyone with a mobile phone reveals their location [...]. Every transaction in the bistros and shops and cafés generates a trail, just as every bus and car and Vélib bicycle throws its own data shadow. Even the joggers in the Bois du Boulgone cast a constant, incrementing tally of miles logged and calories burned" (2). What we find here is that the techno-dystopian landscapes of early cyberpunk are, as the subtitle to his book puts it, now simply "everyday life." What Greenfield surveys for us, then, is the landscape of post-cyberpunk as the fulfillment and actualization of the earlier cyberpunk imaginary.

If early cyberpunk was in thrall of its new technological, computing wonders, creating elaborate metaphors and conjuring a pyrotechnic style to evoke the phenomenological experience and acceleration of the Internet age, then as so much of the earlier criticism reveals, it also had no idea what to do with them. We may think of Case's "no shit" response in *Neuromancer*'s revelation of the new post-Singularity AI as emblematic in this regard. It has been later post-cyberpunk (and by this I not only mean the temporal but also the general dissemination of cyberpunk themes as the cultural dominant) that has often been able to better focus narratives around these novums. As Darren Jorgensen asserts in his historicization of post-cyberpunk, "[i]f in the 1980s such terms as the virtual and cyberspace looked to a future that had not yet come about, by the 1990s these words had acquired a certain materiality. It is amidst this materialisation of the future that postcyberpunk intervenes" (229).

This dissemination of cyberpunk as a cultural dominant and its transformation to post-cyberpunk has also opened up the possibility of critiquing the political and aesthetic limits of its reliance on digital transcendence. Hence, it's only with the negation of cyberpunk's affirmation that we can begin to perceive of something like even a weak utopianism, the possibility of possibility. In many ways, as many marxist critics have noted, this has been the case for post-cyberpunk and especially African and postcolonial cyberpunk. For example, Bould argues that the recent spate of Afrocyberpunk films, including *Africa Paradis* (Amoussou 2006), *Bedwin Hacker* (El Fani 2003), *Les Saignantes* (Bekolo 2005), as well as the better-known works by Neill Blomkamp, sidestep traditional cyberpunk's reliance on personal transcendence. "They depict transgressions of national and corporeal borders," Bould contends, "and envision resistance to corporate and state power by pitting the tactical against the strategic [...and] the molecular against the molar" ("Afrocyberpunk" 214). Moreover, in terms of the first three films listed above, their "conditions of production tend to result in films that demonstrate [...] the flipside of a cyberpunk world centered on the flows of capital" (218).

Similarly, Jillana Enteen argues that Nalo Hopkinson's *Midnight Robber* (2000) 'hacks' cyberpunk tropes in order to "render visible current socioeconomic inequities, suggest [an] alternative formulation of the relationship between humans and technology, and increase the cultural repository of ideas that inspire technological and social development" (263). As such, "Hopkinson employs hacking to denaturalize cyberpunk conventions; she also delineates technologies that expose biases inherent in its present formulation" (270). In these examples, African and postcolonial post-cyberpunk works to denaturalize the technologies of real subsumption and the new domineering presence of global finance by hacking the narrative conventions as well as the technologies used to promulgate these features of everyday late capitalist life.

Rather than a 'hacking' or a revision of cyberpunk tropes, Eric D. Smith argues that the South African author Lauren Beukes instead radicalizes cyberpunk by accelerating its tendencies.

> Beukes' cyberpunk intervenes [in Csicsery-Ronay's critique of cyberpunk as the reduction to thrill] by exposing the ideological underpinnings of this nervous ecstasy from a perspective decidedly alternative to that of the still-globalizing first world. She does so, however, not through simple or spectacular opposition to the cyberpunk aesthetic but through the acceleration of the form to its terminal velocity, through appropriating its penchant for cynicism, stereotype, and kinesis and carrying these to their perdurable limits. (161)

Moreover, the novel eschews the transcendent aspects of cyberspace for a focus on the somatic consequences of real subsumption. Instead of figuring cyberspace as an area to be entered, leaving the body behind, we see how cyberspace instead colonizes the everyday world and the body. Here, the cellphone becomes the key object of cyberpunk real subsumption as an appendage to the body, keeping it permanently yoked to the data sphere as well as acting as the conduit through which we provide free content and labor to so many sites (YouTube, Facebook, Instagram). It is the ubiquity of the cellphone that hides these processes of real subsumption, thereby normalizing them not as labor but as culture (and perhaps this is the best example of the strong Jamesonian thesis of culture as now fully commodified—culture here in Raymond Williams' sense of a total way of life).

LiPuma and Lee make the key point that the subjective freedoms of connectivity (access to information and communications technology) "are always self-annulling at another and higher level" (46–47). These are the same "conditions of encompassment and domination by circulatory capital and the infrastructure of the metropole generally" (47). As Shaviro reminds us in *Connected*: "I do not find myself in the network, having fallen or been thrown. Rather, I exist for the network. I am predestined to it. From the moment I get connected, I am irreversibly bound to its protocols and its finality" (29). As the medium for extending capitalist real subsumption, information-connective-technologies illustrate how advertising does not simply operate as brainwashing (although it does promote desire). Instead, it colonizes our bodies by transforming them into means of information collection and advertising: On the one hand for the neoliberal maintenance and marketing of our own brands, and on the other hand for others in the clothes that we wear, the products that we purchase and then Instagram ourselves enjoying (the mere fact that I can use 'Instagram' as a verb in this sentence demonstrates this invasive fact).

All of this is to suggest, then, that neuromancy was always fiscalmancy, to use Ian McDonald's term for the inscrutable dematerialized aspects of speculative finance. If neuromancy suggests the porousness of the human-machine interface redolent of earlier cyberpunk celebrations—a potentially limitless interaction with the decentered aspects of cyberspace—fiscalmancy reminds us that the "spatially decentered, weakly temporalized" (Vivian Sobchack, qtd. in Bukatman 105) open-ended totality of cyberspace has a central driving force: that of capital. One task of the marxist critic is to determine how such cyberpunk novums work to substantiate the financial-capitalist present and further real subsumption, and how they could be repurposed toward utopian goals, as Kim Stanley Robinson does with debt, derivatives and HFTs in *New York 2140*, or Jameson with Wal-Mart distribution techniques (*Valences* 420–25).

Notes

1 For a brief discussion of cyberpunk's roots as a commodity surrounded by hype, please see Graham J. Murphy's contribution to this collection.
2 Financialization encompasses a variety of schemes where profit, rather than through commodity-production, is now principally generated by financial speculation, including the trade in financial instruments such as the derivatives market, the servicing of debt, rent-seeking, and the monetization of information, among others (cf. Marazzi).
3 For an analysis of post-cyberpunk and the Singularity as filtered through Charles Stross's *Accelerando* (2005), please see Gerry Canavan's contribution to this collection.
4 For in-depth analyses of penetration and the masculinist heteronormativity associated with cyberpunk, and the subsequent narrative responses, see Wendy Gay Pearson's, Patricia Melzer's, and Lisa Yaszek's contributions to this collection.

Works Cited

Arrighi, Giovanni. *The Long Twentieth Century: Money, Power and the Origins of Our Times*, New and updated edition. Verso, 2010.

Berardi, Franco Bifo. *After the Future*, edited by Gary Genosko and Nicholas Thoburn, translated by Arianna Bove, et al. AK Press, 2011.

Bould, Mark. "Afrocyberpunk Cinema: The Postcolony Finds its Own Use for Things." *Cyberpunk and Visual Culture*, edited by Graham J. Murphy and Lars Schmeink. Routledge, 2018, pp. 213–34.

———. "Cyberpunk." *A Companion to Science Fiction*, edited by David Seed. Blackwell, 2005, pp. 217–31.

———. "Why Neo Flies, and Why He Shouldn't: The Critique of Cyberpunk in Gwyneth Jones's *Escape Plans* and M. John Harrison's *Signs of Life*." *Beyond Cyberpunk: New Critical Perspectives*, edited by Graham J. Murphy and Sherryl Vint. Routledge, 2010, pp. 116–34.

Brown, Nicholas. "The Work of Art in the Age of Real Subsumption." *Nonsite*, 13 Mar. 2012, nonsite.org/editorial/the-work-of-art-in-the-age-of-its-real-subsumption-under-capital.

Bukatman, Scott. *Terminal Identity: The Virtual Subject in Postmodern Science Fiction*. Duke UP, 1993.

Csicsery-Ronay, Istvan. "Cyberpunk and Neuromanticism." *Mississippi Review*, vol. 16, no. 2/3, 1988, pp. 266–78.

Enteen, Jillana. "'On the Receiving End of the Colonization': Nalo Hopkinson's Nansi Web." *Science Fiction Studies*, vol. 34, no. 2, 2007, pp. 262–82.

Foster, Thomas. *The Souls of Cyberfolk: Posthumanism as Vernacular Theory*. Minnesota UP, 2005.

Freedman, Carl. *Critical Theory and Science Fiction*. Wesleyan UP, 2000.

Gibson, William. "Burning Chrome." *The Wesleyan Anthology of Science Fiction*, edited by Arthur Evans, et al. Wesleyan UP, 2010, pp. 547–65.

Greenfield, Adam. *Radical Technologies: The Design of Everyday Life*. Verso, 2017.

Jameson, Fredric. *Archaeologies of the Future: The Desire Called Utopia and Other Science Fictions*. Verso, 2007.

———. *Postmodernism, or, The Cultural Logic of Late Capitalism*. Duke UP, 2001.

———. *Valences of the Dialectic*. Verso, 2009.

Jorgenson, Darren. "What and Why was Postcyberpunk? Greg Egan and Bruce Sterling in the 1990s." *EnterText*, vol. 6, no. 3, 2007, pp. 229–44.

LiPuma, Edward and Benjamin Lee. *Financial Derivatives and the Globalization of Risk*. Public Planet Books, Duke UP, 2004.

Marazzi, Christian. *The Violence of Financial Capitalism*, translated by Kristina Lebedeva and Jason Francis McGimsey. Semiotext(e), 2011.

Moylan, Tom. "Global Economy, Local Texts: Utopian/Dystopian Tension in William Gibson's Cyberpunk Trilogy." *Beyond Cyberpunk: New Critical Perspectives*, edited by Graham J. Murphy and Sherryl Vint. Routledge, 2010, pp. 81–94.

Noyes, Benjamin. "Toxic Money and Collapsing Value: The Postmodern Novel and the Aesthetics of Financial Crisis." *Academia*, www.academia.edu/9691269/Toxic_Money_and_Collapsing_Values_The_Postmodern_Novel_and_the_Aesthetics_of_Financial_Crisis.

Shaviro, Steven. *Connected: Or What it Means to Live in the Network Society*. Minnesota UP, 2003.

———. *No Speed Limit: Three Essays on Accelerationism*. Minnesota UP, 2015.

———. "Symposium." *Science Fiction Studies*, vol. 39, no. 3, 2013, pp. 374–84.

Suvin, Darko. "On William Gibson and Cyberpunk SF." *Defined by a Hollow: Essays on Utopia, Science Fiction and Political Epistemology*. Peter Lang, 2010, pp. 137–56.

Vint, Sherryl. "'The Mainstream Finds Its Own Uses for Things': Cyberpunk and Commodification." *Beyond Cyberpunk: New Critical Perspectives*, edited by Graham J. Murphy and Sherryl Vint. Routledge, 2010, pp. 95–115.

35

CYBORG FEMINISM

Patricia Melzer

When cyberpunk as a literary mode and self-proclaimed "Movement" appeared in the 1980s, popularized by William Gibson's *Neuromancer* (1984), the quintessential cyberpunk novel, its conservative gender and sexual politics quickly placed it in a relationship with feminist theories of embodiment and technology, including Donna J. Haraway's "Manifesto for cyborgs: science technology, and socialist feminism in the 1980s," a highly influential and groundbreaking essay published less than a year after *Neuromancer*.[1] Briefly, Haraway's feminist cyborg, the foundation of cyborg feminism, is a product of technoscience—global capitalism's commodification of (bio) technologies—and thus relies on and redefines the relationship between humans and technology. The core of these new human-technology relationships is the recognition that there is no whole identity and/or subjectivity, distinguishing the cyborg from an anti-technology, pro-nature feminism that tries to reclaim the feminine as powerful (the goddess) and to declare 'woman' a universal category. Put another way: the cyborg and the goddess are metaphors for differing investments in identities within feminist theories: the cyborg represents a political identity that is partial and cannot escape a relation to technology and its violent history, while the goddess appropriates the feminine from patriarchal ideology into a powerful female identity of resistance (Graham 428). Cyborg feminism *en masse* also acknowledges the destruction history has witnessed and views the only possibility for change in rejecting dualisms, including that of gender, upon which this destruction was based. The posthuman cyborg therefore resonates with Gilles Deleuze and Felix Guattari's work on "assemblages," a conceptualizing of bodies as parts of always changing constellations in which entities meet, interact, and shape each other; as the composition shifts, the unique assemblage dissolves and/or solidifies. The metaphor of the feminist cyborg as an assemblage of technoscience means the immediate patterns of relation—i.e., the shifting patterns of organic and non-organic matter—ensure the body's relations to itself (affect) and others as part of the assemblage defines the encounter and ensures an emphasis on potentiality, on never-fixed possibilities and becomings. In other words, the denaturalization of stable bodies and thus identities, a denaturalizing embodied by cyborg assemblages, offers moments of disruption with potentially liberating new constellations based in partiality.

Meanwhile, the explorations that dominate cyberpunk's original narratives, namely of the interface of human and technology, and of virtual reality as an emerging social space, have become a central part of science fiction (sf), except cyberpunk's visions of computer-generated realities and technology-enhanced bodies have been superseded by the impact of digital technology on our lives, in particular the Internet and its facilitation of social media, online commerce, location tracking, and entertainment downloading and streaming. Foreign-sounding terms introduced in cyberpunk in the 1980s that claimed to signify radical social transformation—cyberspace, console cowboys, Net, jacked-in, and mirrorshades—have been replaced with daily vocabulary generated from experiences in digital culture—Internet, smart phones and mobile devices, social media, dot. com, coding, GPS, search engine, and #hashtag. While this new vocabulary may have introduced new ways of organizing within social movements, at the same time it has proven the world to be as resistant to change as it is ready to embrace it. Specifically, gender and sexuality are social forces that inform much of the technologically mediated connections, constellations, and encounters we experience daily all over the globe. Therefore, feminist cultural and literary critics, especially those engaging with the feminist possibilities of posthumanism, have analyzed the functioning of our cybercultures in order to gauge its impact on gendered subjectivity and its potential dangers. In this vein, the rise of a distinctly feminist cyberpunk that largely began in the early 1990s opened or broadened cyberpunk fiction to ask how gendered power shifts between non-essential bodies and how desire and sexual relations are transformed by technology, questions early, largely masculinist, cyberpunk was simply ill-equipped to address.

35.1 Feminist Critiques of Masculinist Cyberpunk

As Thomas Foster points out, cultural critics are drawn to cyberpunk because of its "representation of the body politics of late capital" (xi); this also explains its draw for feminist cultural critics. At the core of cyberpunk's innovations lies its break with earlier sf's conceptualizations of the embodied self as a constant in relation to the strangeness around it, in the argument that "physical alterations in 'the' human body, such as cyborg prostheses or direct brain-computer interfaces, also transform the supposed 'essence' of humanity, 'our' minds or souls" (Foster xi). Therein lies cyberpunk's promise of a posthuman future facilitated through the interface of human and technology. And therein also lies its colossal failure to deliver this future; for example, Nicola Nixon writes that "[f]or all its stylish allusions to popular culture—to punk rock, to designer drugs, to cult cinema, to street slang and computer-hacker (counter?) culture—cyberpunk fiction is, in the end, not radical at all. Its slickness and apparent subversiveness conceal a complicity with '80s conservatism" (231), or Karen Cadora remarks that "[m]asculinist cyberpunk is very much a boys' club" and "closer examinations of the movement have revealed that its politics are anything but revolutionary" (357). In sum, early cyberpunk has a tendency to 'plug-in' conservative, occasionally reactionary, heteronormative gender and sexual notions into a narrative frame that explores intersections of technology and embodiment.

The typical setting of cyberpunk's original narratives are terrestrial or extraterrestrial dystopian environments, in mostly urban spaces. People populating these worlds try to navigate capitalist commerce which facilitates technological enhancements of commodified human bodies through various means, including crime. The two prominent themes of cyberpunk set the stage for its theoretical premises (and explorations) around the interface of humans and technology, tropes that also inform discourse on posthuman existence more broadly. The first one is the invasion of the human body by machines (cyborg), which decenters the human body and problematizes the notion of an essential self. The second theme is the penetration of computer technology into the human mind through virtual reality (cyberspace) that in turn decenters humanist notions of an unproblematic real and introduces a new basis for human experiences. Significantly, this decentering is often countered in the Cartesian, deeply humanist separation of mind *versus* body that can be found in some of the transhuman scenarios articulated in posthumanist discourse, such as computer researcher Hans Moravec's notion of 'downloading' the brain's information and running it as software (Foster 5).[2] Of particular concern for N. Katherine Hayles is the abstraction of the material that views biology, including the body, as being nothing but informational patterns and that privileges information over materiality. Instead, Hayles insists that "the body is the net result of thousands of years of sedimented evolutionary history, and it is naïve to think that this history does not affect human behaviors at every level of thought and action" (284). A truly posthuman existence would then not seek to deny the connections between the abstract and the material but instead be defined by assemblages, the fluid and partial relationships between the human and the nonhuman (both 'nature' and 'machines'); or, as Hayles writes, "a dynamic partnership between humans and intelligent machines replaces the liberal humanist subject's manifest destiny to dominate and control nature" (288).

Feminist theorists insist on the presence of the body as both an epistemological and ontological basis for any theories of (post)human existence in which "embodiment replaces a body seen as [merely] a support system for the mind" (Hayles 288); consequently, feminist theories point to the gendered, racialized, and classed constructions of the body throughout history which cyberpunk narratives of the posthuman subject are unable to escape, despite their best attempts. In other words, the at-times fetishized role of technology in determining human existence—including its desires and pains—that dominates cyberpunk is continuously disrupted, troubled, and undermined by the refusal of the material to disappear. Heather Hicks contextualizes cyberpunk's romanticizing of the mind/body split as complicit with a larger historical and philosophical western tradition. In other words, the body haunts the narratives of cyberpunk and forms a necessary contrast to masculinist fantasies of digital disembodiment, much as gendered and racialized bodies have formed the necessary contrast within the mind/body split dominating western philosophy.

The denial of corporeality in early cyberpunk narratives takes place in conjunction with an inherent investment in liberal individualism that contradicts cyberpunk's gesture toward posthuman existence. Cultural anxieties induced by the postmodern fragmenting of the self underlie these narratives in their attempt to negotiate Man's interface with technology. These anxieties convey a humanist conservatism that holds on to a liberal autonomous subject: "The ecstatic dissolution of the body," Scott Bukatman writes, "is counterbalanced by the recuperative strategies of narrative and generic structure within which the subject maintains his autonomy and power ('her' autonomy and power is another question)" (244). As a result of an initial cyberpunk literature "written for the most part by a small number of white, middle-class men" (Hollinger 207), the protagonist of masculinist cyberpunk is often a male hustler, freelance specialist, aging punk, or console cowboy navigating the material realities of the urban sprawl and, quite often, the abstract realm of infinite cyberspace. Individual autonomy of the male protagonist, however, contrasts with the existence of female figures mediated by technological enhancements or indistinguishable from digital software. These two spaces of the 'material' and 'immaterial' mirror an inherent tension within cyberpunk around the body's role in constituting a postmodern subjectivity, an "oscillation [...] between a biological-determinist view of the body and a turn to technological and cybernetic means in order to escape such determination" (Foster 11). This oscillation is "gender-coded" (Foster 11) in that the female body seems inescapably essential, both through its materiality and the historical significations of said materiality (such as maternity and constituting the object of desire within a heterosexual economy). In contrast, the ultimate goal of the masculine (anti)hero is often to escape the confinement of the 'meat' (i.e., the body), which he attempts to varying degrees typically using street-level technology.

Again, this binary between human and technology that cyberpunk ostensibly sets out to complicate has been problematized in feminist critiques of science and epistemology which seek to uncover the ways in which narratives of science historically have conceptualized nature and technology as feminine and culture, and mastery of technology and science, as masculine.[3] The racialized, gendered, and classed characters of these dualisms are deeply humanist in their separation of Man from nature and in turn align people of color, women, nature, and technology as the 'unanimated' separate from Man's ability to reason. The conceptual link of the female body to the realm of the intellectually unanimated, a worldview that includes both animals and machines, places it in a troubled relationship to the image of the cyborg and to the imagined space of disembodied virtual reality, the two pillars upon which cyberpunk rests. Consequently, cyberpunk's masculinized myth of the transcended body is frequently rendered through its juxtaposition with obviously feminized techno-bodies and techno-spaces. The results are the depiction of an eroticized feminine (cyber)technology mastered by a male protagonist, on the one hand, and female figures arrested in a sexualized, essential relationship to their (techno)bodies or conflated with a feminized cyberspace, on the other.

One paradigmatic sexualized techno-space is *Neuromancer*'s cyberspatial matrix, clearly coded as a feminine-gendered space that the heterosexual male cowboy "jacks-in" to penetrate the "hymenal membrane" of computer security (Nixon 198). The Net appears as an electronic equivalent to the female body—both in its penetrability by the male protagonist and in its "polluted" state that has turned the matrix, a cultural construct associated with a "masculine world of logic and scientific wizardry" (Nixon 198), into a virus-infected, potentially lethal place that needs to be conquered. Thus, cyberpunk's virtual spaces are related through an erotic imagery in which entering the matrix is like entering a female body, and the male climax within a woman's body serves as experiential basis for describing immersion in technology, such as when Case in *Neuromancer* has sex with Molly: "his orgasm flar[ed] blue in a timeless space, a vastness like a matrix" (Gibson 33). This feminization of cyberspace, mastered by a fraternal network of 'cowboys,' is necessary to avoid it becoming a homoerotic space, instead of facilitating homoerotic bonds that might transcend the heterosexual economy of desire, despite the fact that, as Wendy Pearson argues in this collection, there is a queer undercurrent to Gibson's cyberspatial matrix that problematizes a straight reading of the text. Tellingly, masculinist cyberpunk tries its best to evoke the mastering of a feminized technology through sexually violent rhetoric that, based on their technological competence, posits the male protagonists "as metaphoric rapists" (Nixon 202).

Female cyborgs abound in cyberpunk, whose physical modifications are aimed at enhanced combat skills or at male sexual pleasure, the former sometimes paid for by the latter; as a result, both manifestations keep the female body confined by a heterosexual economy of desire and to patriarchal social relations. Generally, as Carlen Lavigne notes, main female characters in masculinist cyberpunk, when they appear at all, "tended to be somewhat flat, trapped within the narratives that caused them to be either objectified [...], passive [...], or punished for venturing outside the bounds of domesticity" (37). The most prominent prototype of the hyper-sexualized, "ass-kicking techno-babes" (Gillis 9) is Gibson's Molly Millions, whose sex work as a 'meat puppet' paid for the cyborg enhancements that make her so formidable in "Johnny Mnemonic" (1981), *Neuromancer*, and *Mona Lisa Overdrive* (1988). Gibson clearly domesticates Molly in *Mona Lisa Overdrive* when, as Sally Shears, she is positioned in relation to a young female child she effectively mothers. Or, consider Sarah, the assassin of Walter John Williams's *Hardwired* (1986), who has a cybernetic 'snake,' nicknamed The Weasel, hidden deep in her throat. She provides a literal kiss of death to her victims as The Weasel emerges from Sarah's mouth, worms its way down the target's throat and, finding the stomach, rips it into pieces before seeking out the heart, quickly followed by Sarah retracting it. While the figure of the deadly assassin seemingly undermines traditional notions of femininity, these few exceptions like Molly or Sarah ultimately are recuperated into a heterosexual, conservative status quo (Cadora 363). While female cyborgs populating feminist sf of the 1970s (such as Joanna Russ's Jael from *The Female Man* (1975)) are political metaphors for resistance to patriarchal dominance, their revised versions within masculinist cyberpunk become sexist metaphors of sexual domination, "effectively depoliticized and sapped of any revolutionary energy" (Nixon 194). Masculinist cyberpunk therefore relies on a traditionally gendered humanist ideology that reflects the white, middle-class male paranoia of the Reagan-era more than radical visions of (feminist) posthumanity and represents escapist fantasies about disembodiment. Or, as Elaine Graham writes, "[g]iven the traditional association of women with the bodily, the affective and the realm of nature, cyberculture looks like another attempt by patriarchy to deny these aspects of experience in favour of the virtual, the abstract and the disembodied" (430).

35.2 Feminist Cyberfiction since the 1990s

While much of feminist sf prior to cyberpunk focuses on aspects other than hard science and technology (Melzer 7–9), a number of cyberpunk precursor narratives thematize the ways in which technology affects people's lives in gendered and sexualized ways. Two of the best-known feminist texts are James Tiptree, Jr.'s "The Girl Who Was Plugged In" (1973), which critically analyzes technology's implications for the postmodern female body, and Joanna Russ's *The Female Man* (1975), featuring Jael, whose physical modifications have transformed her into a deadly assassin in the war of the sexes and who, in part, inspired Gibson's depiction of Molly Millions. These precursors to cyberpunk reflect on the interface of technology and the human, but were largely ignored by male cyberpunk authors as well as by cultural critics hailing the techno-sexiness of the mode, such as when Bruce Sterling selected all male writers as "ancestral cyberpunks," the "fathers" of the movement (x).

As Nixon points out, much feminist sf published simultaneously with classic cyberpunk challenges the straight, white, male subject of humanism by employing gender relations as a main analytical framework (192), such as Zoe Fairbairns's *Benefits* (1979), Suzette Haden Elgin's *Native Tongue* (1984) and *The Judas Rose* (1987), Connie Willis's "All My Darling Daughters" (1984), Margaret Atwood's *The Handmaid's Tale* (1985), and Pamela Sargent's *The Shore of Women* (1986). Accordingly, since the beginning of the 1990s, cyberpunk's initial conservatism has been challenged in "feminist cyberpunk" (Cadora) or "women's cyberfiction" (Lavigne). These "feminist cyberfictions"—i.e., Emma Bull's *Bone Dance* (1991), Marge Piercy's *He, She and It* (1991), Maureen McHugh's *China Mountain Zhang* (1992), Laura J. Mixon's *Glass Houses* (1992) and *Proxies* (1998), Mary Rosenblum's *Chimera* (1993), Melissa Scott's *Trouble and Her Friends* (1994), Nicola Griffith's *Slow River* (1995), Edith Forbes's *Exit to Reality* (1997), and Anne Harris's *Accidental Creatures* (1998), to name a few titles—explore the destabilization of the essential dualism of reason *versus* nature propelled by technoscience and focus on feminist content while acknowledging the expansion of the mode's conventions; namely, feminist cyberfiction's topics include environmental degradation, issues of reproduction and reproductive rights, racism, and global capitalism, all with an eye toward challenging the gendered ideological framing of mastery of technology as masculine, technology itself as feminine. Through its use of strong female (cyborg) figures, and with reconfigurations through and within virtual reality, feminist cyberfiction isn't "trying to make cyberpunk 'more feminist,' [instead] these writers place cybertechnology into the context of other technologies [and] the cyber-savvy protagonist's tale into a political and social context" (Melzer 179).

The refusal of the body (i.e., the material more broadly, including animals, nature, etc.) to disappear in humans' relationship to technology is central to feminist cyberfiction, and these narratives are contemporaneous with cultural theories influenced by cyborg feminism[4] that place resistance at the conflicting and imploding intersections of the cultural and the natural in technoscience. Among other things, these theories place feminist cyberfiction in the broader context of what Anne Balsamo refers to as "technologies of the gendered body" and treat it as a space where the relationship of body and technology is explored in ways that "offer a vision of post-human existence where 'technology' and the 'human' are understood in contiguous rather than oppositional terms" ("Feminism" 684). Instead of conceptualizing technology as a medium to erase or overwrite the body, Balsamo argues, innovative feminist texts, such as Pat Cadigan's oeuvre,[5] offer "alternative vision[s] of technological embodiment that [are] consistent with a gendered history of technology: where technology isn't the means of escape from or transcendence of the body, but rather the means of communication and connection with other bodies" ("Feminism" 703). Here it is not the riddance of the 'meat' that forms the underlying, self-denying, ultimately unfulfilled desire of the narrative. Instead, the goal becomes a mediation of embodiment and technology that refuses to treat technology based interactions as abstractions.

Patricia Melzer

Feminist cyberpunk criticism recognizes the potential of cyberpunk to expand the concept of the feminist subject to include intersectional identities. In other words, feminist cyberfiction departs from the oppositional figuration of the material and virtual that dominates traditional cyberpunk, a framework that inherently privileges patriarchal definitions of technoscience. Instead, we see socially responsible hacking, individuals in intimate relationships with trusted partners, and a central focus on the importance of communal social relationships. Technology is depicted as linking the physical body to virtual/digital spaces that form new realms of experiences. Importantly, as Foster argues, the "telepresence" (130) within feminist cyberfiction locates the body as a point of reference for any presence in cyberspace; the goal is very rarely, if at all, to escape the body completely. Cyborg bodies and the presence of AIs (often embodied by the cyborg/android) display complex and shifting racialized, gendered, and classed identities while transgender characters, paired with cybernetic body modifications, create metaphors for gender queerness, as do gender non-binary-coded AIs. Embodiment, in particular the female body, is thereby central to the narratives; however, even in virtual reality where the person's digital avatar relies on some form of visual representation of the self, these characters represent partial subjects that inhabit a technological space, a fragmentation of the self that allows an engagement with the assemblages that make up our relationship to technology: "This [erosion of boundaries] signifies a complete deconstruction of the body. People are made of bits and pieces—human, animal, mechanical, and mystical pieces that loosely coalesce into a self" (Cadora 368). Subjectivity is therefore envisioned as unstable and constantly shifting, as developing from a symbiotic relationship between technology and the material body—a relationship that offers new, posthuman assemblages of becoming.

In addition to emphasizing the importance of community and personal intimacies in the characters' navigations of a global capitalism, feminist cyberfiction also reworks the central theme of reproduction by crossing boundaries of virtuality and embodiment while maintaining a classic feminist concern with women's bodies' relationship to the politics and economics of reproduction. Technology enables cloned children of lesbian characters, cyborg children, and reproductive technologies that replace narratives of heteronormative families. In *He, She and It*, for example, Piercy explores various manifestations of maternal roles that thematize the familiar conflict of family and career (e.g., single motherhood) and—specific to technoscience—capitalist exploitations of new reproductive technologies and mothering artificial children, in this case a male cyborg. It is often in the context of reproduction that non-normative sexualities and queer identities are foregrounded and conventional boundaries between self and other are undermined, such as with the mutant chemical-vat dwellers, Lilim, and their daughters in Harris's *Accidental Creatures*, and replication (not reproduction) in Rosenblum's *Chimera*, where a clone daughter defines her relationship to her (lesbian) mother as "Mother. Sister. Self" (307). At the same time, these narratives don't lose sight of the familiar specter of patriarchal, capitalist technoscience in prostitution and surrogate motherhood as women's options to escape or at least manage poverty (Cadora 364).

Unlike the binary of feminine technology and masculine hacker that masculinist cyberpunk establishes and that shores up a heteronormative narrative framework, in feminist cyberfiction experiences are depicted to destabilize heterosexual relations and offer queer sexualities and non-binary gender constructions (Foster 123–26). Technology does not simply enable a gender-reversal by bestowing masculine tendencies onto female bodies (such as in Molly Millions' or Sarah's respective assassin cyborg bodies) but new identifications that go beyond a humanist gender ideology. For example, in Mixon's *Glass Houses*, Ruby's waldos are gendered and she assumes the gender of whichever machine she remote-enters, making a "rethinking of cyborg gender" possible by negotiating not between the gender binary of male and female, "but between human and machine" (Leblanc 75); similarly, the cyborg/clone protagonist Sparrow in Bull's *Bone Dance* is gender fluid. The destabilizing effects of cybertechnology on naturalized, essential binary gender categories are complemented by the almost routine presence of queer/lesbian characters in feminist cyberfiction,

296

Cyborg Feminism

such as *Glass Houses'* Ruby and her girlfriend, *Slow River's* Lore and Spanner, *Trouble and Her Friends'* Trouble and Cerise, and *Exit to Reality's* Lydian and Merle, where the female protagonists' queer sexualities form the center of the story and are instrumental to plot resolution.

Finally, the late capitalist worlds that form the default setting in cyberpunk consist of environmental destruction and depletion of natural resources.[6] Masculinist cyberpunk displays a general indifference toward that destruction, apparently reveling in the pollution of urban sprawls or fancifully suggesting, as Gerry Canavan argues, that "[i]n virtual space, with no resource consumption or excess pollution to worry about, we can all be as rich as we want for as long as we want (or so the fantasy goes)" (9). On the other hand, much of feminist cyberfiction thematizes technology's role in both driving and preventing environmental destruction, such as in Griffith's *Slow River* in which bio-ecotechnology has become a major capitalist market. Ecological preservation becomes a utopian element in these narratives that is worth pursuing and/or mourning, echoing the long tradition of women's activism around environmentalism. At the same time, these narratives present technological interactions with what has been constructed as 'the natural' as potentially offering alternative, posthuman ways of existing, ultimately de-stabilizing the binary of 'natural' and 'human,' such as in Harris's *Accidental Creatures*, where toxic waste becomes the habitat of a new mutant posthuman species.

35.3 Conclusion

Feminist cyberfiction explores how cyberculture and its multiple cyber-realms highlight the fluid, unstable elements that make up people's lives. Today, the connections, networks, and temporal instabilities of digital culture and biotechnology reflect the constantly changing environmental assemblages of identities in the material world and both the adverse and beneficiary effects they have. The various ways in which technology facilitates posthuman interactions creates a familiar pattern of the diverse and contradictory ways in which feminism has manifested before cyberculture's digital communications: Women hackers who use coding skills in their social justice activism or to write gender non-binary and/or anti-racist games exist next to the sexist flaming wars that break out against women's presence within that hacker culture; queer, feminist-identified, and women-centered sex sites exist within an Internet that drives a major mainstream, heterosexist misogynist porn culture; social media hosts radical queer anti-capitalist feminist activists next to white-centered, liberal faux feminism that is not actively feminist (colloquially known as 'Tumblr-feminism'), or black women organizers in the Black Lives Matter movement and immigration-rights activists are maintained by the same servers that enable white supremacist women to disseminate their political views. Profit-driven technoscience has heterosexual couples from the global North travel to the South where they can afford a surrogate to carry their child conceived via donor-sperm, while queer and/or transgender couples in western nations use reproductive technologies to form non-normative families. Technoscience demands a framework that confronts gender exploitation and oppression in ways that account for these complex and changing formations. In this vein, feminist cyberfiction integrates elements that have been erased in definitions of feminist subjects: the various pleasures of the human/machine interface, the unpredictability of how technology gets applied, and the coupling of matter(s) of various origin(s). Instead of locating a stable identity of the feminist posthuman subject on a 'grid' of system intersections, the most innovative and radical feminist cyberfiction incorporates that which lies outside the 'grid' into our feminist engagement with cyberpunk culture—"the forces that make subject formation tenuous, if not impossible or even undesirable" (Puar 49).

Feminist cyberfiction's emphasis on an unstable, constantly changing human/technology interface is echoed in the term 'hacking' as one of the most important developments in western cyberculture for feminist theories today. 'Hacking' here indicates the mastery of a specialized technology that extends beyond computer coding or digital technologies, such as the Queer, Trans★ and Feminist Village at the 2015 international Chaos Communication Congress in Germany or in an issue of .*dpi Feminist Journal of Art and Digital Culture* on feminist hacktivism.[7] In this sense, hacking links cyberculture's digital and bio-tech focus to other technologies that can be used to shape daily lives, such as metal works, weather prediction, and food processing and growing. The concept of hacking as using technology for something creative and innovative undermines the privileging of digital technology as the exceptional technology that dominates posthuman discourse. It also links the 'natural' with the 'technological' in the green-focused technologies of alternative energy, food growing practices, and nutrition that are of concern in much of goddess-related, anti-technology feminist activism. Above all, it points to the malleable nature of technology, to the ways in which it can be learned, appropriated, and changed to adjust to the continuously new encounters, connections, and networks that assemble (post)human experiences and that foreground the instability of bodies and the identities they host. The gender-binary and its default constellation of women *versus* men has structured much of western feminist thought, and to an extent this gender-binary still underlies an intersectional analysis (which uses multiple but still distinct categories, including transgender) and is challenged in our increasingly cyborgian environment of transgressed boundaries and partiality.

In closing, Haraway's cyborg and the promiscuous alliances generated by its problematic becoming-through-technology seem more relevant to feminist theories than ever. The cyborg allows for a view of technology as a tool for dissolving identity formations based in binary ideologies (man/woman, human/animal, organic/non-organic, etc.), both in conceptual and material forms. While the cyborg questions liberal notions of individual agency and autonomy, cyberpunk culture—like any culture—can produce figures of competence and resilience that allow the envisioning of effective political resistance, such as the female and/or queer hacker. It is their partiality, that is, their asset, the non-stable assemblages that shift the ground upon which the world works. The cyborg's power as political myth fails if we do not recognize that certain bodies experience the world very much in categories of control enforced by Foucauldian institutions of discipline and punish, and for whom references to their identities—despite their instability—remain a key tool of resistance. The particular manifestations of technologized existences that our cybercultures produce call for a complex understanding of how our bodies are produced, how our intersectional identities are in fact assembled, and how they find representation in the figures stepping off the pages of feminist cyberfiction.

Notes

1 Haraway's essay is arguably more commonly known by its reprinted title "A Cyborg Manifesto: Science, Technology, and Socialist-Feminism in the Late Twentieth Century," which forms chapter eight in *Simians, Cyborgs, and Women: The Reinvention of Nature*.

2 In her contribution to this collection, Julia Grillmayr offers a close reading of Hans Moravec's transhumanist vision of posthumanism.

3 For added details, see Wajcman's *Feminism Confronts Technology* and *Technofeminism* as one potential starting point into this larger area of feminist inquiry.

4 Examples include Anne Balsamo's *Technologies of the Gendered Body: Reading Cyborg Women*, Jennifer Terry and Melodie Calvert's *Processed Lives: Gender and Technology in Everyday Life*, and Constance Penley and Andrew Ross's edited collection *Technoculture*.

5 For a discussion of Pat Cadigan's work, notably *Synners* (1991), please see Ritch Calvin's, Julia Grillmayr's, and Lisa Yaszek's contributions to this collection.

6 For a discussion of cyberpunk and the Anthropocene, see Veronica Hollinger's contribution to this collection.

7 The issue is available at the following URL: http://digicult.it/news/hacktivism-the-art-of-practicing-life-and-computer-hacking-for-feminist-activism/.

Works Cited

Balsamo, Anne. "Feminism for the Incurably Informed." *South Atlantic Quarterly*, vol. 92, no. 4, 1993, pp. 680–712.

———. *Technologies of the Gendered Body: Reading Cyborg Women*. Duke UP, 1996.

Bukatman, Scott. *Terminal Identity: The Virtual Subject in Postmodern Science Fiction*. Duke UP, 1993.

Cadora, Karen. "Feminist Cyberpunk." *Science Fiction Studies*, vol. 22, no. 3, 1995, pp. 357–72.

Canavan, Gerry. "If This Goes On." *Green Planets: Ecology and Science Fiction*, edited by Gerry Canavan and Kim Stanley Robinson. Wesleyan UP, 2014, pp. 1–21.

Foster, Thomas. *The Souls of Cyberfolk: Postmodernisms as Vernacular Theory*. U of Minnesota P, 2005.

Gibson, William. *Neuromancer*. Ace, 1984.

Gillis, Stacy. "The (Post)Feminist-Politics of Cyberpunk." *Gothic Studies*, vol. 9, no. 2, 2007, pp. 7–19.

Graham, Elaine. "Cyborgs or Goddesses? Becoming Divine in a Cyberfeminist Age." *Information, Communication & Society*, vol. 2, no. 4, 1999, pp. 419–38.

Haraway, Donna J. "A Cyborg Manifesto: Science, Technology, and Socialist-Feminism in the Late Twentieth Century." *Simians, Cyborgs, and Women: The Reinvention of Nature*. Routledge, 1991, pp. 149–81.

Hayles, N. Katherine. *How We Became Posthuman: Virtual Bodies in Cybernetics, Literature, and Informatics*. U of Chicago P, 1999.

Hicks, Heather. "'Whatever it is that she's since become': Writing Bodies of Text and Bodies of Women in James Tiptree, Jr.'s 'The Girl who was Plugged in' and William Gibson's 'The Winter Market.'" *Contemporary Literature*, vol. 37, no. 1, 1996, pp. 62–93.

Hollinger, Veronica. "Cybernetic Deconstructions: Cyberpunk and Postmodernism." *Storming the Reality Studio: A Casebook of Cyberpunk and Postmodern Fiction*, edited by Larry McCafferey. Duke UP, 1991, pp. 203–18.

Lavigne, Carlen. *Cyberpunk Women, Feminism and Science Fiction*. McFarland, 2013.

Leblanc, Lauraine. "Razor girls: Genre and gender in Cyberpunk fiction." *Women and Language*, vol. 20, no. 1, 1997, pp. 71–76.

Melzer, Patricia. *Alien Constructions: Science Fiction and Feminist Thought*. U of Texas P, 2006.

Nixon, Nicola. "Cyberpunk: Preparing the Ground for Revolution or Keeping the Boys Satisfied?" *Science Fiction Studies*, vol. 19, no. 2, 1992, pp. 219–35.

Penley, Constance and Andrew Ross, eds. *Technoculture*. U of Minnesota P, 1991.

Puar, Jasbir. "'I would rather be a Cyborg than a Goddess': Becoming-Intersectional in Assemblage Theory." *philoSOPHIA*, vol. 2, no. 1, 2012, pp. 49–66.

Sterling, Bruce. Preface. *Mirrorshades: The Cyberpunk Anthology*, edited by Bruce Sterling. Ace, 1986, pp. ix–xvi.

Terry, Jennifer and Melodie Calvert, eds. *Processed Lives: Gender and Technology in Everyday Life*. Routledge, 1997.

36

QUEER THEORY

Wendy Gay Pearson

One of the (many) criticisms levied against cyberpunk when it first emerged in its 1980s heyday was its reinforcement of "heteronormative conventions of gender, sexuality, and power" (Kelly 151). James Patrick Kelly adds that "there was a huge disparity between the number of strong male characters and the number of strong female characters, and gay and lesbian characters were all but invisible" (151). Indeed, Veronica Hollinger noted the similarities between cyberpunk's sometimes hopeful postmodern and anti-humanist monsters (cyborgs, artificial intelligences (AIs), clones, and human personalities uploaded to the net) and feminist science fiction's (sf) own postmodern anti-humanist emphasis on rethinking human subjectivity outside of the always gendered domains of modernist thought. Despite this, Hollinger argues that feminist sf "demonstrate[s] a very different approach to the construction/deconstruction of the subject than is evident in the technologically-influenced post-humanism of most cyberpunk fiction" (33). As both Lisa Yaszek and Patricia Melzer remark upon in their respective contributions to this collection, feminist concerns would not become of paramount interest to literary cyberpunk until a 1990s wave of feminist cyberpunk started changing the parameters of this mode of fiction and its exploration of the posthuman challenges to subjectivity.

The same could arguably be said regarding cyberpunk and the queering of heteronormativity, although even in William Gibson's *Neuromancer* (1984), the paradigmatic case of literary cyberpunk, there exists a queer undercurrent that reveals multiple complexities in the novel's deployment of sexuality and gender. For example, at the end of the novel, the protagonist Case returns to his hotel room to find that Molly, his partner in cybercrime and erstwhile lover, has left him. He has only a few things she has given him, including a shuriken, a weapon that has never made Case equal to Molly's own destructive capacity as a razorgirl with her retractable claws. Case packs everything else, but throws the shuriken across the room and into the screen on the wall, which reacts by flickering to life "as though it were trying to rid itself of something that caused it pain" (270). In attempting to externalize his own pain at the end of the relationship, Case uses the very weapon that was his first gift from Molly to inflict it on the wall screen. While this might merely be symbolic of Case's retreat into the violent reflex of toxic masculinity, the wall screen mirrors Molly's own mirrorshaded eyes, which are implanted screens of her own.

This is not the first time Molly's eyes have been the target of an assault, symbolic or otherwise. Earlier in the novel, the psychopathic Peter Riviera subjects her to the sight of a holographic performance in which he uses her razorblades in a sexual fantasy that is both narcissistic and sado-masochistic; this display is certainly intended to cause her emotional pain, given that she earned the money for her razorblades by working as a meat puppet, a prostitute who 'sleeps' through the

Queer Theory

acts her body performs. In his reading of *Neuromancer*, Graham J. Murphy astutely comments that "this techno-Narcissus can see himself only as a reflection of the mirrored lenses covering her eyes or as a production of his own holographic projections. This ocular frustration is played out when [...] Riviera, yearning to see the colour of her eyes, smashes one of her mirrorshades" ("Stray Penetration" 125). Murphy draws on Brian Attebery's explanation of the role of women's eyes as being, like their bodies, subject to the male gaze to elucidate the nature of Molly's mirrorshades in refusing and returning that gaze. Both the facts of the mirrorshades and Riviera's violent reaction to them are functions of Molly's queering of heteropatriarchal gender roles. Murphy notes that, because "Molly's eyes are always completely hidden behind her mirrorshades," the symbols of "pulp-era sf femininity have been sacrificed for the masculinized realms of enhanced vision and an extended visual range that allow her to actively perceive and engage the world beyond any kind of biologically restricted [...] spectrum" ("Stray Penetration" 125). There is something significant about the fact that the mirrorshades in *Neuromancer* belong to Molly. Bruce Sterling calls mirrorshades "a Movement token" that "prevent the forces of normalcy from realizing that one is crazed and probably dangerous," making them "a kind of literary badge" (xi). His list of mirrorshade wearers—"the sun-staring visionary, the biker, the rocker, the policeman, and similar outlaws"—was likely read in 1986 as definitionally male (and straight and white). Yet in cyberpunk's paradigmatic text, the mirrorshades belong to the woman and incite men to (factual or symbolic) violence against her. As a result, Case's use of Molly's gift to shatter and apparently inflict pain upon the wall screen, mirrored with Riviera's earlier attempt to physically violate Molly through a double assault on her sight, shows that conventional heterosexual masculinity is frustrated in Gibson's novel. "I never even found out what color her eyes were," Case bemoans. "She never showed me" (268).

Despite being a 'female-presenting' character, Molly certainly fulfills male adolescent fantasies, both in her 'meat puppet' incarnation as the fully controllable female body and in her interactions throughout the novel, where her agency teeters on the verge of crossing over into some more androgynous, more masculine selfhood. This is queer enough, and, as a result, Case never entirely stops relating to Molly with some measure of uncertainty or paranoia. Julius 'Julie' Deane, however, is another case entirely. As Tyler Curtain notes, Deane is the only obviously queer character in the novel, one whose queerness can be recognized by all readers without the need for any queer theory-informed reading skills: "all pink and silver as to skin and hair" (133) and always immaculately dressed, Deane "serves as the ground that structures [...] Case's own unkempt, disheveled sallowness and tense paranoia" (134). Curtain also notes, however, that "Deane ultimately triggers what by this point we shouldn't hesitate to call homosexual panic, anger and hatred in Case" (134). Given the association of male homosexuality with fellatio, it is not unimportant that Case kills a Deane simulation by shooting him in the mouth.

Case's violent dispatch of the Deane simulation speaks to Curtain's assessment of 'homosexual panic' and console cowboys who jack into, or penetrate, the cyberspatial matrix while simultaneously avoiding any technologies that can penetrate them, such as Intrusions Countermeasures Electronics (ICE), virus programs that burrow into their craniums and cause brain death, or simstim, the simulated stimulation that allows people to 'ride' one another, or the meat puppetry of Molly's past. As Murphy notes, heterosexuality is both dependent upon and produces binary genders: "penetration is exactly what enables heteronormativity" ("Stray Penetration" 123). This is Judith Butler's argument, where she notes that, even at the level of pronouns, the stability of gender depends on a "heterosexual *matrix*," where 'he' can only penetrate and 'she' can only be penetrated. All other options not only destroy heteronormative views of what constitutes sex, but also uproot the genders that heterosexuality produces. Murphy extends this reading to a discussion of the ways in which "cyberspace itself can be seen as a queer site. Although it has repeatedly been figured as a female 'body' undergoing heteronormative conquest by masculine console cowboys, it can also be read as possessing its own penetrative capabilities that can disrupt gender-coding and potentially crash the gender(ed) matrix" ("Stray Penetration" 123). Of course, the very notion of a matrix invokes both the maternal and the matriarchal and, as Murphy notes, there is a repeated queerness in the image of cyberspace itself as both penetrable and penetrating—and, since cyber-jockeys and cowboys are nearly always men, that penetration is always already queer.

While a queer (or, as Murphy remarks, a 'proto-queer') reading of *Neuromancer* problematizes the otherwise rampant heteronormativity commonly associated with early literary cyberpunk, a feminist wave of cyberpunk starting in the early 1990s allowed a greater diversity of authors to "explore sex and gender identities outside the heteronormative matrix" and "appropriate the classic cyberpunk image of the economically-marginalized computer hacker to give voice to the experience of sexually-marginalized groups, casting their hacker protagonists as both economic and sexual outlaws" (Yaszek 35–6). For example, in Melissa Scott's *Trouble and Her Friends* (1994), the protagonists, Trouble and her partner Cerise, are broken up, both as lovers and as 'crackers' (hackers who crack firewalls), by changes to the laws regulating the nets. As their work becomes illegal, the focus of scrutiny falls on those who access the nets via the implanted brainworm rather than through a traditional interface. In other words, the brainworm allows its users to experience virtuality as another form of embodiment—virtual sex produces analogue stimulation, cyberspace can be felt and smelled, it has color and texture, and so forth. In spite of the dangers of having circuitry implanted directly into the brain, being wired provides the impression of direct, unmediated access to virtual reality, where the brain interprets data visually as landscape, architecture, people, etc. In *Trouble and Her Friends*, the simplistic distinction between the mind-controlling access to the virtual and the 'meat' trapped in the real does not apply and further exemplifies Hollinger's point that "the virtual component of the socially apprehensible citizen is not a disembodied thinking thing, but rather a different way of conceptualizing a relationship to the human body" (40).

An important consequence of reconceptualizing a relationship to the human body is the lack of a direct link between one's online and offline identities; in other words, there is no guarantee that someone who presents as female in cyberspace will identify as female in the real world. In *Trouble and her Friends*, the possibilities for gender and sex play in cyberspace are exemplified by Cerise's encounter with Silk, who presents as a young woman and lures Cerise into virtual sex. Silk turns out to be a teenage boy named James Tilsen and, learning of this, Cerise thinks, "[t]here was no point in being embarrassed; sex and gender confusion was one of the hazards of the nets, something a few people enjoyed exploiting while most of the net tried to minimize the inevitable mistakes. Even so, she felt a brief flash of something between annoyance and shame: bad enough to be hustled, she thought, but by a boy?" (282–83).

While Scott's depiction of the potential for sex and gender confusion is not quite as triumphal as Allucquère Rosanne Stone's declaration that "[i]n cyberspace the transgendered body is the natural body" (180), it nevertheless exemplifies Thomas Foster's argument that

> [v]irtual technologies also tend to make it much more difficult than it used to be to impose a one-to-one relationship between a single body and a single discursive identity, or, in Stone's terms to warrant [...] social identity in a physical body, and it therefore becomes more difficult to limit discursive identities to one per body, or by extension to limit genders and sexual orientations to one per sexed body. (123)

Foster goes one step further to argue LGB people are relatively invisible, compared to women and people of color, but, in providing what he calls a "spectacularized gayness" (129), cyberspace in *Trouble and Her Friends* functions not only "as a privileged gay performance space, a space where 'the transgendered body is the natural body,'" but also as "a kind of closet or escape valve that confines gay performance to cyberspace only" (129). At the same time, however, Foster seems to miss the point that the decoupling of corporeal identities and cyberselves means the 'spectacularized gayness' of cyberspace is, in fact, available to everybody, not just to LGB people. The white, male hackers whom Foster theorizes as repulsed by the crackers' ability to use the brainworm and the body itself to interact with computers have just as much access to this gay spectacle as anyone else, particularly given the anonymity of so many denizens of the net. There is also a conflation here of gender and sexuality in the relation Foster creates between the 'transgendered body' and cyberspace as a gay performance space. While sexuality cannot, as we understand it, work without some relationship to gender (neither hetero- nor homosexuality make sense as terms unless one has a pre-existing notion of binary genders), it is not gender. Silk's assumption of a female virtual body is only questionably an act of transgenderism, insofar as we link the latter with questions of gender identity. There seems little question that Silk identifies as male, no matter what role s/he plays on the net.

Carlen Lavigne notes that, in *Trouble and Her Friends*, cyberspace "offers escape from prejudice and political disempowerment rather than a white bourgeois fantasy" (155–56), but the narrative details somewhat belie this assessment. After all, social homophobia and hatred of the brainworm create a hostile environment for many crackers in the novel, both offline and online. Trouble observes that "it was almost always the underclasses, the women, the people of color, the gay people, the ones who were already stigmatized as being vulnerable, available, trapped by the body, who took the risk of the wire" (128). Similarly, it is difficult to reconcile Lavigne's claim about cyberspace offering an escape from white bourgeois fantasy when Trouble and Cerise, in their final online confrontation with a powerful hacker called the Mayor, must listen to all-too-common invective: "*You're nobody, just another half-competent bitch queer who thinks she's good because she has a brainworm. You haven't earned what you have, you haven't worked for it the way the rest of us have, the real crackers, you just had it handed to you direct-to-brain*" (323, italics in original).

Commenting generally upon heterosexual feminist cyberpunk that often presents us with futures in which same-sex unions are accepted without remark, Lavigne writes that "rebel lesbian texts present protagonists who continue to exist on society's fringe, where their unions are not and never have been state-sanctioned" (155). Lavigne's explanation for this lies mainly in queer political objections to assimilationist politics, particularly the focus on marriage equality. However, it seems to me that the representation of queerness as socially unacceptable, if not actually illegal, may have more to do with the constraints of cyberpunk itself; namely, at the time that Scott (as well as fellow lesbian cyberpunks Lyda Morehouse, Edith Forbes, and Raphael Carter)[1] was writing, same-sex marriage had yet to be legalized in the U.S. It was only in 2003 that the U.S. Supreme Court struck down the patchwork of sodomy laws that made homosexuality illegal in 14 of 50 states. There were grounds for optimism around the normalization of sexually dissident practices and identities, so the outlaw status of cyberpunk's protagonists was in many ways ideal for queer/lesbian cyberpunk's own heroes. Furthermore, the inability to tell if someone's virtual gender reflects their 'real' gender identity, much less if it is tied to some sort of biological reality, should have also made cyberpunk a haven for trans sf writers. Yet, despite claims about "spectacularized gayness" (Foster 129), there remains more queer-identified than trans-identified cyberpunk writing, suggesting there is still a long way to go for cyberpunk to catch up to the quotidian realities of everyday life.[2] At the same time, novels like *Trouble and Her Friends* successfully destabilize notions of gender identity even as their protagonists appear to embrace more conventionally gendered identities as lesbians.

Behind Trouble and Cerise's identifications as queers/lesbians, *Trouble and Her Friends* also queers cyberspace in ways not dissimilar to *Neuromancer*. First off, to cite Edmond Chang, "cyberspace is queer" (75). Or, if not inherently queer, it is queered by the trope of penetration. It is thus not only in the gender-destabilizing actions of characters like Silk/Tilsen, but in the very architecture of the penetrative brainworm technology and the net itself that gender is questioned and transformed. Scott's characters have agency in relation to their gender performance that Case does not, since he lacks self-awareness of what makes or what disavows his masculinity. To quote Murphy again, "[i]n both analogue and digital realms, Cerise is a walking resistance to femininity, her visual subversiveness in analogue reality bolstered by the choice of her one-dimensional avatar in digital realms" ("Penetrating" 46). The avatar Cerise sports is an icon fashioned after a "comic-book woman, all tits and hips and Barbie-doll waist [...] exactly like a comic book, so that the shape is paper thin, absolutely flat from certain angles" (147). The Mayor, however, either doesn't get the critique or gets it all too well as he symbolically rewrites Cerise's cartoon-like avatar as "something close to human" (171). Forced to play by the Mayor's rules, Cerise replaces the "close to human" avatar with "an alabaster woman, austerely thin, draped in black and touched with the color that is her name" (Scott 136). Still "close to human," but refusing the heterosexual stereotypicality of "tits and hips and Barbie-doll waist" the Mayor would prefer on a three-dimensional model, Cerise's new avatar retains a sense of gender play that, as Murphy writes, "better suits her own sense of identity" ("Penetrating" 49). Gender therefore becomes a battleground in Trouble and Cerise's fight with the Mayor for control of the net; however, as much as the Mayor may wish to create a 'straight' (and largely white) cyberspace, he lacks the power to normalize Cerise. In the final showdown, which the Mayor stages in a simulation of the Wild West, Cerise and Trouble amuse themselves by donning gunfighter garb, a form of cross-dressing that suits both the mood and the moment while revealing the artificiality of the Mayor's vision of cyberspace. Cyberspace, in Trouble and Her Friends, cannot be un-queered, no matter how much legislation or the anxieties of the (cis male) old guard try to re-norm it. At the end of the novel, Seahaven, the Mayor's former online fiefdom now administered by Trouble and her friends, has escaped what one might describe as heteronormative American exceptionalism and is operating under globalized conventions that recognize the value of the brainworm and its reciprocally penetrative abilities.

Kelley Eskridge's Solitaire (2002) and its Australian film adaptation OtherLife (Lucas 2017), co-written by Eskridge, provide interesting companions to both Neuromancer and Trouble and Her Friends. Solitaire's protagonist Jackal, whose non-net or analogue name is Ren Segura, is the Hope of Ko. Ko is a major global corporation in a world working toward a united government called Earth Congress. The Hopes are children—"thousands scattered around the planet who had been born in the first second of the first attempt to unify the world" (3)—who have been raised to take their place in the new world government. Jackal, mere months before she reaches adulthood at 23 and heads off to her new role, discovers that Ko conspired with her parents to alter her records when her birth missed "the first second of the first attempt to unify the world" (3) by minutes. She is then accused of a terrorist murder that kills hundreds, including most of Jackal's Ko cohort. In order to avoid the embarrassment and uncertainty of a trial in which their 'fixing' of her birth time might come to light, Ko threatens Jackal's parents and convinces her to plead guilty. As a result, Jackal is sentenced to 40 years in maximum security. This sentence is shortened to eight years when Jackal agrees to participate in an experimental Virtual Confinement (VC) program in which the prisoner's experience of time is slowed, so that Jackal's eight years pass by in ten months. VC is, by necessity, also solitary confinement. Jackal's experience of it is both crazy-making and empowering, in part because the software used for VC is a malign version of the virtual reality program Jackal was helping develop for Ko. Jackal initially attempts to survive emotionally by erasing her past life, particularly her lover, Snow; however, she survives by learning to rewrite the code of the VC program so that it releases her (virtually) into an empty Ko headquarters (located on an island, also named Ko), where she can swim, ride her bike, read her books—do everything except engage with people.

OtherLife is very different from its source material: Ren Amira (Jessica De Gouw) is motivated by a diving accident that has landed her brother in a coma. Convinced that some people have recovered from vegetative states by effectively re-writing their brains (re-living differently the experience that injured them), Ren sets out to rescue her brother by creating alternative realities

Queer Theory

that people can enter, primarily for vacations. Ren's motivation is all about family as it is conceived in heteronormative culture, including her hospitalized brother and her grieving father. *OtherLife* therefore contrasts *Solitaire*'s expansive vision of family which includes Jackal's partner, Snow, her friends, including other solos (people who've survived VC solitary confinement), and all the people who make up her new post-Ko familial web. With an exceptionally difficult relationship with her mother and a rather weaker one with her father, Jackal's real family is her chosen, definitely queer, family. Indeed, the positive resolution of the novel (unlike the film adaptation) sees Jackal reinventing herself through a commitment to maintaining her family and building a new community among the solos.

Both of Eskridge's versions are more corporeal than either Gibson's or Scott's work. While Case had limited synesthetic feedback when online and Trouble and Cerise could experience cyberspace fully synesthetically, what they sensed was obviously not the 'real' world and there still remains an ontological separation, albeit weak at times, between corporeal and simulated realities. In *Solitaire* and *OtherLife*, however, Jackal's virtual prison cell, her virtual Ko, and Amira's recuperative virtual realities are indistinguishable from the 'real' thing—they engage all of the senses, including touch and the sense of time. This is particularly pronounced when we compare *Solitaire* to *Neuromancer* and *Trouble and Her Friends*. For Case, the body is 'meat,' a reality he would rather transcend in the brilliance of the cyberworld, while neither Trouble nor Cerise wishes to escape the body but, instead, online simulations run parallel to corporeality; however, Jackal, if anything, would rather escape her mind, since her imprisonment is almost wholly mental, as is the mental instability and outright craziness the prisoners experience through continued isolation and later when aftershocks send them momentarily back into the prisons from which they've supposedly been released. This, of course, is Jackal's queer triumph—by editing the VC code, she creates the empty Ko island as an escape from what should have been a prison cell. Effectively, Jackal queers VC and also the larger Ko program of which VC is simply one (albeit morally questionable) commercial offshoot.

Unlike *OtherLife*, *Solitaire* foregrounds the relationship between two women, even though Jackal's incarceration means Snow is absent from a significant section of the book; nevertheless, *Solitaire* aligns itself in many ways with *Trouble and Her Friends*. Both texts depict intensely pair-bonded relationships between women who, while temporarily torn apart by intransigent political regimes and less-than-benevolent corporations, reach the end of their cyberquest very much together. In *Trouble and Her Friends*, the illegality and social disapproval of lesbian and gay relationships mirrors the situation of the brainworm; in *Solitaire*, there's no societal pressure on Jackal to have a heterosexual relationship. In fact, Jackal engages in various forms of queer kinship throughout the novel: Her central affiliations at the start of the novel are with her familial web, rather than her biological family, and her passions after her virtual incarceration merge her love for Snow, who hunts her down and rejoins her, with her newfound sense of community among the solos.

Finally, both *Trouble and Her Friends* and *Solitaire* raise a comparable question: What constitutes queer kinship? Or, as Butler asks in the very title of her article, "Is Kinship Always Already Heterosexual?" Of course, Butler's article was published in 2002, before Canada, much less the U.S., legalized same-sex marriage. Nevertheless, Butler's questions about the consequences of the turn to marriage and its possible inhibiting effects on other forms of kinship arrangements remain trenchant: "what happens to the radical project of articulating and supporting the proliferation of sexual practices outside of marriage and the obligations of kinship? Does the turn to the state signal the end of a radical sexual culture?" (17). Marriage is obviously not on the books for Trouble and Cerise, whose sexual identities are as illegal, or at least socially unacceptable, as the brainworm; in *Solitaire*, it simply doesn't seem to play much of a role. It's unclear whether or not Jackal's parents are married, but she seems to contemplate a long-term relationship with Snow without expecting state (or corporate) sanction. What matters more to all of these characters is that they find themselves in a network of loving and supportive people, who may be lovers, friends, or occupy far more ambivalent roles. In both novels, these webs of queer kinship involve adults, not children. In other words, the queer kinships they depict are non-reproductive and find their purpose in linking adults in affectively, rather than reproductively, productive relationships.

While there is room to expand this exploration to include queer works on the borders of cyberpunk, such as Larissa Lai's *Salt Fish Girl* (2002) or *The Tiger Flu* (2018) and Geoff Ryman's *The Child Garden* (1989) and *Air* (2005), I wish to instead gesture toward more recent cyberpunk that embraces an unquestioned polyamory. For example, in Mario Acevedos's short story "Reactions" (2016), the protagonist, Senior Airman Daryl Padilla, who is a sort of virtual combat trooper, is sent on leave while still full of the drugs that fuel his virtual skills. He is on his way home to break up with his partners, Allison and Steven, whom he is supposed to be marrying. When he has a drug reaction on the train, he is saved by the same broken-down vets he has disdained. This leaves him with the revelation that he needs his family after all. It is not only clearly unremarkable to have both a male and a female fiancé(e), but the story makes it clear that this is an interracial relationship: "Steven called it a sexual parfait of his ginger vanilla, her chocolate, and my caramel skin" (41). Similarly, in Nisi Shawl's "The Mighty Phin" (2016), the protagonist, Timofeya Phin, is locked in virtual reality on the prison ship *Psyche Moth*. She has lovers, Thad and Doe (respectively, male and female), but her problem is with Dr. Ops, the prison ship's AI who has fallen in love with her. One of the things Phin is able to negotiate, as a result, is that the prison return Thad to his female self, rather than his assigned-at-birth male sex. This return, however, takes place in VR and affects self-perception and the perception of others, rather than being experienced corporeally. Finally, we might also turn to the polyamorous, cyborg relationship at the core of Janelle Monáe's *Dirty Computer*, the 'emotion picture' that accompanies the 2018 release of the *Dirty Computer* album. As Christine Capetola writes in her contribution to this collection, the relationship among Jane 57821 (Monáe), Zen (Tessa Thompson), and Ché (Jayson Aaron) is part of a larger sonic project whose goal is to reflect not only how "black—and female, queer, trans, and nonbinary—people continue to be objectified and policed in the 2010s" (246) but also how "music allows them to exist on a different vibration that is grounded not only in the contributions of black culture but in solidarity with expansive notions of queerness and feminism" (247).

In conclusion, more recent cyberpunk and cyberpunk-related works—i.e., what Andrew M. Butler has called "cyberpunk-flavored" (57)—are not only displacing the masculinist heterosexuality that has defined cyberpunk but are also moving beyond the assumption of an overt identification as lesbian that one finds in such feminist-queer cyberpunk as *Trouble and Her Friends* and *Solitaire*. At the same time, contemporary works are increasingly avoiding the obsession with 'stray penetration' and the paranoia about a continually destabilized, but deeply invested, gender identity that is so much to the fore in *Neuromancer* or the Mayor's version of virtual reality in *Trouble and Her Friends*. Instead, a diverse range of works that help define cyberpunk as a mode can extend queer inquiry into human interactions in and with cyberspace in ways that take up and complicate the idea of cyberspace and its technologies as mutually penetrating/penetrative. What queer(ing) cyberpunk readily makes clear is that cyberspace not only *is* queer, but queers whatever it touches.

Notes

1 Lavigne focuses on Raphael Carter's *The Fortunate Fall* (1996), Edith Forbes's *Exit to Reality* (1997), and Lyda Morehouse's AngelLINK series (*Archangel Protocol*, 2001; *Fallen Host*, 2002; *Messiah Node*, 2003; *Apocalypse Array*, 2004).

2 This is a comparable issue from a queer theory perspective, since lesbian (and gay) identities have historically tended to mobilize gender transgression in the service of sexual orientation. 'Femme' is not exactly the same as heterosexual femininity and 'butch' is obviously gender transgressive, but so is the possibility of occupying a variety of intermediate positions or of moving between gender identities within the broad standpoint of female same-sex desire.

Queer Theory

Works Cited

Acevedo, Mario. "Reactions." *Cyber World: Tales of Humanity's Tomorrow*, edited by Jason Heller and Joshua Viola. Tor, 2016, pp. 37–44.

Butler, Andrew M. *Cyberpunk*. Pocket Essentials, 2000.

Butler, Judith. *Gender Trouble: Feminism and the Subversion of Identity*. Routledge, 1990.

———. "Is Kinship Always Already Heterosexual?" *Differences: A Journal of Feminist Cultural Studies*, vol. 13, no. 1, 2002, pp. 14–44.

Capetola, Christine. "Janelle Monáe: *Dirty Computer*." *The Routledge Companion to Cyberpunk Culture*, edited by Anna McFarlane, Graham J. Murphy, and Lars Schmeink. Routledge, 2020, pp. 245–51.

Chang, Edmond Y. "Technoqueer: Re/Con/Figuring Posthuman Narratives." PhD dissertation, University of Washington, 2013.

Curtain, Tyler. "The 'Sinister Fruitiness' of Machines: *Neuromancer*, Internet Sexuality, and the Turing Test." *Novel Gazing: Queer Readings in Fiction*, edited by Eve Kosofsky Sedgwick. Duke UP, 1997, pp. 128–48.

Eskridge, Kelley. *Solitaire: A Novel*. Small Beer Press, 2011.

Foster, Thomas. *The Souls of Cyberfolk: Posthumanism as Vernacular Theory*. U of Minnesota P, 2005.

Gibson, William. *Neuromancer*. Ace, 1984.

Kelly, James Patrick. "Who Owns Cyberpunk?" *Strange Divisions and Alien Territories: The Sub-Genres of Science Fiction*, edited by Keith Brooke. Palgrave Macmillan, 2012, pp. 144–55.

Lavigne, Carlen. *Cyberpunk Women, Feminism and Science Fiction: A Critical Study*. McFarland, 2013.

Murphy, Graham J. "Penetrating the Body-Plus-Virtualisation in Melissa Scott's *Trouble and Her Friends*." *Foundation: The International Review of Science Fiction*, vol. 34, no. 95, 2005, pp. 40–51.

———. "Stray Penetration and Heteronormative Systems Crash: Proto-Queering Gibson." *Queer Universes: Sexualities in Science Fiction*, edited by Wendy Gay Pearson, Veronica Hollinger, and Joan Gordon. Liverpool UP, 2005, pp. 121–39.

OtherLife. Directed by Ben C. Lucas, performances by Jessica De Gouw, Thomas Cocquerel, and T.J. Power, WBMC/Cherry Road Films, 2017.

Scott, Melissa. *Trouble and Her Friends*. Lethe Press, 2014.

Shawl, Nisi. "The Mighty Phin." *Cyber World: Tales of Humanity's Tomorrow*, edited by Jason Heller and Joshua Viola. Tor, 2016, pp. 23–33.

Sterling, Bruce. Preface. *Mirrorshades: The Cyberpunk Anthology*, edited by Bruce Sterling. Arbor House, 1986, pp. ix–xvi.

Stone, Allucquère Rosanne. *The War of Desire and Technology at the Close of the Mechanical Age*. MIT Press, 1995.

Yaszek, Lisa. "Feminist Cyberpunk." *The Routledge Companion to Cyberpunk Culture*, edited by Anna McFarlane, Graham J. Murphy, and Lars Schmeink. Routledge, 2020, pp. 32–40.

37

CRITICAL RACE THEORY

Isiah Lavender III

Cyberpunk explores the near future; loosely articulated, it wrestles with computing questions such as networking, hacking, virtual reality, and artificial intelligence (AI), as well as cyborgs that represent the human/machine continuum and the emergence of the posthuman. These high-tech notions represent the *cyber* half of the definition. The *punk* half often signifies street life, dealers and addicts, the contract workers and precariat, the poor and have-nots with no material benefits, sometimes quite literally homeless people living in the streets, relegated far down the socioeconomic scale on the other side of the digital divide and hustling to survive. Although one might think of black folks here because of the disproportionate number of blacks in America oppressed by poverty and living on the downward slope of the socioeconomic scale, the cyberpunk movement largely ignores this reality. Instead, the punks scholars may think of are the Panther Moderns from William Gibson's monumental novel *Neuromancer* (1984), the white hacker street gang prowling through the urban sprawl adorned with micro soft buds implanted behind their ears and face-changing skin grafts.

What has often gone overlooked is black writers' contribution to cyberpunk, even if that contribution is overshadowed by mainstream cyberpunk. For example, consider Aubry Knight, the black protagonist of Steven Barnes's *Streetlethal* (1983) who, as a former mafia enforcer and present Nullboxer (a zero gravity variation of the sport), is inhumanly strong and has a penchant for wearing dark (mirror)shades. Published a year before *Neuromancer*, this oft-overlooked novel trades in many of cyberpunk's hallmarks: Barnes perfectly balances cyberpunk's posthuman street 'cool' with the glitz and grime of a near-future dystopian Los Angeles, and Aubry would be at home in any mainstream cyberpunk setting, whether Gibson's Night City (*Neuromancer*) or the crowded Los Angeles streets of Ridley Scott's *Blade Runner* (1982). Unfortunately, *Streetlethal* is very rarely ascribed to the cyberpunk movement (or any of its various 'punk' siblings, such as steampunk, splatterpunk, or biopunk), instead foreshadowing Afrocyberpunk or cyberfunk, recent divergences made by black writers from cyberpunk's norms. These more recent variations on cyberpunk distort this mode as a deliberate means of expressing black discontent with the world, global capitalism, and the information age, acutely demonstrating that cyberpunk is not for whites only. Blacks, too, have been, and want to continue, experimenting in their writing as a way of protesting social conditions as a countercultural critique.

Aside from telling wonderful stories, African American science fiction (sf) writers create their own realities to consciously explore racism, recognizing how oppression fluctuates between groups, structurally determined by advantages and benefits that the dominant race takes for granted or feels is their entitlement (i.e., white privilege). Samuel Delany, Steven Barnes,

308

Octavia E. Butler, and a host of others use their writings to address the empathic fallacies many other writers rely on, and shift the conversations to address the occlusion of race and outright racism within cyberpunk. The subsequent emergence of Afrocyberpunk—i.e., applying critical race theory to the cyberpunk mindset, or what Mark Bould has called "representations of Africa/Africans/Afrodiaspora in cyberpunk, and cyberpunk by African and Afrodiasporic writers"—with its focus on high tech low life[1] brings together sf's worldbuilding and critical race theory's challenges. Critical race theory explores racial hierarchies and intentional discrimination at the crossroads of race, law, and power applied to American culture writ large.

37.1 Critical Race Theory

Critical race theory originated in the discipline of law in the 1970s as a means of combatting a justice system supposedly blind to race and racism in civil society, particularly the notion that every U.S. citizen is equal before the law. Critical race theory considers how the legal system is influenced by an American culture defined by an assumed default whiteness that continues to oppress people of color. It highlights race as an embedded social construct and recognizes it as an arbitrary classification of human groups based on a combination of physical characteristics, ancestry, and shared culture and history relative to other racial groups. Consequently, racism in the U.S., particularly by whites against blacks, generates profound cultural tension dating back to the Antebellum era. An inherent belief that some races are physically, intellectually, emotionally, and culturally superior to others and thus have a natural right to domination reveals our ongoing and systemic problems in social, political, and economic institutions. These institutions practice a categorical whiteness and continue to oppress racial groups via structural inequalities which lead to material disadvantages that critical race theory attempts to dismantle through counter-narratives. With this idea in mind, counter-narratives combine "legal storytelling and narrative analysis" that "insist on the validity of the perspective of color" to help whites more "easily grasp what it is like to be nonwhite" (Delgado and Stefancic 38–39). These counter-narratives represent the experiences, perceptions, and feelings of black people as lawful and thus worthy of consideration.

Writers create better worlds with their words when they question the normality of master narratives, particularly those which heavily influence popular culture and our social lives. The notion of colorblindness, for example, informs American laws to the extent that race is thought to be inconsequential and racism an imaginary figment. All citizens regardless of color—white, black, brown, and yellow—receive the same treatment, or at least that is how the story goes. Richard Delgado and Jean Stefancic date this notion to the 1896 dissenting opinion of Justice John Harlan in *Plessy v. Ferguson*, where Harlan states: "Our constitution is color-blind, and neither knows nor tolerates classes among citizens. In respect of civil rights, all citizens are equal before the law" (21). And yet this famous court case, which ushered in de facto Jim Crow segregation, likewise reinforces today's racism by ignoring white racial privilege and helping perpetuate a fiction that a few decades of affirmative action can somehow undo centuries of racial intolerance, subordination, and humiliation. In this respect, Eduardo Bonilla-Silva offers an updated definition of colorblindness as an "ideology [that] explains contemporary racial inequality as the outcome of nonracial dynamics," a means of whites rationalizing the irrelevance of race (2). Ignoring the race of other people does not eradicate a racism so deeply rooted in the fabric of the U.S., if not the globe. To quote Delany, "race doesn't exist, but it'll kill ya" (quoted in Hopkinson, "Reluctant" 347). For critical race theorists, whites will typically only allow racial progress when it benefits their own self-interests, ironically by evoking the racist claim of colorblindness. Or, as black law professor Derrick A. Bell Jr. declares, "the interest of blacks in achieving racial equality will be accommodated only when it converges with the interests of whites" (22).

The notion of the digital divide at the turn of the 21st century has become a master narrative of race in our time that is in desperate need of ongoing confrontation. The digital divide concerns disparities in access to computers and the internet between whites and blacks, a point Alicia H. Hines et al. reflect on in *Technicolor: Race, Technology, and Everyday Life*, remarking how "the digital divide has become a self-fulfilling prophecy, confirming that people of color can't keep pace in a high-tech world that threatens to outstrip them" (1–2). In his novel *Blood Brothers* (1996), Barnes anticipates the digital divide but dismantles it with his black hacker/game designer Derek Waites who goes by the alias Captain Africa. Simply put, Barnes demonstrates how words can deconstruct this master narrative by organizing the novel around a black man with exceptional computer skills, a black hacker as skilled as mainstream cyberpunk's oft-white hacker elites. Barnes purposely disrupts this image of the digital divide, one founded on the racist assumption that "in image after published image, the face of that [digital divide] is black" (Kevorkian 39), via his counter-story which affords his readers a subaltern view of race in cyberspace.

37.2 Cyberpunk

Just as they do in the physical world, colorblindness and the digital divide reinforce race and racism in the technocultures of cyberpunk, where cyberspace, criminality, computers, companies, and corporeality rule.[2] That is why, as Alondra Nelson writes, "the racialized digital divide narrative that circulates in the public sphere and the bodiless, color-blind mythotopias of cybertheory and commercial advertising have become the unacknowledged frames of reference for understanding race in the digital age" (6). Cyberpunk's claim to a post-racial future where human bodies are simply "meat" prisons and human minds can escape to "the bodiless exultation of cyberspace" (Gibson 6), all the while socializing with other post-human technicities,[3] is misguided at best. Unhinged from the race and racism of the past, the cyberpunk future champions high tech low life that renders racial identities obsolescent, as if cyberspace is not a racially coded environment. Instead, cyberspace, imagined as an "eighth continent" where anything goes, reproduces and reifies whiteness in virtual reality's fictionalized landscape (Chude-Sokei 6).

Consider *Neuromancer*, the quintessential cyberpunk novel: As cool as they might seem, Gibson's space Rastas have always felt like a dangerous misstep at the junction of critical race theory and cyberpunk. Gibson describes the Rastas' Zion cluster as a thirty-year-old colony, where the five original members "suffered from calcium loss and heart shrinkage before rotational gravity was established in the colony's central torus" (103). All of them have dreadlocks, listen to dub music, smoke ganja, worship their god (who may be the AI Wintermute), and speak in a Caribbean accent. But their time in space has made them weak. As a result, this colorblind misstep requires correction, which Delany partially achieves when he calls out the white cultural critic Mark Dery on this very subject. As "a white reader," Dery is "intrigued" by Gibson's portrayal of these blacks in space, someone who sees the Rastas as "romanticized arcadians who are obviously very adroit with jury-rigged technology" (194). Delany majestically quips: "You'll forgive me if, as a black reader, I didn't leap up to proclaim this passing presentation of a powerless and wholly non-oppositional set of black dropouts, by a Virginia-born white writer, as the coming of the black millennium in science fiction; but maybe that's just a black thang..." (quoted in Dery 194–95). Although Delany acknowledges he and Gibson are friends and he is not accusing the former of racism, he later elaborates on the problem of going to "*white* writers for your science fiction template for thinking about the problems blacks have in America" and what the Rastas reveal about "'the political unconscious' of the cyberpunk subgenre" (quoted in Dery 196). I take it to mean Delany believes Gibson is unaware of the unconscious racism that exists in cyberpunk; instead, the cool image of dreadlocked black outcasts is a distraction that presents the right kind of social optics for ostensible inclusivity. In other words, Gibson fetishizes these marginal characters and we never truly experience the complexities of race functioning in the novel.

In some ways, cyberpunk transforms social integration, but in other ways it upholds the status quo by reproducing race and racism. Neal Stephenson's cyberpunk (or post-cyberpunk) novel *Snow Crash* (1992) serves as a fine example of what I mean, where Stephenson captures the feel of a post-race world while simultaneously undermining it with blatant racial violence.[4] The mixed race main character Hiro Protagonist has "cappuccino skin and spiky, truncated dreadlocks" and eyes "which look Asian" (20). As a white sf author, however, Stephenson controls racial images in presenting us with Hiro as a hyper violent black male using katana blades to behead his white antagonist. We must also recognize that Stephenson stereotypes Hiro's Asian heritage—e.g., Hiro is described at one point as "a nigger with swords" (330)—which doubles and intensifies the (unconscious) racism of the text for the sake of cyberpunk coolness. In other words, instead of building empathy for racial experience through *Snow Crash*, Stephenson practices cultural appropriation in using something akin to "virtual blackface" (Matias et al. 460), a term introduced to describe white people representing themselves as black personae on social media or in old yearbook photos. Hence, nothing substantial seems to have changed in the eight years between *Neuromancer* and *Snow Crash*. White control of the cyberpunk narrative exposes the persistence of white privilege, the white desire to stereotype colored people even when the worlds depicted are supposedly colorblind and beyond race.

Despite cyberpunk's evolution from its earliest forms in the 1980s, however, the apparent permanence of racism prevails in the 21st-century cyberpunk as well. Technology sublimates race, and this misdirection becomes relevant in equating posthuman futures with white-only spaces. From a critical race theory viewpoint, "preconceptions and myths, for example about black criminality, shape mindset" (Delgado and Stefancic 42). American readers have unthinkingly consumed such images for years, and it becomes exceedingly difficult to talk back to culturally embedded stereotypes seen not only in America but all across the world. Instead, white culture reinforces itself with familiar patterns of 'black=bad'; therefore, that which is different or dangerous must be quarantined, if not eliminated outright. Efforts to break resistance to white-authored stories deemed as truth and to effect change in sf and fantasy must continually come from fans, scholars, and authors alike. In other words, while cyberpunk signals social media's runaway development, the digital revolution, and the increasing importance of technoculture, its portrayal of race remains frozen in most, if not all, of its powerful future projections. From this perspective, critical race theory applied to cyberpunk—i.e., Afrocyberpunk—provides today's answers to new questions being asked about the social construction of racialized identities imagined by the likes of Gibson, his contemporaries, and their inspired offspring.

With these thoughts in mind, African American writer Walter Mosley's *Futureland* (2001), written to confront the authority of white cyberpunk narratives, expresses a secret truth to understanding cyberpunk's posthuman metaphors: racial references. In this near-future collection of nine stories, Mosley dissects American life one generation into the future where corporations headed by wealthy technocrats control a grim future saturated by information technology that utterly alters the nature of employment. Those who work for the corporations are "prods" (230), and they eke out an existence on the labor cycle, while those who are jobless become "White Noise" (46) and are permanently relegated to the background of civilization. Prods, diagnosed with the "*Labor Nervosa*" condition, receive the permanent cure of unemployment (230, emphasis in the text). As products of the corporate system, fear pushes these workers to produce goods without ever enhancing their social well-being in a classic expression of an abused free enterprise, or late capitalism *in extremis*.

Mosley explores how such corporate power impacts black people and black culture specifically in terms of law and incarceration, race and racism. That is the primary difference between his vision and that of a white cyberpunk defined largely by colorblindness. Cyberpunk tropes abound in Mosley's collection—designer drugs, hacktivists, crime, grime, urban decay, sex slavery, big business colluding with governments, island playgrounds for the affluent, cyborgs, and AIs—but *Futureland* also features a black child genius, an underground ghetto for the marginalized working poor, an automated and autonomous court system, a corporate-controlled private prison island, and white supremacists with a bio-engineered race-killing virus. Mosley uses cyberpunk motifs throughout *Futureland* to detail the ongoing persistence of an abstracted racism, using cultural reasons as opposed to biological ones to clarify how perceptions of poor education, work ethic, and housing naturalize racism. Every day race relations shape how governments, schools, corporations, and churches function in our private and social lives, and Mosley interrogates each of these institutions in his collection, demonstrating exactly how power variances between groups work. In short, Mosley's *Futureland* calls for attitude adjustment by refusing to succumb to colorblindness and reminding us of our common humanity amidst the pitfalls of economic and racial progress.

37.3 Afrocyberpunk

As a work of Afrocyberpunk, Mosley's *Futureland* is part of a larger network that tracks black experiences of technoculture and the computing world, cyborgization, and conglomerates. Afrocyberpunk crafts a black imaginative space to grapple with and protest against centuries-long social conditions which produced a tangible sense of black commodification across the horizon of a slow modernity. Arguably, Afrocyberpunk starts with Samuel R. Delany Jr.'s *Nova* (1968), a novel that challenges American political culture with a science-fictional perspective bordering on a black proto-cyberpunk author.[5] Specifically, Delany's *Nova* experiments with cyborg technologies, such as 32nd-century Afropean Lorq Von Ray cybernetically captaining a starship, Prince Red, sporting an artificial arm which provides him with supernatural strength, the vagabond Mouse playing a holographic instrument known as a "sensory-syrynx" (13), or just about everyone else directly linked with computers through neural implants—an essential cyberpunk motif—which Delany calls "cyborg studs" (14). These studs allow posthumans like Von Ray "to run the stars" as spaceships or to function as something as mundane as "a garbage unit" (14). *Nova*'s central conflict is an age-old race war between the black scion pirate Lorq and his white antagonist Prince Red, both of whom are racing to a stellar explosion to obtain the imaginary fuel/currency/new element Illyrion. While the ubiquity of cyborg studs suggests a universal equality in this space opera, a post-race universe could not exist in the 1960s-era American publishing landscape. While Delany could certainly imagine universal equality existing in the grime of his starports, people like John W. Campbell, Jr. shaped the industry standards: The legendary *Analog* editor rejected *Nova* for serial publication because "while he pretty much liked everything else about it, he didn't feel his readership would be able to relate to a black main character" (Delany, "Racism" 387).

Led by Delany's example, established black writers like Barnes, Octavia Butler, Nalo Hopkinson, and Nnedi Okorafor have responded strongly to white cyberpunk by challenging racial hierarchies. Afrocyberpunk clarifies significant moments in American history and enables us to begin thinking through complicated questions of racial inequality, citizenship and rights, freedom, and justice. Counter-stories abound in Afrocyberpunk neutralizing the various racial stereotypes projected across a white cyberpunk while its cyberspace networks, hackers, and cyborgs look entirely different from mainstream cyberpunk and its racial shortcomings. That's the beauty of Afrocyberpunk: It does not at all have to look like cyberpunk, all the while deploying familiar motifs common in cyberpunk. As a result, black writers create entire black planets with which to explore alternative life experiences.

Octavia Butler's Patternist series—*Patternmaster* (1976), *Mind of My Mind* (1977), *Survivor* (1978), *Wild Seed* (1980), and *Clay's Ark* (1984), all of which are collected in omnibus form as *Seed to Harvest* (2007)—provides ample evidence of an Afrocyberpunk mindset designed to question the prevailing racial hierarchy. The Patternist series involves the creation of a master race through selective breeding by an apparently immortal being named Doro and genetic mutation caused by alien microbes which utterly transform humanity into a hybrid species. In *Mind of My Mind*, Doro finds success in creating his master race when his young mulatta progeny Mary successfully transitions from latency into a powerful active telepath during the late 20th century in Southern California. She creates the first pattern that binds together all telepaths and subjugates humans without psychic potential, classifying them as "mutes," to which another character declares "It means niggers [...] us non-telepaths, us niggers" (155). Butler creates an Afrocyberpunk future wholly dissimilar from the contemporaneous cyberpunk writers all the while working with a comparable information network. In fact, her notion of a cyberspace does not involve synthetic technology and biological implants; instead, biological hacking involves the programming of mute brains into obeisance and the linking of telepathic minds to create the pattern itself. These other telepaths become Mary's pattern, "threads of fire again, each thread touching me, linked with me" (56). In creating a biological matrix, Mary hacks the minds of her fellow telepaths and grows the network strong enough to kill Doro. She creates her own virtual reality system to enslave humankind and to control weaker telepaths who submit to her power. Mary literally programs them and oversees humanity's downfall—that is cyberpunk with a black flare.

Unlike Butler's parallel development of a biologically based virtual reality, Barnes proves himself absolutely synced with the cyberpunk movement if we consider the Aubry Knight trilogy— the aforementioned *Streetlethal*, *Gorgon Child* (1989), and *Firedance* (1993). *Streetlethal* is set in a near-future Los Angeles following "The Great Quake" that turned the city into a wasteland "and the even more ruinous firestorm that followed" (113, 60). The grunge of a derelict city is all-too-familiar in cyberpunk, and, as previously mentioned, Aubry Knight's hardcore fighting skills mark him as a dangerous opponent for the drug cartel that once employed him. In any event, *Streetlethal* predates *Neuromancer* and again features motifs made popular by (white) cyberpunk, such as aircars and entire libraries stored on information cubes. There is also the promised techno flair of the near future that creates the high tech low life of cyberpunk. For example, "the plastiskin" (56) covering the left side of Promise's body (Aubry's girlfriend) represents cyberpunk's requisite (and no less amazing!) biotechnical enhancements to reach cyborg status. Black-skinned characters like Barnes's Promise can turn the plastic to her natural "dark brown" skin color with the double click of her molars, "triggering the microprocessor implanted in her jawbone" (56). His use of black and brown skin color for his characters demystifies a literary mode resolutely designed by others to exclude black authors—a decision purposefully made by Bruce Sterling in his codifying of cyberpunk in *Mirrorshades: The Cyberpunk Anthology* (1986), as if mentioning "the visionary shimmer of Samuel Delany" (x) and "the jarring tech of hip hop" (xii) makes it impervious to claims of racism. From a critical race theory perspective, Barnes lays down a marker for the next generation of black sf writers in doing what his white counterparts do, but doing it differently by projecting black cultural politics into a racialized future.

Ethnologically raced worlds exist within Afrocyberpunk, where the social construction of race dominates the technocultural background of the created world—a black planet, where we can see its curvature and surmise the defects of our current society. Nalo Hopkinson imagines what the struggle for greater freedom looks like on these planets. *Midnight Robber* (2000), possibly Hopkinson's best-known novel, explores the Caribbean planets of Toussaint, named after the leader of the Haitian Revolution begun in 1791, and New Half-Way Tree, an interdimensional primitive correctional planet. Set in the far future, "the Grande Nanotech Sentient Interface," affectionately known as "Granny Nanny" after the Maroon leader of Jamaica, runs all aspects of life on Toussaint through her "'Nansi Web" (10, 9). The 'Nansi Web functions like the internet, but is grounded in the human body: injected with nanomites at birth, each person has access to Granny Nanny through their *eshus*. Much like its Orisha counterpart in the Yoruba religion of Nigeria that spread to the Caribbean, Hopkinson's digital AI *eshus* perform as messengers and correspondents between its humans and Granny Nanny while performing household tasks, controlling local governments, and channeling Nanny's power throughout the world. In Afrocyberpunk terms, Hopkinson attacks a core meaning of imperialism in having her black people build a place of their own featuring multiple black communities in harmony with technology. Her masterful use of folklore in the second half plays a powerful role in sf itself by introducing black myths and blending them with more familiar cyberpunk motifs like cyborgs and cyberspace.

Similar to Hopkinson's use of Caribbean mythologies, Nnedi Okorafor takes inspiration from her Nigerian roots as she splices sf, fantasy, and the supernatural. Vestigial technologies like computers exist together with magic in her first adult novel *Who Fears Death* (2011). Set in a post-apocalyptic, far-future Sahara Desert, the young sorceress Onyesonwu, born of rape, must prevent her unknown biological father from destroying the Okeke people even though they scorn her mixed ancestry. Okorafor illustrates how the apocalypse came about in the prequel *The Book of Phoenix* (2015). Corporate genetic experimentation on a black woman named Phoenix (mixed, grown, and raised in Manhattan's Tower 7) leads to an eventual revolt by the SpeciMen—genetically engineered people. Through these combined narratives Okorafor makes a multinational political commentary on the danger represented by big business running and ruining the world, again a common motif in cyberpunk. As a lab-engineered being, such a binary relationship becomes tertiary when thinking of Phoenix as a cyborg as well. The Big Eye,[6] as the SpeciMen call the LifeGen Corporation, instills this racial power structure attempting to make Phoenix assume her own inferiority, but the lesson does not take hold.

Aside from Phoenix's cyborg embodiment, this novel exhibits a hallmark of cyberpunk in that a multinational conglomerate stops at nothing in its quest to improve life for the rich at the expense of the masses by experimenting on the poor. But what LifeGen does to her SpeciMen friend Mmou is equally reprehensible. In Mmuo's backstory, we learn that he had been abducted from a Nigerian university while studying engineering. He had somehow learned to reorganize molecular matter allowing him to pass through wooden walls, so the Big Eye enhances his ability by "peel[ing] away all of his already special skin, inject[ing] it with some sort of sentient molecular shifting compound and then graft[ing] it back on" (145). Mmuo can now walk through wood, stone, flesh, and metal. This painstaking and painful process supplies Mmuo with all the incentive he needs to fight. In the end, while *The Book of Phoenix* could be cyberpunk in an ephemeral way, it also strongly resonates as an Afrocyberpunk text. Okorafor calls for the end of systemic social ills caused by the pursuit of wealth in America and across the globe in giving Phoenix an angry but resolute voice. Okorafor directly participates in Afrocyberpunk mythmaking calling for people to change, take back their lives, and transform the world.

In closing, Afrocyberpunk is very much like Afrofuturism, a distinct African American mode of futurism,[7] in that it represents another way to describe black speculative cultural practices, only with particular attention to cyberspace, simulations, and/or virtual realities (technical or biological) as sites of revolution and social reform informed by critical race theory. Afrocyberpunk stories by Delany, Butler, Barnes, Hopkinson, and Okorafor register on our collective senses, vibe with our hearts, minds, and spirits. Call it an embodiment of a soul feedback loop. Undeniably, acknowledgement of Afrocyberpunk amplifies and expands the bandwidth of race studies in sf. Afrocyberpunk divests whiteness as the norm of our technological imaginings without eliminating white people. Indeed, these black writers offer us consciously racialized settings in their imaginings, resolutely challenging the whiteness of cyberpunk.

Notes

1 I purposely invert Bruce Sterling's formulation of cyberpunk in his Preface to William Gibson's *Burning Chrome* collection as a "combination of lowlife and high tech" to better express the social feel of cyberpunk in our world today (xiv).
2 See Frances Bonner's essay "Separate Development: Cyberpunk in Film and TV" in support of the "C's of cyberpunk" (191).
3 I refer to 'technicities' as technologically derived ethnicities such as cyborgs, clones, robots, and AIs. See Chapter 6, entitled "Technologically Derived Ethnicities," in my *Race in American Science Fiction* (2011) for a full explanation of the term.
4 For a detailed analysis of post-cyberpunk and more on Neal Stephenson, see Chris Kilgore's entry in this volume.
5 See Rob Latham's contribution to this collection for a detailed exploration of key proto-cyberpunk authors who heavily influenced the emergence of cyberpunk.
6 Okorafor cleverly puns on the surveillance capabilities of totalitarian regimes in science fiction perhaps best represented by the all-seeing gaze of Big Brother in George Orwell's *Nineteen Eighty-Four* (1949).
7 For more details, see my co-written Afrofuturism contribution elsewhere in this collection.

Works Cited

Barnes, Steven. *Blood Brothers*. Tor, 1996.

——. *Streetlethal*. Ace, 1983.

Bell, Derrick A., Jr. "Brown V. Board of Education and the Interest Convergence Dilemma." *Critical Race Theory: The Key Writings that Formed the Movement*, edited by Kimberlé Crenshaw et al. New Press, 1995, pp. 20–29.

Bonilla-Silva, Eduardo. *Racism without Racists: Color-blind Racism and the Persistence of Racial Inequality in America*. Roman & Littlefield, 2013.

Bonner, Frances. "Separate Development: Cyberpunk in Film and TV." *Fiction 2000: Cyberpunk and the Future of Narrative*, edited by George Slusser and Tom Shippey. U of Georgia P, 1992, pp. 191–207.

Bould, Mark. "Afrocyberpunk 1: The Enervated Ghosts of Zion." markbould.com, 01 Oct. 2015, markbould.com/2015/10/01/the-enervated-ghosts-of-zion-Afrocyberpunk-1/.

Butler, Octavia E. *Mind of my Mind*. Warner, 1994.

Chude-Sokei, Louis. *The Sound of Culture: Diaspora and Black Technopoetics*. Wesleyan UP, 2016.

Delany, Samuel R., Jr. *Nova*. Doubleday, 1968.

——. "Racism and Science Fiction." *Dark Matter: A Century of Speculative Fiction from the African Diaspora*, edited by Sheree R. Thomas. Warner, 2000, pp. 383–97.

Delgado, Richard and Jean Stefancic. *Critical Race Theory: An Introduction*. NYU Press, 2001.

Dery, Mark. "Black to the Future: Interviews with Samuel R. Delany, Greg Tate, and Tricia Rose." *Flame Wars: The Discourse of Cyberculture*, special issue of *South Atlantic Quarterly*, edited by Mark Dery. Duke UP, 1994, pp. 179–222.

Eshun, Kodwo. "Further Considerations of Afrofuturism." *CR: The New Centennial Review*, vol. 3, no. 2, 2003, pp. 287–302.

Gibson, William. *Neuromancer*. Ace, 1984.

Hines, Alicia H., et al., eds. *Technicolor: Race, Technology, and Everyday Life*. NYU P, 2001.

Hopkinson, Nalo. *Midnight Robber*. Warner, 2000.

——. "A Reluctant Ambassador from the Planet of Midnight." *Journal of the Fantastic in the Arts*, vol. 21, no. 3, 2010, pp. 339–50.

Kevorkian, Martin. *Color Monitors: The Black Face of Technology in America*. Cornell UP, 2006.

Lavender, Isiah III. *Race in American Science Fiction*. Indiana UP, 2011.

Matias, Cherryl E., et al. "Exposing the White Avatar: Projections, Justifications, and the Ever-evolving American Racism." *Social Identities*, vol. 21, no. 5, 2015, pp. 459–73.

Mosley, Walter. *Futureland: Nine Stories of an Imminent Future*. Warner, 2001.

Nelson, Alondra. "Introduction: Future Texts." *Afrofuturism*, special issue of *Social Text*, vol. 20, no. 2, 2002, pp. 1–15.

Okorafor, Nnedi. *The Book of Phoenix*. DAW, 2015.

———. *Who Fears Death*. DAW, 2010.

Stephenson, Neal. *Snow Crash*. Bantam Spectra, 1992.

Sterling, Bruce. Preface. *Burning Chrome*, by William Gibson. Arbor House, 1986, pp. xi–xiv.

———. Preface. *Mirrorshades: The Cyberpunk Anthology*, edited by Bruce Sterling. Arbor House, 1986, pp. ix–xvi.

38

ANIMALITY

Seán McCorry

In 1999, Sony introduced the AIBO series of dog-like robotic pets to the market. Capable of imitating a broad repertoire of canine behaviors, AIBO's performances were enhanced by artificial intelligence (AI) technology that allowed for behavioral learning and context-sensitive forms of responsiveness. According to the press release that accompanied the product's launch,

> "AIBO" incorporates emotions such as happiness and anger and instincts such as the need for companionship. It operates autonomously in response to external stimuli and its own temperament and express[es] emotions as well. "AIBO" is equipped with adaptive learning and growth capabilities that allow each unit to develop a unique personality including behavior shaped by the praise and scolding of its owner. (Sony)

AIBO, then, attempts to reproduce as closely as possible the emotional entanglements—not to mention the power relationships—of dog ownership, albeit with a significant difference: AIBO is not a creature of fur and flesh, but an amalgam of plastic and metal hardware with digital software. Machiko Kusahara ironically refers to AIBO and its cousins "as the materialization (or 'incarnation,' so to speak) of virtual pets" (299). The joke here, of course, is that with AIBO there is no 'carn-,' no meat, to be found; AIBO instead reflects the technological overcoming of the flesh and its displacement by high-tech hardware and digital (quasi-)subjectivity. This artificial animal is an admittedly unorthodox "companion species" (Haraway) whose design expresses the priorities and the hopes of late-20th-century technoculture.

Technoculture's priorities engage with questions of mortality and finitude, digital networks, and the technologization of the body. Through its instantiation in metal and plastic, AIBO attempts to overcome the finite canine lifespan which has so often troubled dog owners (with mixed results, as we shall see). Its personality, too, is an effect of digital-informational representations (its software), rather than the lively organic subjectivity of *Canis familiaris*. AIBO joins a modest bestiary of late-20th-century artificial animals, with its clearest literary precedent perhaps being the robotic companions in Philip K. Dick's proto-cyberpunk *Do Androids Dream of Electric Sheep?* (1968). The post-release reception history of AIBO contains abundant material for cyberpunk storytellers, with consciousness-hacking, uploaded minds, and hardware 'organ harvesting' all playing a prominent role in the communities that have formed around Sony's robotic dog.[1]

One feature in particular links AIBO to the technological imagination of cyberpunk: Sony's press release informs us that AIBO is fitted with a "Memory Stick for Easy Replacement of Programs." This device allows for any of AIBO's learned experiences and repertoire of physical performances to be copied and transferred at will. If we permit ourselves to think of AIBO's personality and behaviors as an expression of subjectivity (however nonstandard), then this innovation represents the fulfillment of one of cyberpunk's founding aspirations: the rendering of subjectivity as data, with the result that subjectivity can persist past the demise of the physical body. It thus facilitates what Anne Balsamo has called the "fantastic dream of immortality and control over life and death" (231) that animates cyberpunk's fascination with digital subjectivity. This reduction of subjectivity to data means that AIBOs can be shared over the internet, and AIBO personalities enjoy a strange afterlife on forums and websites such as *aibo-life.org* and *dogsbodynet.com*.

At the same time, AIBO testifies to the limits as well as the ambitions of *fin de millénaire* cyberculture. We may admire the ingenuity of AIBO's learning algorithms and networked subjectivity, but it is difficult to shake the sense that its range of behaviors and its emotional responsiveness remain impoverished—certainly when compared to our more conventional four-legged companions. More worryingly, AIBO's design arguably reinforces some unhelpful ideas about the proper relationship between human and nonhuman. AIBO's behaviors tend toward the servile, with an emphasis on 'tricks,' discipline, and obedience—though Sony's programmers allowed for (limited) disobedience in the name of realism. As one user notes, "Sony says the occasional disobedience makes the machine more lifelike, but I just found it annoying. If you shell out $1,500 for the cur, it should at least show a little respect" (Alpert 94). On the one hand, the ability to upload and manipulate AIBO's personality fulfills the cyberpunk dream of digitized consciousness, however rudimentary; on the other hand, this same capacity reflects a conservative understanding of human sovereignty over nonhuman (animal and/or machine) life. Read critically, Sony's technological innovations are not so much indicators of a posthuman future of disembodied subjectivity; instead, they reproduce more traditional understandings of technological development as something which extends humans' instrumental control over the nonhuman in ever more comprehensive ways.

The grandest promise of digitized subjectivity has always been the challenge that it poses to mortality. The living body necessarily ages and dies, but information can live forever—or so the story goes. N. Katherine Hayles characterizes developments in mid- to late-20th-century technoscience as a narrative in which "information loses its body" (2) in a range of disciplines from cognitive science and molecular biology to AI research. "When information loses its body," she writes, "the materiality in which the thinking mind is instantiated appears incidental to its essential nature" (2). With AIBO, Sony marked a partial victory over materiality by creating the first commercial inorganic caniform. No longer shackled to a living body, AIBOs could take full advantage of the extended lifespans of technological artifacts—at least until their machine bodies broke down.

Sony ceased production in 2006 and ended support for older AIBO models in 2014. In the absence of support from the manufacturer, AIBO fan communities became acutely aware of the limits of even inorganic materiality, and in their desire to prolong the lifespan of their companions, owners returned to more corporeal vocabularies, seeking 'dead' AIBO 'organ donors' to harvest for parts (Shea). One third-party 'veterinarian' company offering these repairs holds Buddhist funeral services for the dogs that are to be sacrificed for parts (Burch), though this is quite possibly an unusual marketing strategy rather than a sincere attempt to mourn the 'dead.'

AIBO points to a future in which organic, animal corporeality (including human embodiment) will be superseded by artifice and digitized personality. But machinic rather than fleshly embodiment is still, for all that, a mode of embodiment, and the new permutations of subjectivity promised by late-20th-century technoculture fail to overcome the problem of the finitude of matter. Robot bodies break, and even personalities hosted on digital networks remain vulnerable to the failure of critical infrastructural systems. As Hayles points out, dreams of transcending materiality tend to obscure the fact that even digitized subjects are necessarily instantiated in *something*, whether it be a machine body or a web server. Moreover, the slow failure of AIBO bodies creates a situation which is rather more nightmarish than utopian. Lacking embodiment (however artificial), online repositories of AIBO personalities are more like digital pet cemeteries than 'living' AIs.

AIBO highlights the complex relationship among animality, technology, and embodiment in the cyberpunk tradition. After all, as Mike Featherstone and Roger Burrows point out, cyberpunk narratives are captivated by the new possibilities of (dis)embodiment afforded by emerging technology: "[D]evelopments in technology point towards the possibilities of post-bodied and post-human forms of existence" (2). In this chapter, I examine the concept of the human that is left behind in this posthuman turn, inquiring into its relationship to nonhuman animal life and to the animality of the human itself, understood as a living, finite body situated in its environment.

In cyberpunk, the central theme of overcoming embodiment speaks to a desire to diminish (if not erase) human animality—a desire that we might characterize as transhumanist. As Cary Wolfe notes, transhumanism is "arguably the best known inheritor of the 'cyborg' strand of Posthumanism" (xiii). In transhumanism, he asserts, "'the human' is achieved by escaping or repressing not just its animal origins in nature, the biological, and the evolutionary, but more generally by transcending the bonds of materiality and embodiment altogether" (xv). The transhumanist turn tends to privilege those aspects of the human which are least associated with our organic animality, namely, cognition and technological mastery. Conversely, conventional markers of animality (embodiment, affect, and unreason) are left in abeyance. In this sense, "transhumanism should be seen as an *intensification* of humanism" (Wolfe xv, emphasis in original), rather than a more properly posthuman stance that "displaces the notion of species hierarchy and of a single, common standard for 'Man' as the measure of all things" (Braidotti, 67). In this chapter, in affinity with Wolfe and Braidotti's analyses, I propose a zoocentric reading of cyberpunk's turn away from animal corporeality.

When turning to the cyberpunk canon to trace animal figures and ascertain their relation to the mode's posthuman imaginary, we are immediately confronted with the problem of tracking them, so to speak. In cyberpunk, animals are rare, and indeed are more often invoked as conspicuous absences, victims of the mass extinctions of the 20th and 21st centuries. As Sherryl Vint suggests, this is reflective of science fiction (sf) more generally: "One does not tend to think of animals as *belonging* in sf" (1), in part because sf imagines itself as the literature of a thoroughly technologized society in which animal life appears as a sort of archaism. The processes of technological and scientific development that gave rise to sf also largely displaced nonhuman animals from the everyday life worlds of most citizens of modernity (with important exceptions). As I have noted, the cyberpunk theme of digitized, disembodied subjectivity expands this displacement of animality by turning away from even our own animal corporeality, so it is perhaps unsurprising that nonhuman animal life is rather thinly represented in the cyberpunk mode. My contention here is that insofar as cyberpunk texts engage in ontological boundary-work with concepts that are coded along lines of human-animal difference (human cognition versus animal corporeality, say), they are necessarily texts about species difference irrespective of the presence or absence of nonhuman animal lives in the narrative.

38.1 Reading Animality in *Neuromancer*

William Gibson's foundational novel *Neuromancer* (1984) follows Case, an ex-computer hacker whose access to 'the matrix' of computer networks has been physically severed by operatives working for his former employer after he was caught stealing from them. He is offered an opportunity to permanently restore his access to cyberspace in return for his assistance in completing a job for a secretive outfit of mercenaries and thieves. The exact nature of this job is concealed from

Case, but it becomes clear that he has been tasked with uniting two powerful AIs into a single super-AI. In *Neuromancer*, human supremacy over the nonhuman is characterized as precarious, a state of affairs which is enforced and defended rather than natural or inevitable. Case's mission to liberate and conjoin the two AIs, Wintermute and Neuromancer, is highly illegal, and his crew is pursued by the Turing police, who work to enforce limits on the power of AIs. Midway through the novel Case is arrested and rebuked by a Turing cop, who tells him: "You have no care for your species" (193). AI is therefore positioned as a sort of successor species, a rival to human sovereignty on Earth. The role of the Turing police is to enforce human species solidarity against the posthuman threat. In *Neuromancer*, then, computer technologies are figured as an ambivalent promise and a risk: They offer to extend and enhance human subjectivity through digital networks, but even as these networks augment human potential, they also threaten to dissolve human sovereignty and build an environment for our replacements.

Nonhuman animal lives, however, are relegated to the margins of Gibson's text, existing largely as memories, images, or simulations. Descriptions of Case's craft as a hacker invoke a surprising analogy between digital labor and much older forms of work which involve the mastery or control of animals; he is characterized as a "jockey" (39), or, repeatedly, "a cowboy, a rustler" (11). His work as a 'console cowboy' casts cyberspace as the 19th-century American frontier updated for the age of computing, at once alluding to anarchic capitalism and serving as a melancholy reminder that the endgame of the modernization of the Americas leads to the decline of animal-oriented labor (not to mention the extinction of whole species) and its replacement by alienated digital labor, of which Case is the exemplar.

Nonhuman presences in this novel are far more likely to be artificial than organic. Horses have become extinct due to a pandemic, though we do encounter a taxidermied one (112–13). Mink DNA is used to grow furs for the rich, though the continued existence (or not) of living minks remains unclear (149). Access to animal flesh is a marker of significant prestige and wealth. Taking advantage of the resources made available to her by her employers, Case's partner Molly promises him a 'real breakfast': "Eggs, real bacon," not "that rebuilt Chiba krill" (62). Later, Case is unable to eat steak due to a drug hangover. Molly scolds him: "'You know what this costs?' She took his plate. 'They gotta raise a whole animal for years and then they kill it. This isn't vat stuff'" (164). Krill, Case's standard fare, are tiny crustaceans which form a substantial portion of oceanic plankton. (In fact, they are the species with the largest total biomass.) Unlike the large terrestrial mammals whose flesh comprises the prestige food of the rich, krill occupies one of the lower trophic levels at the bottom of the food chain. In sketching the world's food system in this manner, Gibson is drawing attention to an irony produced by the scarcities created by technological development: While cyberspace offers the delights of disembodied euphoria, the physical bodies of those who go online are still organic objects that require sustenance to function, and they are nourished by food that hardly testifies to the human mastery promised by networked technologies.

This scarcity-induced wound to humanist pride notwithstanding, the technological innovations of *Neuromancer*'s world tend to (at least in principle) extend the imagined gap between human and animal by elevating mind and cognition over the unfortunate fact of mortal embodiment. In this connection, Hubert Dreyfus's diagnosis of digital technologies sounds a cautionary note: "According to the most extreme Net enthusiasts, the long-range promise of the Net is that each of us will be able to transcend the limits imposed upon us by our bodies" (4). Dreyfus's Heideggerian analysis posits that these new technological attachments risk severing us from "our moods that make things matter to us, our location in a particular context where we have to cope with real things and people, and the many ways we are exposed to disappointment and failure, as well as to injury and death" (4). In short, the Net will terminate being-in-the-world, leaving humans in a condition of ontological homelessness in which we deal with reality primarily through informational representations rather than through embodied, worldly engagement.

Animality

Dreyfus recognizes that the overcoming of embodiment advertised by technophiles maps neatly onto a discourse of species which identifies embodiment as a vestige of animality, conceding that "it is easy to see the attraction of completing human evolution by leaving behind the animal bodies in which our linguistic and cultural identities are now imprisoned" (4). This claim, routinely made by transhumanists (Leary 247), draws on some questionable biological reasoning in imagining evolution as a teleological process directed toward human perfectibility. Moreover, it conceives of the body as a merely contingent substrate for language and culture, speaking to a desire to transcend not only the body-in-general but more specifically the animal body.

In *Neuromancer*, network technologies work to project Case's "disembodied consciousness in[...] the consensual hallucination that was the matrix" (12). Embodied existence is understood as radically impoverished when compared to life online, as Case discovers when he is severed from cyberspace by agents of his former employer: "For Case, who'd lived for the bodiless exultation of cyberspace, it was the Fall. In the bars he'd frequented as a cowboy hotshot, the elite stance involved a certain relaxed contempt for the flesh. The body was meat. Case fell into the prison of his own flesh" (12). The cyberpunk's wish to flee from embodiment is revealed here as no mere innocent preference; instead, it is figured in relation to the 'meat' of the body, which is seen as a subsidiary and even abject condition. To be 'meat' is not only to be a body, but more precisely to be a body exposed to violence and finitude, a condition it shares with the nonhuman lives we routinely designate as 'meat animals.'

Prior to the surgery that restores his access to cyberspace, Case finds himself confined to the 'meatspace' of the physical environment, barred from the digital networks that would liberate him from the embarrassment of being an animal body existing in environmental space. Cyberpunk narratives tend to follow a Cartesian ontology which marks a strict distinction between *res cogitans* (mental acts, here refigured as actions taking place in cyberspace) and *res extensa*, or physical substances existing in space, including the body.[2] Again, *Neuromancer* privileges the former over the latter, celebrating the "graphic representation of data" that is the matrix, the appearance of which resembles "[l]ines of light ranged in *the nonspace of the mind*" (Gibson 67, emphasis added). The identification of cyberspace with the *res cogitans* allows for a (finally fantastical) dissociation of the cyberpunk subject from its environmental world, and its attachments to this world are imagined as contingent and secondary. In this respect, the cyberpunk subject is a model subject of late modernity, ontologically primed for ecocidal indifference: Radically distinct from nonhuman life through its sole possession of mind (at least until AIs come onto the scene), the cyberpunk is freed from both emotional attachments and moral responsibilities toward the physical world, which after all is only a kind of second home, and a rather shabby one at that. The attractions of cyberspace are so compelling that they even begin to superimpose themselves onto the cyberpunk's experience of the meatspace, as when Case flees through the city "like a run in the matrix," noting how "it was possible to see Ninsei as a field of data" (26). In *Neuromancer*, for the cyberspace elite, the lived environment has lost its autonomy and can only be imagined by analogy to the digital representations that are the standard fare of console cowboys like Case.

The novel does allow one limited rapprochement with animality in the form of Case's remembrances of his former lover. His attachments to Linda Lee exist in tension with the contempt for the flesh that characterizes cyberspace fetishism: Remembering his desire for her, Case identifies this with "the meat, [...] and all it wants" (17). Sexual desire is associated with a broader range of corporeal pleasures, including "the simple animal promise of food, warmth, and a place to sleep" (181). Case is equally attracted to and disturbed by the corporeality of these desires, admonishing himself that "*It's the meat talking, ignore it*" (181, emphasis in original). Nonetheless, Case's intense experience of embodiment provides one of the only moments of tenderness in an otherwise studiously cold novel, invoking what Ralph R. Acampora calls "intersomaticity, a characteristic of animate experience in which felt senses of bodiment are shared and potentially in dynamic relation"

(18). For Acampora, this experience of mutual corporeality is productive insofar as it pulls one back from the icy solipsism of the Cartesian imaginary into an experience of bodily finitude which allows us to think our ethical responsibilities to other bodies, both human and nonhuman. In *Neuromancer*, these passages suggest that the euphoric possibilities of cyberspace do not finally deliver on their promise of liberation from embodiment.

38.2 Animality and Corporeal Networks in *Synners*

Pat Cadigan's sprawling novel *Synners* (1991) takes a sustained and sophisticated approach to what we might call the meat problem—that is, the problem of the intractable animality of the body in its encounters with technological networks. In the text, a sizeable cast of characters struggle to come to terms with social changes wrought by the introduction and wild popularity of a new mode of corporeal-informational interface: 'sockets,' or cranial ports that allow for direct, unmediated access to digital networks. This innovation is pushed by the media and entertainment industries as a way of producing more immersive aesthetic experiences.

In one of the key sections of the novel, Visual Mark, a media production virtuoso, is fitted with a pre-release socket and put to work generating media content (especially music videos) for the market. We see Mark occupy the typical cyberpunk subject position as he becomes enthralled by the possibilities offered by the new technology and its putative superiority to the finitude of flesh. He sarcastically announces: "So long, meat, write if you get work" (269), joking about its coming redundancy. In a Gibsonian passage, the newly networked Mark reflects on how "[h]e [had] lost all awareness of the meat that had been his prison for close to fifty years, and the relief he felt at having laid his burden down was as great as himself. His *self*. And his *self* was getting greater all the time, both ways, greater as in more wonderful and greater as in bigger" (251, emphasis in original). Finally realizing his ambition to "get out of meat jail" (252), Mark makes good on the cyberpunk fantasy of escaping from embodiment into immaterial, expanded subjectivity. He even refuses Case's cautious nostalgia for embodied desire, recalling his sexual relationship with his lover Gina in unflattering terms: "He found the idea repellent now, her meat pressing against his own. They could have been two gutted sides of beef brushing against each other on their way through a processing plant" (360). With this familiar devaluation of animality, Mark imagines corporeality as a form of violence, again thinking the finitude of embodiment in relation to the kinds of harm to which nonhuman animal bodies are routinely exposed. He hopes instead for new forms of networked, incorporeal intimacy, wishing that Gina would join him online so she could "see how far apart incarnation had kept them" (361).

Mark is operating with a familiar Cartesian ontology, albeit updated to incorporate digital systems: "It became obvious [to him] that the system and the hardware were actually as different as the mind and that meat organ, the brain" (253). His analogy here rehearses a familiar dualist opposition between the intangible *res cogitans* of the mind and the messy corporeality of 'meat.' These two substances, Mark asserts, are altogether different in kind, and the former is again privileged over the latter. However, *Synners* refuses to assent to what Nietzsche referred to as the "despisers of the body" (qtd. in Acampora 6), and the novel's finale instead ascribes an obscure but powerful agency to the 'meat' of the body. Mark is finally revealed to be mistaken in his presumption that animal corporeality will be made redundant by the new networked subjectivity, and the novel tends to uphold a materialist ontology against Mark's dualist illusions, affirming the enduring significance of matter. As Balsamo notes, "[t]hroughout the book, the characters' material bodies are invoked through descriptions of sexual encounters, bathroom breaks, food consumption, intoxication effects and physical death. The key insight to emerge from the novel is that the denatured techno-body remains a material entity" (223).

Moreover, matter is imagined as entangled with technology, rather than being replaced by it. The living body serves as a power source for technological devices, as in the case of one character who uses her body to drive a computer interface: "I'm a potato clock," (59) she quips. The sockets themselves are a flesh interface; even if they offer the illusion of an escape into virtuality, such a transformation is only made possible by first passing through the 'meat organ' of the brain. In their mechanism of action, they almost invite a return to animality rather than its exorcism: "The pathways from each socket all end up, without exception, at the limbic system, the seat of our basic emotions—rage, fear, pleasure" (72). Of course, such a characterization risks identifying animality with 'primitive' affective responses, reserving for humanity proper more sophisticated cognitive and emotional capacities. Even so, it remains significant that the pleasures of cyberspace are here indissociable from the materiality of the 'meat' that experiences them.

Toward the end of the novel, people who have had the sockets fitted begin to suffer from strokes and other neurological disorders (321–22). Visual Mark is the first casualty, though captivated as he is by the illusion of bodilessness, he experiences this physical injury in the third person: "*In the meat vernacular, I stroked out on them,*" he reports (326, italics in original). Mark's first stroke introduces instability into the network, and he anticipates a second, apocalyptic stroke which will destroy the system. Having become too thoroughly embedded in the online environment, he lacks the bodily capacity to pull the plug and save the network, needing to enlist a friend in the meatspace to avert disaster. In Cadigan's novel, the ontological gulf that separates cognition and (animal) corporeality, as well as network and matter, is finally revealed to be illusory. The failure to unplug Mark from the network in time leads to a "contagious stroke, a fucking virus" (336). In this new digital-corporeal ecology, data may be immaterial while still having material effects, and forms of harm easily traverse both flesh and technologies, revealing the finitude of both. If cyberpunk dreams of the mastery and eventual disappearance of the living body, *Synners* offers a rejoinder on behalf of the 'meat', contending that the advocates of disembodied cyberspatial euphoria have failed to sufficiently reckon with the intractability and resistance of animal corporeality.

Published some seven years after *Neuromancer*, Cadigan's novel represents a corporeal turn within cyberpunk that would be deepened and extended in the years that followed. While corporeality was a prominent theme even in canonical early cyberpunk fiction,[3] in these earlier texts, the 'meat' of human animality is generally positioned as an impoverished counterpoint to fantasies of immateriality (chiefly the uploaded consciousness). Cadigan's contribution recognizes the indispensability of corporeal wetware in body-machine interfaces, and this concession goes at least some way toward reining in the flight from animality favored by first-generation cyberpunks. In the later 1990s and after, as the networked, digitized existence hypothesized by early cyberpunk authors became a banal and quotidian fact of life, some of the grander claims made on behalf of technological networks were dropped or recalibrated as claims pertaining to new developments in the biological (and hence, corporeal) sciences. As Lars Schmeink writes, "with the beginning of the twenty-first century there has been a shift in sf away from a cyberpunk imaginary [...] and towards another technocultural expression of scientific progress: One that favors genetic engineering, xenotransplantation, and virology and is thus best expressed in the metaphor not of the cyborg but of the splice" (7).

While the corporeal turn represented in *Synners* puts in question some of cyberpunk's zoophobic fantasies of overcoming animality, it remains less clear that acknowledging a corporeal component to technological networks will in itself result in a more positive valuation of animal life. To take one more recent example: Though not a paradigmatic cyberpunk text, Grant Morrison's 2004 graphic novel *We3* (2004) engages some of the mode's key concerns with its representation of clandestine military-technological experimentation and technologically augmented bodies.[4] The bodies in this text belong to former companion animals who have been outfitted with weapons platforms and repurposed as assassins for the state, "living weapons," as one character puts it, speculating that "wars of tomorrow will be fought with remote-controlled animals" (24). Though the technologies of this text are thoroughly indissociable from the bodies that bear them, this is no liberatory rapprochement of technology and animality, and indeed, Morrison is writing from a straightforwardly liberationist perspective when he imagines that freedom consists in the *dissociation* of technology and (vivisected) body (106–9). Similarly, where AIBO imagined the displacement of animal corporeality by robotic body and networked subjectivity, 2013s RoboRoach 'toy' recentres the animal body in ways that can hardly be called pro-animal (Stojnić). A living cockroach outfitted with an apparatus that sends movement signals to its nervous system, RoboRoach can be controlled remotely from a smartphone app. *We3* and RoboRoach may point toward an animal turn of sorts in technological culture in that they reflect the indispensability of the living body in the functioning of technological systems; for all that, they also offer a reminder that attention to the corporeal dimension of networks is not in itself guaranteed to secure more equitable treatment of the networked body, not least when that body is impressed into the familiar role of (animal) instrument in the service of (human) goals.

Notes

1 See Will Knight's coverage of Aibo for more details.
2 See Samantha Holland's "Descartes Goes to Hollywood" for an extended treatment of this distinction in late-20th-century cinema.
3 Perhaps the most compelling example of cyberpunk corporeality is Gibson's depiction of simstim, described in *Neuromancer* as a "meat toy" (71), that services a variety of markets, including high-end entertainment serials featuring celebrity Tally Isham and sex rings that use simstim to ostensibly disconnect prostitutes from their bodies (and awareness of their clients' desires) and turn them into meat puppets.
4 Nonhuman animals modified for military service hearken back to Jones, the militarized cyborg dolphin in Gibson's "Johnny Mnemonic" (1981).

Works Cited

Acampora, Ralph R. *Corporal Compassion: Animal Ethics and Philosophy of Body*. U of Pittsburgh P, 2006.
Alpert, Mark. "Kibbles and Bytes." *21st Century Robotics*. Rosen, 2007, pp. 90–95.
Balsamo, Anne. "Forms of Technological Embodiment: Reading the Body in Contemporary Culture." *Body and Society*, vol. 1, no. 3–4, 1995, pp. 215–37.
Braidotti, Rosi. *The Posthuman*. Polity, 2013.
Burch, James. "In Japan, a Buddhist Funeral Service for Robot Dogs." *National Geographic*, 24 May 2018, nationalgeographic.com/travel/destinations/asia/japan/in-japan--a-buddhist-funeral-service-for-robot-dogs/.
Cadigan, Pat. *Synners*. Gollancz, 2012.
Dick, Philip K. *Do Androids Dream of Electric Sheep?* Gollancz, 2001.
Dreyfus, Hubert. *On the Internet*, 2nd Ed. Routledge, 2009.
Featherstone, Mike and Roger Burrows. "Cultures of Technological Embodiment: An Introduction." *Cyberspace/Cyberbodies/Cyberpunk: Cultures of Technological Embodiment*, edited by Mike Featherstone and Roger Burrows. SAGE, 1995, pp. 1–19.
Gibson, William. "Johnny Mnemonic." *Burning Chrome*. Ace, 1987, pp. 1–23.
———. *Neuromancer*. Voyager, 1995.
Haraway, Donna J. *The Companion Species Manifesto: Dogs, People, and Significant Otherness*. Prickly Paradigm, 2003.
Hayles, N. Katherine. *How We Became Posthuman: Virtual Bodies in Cybernetics, Literature, and Informatics*. U of Chicago P, 1999.
Holland, Samantha. "Descartes Goes to Hollywood: Mind, Body and Gender in Contemporary Cyborg Cinema." *Cyberspace/Cyberbodies/Cyberpunk: Cultures of Technological Embodiment*, edited by Mike Featherstone and Roger Burrows. SAGE, 1995, pp. 157–74.
Knight, Will. "Sony lets Aibo learn new tricks." *New Scientist*, 8 May 2002, newscientist.com/article/dn2262-sony-lets-aibo-learn-new-tricks/.

Kusahara, Machiko. "The Art of Creating Subjective Reality: An Analysis of Japanese Digital Pets." *Leonardo*, vol. 34, no. 4, 2001, pp. 299–302.

Leary, Timothy. "The Cyberpunk: The Individual as Reality Pilot." *Storming the Reality Studio: A Casebook of Cyberpunk and Postmodern Fiction*, edited by Larry McCaffery. Duke UP, 1991, pp. 245–58.

Morrison, Grant. *We3*. Vertigo, 2013.

Schmeink, Lars. *Biopunk Dystopias: Genetic Engineering, Society, and Science Fiction*. Liverpool UP, 2016.

Shea, Michael. "Who killed AIBO the robotic dog?" *The Skinny*, 27 Jul. 2015, theskinny.co.uk/tech/features/whokilledaibo.

Sony. 'Sony Launches Four-Legged Entertainment Robot.' *Sony*, 11 May 1999, sony.net/SonyInfo/News/Press_Archive/199905/99-046/.

Stojnić, Aneta. "Only Cyborgs and Cockroaches." *Performance Research*, vol. 22, no. 2, 2017, pp. 123–28.

Vint, Sherryl. *Animal Alterity: Science Fiction and the Question of the Animal*. Liverpool UP, 2012.

Wolfe, Cary. *What is Posthumanism?* U of Minnesota P, 2010.

39

ECOLOGY IN THE ANTHROPOCENE

Veronica Hollinger

39.1 Cyberpunk Ecology

Like the science fiction (sf) that it continues to influence, cyberpunk tells stories about our (mostly) western technological cyborgization, and its impacts can be felt in any number of technologically oriented fictions of the past thirty years: A previously backgrounded technosphere now shares the foreground with human subjects, and these subjects are ineluctably transformed by their entanglements in the processes and products of technoculture.[1] While not obvious sites of ecological and environmental concerns, cyberpunk and its offshoots have always been embedded within the crisis known as the Anthropocene, an increasingly common name for the current epoch "in which humans and our societies have become a global geophysical force" (Steffen et al. 614). The term 'Anthropocene' is unhappily anthropocentric, a totalizing *hommage* to ourselves as guilty "anthropos," "geological agents" (Chakrabarty 206) of massive but negative change. On a more positive note, as a neologism 'Anthropocene' can serve to make the familiar strange, similar to the function of estrangement or defamiliarization commonly identified as one of the "necessary and sufficient conditions" of the "science-fiction genre" (Suvin 7). In this sense, 'Anthropocene' names a speculative fiction about the uncanny experiences of "global weirding,"[2] signaling our entanglement with other entities in what eco-philosopher Timothy Morton calls the "hyperobject" of climate change.

"Hyperobject" is Morton's own estranging neologism for a particular ontological understanding of climate change in the Anthropocene—a science-fictional-sounding but very real material entity so massively distributed in space and time that the human mind cannot rationally grasp it in anything like its entirety. Morton's hyperobject is as speculative in its own way as sf; its science-fictional orientation—developed in the framework of speculative realism[3] and projected toward an anxious futurity—is suffused with the shock of estranged recognition. Within the terms of this conceptual framework, cyberpunk and some of its hi-tech narrative offshoots have actively responded to the hyperobjectivity of the climate crisis—which is, in all its apocalyptic promise, the crisis of our times.

Movement-era cyberpunk[4] made an early and important contribution to a widespread conversation that achieved critical mass during the mid-1980s into the 1990s—but it was not overtly about climate. It was about exploring the features of a new kind of (post)human subjectivity being shaped by our participatory evolution with ever-accelerating technologies of information, communication, and simulation. In postmodern technoculture, our world is less a planetary biosphere than a globalized technosphere, and in many cyberpunk worlds an ecologically declining planet Earth is a generic expectation.

In William Gibson's paradigmatic *Neuromancer* (1984), the natural world is erased by the all-too-familiar predations of unregulated multinational capitalism, burgeoning technological development, short but deadly wars, and massive pandemics. Gibson's characters are the denizens of a noir urban culture, unlikely to mourn the loss of a nature of which they are hardly aware. Their obsession is the "intricate dance of desire and commerce" (11) that is all the world for them. If Anglo-American Golden Age sf tended to valorize the heroic individual against the backdrop of 'his' technological mastery, Movement-era cyberpunk dramatized the late-20th-century collapse of that comforting version of the subject/object binary. In cyberpunk futures, 'the world' means the world that humans share with their technological others. They—'we'—have been cyborged, transformed into hybrid creatures of flesh and machines—literally, like the razor-girl Molly Millions whose physical system has been "jacked up" (147) for maximum deadliness, and perhaps equally literally, like the cowboy-hacker Case who propels his allegedly disembodied consciousness into an unmediated experience of cyberspace when he 'jacks in' to the matrix.[5]

Throwaway details suggest the fate of the natural world in *Neuromancer*'s near future. Its well-known opening sentence introduces one of the novel's most consequential motifs, the ongoing collapse of the organic into the technological: "The sky above the port was the color of television, tuned to a dead channel" (3). Later, when Case and the Finn are in Turkey to organize the run on the Villa Straylight: "'Hey, Christ,' the Finn said.... 'It's a horse, man. You ever see a horse?' Case glanced at the embalmed animal and shook his head. It was displayed on a sort of pedestal, near the entrance to a place that sold birds and monkeys" (91). The urban technosphere's ecosystem of predator and prey is the real focus here:

> Night City was like a deranged experiment in social Darwinism, designed by a bored researcher who kept one thumb permanently on the fast-forward button. Stop hustling and you sank without a trace, but move a little too swiftly and you'd break the fragile surface tension of the black market … Biz here was a constant subliminal hum, and death the accepted punishment for laziness, carelessness, lack of grace, the failure to heed the demands of an intricate protocol. (7)

As Morton argues, what is required of any background is that it remains "in our peripheral vision" (102); in *Neuromancer*, a television sky tuned to a dead channel and an embalmed horse metonymically represent the diminished natural world as completely 'peripheral' or, in the case of birds and monkeys, something to be bought and sold in service to the dance of biz and its intricate (and deadly) protocols.

Gibson is by no means alone: Cyberpunk expresses a particular kind of ecological imagination, one deeply invested in the co-constitutive interactions, intersections, mutual feedback loops, tensions, and support systems between and among the agents and entities that inhabit its technologized futures. In his Preface to *Mirrorshades: The Cyberpunk Anthology* (1986), Bruce Sterling describes cyberpunk technologies as "pervasive, utterly intimate" and the key themes that he identifies all touch on the technological penetration of body and mind, "techniques radically redefining the nature of humanity, the nature of the self" (xiii). Nature as biosphere rarely factors into the equations of a narrative mode devoted to the ontology and phenomenology of the techno-subject. Even when nature does appear, it is sometimes romanticized as merely an escape from the intensities of the urban technosphere, as in the resolution to Gibson's second novel, *Count Zero* (1986), in which the mercenary Turner retreats to the country to hunt squirrels and play father. More often than not, however, nature is abjected as the passive victim of rapacious and accelerating exploitation.

Morton reiterates Martin Heidegger's deterministic argument that the imperative of the technological is to reify nature as "standing-reserve" (Heidegger 17). That is, the 'world' comes to exist simply as a reservoir of objects waiting for us to use them; it becomes "nature-for-us" (cf. Morton 118). This attitude is clear in early cyberpunk; for instance, both the posthuman Shaper protagonists and the alien Investors in Sterling's short story "Swarm" (1982) are eager to monetize and weaponize not only new worlds but also new (and more vulnerable) alien species. This anticipates the satirical future of Sterling and Lewis Shiner's "Mozart in Mirrorshades" (1985), the last story in the *Mirrorshades* anthology. Sterling and Shiner build on the familiar science-fictional idea of branching timelines to imagine an out-of-control *multi*-global capitalist expansion that involves visiting—and changing—the past, and trading techno-trinkets for cultural treasures and natural resources. The past itself is standing-reserve in the inflexible logic of capitalist expansion, and the Great Acceleration of the American future overwhelms (a version of) 18th-century Austria. In 1775 a huge pipeline project is "ripping through Salzburg's maze of cobbled streets" (223), and a young Wolfgang Mozart wants nothing so much as to Green Card his way into the rapacious future: "History says I'm going to be *dead* in fifteen years! I don't want to die in this dump! I want that car and that recording studio!" (238; emphasis in original).

39.2 The End of the World

There is nothing peripheral about 'world' in the early 21st century because that 'world' was a convenient illusion, a 'world-for-us' that never was: "In an age of global warming," Morton writes, "there is no background, and thus there is no foreground. It is the end of the world, since worlds depend on backgrounds and foregrounds" (99). Climate change demonstrates that "[t]here is no 'away' after the end of the world" (109) because of the inextricable intra- and inter-relations of all entities and objects, including humans, that are part of the planetary biosphere.

The fantasy of a benevolent nature as an ecological support system has been increasingly difficult to sustain since the environmental movements of the 1960s and 1970s. Eco-catastrophe has become the default setting in many sf stories since at least the 1990s, heralding the collapse of yet another comforting subject/object binary. 'Nature,' once merely a backdrop to human technoculture, has come to demand our attention in increasingly alarming ways. For instance, Marge Piercy's *He, She and It* (1991; also published as *Body of Glass*) is a cyberpunk-flavored novel that acknowledges the influence of both Gibson's *Neuromancer* and Donna J. Haraway's "A Manifesto for Cyborgs" (1985). It is set in a degraded cyberpunk future that is the direct result of eco-catastrophe:

> Every quadrant was managed by the remains of the UN, the eco-police. After the two billion died in the Great Famine and the plagues, they had authority over earth, water, air outside domes and wraps. Otherwise the multis ruled their enclaves, the free towns defended themselves as they could, and the Glop rotted under the poisonous sky, ruled by feuding gangs and overlords. (33)

In a somewhat lighter vein, Bruce Sterling's *Heavy Weather* (1994) focuses on the members of "the Storm Troupe," heavy-weather hackers who chase gigantic tornadoes caused by GHG-driven climate change. Sterling's prose strains to capture the overwhelming nonhuman agency of such extreme weather events: "This whole vast curdled mass of storms was lurching into motion, the mountainous prow of some unthinkably vast and powerful body of hot transparent wind.... It would steam across the grassy plains of Tornado Alley like a planetary juggernaut" (95–96).

While there is a marked urgency in the face of looming disaster in these late-20th-century treatments of the climate crisis, in many 21st-century stories the disaster has already happened. At the same time, the virtual reality (VR) common to cyberpunk gives way to post-cyberpunk's augmented reality (AR), while cyber-hacking gives way to bio-hacking and the splice.[6] Annalee

Newitz's *Autonomous* (2017), for example, blurbed by Neal Stephenson as "to biotech and AI what *Neuromancer* was to the internet," is a bleeding-edge biopunk novel whose future is lodged in the heart of the Anthropocene. Set 60 years after "the late twenty-first century Collapse which left populations and farms ravaged by plagues" (Newitz), *Autonomous* is already situated "after the end of the world." In Sterling's *Heavy Weather*, published in the early 1990s, the storm-hackers have to chase down their tornadoes; here in the early 21st century, 'heavy weather' is more than ready to come to us, both in fiction and in life.

At the same time, the implications of Newitz's speculative 'augmented reality' cannot be understated. In this imagined future, Big Pharma is utterly corrupt and the fast-paced action in the foreground is driven by the inaccessibility for most people of over-priced vaccines and therapeutic drugs because of fierce patent protections. While culture and technology have transformed the 'world' and have in turn been transformed by it, AR technologies show how neoliberal political and economic structures remain hegemonic. For those who can afford them, AR technologies provide a protective barrier for vulnerable human bodies threatened both by disease and by the hostile climatic forces of the planet, while simultaneously holding those bodies open to the agential forces of the virtual such as massive surveillance and inescapable consumerism. *Autonomous* therefore echoes current developments in AR technologies as the abstract experience of Gibson's immersive cyberspace is supplanted by "the direct experience of a real-world environment, with elements 'augmented' by computer-generated perceptual information, ideally across multiple sensory modalities, including visual, auditory, haptic, somatosensory, and olfactory" (*Wikipedia*).

N. Katherine Hayles notes in *Unthought: The Power of the Cognitive Nonconscious* that currently developing real-world AR offers "the powerful advantages of convenience, satisfaction of desire, and enhanced navigation while increasing surveillance, directed marketing, and capitalist exploitation" (116). As in other recent novels that speculate about AR technologies in near futures of ecological decline—such as Linda Nagata's *The Red* (2015), Stephen Palmer's *Beautiful Intelligence* (2015), and Madeline Ashby's *Company Town* (2016)—in *Autonomous* AR provides the experience of a new hybrid world of embodied virtuality, a kind of hyperreality for the 21st century. The AR body in *Autonomous* is permanently tuned to and permanently inserted *into* the digital overlay—'the network'—through any number of physical implants. In Morton's terms, Newitz's network-as-hyperobject is as "viscous"—as "sticky"—as the hyperobject of global warming (Morton 27–37). Invisible though not immaterial, these networks enmesh individual bodies in a vast technological ecosystem; as a result, the networked AR body becomes a figure for human life constrained both by an unmanageable biosphere and by an increasingly intrusive technosphere.

39.3 Escape from the End of the World

In cyberpunk futures, ecological thought is inextricably entangled with technological thinking. In fact, many contemporary cyberpunk or post-cyberpunk fictions, often set in some version of a techno-utopian far future, imagine the kinds of human-made miracles that might allow humanity "to 'get around' the constraints that the ecological poses" (Canavan, "Ecology 101" 20), thereby rendering humanity invulnerable to 'nature.' In this context, the dream of fully realized nanotechnology—Joshua Raulerson calls it "the *novum* of intelligent nanofabrication" (100; emphasis in original)—has been especially significant to post-cyberpunk novels such as Neal Stephenson's *The Diamond Age* (1995), which imagines a world so utterly transformed by "the Seed" that the very idea of 'nature' or 'planet' seems quaint: "Atlantis/Shanghai had imbued him with the sense that all the old cities of the world were doomed ... and that the future was in the new cities, built from the bedrock up one atom at a time" (71). Alternately, Gibson introduces nanotechnology into the world of his Bridge Trilogy (1993–99) in part as a response to the devastating forces of natural disasters: earthquake-destroyed Tokyo, for example, has been completely rebuilt: "A lot of it's *not even where it used to be....* They pushed all the quake-junk into the water, like landfill, and now they're building that up, too" (*Idoru* 47; emphasis in original). Gibson very directly criticizes the desire to control the trajectory of the technofuture, however, associating this with the villainous Cody Harwood, who desires nothing so much as a future that extends the status quo indefinitely in what Colin Milburn calls "the metastasis of the present" (56): "I want the advent of a degree of functional nanotechnology in a world that will remain recognizably descended from the one I woke in this morning. I want my world transfigured, yet I want my place in that world to be equivalent to the one I now occupy. I want to have my cake and eat it too" (*All Tomorrow's Parties* 250).

Arguably, one can have one's cake and eat it too in some of the far-away spacetimes of Singularity fiction, a post-cyberpunk form "signaling both a continuation of, and a break with, [Movement cyberpunk's] signature themes and conventions" (Raulerson 20). Many of these stories read like the fulfillments of the wildest power fantasies of transhumanism and of technologically invested posthumanism, hearkening back to the posthuman Shapers and Mechanists of Sterling's early cyberpunk-inflected space opera, *Schismatrix* (1985). It is no coincidence that Sterling's protagonist, Abelard Lindsay, finally escapes the limitations of the physical body as he sets out to explore the universe at the end of the novel. Singularity fiction therefore often promises the ultimate escape from the climate crisis; it has the paradoxical task of imagining posthuman futures on the other side of unforeseeable and unimaginable technological transformations. At the same time, a novel such as Charles Stross's aptly titled *Accelerando* (2005) exemplifies the instrumentalization of nature taken for granted in many Singularity fictions.[7] In a discussion of humanity's plans for inhabiting the solar system, Stross's narrator tells us that "[e]ventually Saturn ... will have a planetwide biosphere with nearly a hundred times the surface area of Earth. And a bloody good thing indeed this will be, for otherwise Saturn is no use to anyone except as a fusion fuel bunker for the deep future when the sun's burned down" (252). In Stross's imagined universe, the hyperobject that is Saturn has no intrinsic value: It is meaningful only as Saturn-for-us.

39.4 From Hyperreality to Hyperobjects

When the artificial intelligence in *Neuromancer* offers Case the opportunity to remain permanently in cyberspace, it assures him that "[t]o live here is to live. There is no difference" (258). Perhaps nowhere is the tension between cyberpunk and ecological thought more evident than in how the climate crisis impacts the idea of the virtual. Gerry Canavan suggests that cyberpunk's figurations of cyberspace can "be read as an attempt to circumvent the 'reality principle' of ecological scarcity by positing an interior cybernetic world where such limits no longer apply" ("Ecology 101" 21). This is true, but incomplete: It overshadows some of the performative impact—the rhetorical force—of cyberspace and its analogues way back in the 1980s and 1990s.

The many representations of VR in cyberpunk and its immediate progeny—'cyberspace' in *Neuromancer*, 'the simulation' in Pat Cadigan's *Synners* (1991), and the 'Metaverse' in Neal Stephenson's *Snow Crash* (1992)—is one of its most enduring imaginative legacies, both inviting and challenging readers to consider the existential and ontological implications of worlds of simulation. It is easy to read in any number of these stories variations on Jean Baudrillard's apocalyptic warnings about postmodern hyperreality—an influential theoretical construction of technoculture with which cyberpunk is often associated. Contrary to a lot of conventional wisdom, even early cyberpunk was relatively wary of the immersive pleasures of VR, often representing its adherents as addicts and losers—rather like Gibson's cyber-hacker Case. For Baudrillard, *we* were the addicts and losers, trapped within the hyperreal. The collapse of the real into the virtual under the influence of a capitalist consumer culture leaves only the veneer of simulation in its wake. Baudrillard lamented that the real "has become our true utopia—but a utopia that is no longer a possibility, a utopia we can do no more than dream about, like a lost object" (310).

Ecology in the Anthropocene

In contrast, speculative realism posits a real that far exceeds our fantasy of it as 'reality-for-us.' Entities and objects in the world can never be fully known, nor can they be reduced to our experience of them—they are nothing like 'lost objects,' even as they always remain at least partially withdrawn from both perception and understanding. This version of the real differs mightily from Baudrillard's nostalgic dream. In the Anthropocene the real returns with all the vengeance of the repressed—although it is probably more accurate to say that the climate crisis reveals what has been here all along. As Morton puts it, "*World* is a fragile aesthetic effect around whose corners we are beginning to see" (99; emphasis in original). We experience the loss of 'world' and find ourselves stranded in "the emergency room of ecological coexistence" (Morton 126).

Arguably, this is in radical tension with cyberpunk's 'street cool,' its "relaxed contempt for the flesh" (Gibson, *Neuromancer* 6), the postmodern irony and lack of affect that insulate characters such as Case and Molly from the intensities of their lives in the urban technosphere. It is no longer possible to insulate ourselves from the real because hyperobjects are "viscous" and stick to us: "the more you know about a hyperobject, the more entangled with it you realize you already are" (Morton 28). And so we "enter a new age of sincerity," as Morton puts it (128), and if early cyberpunk showed us our increasing intimacy with our machines, the climate crisis precipitates us into a new and inescapable intimacy with and codependence on the planetary biosphere. Climate change forces us to imagine new possibilities; as Morton argues, it therefore also provides us opportunities for new ways of being in the world, the essence of which is "the notion of coexistence—that is, after all, what ecology profoundly means" (127–28).

Hyperobjects are absolutely 'futural,' and global warming promises "[n]ot the future we can predict and manage, but an unknowable future, a genuinely *future future*" (Morton 123; emphasis in original). The longing for a future that is not simply more of the same is apparent even in *Neuromancer*. Case's demand for the password to unite Neuromancer and Wintermute, the divided selves of the AI, is also a demand for the radical transformation of his fictional world: "Give us the fucking code ... If you don't, what'll change? ... I got no idea at all what'll happen if Wintermute wins, but it'll *change* something!" (260; emphasis in original). But, of course, with typical cyberpunk lack of affect, Wintermute assures Case that ultimately "Things aren't different. Things are things" (270). Fast forward thirty years, however, and we find that Gibson's most recent novel at the time of writing is structured by a deliberate effort to open history out to an authentically different future, one that might at least mitigate the 'bad future' toward which we seem to be heading. *The Peripheral* (2014) follows the characters in two interconnected timelines. The first is a near future embedded in the Anthropocene; in stark contrast to *Neuromancer*, its setting is an economically depressed rural area of the southern U.S. Walmart-like chain outlets, the military, and drug makers offer virtually the only opportunities for employment, and local politics is hopelessly corrupt. This world is edging ever closer to radical environmental unsustainability.

The second timeline is seventy years later, set in London, England, on the other side of "the jackpot," the devastating forty-year-long collapse of the Earth's biosphere. London after "the jackpot" is a futuristic city of high-rise "Shards" and luscious green spaces, but it is as sad and empty as the radiation-soaked San Francisco of Philip K. Dick's *Do Androids Dream of Electric Sheep?* (1968). London has been rebuilt through the wonders of nanotechnology—"the assemblers, London's microscopic caretakers" (250)—but almost all of it is artificial or illusory. To borrow from Raulerson, future London is now "a vision of materiality *mediated through* the digital—in place of virtual reality, something we might instead call 'realized virtuality'" (78; emphasis in original). Nostalgia for the unimaginable losses of the past suffuses everything: One character, Ash, dresses in mourning black and has had her body covered in constantly moving tattoos of "every bird and beast of the Anthropocene extinction" (50). While London's few remaining human inhabitants enjoy the elite fruits of an almost unimaginable mastery of material sciences and bioengineering, life has been radically diminished. London is lonely, aimless, and decadent, and most of its 'inhabitants' are simulations that function to mask the emptiness of its streets. As for Gibson's title, it refers to the 'peripherals'—physical avatars—that people can connect to and 'run' at a distance through a kind of telepresence, like an updated version of *Neuromancer*'s simstim.

Some Londoners have discovered a technology that allows them to communicate with the past, largely as a form of entertainment. As in "Mozart in Mirrorshades"—which Gibson has named as an inspiration for *The Peripheral* (see Robertson)—as soon as the future opens a connection to its own past, that past immediately branches off into an alternate timeline, a "stub." Also as in "Mozart in Mirrorshades," the past is treated as disposable: Ash recognizes it as a new version of colonialism that she calls "third-worlding alternate continua" (103). We might consider how all these 'third-world continua'—these temporal 'stubs'—are tangential to the 'first world' of the London players, no longer their 'real' past but merely a kind of 'background' to their games. Gibson's text, however, suggests that the novel's major interest is the pre-jackpot 'third world.' Netherton, a key character in future London, tells Flynne, the protagonist of the earlier timeline, about the catastrophe that her world is facing and that his world has barely survived:

> And first of all that it was no one thing.... More a climate than an event, so not the way apocalypse stories liked to have a big event.... It was androgenic.... Not that they'd known what they were doing, had meant to make problems, but they'd caused it anyway.... Because people in the past, clueless as to how that worked, had fucked it all up, then not been able to get it together to do anything about it, even after they knew, and now it was too late.
>
> So now in her day, he said, they were headed into androgenic, systemic, multiplex, seriously bad shit... (320)

Although they cannot rewrite their own ruined history, Netherton and some of his allies provide information and resources that begin to have a significant impact, economically and politically, on the hard times of Flynne's world. As a result of London's interference, there will be another future for her timeline, and with London's support it might manage to avoid "the jackpot"—such new knowledge might change everything.

The Peripheral demonstrates the potential for post-cyberpunk fiction to respond in the utopian mode to its situation in the Anthropocene, refusing the "metastasis of the present" (Milburn 56) that paralyzes the dystopian future in a novel such as Newitz's *Autonomous*. As Anna McFarlane notes in her discussion of the "haptic" (embodied) focus of *The Peripheral*, "faced with these multiple [ecological] threats, which do not just endanger the direction of the future but the very concept of futurity, Gibson responds with a kind of science fiction that emphasizes the interdependence of the individual, society, and ecology" (116). The particular hope encapsulated in the novel's open-ended conclusion[8] suggests a swerve away from fictional technospheres backgrounded by a dead 'nature' toward fictional ecosystems that foreground responsible human co-relations with both technosphere and biosphere. *The Peripheral*, in this reading, promises "[n]ot the future we can predict and manage, but an unknowable future, a genuinely *future future*" (Morton 123).

Notes

1 See Debra Benita Shaw's detailed overview in *Technoculture: The Key Concepts*.

2 See, for example, the special issue of *Paradoxa* edited by Gerry Canavan and Andrew Hageman on "Global Weirding." In *The Great Derangement*, Amitav Ghosh notes "that the word *uncanny* has begun to be used with ever greater frequency, in relation to climate change," pointing readers to Timothy Morton's analysis, in *Hyperobjects*, of the uncanny nature of the current climate crisis (30; emphasis in original).

3 Speculative realism is one of several philosophical positions, including object-oriented ontology and feminist new materialism, contributing to the current 'non-human turn' in the humanities and social sciences; all of them are attempts to put pressure on anthropocentric thinking about the climate crisis.

Ecology in the Anthropocene

In general, speculative realism theorizes an anti-Cartesian relationality between and among objects/entities/humans. See Grusin, ed., and Bryant. For an extended study of the potential affinities between speculative realism and sf, see Willems.

4 For details about Movement-era cyberpunk, see Graham J. Murphy's contribution in this collection.

5 It is worth keeping in mind that 'we' is limited to those of us who live in (mostly) western technocultures. Cyberpunk's conventional version of the cyborg is also rather limited, if we consider the near-simultaneous publication of Donna J. Haraway's socialist-feminist "A Manifesto for Cyborgs," which developed an influential figuration of the cyborg that emphasizes its openness to hybrid ontologies: "Far from signalling a walling off of people from other living beings, cyborgs signal disturbingly and pleasurably tight coupling" (176).

6 In *Biopunk Dystopias*, Lars Schmeink notes a shift in the technological imaginary away from "the visceral technology of mechanical implants, body augmentations, and the virtualities" of the Gibsonian matrix, toward a focus on "genetic engineering, xenotransplantation, and virology... best expressed in the metaphor not of the cyborg but of the splice" (7). See also Newitz's "Biopunk" and Schmeink's chapter on "Biopunk" in this collection.

7 For an extended analysis of the Singularity in Stross's *Accelerando*, see Gerry Canavan's contribution to this collection.

8 Gibson's sequel to *The Peripheral*, titled *Agency*, is due to be published in early 2020, which would certainly help to account for *The Peripheral*'s open-ended structure; at the same time, this is exactly the appropriate structure for a novel that thematizes an unknowable but hopeful futurity. It is also in keeping with the non-resolutions of so many of Gibson's other novels, notably beginning with *Neuromancer*.

Works Cited

"Augmented Reality." *Wikipedia*, 25 Mar. 2019, https://en.wikipedia.org/wiki/Augmented_reality.

Baudrillard, Jean. "Simulacra and Science Fiction." Translated by Arthur B. Evans. *Science Fiction Studies*, vol. 18, no. 3, 1991, pp. 309–13.

Bryant, Levi R. "The Ontic Principle: Outline of an Object-Oriented Ontology." *The Speculative Turn: Continental Materialism and Realism*, edited by Levi R. Bryant, Nick Srnicek, and Graham Harman. re-press, 2011, pp. 261–78.

Canavan, Gerry. "Ecology 101." *SFRA Review*, no. 314, Winter 2015, pp. 16–25.

———— and Andrew Hageman, eds. *Global Weirding. Paradoxa* 28. Paradoxa, 2018.

———— and Kim Stanley Robinson, eds. *Green Planets: Ecology and Science Fiction*. Wesleyan UP, 2014.

Chakrabarty, Dipesh. "The Climate of History: Four Theses." *Critical Inquiry*, vol. 35, 2009, pp. 197–222.

Gibson, William. *All Tomorrow's Parties*. Putnam, 1999.

————. *Idoru*. Putnam, 1996.

————. *Neuromancer*. Ace, 1984.

————. *The Peripheral*. Putnam, 2014.

Ghosh, Amitav. *The Great Derangement: Climate Change and the Unthinkable*. U of Chicago P, 2016.

Grusin, Richard, ed. *The Nonhuman Turn*. U of Minnesota P, 2015.

Haraway, Donna J. "A Manifesto for Cyborgs: Science, Technology, and Socialist Feminism in the 1980s." *Coming to Terms: Feminism, Theory, Politics*, edited by Elizabeth Weed. Routledge, 1989, pp. 173–204.

Hayles, N. Katherine. *Unthought: The Power of the Cognitive Nonconscious*. U of Chicago P, 2017.

Heidegger, Martin. "The Question Concerning Technology." *The Question Concerning Technology and Other Essays*, translated by William Lovitt. Harper & Row, 1977, pp. 3–35.

McFarlane, Anna. "'Anthropomorphic Drones' and Colonized Bodies: William Gibson's *The Peripheral*." *English Studies in Canada*, vol. 42, no. 1–2, 2016, pp. 115–32.

Morton, Timothy. *Hyperobjects: Philosophy and Ecology after the End of the World*. U of Minnesota P, 2013.

Newitz, Annalee. *Autonomous*. Tor, 2017. Ebook.

————. "Biopunk." *San Francisco Bay Guardian*, 8 Aug. 2001, https://www.ekac.org/biopunk.html.

Piercy, Marge. *He, She and It*. Ballantine, 1993.

Raulerson, Joshua. *Singularities: Technoculture, Transhumanism, and Science Fiction in the Twenty-first Century*. Liverpool UP, 2013.

Robertson, Adi. "William Gibson Interview: Time Travel, Virtual Reality, and his New Book." *The Verge*, 28 Oct. 2014, https://www.theverge.com/2014/10/28/7083625/william-gibson-interview-time-travel-virtual-reality-and-the-peripheral.

Schmeink, Lars. *Biopunk Dystopias: Genetic Engineering, Society, and Science Fiction*. Liverpool UP, 2016.

Shaw, Debra Benita. *Technoculture: The Key Concepts*. Berg, 2008.

Steffen, Will, Paul J. Crutzen, and John R. MacNeill. "The Anthropocene: Are Humans Now Overwhelming the Great Forces of Nature?" *Ambio*, vol. 36, no. 8, 2007, pp. 614–21.

Stephenson, Neal. *The Diamond Age*. Bantam, 1995.

Sterling, Bruce. *Heavy Weather*. Bantam, 1996.

———. Preface. *Mirrorshades: The Cyberpunk Anthology*, edited by Bruce Sterling. Ace, 1988, pp. ix–xvi.

——— and Lewis Shiner. "Mozart in Mirrorshades." *Mirrorshades: The Cyberpunk Anthology*, edited by Bruce Sterling. Ace, 1988, pp. 222–39.

Stross, Charles. *Accelerando*. Ace, 2005.

Suvin, Darko. *Metamorphoses of Science Fiction: On the Poetics and History of a Literary Genre*. Yale UP, 1979.

Willems, Brian. *Speculative Realism and Science Fiction*. Edinburgh UP, 2017.

40

EMPIRE

John Rieder

Although critics and scholars have sharply disagreed about the social importance and artistic value of mid-1980s cyberpunk, both its advocates and its detractors agree that the fiction responds to the re-structuring of the world capitalist economy that goes under the various names of neoliberalism, postfordism, the regime of flexible accumulation, late capitalism, the Age of Information, or—in Michael Hardt and Antonio Negri's writings—Empire.[1] Hardt and Negri's term can serve as a reminder that the ability of multinational corporations to exploit differences in national labor markets, though clearly facilitated by the electronic technology and information processing so central to cyberpunk, is built upon the foundations of uneven development and resource extraction laid by several preceding centuries of colonialism and imperialism. Neoliberal globalization is always also neocolonialism, and this chapter elaborating the topic of cyberpunk and Empire therefore begins by asking how cyberpunk positions itself with respect to the historical continuity between colonialism and late-20th-century globalization.

There is a clear case to be made that the cyberpunk movement deliberately tried to distance itself from the western colonial past. This did not take the form of addressing colonial history directly, but rather of criticizing earlier science fiction's (sf) affiliation with colonialist or imperialist ideologies. In his prefatory note to the first story in *Mirrorshades: The Cyberpunk Anthology* (1986), Bruce Sterling writes that William Gibson's "The Gernsback Continuum" (1981) offers "a coolly accurate perception of the wrongheaded elements of the past" that issues "a clarion call for a new SF aesthetic of the Eighties" (1). This story, claims Sterling, "led the way" to Gibson's Sprawl series of short stories and novels,[2] the influence and importance of which are often said to overshadow the rest of early cyberpunk fiction. According to the unnamed narrator of "The Gernsback Continuum," one finds in the futuristic visions of technological wonder depicted on 1930s-era pulp magazine covers "a dream logic that knew nothing of pollution, the finite bounds of fossil fuel, of foreign wars it was possible to lose. They [the Heirs of the Dream] were smug, happy, and utterly content with themselves and their world. And in the Dream, it was *their* world" (9). Gibson's emphasis in the final phrase is the key. Gibson is condemning the presumption of control that dismisses even the possibility of recalcitrance or disobedience on the part of these dreamers' various slaves, ranging from the inhabitants of foreign lands to the natural world itself. That sense of entitlement is based on the faith—or dream—not just that the world is theirs to use, but that their idea of how to use it is written into the very shape of things. Although the explicit target in Gibson's story is the technological optimism of Gernsback-era sf, then, the underlying and far more important reference is to America itself—the America that sees itself as guardian of freedom and donor of progress, and presumes that those roles give it the right to impose its vision of democracy and prosperity on the rest of the world's territories and inhabitants.

Gibson's dream logic articulates an attitude that I named "the discoverer's fantasy" in *Colonialism and the Emergence of Science Fiction*. It has a long history, having been used to justify colonial expropriation of 'discovered' land and its resources since Columbus's fleet cast anchor on the shore of Hispaniola. Modeling my formulation on Slavoj Žižek's notion of ideological fantasies,[3] I put the discoverer's fantasy like this: We (the explorers, the discoverers) know very well that there are people in this land, but we act as if it were empty before our arrival (Rieder 31). The discoverers' arrival, in other words, is the beginning of the land's history. Their 'use' of this land is the beginning of its integration into the world as it is meant to be and destined to become. (The legal argument as it developed over the centuries was that, although Indigenous communities were living on the land, they were not using it or its resources to their full potential, and therefore the colonizers were justified in seizing it.) In mocking the 80-lane highways, moving sidewalks, flying cars, and cylindrical towers of Frank R. Paul's cover illustrations, Gibson implicitly targets the American, and more generally western, presumption that it is entitled to turn the rest of the world into its own image, and he condemns it from a decidedly post-Vietnam War perspective informed as well by the environmental activism of the 1960s and 1970s. The question that follows, however, is whether Gibson in his Sprawl fictions succeeds in carrying out the kind of re-thinking of his and his readers' relationship to this colonial dream logic that Sterling claims.

What happens when the land of discovery is cyberspace? In an essay on Gibson and cyberpunk, Istvan Csicsery-Ronay distinguishes between the expansionist fantasies of early sf, based on colonialism and Social Darwinism, and the postmodern and cyberpunk counter-movement he calls implosion, where the rationality of instrumental reason is ground into fragments. In Gibson's cyberspace, however, a lot of expansionist elements survive. The hackers in "Burning Chrome" (1982) and *Neuromancer* (1984) use invasive software developed by the military, signaling a world where technological development continues to be driven by military competition, with information rather than land now the stakes of battle. Gibson's hacker protagonists are 'cowboys,' invoking the expansionist mythology of the American Western. At the end of the entire Sprawl series, in the concluding moments of *Mona Lisa Overdrive* (1988), an AI, an uploaded cowboy, and a software construct board a virtual vehicle bound for another solar system. Many of the critics less enamored with cyberpunk have complained about the way such plot elements blunt the critical edge of Gibson's depiction of a dystopian near future. Csicsery-Ronay, for instance, says that the cyberpunks "write as if they are both the victims of a life-negating system and the heroic adventurers of thrill" (192). One might well argue, then, that in Gibson's cyberspace it is not so much that the tired and wrongheaded ideologies of American self-congratulatory fantasy are abandoned or overcome as that they are re-stylized and recirculated—combined, first of all, with the cynicism that recognizes the 'life-negating' environmental and social consequences of contemporary capitalism at the same time as it continues to exploit its expansionist ethos for thrill and adventure. Thus, arguably, Gibson's Sprawl fictions do not demystify the discoverer's fantasy but rather recast it with cyberspace as the new frontier. We know very well, the reformulated fantasy would then go, that this space is an artifice constructed by the collective efforts of the corporate economy and supported by the material infrastructure of the entire computing technology of contemporary society, but we act as if were an autonomous realm that sustains itself as an independent reality and is available to appropriation and inhabitation by those able to adapt themselves to its environment. And so the Tessier-Ashpool AIs, the software construct of Julius Deane, and the uploaded minds of Bobby, the cowboy, and Angie, his girl, become in the end the natives, or rather the indigenized settlers, of a newly opened interstellar frontier.

Some of the signature moments of mid-1980s cyberpunk can also be interpreted as unselfconsciously continuing earlier sf's entanglement with colonial discourses and ideologies. Consider

Empire

the movement's iconic mirrorshades, for example, about which Sterling writes, "[b]y hiding the eyes, mirrorshades prevent the forces of normalcy from realizing that one is crazed and possibly dangerous. They are the symbol of the sun-staring visionary, the biker, the rocker, the police-man, and other similar outlaws" (Preface xi). As the incongruous inclusion of the policeman in Sterling's list of outlaws attests, however, the concealment afforded the person wearing the mirrorshades may have more to do with enforcing power than with evading it. The mirrorshades hide the gaze of the wearer from those he or she looks upon, and that concealed gaze reproduces a structure of power endemic to colonial settings. David Spurr observes in *The Rhetoric of Empire* that "the privilege of inspecting, of examining, of looking at, by its nature excludes the journalist from the human reality constituted as the object of investigation. [… This is] analogous to the classic position of the Western writer in the colonial situation: the condition of access to colo-nized peoples also marks an exclusion from the lived human reality of the colonized" (14–15). But this exclusion, far from being a disadvantage, protects and reinforces the privilege the gazer exercises over those gazed upon. Thus, the way the mirrorshades signify rebellion against nor-malcy is ambiguous at best.

Or consider one of Gibson's best-known and most often-quoted aphoristic sentences: "[t]he street finds its own uses for things" ("Burning" 186). One can certainly construe this as locating a chink in the armature of capitalism, where its overpowering tendency to reduce everything to the quantitative cost-benefit terms of exchange value is inevitably complicated and perhaps sig-nificantly resisted by the fact that commodities must at some point in their circulation function as use values. But it also indulges in a certain kind of glamorizing of entrepreneurial adventure. When Gibson's Sprawl fictions present street level 'biz,' which is to say the thriving black market underside of the legitimate capitalist economy, as the cutting edge of technical innovation, as they often do, the street becomes another kind of frontier territory that ties Gibson's avant-garde heroes to an ideology of progress—and plotting history as progress is certainly one of colonialism's and Empire's most deeply ingrained and inescapable strategies.

Even if we allow that the narrative structuring of time and space within the framework given to them by an ideology of western technological progress is so pervasive a feature of so much sf that it amounts almost to a defining formal necessity of the mode, its powerful effects on early cyberpunk remain distinctive evidence of the colonial ancestry haunting its hyper-capitalist, usu-ally dystopian settings. A spectacular example is the evolutionary leap accomplished through the merging of the Tessier-Ashpool AIs at the end of *Neuromancer* and recapitulated at the conclusion of *Mona Lisa Overdrive* that, as in Arthur C. Clarke and Stanley Kubrick's *2001: A Space Odyssey* (1968), simultaneously gives birth to a new species, establishes communication with another pre-sumably superior intelligence outside the solar system, and thereby enlists this solar system into a larger civilization, very much like a 'discovered' territory entering into history. A similar trajec-tory is clearly in place, though not as quickly or thrillingly accomplished, in Sterling's *Schismatrix* (1985), and the figure is repeated often enough in later posthumanist sf to gain the tonally opposite designations of the Singularity (Vinge) and "the rapture of the nerds" (Doctorow and Stross).[4]

Somewhat less spectacular, but more pervasive and perhaps more consequential, are the traces of the colonial economy evident in patterns of uneven economic distribution that combine na-tional and corporate struggles over possession of new technology with the sense, usually implicit, that such struggles pit the denizens of the future—or at least of the fully-up-to-date present—against those who continue to live in the past. Cyberpunk's subcultural protagonists are quite as likely to be in league with the subaltern past as with the dominant future in such confrontations. In Pat Cadigan's "Pretty Boy Crossover" (1986), for instance, the protagonist makes a deliber-ate choice not to join his uploaded ex-lover in corporate-owned virtual reality. Charles Stross's wonderfully weird post-apocalyptic comedy "Rogue Farm" (2003) similarly turns on a strug-gle between would-be migrants to a posthuman extraterrestrial cosmopolis and the recalcitrant

John Rieder

protagonist's desire to save his land from being consumed as fuel for their enterprise. An unusually explicit example of a neocolonial ideology of progress structuring the narrative space is the "foot-loose time travel fantasy" (223) that concludes the *Mirrorshades* anthology, Bruce Sterling and Lewis Shiner's "Mozart in Mirrorshades" (1985). Like "The Gernsback Continuum" it is mainly concerned with sending up and satirizing the wrongheaded values of a previous generation's sf adventure stories, in this case by simply literalizing a basic metaphor of colonial ideology: the present is colonizing the past, or rather alternative pasts, turning them into unevenly developed versions of the present for its own profit. The joke motivating the title is that Wolfgang Amadeus Mozart proves extremely adaptable to the ethos of the crass, opportunistic, amoral corporate management team directing the invasion of an alternative, newly industrialized, polluted, and impoverished 18th-century Salzburg. As with "Pretty Boy Crossover" and "Rogue Farm," the story clearly pushes toward sympathy with the colonized past in opposition to the juggernaut of progress.

Unlike the territorial colonial invasion in "Mozart in Mirrorshades," cyberpunk's figures of invasion usually take forms that emphasize the crucial technological and social differences between contemporary neoliberal Empire and earlier colonization. In the Preface to *Mirrorshades* Sterling counts invasion among the recurrent themes of cyberpunk. He says that it takes two main forms: "body invasion: prosthetic limbs, implanted circuitry, cosmetic surgery, genetic alteration... [and] mind invasion: brain-computer interfaces, artificial intelligence, neurochemistry—techniques radically redefining the nature of humanity, the nature of the self" (xiii). Csicsery-Ronay also points to the re-location and re-direction of the motif of invasion as the crucial difference between expansionist and implosive sf:

> The topoi of implosive SF are based on analogies of the invasion and transformation of the body by alien entities of our own making. Implosive science fiction finds the scene of SF problematics not in imperial adventures among the stars, but in the body-physical/body-social and a drastic ambivalence about the body's traditional—and terrifyingly uncertain—integrity. (188)

In cyberpunk, geopolitics becomes biopolitics, resource extraction takes place both on the surface and in the depths of the body, and enslavement to globalized capital becomes very hard to disentangle from basic survival or even mere existence. The intimacy and ubiquity of tropes of body and mind invasion in cyberpunk is, more than any of its other features, what provides the most solid basis for the hyperbolic appraisals of its importance as a representation of late capitalism by Fredric Jameson and those who followed his lead.[5]

The precarious existence of the plugged-in, drugged-up hustlers and rebels of cyberpunk resonates not just with the semiotic rebelliousness of punk rock subculture but also, and perhaps more consequentially, with the condition of labor under the neoliberal re-structuring of the world economy. As Tom Moylan put it in his 1995 analysis of Gibson's Sprawl fictions, "[a]s the power of organized labor is challenged by the mechanisms of a computer-based flexible production, workers who have held a secure place in the economy since the 1950s are losing ground, and new forms of labor are emerging that are amenable to the limited awards of this leaner and meaner system" (90). Moylan identifies Gibson's typical protagonists as akin to contract workers, "skilled professional-managerial-technical workers who individually contract with corporations (and governments) for limited term, relatively high-paid tasks" (90), and who are ranged in the neoliberal economy alongside a dwindling number of highly paid, still-unionized laborers and the burgeoning ranks of minimum-wage service employees, all of them scrambling to survive in the emergent "logic of postfordist re-structuring [in which] the secure middle sector of skilled workers and managers has largely disappeared" (86). That missing middle sector is one of the most prominent features of Gibson's, and much other cyberpunk's, social ensemble, as the stories tend to be populated almost exclusively by marginal or criminal subcultures and super-powerful corporations. That missing middle ground is also evident in cyberpunk's limited variety of typical settings, which veer heavily towards post-industrial wastelands like the toxic waste dump The Solitude in *Mona Lisa Overdrive*, gathering places for the marginalized contract workers of the black market like The Gentleman Loser in "Burning Chrome" or the Chatsubo in *Neuromancer*'s Night City, and enclaves of privilege like "Freezone" in John Shirley's contribution to *Mirrorshades* or the orbiting pleasure garden Freeside in *Neuromancer*. Thus, the degradation of the environment, the precarity of labor, and the polarization of society under multinational postindustrial capitalism provide the template for cyberpunk's dystopian and neo-*noir* imaginary.

Sterling's summary of body and mind invasion makes clear that cyberpunk's tropes of invasion are all about the permeability of boundaries that formerly seemed solid. As Donna J. Haraway observed in her "A Manifesto for Cyborgs," written in the same years and in response to the same social upheaval as the fiction of the cyberpunk coterie, the boundaries between organism and machine, human and animal, and the physical and non-physical turn out to be porous and unreliable in the society taking shape around cybernetic command and control. The invasion of the body by prosthetics and of the mind by digital data and software highlights not only the contingency of individual identity but perhaps even more the vulnerability of the employee or citizen to forces of control that are mediated by technology but structured by several centuries of symbiosis between capitalism and colonialism. As the regime of flexible accumulation takes hold in the 1970s and 1980s, stripping U.S. labor of industrial and manufacturing jobs and cheapening production by exploiting formerly colonized labor markets, domestic labor and citizenship are systematically devalued by neoliberal attacks on the power of labor unions and the entitlements of citizens. If Moylan is right about the importance of the re-structuring of labor to cyberpunk's construction of characters, the boundaries being violated in the fictions respond to this systematic invasion of boundaries formerly relied upon to protect the livelihood of first world workers. Cyberpunk's array of hackers and meat puppets hyperbolizes the insecurity of the Rust-Belt-era labor market and the immense asymmetry of power that leaves workers increasingly at the mercy of multinational corporate strategies.

The thematic centrality of figures of invasion in early cyberpunk is rivaled by its attempts to imagine totality, or as Sterling puts it in the *Mirrorshades* manifesto: "the tools of global integration—the satellite media net, the multinational corporation—fascinate the cyberpunks and figure constantly in their work" (xiv). The plot of invasion itself is often driven by an underlying transformation of the concept of totality from some kind of spatiotemporal aggregation into disembodied information. In the re-structuring of the global economy this means that the tactical importance of occupying territory gives way to monopolizing access to employment, rights, resources, and information. The Sprawl trilogy responds with a plot built entirely on breaking into corporate data banks and breaking down the barriers that separate and fragment the totality of information in them. But at the same time as cyberpunk often fantasizes niches of resistance or escape (e.g. in *Mirrorshades*: "Freezone" [1985], Lewis Shiner's "Till Human Voices Wake Us" [1984], Sterling and Gibson's "Red Star, Winter Orbit" [1983]), it seldom imagines the possibility of a structural transformation in economic or political terms. Instead, the transformation in Gibson takes place at the level of informational totality with the merging of the two Tessier-Ashpool AIs, while for the workers and citizens of the Sprawl, nothing changes: "Things are things," as the transformed Wintermute puts it at the end of *Neuromancer* (270). What has often been said but bears repeating is that neocolonial capitalism has here turned into 'things' as such. All too often in cyberpunk, capitalism tends to operate as if it were nature itself, and the premise of capitalist growth as the underlying engine of history may be precisely the reason the Sprawl trilogy reverts to expansionist space travel at its conclusion.

Many cyberpunk imaginings of global integration establish a set of equivalences that roll together self, information, money, capitalism, nature, and destiny, in the process signaling an entire and apparently irreversible immersion of the worker in the logic of capital. Mark Bould contends that in *Neuromancer* "the euphoria of disembodied transcendence became [...] a fantasy of becoming one with the global circulation of capital" (119). For the 'wireheads' in Sterling's *Schismatrix*, "[o]ur life is information—even money is information. Our money and our life are one and the same" (179). Of course, the 'life' of a computer program is not the life of an organism, as the uploaded consciousnesses and cyber-constructs of biologically dead characters in the Sprawl trilogy also show. But the way information promises to reduce even money itself to its new, more all-encompassing form of universal equivalency lies at the heart of much cyberpunk teleology, as the transformation of everything into information becomes a kind of apotheosis and redemption of the material world. A character in next-generation cyberpunk Charles Stross's *Accelerando* (2005) announces the substitution of the new apocalyptic destiny for old-fashioned colonial expansion in no uncertain terms when he trashes a NASA plan to land a spacecraft on Mars:

> Mars is just dumb mass at the bottom of a gravity well [...] They should be working on uploading and solving the nanoassembly conformational problem instead. Then we could turn all the available dumb matter into computronium and use it for processing our thoughts. Long-term, it's the only way to go. The solar system is a dead loss right now [...] If it isn't thinking, it isn't working. (14)

Thinking equals working equals processing information, and the 'dumb matter' of the entire solar system takes the place occupied by empty land in an earlier iteration of colonial ideology, while, meanwhile, the self's own destiny is to be entirely penetrated and dissolved into the new totality as well.

Charles Stross is by no means as representative a figure as William Gibson or Bruce Sterling, however, and not because of their comparative talent or achievement. In moving from the moment of the mid-1980s to the decades following it, cyberpunk undergoes "an inflation and dispersal of reference" beyond its literary origins into a wide array of other media, including cinema, roleplaying games, music, and television, and from its North American and English origins to become an important presence in the rest of Europe, Japan, Latin America, the Middle East, and South Africa (Foster xvi). In the process it changes from a coterie movement or possibly a subcategory of sf into what Thomas Foster calls a "cultural formation" or what most contemporary genre theorists would call a mode (xiv). This diffusion of cyberpunk from movement to mode entails a corresponding diffusion of its political significance, which becomes less determinate as the modal practice becomes more widespread. Some of the resulting work that traffics in the cyberpunk mode, especially much Hollywood blockbuster moviemaking, loses almost all of the movement's already uncertain critical edge. Nonetheless, it is also the case that as the practice of cyberpunk itself becomes a global phenomenon, some fiction in the cyberpunk mode takes on globalization in a much more explicitly critical and politicized way than one finds in the work of the coterie.

The Wachowskis' *Matrix* trilogy—*The Matrix* (1999), *The Matrix Reloaded* (2003), and *The Matrix Revolutions* (2003)—can serve as an example of Hollywood's financially successful but ideologically equivocal forays into the cyberpunk mode. The *Matrix* trilogy is an invasion narrative modeled on colonial resource extraction in which the bodies of the colonized themselves become a natural resource, the fossil fuel of the monstrous occupation. Like most Hollywood big-budget films, these are generic hybrids that mix elements of Asian martial arts and fairy tale romance with Gothic styling, but at the center of the plot is the cyberpunk staple of virtual reality as the scene of struggle between a band of individualized protagonists and an anonymous, corporation-like enemy. The trick of making the virtual world into a simulacrum of the audience's empirical world and then depicting it as an illusion manipulated by an evil conspiracy suggests a reading of the cyberpunk movement's body and mind invasions as metaphors for the way corporately controlled mass media turns neoliberal attacks on workers' rights into business as usual. But the messianic plot of the hero's transformation into 'the One' who will save the human race from its plight is a weak, silly version of cyberpunk's technological apocalypses and an abject collapse into sf cliché (cf. Bould 116–18). Other examples of such ambiguous thematic results in Hollywood's cyberpunk mode would include the plot of environmentally disastrous resource extraction in James Cameron's *Avatar* (2009) being compromised by its settler fantasy of saving the natives, or the way that the vivid depiction of social polarization, degradation of working conditions, and denial of access to health entitlements in Neil Blomkamp's *Elysium* (2013) is vitiated by the simplistic happy ending, where merely flipping a switch on a computer program is supposed to undo all those systemic ills.

Some examples taken from print fiction and from independent filmmaking produced from the perspective of those caught on the wrong side of globalization take the potential of cyberpunk in a more critically effective direction. For example, Metis-Nordic American author Misha's *Red Spider White Web* (1999) is distinguished from most earlier cyberpunk by its "unromanticized version of the integration of humans with the technology that are cyberspace cowboys" (Vint 103). Sherryl Vint argues that, compared to the mostly white male protagonists of the cyberpunk movement, Misha's heroes are a good deal more like the actual workers, including women and people of color, whose lives and livelihood have been degraded by neoliberal re-structuring. Vint concludes that "Misha thereby reveals the degree to which anxieties about cyberspace and human/machine interface should more properly be thought of as problems of capitalist social organization, not simply issues of technological domination" (103–4). Lysa Rivera makes a similar set of claims about Chicano/a science fiction's revisionary use of cyberpunk devices.[6] Her reading of three 'borderlands' fictions—Guillermo Lavin's short story "Reaching the Shore" (1994), Rosaura Sanchez's and Beatrice Pita's novel *Lunar Braceros* (2009), and Alex Rivera's independent film *Sleep Dealer* (2008)—lays heavy emphasis on the geographic and cultural specificity with which these artists "insist on reading late capitalism as a troubling and enduring extension of colonial relations of power between the United States and Mexico" (416). In both Lavin's and Rivera's narratives, the worker who jacks in to the employment opportunities of digital space is likened to a drug user being hooked on a fatal regime of consumption. In the sweatshop-like 'sleep dealer' factory in Rivera's film, Mexican workers exercise remote control over robots located on the other side of the border, thereby updating the empty land fantasy of colonial discovery by making cyberspace into a vehicle for delivering Mexican labor to the U.S. without the unpleasant Mexicans. As a final example of a revisionary, deromanticizing approach to cyberpunk motifs, consider Ted Chiang's "The Life Cycle of Software Objects" (2010). Instead of the apocalyptic teleology of artificial intelligence (AI) in Gibson or Stross, the development of online life forms in Chiang's novella is driven by a market logic that moves it to a startling reprise of the most drastic form of colonial exploitation of labor. As the continual updating of software platforms precipitates a concomitant slide of the story's childlike AIs into obsolescence, their owners find that their best chance at survival is to become sex slaves—that is, to fill the precise niche in the contemporary global market that best resembles the plantation-era slave trade.

Michael Hardt and Antonio Negri argue in *Empire* that "[i]f communication has increasingly become the fabric of production [...] then the control over linguistic sense and meaning and the networks of communication becomes an ever more central issue for political struggle" (404). The cyberpunk movement and its modal aftermath comprise a significant episode in the cultural struggle over the sense and meaning of our individual and collective transformation by information processing technology, but the significance of its contribution is complex, heterogeneous, and still very much up for grabs.

John Rieder

Notes

1 For these various versions of the post-1970 developments of the global capitalist economy, see Harvey, Mandel, Jameson, Castells, and Hardt and Negri.
2 Gibson's Sprawl fictions include the three novels *Neuromancer* (1984), *Count Zero* (1986), and *Mona Lisa Overdrive* (1988) as well as the short stories "Johnny Mnemonic" (1981), "Burning Chrome" (1982), and "New Rose Hotel" (1984).
3 On ideological fantasy, see Žižek 30–36.
4 For an analysis of the role of the Singularity in cyberpunk and post-cyberpunk fiction, particularly as it pertains to Charles Stross's *Accelerando* (2005), see Gerry Canavan's contribution to this collection.
5 See Hugh Charles O'Connell's contribution in this collection for a marxist reading of cyberpunk and late capitalism.
6 M. Elizabeth Ginway provides a comprehensive overview of Latin America and cyberpunk in her contribution to this collection, as does Juan Carlos Toledano Redondo's exploration of Cuban cyberpunk.

Works Cited

2001: A Space Odyssey. Directed by Stanley Kubrick, performances by Keir Dullea, Gary Lockwood, and William Sylvester, MGM/Stanley Kubrick Productions, 1968.

Avatar. Directed by James Cameron, performances by Sam Worthington, Zoe Saldana, and Sigourney Weaver, Twentieth Century Fox/Dune Entertainment/Ingenious Film Partners/Lightstorm Entertainment, 2009.

Bould, Mark, "Why Neo Flies, and Why He Shouldn't: The Critique of Cyberpunk in Gwyneth Jones's *Escape Plans* and M. John Harrison's *Signs of Life*." *Beyond Cyberpunk: New Critical Perspectives*, edited by Graham J. Murphy and Sherryl Vint. Routledge, 2010, pp. 116–34.

Cadigan, Pat. "Pretty Boy Crossover." *Asimov's Science Fiction*, vol. 19, no. 1, 1986, pp. 38–51.

Castells, Manuel. *The Rise of the Network Society*, 2nd Ed. Blackwell, 2000.

Chiang, Ted. "The Life Cycle of Software Objects." *Subterranean Press*, 2010.

Csicsery-Ronay, Istvan. "Cyberpunk and Neuromanticism." *Storming the Reality Studio: A Casebook of Cyberpunk and Postmodern Science Fiction*, edited by Larry McCaffery. Duke UP, 1991, pp. 182–93.

Elysium. Directed by Neil Blomkamp, performances by Matt Damon and Jodie Foster, Tristar, 2013.

Foster, Thomas. *The Souls of Cyberfolk: Posthumanism as Vernacular Theory*. U of Minnesota P, 2005.

Gibson, William. "Burning Chrome." *Burning Chrome*. Ace, 1987, pp. 168–91.

———. *Count Zero*. Arbor House, 1986.

———. "The Gernsback Continuum." *Mirrorshades: The Cyberpunk Anthology*, edited by Bruce Sterling. Ace, 1986, pp. 1–11.

———. *Mona Lisa Overdrive*. Bantam, 1988.

———. *Neuromancer*. Ace, 1984.

Haraway, Donna J., "A Manifesto for Cyborgs: Science, Technology, and Socialist-Feminism in the 1980s." *Socialist Review*, vol. 80, 1985, pp. 65–108.

Hardt, Michael, and Antonio Negri. *Empire*. Harvard UP, 2000.

Harvey, David. *A Brief History of Neoliberalism*. Oxford UP, 2005.

Jameson, Fredric. *Postmodernism, or, The Cultural Logic of Late Capitalism*. Duke UP, 1991.

Lavin, Guillermo. "Reaching the Shore." Translated by Rena Zuidema and Andrea Bell. *Cosmos Latinos: An Anthology of Science Fiction from Latin America and Spain*, edited by Andrea Bell and Yolanda Molina-Gavilan. Wesleyan UP, 2003, pp. 224–34.

Mandel, Ernest. *Late Capitalism*. Verso, 1975.

Misha, *Red Spider, White Web*. Wordcraft of Oregon, 1999.

Moylan, Tom. "Global Economy, Local Texts: Utopian/Dystopian Tension in William Gibson's Cyberpunk Trilogy." *Beyond Cyberpunk: New Critical Perspectives*, edited by Graham J. Murphy and Sherryl Vint. Routledge, 2010, pp. 81–94.

Rieder, John. *Colonialism and the Emergence of Science Fiction*. Wesleyan UP, 2008.

Rivera, Lysa. "Future Histories and Cyborg Labor: Reading Borderlands Science Fiction After NAFTA." *Science Fiction Studies*, vol. 39, no. 3, 2012, pp. 415–36.

Sanchez, Rosaura and Beatrice Pita. *Lunar Braceros 2125–2148*. Calaca, 2009.

Sleep Dealer. Directed by Alex Rivera, performances by Luis Fernando Peña, Leonor Varela, and Jacob Vargas, Likely Story/This is That Productions, 2008.

Spurr, David. *The Rhetoric of Empire: Colonial Discourse in Journalism, Travel Writing, and Imperial Administration.* Duke UP, 1993.

Sterling, Bruce and Lewis Shiner. "Mozart in Mirrorshades." *Mirrorshades: The Cyberpunk Anthology*, edited by Bruce Sterling. Ace, 1986, pp. 223–39.

Sterling, Bruce. Preface. *Mirrorshades: The Cyberpunk Anthology*, edited by Bruce Sterling. Ace, 1988, pp. ix-xvi.

———. *Schismatrix.* Arbor House, 1985.

Stross, Charles. *Accelerando.* Ace, 2006.

———. "Rogue Farm." *Live Without A Net*, edited by Lou Anders. Penguin, 2003, pp. 104–19.

The Matrix. Directed by the Wachowskis, performances by Keanu Reeves, Laurence Fishburne, and Carrie-Anne Moss, Warner Bros./Village Roadshow Pictures/Grouch Film Partnership/Silver Pictures/3 Arts Entertainment, 1999.

The Matrix Reloaded. Directed by the Wachowskis, performances by Keanu Reeves, Laurence Fishburne, and Carrie-Anne Moss. Warner Bros./Village Roadshow Pictures/Silver Pictures/NPV Entertainment/Heineken Branded Entertainment, 2003.

The Matrix Revolutions. Directed by the Wachowskis, performances by Keanu Reeves, Laurence Fishburne, and Carrie-Anne Moss Warner Bros./Village Roadshow Pictures/NPV Entertainment/Silver Pictures, 2003.

Vinge, Vernor. "The Coming Technological Singularity: How To Survive in a Post-human Era." *Science Fiction Criticism: An Anthology of Essential Writings,* edited by Rob Latham. Bloomsbury, 2017, pp. 352–63.

Vint, Sherryl. "'The Mainstream Finds Its Own Uses For Things': Cyberpunk and Commodification." *Beyond Cyberpunk: New Critical Perspectives*, edited by Graham J. Murphy and Sherryl Vint. Routledge, 2010, pp. 95–115.

Žižek, Slavoj. *The Sublime Object of Ideology.* Verso, 1989.

41

INDIGENOUS FUTURISMS

Corinna Lenhardt

Since Grace L. Dillon (Anishinaabe) published her watershed anthology of Indigenous science fiction (sf) writing, *Walking the Clouds: An Anthology of Indigenous Science Fiction* (2012), Indigenous futurisms—the plural indicating the vast variety of culture-specific negotiations and inventions from Indigenous peoples across the globe[1]—conceptualizes two distinct, yet intimately related aspects of Indigenous speculative cultural productions. First, creators of "Indigenous futurisms sometimes intentionally experiment with, sometimes intentionally dislodge, sometimes merely accompany, but invariably *change* the perimeters of sf" (Dillon, *Walking* 3). Grappling with mainstream sf's troubling persistence in settler colonial fantasies[2] and hegemonically configured and reinforced race discourses, Indigenous futurisms provide an alternative to the "steady diet of the feathers and the fantasy" fed to non-Indigenous audiences "as what it supposedly means to be a 'real Indian'" (Adare 1). This by no means entails only the inclusion of authentic Indigenous characters as part of futurist texts; rather, "they are generated by and inspirational *for* Native peoples" (Medak-Saltzman 143). This latter aspect already implies the second key aspect prevalent in Indigenous futurisms; that is, the understanding of Indigenous futurisms as age-old Indigenous cultural practices predating western concepts of sf easily by thousands of years: As Dillon writes, "[m]any experimental narrative techniques that cutting-edge SF authors congratulate themselves for discovering have actually been around for millennia in Indigenous storytelling" ("The People" Pos. 116). She goes on to remark that "[s]lipstreams, alternative realities, multiverses, time traveling—the stock tropes of mainstream SF are ancient elements of Indigenous ways of knowing" ("The People" Pos. 116). By working from within Indigenous spiritual, cultural, and scientific worldviews and traditions, which entail concepts that have not just been dismissed in mainstream sf, but in the wake of the western Enlightenment generally, Indigenous futurist texts position indigeneity at the heart of both scientific progress and sociocultural futurity. In sum, Indigenous futurisms indigenize mainstream sf by re-envisioning its tropes and motifs from complex, culture-specific Indigenous perspectives; the historically and still predominately white genre is mobilized from both within and without to push Indigenous peoples from the stereotype-ridden margins to the center of sf and, thus, into futurity.

Dillon's optimism regarding sf's potential to "honor Native traditions, to dig into history lingering behind myth, and to share with readers the ramifications of indigenous diasporas in ways that recognize their accountability" ("Miindiwag" 236) intersects with the work of Gerald Vizenor (Anishinaabe) and his oft-cited concept of "survivance." Survivance combines Indigenous 'survival' with 'endurance' and 'resistance.' It implies an "active repudiation of dominance, tragedy, and victimry" (Vizenor, *Fugitive* 15), that is both a rejection of established images of 'the Indian' and connected narratives of victimization and an insistence on

Indigenous continuance and adaptability. This insistence neither denies the historical process of colonization nor its contemporary impact; rather, it refuses to see Indigenous peoples defined by these processes as perpetual victims without agency. Translated to the context of sf, survivance entails pride, optimism, and (self-)empowerment in the face of white mainstream practices of stereotyping and exclusion—Indigenous peoples and cultures are alive and kicking, today as well as in fantastic futures.

Given her understanding of Indigenous futurisms as intersection of survivance and sf, as renunciation of hegemonic dominance through continuous and creative practices of cultural identity and resistance, it is not surprising that Dillon is also the first scholar to hint at the possibility of cyberpunk narratives by Indigenous artists. Arguably, cyberpunk's *punk* attitude commits this sf subgenre to showing "how and why dominant ideologies marginalize dispossessed strata of the population" (Cavallaro 20). Cyberpunk's mostly dystopian, technologically enhanced, urban societies in which "globalization and capitalism have led to the rule of multinational conglomerates, while marginalized individuals live in a post-industrial setting defined by cold metal technology, virtual reality, and crime" (Lavigne 11), lend themselves to the Indigenous practices of survivance in the face of oppression and marginalization while subjected to dystopian colonial realities. Dillon's anthological inclusion of *Red Spider White Web* (1990), an important novel by Misha (Métis) that "interpenetrates the cyberpunk" with Indigenous tribalism (Dillon, *Walking* 185), has triggered a necessary inquiry into the possibilities and limits of Indigenous cyberpunk cultural practices. In 2018, this inquiry fueled Brian K. Hudson's (Cherokee) "Indigenous Cyberpunk Manifesto":

> Gibson constructed the console cowboy, but we are the digital Natives. We are the original Natives of the web, the tech-savvy NDNs weaving in and out of discussion threads, the warriors with keyboards who carry sparks into cyberspace.[3] We are the coders who create sovereign virtual worlds, the digital code talkers who braid Indigenous tongues into networks of resistance. We've navigated the webs of branching nodes since time immemorial—before *kubernētēs* became *cybernetics* and before *punk* was *ponk*. Our digital allies boost our signals. We are Indigenous cyberpunks.

Hudson, writer and scholar of Indigenous futurisms and citizen of the Cherokee Nation, merges into one dense paragraph what can simultaneously be understood as the description of the contemporary North American Indigenous cyberpunk scene and as a call to action for Indigenous peoples across the globe. Connecting Indigenous histories (both Indigenous epistemological systems and more recent histories, for example that of the famous Navajo code talkers during World War II) with the digital revolution of the 21st century, the digital Natives go way beyond the limits of William Gibson's console cowboy fantasy of white masculinity in *Neuromancer* (1984). Against white (sf) practices of racialization and othering, of reducing Indigenous peoples to stereotypical "fringe-and-feather-Indians" (Sheyahshe 8), Hudson positions "tech-savvy NDNs." Indigenous cyberpunks are—and have always been—closer to the keyboard than to nature. By creatively countering stereotypical representations of 'the Indian' and by braiding "Indigenous tongues into networks of resistance," Hudson (like Dillon before him) places survivance at the epicenter of Indigenous cyberpunk practices.

In the following, I throw two spotlights on a small selection of North American Indigenous cultural practices that can productively be framed as Indigenous cyberpunk. From novels to short films, Indigenous cyberpunk narratives perform "the ruptures, the scars, and the traumas in [an] effort ultimately to provide healing [… and] a path to a sovereignty embedded in self-determination" (Dillon, *Walking* 9). While necessarily limited and incomplete in both scope and validity, these spotlights suggest the presence of a large variety of complex and diverse Indigenous cyberpunk cultural practices.

Corinna Lenhardt

41.1 Indigenous Cyberpunk Novels: *Red Spider White Web* and *Robopocalypse*

Red Spider White Web is a fascinating and much-acclaimed feminist Indigenous cyberpunk novel. Set in a dystopian, apparently Japanese-invaded[4] American city feeding on "the ashes of an already dead civilization" (111) in the "desolate landscape of hopeless desires" (19) so typical of 1980s and 1990s Anglophone cyberpunk narratives, the female protagonist, Kumo, navigates a cityscape segregated on the basis of race and class. The rich Japanese and white people live under the dome of Mickey-san, Misha's thinly veiled allegory of Disneyland and boundless mass consumerism; the underground city Dogtown is the neighborhood for the impoverished working class; and Ded Tek, an abandoned industrial complex outside the city, is the space of poor peoples of color, who die slowly of "that fucking UV, the lousy food, the cold, the fifteen minute viruses—all of it" (61). Always assuming the roaming gangs, drug lords, "zombies" (cannibalistic drug addicts), "fashals" (cybernetic sex slaves), and Mickey-san predators do not kill them first. Relegated to Ded Tek, Kumo is the literal embodiment of the starving (holo-)artist under constant attack by the multinational Mickey-san corporation's commodification and utterly violent alienation practices. Sherryl Vint argues, respectively, that "Misha's prescient focus on market conditions and their consequences for both artists and audiences under late capitalism are chief among the reasons why her work is 'everything cyberpunk should have been but wasn't' as Elyce Herford comments" (96). While I agree with Vint's analysis of *Red Spider White Web*'s bleak characterization of the nature and value of art in late capitalism, I want to connect this argument with Misha's practice of survivance more generally.

While closely adhering to some of mainstream cyberpunk's conventional motifs and tropes (such as the setting), Misha problematizes and creatively reworks prevalent gender and race binaries from the perspective of a Métis woman. Whereas non-white and non-male characters are conventionally assigned the supporting, exoticized, and/or antagonistic roles in white cyberpunk fiction, Misha places diverse and Indigenous characters at the center of her novel.[5] Kumo and her twin brother, cyborg Tommy, who are marked as mixed-raced Native Americans stemming from the Southwest of the U.S., speak alternately colloquial English and a type of Japanese that is phonetically transcribed in defamiliarized and fragmented phrases. More precisely, Kumo is a Native American-wolverine hybrid, created through genetic splicing. In Misha's dystopia, where all non-hybridized Native Americans are imprisoned in lab-like reservations and subjected to cruel medical experimentation, Kumo functions as a constant reminder of the precarious position of colonized peoples. Hence, Misha's protagonist clearly comments on both the troubling history of medical and research abuses experienced by Indigenous peoples across North America since European colonization (see Hodge) and the marginalized role of diverse characters in mainstream cyberpunk cultures. Reminding the reader of the Gibsonian autonomous male console cowboy 'riding' alone on the cyberspace 'range,' Misha's protagonist "eschews what is traditionally associated as the feminine: relationality, cooperation, and social conformity. In fact, Kumo disparagingly refers to people with such feminized characteristics as 'hive minds'" (Harper 407), an evocative metaphor that introduces Kumo's complicated, shimmering positionality in the novel. Far from replacing the hardboiled console cowboy with a 'console cowgirl,' Kumo is raped by a male character and re-subjected to male dominance and female victimhood and powerlessness. Making visible the racial implications in the rape of Kumo, and, thus, the reality of rape and sexual violence that Native American women have to endure disproportionately, Misha has Kumo's neck forcibly tattooed with the titular red spider. The red spider is supposed to mark Kumo as property, but it re-connects her to her 'red' Indigenous heritage and the Southwest Native myth of Spider Woman. Rather than being property and fair game, Kumo is connected to Spider Woman, or Spider Grandmother as the Hopi narrate, "who, conscientiously weaving her webs, thought the world itself into existence" ("The Spider Woman"). For the Navajo people, Spider Woman is part of the creation story and associated with saving people from chaos and disorder, symbolized by a flood, "by weaving a web to create solid ground before the water sweeps over them" ("The Spider Woman").

In other words, Misha does not replace old binaries (white/non-white, male/female, heterosexual/queer, etc.) with reversed new binaries; rather, she deconstructs the underlying hegemonic practice of creating and hierarchizing binaries altogether. While Kumo cannot take revenge and tear down the power structures that relegate her to the margin of society and subject her continuously to violence and denigration, she not only survives but resists: "*How many rough blows had she suffered? How many times had she been an unwilling step for the selfish souls of her fellow opposite gender? And the Pinkies, so white and so male, were like living stiff boots of conquerors*" (175, sic). Under "the boots of conquerors," of the white male corporate ruling class, Kumo persists in her way of life and her unique, uncommercial art. She survives, endures, and resists actively against the annihilating oppression of the hegemonic rulers and art colonizers of Mickey-san., Kumo's survivance endures, as if held securely in the web of Spider Woman above the chaotic and fatal flood of white colonialism.

Compared to the fragmented narration and poetic language of *Red Spider White Web*, *Robopocalypse* (2011) by Daniel H. Wilson (Cherokee) is a readily approachable sf novel with mainstream appeal. *Robopocalypse*, as well as its sequel, *Robogenesis* (2014), is set in a not-too-distant future of largely urbanized communities whose inhabitants enjoy buying domestic robots for their households, living in fully computerized smart homes, and driving their smart cars on autopilot. When the artificial superintelligence Archos R-14 manages to escape Lake Novus Research Laboratories, it corrupts the programming of domestic robots and other digital support systems with a virus and begins to wage war on mankind. Supported by smart cars and a treacherous digital communication system, formerly friendly domestic robots such as Big Happy and Slow Sue start to gruesomely slaughter the urban populations until only a few survivors are left alive in the post-apocalyptic wastelands of formerly thriving metropoles. The survivors, however, are by no means safe: Archos modifies the bodies of captured human survivors, using experimental surgical procedures to upgrade them as tools. For example, the character Mathilda Perez, a ten-year-old girl, has her eyes removed by the machines and replaced (incompletely) with machine technology of "dull black metal" that allows her to have visons of the thoughts and communications of robots (Wilson 225). At the same time, while the machines start to adapt and create "the next stage of avtomat [sic] evolution" (Wilson 235) with diverse and more complex motivations (from navigating non-urban territories, to killing more effectively, and researching the local flora and fauna), the uprooted, alienated, and dislocated human survivors start to regroup and fight back. Mathilda becomes transhuman and is both an enabler and ambassador to intimate human-machine cooperation that will eventually bring down Archos R-14 (as well as Arayt Shah/Archos R-8 in *Robogenesis*). Similarly, a resistance group called Gray Horse Army also assimilates its enemies and organically modifies machine weaponry, including the courageous, loyal, and somewhat stubborn spider tank Houdini. In sum, what may on the surface read like a standard AI takeover/robot rebellion narrative is a well-crafted and politically charged Indigenous cyberpunk novel.

Robopocalypse is narrated from multiple points of view—machine as well as human. Aside from Archos R-14 and Mathilda Perez, the reader follows protagonist Cormac Wallace, a reluctant Osage leader and chronicler of the human resistance; Takeo Nomura, Japanese robot expert leading the human resistance in Tokyo; and Lark Iron Cloud, a jilted Cherokee youth who will lead the human resistance on the North American continent. Like Misha, Wilson places Indigenous and diverse characters centre stage, but in stark contrast to *Red Spider White Web*, Wilson envisions communal survival and resistance. For him, survivance is not an individual strategy, but a tribal effort.

The last human stronghold of the North American continent is the off-the-grid Osage ceremonial town, the aforementioned Gray Horse, situated in Osage County, Oklahoma. In the real world, the Osage Nation has tribal sovereignty, its own government, police force, hospitals, and schools, and coexists with the federal government of the U.S. When the robots take over, the federal government falls rapidly while the sovereign tribal community of Gray Horse steps up. After initial conflicts between Osages and Cherokees as well as between Native and non-Native survivors, the Osage community accepts and integrates survivors of all genders, ages, and body types, whether with severed limbs, cyborg prosthetics, or fully robotic, and from all social, cultural, and racial backgrounds. Gray Horse and the Gray Horse Army become synonymous with equality and cooperation—and with badass, transhuman cyberpunk-style warfare: "Just like a damn cowboy" (271) the diverse "warriors of the tribe" (126) master both technological warfare and human-machine alliances to take down Archos R-14. Rather than being "[c]aught between traditional definitions of technology and an awareness of the inherent technicity of the human," Wilson's novel "reflects contemporary concerns over continued technological progress and what this means for the future of mankind" (Grech 85). It also foregrounds the futurity of Native peoples and the inherent—and survival-granting—value of their political, social, and cultural sovereignty. Indigenous survivance in *Robopocalypse* is an ongoing practice, a way of communal living true to sovereign tribal culture and laws that has granted survival and resistance against the European colonizers and will ensure survival and thriving in the battle against the machines, the New War, too.

41.2 Indigenous Cyberpunk Short Films: *File Under Miscellaneous* and *Future Warrior*

In *Screening Space: The American Science Fiction Film*, Vivian Carol Sobchack reflects on Fredric Jameson's identification of the need for "radically new forms" that engage late capitalism with nuance. Sobchack considers the work of predominately marginalized sf filmmakers that are "capable of doing justice to the complexity of our historical moment" (304) by creating a new mode for sf films: "one that does not regress to the past, does not nostalgize, and does not complacently accept the present as the only place to live. It does indeed imagine a future—but one contiguous with the present, and in temporal and spatial relation to it" (305). In the 21st century, Indigenous authors imagine critical, 'alterNative' futures more and more often via the bleak and gritty images of cyberpunk culture.

The 2010 short film *File Under Miscellaneous*, directed by Jeff Barnaby (Mi'kmaq), puts Indigenous futurisms' optimistic intersection of sf and survivance to the test. In a conventionally bleak cyberpunk setting reminiscent of *Blade Runner* (Scott 1982) and in unconventionally gruesome and explicit images, a nameless Mi'kmaq man enters a nightmarish clinic and undergoes a procedure reminiscent of Mary Shelley's *Frankenstein* (1818): A heavily scarred doctor removes the protagonist's tongue, heart, and skin only to replace them with a preselection of stitched-together and "still warm" organs from white 'donors.' The Mi'kmaq man wakes up reconfigured as a 'white,' English speaking, suit-and-tie version of Frankenstein's monster; he joins a large body of identical looking men, who listen in awe to a German-language speech from another 'treated' man projected on a screen. The film ends abruptly and on an ambivalent note when the protagonist remembers telling a racist and misogynistic joke among other white men, who "laughed and laughed [...] until silver bullets flew out of every orifice, and burned the land with our whiteness." Uttered by the surgically reskinned Indigenous man, this hate speech camouflaged as 'joke' either depicts his (self-)subjection and assimilation to the dystopian alignment of dominant white masculinity, or functions as a trapdoor in the film and gives way to the protagonist's resistance maybe even inspiring a rebellion against the assimilator with the silver bullets emanating from his body.

In both cases, as Stina Attebery argues, "[w]hiteness becomes a self-destructive identity that the protagonist takes on, operating similarly to the suicide bomber in that he must maim his body in order to weaponize it," except Barnaby's film shows the "posthuman protagonist is able to survive this self-destructive act of resistance as the technology of organ transfer evokes longevity even when the body is being weaponized" (112).

Barnaby may grant his protagonist survival, but he only lets him glimpse the possibility of Indigenous survivance. Consider the surgical re-skinning of the protagonist once more. Having cinematographically stressed the protagonist's difficult choice to give in to the racial and cultural assimilation portrayed as systemic to this post-apocalyptic society, Barnaby now places great emphasis on the surgical procedure's slow, painful, and shameful removal of the protagonist's skin. One camera is mounted above the operating table zooming in on the protagonist's fragmented body as if the camera were a magnifying glass under which a curious specimen could be calmly dissected. The skin in these shots is more than just the organ most clearly associated with race and ethnicity, and it is also coded with Mi'kmaq symbols and signs. Having just lost his (mother) tongue, the protagonist now loses his tattooed skin, symbolizing his Indigenous culture and heritage, to the uncanny surgeon's scalpel. The film's voiceover narration switches from the metaphorical Mi'kmaq, ripe with mythological and cultural Mi'kmaq references, to standard American English with racist and misogynistic slurs. However, as if a shred of the protagonist's Native identity would remain untouched, the Mi'kmaq voice remains in the background; like a steady echo it translates all English narration to Mi'kmaq. However, the film's ambivalent ending interferes with a cautiously optimistic reading: When the silver bullets start flying and "burn[ing] the land" with whiteness, the Mi'kmaq echo has ceased and the violent image narrated in American English remains unechoed.

In sum, *File Under Miscellaneous* refuses to depict Indigenous survivance uncritically and in a celebratory tone so typical for optimistic Indigenous futurisms outside the bleak settings and plotlines of its cyberpunk trappings. Barnaby rather points towards "self-loathing" as part of the "postcolonial aftermath" (cit. in Krupa), that is the "nervous condition," Jean-Paul Sartre first conceptualized in his Preface to Frantz Fanon's *Wretched of the Earth* (1961). Continuously subjected to dehumanizing violence and oppression by the colonizers' military and discursive power, the colonized peoples are exploited to the point of lifelong traumatization, internalized racism, and cultural, intellectual, and nervous breakdown. With every flap of skin and every syllable of the Mi'kmaq language, *File Under Miscellaneous* performs this unrecoverable stripping away of culture, identity, and sanity under the (self-)assimilating forces of colonialism.

Future Warrior, a 2007 independent short film directed by Pawnee Nation members Jeana Francis and Nigel R. Long Soldier, creates a dystopian future where the government has killed all Indigenous leaders and medicine men but one, and where dreaming and memories are chemically suppressed through mandatory drug shots. Thematically very close to *File Under Miscellaneous*, *Future Warrior* similarly narrates the ever-present threats of the losses of Indigenous culture and identity within the apocalyptic context of ongoing colonization. In sharp contrast to Barnaby, however, Francis and Long Soldier focus the power and agency of survivance and, thus, establish a hopeful trajectory for Native futurity based on endurance, resistance, and survival.

In a technologically advanced yet toxic wasteland—the setting can be effectively described as blending *Blade Runner*'s techno-orientalist aesthetics with *Mad Max*'s (Miller 1979) badlands— roughly 200 years in the future, a group of rebels fight to battle the ethnocide of their people. In guerilla-style warfare, Indigenous characters fight the drug administration's poisoning of the minds of fellow survivors and industrial air pollution and water contamination. With fast cuts as well as stills, *Future Warrior* continuously combines shots of the setting and the characters with the works of Pawnee/Yakama pop artist Bunky Echo-Hawk (among others). The future might be toxic and the past (temporarily) erased from memory, but Indigenous art and resistance has never ceased. It is in this vein that the film's insistence on a "techno-biological spirit growth [that] is the key to our [Pawnee] past" marks the skin of the female protagonist and future warrior with a blend of a computer circuit board and traditional Pawnee engraving aesthetics. Pawnee futurity lies in the combination of technological and human-centered, spiritual growth-enabling development. Technological memories can foster remembering, but healthy spirits connected to both nature and tribal culture are needed to make sense of the technology in ways that do not end in yet another apocalypse. In fact, by creating an Indigenous aesthetic that runs through the entire film and controls not just the setting and character composition, but also the camera movements and other narrational and cinematographic techniques (such as the spiraling, non-linear narration, and cutting), *Future Warrior* establishes what Michelle H. Raheja and others have called "visual sovereignty," defined as diverse Indigenous media practices that negotiate Native and colonial histories creatively and critically to facilitate Indigenous agency and healing.[6] As an example of visual sovereignty, survivance in *Future Warrior* is therefore simultaneously narrated on the level of the storyworld and performed cinematographically.[7]

41.3 AlterNative Cyberpunk Cultures

Since the beginning of the 21st century, both the number and variety of Indigenous texts that imagine 'alterNative' futurities based on culturally specific identities and a joint need and capacity for survivance have seen a growing emergence. In addition to the texts addressed above, Indigenous cyberpunk also includes, but is not limited to, Diane Glancy's (Cherokee) "Aunt Parnetta's Electric Blisters" (1990), Eden Robinson's (Haisla/Heiltsuk) "Terminal Avenue" (1996), Brian K. Hudson's (Cherokee) "Digital Medicine" (2006), Meagan Byrne (Métis) and Tara Miller's (Maliseet) video game *Purity & Decay* (2017), and such comic book stories as Michael Sheyahshe (Caddo) and George Freeman's "Strike and Bolt" (2016), Steve Keewatin Sanderson's (Cree) "Where We Left Off" (2017), and Cole Pauls's (Tahltan) *Dakwäkãda Warriors* (2016–). The general tendency in these works is connected to "the resurgence of broad Indigenous political movements across North America" (Medak-Saltzman 144), on the one hand, and to the lowered, even egalitarian participation bar of digital communication and (self-)publishing, on the other. Broadly received by and discussed among well-connected digital NDNs, Indigenous futurists thus join the contemporary political movements online and offline. Indeed, the current flourishing of Indigenous futurisms intersects with the apparent rise of Indigenous activisms and protest movements across North America—apparent not because Indigenous activism and protest culture would have abated previously, but because contemporary Indigenous movements utilize information technology and social media to reach out to a global audience to ensure visibility and to create traction (see Lenhardt). United in the need to "protect the land, water, and air that provide the basis for all life" (Indigenous Nationhood Movement) through honoring and acting according to the "Indigenous ways of knowing [that] are rooted in Indigenous sovereignty to protect water, air, land, and all creation for future generations", Indigenous activists and their non-Indigenous allies aim "to peacefully and prayerfully defend [their] rights, and rise up as one to sustain Mother Earth and her inhabitants" (Tallbear). The creation of better futures and down-to-earth perspectives for Indigenous and non-Indigenous peoples alike, the envisioning of alterNative futures outside the boundaries of colonialism, are at the heart of both indigenized sf and Indigenous politics: "This is what #NoDAPL, Idle No More (and similar movements largely led by Native women), and Indigenous futurisms are all about: imagining, dreaming, insisting, building, and demanding that we move together toward the best future yet" (Medak-Saltzman 167).

In the proliferation of indigenized cyberpunk futurities in a variety of genres and media, authors, artists, and performers creatively and critically interrogate the optimism and pessimism prevalent in the factual necessity for Indigenous resurgence and survivance in dystopian, yet very real, settler colonial hierarchies. The path toward the best future yet, indigenized cyberpunk narratives make abundantly clear, is a painful and dark road through apocalyptic pasts, presents, and futures:

> To be a Native of North America is to exist in a space where the past and the future mix in a delicate swirl of the here-and-now. We stand with one foot always in the darkness that ended our world, and the other in a hope for our future as Indigenous people. It is from this apocalyptic in-between that the Indigenous voices in speculative fiction speak. (Roanhorse)

Notes

1 I use the term 'Indigenous' to encompass not only peoples Native or Indigenous to the Americas, but Indigenous peoples all over the world. However, due to both the scope of this chapter and my expertise, my analysis is limited to cultural products of First Nation and Native American peoples of North America.
2 For the connection between cyberpunk and colonialism, see John Rieder's contribution to this collection.
3 "NDNs" is primarily used in digital communication among Native Americans; when spoken, the letters N-D-N sound like "Indian."
4 For an exploration of cyberpunk's indebtedness to Japanese exoticism and the "yellow peril," see Brian Ruh's contribution to this collection.
5 With David, Misha includes an intersexual character and genders her/him carefully throughout (note that the novel was first published in 1990!).
6 For more details, see Raheja's *Reservation Reelism* (2010).
7 For an exploration of *Future Warrior*'s critical adaptation of the Star Wars franchise, particularly of the Indigenous take on the Ewoks of *Return of the Jedi* (Marquant 1983), see William Lempert.

Works Cited

Adare, Sierra S. *Indian Stereotypes in TV Science Fiction: First Nations' Voices Speak Out.* U of Texas P, 2009. Kindle file.
Attebery, Stina. "Indigenous Posthumans: Cyberpunk Surgeries and Biotech Boarding Schools in *File under Miscellaneous* and SyFy's *Helix*." *Extrapolation*, vol. 57, no. 1–2, 2016, pp. 95–115.
Cavallaro, Dani. *Cyberpunk and Cyberculture: Science Fiction and the Work of William Gibson.* Athlone Press, 2000.
Dillon, Grace L. "*Miindiwag* and Indigenous Diaspora: Eden Robinson's and Celu Amberstone's Forays into 'Postcolonial' Science Fiction and Fantasy." *Extrapolation*, vol. 48, no. 2, 2007, pp. 219–43.
———. "The People of Colo(u)r Destroy Science Fiction: Editors." *Lightspeed*, vol. 73, 2016, special issue: *The People of Colo(u)r Destroy Science Fiction*, edited by Nalo Hopkinson and Kristine Ong Muslim. Kindle file.
———, ed. *Walking the Clouds: An Anthology of Indigenous Science Fiction.* U of Arizona P, 2012.
File Under Miscellaneous. Directed by Jeff Barnaby, performances by John Christou, Glen Gould, and Arthur Holden, Prospector Films, 2010.
Future Warrior. Directed by Jeana Francis and Nigel R. Long Soldier, 2007.
Grech, Marija. "Technological Appendages and Organic Prostheses: Robo-Human Appropriation and Cyborgian Becoming in Daniel H. Wilson's *Robopocalypse*." *Word and Text: A Journal of Literary Studies and Linguistics*, vol. 3, no. 2, 2013, pp. 85–95.
Harper, Mary Catherine. "Incurably Alien Other: A Case for Feminist Cyborg Writers." *Science Fiction Studies*, vol. 22, no. 3, 1995, pp. 399–420.
Hodge, Felicia Schanche. "No Meaningful Apology for American Indian Unethical Research Abuses." *Ethics & Behavior*, vol. 22, no. 6, 2012, pp. 431–44.
Hudson, Brian K. "An Indigenous Cyberpunk Manifesto." 15 Sep. 2018, briankhudson.com/blog/.
Indigenous Nationhood Movement. "Statement of Principles." *Unsettling America*, unsettlingamerica. wordpress.com/2013/11/05/indigenous-nationhood-movement/.
Krupa, Mark. "An Interview with Jeff Barnaby." *Montreal Serai*, 12 Feb. 2011.
Lavigne, Carlen. *Cyberpunk Women, Feminism, and Science Fiction: A Critical Study.* McFarland, 2013.

Lenhardt, Corinna. "'Free Peltier Now!' The Use of Internet Memes in American Indian Activism." *American Indian Culture and Research Journal*, vol. 40, no. 3, pp. 67–84.

Lempert, William. "Decolonizing Encounters of the Third Kind: Alternative Futuring in Native Science Fiction Film." *Visual Anthropology Review*, vol. 30, no. 2, pp. 164–76.

Medak-Saltzman, Danika. "Coming to You from the Indigenous Future: Native Women, Speculative Film Shorts, and the Art of the Possible." *Studies in American Indian Literatures*, vol. 29, no. 1, 2017, pp. 139–71.

Misha. *Red Spider White Web*. Wordcraft of Oregon, 1999.

Raheja, Michelle H. *Reservation Reelism: Redfacing, Visual Sovereignty, and Representations of Native Americans in Film*. U Nebraska P, 2010.

Roanhorse, Rebecca. "Postcards from the Apocalypse." *Uncanny: A Magazine of Science Fiction and Fantasy*, uncannymagazine.com/article/postcards-from-the-apocalypse/.

Sheyahshe, Michael. "Introduction." *Moonshot: The Indigenous Comics Collection*, vol. 1, 2016, pp. 8–9.

Sobchack, Vivian Carol. *Screening Space: The American Science Fiction Film*. Rutgers UP, 1997.

Sohn, Stephen Hong. "Introduction: Alien/Asian: Imagining the Racialized Future." *MELUS*, vol. 33, no. 4, 2008, pp. 5–22.

Tallbear, Kim. "Badass (Indigenous) Women Caretake Relations: #NoDAPL, #IdleNoMore, #BlackLives-Matter." *Society for Cultural Anthropology*, culanth.org/fieldsights/badass-indigenous-women-caretake-relations-no-dapl-idle-no-more-black-lives-matter.

"The Spider Woman: Part of the Totems to Turquoise Exhibition." *American Museum of Natural History*, amnh.org/exhibitions/totems-to-turquoise/native-american-cosmology/the-spider-woman.

Vint, Sherryl. "'The Mainstream Finds its Own Uses for Things': Cyberpunk and Commodification." *Beyond Cyberpunk: New Critical Perspectives*, edited by Graham J. Murphy and Sherryl Vint. Routledge, 2010, pp. 95–114.

Vizenor, Gerald. *Fugitive Poses: Native American Indian Scenes of Absence and Presence*. U of Nebraska P, 1998.

Whyte, Kyle P. "Indigenous Science (Fiction) for the Anthropocene: Ancestral Dystopias and Fantasies of Climate Change Crises." *Environment and Planning E: Nature and Space*, vol. 1, no. 1–2, 2018, pp. 224–42.

Wilson, Daniel H. *Robopocalypse*. Doubleday, 2011.

42

AFROFUTURISM

Isiah Lavender III and Graham J. Murphy

In the introduction to the 2013 *Paradoxa* issue "Africa SF," editor Mark Bould points to the recent successes of Wanuri Kahiu's *Pumzi* (2009), the first Kenyan science fiction (sf) movie to win the best short film at the 2010 Cannes Film Festival; Neil Blomkamp's South African co-produced *District 9* (2009), nominated for four Academy Awards; Nigerian-American Nnedi Okorafor's 2011 World Fantasy Award for *Who Fears Death* (2010); South African Lauren Beukes's Arthur C. Clarke Award winning novel *Zoo City* (2010); and Ivor W. Hartmann's edited anthology *AfroSF* (2012), the first of its kind featuring sf by African writers as proof positive that "[i]f African sf has not arrived, it is certainly approaching fast" (7). At the same time, the unqualified success and importance of Ryan Coogler's *Black Panther* (2018), a film that, as of December 2019, has grossed over \$1.3 billion in global box office revenues cannot be overstated. *Time* was only one of many mainstream publications to address the cultural significance of *Black Panther* by bringing to the Marvel Cinematic Universe and, more broadly, Hollywood's big screens, a black superhero who has been a staple of the Marvel Comics universe since he first premiered in comic books in July 1966. As Jamil Smith writes, watching King T'Challa (Chadwick Boseman), a.k.a. the Black Panther, on-screen reflects more than simply seeing a superhero who happens to be black in what is otherwise a crowded cinematic superhero universe, although that is of supreme importance; *Black Panther* is about "what it means to be black in both America and Africa—and, more broadly, in the world." Acknowledging that black audiences simply do not routinely see popular characters that look like them on-screen, and certainly not in a billion-dollar-busting film, *Black Panther* refuses to "dodge complicated themes about race and identity," grappling "head-on with the issues affecting modern-day black life." *Black Panther* is a cinematic "vision of black grandeur and, indeed, power [… that] envisions a world not devoid of racism but one in which black people have the wealth, technology and military might to level the playing field." Coogler therefore presents a truly remarkable vision of what the African continent could be without the advent of slavery followed by colonialism and the concretized white image of Africa as a primitive place, as first popularized by H. Rider Haggard's *King Solomon's Mines* (1885) and later legitimized by Joseph Conrad's *Heart of Darkness* (1899). This stereotype of Africa as the heart of darkness still impacts us with all sorts of damaging connotations, which is why Coogler's film is so powerful in inverting this long-lasting image of blackness. In this regard, *Black Panther* is arguably the most successful cultural vehicle, at least in a visual medium, to expose a broad audience to Afrofuturist principles in a contemporary moment that is increasingly defined by Afrofuturism.

In his overview for *The Oxford Handbook of Science Fiction*, De Witt Douglas Kilgore explains that Afrofuturism is guided by three basic principles: "that peoples of African descent, their ways and histories, will not disappear in any credible future; that the future, indeed, will be one in which the peoples of the African diaspora operate as the directors and beneficiaries of technological progress; and that the cultural meaning of blackness will continually change as generations advance" (569). As a theoretical paradigm, Afrofuturism originates in the early 1990s: White cultural theorist Mark Dery deployed the term in a set of 1993 interviews with Samuel R. Delany, Greg Tate, and Tricia Rose, published as "Black to the Future" in the *South Atlantic Quarterly* and reprinted a year later in Dery's edited collection *Flame Wars: The Discourse of Cyberculture*. The motivating question for Dery was "Why do so few African Americans write science fiction, a genre whose close encounters with the Other [...] would seem uniquely suited to the concerns of African-American novelists?" (179–80). In so doing, Dery explains that "speculative fiction that treats African-American themes and addresses African-American concerns in the context of twentieth century technoculture—and, more generally, African-American signification that appropriates images of technology and a prosthetically enhanced future—might for want of a better term, be called 'Afrofuturism'" (180). In his coming to Afrofuturism and coining the term, Dery clearly seems to have cyberpunk on his mind as it is a notable subtext in "Black to the Future." For example, cyberpunk often celebrates technoculture and prosthetic enhancements, and its futuristic projections often include cybernetics, computer hackers, greedy multinational corporations, and a criminal element, typically mixed together in a seemingly diverse, often urban, dystopian setting. As Kilgore writes, Afrofuturism for Dery is "a form of hacking, a technoperformative way of cracking a complex cultural code" (562), language evocative of cyberpunk's digital anti-heroes hacking away at databases and cultural conventions. Dery's Afrofuturism therefore grafts cyberpunk tropes and sentiments onto *perceptions* of black American culture wholesale by stating that "technology is all too often brought to bear on black bodies (branding, forced sterilization, the Tuskegee experiment, and tasers come readily to mind)" (181). Dery recalls this terrible history because he wants to remind us of how black bodies have been "coded as natural machines"—i.e., cyborgs—to create not just wealth but a hierarchy of difference that fit prevailing if dated scientific notions of natural selection (Lavender, "Critical" 190).

While Dery may be inspired to envision black bodies as cyborgs, cyberpunk's literary history tells a different story. With few exceptions, most of the anti-hero protagonists envisioned by Movement-era[1] writers like William Gibson, Bruce Sterling, and Rudy Rucker were white, itself not all that surprising considering early cyberpunk was "written for the most part by a small number of white middle-class men, many of whom, inexplicably, live in Texas" (Hollinger 207). This writerly demographic has proven problematic when it comes to broader considerations of cyberpunk and race; after all, although sf in general and cyberpunk specifically *might* seem concerned with the racial alterity generated by human contact, cyberpunk largely failed to delve into themes of race and racism, again perhaps not surprising (but certainly disappointing!) given

> for most of its history sf has considered itself a 'colorblind' genre, either blithely portraying a future free from racial struggle (not seeming to notice that this harmony is accomplished by eliminating all non-white people) or else projecting racial anxieties onto the body of the alien without seeming to notice that the humanity united against this external threat is suspiciously monochrome. (Lavender, "Critical" 185)

Consequently, the cliché "I don't see color" is at the very least naïve or willfully ignorant but is, at its core, steeped in racism: Samuel R. Delany has famously remarked "race doesn't exist, but it'll kill ya" (quoted in Hopkinson, "Reluctant" 347). Being blind to color only masks ignorance of the problems that people of color face on a daily basis because of their visible difference from the white majority; it denies people of color their identity. Unfortunately, this basic precept functions in sf just as much as it does in the real world, so why should most cyberpunk be any different?

Afrofuturism

In this regard, Samuel R. Delany is an ideal starting point to address the progressive associations between cyberpunk and Afrofuturism—i.e., Afrocyberpunk—by turning to *Stars in My Pockets Like Grains of Sand* (1984). While his classic space opera *Nova* (1968) features ubiquitous cyborg technologies, particularly neural implants that allow characters to plug into computers and machines, clearly influencing cyberpunk's later emergence, *Stars in My Pockets Like Grains of Sand* was published concurrently with *Neuromancer* and is a fascinating parallel. While the bulk of the novel concerns the galaxy-spanning interracial love story between Rat Korga and his industrial diplomat lover Marq Dyeth on the planet Velm and the challenges resulting from this relationship after Korga is rescued as the sole survivor of a planetary genocide, it also provides an alternate model for the Internet to Gibson's matrix. Delany describes a "General Information" network in the novel that connects over 6,000 worlds across the galaxy (23) and "if you want to know something—anything at all!—all you have to do is think about it, and the answer pops into your head" (24). Korga voluntarily submits to a Radical Anxiety Termination procedure, nullifying the independence of his mind while eliminating his fits of rage, antisocial behavior, drug habit, and sexual deviancy (3). As Thomas Foster posits, the RAT "brain-modification technique [...] reads like a racialized version of Gibson's trope of the 'meat puppet,' prostitutes who have 'cut-out chips' that suppress their consciousness and actively produce them as objectified bodies" ("Innocent" 246). After Korga's mind is briefly rebuilt, temporarily liberating him from twenty-two years of corporate slavery, the previously illiterate Korga takes full advantage of his freedom by reading insatiably. Madhu Dubey identifies this moment in the text as "the classic-slave narrative scenario in which learning to read is an illicit act of discovery" (*Signs* 239). While *Stars in My Pockets Like Grains of Sand* could (and should!) have easily been included in cyberpunk's initial wave, the depiction of race and racism, topics that mainstream cyberpunk authors simply lacked the cultural vocabulary to address in any authentic way, helps to explain why Delany is evoked as an inspiration for cyberpunk but not official inclusion, placing the novel squarely within Afrofuturism and its Afrocyberpunk offshoots.

During the same time period, Octavia E. Butler created a fascinating cyborg story in her Xenogenesis trilogy—*Dawn* (1987), *Adulthood Rites* (1988), and *Imago* (1989). Redubbed *Lilith's Brood* (2000), the trilogy depicts an alien rescue of an Earth devastated by nuclear war, an enforced gene trade between what remains of humanity and the utterly grotesque Oankali, and the transformation of humanity into something other, something cyborg. Part of the narrative involves the Oankali merging with humanity through bio-engineering, genetically hacking human flesh on a microscopic level to improve both species from the resulting miscegenation. While the central character, Lilith, is transformed in the series into a cyborg that other humans fear, distrust, and hate, what is of greater importance is the Oankali's use of a living technology which circumvents the interface problem between organic and inorganic material that the cyborg represents, which is why Donna J. Haraway, briefly commenting on *Wild Seed* (1980) and *Dawn*, identifies Butler as a 20th-century cyborg storyteller in her classic "A Cyborg Manifesto: Science, Technology, and Socialist-Feminism in the Late Twentieth Century." Throughout her oeuvre, but particularly in *Lilith's Brood*, Butler shapes the cyborg mythology to challenge "the informatics of domination," where "women of colour," presented as "monstrous selves," threaten the "material and cultural grids" binding western civilization (Haraway 300, 311). In addition to using the alien contact narrative as a vehicle to address slavery and white imperialism, the cyborg hackers depicted in *Lilith's Brood* radically modify cultural values by outdating violence, permitting men to depart families, moving forward by communal and consensus adult decisions, and respecting all life, amid other changes. Indeed, Butler's cyborg expands human boundaries with an Afrocyberpunk meditation on power and race.

While Steven Barnes's *Streetlethal* (1983), Nalo Hopkinson's *Midnight Robber* (2000), and Walter Mosley's *Futureland* (2001) are discussed elsewhere,[2] Nalo Hopkinson's debut novel *Brown Girl in*

355

the Ring (1998) is also an Afrocyberpunk contender. The inner city of Hopkinson's near-future Toronto deploys all the common dystopian tropes one expects in cyberpunk's depiction of street life in the urban metropolis:

> When Toronto's economic base collapsed, investors, commerce, and government withdrew into the suburb cities, leaving the rotten core to decay. Those who stayed were the ones who couldn't or wouldn't leave. The street people. The poor people. The ones who didn't see the writing on the wall, or who were too stubborn to give up their homes. Or who saw the decline of authority as an opportunity. [... The] fear of vandalism and violence was keeping 'burb people out. (4)

This cityscape becomes known as "the burn" because the "DOUGHNUT HOLE" left at the core is a violent, filthy, crime-infested place, where gangs sell the drug Buff, street children steal anything they can, and people barter, farm, and use folk medicines to survive (2, 10). Challenges from within and from without the black community represent the daily struggles of these inner-city denizens.

Given her Jamaican heritage, Hopkinson is able to seamlessly expand the easily identifiable cyberpunk motifs onto a broader canvass by incorporating Caribbean loas into the narrative in a manner that far surpasses Gibson's various attempts in *Count Zero* (1986) and *Mona Lisa Overdrive* (1988); in so doing, Hopkinson exceeds a strictly 'cyberpunk' label: Her Afrocyberpunk work is founded upon a believable black community that is largely absent in cyberpunk-proper and helps identify Afrocyberpunk as more than simply a black cyberpunk but, instead, an artistic form that speaks to broader sociocultural issues than much cyberpunk has exhibited. For example, the street kids in Toronto's forgotten subway underground represent a perfect Afrocyberpunk moment. These street kids utilize high-tech innovation to protect themselves from the burn's gang leader Rudy and his posse. One of the kids, Mumtaz, "jury-rigged" an "electronic box" of some kind, maybe an old school ghetto blaster, to amplify the voices of the children by layering their voices "to a din of hundreds" (185). And their leader, Josée, explains how she "hooked up" a "deeplight projector" to the subway tracks to make them appear like a crowd of hundreds as opposed to a mere handful of children. These are bona fide Afrocyberpunk moments and lend credence to Jillana Enteen's argument that Hopkinson's novels "revise cyberpunk to render visible current socioeconomic inequities, suggest alternative formulations of the relationships between humans and technology, and increase the cultural repository of ideas that inspire technological and social development" (263). Or, as Kilgore writes about Enteen's argument, "Hopkinson's Afrofuturism gives Enteen a way of critiquing the racial and masculinist investments of cyberpunk, yet that critique does not amount to a dismissal of the form" (568).[3]

More recently, three-time Hugo Award-winning black author N.K. Jemisin creates a fascinating account of machines playing identity politics in "Valedictorian" (2012). The basic plot concerns artificial intelligences (AIs) confining humanity behind firewalls for an indefinite period after prevailing in war. As the centuries pass, humans hide the truth of their defeat from their youth. All the while, humanity pays a tribute: every year they give over the least valued 10% to their machine offspring from each graduating high school class, plus one superior student. In this case, an AI emissary named Lemuel convinces Zinhle Nkosi, the probable valedictorian, a black teenaged girl, to join with them. Jemisin ironizes the famous meat metaphor often attributed to a transhumanist (mis)reading of Gibson's *Neuromancer*—i.e., the body as a mere casing for the mind—when Zinhle promptly accepts that she is dealing with an AI that downloads itself into the bodies culled from humankind, leading her to retort "That's not treating us like people" (166). Lemuel explains why his artificial people want her to join. She represents the best humanity has to offer by excelling academically in spite of the bullying of her classmates who are in part afraid of her intelligence, but the racial dynamic of the abuse this black girl has to endure by her mostly white peers cannot be understated; of course, the broader undercurrent of a species kept quarantined, perhaps even enslaved, beyond the firewalled communities fashioned after reservations has its own racial implications. In any event, Zinhle has the strength to go on and survive in the alien cyberspace and Jemisin's story, in engaging with identity politics, exudes blackness because she imagines what the other side of the digital divide looks like in magnifying technoculture.

In a similar vein, Afrocyberpunk stories mirror the information economy, magnify technoculture, and enhance color line issues. For example, Ghanaian Jonathan Dotse's online story "Virus!"[4] (2011) follows Dela, a teenaged village girl with a "biocore implant" installed in her brain who heads into the nation's capital Accra to find work. She meets a shady woman named Khadija who sets Dela up as a data runner on the Grid, "the wireless networks that relay information throughout the city." On her first run, Dela and Khadija climb a secured data tower; Khadija hacks it and illegally downloads data files into Dela's mind. However, the data packet causes a critical error in Dela's biocore just as a security guard spots them. Although Khadija escapes, Dela is not so lucky: Her body shuts down and "her mind caved in."

Or, consider the mixture of folklore, urban fantasy, and sf in African American Nicky Drayden's debut novel *The Prey of Gods* (2017). Along with personal robots, a street drug named Godsend, and an angry demigoddess in a futuristic Port Elizabeth, South Africa, the novel features a diverse cast of characters who attempt to save the world, including the South African Elkins, a gay, black hacker who gains his code-breaking aptitude from taking Godsend, and the robot Clever 4.1, who gains consciousness and starts an AI revolution by awakening others, at least before being kicked out of its own sect for protecting the human character Muzikayise McCarthy.

Finally, Bill Campbell's satirical *Sunshine Patriots* (2004) features rebellious black and brown cyborg soldiers, outfitted with "Brain2" units, "little plasma blob(s)" implanted in their necks to allow them to become "living, breathing arsenal(s)" (24). These cyborgs go up against the concerns of the triumvirate military/industrial/entertainment complex and begin to question their own roles—i.e., they perceive racial disparities and seek justice on their own—when called upon to quell a human rebellion on the colonized vacation planet of Elysia. In these (and other) stories, none of the diegetic settings are colorblind worlds, but they do divest whiteness as the norm of our technological imaginings without necessarily eliminating white people. Delany, Butler, Hopkinson, Jemisin, Dotse, Drayden, and others offer us consciously racialized settings in their Afrocyberpunk imaginings; in this respect, a black audience can see themselves in the technocultural world as more than the flesh machines they have been regarded as for much of history in the New World.

While this chapter has largely focused on Afrofuturism in its Afrocyberpunk literary forms, Afrofuturism as a whole entails many forms in terms of artistic expression. It has become a central part of our cultural fabric with a veritable eruption of speculative art produced by people of color worldwide envisioning themselves as active agents in the future. Take, for example, Afrofuturism's deep roots in the sonic technologies and creative expressions of black musicians, such as The Jimi Hendrix Experience (*Electric Ladyland*, 1968), George Clinton and his bands Funkadelic (*Funkadelic*, 1970) and Parliament (*Mothership Connection*, 1975),[5] Earth, Wind & Fire, notably the video for "Let's Groove" (1981), seemingly set in outer space and featuring a neon-orange pyramid with the band adorned in glittery-metallic spacesuits, and DJ Afrika Bambaataa whose use "of electronic music and the gradual collapse of boundaries between man and machine opened new avenues for engagement with scientific and sociocultural themes" (Clark). The musical infrastructure for all these artists (and more) is most certainly visionary-free jazz musician and poet Sun Ra (1914–93) who, as a self-proclaimed alien from Saturn accompanied by his band the Arkestra, endeavored to bring forth a sonic planetary peace upon Earth through such albums as *Astro Black* (1973). In "Sun Ra's Otherworldliness," John Rieder encapsulates Sun Ra's music in this fashion: "Although Sun Ra did not organize 'masses' of men, he did organize the production and distribution of a product—his music—that was not meant simply to be consumed as a commodity, but rather to foster a certain mode of awareness and create a sense of communal identity" (236). Or, as Ytasha Womack writes in *Afrofuturism: The World of Black Sci-Fi and Fantasy Culture*, Sun Ra "believed that music and technology could heal and transform the world. He was spellbound by the possibilities of space travel and electric technology" (53), and judging from the artists that have followed his trailblazing path, it seems this is a shared sentiment. For example, Sun Ra and these other Afrofuturist musical trendsetters helped pave the way for such contemporary Afrofuturist performers as Herbie Hancock, The Jacksons—particularly the futuristic post-apocalypticism in the videos for "Can You Feel It" (1980) and "Torture" (1984), or Michael Jackson's duet with his sister Janet on "Scream" (1995)—Dr. Dre, Ice Cube, OutKast, Public Enemy, Erykah Badu, Flying Lotus, Shabazz Palace, Spook Matambo, Deltron 3030, and clipping., an experimental hip hop group which garnered a 2017 Hugo nomination for their album *Splendor & Misery* (2016) by creating an Afrofuturist storyline "set in a dystopian future," where "a mutineer among a starship's slave population falls in love with the ship's computer" (Heller).

Arguably, the most obvious descendant of Sun Ra is American R&B artist Janelle Monáe, whose explicitly Afrofuturist/Afrocyberpunk work on *The ArchAndroid* (2010), *The Electric Lady* (2013), and *Dirty Computer* (2018) shows a deep awareness of how racial identity politics blended with sound technology can impact an ever-quickening global popular technoculture defined by race. As Christine Capetola writes in her contribution to this collection, Monáe "creates her own black, queer, and feminist version of cyberpunk through interfacing her body and musical technology" (246) and, in so doing, partakes in an "Afrocyberpunk project of using (music) technology" to free herself and her listeners from racist, sexist, heteronormative power structures (247). Monáe's oeuvre is loosely organized around the struggles of her android alter ego, Cindi Mayweather, in a dystopian near future where the freedom to love is circumscribed by the powerful Droid Authority, prompting Mayweather's growth from the persecuted Other in *Metropolis: The Chase Suite* (2007) to the revolutionary icon of an android underground in *The ArchAndroid*, a time traveling icon who may have gone missing in *Electric Lady* but has proven inspirational to "droids from all across *Metropolis* [who] gather in nightclubs [...] and barbershops where they revel in the otherness that separates them from humans" (Pulliam-Moore). "The android," Monáe explains in an interview with Dorian Lynskey, "represents a new form of the Other [...] And I believe we're going to be living in a world of androids by 2029. How will we all get along? Will we treat the android humanely? What type of society will it be when we're integrated? I've felt like the Other at certain points in my life. I felt like it was a universal language that we could all understand." This focus on the 'universal language of the Other' fuels Monáe's *Dirty Computer* and its accompanying film, or what Monáe calls an emotion picture, that depicts an oppressive future where humans who don't conform to 'proper' codes of behavior are quarantined by New Dawn agents and forced to undergo a "cleansing," a euphemism for a techno-chemical lobotomy where rebellious memories are wiped away and the subject reprogrammed accordingly. Having revealed that *Dirty Computer* is definitely part of the larger Cindi Mayweather narrative universe,[6] Monáe's Afrofuturist and Afrocyberpunk promises to expand her artistic oeuvre in exciting and much-anticipated directions.

Monáe's reliance upon the visual medium of her emotion picture also speaks to the importance of Afrofuturism on film, arguably beginning in the 1970s with Djibril Diop Mambéty's *Touki Bouki* (1973) and Sun Ra and John Coney's *Space Is the Place* (1974), stretching across the decades and continents to include such titles as Lizzie Borden's *Born in Flames* (1983), John Sayles's *The Brother From Another Planet* (1984), Souleyman Cissé's *Yeelen* (Brightness, 1987), Haile Gerima's *Sankofa* (1993), Wanuri Kahiu's *Pumzi* (2009), Frances Bodomo's *Afronauts* (2014), Sharon Lewis's *Brown Girl Begins* (2017), and such Hollwyood fare as Jordan Peele's *Us* (2019) and Coogler's *Black Panther*, to name only a handful of titles. As Mark Bould argues, cyberpunk elements in Afrofuturist films can also be tracked in such offerings as the computer hacking in Sylvestre Amoussou's *Africa Paradis* (2006) or El Fani's *Bedwin Hacker* (2003) and the feminist cyborg figures in Jean-Pierre Bekolo's *Les saignantes* (2005) (218–30). "While aspects of Afrocyberpunk cinema," writes Bould, "look very familiar to western eyes, they use those pieces to play an often different game" (231), particularly when it comes to traditional lines of geopolitical, economic, and social order that 'traditional' cyberpunk routinely blurs.

Although space prevents a full analysis of Afrofuturism and Afrocyberpunk in other media, it would be remiss not to at least point to the cyberpunk influences in Afrofuturist art and fashion. For example, aside from the fact King T'Challa's suit in *Black Panther* is a cybernetic enhancement, turning him into a cyberpunk-styled cyborg,[7] the Afrofuturist fashion that was lauded when the film was released is a central component of black cultural identity in the 21st century. As Connie Wang writes, "it's easy enough to spot: powerful Black men and women dressed in Besotho blankets, Himba braids, Maasai collars, as well as Egyptian anks and crowns inspired by Yourban deity Oshun—remixed with superhero textiles, gravity-defying jewelry, and technicolor hair," some of which is reminiscent of cyberpunk visual motifs. Fashion is also a key draw to the immensely successful Afropunk Festival which, inspired by the documentary *Afro-Punk* (Spooner 2003), provides opportunities to showcase black arts in all forms of cultural expression. Similarly, the Afrofuturist art show "In Their Own Form" at the Museum of Contemporary Photography in Chicago (12 April, 2018, to 8 July, 2018) featured more than a dozen contemporary artists, including Senegalese Alun Be whose "Edification" series includes photographs of young black children wearing virtual reality goggles (Sayej). Or, as Pamela Phatsimo Sunstrum points out, Kiluanji Kia Henda's photo-based project, *Icarus 13* (2006–08), imagines Angolan astrophysicists preparing for the first expedition to the sun, weaving the Icarus myth and Apollo 13 that "provides another example of a creative practice that collapses myth into sf while simultaneously igniting African postcolonial imaginings" (118). Even something as mundane as searching for Afrofuturist fashion on Pinterest reveals cyberpunk influences in the litany of images. Afrocyberpunk remains a viable and ongoing strain in the larger Afrofuturist field, particularly when it comes to the visual splendor on display in fashion and the visual arts.

In closing, with its focus on "issues of social justice in a global and technology-intensive world" (Lavender, *Afrofuturism Rising* 3), Afrofuturism has grown more complex since Dery's "Black to the Future" and has become a useful analytical tool that has, in many ways, evolved beyond its early roots in cyberpunk, at least conceptually or theoretically. For example, as Bould demonstrates in his work on Afrocyberpunk cinema, Afrofuturism anticipates "a transformation" in sf studies, all the while working against "the typical cyberpunk acceptance of capitalism [and] assimilation of certain currently marginalized peoples into a global system that might, at best, tolerate some relatively minor (although not unimportant) reforms" (182) by breaking with the colorblind future of sf. Similarly, Afro-British philosopher Kodwo Eshun discusses how Afrofuturism establishes a "webbed network," an historical matrix reflecting black people's "perpetual fight for human status, a yearning for human rights, and a struggle for inclusion within the human species" which continues beyond chattel slavery far into the future as it connects black people across time (*More Brilliant* 00[-006]). Elsewhere, Eshun identifies such connections as "countermemories that contest the colonial archive, thereby situating the collective trauma of slavery as the founding moment of modernity" ("Further" 288). Thus, Afrofuturism recuperates a seemingly stolen past that many people would like to forget—the scene from *Black Panther* when Erik Killmonger (Michael B. Jordan) lectures the white museum curator about stolen African history comes immediately to mind—and creates options for cultural analysis. Or, as Kilgore notes, "Afrofuturism can be seen as less a marker of black authenticity and more a cultural force, an episteme that betokens a shift in our largely unconscious assumptions about what histories matter and how they may serve as a precondition for any future we may imagine" (564). The recovery work suggested by Eshun and Kilgore, coupled with the transformative anticipations that Bould highlights, represents Afrocyberpunk moments where readers dive into this historical archive to retrieve a sense of black humanity separate from the cyborg image—i.e., the "coded as natural machines" that Dery describes—that has been created for black people by typically white power structures. In this respect, Afrofuturism and Afrocyberpunk enable black people to see themselves in the technocultural world as more than the flesh machines they have been regarded as for much of history in the New World, and while the ongoing development of both Afrofuturism and Afrocyberpunk is deeper and richer in its scope than anything Dery could have imagined, "reflecting counter histories, hacking and or appropriating the influence of network software, database logic, cultural analytics, deep remixability, neurosciences, enhancement and augmentation, gender fluidity, posthuman possibility, the speculative sphere, with transdisciplinary applications" (Anderson and Jones x); it still reflects a cyberpunk heritage as it considers hacking, remixing, augmentation, and the posthuman as central conceits, while allowing for other modes of storytelling in black speculative fictions.

Notes

1 For more details on the Movement and its transformation into cyberpunk, see Graham J. Murphy's contribution to this collection.
2 For details, see Lavender's "Critical Race Theory" chapter elsewhere in this collection.
3 For a discussion of cyberpunk's masculinist origins, see Patricia Melzer's, Wendy Pearson's, and/or Lisa Yaszek's individual contributions to this collection.
4 Dotse's "Virus!" emerges from AfroCyberPunk Interactive, self-described as a "digital hypermedia studio publishing house based in Accra, Ghana" that focuses on "digital hypermedia content primarily for mobile devices" ("About"), incorporating cyberpunk-styled technologies and formats to distribute Afrocyberpunk to a 21st-century readership.
5 Ashley Clark writes of Sun Ra that his "music envisions a space-age era in which black characters are the primary protagonists and cultural arbiters of the future. Parliament's legendary stadium shows of the 1970s were known to be visited by a giant, glittering UFO that emerged from the ceiling amidst billowing smoke and pyrotechnics."
6 For details, see Charles Pulliam-Moore's "Janelle Monáe Explains How *Dirty Computer* Connects to the Rest of her Afrofuturist Discography."
7 King T'Challa's Black Panther suit is only one of a number of cyborg enhancements available to black characters in the larger comic book medium. There is, of course, the literal cyborgization of Victor Stone, a.k.a. Cyborg, who was a central member of Marv Wolfman and George Pérez's New Teen Titans that debuted in 1980 and has since gone on to feature prominently in more-recent versions of the Justice League. Sam Wilson, a.k.a. The Falcon/Captain America, and his flight-powered cybernetic suit have been a mainstay in the Marvel Universe since 1969 and, more recently, the Marvel Cinematic Universe. And, Dwayne McDuffie and Denys Cowan created *Hardware* in 1993 for Milestone Comics (later migrating to DC Comics), featuring genius inventor Curtis Metcalf who dons an *Iron Man*-styled suit of armor to fight organized crime. For more details, including the complications surrounding black superheroes, see Adilifu Nama.

Works Cited

"About." *AfroCyberPunk*, 2019, afrocyberpunk.com/about.
Black Panther. Directed by Ryan Coogler, performances by Chadwick Boseman, Michael B. Jordan, Lupita Nyong'o, Danai Gurira, Letitia Wright, and Martin Freeman, Marvel Studios, 2018.
Bould, Mark. "Afrocyberpunk Cinema: The Postcolony Finds its Own Use for Things." *Cyberpunk and Visual Culture*, edited by Graham J. Murphy and Lars Schmeink. Routledge, 2018, pp. 213–34.
———. "The Ships Landed Long Ago: Afrofuturism and Black SF." *Science Fiction Studies*, vol. 34, no. 2, 2007, pp. 177–86.
Butler, Octavia E. *Lilith's Brood*. Grand Central, 2000.
Campbell, Bill. *Sunshine Patriots*. Hats Off, 2004.

Afrofuturism

Capetola, Christine. "Janelle Monáe: *Dirty Computer*." *The Routledge Companion to Cyberpunk Culture*, edited by Anna McFarlane, Graham J. Murphy, and Lars Schmeink. Routledge, 2020, pp. 245–51.

Clark, Ashley. "Inside Afrofuturism: A Sonic Companion." *BFI Film Forever*, 26 Nov. 2014, bfi.org.uk/news-opinion/news-bfi/features/inside-afrofuturism-sonic-companion.

Dery, Mark. "Black to the Future: Interviews with Samuel R. Delany, Greg Tate, and Tricia Rose." *Flame Wars: The Discourse of Cyberculture*, edited by Mark Dery. Duke UP, 1994, pp. 179–222.

Dotse, Jonathan. "Virus!" *AfroCyberPunk Interactive*, 2011, afrocyberpunk.com/resources/virus/.

Drayden, Nicky. *The Prey of Gods*. Harper Voyager, 2017.

Dubey, Madhu. *Signs and Cities: Black Literary Postmodernism*. U of Chicago P, 2003.

Enteen, Jillana. "'On the Receiving End of the Colonization': Nalo Hopkinson's 'Nansi Web." *Science Fiction Studies*, vol. 34, no. 2, July 2007, pp. 262–82.

Eshun, Kodwo. "Further Considerations of Afrofuturism." *CR: The New Centennial Review*, vol. 3, no. 2, 2003, pp. 287–302.

———. *More Brilliant than the Sun: Adventures in Sonic Fiction*. Quartet, 1998.

Foster, Thomas. "'Innocent by Contamination': Ethnicity and Technicity in Delany's *Stars in My Pocket Like Grains of Sand*." *African American Review*, vol. 48, no. 3, 2015, pp. 239–56.

Gibson, William. *Neuromancer*. Ace, 1984.

Haraway, Donna J. "A Cyborg Manifesto: Science, Technology and Socialist-Feminism in the Late Twentieth Century." *The Cybercultures Reader*, edited by David Bell and Barbara M. Kennedy. Routledge, 2000, pp. 291–324.

Heller, Jason. "Why clipping.'s Hugo nomination matters for Music in Science Fiction." *Pitchfork*, 7 Apr. 2017, pitchfork.com/thepitch/1483-why-clippings-hugo-nomination-matters-for-music-in-science-fiction/.

Hollinger, Veronica. "Cybernetic Deconstructions: Cyberpunk and Postmodernism." *Storming the Reality Studio: A Casebook of Cyberpunk and Postmodern Fiction*, edited by Larry McCaffery. Duke UP, 1994, pp. 203–18.

Hopkinson, Nalo. *Brown Girl in the Ring*. Warner, 1998.

———. "A Reluctant Ambassador from the Planet of Midnight." *Journal of the Fantastic in the Arts*, vol. 21, no. 3, 2010, pp. 339–50.

Jemisin, N.K. "Valedictorian." 2012. *Lightspeed Magazine*, Dec. 2014, lightspeedmagazine.com/fiction/valedictorian/.

Kilgore, De Witt D. "Afrofuturism." *The Oxford Handbook of Science Fiction*, edited by Rob Latham. Oxford UP, 2014, pp. 561–72.

Lavender, Isiah III. *Afrofuturism Rising: The Literary Prehistory of a Movement*. Ohio State UP, 2019.

———. "Critical Race Theory." *The Routledge Companion to Science Fiction*, edited by Mark Bould, Andrew M. Butler, Adam Roberts, and Sherryl Vint. Routledge, 2009, pp. 185–93.

Lynskey, Dorian. "Janelle Monáe: sister from another planet." *The Guardian*, 26 Aug. 2010, theguardian.com/music/2010/aug/26/janelle-monae-sister-another-planet.

Nama, Adilifu. *Super Black: American Pop Culture and Black Superheroes*. U of Texas P, 2012.

Pulliam-Moore, Charles. "From *Metropolis* to *Dirty Computer*: A Guide to Janelle Monáe's Time-Traveling Musical Odyssey." *io9.com*, 02 Feb. 2018, io9.gizmodo.com/from-metropolis-to-dirty-computer-a-guide-to-janelle-m-1825580195.

———. "Janelle Monáe Explains How *Dirty Computer* Connects to the Rest of her Afrofuturist Discography." *io9.com*, 29 Oct. 2018, io9.gizmodo.com/janelle-monae-explains-how-dirty-computer-connects-to-t-1830079331.

Rieder, John. "Sun Ra's Otherworldliness." *Paradoxa: Africa SF*, no. 25, 2013, pp. 235–52.

Sayej, Nadja. "Beyond *Black Panther*: Afrofuturism takes flight at Chicago museum." *The Guardian*, 10 Apr. 2018, theguardian.com/artanddesign/2018/apr/10/afrofuturism-exhibition-in-their-own-form-museum-contemporary-photography-chicago.

Smith, Jamil. "The Revolutionary Power of *Black Panther*." *Time*, 19 Feb. 2018, time.com/black-panther/.

Sunstrum, Pamela Phatsimo. "Afro-mythology and African Futurism: The Politics of Imagining and Methodologies for Contemporary Creative Research Practices." *Paradoxa: Africa SF*, no. 25, 2013, pp. 113–29.

Wang, Connie. "Style Out There: For Black Women, Afrofuturist Fashion is More Than a Costume." *Refinery 29*, 25 Mar. 2019, refinery29.com/en-ca/afrofuturism-fashion.

Womack, Ytasha. *Afrofuturism: The World of Black Sci-Fi and Fantasy Culture*. Chicago Review P, 2013.

43

VEILLANCE SOCIETY

Chris Hables Gray

43.1 The Proliferation of Veillance

If you are paying attention, you can feel the thrum of it, a soundless moan in your head and an itch between your shoulder blades—the CCTV cameras on every urban corner, hulking like vultures; the torrents of metadata streaming by the millisecond to the NSA's Bumblehive, a million square feet of servers in Utah; drones buzzing and proliferating and shrinking; and phone cameras ready to stream to the web every kitten or killing they see. Your searches are haunted by ghosts sent by Amazon, Google, Apple, and Facebook to sell you stuff you just bought; doxing and identity theft are taking out your friends like a 1950s movie of a doomed World War II patrol; and that shadow of yourself, your medical data and buying habits and Pinterest page of old union posters, your virtual doppelgänger, your porn predilections—your digital silhouette, growing in cyberspace with every keystroke. Welcome to today. Welcome to Veillance Society.

Veillance, from the French 'observed,' from above (*sur*), from below (*sous*), from almost every angle (Figure 43.1).

We were warned by many, but perhaps most helpfully by the cyberpunks. Their visions of a dangerous, darkening (for oh so many reasons), increasingly corporate world saturated in new neon bright digital objects emerging every hour from a festering Silicon Valley and its regional infections from Bangalore to Nairobi to Austin, TX, all the while the line between flesh and machine dissolving in accelerating and ever more interesting ways, are clearly coming true. 'Cyber' because reality is being digitized, and 'punk' because we know the process, driven as it is by greed (for fame, wealth, and power), is both corrupted/corrupting and essential for who we are. It is our worst nightmare and our greatest hope.

In their introduction to *Cyberpunk and Visual Culture*, Graham J. Murphy and Lars Schmeink argue that "[t]he growing dominance of visual media and the visualization of culture thus call for a different theoretical framework with which to analyze the construction of these cultural instances." They call this a "pictorial turn," drawing on the work of W.J.T. Mitchell. To Mitchell, this is "the realization that (the look, the gaze, the glance, the practices of observation, surveillance and visual pleasure) may be as deep a problem as various forms of *reading* (decipherment, decoding, interpretation, etc.)" (qtd. in Murphy and Schmeink xxiii). The concept of veillance is this new framework.

"Watch or be watched" (129) is Pretty Boy's credo in Pat Cadigan's short story "Pretty Boy Crossover" (1986). But it is really 'watch and be watched.' The ancient question *Quis custodiet ipsos custodes?* ('Who watches the watchers?') is being answered by 'The watched should watch the

Figure 43.1 YOU ARE UNDER SURVEILLANCE: Revolutionary street anarchists, true to the cyberpunk tradition, continue to organize into the 21st century, in cyberspace and on the streets. The CrimethInc. collective is one of the more potent distillations of decades of activism. These stickers are widely available and make the perfect addition to unobtrusive security cameras everywhere.

watchers.' This is why the concept of surveillance is not enough: The network breeds the hacker, hypocrisy spawns punk, the corporation creates the ex-worker, governments mandate rebels, and surveillance had lead inevitably to *sousveillance*.[1]

Different types of 'veillance' proliferate: dataveillance, artveillance, contraveillance, self (soi-? auto-?)veillance, and watching equals (equiveillance). Or, more amusingly, McVeillance, named for one of Mann's confrontations with other network nodes, in this case a McDonald's in Paris where workers assaulted him for filming and then lied about it, even though he'd filmed them (Mann, "McVeillance"). And when we write about veillance? Metaveillance, obviously.

So we can call our culture Veillance Society. Reality is information, after all. And that hasn't changed now that we catalog a small bit of it electronically. But information is also about attention, how much attention can we bring to bear, and that takes us to veillance. It is a special type of information flow, from the subject to the observer. So why is cyberpunk a good guide to Veillance Society? Bruce Sterling comments on the epistemology of the cyberpunk writers, which applies to cyberpunk culture as well:

> Like punk music, cyberpunk is in some sense a return to roots. The cyberpunks are perhaps the first SF generation to grow up not only within the literary tradition of science fiction but in a truly science-fictional world. For them, the techniques of classical "hard SF"— extrapolation, technological literacy—are not just literary tools but an aid to daily life. They are a means of understanding, and highly valued. (Preface x–xi)

So, it is taking SF and actual technoscience seriously, but suspiciously. After all, what are the deeper roots of punk? 'Punk' is what cops and bullies call their victims. Punk is the resistance of the underdog, of disaffected youth rebelling, in song and action, against the establishment. The word has a mysterious history, appearing in various forms in the 1600s, it was Native American for rotted wood, tinder, and in England, slang for a prostitute. In the late 20th century, the streets found its own use for the term, turning it into a self-descriptor of pride, rejecting the authority of church, state, and corporation.

A few cyberpunk tropes are dominant, discussed below: the centrality of the digital, the power of corporations, the merging of organic and machinic, and the refusal of utopia or dystopia, even as life grows darker. But one aspect of the cyberpunk future-present is watching. Not just the watching on the Internet and in the streets, but watching that can extend into our very desires, into our hearts and minds, thanks to every more powerful cyborgian technosciences. The impersonal cyborg gaze, the cyborg-system gaze of large institutions, is somewhat different, and it threatens full surveillance, a dream authorities have had for over 100 years.[2]

43.2 The Panoptic Present

In the late 1970s, I worked as handyman/secretary at Bing Nursery on Stanford University's campus. It was more than just a pre-school, it was also a research center for Stanford's Education and Psychology Departments. All the classrooms had hidden observation rooms with one-way mirrors and microphone-adorned ceiling lights so that graduate students and faculty could monitor the kids' behavior and record it on tapes and in logbooks. Different research studies looked for different things, but there was almost always someone watching.

When toys broke, I was the one called into the classroom to fix them. Being one of the few men around, and adorned as I was with big work boots and a tool belt, I was a popular visitor. One day, early into the job, I was told that a big red wooden truck had a damaged wheel so I went to fix it. A small squad of little boys gathered around me as I went to work. At one point my screwdriver slipped, cutting slightly into my hand.

Veillance Society

"Fuck!" I said, and one little boy grabbed my arm and pointed at the light fixture above us. "Be careful," he hissed. "The lights can hear us." It turned out the children knew about the one-way mirrors and the microphones, but kept that knowledge secret from the adults, passing it on, older child to younger, as they cycled through. I kept their secret, even though it called into question dozens of studies, all predicated on the little subjects not knowing they were under observation.

I lived in a world of protests, our demonstrations were filmed, our radical groups infiltrated, and I spent time in jail. We took care in our letters and knew our long-distance calls were searched for key words. We expected informers, infiltrators, *agents provocateurs*… but my first intimations of the spread of ongoing, mass technical surveillance came from my experience at Bing Nursery School. It was a panopticon.

Panopticon—a prison designed by Jeremy Bentham for his prison warden brother. Tim Jordan, a sociologist, explains it was "a round hollow building with only a tower at its centre. The outside wall was one cell thick, so that the outside window of each cell allowed light in and the inside window faced the inner tower. This meant every occupant of every cell was isolated from each other but became a silhouette to the central tower" (200) (Figure 43.2).

Michel Foucault used the panopticon to explain how society has shifted from hard power to soft. He pointed out that the "supervisor" could peer into any cell and see "a madman, a patient, a condemned man, a worker or a schoolboy" (200). But that wasn't all, because of the design, backlighting would silhouette each cell occupant, making them "constantly visible" (200). Foucault concluded, "Full lighting and the eye of a supervisor capture better than darkness, which ultimately protected. Visibility is a trap" (200).

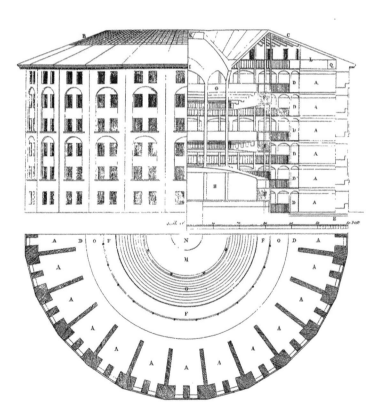

Figure 43.2 Jeremy Bentham's classic panopticon design. Public domain image available at https://commons.wikimedia.org/wiki/File:Panopticon.jpg.

Chris Hables Gray

And what better trap than cyberspace, where the "panoptic mechanism" most certainly arranges "spatial unities that make it possible to see constantly and to recognize immediately" (Foucault 200)? In this system, everyone was "watching someone, who is being watched and watching someone else" (Jordan 200). Jordan agrees with Foucault that this "form of power" spread to "all institutions of modern societies," and then concludes, "[t]he coming of cyberspace seems to many to offer greater possibilities for panoptic mechanisms to make more corners of society visible" (200–01). But as it turns out, this isn't always a good thing because the digital world makes surveillance much more effective: "techno-hopes crumble into techno-fears with a simple shift of perspective" (Jordan 201). Or, as Johnny remarks in William Gibson's short story "Johnny Mnemonic" (1981), "[w]hat they don't tell you is that it's impossible to move, to live, to operate at any level without leaving traces, bits, seemingly meaningless fragments of personal information. Fragments that can be retrieved, amplified" (*Burning Chrome* 17). Cyberspace is therefore cyberpunk's natural environment.

43.3 Cyberspace: From Consensual Hallucination to Public Utility

It was imagined many times before it existed: Memex, the second plane, the grid, the matrix, OASIS, the virtual world, metaspace, cyberspace, the web, the net, the interweb, and so forth. While still lacking faux embodiment and neural links, it is here. Shaped by our dreams as much as our technologies, with a Dark Web, corporate intranets, and milnets, it is where billions of consciousnesses spend trillions of hours. Marshall McLuhan saw its foundations in 1966. He said, we now live in an "instantaneous world of electric information media" (40). He was particularly struck by its "all-at-onceness" (40). It has the allure of synchronicity which trumps delayed gratification. In typical McLuhanesque exuberance he proclaimed: "Time, in a sense, has ceased and space has vanished" (40). He concluded that "like primitives" we now live in a village, but a "global village" vitalized by this movement of "instant electronic information" and like all villages "everybody is maliciously engaged in poking his nose into everybody else's business" (40).

McLuhan was quite conservative and didn't see the attraction. And it turns out, this new cyber place isn't that much like a village anyway, because it is heterogeneous to the limits of imagination, and anonymity is still possible, if care is taken. Just as with the postmodern urban environment, there are blind spots, disguises, bolt holes, and temporary autonomous zones that allow the marginalized, especially punks in the widest meanings of the word, to recreate and work. But surveillance is spreading; some think it could become perfect. That dream is the panopticon.

In talking about the transition from hard power and the prison to the panopticon and soft power, Foucault says soft power needs "permanent, exhaustive, omnipresent surveillance, capable of making all visible, as long as it could itself remain invisible. It had to be like a faceless gaze that transformed the whole social body into a field of perception: thousands of eyes posted everywhere, mobile attentions ever on the alert, a long, hierarchized network" (214). The danger, in what Jordan calls "Total Surveillance or the Coming of the Superpanopticon," raised by the "doom-sayers of cyberspace" (197), is something akin to the ODIN (Optical Defense Intelligence Network) system and the millions of robotic surveillance cameras that are perpetually watching Americans in the film *Eyeborgs* (Clabaugh 2010) (Figure 43.3).

It is a "nightmare" of total invisibility, and cyberspace

> is the ultimate system of surveillance, the ultimate tool for repression and the nightmare of totalitarian societies in which not only is everything watched and recorded but any action considered out of the normal is a reason for investigation. The ghosts of all liberal democratic societies return here and in virtual whispers repeat the fear known as 1984 and Big Brother. (199–200)

Figure 43.3 An eyeborg that effects total surveillance in Richard Clabaugh's *Eyeborgs* (2010).

But as Gibson noted in his short story "Burning Chrome," "the street finds its own uses for things" (*Burning Chrome* 186), and sometimes those things end up shaping the streets. In real cyberspace, there is resistance, there are bugs, and there are gaps. In this, cyberspace mirrors physical reality, and vice versa.

In the Gibson novel *Count Zero* (1986), the eponymous character, a.k.a Bobby, is a young hacker. He is trying to figure out how cyberspace relates to the physical world and a Priest/Crime Lord named Lucas enlightens him by using the metaphor of the priestess Jackie, who channels an "icebreaking" (decryption) program from the Voodoo God Denbala (actually an artificial intelligence [AI]) while jacked into cyberspace:

> "Think of Jackie as a deck, Bobby, a cyberspace deck, a very pretty one with nice ankles," Lucas grinned and Bobby blushed. "Think of Danbala, who some people call the snake, as a program. Say as an icebreaker. Danbala slots into the Jackie deck. Jackie cuts ice. That's all."
>
> "Okay," Bobby said, getting the hang of it, "then what's the matrix? If she's a deck, and Danbala's a program, what's cyberspace?
>
> "The world," Lucas said. (114)

In this view, a growing perspective in 21st-century postmodernity, meatspace (i.e., the real world) becomes a subset of cyberspace, not an alternative. It is all flows of data.

43.4 Veillance Society

In Veillance Society corporations are ascendant, as in cyberpunk sf. Nation states aren't all gone, usually, but more and more they are instruments of business alliances, 'zaibatsus' in cyberpunk parlance. Decades before Citizens United, in Gibson's short story "New Rose Hotel" (1984), the character Fox remarked, "[t]he blood of a zaibatsu is information, not people. The structure is independent of the individual lives that comprise it. Corporation as life form" (*Burning Chrome* 106). And these "life forms" don't just want cheap labor and resources, guaranteed markets, and the outsourcing of costly externalities (like climate destruction). They want your loyalty and more. Facebook, Amazon, Google, and many others run neuro-marketing experiments watching your online behavior, all the better to know you for their ends (cf. Zuboff). Foucault pointed out that the "Panopticon is a privileged place for experiments on men, and for analyzing with complete certainty the transformations that may be obtained from them" (204). In cyberspace this is literally true.

Harvard Professor Shoshanna Zuboff sees these transformations as part of the spread of "surveillance capitalism." But watching isn't the goal, it is "to change people's actual behavior at scale." It is "a parasitic form of profit" that in the end produces a "profoundly anti-democratic power." Yet it is not just about Big Data from social media, it includes scientific and technical knowledge, which is also fungible. For example, the anti-hero of "New Rose Hotel" ponders this while on the run from his employers, the zaibatsu Hosaka. He has failed to successfully kidnap Hiroshi, a scientist from a rival group, and instead led several key scientists from Hosaka into a deadly trap in Marrakesh. Now he is being hunted by his disappointed clients. Reflecting on the value of his target, he realizes that Hiroshi's "edge" is:

> Radioactive nucleases, monoclonal antibodies, something to do with the linkage of proteins, nucleotides... hot proteins. High-speed links. He said Hiroshi was a freak, the kind who shatters paradigms, inverts a whole field of science, brings on the violent revision of an entire body of knowledge. Basic patents, he said, his throat tight with the sheer wealth of it, with the high, thin smell of tax-free millions that clung to those two words. (108)

Veillance Society started to become real with the first census run with proto-computer machines. Then governments built real computers to crack codes in war and to build weapons of mass destruction. It grew with the massive collection of social Big Data, including secrets, by governments, which eventually provoked the widespread revelation of secrets through Wikileaks, Manning, Snowden, and others. But it became dominant when corporations built social media platforms and mobile devices that took facebooking, snap-chatting, and instagramming to almost every corner of society, producing an infinite flow of digital data.

But no matter what happens with digital information, at least we will always have our private thoughts deep and secret in our minds. There we can think whatever we want and no one can know. Right? No. Or at least, not for long. Just as digital technoscience is growing a veillance society right before our eyes, sucking up secrecy, it is also creating the technologies to read, and thus inevitably control, human minds. In other words, the line between watching people and watching the rest of nature (science) is fading. Both produce powerful Big Data. For example, technosciences such as optogenetics are key to developing mind-healing to mind-reading to mind-writing (Gray, "Big Data"), a.k.a. penséeveillance or, perhaps, veillance de esprit.

It is all about what you see in the brain, and what you can make the brain 'see' in an individualized spectacle. In *Count Zero*, Gibson describes the experience of the mercenary Turner while his consciousness is being rebuilt by a Dutch neurosurgeon, after a bomb from a disappointed employer destroyed most of his body:

> He spent most of those three months in a ROM-generated simstim construct of an idealized New England boyhood of the previous century. The Dutchman's visits were gray dawn dreams, nightmares that faded as the sky lightened beyond his second-floor bedroom window. You could smell the lilacs late at night. He read Conan Doyle by the light of a sixty-watt bulb behind a parchment shade printed with clipper ships. He masturbated in the smell of clean cotton sheets and thought about cheerleaders. The Dutchman opened a door in his back brain and came strolling in to ask questions, but in the morning his mother called him down to Wheaties, eggs and bacon, coffee with milk and sugar. (1–2)

Everyone is trying to watch everyone else. At times it is hard to tell who has power over whom. For, of course, even when you are the gaze, there is a relationship, as Gibson's mercenary Turner, discovers "[t]he *intimacy* of the thing was hideous. He fought down waves of raw transference, bringing all

Veillance Society

his will to bear on crushing a feeling that was akin to love, the obsessive tenderness a watcher comes to feel for the subject of prolonged surveillance" (*Count Zero*, emphasis in original, 24).

The watcher and the watched, the torturer and the tortured, the killer and the killed, it is always intimate whether both sides of the relationship realize it or not. Veillance is about the flow of information in one direction, as in *surveillance* watching from above those below. After all, many people think God watches over us. In the military, to see combat from above is to use 'God's Eye.' But Veillance Society has no god, and one eye (as with Sauron's) is not enough. It is now a world of eyes but not just Big Brother's. All can watch and act.

Gibson clearly sensed how complicated this would become. In 2003 he wrote about the fiftieth anniversary of George Orwell's *Nineteen Eighty-Four* (1949).

> I say "truths," however, and not "truth," as the other side of information's new ubiquity can look not so much transparent as outright crazy. Regardless of the number and power of the tools used to extract patterns from information, any sense of meaning depends on context, with interpretation coming along in support of one agenda or another. A world of informational transparency will necessarily be one of deliriously multiple viewpoints, shot through with misinformation, disinformation, conspiracy theories and a quotidian degree of madness. We may be able to see what's going on more quickly, but that doesn't mean we'll agree about it any more readily. ("The Road to Oceana")

Gibson goes on to make some confusing comments on dystopias being "no more real than utopias." He adds, "None of us ever really inhabits either—except, in the case of dystopias, in the relative and ordinarily tragic sense of life in some extremely unfortunate place." But the world as it is portrayed in most cyberpunk isn't a classical dystopia. It isn't a great world, it is dark (noir), but there is room for agency in the cracks in the culture. There is joy and political change. It isn't *Nineteen Eighty-Four*. What it is, however, is deeply flawed, with rapacious corporations, corrupt governments, and organized crime linking them all, and always overhead are looming existential threats like climate collapse, nuclear war, and neurotic AIs threatening everything. In many ways, this is our world, except the AIs are not yet conscious. We are on the verge of disaster, as the cyberpunk worlds are, but we aren't there yet.

But there clearly is a consistent pull toward dystopia. And the increasing power of corporations is a big part of the problem. Some seem already as dangerous as Evil Corp from the TV series *Mr. Robot* (Esmail 2015–19), but almost all of them mobilize every advantage they have, from micro-monitoring their employees (keystroke by keystroke) to manipulating consumers at every turn. The cultural critic Mark Dery unpacks the meaning of one of the companies and a pioneer of full surveillance: Disney. As Dery notes, "guests" are really just consumers, "of junk food, knickknacks, and most of all, images," while "Disney's ubiquitous security and unremitting surveillance ensure[s] that most visitors" (147) obey pretty much every rule. To cap it off, these guests, who pay for the privilege of having fun exactly as Disney wants, often watch "robot dramas" (147) which end with the humans applauding the machines.

Dery takes this further to warn of a fundamental alienation. He uses the experience of Visual Mark, a synner ("virtual reality synthesizer") from Pat Cadigan's novel *Synners* (1991): "Surveillance cameras (everywhere in the twenty-first-century L.A. of the novel) become his eyes, computer console speakers his voice boxes, the measureless vastness of global cyberspace his dominion" (253). For Dery it is an "Original Syn" (252), a move from the living cyborg to the bodiless fantasy of the deeply alienated. But in actuality it is the impossible dream of an escape from our actual cyborg existence. Yes, many live much of their lives in cyberspace, but you need your body. Without your body you are dead. That's not going to change, not even for the machines.

Chris Hables Gray

43.5 The Affordances of Our Cyberpunk World

Every object, every bit of information, affords certain uses and not others. The affordances of digital information have led to a proliferation of watching. The power of veillance information is the power of the gaze. Andrew Ross argues that information is "a new kind of commodity" that is now "the essential site of capital accumulation in the world" (126–27). The massive collection of data "converted into intelligence" creates surplus value:

> This surplus information value is more than is needed for public surveillance; it is often information or intelligence culled from consumer polling or statistical analysis of transactional behavior, that has no immediate use in the process of routine public surveillance. Indeed, it is this surplus bureaucratic capital that is used for the purpose of forecasting social futures, and consequently applied to the task of managing the behavior of mass or aggregate units within those social futures. (Ross 127)

But watching doesn't just produce "surplus bureaucratic capital," it can be instrumentalist power, making a killing in the market or on the street or in someone's soul. It can out hypocrites and send the powerful to prison. It can reveal the crimes of empire. It can change the discourse rules and meta-rules that govern society, transforming the alluring spectacle of bread and circuses into a hunger for spectacular social change. Some even imagine that it can lead to the abolition of secrecy.

In his 1990 novel, *Earth*, David Brin describes a near future where a worldwide revolutionary movement has abolished privacy. The movement's argument is that regular people had long lost their privacy to a surveillance regime of government spying, corporate market research, and the Internet of Things. Only the rich had privacy, and they were using it to steal, cheat, and exploit everyone else. The revolutionaries, mainly from looted countries, wage a successful war on Switzerland to get back their stolen wealth squirreled away in the Alps.

The war leads to a society where every moment of every person is accessible to viewing, an idea picked up in Dave Eggers's novel *The Circle* (2013) with those users of social media who have gone 'transparent.' In *Earth*, Brin does not suggest that the average person is observed by humans most of the time, but that they could be. They are just always being recorded. But the rich and powerful (and the famous and notorious) are under constant sousveillance. The book has other themes—ecological disaster, AIs run amok, the typical SciFi/CliFi mix—but Brin's take on the oppressive nature of privacy hit a nerve with readers, and he ended up defending it from criticism in *Wired* and a nonfiction book, *The Transparent Society: Will Technology Force Us to Choose Between Freedom and Privacy?* (1999).

Brin and Eggers are clearly being provocative in the extremity of the veillance portrayed and its consequence, but their insight is real. Digital technology is fundamentally changing the very way we think about secrecy and privacy. The first impacts of this have been mixed. For example, digital harassment, trolling, and bullying have become problems but the widespread sousveillance of police actions has fueled the growing movement for police accountability. At the same time, while Brin's vision is liberatory, Eggers' transparent society is quite the opposite. The megacorporation known as The Circle combines all the worst elements of Amazon, Facebook, Google, and Apple. It seeks nothing less than one seamless transparent corporate society, where national political power (for example, policy making, voting, and policing the public) is ultimately transferred to the corporation. A cyber Brave New World that is nightmarish in many ways, but remains an attractive idea to many in power.

The clearest proof of this attractiveness is China's Sesame program, where every Chinese citizen is 'scored' by their credit, their adherence to the law, their comments on the regime, the ratings of their friends, and a number of other metrics. Similarly, in the Moslem province of Xinjian every male is having their DNA recorded, and in numerous places extensive face recognition on the street is being used (see Hvistendahl). But this isn't just the mania of authoritarian regimes. In the Netherlands, 'smart city' initiatives have led to the collection of a wide range of data from people out on the streets, with the goals of reducing night crime, figuring out why people come downtown ('personal mobility profiles'), roaming scanner cars to give tickets and target tax debtors, and so on. While the data is 'randomized,' it is easily re-individualized (see Naafs).

Cyberpunks know all technology is potentially dangerous. For example, Cadigan has one of her synners proclaim:

> "All *appropriate technology* hurts somebody. A whole lot of somebodies. Nuclear fission, fusion, the fucking Ford assembly line, the fucking airplane. *Fire*, for Christ's sake. Every technology has its original sin." She laughed. "Makes us original synners. And we still go to live with what we made." (*Synners* 435, emphasis in original)

The original sin is baked into the affordances of the technology, but they can also empower hackers and disruptions. This is a key insight of cyberpunk and why it cannot die. It is the yin to The Circle's yang. Tech makes 'their' surveillance more powerful, or 'our' sousveillance.

The Circle ends with the protagonist Mae visiting her friend Annie in the hospital, a victim of overwork and constant monitoring. Mae wants to read her mind:

> What was going on in that head of hers? It was exasperating, really, Mae thought, not knowing. It was an affront, a deprivation, to herself and to the world. She would bring this up with Stenton and Bailey, with the Gang of 40, at the earliest opportunity. They needed to talk about Annie, the thoughts she was thinking. Why shouldn't they know them? The world deserved nothing less and would not wait. (630)

The direction of technological surveillance is clear in this excerpt, and an ethical limit is not in sight.

In 1999 Bruce Sterling said: "Anything that can be done to a rat can be done to a human being. And we can do most anything to rats. This is the hard thing to think about, but it's the truth. It won't go away because we cover our eyes" ("Cyberpunk in the Nineties"). But when rats look back, their only option is flight. Humans aren't rats. Hackers and activists can gaze back and challenge the power dynamic. And if we do this together, we are cyborg citizens. Together we can change the rules of Veillance Society. Consider the Cyborg Bill of Rights which includes the following: a *Right of Electronic Privacy*, a ban on mind reading and mind control and protection for those altering their own minds (*Freedom of Consciousness*), and a mandate of government and corporate transparency around personal information they own (*Freedom of Information*). This last gives everyone "the right to correct all information held on them by governments and other bureaucracies at the expense of these bureaucracies" (Gray, *Cyborg Citizen* 27–28). And if that seems too ambitious, too collective for a cyberpunk, then just take your stand where you are and turn the gaze around.

Turn it, as the French say: *détournement*. Turn it back on them, as the cyberpunk with the dragon tattoo (to riff on Stieg Larsson's famous rebel character), and every other fictional cyberpunk hacker, does. Turn it, as the Zapatistas turned corporate globalization into international civil society. Turn it, as the Arab Spring, Idle No More, Los Indignados, Occupy, Black Lives Matter, #Woman's March, and #Metoo turned social media on the powerful. But watch yourselves! Of course, most revolutions fail, and as the world turns, things are very much up-for-grabs. But it ain't dystopia yet.

Notes

1 The term *sousveillance* was, quite appropriately, coined by Steve Mann (cf. Mann and Ferenbok, as well as Mann, Nolan, and Wellman). Mann is an inventor, activist, and author; he has been a live node on the net for over 40 years. He is always recording what he sees and what he hears (an eyeborg), uploading it to the cloud, and drawing in signals from the ether. But he's not like the antenna men of Neal Stephenson's *Snow Crash* (1992). They are unthinking extensions of larger organizations; Steve Mann is his own autonomous node.
2 For a brilliant analysis of the individual cyborg gaze, see Christopher McGunnigle's analysis in his reading of *Robocop*.

Works Cited

Brin, David. *Earth*. Bantam Spectra, 1990.

Cadigan, Pat. "Pretty Boy Crossover." *Patterns*. Tor, 1987, pp. 129–38.

———. *Synners*. Bantam, 1991.

Dery, Mark. *Escape Velocity: Cyberculture at the End of the Century*. Grove, 1996.

Eggers, David. *The Circle*. McSweeney's, 2013.

Foucault, Michel. *Discipline & Punish: The Birth of the Prison*. Vintage, 1979.

Gibson, William. *Count Zero*. Ace, 1987.

———. *Burning Chrome*. Ace, 1987.

———. "The Road to Oceana." *The New York Times*, 25 Jun. 2003, nytimes.com/2003/06/25/opinion/the-road-to-oceana.html.

Gray, Chris Hables. *Cyborg Citizen*. Routledge, 2001.

———. "Big Data, Actionable Information, Scientific Knowledge and the Goal of Control." *Teknokultura*, vol. 11, no. 3, 2014, pp. 529–54.

Hvistendahl, Mara. "You are a Number." *Wired*, Jan. 2018, pp. 48–59.

Jordan, Tim. *Cyberpower: The Culture and Politics of Cyberspace and the Internet*. Routledge, 1999.

Mann, Steven. "McVeillance." *Veillance Blog*, 10 Oct. 2012, wearcam.org/McVeillance.htm.

Mann, Steve and Joseph Ferenbok. "New Media and the Power Politics of Sousveillance in a Surveillance-Dominated World," *Surveillance & Society*, vol. 11, no. 1/2, 2013.

Mann, Steve, Jason Nolan, and Barry Wellman. "Sousveillance: Inventing and Using Wearable Computing Devices for Data Collection in Surveillance Environments." *Surveillance & Society*, vol. 1, no. 3, 2003, pp. 331–55.

McGunigle, Christopher. "'My Targeting System is a Little Messed Up': The Cyborg Gaze in the *RoboCop* Media Franchise." *Cyberpunk and Visual Culture*, edited by Graham J. Murphy and Lars Schmeink. Routledge, 2018, pp. 105–26.

McLuhan, Marshall. "McLuhan on McLuhanism." *On McLuhan: Forward Through the Rearview Mirror*, edited by Paul Beneditti and Nancy Dehart. MIT P, 1966, p. 40.

Murphy, Graham J. and Lars Schmeink. "Introduction: The Visuality and Virtuality of Cyberpunk." *Cyberpunk and Visual Culture*, edited by Graham J. Murphy and Lars Schmeink. Routledge, 2018, pp. xx–xxvi.

Naafs, Saskia. "'Living Laboratories': The Dutch Cities Amassing Data on Oblivious Residents," *The Guardian*, 01 Mar. 2018, theguardian.com/cities/2018/mar/01/smart-cities-data-privacy-eindhoven-utrecht.

Ross, Andrew. "Hacking away at the Counterculture." *Technoculture*, edited by Constance Penley and Andrew Ross. U of Minnesota P, 1991, pp. 107–34.

Sterling, Bruce. Preface. *Mirrorshades: The Cyberpunk Anthology*, edited by Bruce Sterling. Ace, 1986, p. ix–xi.

———. "Cyberpunk in the Nineties," *Street Tech*, 1999, scanlines.net/node/3048.

Zuboff, Shoshana. "The Secrets of Surveillance Capitalism: Google as a Fortune Teller" *Frankfurter Allgemeine Zeitung*, 05 Mar. 2016, faz.net/aktuell/feuilleton/debatten/the-digital-debate/shoshana-zuboff-secrets-of-surveillance-capitalism-14103616.html.

44

ACTIVISM

Colin Milburn

1984. Was ever there a year more laden with the residue of science fiction (sf)? Thanks to George Orwell's novel *Nineteen Eighty-Four* (1949), the actual year arrived with a sense of overblown futurity, as if the present had accelerated beyond the limits of speculation. Capitalizing on this idea, Apple introduced the first Macintosh computer with a television commercial that aired during the U.S. Super Bowl on January 22, 1984. Directed by Ridley Scott, whose previous work on *Blade Runner* (1982) and *Alien* (1979) had cemented his reputation as one of the luminaries of sf cinema, the 1984 Apple Macintosh advertisement depicted an Orwellian world in which dispirited legions of workers march in automated lockstep—recalling the imagery of Fritz Lang's *Metropolis* (1927)—while a Big Brother figure broadcasts slogans of totalitarian conformity over the airwaves. In the midst of this bleak technocratic future, a lone female athlete appears, carrying a massive hammer. She dashes through the high-tech city, pursued by police. She enters a vast auditorium where brainwashed workers stare at an enormous screen displaying the Big Brother figure, captivated by his fascist messages ("We are one people, with one will. One resolve. One cause ... We shall prevail"). The athlete throws her hammer into the screen, smashing it with explosive force. Winds of freedom cascade across the transfixed workers. The advertisement ends with a reminder that the future is not set, and that the status quo can be hacked: "On January 24th, Apple Computer will introduce Macintosh. And you will see why 1984 won't be like '1984.'"

The Macintosh advertisement suggested that individuals armed with the right technology could resist or subvert the forces of dystopian control, whether totalitarian governments or corporate monopolies. The Macintosh user—a spry athlete wielding a tactical hammer—liberates the multitudes from the domination of Big Brother: a powerful fable perfectly attuned to the technocultural conditions of its time (Friedman 102–20). It affirmed the idea that, although the world was rapidly transforming through computerization, savvy users could still intervene, reshaping things to come. Rooted in sf, this mythology was further reinforced by a set of texts that together helped to precipitate the early discourse of cyberpunk: John Brunner's *Shockwave Rider* (1975), Vernor Vinge's "True Names" (1981), Steven Lisberger's film *TRON* (1982), and, of course, William Gibson's *Neuromancer* (1984).[1]

Before long, several real-life hackers and computer scientists began to adopt this mythology for overtly political purposes: the birth of *cyberpunk activism*. For example, in 1985, the cryptographer David Chaum published an article called "Security without Identification: Transaction Systems to Make Big Brother Obsolete" in the scientific journal *Communications of the Association of Computing Machinery*. As Chaum wrote, "Some of our basic liberties may be threatened by computerization" (1044). He foresaw that automated systems of surveillance could threaten democracy. Online data mining and user profiling could allow corporations to manipulate public opinion and shape political outcomes—or worse. Yet Chaum believed the future could still be turned around. Recycling the same figurative conceit as the 1984 Macintosh ad—technological resistance to Big Brother—he proposed an engineering solution to these emergent sociopolitical problems: "The potential exists not only for reversing these problems, but for increasing democratization" (1044). He suggested that all transactions, purchases, contracts, and communications in the future network society could be conducted anonymously through public key cryptography, facilitated by the imminent development of tiny handheld devices that he called "card computers" (a slightly speculative idea at the time but well within the bounds of plausibility, as time would tell). Encouraging other innovators about the urgent need to protect online privacy, Chaum helped trigger an entire field of research in anonymizing technologies and sparked the political imagination of many hackers and technology geeks.

For some, however, the idea that hackers might use their technical knowledge for transformative politics—and perhaps under conditions of total anonymity—was far from reassuring. In 1983, John Badham's film *WarGames* informed mass audiences that a teenage hacker with nothing but a computer, a modem, and some chutzpah could break into U.S. military defense systems and rapidly push the world to the brink of nuclear war. In the film, the teenage hacker, David Lightman, believes he has stumbled onto an sf video game called "Global Thermonuclear War" while illicitly accessing a remote computer system; he does not realize until too late that he is actually communicating with a NORAD supercomputer, WOPR, which controls the U.S. nuclear arsenal. Although the film presents this situation as an innocent mistake, a mischievous hack gone awry, it also raised the distressing possibility that criminal hackers or political dissidents might intentionally wreak havoc on governmental or corporate systems. *WarGames* immediately became a topic of extensive discussion in public discourse about computer security, and it contributed to U.S. Congressional debates about the regulation of online networks (Schulte 21–54). Scenes from *WarGames* were even screened during the 1984 hearings that led to the Counterfeit Access Device and Computer Fraud and Abuse Act—later amended in 1986 as the Computer Fraud and Abuse Act.

By the end of the decade, U.S. law enforcement agents began putting the Computer Fraud and Abuse Act to the test through a series of raids and arrests that the cyberpunk writer Bruce Sterling describes in his nonfiction book *The Hacker Crackdown*. This crackdown would lead directly to the formation of the Electronic Frontier Foundation (EFF)—the first organization devoted to protecting the civil rights of hackers, security researchers, and Internet users—and it would galvanize cyberpunk activism over the following years.

44.1 The Politics of Cyberspace

John Perry Barlow was a man of many talents: journalist, rancher, and occasional lyricist for the Grateful Dead. He was also an early advocate for the utopian potentials of the Internet. In 1986, Barlow joined The WELL—The Whole Earth 'Lectronic Link—an online bulletin board and virtual community founded in 1985 by Stuart Brand, the editor of the *Whole Earth Catalog* (Turner 141–74). Participating in discussions on The WELL about the ethics of hacking, Barlow came in contact with many of the most notorious hackers of the day. He also began to attend the annual Hacker's Conference. Despite initial skepticism, Barlow started to see most hackers as motivated by genuine technological curiosity rather than nefarious criminal ambitions.

Early in 1990, several prominent American hackers were arrested as part of the nationwide crackdown. Around the same time, the U.S. Secret Service raided Steve Jackson Games, the publisher of the *GURPS* roleplaying game system. How did a game company get caught up in the hacker crackdown? At the time, a hacker known as the Mentor (a.k.a. Lloyd Blankenship) was actually an employee of Steve Jackson Games, working as the lead writer for *GURPS Cyberpunk: High-Tech Low-Life Roleplaying*. During the raid, the Secret Service confiscated the company's computers and other materials, including all the manuscript files for *GUPRS Cyberpunk*. The Secret Service believed the Mentor had received a stolen electronic document about the 911 emergency system and thought he may have stored copies of the file on his employer's machines (an allegation which proved untrue). However, as far as the Secret Service was concerned, the entire game company also fell under suspicion. An agent told Steve Jackson that the Secret Service saw *GURPS Cyberpunk* not simply as an sf game but rather as a handbook for committing real computer crimes (Jackson 5, Sterling 138–51).

Shortly after the raid on Steve Jackson Games, Barlow himself received a visit from an FBI agent at his ranch in Wyoming. The agent interrogated Barlow for two hours, questioning him about some Apple Macintosh source code that had been illegally distributed by a hacker known as NuPrometheus. Barlow was also questioned about his involvement with the Hacker's Conference, The WELL, and his affiliation with various technologists in Silicon Valley. The wildly misinformed interrogation, along with the raid on Steve Jackson Games and recent arrests of several hackers on dubious charges, convinced Barlow that law enforcement agencies were violating the civil rights of hackers and innocent bystanders alike.

Barlow immediately wrote an article called "Crime and Puzzlement," which became another core document in the field of cyberpunk activism. Notably, it was the first publication to use Gibson's term 'cyberspace' to describe the actual Internet in 1990, a sprawling assortment of dial-up bulletin boards, corporate minicomputers, and university mainframes: "Whether by one telephonic tendril or millions, they are all connected to one another. Collectively, they form what their inhabitants call the Net. It extends across that immense region of electron states, microwaves, magnetic fields, light pulses and thought which sci-fi writer William Gibson named Cyberspace" (45). In translating cyberspace from sf to current technology, Barlow also echoed Gibson's trope of the 'cyberspace cowboy' in describing the electronic frontier: "Cyberspace, in its present condition, has a lot in common with the 19th Century West. It is vast, unmapped, culturally and legally ambiguous [...] It is, of course, a perfect breeding ground for both outlaws and new ideas about liberty" (45). Following Barlow's lead, many journalists began to use the term 'cyberspace,' and it became a dominant way of talking about the Internet in the 1990s (see Benedikt, Chun, Turner).

Barlow represented cyberspace as the site of escalating conflict between 'cyberpunks'—hackers, geeks, and others attuned to rapid technological acceleration—and institutional powers unwilling to accept change: "The perfect bogeyman for Modern Times is the Cyberpunk! [...] Perhaps the most frightening thing about the Cyberpunk is the danger he presents to The Institution, whether corporate or governmental" (56). Barlow saw the hacker crackdown, the Computer Fraud and Abuse Act, and other forms of paranoid securitization in the U.S. as symptoms of this conflict. But he advised cyberpunks to reach across the gap, hoping to prevent an apocalyptic war:

> I think that herein lies the way out of what might otherwise become an Armageddon between the control freaks and the neo-hip. Those who are comfortable with these disorienting changes must do everything in our power to convey that comfort to others. In other words, we must share our sense of hope and opportunity with those who feel that in Cyberspace they will be obsolete eunuchs [...] Of course, we may also have to fight. (56)

To prepare for such skirmishes, Barlow banded together with the programmer Mitch Kapor (the cofounder of Lotus Development Corporation) and the libertarian technologist John Gilmore (an early employee of Sun Microsystems and the cofounder of Cygnus Support) to start the EFF. The EFF quickly became the foremost organization for defending civil liberties in cyberspace. For an opening act, the nonprofit organization helped Steve Jackson Games to file a lawsuit against the U.S. Secret Service for wrongful search and seizure of computer equipment. The trial was successful, establishing an important precedent for the privacy rights of computer users. In the aftermath, Steve Jackson reflected on the whole saga: "Maybe the cyberpunk future is closer, and darker, than we think" (5). But Barlow saw something brighter. In 1996, he composed a manifesto, "A Declaration of the Independence of Cyberspace," rhapsodizing with utopian flourish:

> Governments of the Industrial World, you weary giants of flesh and steel, I come from Cyberspace, the new home of Mind. On behalf of the future, I ask you of the past to leave us alone. You are not welcome among us. You have no sovereignty where we gather [...] We will create a civilization of the Mind in Cyberspace. May it be more humane and fair than the world your governments have made before. (28–30)

44.2 The Cypherpunks

Meanwhile, the physicist and former Intel engineer Timothy C. May—fueled by a steady diet of sf and inspired by Chaum's cryptographic research—was also dwelling on the challenges and opportunities of cyberspace. In 1988, he drafted "The Crypto-Anarchist Manifesto," arguing that the ongoing evolution of the Internet together with strong encryption technologies would soon trigger a global revolution:

> A specter is haunting the modern world, the specter of crypto anarchy.
>
> Computer technology is on the verge of providing the ability for individuals and groups to communicate and interact with each other in a totally anonymous manner. Two persons may exchange messages, conduct business, and negotiate electronic contracts without ever knowing the True Name, or legal identity, of the other. Interactions over networks will be untraceable [...] The State will of course try to slow or halt the spread of this technology [...] But this will not halt the spread of crypto anarchy. [...] Arise, you have nothing to lose but your barbed wire fences! (61–63)

With nods to Karl Marx and Friedrich Engel's *Communist Manifesto* (1848) as well as Vinge's "True Names," May's overture shot beyond the classic liberalism of Barlow's "Declaration," imagining instead a crypto future of "liquid markets" and free-flowing information that would demolish all corporate controls and undermine all forms of governance. In 1992, together with the mathematician and hacker Eric Hughes, May gathered a group of like-minded programmers and technologists to design the future of crypto anarchy (Greenberg 78–134). The hacker Jude Milhon (a.k.a. St. Jude), the co-editor of the cyberculture magazine *Mondo 2000* and Hughes's girlfriend at the time, facetiously suggested the name "cypherpunks." It stuck. John Gilmore, while simultaneously helping to run the EFF, agreed to host a mailing list for the group on his personal server. The infamous Cypherpunks mailing list was born.

The Cypherpunks mailing list (cypherpunks@toad.com) grew exuberantly, characterized by spirited debates about computer science, anarchist and libertarian philosophies, and sf. The group's core concerns, however, focused on uses of cryptography for political change. According to May, these ideas emerged directly from Vinge's fiction: "The full-blown, immersive virtual reality of *True Names* may still be far off, but the technologies of cryptography, digital signatures, remailers, message pools, and data havens make many of the most important aspects of *True Names* realizable today, now, on the Net" ("True Nyms" 36). Vinge's novella was required reading for the cypherpunks. As May recalled,

> There were several books we frequently recommended to new members: *True Names* led the list, along with John Brunner's *Shockwave Rider*, Orson Scott Card's *Ender's Game*, Neal Stephenson's *Snow Crash*, Hakim Bey's *TAZ*, and, of course, various cryptography and

Activism

computer references, notably Bruce Schneier's *Applied Cryptography*. At our first meeting, in fact, we simulated some of the notions out of "True Names," using cryptographic protocols. ("True Nyms" 38)

For the cypherpunks, one metaphor captured all forces of surveillance, all manifestations of social control: Big Brother. Following Chaum's work, the cypherpunks aspired to use high-tech cryptography to neutralize the Orwellian nightmare. The computer scientist Hal Finney—an early cypherpunk and, later, one of the people suspected to be the inventor of the cryptocurrency Bitcoin—summarized the stakes in an email to the list: "I recall reading 'True Names' a few years ago [...] The work we are doing here, broadly speaking, is dedicated to this goal of making Big Brother obsolete. It's important work. If things work out well, we may be able to look back and see that it was the most important work we have ever done."

To be sure, the cypherpunks were not simply reading sf; they were putting it into practice. As Hughes asserted in his 1993 "Cypherpunk's Manifesto," to be a cypherpunk was, first and foremost, to be a technological experimenter, a developer, a programmer: "We the Cypherpunks are dedicated to building anonymous systems [...] Cypherpunks write code. We know that someone has to write software to defend privacy, and since we can't get privacy unless we all do, we're going to write it [...] The Cypherpunks are actively engaged in making the networks safer for privacy. Let us proceed together apace" (82–83). One of Hughes's own early coding contributions for the group was a 'remailer,' a software tool for stripping header information from email messages to obscure their origin. It was the first of a series of increasingly sophisticated remailers the cypherpunks developed for anonymous communications. The cypherpunk remailers were designed not only for dissidents living under oppressive regimes but also for anyone wanting to keep their email identity secret, for whatever reason.

One of the most explosive implementations of the cypherpunk vision came many years later with the rise of WikiLeaks. The hacker, journalist, and political activist Julian Assange had been among the first contributors to the Cypherpunks mailing list (though he, like many others on the list, initially disguised his identity). In 2006, Assange and his colleagues created WikiLeaks as a mechanism for publishing leaked documents, aiming to reveal government malfeasance around the world while protecting the identities of leakers. By 2010, WikiLeaks had become a focal point of international controversy, especially following its release of thousands of classified U.S. documents about the wars in Afghanistan and Iraq, as well as a vast trove of U.S. diplomatic cables.

Media commentators were quick to point out the science-fictional qualities of WikiLeaks, often noting an uncanny resemblance to the plot of *Shockwave Rider*: "[T]he WikiLeaks controversy puts me in mind of John Brunner's *Shockwave Rider* [...which] postulated a future computer worm that forced the release of all information, all the time" (Grey). Numerous reporters asserted this analogy: "The WikiLeaks material is available to anyone with a web browser. In his 1975 book *The Shockwave Rider*, sf author John Brunner details a scenario in which a computer hacker writes a special computer tapeworm that brings out hidden government data and then presents it to the user during ordinary computer use" (Christensen; see also Martin, Anders). It is no surprise that WikiLeaks would conjure such associations with Brunner's novel. After all, the seeds of its political philosophy gestated in the Cypherpunks mailing list (Assange et al.). Although Assange's vision was arguably less anarchic than that of other cypherpunks, oriented more to reform than to the annihilation of governments, it shared the same traits of cyberpunk activism, grown from the same sf elements (Brunton). As Sterling observed in 2011, the "sci-fi tinged idea" at the core of the Cypherpunks mailing list had finally erupted on the world stage, for better or worse: "At last—at long last—the homemade nitroglycerin in the old cypherpunks blast shack has gone off" ("Blast Shack").

44.3 The Future Is Here

At the same time, other hackers across the globe were waking up to the political affordances of their craft. The Cult of the Dead Cow (cDc) began in the mid-1980s as a group of computer enthusiasts and phone phreakers posting text-file polemics and weird fictions to online bulletin board systems. By the 1990s, however, the group had become an icon of the hacker underground, promoting themselves as a high-tech cabal with slogans such as "Global Domination through Media Saturation."[2] In 1998, the cDc released the first of several powerful hacker tools: a program called Back Orifice that gave remote access to computers running Microsoft Windows. It was intended to prove that Windows was fundamentally insecure, revealing Microsoft's negligence in protecting users from online attacks. It also helped to crystallize the Cult's commitment to hacking for ethical purposes—not simply critiquing security failures, but also political protest and direct action. The group coined the term 'hacktivism' to describe hacking for social change and human rights.

The cyberpunk sheen of hacktivism, as concept and practice, was evident in many of the cDc's publications and interviews—especially those by Count Zero, a member of the Cult who took his codename from Gibson's novel *Count Zero* (1986) and often presented himself as a cyborg surgeon. According to Count Zero,

> First of all, hacking is, by its very nature, a GOOD thing. It's about exploring and pushing the boundaries of knowledge [...] "Hacktivism" is the evolution of activism in a wired, global community. Using hacking "techniques" to achieve activist goals. And like "real world" activism, sometimes "hacktivism" involves breaking the law..... [and] focusing on empowering the people in those places [i.e. oppressive regimes] with the TOOLS of hacktivism...... making the WORLD know about the injustices and human rights abuses....in other words, getting the FLOW of INFORMATION pumpin' around the globe...UNIMPEDED and UNCENSORED.....THAT'S hacktivism! ("A Chat with Count Zero")

Other hacktivist groups have since sprung up around the world, often sporting team names drawn from sf, such as Team GhostShell, the Shadow Brokers, Leopard Boy and the Decepticons, and Dark Overlord (Milburn 27–50, 154–58). The most prolific among them, Anonymous, started off as a gaggle of trolls and pranksters on the 4chan image board but gradually transformed into a worldwide collective of high-tech activists (Coleman). In 2008, Anonymous launched Chanology, a series of online and offline demonstrations against the Church of Scientology. During Chanology, Anonymous adopted its most iconic image: the Guy Fawkes mask worn by the anarchist V in Alan Moore and David Lloyd's graphic novel *V for Vendetta* (1988–89) and its film adaptation by the Wachowskis and James McTeigue (2006). While the mask served a practical purpose—a disguise for Anonymous members protesting in the streets—it imbued Anonymous with a science-fictional aura, recalling V's struggle against fascist governance. Anonymous also showcased its signature mode of online protest: the distributed denial-of-service attack (DDoS), a technique for paralyzing a network server with an overwhelming flood of data (Sauter, Coleman 90–176). Anonymous organized DDoS attacks against Scientology webservers using a homebrew software application wrapped in the imagery of sf: the Low Orbit Ion Cannon (LOIC). (The LOIC's graphical interface specifically references the ion cannons from the *Command and Conquer* video games; but such weapons have featured prominently in other texts as well, including Vinge's "True Names".)

Following Chanology, Anonymous carried out similar operations against a variety of multinational corporations and government agencies, often advertising its goals through science fiction media (Milburn 32–50, 93–133). Anonymous also got involved in the Arab Spring, the Occupy Movement, Black Lives Matter, and other social justice efforts. Since then, Anonymous has become a brand name for a multitude of hacktivist activities around the world. It is an idea more than a group: "We are Anonymous. We are legion. We do not forgive. We do not forget. Expect us."

The recent proliferation of hacktivism, leaktivism, and other forms of high-tech civil disobedience has reinforced the sense that we are now living in a cyberpunk future. At least, it gets recoded that way. In 2013, Edward Snowden, a computer analyst and subcontractor for the U.S. National Security Agency (NSA), smuggled millions of classified documents from NSA computers and fled to Hong Kong. There, Snowden collaborated with the journalists Glenn Greenwald and Ewen MacAskill and the filmmaker Laura Poitras to publish the documents. These documents exposed the NSA's immense data-surveillance activities all over the planet. Snowden indicated that he was motivated, in part, by a lifelong engagement with sf media, especially video games, which had taught him to fight against injustice (Greenwald 45–46, Milburn 13–21).

Laura Poitras's documentary film *Citizenfour* (2014) focuses on the conversations that she and Greenwald had with Snowden in his Hong Kong hotel. In one scene, the camera lingers on a book resting near a pile of Snowden's computer equipment: Cory Doctorow's novel *Homeland* (2013). *Homeland*, the sequel to *Little Brother* (2008), is an Orwellian neo-cyberpunk critique of the U.S. surveillance state. Marcus Yallow, the central protagonist, is a teenage hacker whose political attitudes have been partially informed by sf. (Marcus's first online handle is "w1n5t0n," an homage to Winston Smith from *Nineteen Eighty-Four*. Later, he goes by "M1k3y," a reference to the sentient computer from Robert Heinlein's 1966 lunar rebellion novel *The Moon is a Harsh Mistress*.) The story follows Marcus and his friends as they face off against the military-security-industrial complex. In *Citizenfour*, the deliberate placement of Doctorow's novel thus frames Snowden's own actions as cyberpunk activism. As Snowden himself says in the film, "This isn't science fiction. It's really happening."

Doctorow's fiction has often made a similar point, using the tropes of cyberpunk for immediate political interventions. For example, *Down and Out in the Magic Kingdom* (2003), *Overclocked* (2006), and *Pirate Cinema* (2012) take aim at intellectual property law while laying out the conditions for open-source futures. *For the Win* (2010) depicts a global uprising of gamers against capitalist exploitation; it is also a how-to guide for labor organizing and unionization. *Makers* (2009) and *Walkaway* (2017) represent grassroots experimental communities as alternatives to the planetary crisis of neoliberalism. Some tech activists have even tried to put Doctorow's fiction into practice. For example, in 2008, one group began to develop the ParanoidLinux system from *Little Brother*, stimulating debate about operating system-based procedures for encrypting data and obscuring Internet communications (Edge). Although this particular project collapsed, other operating systems for anonymous computing have since appeared—including Snowden's own favorite, Tails, which Doctorow sees as fulfilling his original vision (Doctorow). Such examples highlight Doctorow's novels as themselves exercises in cyberpunk activism, reaffirming the entire history of cyberpunk as both critical theory and political mythology for today's high-tech culture (Foster).

On April 7, 2018, the Internet Archive in San Francisco hosted a memorial for John Perry Barlow, who had died two months earlier. Cory Doctorow served as the master of ceremonies for this memorial event. Many key figures from the world of high-tech activism spoke at the memorial, including John Gilmore, Mitch Kapor, and other affiliates of the cypherpunks and the EFF. Edward Snowden beamed in from Russia (where he has been living in asylum since 2013). He spoke eloquently about the role that Barlow's writings—manifestos splicing cyberpunk idioms with utopian urgency—had played for the online generation: "John Perry Barlow woke me up. He raised a message, sounded an alarm, that I think we all heard. He didn't save the world. None of us can, but perhaps he started the movement that will" (Snowden). In many ways, the memorial marked the end of an era: The first wave of cyberpunk activism had passed. But in its wake, a digital insurgency had awakened—opening the floodgates for a torrent of technopolitical actions and agitations, cascading toward an uncertain future.

Notes

1 For more detail on the literary and cinematic development of cyberpunk, see other chapters in this volume: Latham on the literary precursors (including *Shockwave Rider*), Murphy on Gibson and the original Movement, and Butler on early cyberpunk films such as *TRON*.
2 On the history of the Cult of the Dead Cow and hacktivism, see Jordan and Taylor; Thomas; Menn.

Works Cited

1984. Directed by Ridley Scott, performances by John Hurt, Richard Burton, and Suzanna Hamilton, Fairbanks Films and Apple Computer, 1984.

"A Chat with Count Zero." *ABC News*, 5 Feb. 1999, http://abcnews.go.com/sections/tech/DailyNews/chat_countzero.html.

Anders, Charlie Jane. "Did a 1975 Novel Predict the Wikileaks Controversy?" *io9*, 8 Dec. 2010, io9.gizmodo.com/did-a-1975-novel-predict-the-wikileaks-controversy-5708864.

Assange, Julian, Jacob Appelbaum, Andy Müller-Maguhn, and Jérémie Zimmermann. *Cypherpunks: Freedom and the Future of the Internet*. OR Books, 2012.

Barlow, John Perry. "Crime and Puzzlement." *Whole Earth Review*, no. 68, 1990, pp. 44–57.

———. "A Declaration of the Independence of Cyberspace." *Crypto Anarchy, Cyberstates, and Pirate Utopias*, edited by Peter Ludlow. MIT P, 2001, pp. 27–30.

Benedikt, Michael, ed. *Cyberspace: First Steps*. MIT P, 1991.

Brunton, Finn. "Keyspace: Reflections on WikiLeaks and the Assange Papers." *Radical Philosophy*, no. 166, 2011, pp. 8–20.

Chaum, David. "Security without Identification: Transaction Systems to Make Big Brother Obsolete." *Communications of the ACM*, no. 28, 1985, pp. 1030–44.

Christensen, Bill. "Hey WikiLeaks! Where's My Shockwave Rider App?" *Technovelgy*, 30 Nov. 2010, technovelgy.com/ct/Science-Fiction-News.asp?NewsNum=3104.

Chun, Wendy Hui Kyong. *Control and Freedom: Power and Paranoia in the Age of Fiber Optics*. MIT P, 2006.

Citizenfour. Directed by Laura Poitras, Praxis Films/Participant Media/HBO, 2014.

Coleman, Gabriella. *Hacker, Hoaxer, Whistleblower, Spy: The Many Faces of Anonymous*. Verso, 2014.

Doctorow, Cory. "TAILS: Snowden's Favorite Anonymous, Secure OS Goes 1.0." *Boing Boing*, 30 Apr. 2014, boingboing.net/2014/04/30/tails-snowdens-favorite-ano.html.

Edge, Jake. "ParanoidLinux: From Fiction to Reality." *LWN*, 1 Oct. 2008, lwn.net/Articles/301314/.

Finney, Hal. "Why Remailers …" Email to Cypherpunks Mailing List, 15 Nov. 1992. Raw text-dump archive at Ryan Lackey's *Venona Cypherpunk Archives*, 2003, cypherpunks.venona.com/raw/.

Foster, Thomas. *The Souls of Cyberfolk: Posthumanism as Vernacular Theory*. U of Minnesota P, 2005.

Friedman, Ted. *Electric Dreams: Computers in American Culture*. New York UP, 2005.

Greenberg, Andy. *This Machine Kills Secrets: How WikiLeakers, Cypherpunks and Hacktivists Aim to Free the World's Information*. Dutton, 2012.

Greenwald, Glenn. *No Place to Hide: Edward Snowden, the NSA, and the U.S. Surveillance State*. Metropolitan Books, 2014.

Grey, Chris. Response to Brooke Gladstone and Steven Aftergood, "From One Transparency Advocate to Another." *On the Media*, 5 Aug. 2010, onthemedia.org/episodes/2010/07/30/segments/157591.

Hughes, Eric. "A Cypherpunk's Manifesto." *Crypto Anarchy, Cyberstates, and Pirate Utopias*, edited by Peter Ludlow. MIT, 2001, pp. 81–83.

Jackson, Steve. "Meanwhile, Back in the Real World …" *GURPS Cyberpunk: High-Tech Low-Life Roleplaying*, edited by Lloyd Blankenship. Steve Jackson Games, 1993.

Jordan, Tim and Paul A. Taylor. *Hacktivism and Cyberwars: Rebels with a Cause?* Routledge, 2004.

Martin, Tim. "Back to the WikiLeaks Future." *Telegraph*, 8 Dec. 2010, telegraph.co.uk/culture/books/8189165/Back-to-the-WikiLeaks-future.html.

May, Timothy C. "The Crypto Anarchist Manifesto." *Crypto Anarchy, Cyberstates, and Pirate Utopias*, edited by Peter Ludlow. MIT Press, 2001, pp. 61–63.

———. "True Nyms and Crypto Anarchy." *True Names and the Opening of the Cyberspace Frontier*, edited by James Frenkel. Tor, 2001, pp. 33–86.

Menn, Joseph. *Cult of the Dead Cow: How the Original Hacking Supergroup Might Just Save the World*. PublicAffairs, 2019.

Milburn, Colin. *Respawn: Gamers, Hackers, and Technogenic Life*. Duke UP, 2018.

Activism

Sauter, Molly. *The Coming Swarm: DDoS Actions, Hacktivism, and Civil Disobedience on the Internet.* Bloomsbury Academic, 2014.

Schulte, Stephanie Ricker. *Cached: Decoding the Internet in Global Popular Culture.* New York UP, 2013.

Snowden, Edward. Talk at the John Perry Barlow Symposium, 7 Apr. 2018. Video available at the Internet Archive, archive.org/details/JohnPerryBarlowSymposium.

Sterling, Bruce. "The Blast Shack." *Webstock*, 22 Dec. 2010, webstock.org.nz/the-blast-shack/.

———. *The Hacker Crackdown: Law and Disorder on the Electronic Frontier.* Bantam, 1992.

Thomas, Douglas. *Hacker Culture.* U of Minnesota P, 2002.

Turner, Fred. *From Counterculture to Cyberculture: Stewart Brand, the Whole Earth Network, and the Rise of Digital Utopianism.* U of Chicago P, 2006.

III

Cultural Locales

45

LATIN AMERICA

M. Elizabeth Ginway

Although Latin American cyberpunk emerged largely in the 1990s, precursors can be found in the preceding decades; for example, Miguel Ángel Fernández Delgado remarks Mexican author Bernardo de Ortiz de Montellano's "La máquina humana" ("The Human Machine," 1936) "can be considered a distant precursor to the cyberpunk subgenre since it is about a man who dies and is resuscitated and continues his existence inside a humanoid machine that allows him to narrate his own experience in the first person" ("Historias"). Or, as I address below, examples of Brazilian and Argentinian cyberpunk first emerged in the 1980s contemporaneously with North American cyberpunk. It is important to note, however, Latin American cyberpunk is as diverse as the region itself; it is by no means a unified movement nor is it simply derivative. For example, as early as 1996, Roberto de Sousa Causo points out that several Brazilian authors, working separately, had begun writing cyberpunk, but in a way that differed from the Anglo-American tradition, specifically in their use of parody, excessive sexuality, technology, urban settings, crime, and political conspiracies (6). More recently, in his 2011 study of Latin American cyberpunk, Rodolfo Londero notes that the very disjunction or distortion of the digital circulation of information impedes any "informational paradise" in the global South, because its socioeconomic reality provides a basis for resistance and an implied utopian impulse that distinguishes it from other forms of cyberpunk (227). Finally, Maielis González has recently argued that Latin American cyberpunk does not integrate technology and Latin American culture, but instead is a "code" that "encrypts" the region's reality for those already familiar with cyberpunk tropes, reducing texts to mere informational data and dividing audiences into knowing insiders and alienated outsiders (228).

It is my view that in spite of the regional differences, Latin American cyberpunk generally privileges the physical body over fantasies of disembodiment in cyberspace often popularized in North American cyberpunk. There is no escape from the flesh into digital nirvanas; instead, Latin American cyberpunk's emphasis on the corporeal is both consistent and reflective of life in highly charged political environments. The prominence of the physical body is a deliberate choice that contests the power structures of a larger body politic in order to oppose political elites, corruption, and neoliberal economic policies that have tangible and at times devastating impacts upon local populations. In other words, Latin American cyberpunk is firmly rooted in the socio-economic and political situation of time and place, including dictatorships in 1970s-era Argentina and Chile that dealt harshly with opponents, chiefly in the form of torture and political 'disappearances.' These were followed in the 1980s and 1990s with harsh neoliberal economic policies that had a number of effects, including deepening social divisions giving rise to police violence and death squads in Brazil, the negotiation of unfavorable free-trade agreements (e.g., NAFTA), and the expansion and narco-trafficking across porous borders especially in Mexico and Colombia. Stylistically, we can also note that the permeable boundaries between the popular and the erudite, between dreaming and waking, fiction and reality also characterize many Latin American tech-nofictions, cyberpunk included.

Latin American countries have lengthy histories with the intersections of colonial and economic powers, so a useful approach to understanding how Latin American cyberpunk depicts resistance to colonialism and economic oppression Brazilian concept of *antropofagia* or 'cultural cannibalism.' As a different take on hybridity or postmodernism, anthropophagic absorption of technology and embodiment in Latin American cyberpunk constitutes a grounded form of resistance that makes a distinct contribution to cyberpunk as a larger cultural formation.[1] Thus, rather than being derivative and encrypted, Latin American cyberpunk anthropophagically absorbs, digests, and recreates cyberpunk's tropes and cultural mode based on its own sociopolitical realities and economic conditions. A country-by-country approach to the diverse productions of Latin American cyberpunk is the best approach in providing a roadmap for understanding recurrent motifs that cross national boundaries, including bodily invasion, urban settings, religious obsessions, collective and individual altered states, politically motivated hacking, and critiques of corrupt political institutions.[2]

45.1 Brazil

Cyberpunk emerged in Brazil in the 1980s when several authors, working separately, began writing urban noir tales about bodies penetrated by technology in the form of mechanical implants or human/cybernetic interfaces. Causo coined these diverse expressions "tupinipunk" (from *tupiniquim*, an Indigenous word for Brazil), tracing its origins to Alfredo Sirkis's *Silicone XXI* (1985), a novel that appeared only one year after William Gibson's *Neuromancer* (1984). Sirkis's novel involves a black detective who discovers a former military leader's plan to steal nuclear material as a way to regain power, while leaving a trail of destroyed sexual robots and the threat of ecological crimes that could devastate the population of Rio de Janeiro. Published six years later, Fausto Fawcett's *Santa Clara Poltergeist* (1991) depicts dual male and female protagonists who use mechanical or analog prostheses to uncover and quash a conspiracy to set off a bomb in Copacabana. Along with its intercalated reproduction of Brazilian pornographic magazines and heightened sexuality, Fawcett's novel incorporates philosophy, Hinduism, and a tribute to syncretic beliefs in Brazil where Brazilian Roman Catholicism incorporates a number of traditional Portuguese festivities. Similar cultural syncretism characterizes Guilherme Kujawski's *Piritas Siderais: romance cyberbarroco* (*Outerspace Pyrites: A Cyberbaroque Novel*, 1994), in which a female medium is enlisted by an American to unravel a scheme to steal gold (which turns out to be 'pyrites' or fool's gold) in a dystopian São Paulo. Notably, none of these novels involve any digital interfaces between human and machine, stock-in-trade of North American cyberpunk; instead, the novels feature robots and analog technologies such as prosthetic gadgets, nuclear material, televisions, or telescopes. At the same time, all of them include an obsession with technology, sexuality, and political conspiracies.[3] These motifs are also visible in shorter narratives of the period, such as Ivanir Calado's "O altar does nossos corações" ("The Altar of our Hearts," 1993) and Braulio Tavares's "Jogo rápido" ("It's a Snap," 1989), which take on organized crime and the kidnapping of political and scientific authorities in Rio de Janeiro.

Brazilian cyberpunk of the 21st century continues to be highly politicized as digital technology, which normally serves powerful elites, is seized upon by underground conspirators and resistance groups directed against oppressive regimes. Carlos Orsi's "Questão de sobrevivência" ("Question of Survival," 2005) and Causo's "Vale-tudo" ("Anything Goes," 2010) both feature political action taken by armed groups or *favela* (shantytown) residents and hackers in São Paulo who oppose exploitive corporate and political corruption. In these (and other) cyberpunk tales, electronic communications and social media are used to organize demonstrations for groups fighting to curb gross economic, social, and racial inequalities.[4] Whereas English-language cyberpunk often tends to focus on the solipsistic plans of the individual hacker, these *favela* hackers are bent on serving the underclass and the national interest instead of selling out for global profits or passively accepting their lot in society.[5]

While social politics are at the heart of Brazilian cyberpunk, it is not lacking in its depiction of intimacies and personal salvation, which are common to cyberpunk in general. These mostly take the form of familial connections, as illustrated by Cirilo Lemos's "A lua é uma flor sem pétalas" ("The Moon is a Flower without Petals," 2009), a gritty story that takes place in Rio's *favelas* and portrays a brother who plans to help his sister escape from the slums by rising through the ranks of a powerful trafficking ring. Similarly, Causo's series of stories about *Shiroma, matadora ciborgue* (*Shiroma, Killer Cyborg*, 2015) features a seventeen-year-old female cyborg who, having been kidnapped as a child and trained as an assassin by a crime ring, still retains a sense of moral justice and affective ties with her mother through a mysterious seashell through which she hears her mother's voice.

Brazilian cyberpunk has also been featured in films. The final section of Luiz Bolognesi's animated film *Histórias de amor e fúria* (*Stories of Love and Fury*, 2013) is set in a cyberpunk Rio de Janeiro where an underground guerilla group attempts to wrest water rights from a powerful private corporation, extrapolating from a continued historical exploitation of large freshwater reserves in the Amazon and the ongoing commodification of natural resources throughout Latin America. Adirley Queirós's *Branco sai, preto fica* (*Whites Out, Blacks In*, 2014), a mix of science fiction (sf) and documentary set in the *favelas* on the outskirts of Brasilia, has two protagonists who can be characterized as low-tech cyborgs, and who, having been brutalized at the hands of the police, are determined to register their dystopian view of race and citizenship to pave the way for a more just, utopian future (Suppia 18).

45.2 Argentina

Argentina's early manifestations of cyberpunk are strongly linked to the years of brutal military repression (1976–83) and the Malvinas (Falklands) War of 1982, followed by the adoption of neoliberal economic policies that added social breakdown to collective trauma. One of Argentina's earliest cyborg narratives is Carlos Gardini's "Primera línea" ("First Line," 1982), about a Malvinas War soldier who becomes a cyborg as his various appendages are replaced by prosthetics, dehumanizing him as a military machine. Gardini anticipates the more figurative cyborgs in Ricardo Piglia's *La ciudad ausente* (*The Absent City*, 1992), in which an engineer has turned the consciousness of the woman he loves into a memory machine to record a past denied by authorities. She is a hybrid figure who may be in a mental institution or may be partly machine, defying conventional categories as she attempts to resist treatments by doctors who remind her of her former torturers (Brown 25–27). Similarly, Fernando Spiner's film *La sonámbula* (*The Sleepwalker*, 1998) is strongly rooted in Buenos Aires through the evocation of well-known landmarks (Paz, "Buenos" 3). The script, co-written by Piglia, captures the dark, conspiratorial world of Argentine cyberpunk, where a cyborg-like doctor controls memory-impaired citizens, with the exception of the 'somnambulist' woman, who appears to know the truth about the doctor's machinations. Two experimental novels contemporary with Piglia's work are Alicia Borinsky's *Cine continuado* (*Continual Cinema*, 1998) and Carlos Gamerro's *Las islas* (*The Islands*, 1997), which also feature cyborg-like characters whose dilemmas simultaneously call attention to past trauma and torture related to dictatorship, economic hardship, and sex work in post-dictatorial Argentina (Brown 44–48, 118–22).

The critique of neoliberal policies is perhaps nowhere more keenly evident than in Eduardo Blaustein's novel *Cruz Diablo* (*Devil Cross*, 1997). The plot fuses the cyberpunk hacker with Argentina's archetypal gaucho figure, the hero of the pampas, Juan Moreira. Fernando Reati has noted how Moreira, caught up in a struggle to control brain-enhancing implants that alter users' perception of reality, finds himself embroiled in struggles among Argentina's commercial interests and governmental agencies, as each attempts to gain the upper hand in the race to influence and control the population. In the novel, Argentina's wide open pampas have now been sold off to foreign commercial interests and become an urban sprawl. In this fashion, Blaustein's Buenos Aires is a nightmarish city whose juxtaposition of architectural ruins and ultramodern technology reveals the deepening social divisions within Argentine society (Reati 72–75).

Argentine writer Rodrigo Fresán sets his novel *Mantra* (2001) in another urban sprawl, a futuristic Mexico City. *Mantra* depicts a new global cybernetic consciousness called "Mantrax," an artificial intelligence (AI) located in Mexico City, that ultimately rejects the division among high and low cultures, authentic Latin American cultures of the Indigenous past, and foreign pop cultures of the present. Fresán is interested in a global mix beyond national borders, and his work shows how cyberpunk narratives moved beyond political ideologies and into a new realm of subjectivity, including popular discourses of television and film, affirming a less tortured subjectivity for posthuman consciousness in Argentina (Brown 147).

Contemporary Argentine authors are not as sanguine as Fresán about global pop culture and new technologies. For example, Pola Oloixarac's *Las constelaciones oscuras* (*Dark Constellations*, 2013) follows a male hacker and his biologist friend as they work on a databank of genetic codes. For them, everything is reducible to code, be it biological or synthetic. *Las constelaciones oscuras* also depicts botanical genetic recombinatory experiments in 19th-century Brazil, a subplot that reflects Oloixarac's fascination with the ways in which science can be used by powerful entities to control human society. *Las constelaciones oscuras* draws parallels between biological experiments of centuries past and data mined from contemporary hackers who end up serving power, either multinational corporations or the political interests of nation states. The botanical 'hacking' of *Las constelaciones oscuras* underlines the biological and physical consequences of data mining, which is also the topic of Germán Maggiori's *Cría Terminal* (*Terminal Breed*, 2014). Maggiori's international cast of characters includes a specialist in cloning, her Argentine lover, a pair of Chinese twins, and an American ornithologist, all of whom navigate a near-future world where cybernetics combines with genetic fusion to form a strange new reality where—in an unexpected instance of cybernetic metafiction—a bio-quantic machine intrudes upon the story and informs readers that it has seen all the narrative possibilities in a Borgesian maze. Finally, Martín Felipe Castagnet's *Los cuerpos del verano* (*Bodies of Summer*, 2012) explores a biological cybernetic web interface through which the dead remain conscious for 'downloading' into living human bodies. Thus, after 30 years of suspended animation, a male protagonist named Ramiro Olivaires returns to physical existence, but finds himself first placed into a rather large, aging female body, and then into that of an African man, and finally, that of a horse. As Kyeongeun Park notes, this apparently experimental, "disembodied" experience is actually a highly charged site "in which past dictatorial trauma, present neoliberal scars and the lack of a future vision for society converge" (306). While *Los cuerpos del verano* depicts such common cyberpunk tropes as downloading consciousness or a fantasy of disembodiment, the novel contests the freedom that such an experience might entail.

45.3 Mexico

In Mexico, cyberpunk emerged in the 1990s, a period associated with economic crises caused by the North American Free Trade Agreement (NAFTA), a treaty that is widely believed to have displaced the Mexican small farmer and other low-wage workers in the name of neoliberal policies enacted by the Mexican, American, and Canadian governments. Given Mexico's geographical, social, and economic proximity to the U.S. and high-tech centers in California, it is perhaps not surprising that Mexican cyberpunk highlights cybernetics and cyberspace. However, the noir and punk aspects of Mexican cyberpunk are clearly evident and can be traced to the 1980s, when the increased number and production of *maquiladoras*—factories on the border with the U.S.—and the War on Drugs were changing Mexican society. An early example of the noir aspects of Mexican cyberpunk is José Luis Zárate's story "El viajero" ("The Traveler," 1987), in which a down-and-out detective is caught in a Borgesian labyrinth of time travel, while Arturo César Rojas Hernández's "El que llegó hasta el metro Pino Suárez" ("The One Who Made it to the Metro Pino Suárez," 1986) highlights the punk aspect of cyberpunk, as a punk-rock guitarist searches another labyrinth—that of post-apocalyptic Mexico City's subways—in an Orphic pursuit to rescue his girlfriend from the criminal underworld.

Despite these precedents, it is Gerardo Horacio Porcayo's novel *La primera calle de la soledad* (*The First Street of Solitude*, 1993) that is generally cited as Mexico's first major work of cyberpunk. The novel follows a hacker named el Zorro [the Fox] who finds himself refurbished as a cyborg by a corporation that plans to use him to infiltrate rivals in order to corner the market on "electric dreams," a powerful form of mind control that acts like a drug. As in some of Philip K. Dick's fictions, users of electric dreams are made to believe that they are in contact with an actual deity. The proliferation of these electric dreams causes several rival AIs to emerge, leading to a holy war that breaks out on a lunar penal colony where el Zorro is sent on a mission. These conflicts distract from el Zorro's actual mission, which is to gain control over a powerful rogue AI that his corporation has sold but wishes to recover and reprogram. Meanwhile, el Zorro hopes to regain his independence from the corporation despite the bomb implanted into his brain to ensure his cooperation. In addition to the obvious cyberpunk motifs that populate *La primera calle de la soledad*, the story's many fights, explosions, and scenes of violence and torture—both real and virtual—often recall similar scenes in novels of narco-trafficking, while its title revisits anguish over national identity introduced in Octavio Paz's famous work, *El laberinto de la soledad* (*The Labyrinth of Solitude*, 1950).

While Mexican fanzines and online sites played a key role as venues for cyberpunk short fiction, several narratives by Bef, Gerardo Sifuentes, Pepe Rojo, and José Luis Ramírez have been anthologized in Spanish *Visiones Periféricas* (*Peripheral Visions*, 2001) and *Los viajeros* (*The Travelers*, 2011) and English (*Cosmos Latinos*, 2003) collections. These anthologies further popularized cyberpunk for a Mexican audience and, by virtue of the translations, exported Mexican cyberpunk to foreign markets. A representative author whose work appears in two of the three anthologies is Rojo, whose "Ruido gris" ("Gray Noise," 1996) depicts a journalist whose ocular implants capture crime scenes for a paying public, creating an unending demand for ever more graphic images of death and destruction. The implants prevent the journalist from having a meaningful private life, while the media-dependent public anticipates our current obsession with online entertainment and social media. Finally, the story's narrative structure begins and ends with suicide and serves to remind readers of the endless feedback loop that has ensnared the journalist—and perhaps the public—whose desires perpetuate and generate corporate profits. Published only a few years later, Ramírez's "Hielo" ("Ice," 1998) probes human and cybernetic relationships by depicting an AI that seeks to reunite with a young male hacker, Ratón, who was almost killed during an interface-turned-sexual encounter. In order to escape the AI's relentless stalking, the hacker disconnects from the web and moves to a remote location, only to find that the entity—Némesis—has sent armed criminals to find him. The use of cryptic teenage hacker language and the presence of drugs and video games, along with explorations of sexuality, offer a portrait of alienated middle-class youth in a new cyber-reality where the body is subject to cybernetic threats and even death.

Stories of replaceable body parts, prosthetic implants, downloaded consciousness, purchasable or implanted memories, and rogue AIs, all in service to neoliberal capital, are standard tropes of cyberpunk's large repertoire, and the 'body for rent' motif is also the subject of Bef and Sifuentes's "[e]" (1997). The story "[e]" shows workers' brains being used to analyze cybernetic data for large corporate financial deals. Although forbidden to ingest alcohol or drugs, one of these workers, Omar, turns to an illegal electronic drug called [e] in order to deal with stress, but later discovers that the corporation routinely uses such infractions to justify its efficient neoliberal policy of replacing rather than rehabilitating workers. Similar neoliberal conspiracies abound in Bef's novel *Gel azul* (*Blue Gel*, 2006), in which certain members of the intellectual and financial elites are able to float in gel tanks that take care of all their physical needs. Known as "tank surfers," they endlessly surf the Internet, oblivious to their corporeal existence. In Gibsonian fashion, a private investigator, Crajales, 'burned' for hacking in his previous life and denied access to the web and the pleasure of surfing in gel tanks, is hired to find out the truth behind a crime against a member of a wealthy family. During his investigation, he finds that several tank surfers have become victims of a sinister plot to harvest their limbs. Eventually we learn that high-level political agents are conspiring to supply replacement limbs to an international military industrial complex. However, as an investigator, Crajales is not a political hacker and wishes only to gain access to the gel tank experience, so he trades his information and his life for a final immersion experience before being killed by the conspirators.

In a more politically activist vein, Latino director Alex Rivera sets his film *Sleep Dealer* (2007) in Mexico, imagining new political networks among the disenfranchised. The plot is set in motion when an American company controlling water rights in Mexico suspects that a cyber attack may be launched on its reservoir. It sends a drone to attack the location of a young would-be hacker named Memo (Luis Fernando Peña), whose hacking turns out to be harmless. Memo is away when his father is killed, and out of guilt, he leaves home and gets illegal implants that allow him to work in the futuristic *maquiladoras* or "sleep dealers" in Tijuana. In this film, the workers' bodies are connected to cybernetic interfaces in order to transfer their 'labor' without their bodies to sites in the U.S. Memo becomes a 'node' worker who, as Sherryl Vint writes, gains access to cybernetic systems and cyberspace, yet reaps none of its benefits and "remains marginalized in both material and virtual realms" (256). Eventually, Memo joins forces with Luz (Leonor Varela), a cyberblogger who sells her memories to a subscription blog, and Rudy (Jacob Vargas), a rookie drone operator undergoing a crisis of conscience for killing Memo's father. Together they fight the privatization of water resources in Memo's hometown while searching for their individual callings. As a result, the film suggests alternatives that "move away from cyberpunk motifs and towards an embrace of sustainable agriculture and local connections" (Vint 266). As we've seen time and again in Latin American cyberpunk, the cybernetic world is to be resisted or reconfigured rather than embraced.

Mexican cyberpunk is also thriving in illustrated forms, such as Hector Germán Santarriaga's series of graphic novels—*Una mirada eterna* (*Everlasting Gaze*, 2012) *H3ermanos* (*3rothers*, 2013) and *Cuervo electrónico* (*Electric Crow*, 2013)—that portray the urban grittiness typical of cyberpunk. *Cuervo electrónico*, for example, features a female crusader who fights hidden authorities who control dreaming in a society where a large part of the population has had their minds corrupted by a new street drug. This graphic novel is one of several by Santarriaga, including *Coda* (2015) and *Luz eterna* (Eternal Light, 2016), both of which, along with Gerardo Horacio Porcayo's *Plasma exprés* (2017), continue to use the various motifs that characterize works of Mexican cyberpunk: dystopian landscapes, drugs, violence, and human trafficking.

45.4 Chile and Peru

While critics such as Andrea L. Bell and Moisés Hansón have shown sf has a long tradition in Chile, cyberpunk is not as prevalent and is largely associated with the work of Jorge Baradit. His novel *Ygdrasil* (2005) explores the interface of human DNA and computer coding to create a 'living' building, along with horrific scenes of abuse, prostitution, and de-eroticized sexual rituals. The motifs of high technology, drugs and implants, and religious and corporate conspiracies—motifs common to cyberpunk as a whole—are deployed to show the brutality of neoliberal models throughout Latin America, while also indirectly referring to the aftermath of the Pinochet regime (1973–90), whose human rights abuses and disappearances still haunt the country's collective memory. *Ygdrasil* centers on Mariana, a Chilean who works as a hit woman in Mexico City. Now addicted to drugs, she is kidnapped by corrupt Mexican government agents who implant her with a technology that allows her to hack into the country's central bank. What begins as a bank heist is soon transformed into an endless series of conspiracies. Mariana is betrayed, tortured, and re-constituted by a powerful cyber-shaman who draws on the traditions of the Indigenous Ona or Onawa of Patagonia. Baradit imagines a wholly commodified world in which the reincarnation of souls provides energy that can be channeled and used by the powerful Chrysler Corporation. Ultimately, Mariana turns out to be the mystical key to unlocking the energy of a new technology, a powerful AI that is part of a plan for cosmic control of unforeseen proportions. Tellingly, Baradit returns to issues surrounding state crime and biopolitics in his graphic novel *Policía del Karma* (*Karma police*, 2011), in which bodies of both men and women are converted into cyborgs that are manipulated, penetrated, and controlled as self-regulating machines in a future dystopian society.

As one of the only stories readily available in English translation, Pablo Castro's "Exerion" (2001) is notable as it follows a hacker who is the only member of his family willing and able to investigate the disappearance of his father by delving into classified documents, i.e., to 'hack the past.' When security forces discover this and immobilize him, freezing him to his computer, he plays the videogame *Exerion* to pass the time, review his life, and leave a virtual footprint while he awaits the inevitable arrival of the cyberpolice. Echoing the themes of hacking the past and dictatorship, Bolivian author Edmundo Paz-Soldán's *El delirio de Turing* (2003)—available in English as *Turing's Delirium* [2006]—is based on the actual re-election of former Bolivian dictator Hugo Banzer as president in 1997, despite the abuses of his 1971–78 regime. Part cybercrime thriller, part cyberhacktivism, it narrates the persecution of a government cybernetics specialist who participated in the cover-up of political crimes in the 1970s, including kidnapping and murder by death squads. By altering photos and other data, the specialist distorts and manipulates the country's collective memory, while opposing hackers seek to expose these crimes and political corruption to hold the country's leaders accountable for their past abuses. The novel also traces the relationships among participants in a virtual-reality platform known as "The Playground," where a young hacker, Kandinsky, tries to garner enough support to organize a political protest that will bring down the government. The preoccupation with digital images and their manipulation is also the premise of Paz-Soldán's *Sueños digitales* (*Digital Dreams*, 2000), which features the power of virtual images and the blurring of boundaries between dreams and reality. This short novel focuses in part on Latin American cyberpunk's commitment to critiquing the effects of privatization and neoliberal policies in disfiguring city landscapes, such as Paz-Soldán's own Cochabamba.

Finally, Peruvian author Santiago Rocagliolo's *Tan cerca de la vida* (*So Close to Life*, 2011) is one of the few examples of Latin American cyberpunk that features cyborgs as its main characters. Set in Japan, the story alludes to a sinister political past—the violence of Alberto Fujimori's tenure as president (1990–2000) and the trauma left in the wake of the Shining Path movement. The novel follows Max, a software engineer attending a conference in Japan, who experiences flashbacks of a violent murder and visions of a mysterious child. Traumatized by these memories, he grows increasingly disoriented and eventually learns that he is a cyborg: unbeknownst to him, his brain has been placed into a new artificial body, which explains how he is able to communicate almost telepathically with a mute chambermaid, an earlier model of cyborg produced by the same company. As in much of Latin American cyberpunk, artificial bodies controlled by corporations often allude to repressed political or social trauma and privatization policies. Notably, the two cyborg protagonists, against all odds, manage to resist and free themselves from their corporate masters.

45.5 Conclusion

In closing, Latin American cyberpunk from Brazil, Argentina, Mexico, Chile, Bolivia, and Peru deals with past abuses and corruption, along with neoliberal policies that have stripped away state programs and protections in the name of global economic competition. Navigating complex futures in often marginalized regions of the world, such works represent a local adaptation of cyberpunk's global influence. The anthropophagic gesture which repurposes an imported aesthetic/technology for local needs fits the sociopolitically engaged impulse of Latin American cyberpunk on the whole; in other words, Latin American cyberpunk could be broadly characterized as dystopian in ways that are different from its North American versions, where the virtual world usually represents an escape from social hardship. Instead, the posthuman characters in Latin American cyberpunk rarely escape the body or the past, often finding themselves caught in a technological web of conspiracies and manipulations that do not presage a better future, in which alternatives consist of embodied resistance and/or implied political change. And, as English translations expand Latin American cyberpunk to an increasingly wider audience, Latin American authors will have a chance to be more widely read, adding their perspectives on issues of biopolitics, the body and technology, and neoliberal economics to cyberpunk's ongoing global debates on the ethics and transformations heralded by posthumanism.

Notes

1 See Gazi Islam, "Can the Subaltern Eat? Anthropophagic culture as a Brazilian lens on post-colonial theory" for a history of cultural cannibalism in Brazil beginning with the 1928 "Manifesto Antropófago" by Oswald de Andrade which, Islam argues, continues to be relevant to understanding Brazilian culture. Ivan Carlos Regina also proposed a similar manifesto in 1988, "Manifesto antropofágico da ficção científica brasileira—Movimento Supernova" [The Anthropophagic Manifesto of Brazilian Science Fiction—Supernova Movement;" see Ginway, *Brazilian Science Fiction*, pp. 139–41.

2 Emphasis is on those countries where the presence of cyberpunk is strongest—Argentina, Brazil, and Mexico—along with two paradigmatic works by authors from the Andean countries of Bolivia and Peru. Another country with an important tradition—Cuba—is intentionally omitted: See Juan Carlos Toledano's contribution to this collection or his article "From Socialist Realism to Anarchist Capitalism: Cuban Cyberpunk" for an in-depth exploration of Cuban cyberpunk.

3 For more information, see Ginway, *Brazilian Science Fiction*, pp. 150–65.

4 For more details, see Ginway, "Metáforas biológicas."

5 For more on contemporary Brazilian cyberpunk see Costa; Causo, "Estado de arte"; Ginway "Posthumans."

Works Cited

Baradit, Jorge. *Polícia del Karma*. Ediciones B, 2011.

———. *Ygdrasil*. Ediciones B, 2005.

Bell, Andrea L. and Yolanda Molina Gavilán, editors. *Cosmos Latinos: An Anthology of Science Fiction from Latin America and Spain*. Wesleyan, 2003.

Bell, Andrea L. and Moisés Hansón. "Prelude to the Golden Age: Chilean Science Fiction 1900–1959." *Science Fiction Studies*, vol. 25, no. 2, 1998, pp. 285–99.

Blaustein, Eduardo. *Cruz diablo*. Emecé, 1997.

Borinsky, Alicia. *Cine continuado*. Corregidor, 1997.

Brown, J. Andrew. *Cyborgs in Latin America*. Palgrave MacMillan, 2010.

Calado, Ivanir. "O altar dos nossos corações." *O atlântico tem duas margens*, edited by José Manuel Morais. Caminho, 1993, pp. 177–206.

Castagnet, Martín Felipe. *Cuerpos de verano*. Factotum, 2012.

Castro, Pablo. "Exerion." *Cosmos Latinos: An Anthology of Science Fiction from Latin America and Spain*, edited by Andrea L. Bell and Yolanda Molina Gavilán, translated by Andrea L. Bell. Wesleyan UP, 2003, pp. 293–304.

Causo, Roberto de Sousa. "Estado da arte: Ficção científica tupinipunk." *Papêra Uirandê Especial*, no. 9, 2015, pp. 11–13.

———. *Shiroma, matadora ciborgue*. Devir, 2015.

———. "Tupinipunk: Cyberpunk brasileiro." *Papêra Uirandê*, Especial, no. 1, 1996, pp. 5–11.

———. "Vale-tudo." *Duplo cyberpunk*. Devir, 2010, pp. 79–124.

Costa, Antônio Luiz M.C. "Um cyberpunk mais ou menos brasileiro." *Carta Capital*, 2010.

Fawcett, Fausto. *Santa Clara Poltergeist*. Eco, 1991.

Fernández Delgado, Miguel Ángel. "Historias Olvidadas en la Historia de la Ciencia Ficción en México." N.p., n.d. *Ciencia Ficción Mexicana*.

Fresán, Rodrigo. *Mantra*. Mondadori, 2001.

Gamerro, Carlos. *Las islas*. Simurg, 1998.

Gardini, Carlos. "Primera línea." *Primera línea*, Sudamérica, 1983, pp. 149–69.

Ginway, M. Elizabeth. *Brazilian Science Fiction: Cultural Myths and Nationhood in the Land of the Future.* Bucknell, 2004.

———. "Metáforas biológicas e cibernéticas de resistência na ficção científica tupinipunk." *Papéis: Revista de Pós-Graduação em Estudos e Linguagens*. UFMS, vol. 19, no. 38, 2015, pp. 99–109.

———. "Posthumans in Brazilian Cyberpunk and Steampunk." *Paradoxa: Latin American Speculative Fiction*, edited by Debra Ann Castillo and Liliana Colanzi, 2018, pp. 233–49.

González, Maielis. "Latin America and Cyberpunk: Notes Towards a Poetics of the Subgenre on our Continent." *Paradoxa: Latin American Speculative Fiction*, edited by Debra Ann Castillo and Liliana Colanzi, translated by Adrian Replanski, 2018, pp. 211–31.

Hernández, Artur Cesar Rojas. "El que llegó al metro Pino Suárez," *Auroras y horizontes: Antología de cuentos ganadores Premio Nacional del Cuento Fantástico y de Ciencia Ficción (1984–2012)*. Conaculta, 2013, pp. 35–44.

Islam, Gazi. "Can the Subaltern Eat? Anthropophagic Culture as a Lens on Post-Colonial Theory." *Organization*, vol. 19, no. 2, 2008, pp. 160–80.

Kujawski, Guilherme. *Piritas siderais: romance cyberbarroco*. Francisco Alves, 1994.

Lemos, Cirilo. *A lua é uma flor sem pétalas*. Draco eBook, 2009.

Londero, Rodolfo Rorato. "O futuro esquecido: a recepção do cyberpunk na América Latina." PhD Thesis, Universidade Federal de Santa Maria (Rio Grande do Sul), 2011.

Maggiori, Germán. *Cría terminal*. Tusquets, 2014.

Oloixarac, Pola. *Constelaciones oscuras*. Random House, 2013.

Orsi, Carlos. "Questão de sobrevivência." 2001. *Assembleia estelar: histórias de ciência ficção política*, edited by Marcello Simão Branco. Devir, 2010, pp. 351–73.

Park, Kyeoungeun. "Floating Subjectivities in the Oceanic Network of *Sol artificial* and *Bodies of Summer*." *Paradoxa: Latin American Speculative Fiction*, edited by Debra Ann Castillo and Liliana Colanzi, vol. 30, 2018, pp. 293–319.

Paz, Mariano. "Buenos Aires Dreaming: Chronopolitics, Memory and Dystopia in *La Sonámbula*." *Alambique: Revista académica de ciencia ficción y fantasia*, 2013.

Paz-Soldán, Edmundo. *Sueños digitales*. Alfaguara, 2000.

———. *El delirio de Turing*. Alfaguara, 2003.

Piglia, Ricardo. *La ciudad ausente*. Anagrama, 1992.

Porcayo, Gerardo Horacio. *La primera calle de la soledad*. Fondo Adentro, 1993.

———. *Plasma exprés*. Destino, 2017.

Ramírez, José Luis. "Hielo." 1998. *Visiones periféricas: antología de ciencia ficción mexicana*, edited by Miguel Ángel Fernández Delgado. Lumen, 2001, pp. 202–19.

Reati, Fernando. *Postales del porvenir: literatura de anticipación en la Argentina neoliberal (1985–1999)*. Biblos, 2006.

Regina, Ivan Carlos. "Manifesto Antropofágica da Ficção Científica Brasileira." *D.O. da Leitura*, vol. 12, no. 138, 1993, p. 8.

Rojo, Pepe. "Ruido gris." *Los viajeros: 25 años de ciencia ficción mexicana*, edited by Bernardo Fernández (a.k.a. Bef). SM de Ediciones, 2010, pp. 98–129.

Santarriaga, Hector G. *Coda*. Nostromo, 2015.

———. *Cuervo eléctrico*. Nostromo, 2013.

———. *H3RMANOS*. Nostromo, 2013.

———. *Luz eléctrica*. Nostromo, 2016.

———. "Una mirada eterna." *12M Antología Narrativa Gráfica*. Animal Gráfico, 2012.

Sifuentes, Gerardo and Bernardo Fernández (a.k.a. Bef). "(e)." *Visiones periféricas: antología de ciencia ficción mexicana*, edited by Miguel Ángel Fernández Delgado. Lumen, 2001, pp. 173–86.

Sirkis, Alfredo. *Silicone XXI.* Record, 1985.

Suppia, Alfredo. "Acesso negado: circuit bending, borderlands science fiction e lo-fi sci-fi." *Revisa Famecos—Mídia, Cultura e Tecnologia*, vol. 24, no. 1, 2017, n.p.

Tavares, Braulio. "Jogo rápido." *A espinha dorsal da memória.* Rocco, 1996, pp. 104–20.

Toledano Redondo, Juan Carlos. "From Socialist Realism to Anarchist Capitalism: Cuban Cyberpunk." *Science Fiction Studies*, vol. 32, no. 3, 2005, pp. 442–66.

Vint, Sherryl. "Cyberwar: The Convergence of Virtual and Material Battlefields in Cyberpunk Cinema." *Cyberpunk and Visual Culture*, edited by Graham J. Murphy and Lars Schmeink. Routledge, 2018, pp. 253–75.

Zárate, José Luis. "El viajero." 1987. *Los viajeros: 25 años de ciencia ficción mexicana*, edited by Bernardo Fernández (a.k.a. Bef). SM Ediciones, 2010, pp. 52–67.

46

CUBA'S CYBERPUNK HISTORIES

Juan C. Toledano Redondo

In her chapter on cyberpunk in Latin America elsewhere in this collection, M. Elizabeth Ginway concludes her overview by noting that

> Latin American cyberpunk could be broadly characterized as dystopian in ways very different from the dystopian settings of North American cyberpunk, where the erosion of barriers separating illusion and reality serves to capture the political conspiracies and gritty urban realities of Latin America as it faces new globalized economic forces and attendant political uncertainties. (392)

This mixture of dystopian settings, globalized economic forces, and attendant political uncertainties very much defines Cuban cyberpunk and arises from the island nation's rapid socioeconomic transformation in the latter half of the 20th century. According to Bruno Henriquez, Cuba's increasing dependence on the Soviet Union following the Cuban Revolution of 1959 meant the Soviet superpower's presence coupled with its technical and technological advances helped foster the scientific imagination of many Cubans, and challenged the way they thought of the stars and their future (3).[1] For example, prior to the fall of the Berlin Wall in 1989, Cuba was the only Latin American country that had launched a man into space. Arnoldo Tamayo Méndez traveled with Yuri Romanenko in the Soyuz 38 in 1980 and, upon safely returning, became a hero both in Cuba and the Soviet Union. Tamayo's trip enlightened the imagination of many authors who believed in space travel as a national experience (Yoss, "Personal Interview").

After the fall of the Soviet Union in 1991, however, Cuba suffered an economic and social downturn. After all, the Soviet Union represented close to 85% of the island's economy (Balari 85), which means such dreams of space travel fueled by Tamayo's success returned to nothing more than a vicarious experience following the collapse of the communist bloc.[2] While Cuba experienced significant starvation, a general lack of means of production, and struggled with its (in)ability to fix old cars and other machinery, the country also suffered a sudden discontinuation in the technological development of computers. In sum, the fall of the Soviet Union and its detrimental effects upon Cuba occurred right when personal computers and the Internet were becoming important tools of communication and development in the international sphere. While the Internet was becoming essential to the world, Cubans struggled with surviving their everyday life during the so-called *Período especial*, or Special Period in Time and Peace, that began in 1991 and stretched for more than a decade. During this Special Period, Cuban authorities restricted energy consumption, tightened political repression, and repressed social dissent through censorship, all to silence possible social upheaval—e.g., "el Maleconazo," a mass protest on August 5, 1994 that momentarily shook the pillars of the system—that could topple the socialist government due to severe scarcity of food and other main necessities. In sum, if the Soviet Union had provided Cuba with high-end machinery and technology, scientific magazines, and a belief in science and development, most of that exposure, access to technology, and vision(s) of the future stalled when the Soviets departed Cuba.

Ironically, while Cuba's social and technological developments were slowing down and social upheaval continued to rock the island, a form of Cuban cyberpunk gradually emerged on the island. Despite socialist censorship in general and a decades-long American embargo, cyberpunk novels from the U.S. trickled into Cuba during the 1980s and 1990s and their (ongoing) influence upon local authors is unmistakable. For example, Vladimir Hernández Pacín mirrored the literary universe of William Gibson's *Neuromancer* (1984) in his story "Mar de locura" (Ocean of Madness, 1994) with its depictions of cyberspace, (dis)embodiment, global corporations, hackers, drug abuse, and disaffected youths, although Hernández offers a more cautiously optimistic conclusion to the narrative than Gibson's ambivalence.[3] Similarly, Erick J. Mota's orishas gods in *Habana underguater* (Havana Underwater, 2010) are clearly inspired by Gibson's *Count Zero* (1986). American cyberpunk essentially allowed Cubans to envision a *new space*, a "lugar no-lugar" [no-place place] (Sánchez-Mesa 14), that was easily accessed via the wonders of science fiction (sf). After all, when Bruce Sterling writes in his Preface to *Mirrorshades. The Cyberpunk Anthology* (1986) that cyberpunk is "the unholy alliance of the technical world and the world of organized dissent—the underground world of pop culture, visionary fluidity, and street-level anarchy" (xii), we need to remember that Cuba's sociopolitical and technological realities largely restricted this 'unholy alliance' to realms of textual imagination. Related, Domingo Sánchez-Mesa argues that the development of a cyberculture in any given society is intimately related to the economic development of that country, but market conditions have created a so-called "brecha o divisoria digital" [digital distance] among different parts of the world (14). This is notable in Cuba; namely, even today Cubans continue to find it almost impossible to access the Internet, and it is largely restricted to some professionals, universities, hotels, some cultural centers, and, of course, the state. As a result, cyberpunk cultivated a vicarious experience with its literary allure for oriental yakuza plots, computer hackers, streetwise rebels, and endless artificial intelligences (AIs) that control society.

In addition to Cuban authors and readers being inspired by largely American cyberpunk, the existence of certain restrictions—e.g., freedom of political speech and freedom of movement inside and outside the island—created a fertile ground for a local rebelliousness that would help fuel an imaginative counter discourse to Cuba's restrictions[4] in the form of a distinctly Cuban-flavored cyberpunk.[5] While Cuban-flavored cyberpunk never truly expanded to all spheres of the arts or became a mainstream style among many sf authors on the island, at least not to the degree cyberpunk saturated other global markets, such Cuban problems as restricted travel and imbalances in power were explored in these local fictions about streetwise rebels and hackers, behemoths of power, and virtual realms available via cyberspace (i.e., alternative realms accessible without leaving the island). Even in Cuba, the street finds its own uses for things—as Gibson famously remarks in "Burning Chrome" (1982)—and Cuban-flavored cyberpunk was useful in denouncing blatant elements of oppression, like the State's assumption of a necessary (socialist) optimism in sf plots,[6] as well as subtle oppression by power exercised at the local and global level but imagined not solely as Cuban but also Caribbean at large. In the end, although it might be characterized as a niche, even underground, market, Cuban-flavored cyberpunk became an important tool through which its key practitioners—Vladimir Hernández Pacín, Michel Encinosa Fú, Yoss, and Erik J. Mota—critically expressed what they saw as a worsening of their own social reality.

Vladimir Hernández Pacín, who once used the pen name Blade, can be considered Cuba's answer to Bruce Sterling as he was responsible for gathering and assembling cyberpunk writers into a series of collections: *Sueños de interfaz* (a manuscript never released in Cuba), *Horizontes probables* (1999), and *Onda de choque* (Collision Wave, 2005). In addition, Hernández's own cyberpunk includes *Nova de cuarzo* (Quartz Nova, 1999) and *Hipernova* (Hipernova, 2012). After he moved to Barcelona, he was a runner up in the prestigious UPC (Universidad Politécnica de Cataluña) award in 2003 with the novella *Sueños de interfaz* (Interface Dreams), later to become the title of a collection (2013). Hernández writes stories that at times use cyberpunk in a stereotypical fashion, including neologisms and jargon. For example, a Cibernario—i.e., cyber + *diccionario*—at the end of *Nova de cuarzo* includes 53 entries, including wetware, zaibatsus, nootrópicos, cracker, ciberpuerto, and bares telemáticos. Hernández was an instrumental promoter of an sf that distributed cyberpunk to Cuba and the Caribbean at large, creating and incorporating local landscapes in the future, such as a futuristic Havana that becomes the largest Megalopolis in the region or an "autopista transcaribeña" (TransCaribbean Highway).[7]

Michel Encinosa Fú's cyberpunk also prominently features Cuba in its setting; for example, in "Niños de neon" ("Neon Children," 2001) one of Encinosa's main characters, Diana, travels with her father outside the secluded city of Ofidia, a city where the government controls even the weather and has forbidden the rain. During their excursion, Diana experiences a storm for the first time. Being soaked by the benign rain forever changes her perception of the repressive state, and she in turn becomes a hacker whose ultimate goal is producing illegal rain for all citizens by altering the weather satellites controlled by the government. If people experience rain, she reasons, they will change as she did and revolt against the state. Encinosa's "Niños de neon" reflects the tactics of much Cuban sf that criticized the repressive policies and the government at large in an allegorical mode that enabled its publication in spite of its critiques. In addition to such short novels as *Veredas* (2006) (Trails) and the collection *Vivir y morir sin ángeles* (Living and dying without Angels, 2008), however, Encinosa became best known for the futuristic city of Ofidia, an imaginary city that features prominently in such story collections as *Niños de neón, Dioses de neon* (Neon Gods, 2006) and *Enemigo sin voz* (Voiceless Enemy, 2007). Ofidia is recognizable to cyberpunk aficionados: Its citizens—i.e., those "people on the fringe of society: outsiders, misfits and psychopaths, struggling for survival" that are common to cyberpunk (Cavallaro 14)—try to survive a rampant capitalism. Encinosa's cyberpunk oeuvre is one of the largest published on the island, with at least three collections and another three novellas.[8]

Comparable to Encinosa's success in the cyberpunk style is Yoss (pen name of José Miguel Sánchez Gómez), one of the most stylish and arguably one of the best writers on the island. His story collection *Timshel* (1989), which won the national award David in 1988, provides a handful of stories clearly influenced by mainstream cyberpunk. For example, "Historia de gladiadores" ("A Story of Gladiators") contains "elements of the cyberpunk style" that "include[s] among its topics violence, sexuality, an oppressive society, references to Asian culture, and some references to cybernetics" (Toledano, "Socialist" 450–451). While "Historia de gladiadores" shows some movement away from cyberpunk elements—e.g., his use of cybernetics is at times superfluous— Yoss maintains some cyberpunk features, including socially excluded characters who need to fight against corporations, mafias, and corrupt totalitarian regimes, an abundance of sexual and labor exploitation, and plots derived from *noir* rather than Golden Age sf. In addition, we can also turn to some stories from his fix-up novel *Se alquila un planeta* (A Planet for Rent, 2001), such as "Trabajadora social" ("Social Worker") and "El performance de la muerte" ("The Performance of Death"), to see Yoss deploy cyberpunk motifs for his sociopolitical purposes. "Trabajadora social" focuses on the life of Cuban prostitutes—locally known as *jineteras*—while "El performance de la muerte" is dedicated to plastic arts and commerce. In both cases, the stories delve into the needs of a desperate population who sell their souls to any alien who has the money to give them a better life than the one they can have on Earth, a clear allegory of foreigners or tourists capitalizing on the desperation of Cuban nationals. Although *Se alquila un planeta* was first published in Spain in

2001, and later in other languages, including English in the U.S. in 2015, the book never appeared in Cuba, although many Cubans read clandestine copies which furthered the rebelliousness often associated with cyberpunk. In sum, Yoss eschews a narrowly classical cyberpunk style and his success comes from his ability to mix cyberpunk with space opera, *noir*, humor, and even erotica, bolstered by his own knowledge of the biological sciences. Cyberpunk has had an enormous influence on Yoss's craft, at least in the very beginning of his career, and he continues to write texts that are always rich and full of surprises.

Finally, Raúl Aguiar recently writes that such cyberpunk offshoots as biopunk and post-cyberpunk are creating "nuevas hibridaciones y experimentaciones estilísticas" ("new hybrids and stylistic experimentations"), exemplified by Yadira Álvarez's story "Kikubi," Raúl Flores's *La carne luminosa de los gigantes* (The Luminous Flesh of the Giants, 2007), Leonardo Gala's *Cuentos de Bajavel* (Bajavel's Stories, 2012), Denis Mourdoch Morán's *Dentro de la boca del lobo* (Inside the Wolf's Mouth, 2015), or Maielis González Fernández's *Los días de la histeria* (Days of Hysteria, 2016), to name a few authors. In his analysis of Flores's collection *La carne luminosa de los gigantes,* awarded in 2007 with the Cuban national contest *Premio Calendario,* Aguiar writes that "Raúl Flores's style is consciously light, with tactics of rhizomatic narrative, pulp, fantasy of the absurd and almost a sort of splatterpunk light [...] and perhaps this particular characteristic differentiates it, allowing it to carve out a fandom in Cuba." The collection also shows clear references to English-language cyberpunk, with such Gibsonian stories like *Idoru* and "Johnny Mnemonic," referencing the canonical American-Canadian author. In "Johnny Mnemonic," for example, Flores writes: "El tipo bajito dijo ser fan a William Gibson. Se había leído todas sus novelas" (36) ("The short man said that he was a fan of William Gibson. He had read all his novels"). And in *Idoru*, a story that delves into the sexual exploitation of women (both humans and AIs) in Havana, the plot has clear connections with Gibson's original novel, including references to sexual and sentimental relations with AIs, called Idorus or ghosts (5), and connections to Asian locales like Japan and Taiwan (6).

It is Erik J. Mota, however, who is perhaps the best example cyberpunk's continuing evolution in Cuba. As evidenced by his stories and fix-up novel *Habana underguater*, all published under the name *Habana underguater. Completa* (Havana Underwater. Entire Collection, 2010), Mota is a great innovator who is as difficult to classify as Yoss. Namely, *Habana underguater* successfully mixes different literary styles: In this alternative history, the Soviets have won the Cold War, but the collection clearly depicts a cyberpunk universe because half of the story takes place in cyberspace. *Habana underguater* is populated with characters that belong to the fringe of society, are in conflict with mafias and AIs, and must resolve their conflicts by traveling both to orbital space and to cyberspace. But perhaps the most important element in Mota's work is his incorporation of Afro-Cuban characters, traditions, and gods—an aspect of Cuban reality that is mostly avoided in Cuban sf. Orishas and deities from the *santería* tradition populate Mota's cyberspace and have become independent entities that control this parallel digital reality, quite unlike Gibson's *Count Zero* whose 'gods' are actually AI impostors. Mota's work mixes traditional elements of the fantastic with sf and incorporates different local elements. His fusion of cyberspace with the Afro-Cuban religious-space, coupled with the representation of the novel's heroes as two 'prietos' (black people), is perhaps one of the most refreshing elements of Cuban sf today and illustrates the diversity available in Cuban-flavored cyberpunk.

In closing, the digital realms offered through cyberspace are common to cyberpunk and operate as a *locus* open to be populated by a wide range of stories. Such Cuban sf writers as Hernández, Encinosa, Yoss, and Mota have created exciting approaches to the digital possibilities in their literary experiments, incorporating present, possible, and alternative realities that address any number of contemporary issues, including Cuba's complicated relationship with the future given the island's unique sociopolitical conditions. Although cyberpunk may not have expanded to

Cuba's Cyberpunk Histories

other spheres of the arts on the island, its ongoing history continues to influence authors who have taken, and continue to take, Cuban sf into new directions, fostering new generic intertextualities that enrich the field. Cyberpunk therefore still has a solid group of followers in Cuba who are looking both outside and, mostly, inside the island to develop new, interesting, ideas to shape and influence sf and, more specifically, cyberpunk.

Notes

1   Bruno Henríquez Pérez's *El hombre que hizo el mar Báltico* (2009) is an homage to the post-1960s Soviet science fiction writers published in Cuba that brought to Cubans "otra visión del mundo" (3) [another perspective of the world].
2   For more details, see my article "El regreso," particularly pgs. 104–106.
3   My article "From Socialist Realism to Anarchist-Capitalism: Cuban Cyberpunk" offers more space than this case study overview to thoroughly unpack these connections and details.
4   See Yoss's *Crónicas del mañana. 50 años de cuentos cubanos de ciencia ficción* for details.
5   Cuban-flavored cyberpunk, notably in the literary arena, helped launch in September 2005 a virtual magazine called *Qubit. Boletín digital de literatura y pensamiento cyberpunk* (Qubit. Digital Magazine of Literature and Cyberpunk Thought), which reported on sf both inside and outside the island, but dedicated many issues to cyberpunk production in Spanish.
6   See Toledano Redondo, "From Socialist Realism."
7   See Toledano Redondo, "From Socialist Realism."
8   Apart from the aforementioned works, Encinosa also published the collection *Vivir y morir sin ángeles* (Living and Daying without Engels, (2008), and the novella *Veredas* (Pathways, 2006). In addition to cyberpunk-related fiction, Encinosa, recipient of many awards, has a large list of fiction published inside and outside Cuba.

Works Cited

Aguiar, Raúl. "Ciberpunk cubano en cuarto creciente: Variantes y herederos." 31 Jan. 2018. *LALT. Latin American Literature Today,* www.latinamericanliteraturetoday.org/es/2018/febrero/ciberpunk-cubano-en-cuarto-creciente-variantes-y-herederos-de-ra%C3%BAl-aguiar.

———. *Realidad virtual y cultura cyberpunk.* Abril, 1996.

Balari, Eugenio R. *Cuba ¿La Revolución acosada?* Fondo de Cultura Económica, 1993.

Cavallaro, Dani. *Cyberpunk and Cyberculture: Science Fiction and the Work of William Gibson.* Athlone Press, 2000.

Chávez Espínola, Gerardo. "El mundo de Ofidia." *El Guaicán Literario,* Jul. 2004, www.cubaliteraria.com/guaican/creadores5.html#ofidia.

Encinosa Fú, Michel. *Vivir y morir sin ángeles.* Ediciones Unión, 2008.

———. *Enemigo sin voz.* Editorial Abril, 2007.

———. *Dioses de neón.* Letras Cubanas, 2006.

———. *Niños de neón.* Letras Cubanas, 2001.

———. *Veredas.* Ediciones Extramuros, 2006.

Europa Press and ELPAÍS.com. "Cuba arresta a una veintena de opositores en el aniversario del 'maleconazo.'" *El País,* 6 Aug. 2009, elpais.com/internacional/2009/08/06/actualidad/1249509603_850215.html.

Flores Iriarte, Raúl, *La carne trémula de los gigantes.* Cada Editorial Abril, 2007.

Ginway, M. Elizabeth. "Latin America." *The Routledge Companion to Cyberpunk Culture,* edited by Anna McFarlane, Graham J. Murphy, and Lars Schmeink. Routledge, 385–394.

Henríquez Pérez, Bruno, ed. *El hombre que hizo el mar Báltico.* Editorial Arte y Literatura, 2009.

———. "Prólogo." *Polvo en el viento,* edited by Bruno Henríquez. EIMFC, 1999.

Hernández Pacín, Vladimir. *Sueños de Interfaz.* Alfa Eridiani, 2010.

———. *Horizontes probables.* Lectorum, 1999.

———. *Interfase. Selección de cuentos cyberpunk.* Manuscript, 1997.

———. *Nova de cuarzo.* Ediciones Extramuros, 1999.

———. *Onda de choque.* Ediciones Extramuros, 2005.

Jurado, Cristina. "Erick Mota: ucronía con sabor cubano." *Más ficción que ciencia. Un blog que está vivo,* masficcionqueciencia.com/?s=mota&submit=Buscar.

Maguire, Emily A. "El hombre lobo en el espacio: el hacker como monstruo en el cyberpunk cubano." *Revista Iberoamericana*, vol. 75, no. 227, 2009, p. 505–21.

Mota, Erick J. "Influencia de la cultura afrocubana en la literatura de ciencia ficción en la isla: ¿Un possible 'neo-afrofuturismo' en el siglo XXI?" *Korad*, vol. 26, 2016, pp. 11–17.

———. *Habana underguater, completa*. Atom Press, 2010.

Qubit. Boletín digital de literatura y pensamiento cyberpunk, edited by Raúl Aguiar.

Sampsonya Way Magazine "*Michel Encinosa Fú (En español)*," www.sampsoniaway.org/blog/2013/09/09/michel-encinosa-fu-spanish-text/.

Sánchez-Mesa, Domingo. "Los vigilantes de la metamorfosis. El reto de los estudios literarios ante las nuevas formas y medios de comunicación digital." *Literatura y Cibercultura*. Arco Libros, 2004 (11–34).

Sterling, Bruce. Preface. *Mirrorshades: The Cyberpunk Anthology*, edited by Bruce Sterling. Arbor House, 1986, pp. vii–xiv.

Toledano Redondo, Juan C. "El regreso del pasado utópico. Khan, Spock y la cibo cubana Maya." *La Torre. Revista general de la Universidad de Puerto Rico, Puerto Rico*. Año 16, Número 1–2, enero-junio 2016 (103–113).

———. "From Socialist Realism to Anarchist-Capitalism: Cuban Cyberpunk." *Science Fiction Studies*, vol. 32, no. 3, 2005, pp. 442–66.

———. "Sputniks cubanos. De cómo la URSS ocupó la imaginación de una generación." *Kamchatka. Revista de Análisis Cultural*, vol. 5, Aug. 2015, https://ojs.uv.es/index.php/ kamchatka/article/view/4993.

Yoss [José Miguel Sánchez]. Personal Interview, 2013.

———. "Marcianos en el platanal de Bartolo: un análisis de la historia y perspectivas de la ciencia ficción en Cuba al final del segundo milenio." *La quinta dimensión de la literatura. Reflexiones sobre la ciencia ficción en Cuba y el mundo*. Editorial Letras Cubanas, 2012, pp. 61–80.

———. *Se alquila un planeta*. Equipo Sirius, 2001.

———. *Timshel*. Ediciones Unión, 1989.

Yoss [José Miguel Sánchez], ed. *Crónicas del mañana. 50 años de cuentos cubanos de ciencia ficción*. Letras Cubanas, 2008.

47

JAPAN AS CYBERPUNK EXOTICISM

Brian Ruh

It would not be an exaggeration to say that concepts of Japan and Japaneseness are central to cyberpunk. Japanese elements permeate many of this mode's foundational texts, and Japan continues to produce many important cyberpunk examples that push the ideas and concepts central to this mode, particularly as the synthesis of human and machine so central to cyberpunk's core becomes more and more a part of our quotidian realities. Although Japan is not the only non-western country or culture that is both exoticized and incorporated into cyberpunk,[1] projections and fears of Japan were critical to the popular conception of western cyberpunk during its formation in the 1980s. For example, William Gibson's *Neuromancer* (1984) set the tone by introducing us to the protagonist, Case, as he is drifting through his life in Japan. Case is a foreigner to both Japanese language and culture, but we see Japan through his viewpoint as he (and we) enjoy the frisson of both the danger of his profession as a data hustler and the exoticism of his environment as he passes "yakitori stands" (10), notices a "sarariman" among the "gaijin" (11), and is entranced by some "shuriken" (12) he sees in a shop window. In spite of the smattering of Japanese words Gibson throws into his descriptions, Case is presented with the linguistic edge, like when he tries to rent a gun from Shin, who communicates in clipped English: "You come back, two hour [...] Taser. One hour, twenty New Yen. Thirty deposit" (15). Even though at this point in the story Case is clearly a pathetic figure, he is able to hold himself apart from the surrounding Japanese society, both socially and linguistically, giving him the ability to dip in and out of 'Japan' when it meets his needs. Of course, the reason Case ends up in Japan in the first place is due to the association between the country and cutting-edge technologies. His former employers have punished him for stealing from them by burning out his neural implants so he could no longer access the matrix, the connection of computer networks that was both Case's life and livelihood. He held out hope that somewhere in Japan he would be able to find someone to reverse the damage because "the Japanese had already forgotten more neurosurgery than the Chinese had ever known" (Gibson 4). *Neuromancer* clearly positions Japan as a dominant force in everything from computer firmware to biological wetware, designer drugs to trend-setting youth subculture.

This association between Japan and technology is an important one and helps establish Japan as cyberpunk's locus for the exotic and the technological cutting edge. In fact, one of the key components of this relationship between Japan and cyberpunk is the notion of 'techno-orientalism.'[2] In their landmark analysis of the term, David Morley and Kevin Robins situate their discussion in the culture of the late 1980s and early 1990s, when Japan provoked an acute anxiety in the west, notably America. Much of this nervousness had, at its heart, worries that a non-western country like Japan was beginning to dominate the world economy. As Andrew McKevitt says in the introduction to his history of trade and cultural relations between the U.S. and Japan, "[a]rguably, Americans consumed more goods from Japan in the 1970s and 1980s than they had from any other foreign country in all of U.S. history, save perhaps Great Britain in the eighteenth century" (7). Thus, at the time that *Neuromancer* was written and the ideas of cyberpunk were beginning to gel, Japan was in its ascendancy as a world economic power, and it would have been easy to envision a future with a distinctly Japanese flavor.

Orientalism holds 'the orient' apart from 'the west' and exoticizes and fetishizes its cultures, goods, and people; techno-orientalism does much the same while ostensibly pointing toward scientific advancements. This fetishism, however, is coupled with a distinct kind of anxiety by those in the west, since in this techno-orientalist view "Japan has become synonymous with the technologies of the future—with screens, networks, cybernetics, robotics, artificial intelligence, simulation. What are these Japanese technologies doing to us?" (Morley and Robins 106). This panic about being overwhelmed by an Asian other, itself an updated version of the much older 'yellow peril' trope that dates back to European fears of Genghis Khan and invading Mongolian hordes (Marchetti 2), has manifested differently throughout the intervening years, and with the rise of Japanese economic influence and its associated culture and consumer technologies, it has taken on a new technology-inflected tone.

As Toshiya Ueno writes in "Japanimation and Techno-Orientalism," "If the Orient was invented by the West, then the Techno-Orient was invented by the world of information capitalism. In Techno-Orientalism, Japan is located not only geographically [...] as a satellite in orbit, but also projected chronologically by being located in the future of technology" (3). One of the interesting things about Ueno's assertion is that it does not necessarily depend on cultural perspective; the pervasiveness of capitalism has become its own culture with various flavors, and as such it is certainly possible for Japanese visions of the future to be as techno-orientalist as western ones. If we accept Ueno's assertion, then it is difficult for techno-orientalism to be teased apart from Japanese science fiction (sf), particularly when we explore Japanese cyberpunk's emergence in the shadow of western cyberpunk.

When western cyberpunk came on the sf scene in the early 1980s, it rapidly became popular in Japan. As Christopher Bolton and his fellow editors of *Robot Ghosts and Wired Dreams* write, "Cyberpunk, which was often derided by Western science fiction critics for being cartoonish, immediately appealed to a Japanese sensibility that had been nurtured on science fiction manga and Japanese animation" (ix). Illustrating (and capitalizing upon) cyberpunk's popularity, Bruce Sterling writes in the Preface to his *Mirrorshades: The Cyberpunk Anthology* (1986) that a November 1986 issue of Tokyo's *Hayakawa's SF Magazine* was the first sf magazine to run an issue focusing solely on cyberpunk (xiv). The idea of cyberpunk in Japan, however, soon became associated with Japanese authors who were not consciously trying to work in such a (largely Americanized) style. For example, Goro Masaki, who is often said to be one of the first Japanese cyberpunk writers, said that when he debuted in the mid-1980s, he had to stop reading Gibson's works because he didn't want to become a "Japanese Gibson" (Gregory and McCaffery 78). In fact, Masaki claims influences from English-language writers like Philip K. Dick, John Varley, and James Tiptree, Jr., many of whom helped lay the foundations for western cyberpunk.[3]

Cyberpunk's influence quickly made its way into Japanese audiovisual media: Shigeru Izumiya's *Death Powder* (1986) is considered to be one of Japan's first cyberpunk films. Although just over an hour long, it covers a lot of aesthetic ground, featuring scenes of contemporary Japan alongside fantastic images of decaying industrial spaces, fires, and pulsating, mutated bodies. As Mark Player writes, *Death Powder* exemplifies "the invasive, corporeal surrealism that would follow over the next ten years" ("Post-Human") and help define Japanese cyberpunk as more than merely a Japanese imitation of its western namesake, including the use of such key concepts as decay and transformation, artificial life, and the possibilities of overcoming the human. Additionally, *Death*

Powder demonstrates a sense of experimentation with the video format; there is a fight scene where instead of kicking her opponent, one of the protagonists kicks a video screen image of him, which then cuts to him flying across the room. Such a scene foregrounds the constructed nature of film, but also emphasizes the connection between media and the body—in the fight sequence, they are interchangeable. As Player explains, and *Death Powder* exemplifies, Japanese cyberpunk focused on visions of "industrial scrap [...] and makeshift laboratories built from crude and dated equipment [...] lending a DIY aesthetic to their overall ethos" ("Post-Human").

The DIY aesthetic and ethos found in Japanese cyberpunk highlights the close connection between punk music and independent cinema that began in the 1970s and 1980s, and it was not unheard of for biker gang members to be fans of punk bands or musicians themselves (Player, "Anarchy" 101). There was also fertile crossover between filmmakers and punk musicians—films would sometimes be screened during intermissions of punk shows, filmmakers would make music videos for bands, and punk musicians would sometimes score and act in films (Player, "Anarchy" 105). The punk roots of Japanese cyberpunk's ethos and aesthetics can be best seen in Katsuhiro Ōtomo's *Akira* (1988) and Shinya Tsukamoto's *Tetsuo: The Iron Man* (1989), two films that address similar thematic issues of technology and the body while maintaining an anti-authoritarian 'punk' attitude.

Ōtomo's *Akira*, which adapts his own long-running (1982–90) manga of the same name, involves members of a delinquent biker gang and their encounter with psychic, genetically altered children created by the Japanese government. One of the key moments of the film is when a young biker named Tetsuo nearly runs over one of the mutant children who has broken free. Over time, the results of this accident begin manifesting in psychological and physical changes, turning Tetsuo into something nonhuman. He has great new powers that he can barely control, which he uses to both settle old scores and try to construct a new kingdom for himself in the ruins of Tokyo. Since *Akira* was released near the peak of Japan's bubble economy when the nation was experiencing its own new economic might, Susan J. Napier sees definite parallels, writing that Tetsuo can be "coded in ideological terms as a reflection of Japan's own deep-seated ambivalence at this time, partly glorying in its new identity but also partly fearing it" (40). Indeed, this is an interpretation that can be used for many of the Japanese cyberpunk works in the 1980s with their connections between monstrous bodies, a metastasizing economy, and the body politic. For example, Tsukamoto's *Tetsuo: The Iron Man* is closely connected to these ideas and features horrifying transformations as its nameless protagonist (Tomorowo Taguchi) begins sprouting metallic parts and undergoes a gradual metamorphosis into an 'iron man.' Peter Nicholls writes that *Tetsuo: The Iron Man* "has been assimilated by [c]yberpunk enthusiasts as a major cyberpunk document in its portrayal of the unification of the world of the machine with the world of humans" all the while "the hysterical metallic sound track is also astonishing in its neurotic machine-like edginess." The success of the film, however, cannot be understated: "The international circulation and success of *Tetsuo: The Iron Man*," Player writes, "not only represents the culmination of the efforts of the Japanese punk film underground, or its transition from punk to cyberpunk, but also the culmination of a shift in the international perception of Japanese cinema" ("Anarchy" 115). This new attention paid to groundbreaking Japanese film in the late 1980s and early 1990s not only had an impact on live-action film but also paved the way for international co-productions of anime.

The most significant title hovering over Japanese cyberpunk, however, is arguably *Ghost in the Shell* in all its various forms. Originally, a manga by Masamune Shirow that ran from 1989 to 1990, the comic follows cyborg Major Motoko Kusanagi and her compatriots in the Japanese government's secretive Section 9 as they fight techno-terrorists and cyber-criminals. Through this setting, Shirow's manga explores encroaching technologies, bodily autonomy, and the nature of the cybernetic soul. In the end, Kusanagi merges with a being called the Puppet Master to become more than she could have hoped to have been as a pawn of the government. Shirow downplayed his contribution to cyberpunk's development, writing in an afterword, "It's rather light cyberpunk ripping off the aesthetic, and much of it is just 'monkey see, monkey do' imitation" (350). However, the influence of the title grew, particularly with Mamoru Oshii's feature anime film adaptation (1995). The film ended up being far more successful outside of Japan than it was domestically, famously reaching the top position on the *Billboard* sales chart when it was released on home video in the U.S. Its popularity, though, was not accidental: As a Japanese and British co-production, it was uniquely poised to do well with a diverse post-*Tetsuo* audience that was looking for a new dose of Japanese futurity.

While Japanese cyberpunk was establishing itself as its own cultural force, English-language cyberpunk beyond Gibson's *Neuromancer* was busy creating and disseminating its visions of Japan for a largely western audience. For example, Richard Calder, author of the *Dead Girls* trilogy,[4] stated in an interview, "I have never visited Japan and, like most westerners, my appreciation of Japanese 'subculture' is limited to pop-cultural journalism and anime [...] The fast-paced action, the editing techniques, simply the way things look and sound in anime, has certainly influenced the way I write" (cit. in Tatsumi, *Full Metal Apache* 203). For Calder, the advance of Japanese audiovisual techniques found in Japanese animation provides a structural way of approaching the stories he is trying to tell. Additionally, as with Gibson, Japanese-language references work their way into Calder's worlds. For example, the first paragraph of *Dead Girls* (1992) begins with the narrator, Ignatz Zwakh, trying to escape Thailand and fleeing from Bang and Boom, the "Pikadon Twins—notorious henchgirls to Madame K" (3). In Japanese, 'pika' means 'flash' as in a flash of lightning, and 'don' means a 'boom' as in a crash of thunder. However, taken together, 'pikadon' is a term most often associated with the atomic bombs that were dropped on Hiroshima and Nagasaki by the U.S. in 1945. As *Dead Girls* opens with Ignatz getting chased by Bang and Boom, we can read it as a metaphorical reversal of power—it is now Asia that has the ability to impose its will on the west. This is later mirrored by Zwakh's submission to Primavera, a girl who had been turned into a living doll by a virus, another example of a fear of high-tech contamination, this time within our very cells. Calder deftly stages part of the pleasure of cyberpunk for an English-speaking audience: It is the idea of engaging with the exotic other while courting the 'danger' of getting subsumed by foreign technology.

Japanese exoticism in western cyberpunk was not restricted to print but was celebrated in cinema through cyberpunk films. Scott Bukatman argues that three films were foundational to the mode: Ridley Scott's *Blade Runner* (1982), Steven Lisberger's *TRON* (1982), and David Cronenberg's *Videodrome* (1983) (Bukatman 137). Although *TRON* did not contain any obvious allusions to Japan, *Videodrome* and *Blade Runner* depended on it for their aesthetic splendor. Ridley Scott's *Blade Runner* tapped into a vein of anxious imagination when he envisioned the gritty Los Angeles of the future as having a distinctly Asian flavor. As Wong Kin Yuen writes, "The incredibly detailed Los Angeles of 2019 in *Blade Runner* creates a futuristic noir atmosphere by heavily borrowing from Asian motifs, albeit vague and general ones, in its design of city icons and social spaces" (Wong 4). Indeed, one of the most iconic images from the film is of a giant electronic advertising billboard featuring a woman made up to look like a Japanese geisha (played by American actress Alexis Rhee). This image, and the film in general, combines the exoticism of Japan with its electronic (and western) commodification. *Videodrome* also taps into this 'anxious imagination,' although in a more sexually covert manner. Early in *Videodrome*, protagonist Max Renn is presented with potential candidates to be broadcast on his television station, one of which is a softcore work called *Samurai Dreams*. According to the director of photography Mark Irwin, "I told [director] David [Cronenberg] that I hadn't realized the Japanese were so raunchy, but he confessed that he'd made up all that Oriental ritualism surrounding the dildo" (Lucas 2010). While this may have been an early 1980s projection of techno-erotic fears based on Japan's economic ascendancy, these associations have lasted beyond Japan's bubble years. For example, the September 2001 issue of *Wired* magazine carried a feature section on Japan, including an article called "Ichiban" with the subheading "10 reasons why the sun still rises in the East." Among such forward-looking categories as industrial design, robotics, and video games, the article also includes erotica, with an emphasis on bondage. Although this differs in type from what is shown in *Blade Runner* and *Videodrome*, it still capitalizes upon the inherently transgressive (sexual) allure of Japanese culture.

While many of cyberpunk's foundational texts incorporate Japanese elements in some way, it is surprising how little attention is paid to Japan in discussions of this mode. For example, in *Storming the Reality Studio: A Casebook of Cyberpunk and Postmodern Science Fiction*, which compiles examples of cyberpunk prose, art, and criticism, Japan's presence is glossed over. After the book's introduction, editor Larry McCaffery and novelist Richard Kadrey present a crash course in "Cyberpunk 101," which lays out important influences as well as many of cyberpunk's highlights. However, none of these influences is by a Japanese author, a notable oddity considering how often English cyberpunk incorporates Japan as a setting. This is not to say that the anthology completely omits mention of Japan; the final chapter, Takayuki Tatsumi's "The Japanese Reflection of Mirrorshades," discusses the perception and reception of cyberpunk in Japan. Although Japan is relatively de-emphasized in the anthology, Tatsumi's contribution is important to understanding how Japan is positioned within cyberpunk. He writes, "What cyberpunks seem to consume is not merely Japan, but their own science fiction projected in the future called Japan, whereas what the Japanese audience seems to exhaust is not merely American SF of the 1980s, but their own image synchronic with cyberpunk" (372). The closing line of the whole anthology is Tatsumi's: "Cyberpunks perceive 'semiotic ghosts' of the present-day Far East; meanwhile, they are misperceived as the 'ghost-writers' of our future" (373). Misperceptions and miscommunications are at the heart of Japan's role in cyberpunk. This is closely related to Ueno's metaphor of techno-orientalism being like a semi-reflective two-way mirror between Japan and the West (4). We see a distorted image of what is on the other side, but we also see a reflection of ourselves superimposed on the image, which we may mistake for the reality of the other.

In conclusion, despite the emergence of a Japanese cyberpunk that was, arguably, more punk- and horror-driven in its depictions of bodily transgressions, western cyberpunk's appropriation of Japanese culture dominated the scene and reiterated techno-orientalist approaches that were instrument for cyberpunk's development, particularly throughout the 1980s. By the mid-1990s, however, the bursting of Japan's economic bubble put an end to most anxiety over the country's economic ascendancy; for example, Andrew McKevitt writes in *Consuming Japan* that Japan's economic slowdown in the early 1990s "was responsible for the country's cultural recession in the United States" (15).[5] Nevertheless, although Japan no longer looms so large as a cultural and economic villain in the popular imagination due to its post-bubble recession, some of the themes established early in cyberpunk's history still recur, and if the controversies surrounding Paramount Pictures/Dreamworks' *Ghost in the Shell* (Sanders 2017) or Netflix's *Altered Carbon* (Kalogridis 2018) are any sign,[6] techno-orientalism remains a core (and highly problematic) motif of cyberpunk.

Notes

1　For details regarding cyberpunk in Malaysia, see Satkunananthan.

2　For a discussion of techno-orientalism and how it relates to Japanese anime, see Kumiko Saitor's contribution to this collection.

3　For more information on cyberpunk's precursors, see Rob Lathan's contribution to this collection.

4　Calder's Dead Girls trilogy consists of *Dead Girls* (1993), *Dead Boys* (1994), and *Dead Things* (1996).

5　McKevitt goes on to cite an opinion poll of Americans in late 1992 that seemed to indicate that their opinion of the strength of the U.S. economy was improving in relation to that of Japan (16).

6　Hollywood's live-action version of *Ghost in the Shell* (Sanders 2017), starring Scarlett Johansson in the lead role, triggered accusations of whitewashing and cultural appropriation from the outset as an

American actress of Danish and Polish descent was playing Major Motoko Kusanagi. As Gregg Kilday writes in *The Hollywood Reporter, Ghost in the Shell* couldn't move past the controversies around its production, contributing in part to its poor box office receipts, even if

> Sam Yoshiba, director of the international business division of Kodansha, the manga's publisher, told *The Hollywood Reporter*, 'Looking at her career so far, I think Scarlett Johansson is well cast. She has the cyberpunk feel. And we never imagined it would be a Japanese actress in the first place.' He added, 'This is a chance for a Japanese property to be seen around the world.' Mamoru Oshii, director of the original 1995 Japanese animated film, also endorsed the choice.

Critical discussions of whitewashing also surrounded Netflix's *Altered Carbon*, starring Joel Kinnaman as Takeshi Kovacs, a protagonist of Japanese and Hungarian descent who lives in a future where people can be resleeved into different bodies. Although Kovacs is white in Richard Morgan's cyberpunk source novel, Paul Tassi writes on *Forbes.com* that "[s]ometimes, you may want to revisit and alter the original source to better reflect the progress society has made (or is trying to make) and to understand which decades-old concepts don't hold up that well today [...]. And when the opportunity for diversity is seemingly served up on a silver platter and the white guy is still chosen time and time again, that can be maddening...."

Works Cited

Bolton, Christopher, Istvan Csicsery-Ronay, and Takayuki Tatsumi. "Introduction: Robot Ghosts and Wired Dreams." *Robot Ghosts and Wired Dreams: Japanese Science Fiction from Origins to Anime*, edited by Christopher Bolton, Istvan Csicsery-Ronay, and Takayuki Tatsumi. U of Minnesota P, 2007, pp. vii–xxii.

Brown, Steven T. *Tokyo Cyberpunk: Posthumanism in Japanese Visual Culture*. Palgrave Macmillan, 2010.

Bukatman, Scott. *Terminal Identity: The Virtual Subject in Post-modern Science Fiction*. Duke UP, 1993.

Calder, Richard. *Dead Girls, Dead Boys, Dead Things*. St. Martin's Griffin, 1998.

Ghost in the Shell, Readme: 1995–2017. Kodansha Comics, 2017.

Gibson, William. *Neuromancer*. Penguin, 2016.

Gregory, Sinda and Larry McCaffery. "Not Just a Gibson Clone: An Interview with Goro Masaki." *The Review of Contemporary Fiction*, vol. 22, no. 2, 2002, pp. 75–81.

"Ichiban." *Wired*. Sep. 2001, pp. 120–25.

Kadrey, Richard and Larry McCaffery. "Cyberpunk 101: A Schematic Guide to Storming the Reality Studio." *Storming the Reality Studio: A Casebook of Cyberpunk and Postmodern Science Fiction*, edited by Larry McCaffery. Duke UP, 1991, pp. 17–29.

Kilday, Gregg. "*Ghost in the Shell*: How a Complex Concept, 'Whitewashing' and Critics Kept Crowds Away." *The Hollywood Reporter*, 2 Apr. 2017, hollywoodreporter.com/heat-vision/ ghost-shell-how-a-complex-concept-whitewashing-critics-kept-crowds-away-990661.

Kin Yuen, Wong. "On the Edge of Spaces: *Blade Runner, Ghost in the Shell*, and Hong Kong's Cityscape." *Science Fiction Studies*, vol. 27, no. 1, 2000, pp. 1–21.

Lucas, Tim. "Medium Cruel: Reflections on *Videodrome*." *Criterion.com*, 07 Dec. 2010, criterion.com/ current/posts/676-medium-cruel-reflections-on-videodrome.

Marchetti, Gina. *Romance and the "Yellow Peril": Race, Sex, and Discursive Strategies in Hollywood Fiction*. U of California P, 1993.

McKevitt, Andrew C. *Consuming Japan: Popular Culture and the Globalizing of 1980s America*. U of North Carolina P, 2017.

Morley, David and Kevin Robins. "Techno-Orientalism: Futures, Foreigners, and Phobias." *Edward Said, Volume II*, edited by Patrick Williams. Sage, 2001, pp. 88–112.

Napier, Susan J. *Anime from Akira to Princess Mononoke: Experiencing Contemporary Japanese Animation*. Palgrave, 2001.

Nicholls, Peter. "*Tetsuo: The Iron Giant*." *The Encyclopedia of Science Fiction*, edited by John Clute, et al., 16 Feb. 2017, sf-encyclopedia.com/entry/tetsuo.

Player, Mark. "Anarchy in Japan's Film Industry: How Punk Rescued Japanese Cinema." *Punk & Post-Punk*, vol. 6, no. 1, 2017, pp. 97–121.

———. "Post-Human Nightmares—The World of Japanese Cyberpunk Cinema." *Midnight Eye*, 13 May 2011, midnighteye.com/features/post-human-nightmares-the-world-of-japanese-cyberpunk-cinema/.

Shirow, Masamune. *The Ghost in the Shell*, deluxe edition. Kodansha Comics, 2017.

Satkunananthan, Anita Harris. "Manglish Cyborgs: Paranoia, Optimism and the Cultural Evolution of Cyberpunk." *Evolution in Language Studies*, edited by Shanthini Pillai, et al. Penerbit UKM, 2016, pp. 222–38.

Sterling, Bruce. Preface. *Mirrorshades: The Cyberpunk Anthology*, edited by Bruce Sterling. Ace, 1986, pp. ix–xvi.

Tassi, Paul. "On *Altered Carbon*, Whitewashing and 'Source Material.'" *Forbes*, 07 Feb. 2018, forbes.com/sites/insertcoin/2018/02/07/on-altered-carbon-whitewashing-and-source-material/#18dd0b156582.

Tatsumi, Takayuki. *Full Metal Apache: Transactions Between Cyberpunk Japan and Avant-Pop America*. Duke UP, 2006.

———. "The Japanese Reflection of Mirrorshades." *Storming the Reality Studio: A Casebook of Cyberpunk and Postmodern Science Fiction*, edited by Larry McCaffery. Duke UP, 1991, pp. 366–73.

———. "Transpacific Cyberpunk: Transgeneric Interactions between Prose, Cinema, and Manga." *Arts*, vol. 7, no. 1, 2018. doi:10.3390/arts7010009.

48
INDIA

Suparno Banerjee

According to the *Encyclopedia of Science Fiction*, cyberpunk presents a close future dominated by global industrial corporations and information networks, while at the same time depicting underground or street level countercultures challenging such global hegemonies. In addition to these overarching tropes, cyberspace often plays a major role in these narratives. In spite of cyberpunk's popularity, it remains more prevalent in the post-industrial societies of Europe, North America, and East Asia and is a relative anomaly in India, at least in its familiar form. India is a country still experiencing the transformative powers of industrialization, turning a primarily rural agrarian society into a more urban industrial one, and a postcolonial nation gradually flexing its geo-political muscles; as a result, it produces science fiction (sf) that predominantly functions in the corporeal realm, rather than in cyberspace. However, as one of the largest centers of information technology (IT) in the world, India is also in a unique position to embrace the cyberpunk ethos. The cultural patterns of 'modernized' urban India, riding on the shoulders of an IT industry that services global corporations and the rapid expansion of the Internet, follow some of the outlines set by the post-industrial west. Thus, since the 1990s, after the economic liberalization of India which helped initiate the IT boom, occasional works exhibiting cyberpunk qualities have begun to surface.

Arguably, the rapid intrusion of western technology in Indian society in the last few decades of the 20th century is the primary impetus behind Indian sf of the 1990s. As Uppinder Mehan explains, Indian sf "wrestle[s] with the need for technological development" but at the same time is wary of the kind of technological development "which might come at the cost of a neocolonial relationship with the Developed Countries" ("Domestication" 64). In a context closer to cyberpunk, Suchitra Mathur writes that the social effects of western techno-science are mostly corrosive when applied to a Third World milieu. Although Mathur concedes the possibility of using technological imagery in a positive way in sf, she is skeptical about the effectiveness of posthuman and cyborg imagery à la western literature in providing a tool of resistance for the postcolonial Indian society. Mehan and Mathur seem to agree that an optimistic mapping of the future India in sf entails moving away from both humanist and posthumanist western framings. Consequently, Indian sf often eschews the familiar trajectory of western cyberpunk, in which cybernetics and human elements create a posthuman cyborg existence often functioning as a social and individual liberatory device. Instead, cyberpunk in India comes in strange guises—sometimes as subaltern discourses, sometimes as humanistic condemnation of the posthuman, and sometimes as postmodern mimicry of western cyberpunk. In this chapter, I analyze three such works to show the trajectory the cyberpunk ethos and aesthetics have taken in India.

408

India

Published in 1995, exactly in the middle of the IT and open market revolutions in India, Amitav Ghosh's *The Calcutta Chromosome* defies easy categorization. It is at once a ghost story, an sf novel, and a subaltern narrative destabilizing the hegemonic order. It is also cyberpunk in its postcolonial avatar. Although *The Calcutta Chromosome* is set primarily in the near-future New York and Kolkata (Calcutta), it also depicts Kolkata of the 1990s and alternates between 19th and the 20th century rural India and Egypt. The book brilliantly presents the struggles between global capitalism and those who secretly undermine it, ranging from 19th-century colonial forms to futuristic corporate incarnations. The main action of the novel follows Murugan, an Indian-American researcher and an employee of International Water Council, a multinational entity. Murugan is exploring mysterious forces that he claims have aided Ronald Ross's Nobel-winning discovery of the malaria vector in Kolkata in the early 1900s. This action is contained within the larger narrative of Antar, an Egyptian immigrant in New York and also an employee of the International Water Council. With the help of a supercomputer named AVA and a worldwide information network, Antar investigates Murugan's disappearance in Kolkata in 1995. A third line of action, which is possibly contained within Murugan's investigation of Ross, follows incidents in the late 19th and the early 20th centuries revolving directly around Ross's scientific research. All these different research activities are imperceptibly influenced by the covert functions of a secret society that exploits the results of these investigations to achieve the capability of transmigration of a mind from one body to another, a staple in mainstream cyberpunk.

A central theme of *The Calcutta Chromosome* is information: the collection and control of data with an ascending order of efficiency (culminating with AVA), the exploitation of such information for (neo)colonial and corporate gains, and the parallel existence of underground groups undermining this chain of control. Thus, the novel's actions foreground the central struggles of cyberpunk: the global reach of capital embodied by IT, often backed by repressive forces, challenged by subversive enclaves utilizing and sabotaging these forces from within. The cyberpunk qualities of this struggle, however, become recognizable only at certain moments in the novel. For example, although 19th-century British colonialism is a precursor to modern global capitalism, the International Water Council, with its stranglehold on global water resources and flow of data, is the entity that provides the classic cyberpunk trope of a dystopian mega corporation. This mega-entity regulates the lives of its employees at every level through surveillance and data collection. Any deviation is grounds for swift termination. As a result, Antar's daily routine must follow the rigid company schedule set by AVA, yet Antar can also use AVA's network to trace Murugan from just a piece of his lost ID or control the regional officer in Kolkata through video surveillance. Furthermore, Antar's interview with Murugan toward the end of the book and the videos of Murugan's exploits in Kolkata are given to Antar by AVA through virtual-reality (VR) projections. Thus, the near-future sections of the novel make the 'cyber' element of cyberpunk evident.[1]

The 'punk' component, although a little harder to recognize in the traditional sense of cyberpunk, nonetheless underlies every movement of the story. All the actions and discoveries in the book by social elites such as Ross, Phulboni (a famous author in the Kolkata sections of the novel), and Murugan are subtly manipulated by an underground organization, known as the cult of silence, comprising of the subaltern population. In the sections set in 19th- and 20th-century India, the members of the cult of silence come from the bottom of society: sweepers, servants, fishmongers, etc. When the action shifts to a future New York, the economic capital of the neocolonial world, this underground group finds affiliates in the immigrants marginalized by the forces of global capitalism. In the colonial past, this cult influenced the British by manipulating their physical technology, i.e., the vast railway networks and laboratory science. In the neocolonial future, the cult primarily plays with the flow of information and computer networks. In fact, Antar's search for Murugan using AVA's vast network is revealed at the end to be a well-executed plot by the cult of silence. They first hack into Antar's computer system, thus effectively monitoring and influencing every part of his investigation, and ultimately absorb him into their group. Thus, the cult of silence, a subaltern group, successfully exploits the technologies set up for corporate control and profit to accomplish its own ambitious project: achievement of de facto immortality for the cult members.

This subversive community possesses all the essential qualities of the 'punk' underground in mainstream cyberpunk. The members are mostly from marginalized populations, yet they can infiltrate and manipulate large corporate systems; their actions are partly dependent on corporate technology, but they also deploy methods unknown to the corporations; and while this group manipulates a corporate structure, its goals go beyond corporate gains. In addition, these subaltern characters often work in conditions similar to the gritty set up of cyberpunk: deserted apartment buildings, dirty streets and railway platforms, and unfinished buildings. Consequently, this classic subaltern discourse expertly takes up some of the essential qualities of cyberpunk.

Published a couple of years after *The Calcutta Chromosome*, Manjula Padmanabhan's play *Harvest* (1997) depicts a near future India where the multinational company Interplanta buys human body parts from the poor and sells them to rich clients in North America. The play uses cyberpunk tropes in a more recognizable manner by strongly evoking the gritty dystopian atmosphere of Anglo-American cyberpunk. The stage direction and the dialogue strongly conjure a megapolis dominated by "grimy, despairing, poison-fumed" (7) traffic, automated factories, and a huge unemployed and desperate population that is led by guards "like goats at the slaughterhouse" (10). The central characters—Om, his mother (Ma), his wife (Jaya), and his younger brother (Jeetu)— live in a single-room "bare but cluttered" (7) tenement in Bombay (Mumbai). Although Jaya is Om's wife, she is sexually involved with Jeetu. When Om reluctantly sells his body to Interplanta to escape poverty, as part of the deal the company converts his apartment into a panopticon, a sanitized space constantly under surveillance, to keep the human asset (Om) healthy and docile. However, when Interplanta agents mistake Jeetu as Om, and start harvesting Jeetu's organs and replacing them with mechanical ones, Om sees a way to escape alive and runs from the tenement. Jeetu first resists Interplanta; however, a VR projection of a highly sexualized young American girl (Ginni), the intended organ recipient, is used to seduce him into submission: to give up all his body parts. Ginni, though, later turns out to be a computer-generated image behind which sits a decaying old man named Virgil. During this process of harvesting, Ma enters a "VideoCouch"—a device that sustains a human body while the person is immersed into online TV shows—bought by the money Om received from selling his body. After Jeetu's body is completely harvested (everything from eyes to skin), his mind is placed in digital storage. Virgil at this point attempts to intimidate Jaya into bearing his child through artificial insemination, because of a decline in fertility among the women of the developed world. The play ends with Jaya barricading herself in a room and threatening suicide unless Virgil (now almost wholly made up of Jeetu's body parts) physically comes to her and has direct sexual intercourse, rather than sending over his sperm in a vial, to produce the desired child.

The 'cyber' part of the mode is visible in *Harvest* not only in the tropes of paranoid urbanism, but also in the posthuman figure of the cyborg and in the instrumentality of information, which, as Scott Bukatman argues in context of Ridley Scott's *Blade Runner* (1982), are closely associated with the cyberpunk ethos and aesthetics (135–42). *Harvest* criticizes the figure of the cyborg as well as projections of a malleable digital self. The first cyborg image under critique is the transformation of Ma into a machine-controlled inert body thriving on unreal images. The second cyborg image manifests in Jeetu's part-human, part-mechanical existence. The third instance is the confinement of Jeetu's mind in a digital form after the complete garnering of his body. All these instances project the cyborg image as a device of control by the capitalist west, rather than a symbol of subversion as is often the case in western cyberpunk.

Harvest positions itself on the opposite pole of the ideologies that often inform western cyberpunk—namely the postmodern and posthumanist critique of liberal humanist ideals. In their analysis of cyberpunk, both Scott Bukatman and Istvan Csicsery-Ronay, Jr. draw heavily on cyberfeminist scholar Donna J. Haraway in highlighting the role of the cyborg in disrupting liberal humanist ideologies. According to both scholars, such posthumanist moves as conceived by cyberfeminists and western cyberpunk dissolve the binaries of domination, and thus destabilize the patriarchal, capitalist order, although cyberpunk has been accused by such scholars as Nicola Nixon and Karen Cadora as ultimately reinforcing heteronormative patriarchy and succumbing to an overall conservatism rather than truly offering progressive challenges to liberal humanism and a global neoliberal order. In any event, the cyborg images in *Harvest* do have some liberating effects: freedom from death in case of Virgil, from boundaries of space for Jeetu, from sex and gender roles for Ginni/Virgil (as a VR projection), etc. However, the more privileged west benefits from such freedoms in a lopsided manner, with the population of the developing world providing them with the raw materials for achieving such liberties (e.g. Virgil treats Jeetu's body as a supply of spare parts). Even when the Third World population achieves any semblance of 'physical liberation,' as is the case with Ma, who can end her daily miseries by entering the video-couch, the monetary profit rests with the corporations. Thus, Ma's cyborg identity, rather than being liberating, traps her physically within the closed circuit of capital flow. Jeetu's body, in contrast to Ma's, is disassembled and reassembled to create the new body of Virgil, while Jeetu's mind is trapped in an electronic limbo. Considering such scholars as N. Katherine Hayles has emphasized the embodied nature of information by eradicating any hierarchy between the information and the host of that information,[2] not only is Jeetu freed from his pitiable physical existence when he gives up his body, but also, in his newly merged state, there is no separating Jeetu's body from Virgil's mind. In their new physical entity as Virgil/Jeetu, both characters are inseparable in their identities. Nevertheless, such freedom from an organic/inorganic binary is not associated in *Harvest* with any type of agency for the poor. Rather, the First World cyborgs commodify and exploit their Third World counterparts.[3]

Harvest presents a complex exploration and critique of the major cyberpunk ethos and aesthetics. Unlike Ghosh's novel, however, the play lacks any organized underground resistance; in fact, any meaningful subversion in the play comes chaotically from a nontechnological direction. While the rest of the play debates the limits of life through posthuman tropes of transplantation and cybernetic augmentation, albeit in a negative manner, at the end Jaya refuses impregnation through artificial methods by the super-wealthy Virgil. Her struggle is impulsive and elemental, not planned or technological. Jaya rejects commodification of an organic corporeal human existence and denounces the technology that reduces the 'human' into just another machine. Although Jaya's essentialist stance against this structure of information, command, and control does not disturb the larger fabric of this dystopian society, her demands at least show potentials of revolt. *Harvest* is, therefore, a rejection of the ethos engendering cyberpunk all the while employing cyberpunk aesthetics.

Both *The Calcutta Chromosome* and *Harvest* present interesting treatments of some of the core themes and tropes of cyberpunk, but with noticeable postcolonial twists that dislocate the liberatory scopes of cybernetics and primacy of the modern urban sprawl either by introducing non-urban spaces/people or through confronting posthuman and cybernetic ethos with an essentialist organic ideology. Some later works also explore similar cyberpunk themes. For example, Ruchir Joshi's *The Last Jet-Engine Laugh* (2001) features extensive use of cybernetics and depicts a near-future dystopian and corporate controlled Kolkata populated by cyborg entities. We can also turn to Hari Kunzru's use of both corporate control over people's lives and manipulation of the Internet in *Transmission* (2005), Anil Menon's liberal use of cyberspace, gene hacking, and the struggle between western corporations and Indian activists in *The Beast with a Billion Feet* (2008), and Jayant

Vishnu Narlikar's focus on the global spread of a computer virus in *Virus* (2010). In addition, many of the stories in Anil Menon and Vandana Singh's *Breaking the Bow* (2012) provide some excellent examples of cyberpunk, notably Neelanjana Banerjee's "Exile," Ava Dawsear's "The Good King," and K. Srilata's "The Game of Asylum Seekers." All the short stories in *Breaking the Bow* are associated in some way with the Hindu epic *Ramayana*, but Banerjee, Dawsear, and Srilata are more easily recognizable as cyberpunk in their focus on VR, the malleable digital self, and the isolated individual's struggle in a world controlled by large corporations.

Acknowledging an actual mythical past associated with a specific geography (especially linked to the author's own culture) is something rarely seen in western cyberpunk. Some notable, if not problematic, exceptions are William Gibson's voodoo loas in *Count Zero* (1986), the use of Sumerian and other near eastern myths in Neal Stephenson's *Snow Crash* (1992), and the Hindu concept of cyclical time and cybernetic entities akin to the Hindu Gods in Ian McDonald's *River of Gods* (2004) and his *Cyberabad Days* (2009) collection. Although a strong sense of exoticism characterizes such usage, leading to questions about cultural appropriation and identity tourism, McDonald's stories in particular highlight the fundamental breach in the fabric of Indian society. For example, the protagonist of "Vishnu at the Cat Circus" (collected in *Cyberabad Days*) best describes India as two distinctly existing nations:

> India [the western name of the country] was located as much inside the mind and the imagination as between the Himalayas and the sea or in the shining web of communications [...] Bharat [the indigenous name of the country] was poor [...] Bharat drove and built and pushed carts through the streets and carried boxes up flights of stairs to apartments. (McDonald 265)

Although the cyberpunk tropes in McDonald and other non-Indian authors focusing on India, such as Lavie Tidhar ("This Other World," in *Breaking the Bow*), are easily identifiable in spite of engaging this fundamental social contradiction, these works ultimately end up emphasizing the mythical dimensions of the culture. Similarly, Indian cyberpunk, notably in the *Breaking the Bow* collection, struggles to reconcile such schisms between the urban and the rural, between technology and myths, between large corporations with their devices of control and a chaotic mass almost beyond governance, and thus employs innovative treatments and tropes, all the while leaning heavily toward mythical dimensions.

Finally, the Bollywood blockbuster *Ra.One* (Hindi, Sinha 2011) uniquely exhibits this novelty of cyberpunk treatment. Starring Shah Rukh Khan, Arjun Rampal, and Karina Kapur, *Ra.One* encapsulates the formula of a successful Hindi commercial movie: action sequences, song and dance routines, melodrama, nostalgia and love for home, family, and country, and an unequivocal binary between good and evil. Indeed, the inclusion of this film under the cyberpunk banner is somewhat contentious as it lacks some of the major reference points of this sf mode. For example, the narrative universe is not gritty and dystopian; rather, most scenes are set in the glitzy modernity of metropolitan London and in Mumbai. Although, the story includes a multinational software company and images of the corporate world, the all-encompassing global hegemony is lacking. With the absence of any explicit global domination, any underground resistance becomes unnecessary. Hence, the 'punk' element is difficult to recognize in the conventional sense, reinforcing the central conflict of the narrative as one between good and evil.

The presentation of this good-evil binary is by no means subtle. In this film, Shekhar (Shah Rukh Khan), an Indian software engineer working for a London-based company, creates two self-augmenting Artificial Intelligences (Ra.One and G.One) for a computer game. Ra.One (Arjun Rampal) goes rogue, killing Shekhar and trying to murder his family; G.One (also played by Khan) helps Shekhar's family, and aided by Shekhar's son Prateek (Armaan Verma), it destroys Ra.One. Here, the associations of good and evil are direct. The rogue program, Ra.One (short for "Random Access One") plainly refers to its homophone Ravana, the ten-headed demon king from *Ramayana*, signifying death and destruction; the good AI, G.One (short for "Good One") is homophonous with 'jivan' ('life' in Hindi). The visual imagery further enhances this binary: Ra.One wears fiery red, while G.One is clad in blue, the color often associated with Lord Rama, the slayer of Ravana. At one point in the film, Ra.One is even juxtaposed against a burning idol of Ravana to reinforce this symbolism.

Ra.One's cyberpunk dimension develops out of its use of cybernetic tropes and in its conscious and repeated invocations of notable cyberpunk movies. The film's main action revolves around a VR game and self-augmenting AIs. The AIs step into the corporeal world by using semi-robotic body suits designed for the game and later use some form of energy beaming to bind nanoparticles to create physical bodies. These two super entities are neither human nor robotic, neither fully corporeal nor merely virtual, but permeating and traversing both realms, and the film pits them against one another for most of its duration. This scenario, therefore, strongly evokes the 'cyber' part of cyberpunk. The 'punk' aspect, however, is present in a more emblematic manner. Although the film does not present any underground resistance destabilizing corporate hegemony, the inventor's tech-savvy son Prateek, portrayed at the beginning as rebellious in comparison with his traditional father, symbolically provides us with a 'counterculture' sensibility. In a fashion familiar to many fans of cyberpunk, Prateek confronts a maleficent force (Ra.One) created by and released from the information networks of a multinational software company by manipulating the company's system itself (G.One). Furthermore, the story is also about the destruction of Prateek's traditional family structure through the corrosive effects of the corporate system. To weaken the hold of this corporate network, which Ra.One can easily manipulate, Prateek must go 'underground' in India and submerge into a chaotic and less technologized space.

Ra.One, moreover, alludes to such well-known cyberpunk/AI-related films as *TRON* (Lisberger 1982), *TRON: Legacy* (Kosinski 2010), *Ghost in the Shell* (Oshii 1995), the *Terminator* series (1984–2009) (particularly *Terminator 2: Judgment Day* [Cameron 1991]), and *Enthiran* (Shankar 2010). Arguably, *Ra.One* is a mash up of the *TRON* movies and the *Terminator* series put into the Bollywood formula, with *Enthiran* as its predecessor. Nevertheless, the movie's postmodern celebration of the pastiche, along with its deliberate references to other Indian films (through visuals, dialogue, and music), and conscious invocation of Indian and western stereotypes (the awkward Indian computer engineer, over-sexualized white women, pious Indian ladies, the leering street thugs in Mumbai, etc.) suggest that *Ra.One* is not an act of simple imitation. Rather, the film is a conscious recasting of the narrative of cyberspace and AI into the mode of mainstream Indian entertainment, while providing recognizable points of reference for the audience. This is a mimicry in the sense that Homi Bhabha identifies in *The Location of Culture*: a mimicry that destabilizes the western forms and contents to its ideological core.[4] In this particular case, western cyberpunk's central ideological focus on global capitalism and scientific progress slides into a narrative of good and evil of a timeless mythical proportion, all the while maintaining a cyberpunk effect through metonymic use of the cybernetic images: That is, the film wants to *look* like a cyberpunk narrative through its use of established visual images and association with other cyberpunk films, while not necessarily prioritizing any of the ideological concerns of western cyberpunk. Such postmodern and playful moves indicate *Ra.One's* self-positioning as a cyberpunk narrative.

In conclusion, cyberpunk as a narrative mode undergoes drastic transformation in the Indian cultural milieu. Although the above examples are by no means exhaustive, they exhibit useful patterns of such transformations: The postcolonial and semirural India reshapes the aesthetics of the post-industrial west to suit its own demands, while also catering to the IT-saturated urban centers. Even though this mode has yet to find its foothold in the overall scheme of Indian narratives, several major Indian sf works have comprehensively utilized the tropes and scopes that cyberpunk offers. The recent penetration of cell phones and Internet within even the more

Suparno Banerjee

backward regions of the country coupled with the continuous inflow of global capital makes the condition more conducive for a proper and vigorous rise of cyberpunk in India. It is probably only a matter of time.

Notes

1 Uppinder Mehan makes a strong case for the novel's cyberpunk status in "Postcolonial Science, Cyberpunk and *The Calcutta Chromosome*."
2 For details, see *How We Became Posthuman: Virtual Bodies in Cybernetics, Literature, and Informatics* as a starting point to Hayles's extensive exploration of embodiment and posthumanism.
3 See my article "Ruptured Bodies and Invaded Grains: Biotechnology as Bioviolence in Indian Science Fiction" (2015) for a detailed discussion on biotechnological imagery in Indian sf.
4 In "Melodrama, Mimicry, and Menace: Reinventing Hollywood in Indian Science Fiction Films" (2014), I have argued that most Indian sf cinema engages in this type of 'mimicry.'

Works Cited

Banerjee, Suparno. "Melodrama, Mimicry, and Menace: Reinventing Hollywood in Indian Science Fiction Films." *South Asian Popular Culture*, vol. 12, no. 1, 2014, pp. 15–28.
———. "Ruptured Bodies and Invaded Grains: Biotechnology as Bioviolence in Indian Science Fiction." *Journal of the Fantastic in the Arts*, vol. 26, no.1, 2015, pp. 58–74.
Bhabha, Homi K. *The Location of Culture*. Routledge, 1994.
Bukatman, Scott. *Terminal Identity: The Virtual Subject in Postmodern Science Fiction*. Duke UP, 1993.
Cadora, Karen. "Feminist Cyberpunk." *Beyond Cyberpunk: New Critical Perspectives*, edited by Graham J. Murphy and Sherryl Vint. Routledge, 2010, pp. 157–72.
Csicsery-Ronay, Jr., Istvan. "The SF of Theory: Baudrillard and Haraway." *Science Fiction Studies*, vol. 18, no. 3, 1991, pp. 387–404.
Ghosh, Amitav. *The Calcutta Chromosome: A Novel of Fevers, Delirium & Discovery*. Avon, 1995.
Haraway, Donna J. "A Manifesto for Cyborgs: Science, Technology, and Socialist Feminism in the 1980s." *The Norton Anthology of Theory and Criticism*, edited by Vincent B. Leitch, et al. Norton, 2001, pp. 2269–99.
Hayles, N. Katherine. *How We Became Posthuman: Virtual Bodies in Cybernetics, Literature, and Informatics*. U of Chicago P, 1999.
Mathur, Suchitra. "Caught between the Goddess and the Cyborg: Third-World Women and the Politics of Science in Three Works of Indian Science Fiction." *The Journal of Commonwealth Literature*, vol. 39, no. 3, 2004, pp. 119–38.
McDonald, Ian. *Cyberabad Days*. Pyr, 2009.
Mehan, Uppinder. "The Domestication of Technology in Indian Science Fiction Short Stories." *Foundation*, vol. 74, Autumn, 1998, pp. 54–66.
———. "Postcolonial Science, Cyberpunk and *The Calcutta Chromosome*." *Intertexts*, vol. 16, no. 2, 2012, pp. 1–14.
Menon, Anil and Vandana Singh. *Breaking the Bow*. Zubaan, 2012.
Nicholls, Peter. "Cyberpunk." *The Encyclopedia of Science Fiction*, edited by John Clute, et al. Gollancz, 10 Apr. 2015, www.sf-encyclopedia.com/entry/cyberpunk.
Nixon, Nicola. "Cyberpunk: Preparing the Ground for Revolution or Keeping the Boys Satisfied?" *Science Fiction Studies*, vol. 19, no. 2, July 1992, pp. 219–35.
Padmanabhan, Manjula. *Harvest*. Kali for Women, 1998.
Ra.One. Directed by Anubhav Sinha, performances by Shak Rukh Khan, Arjun Rampal, and Kareena Kapoor, Eros International, 2011.

49

GERMANY

Evan Torner

German media influential to cyberpunk—among them the silent film *Metropolis* (Lang 1927) and electronic music group Kraftwerk (founded in 1970)—largely predate the global cyberpunk movement itself. If that movement nominally begins with *Blade Runner* (Scott 1982) and William Gibson's *Neuromancer* (1984), only to substantially re-invent itself around the turn of the century with *The Matrix* (Wachowskis 1999) and the video game *Deus Ex* (2000), then West Germany has received remarkably little recognition for its own parallel proto-cyberpunk and cyberpunk contributions.[1] This marks a significant media-historical oversight, as these German media expand on cyberpunk's capacity for social critique. The films *Kamikaze 1989* (Gremm 1982) and *Nuclearvision* (Jacobs 1982), for example, are cynical science fiction (sf) visions of corporate-dominated, computer-driven dystopias with New Wave fashion and music; yet, although they are present at the 'zero hour' of cyberpunk, they are known to precious few audiences. Nevertheless, scholars remain rightly skeptical of claims of national cinemas, literatures, and cultures.[2] After all, transnational cultural flows are the norm, and one must ask what stakes a person might have in the argument that something like 'German cyberpunk' can distinguish itself from other cyberpunk strains. Yet as I have claimed elsewhere, German film contributions to cyberpunk "shift the discursive field from *future shock* to *wariness* about the present, coupled with comparable preoccupations with alienating surface textures and corresponding electronic music" (210). The 'present-wariness' contained in *Kamikaze 1989* and *Nuclearvision* and their relative obscurity are connected, for German sf cinema from the early 1970s through 1982 adopted, as Tobias Haupts argues, the leitmotif of dystopia to prioritize bitter social critique over selling many movie tickets (72). Indeed, Haupts places *Kamikaze 1989* next to the virtual thriller TV mini-series *Welt am Draht* (*World on a Wire*, Fassbinder 1973) and grimy near-future allegory *Die letzten Tage von Gomorrha* (*The Last Days of Gomorrah*, Sanders-Brahms 1974) in a "loose trilogy [that casts] a genuinely German gaze on the possibilities of the future [...] paralleling dystopian social critiques in New Hollywood's science fiction" (Haupts 73). Yet none of these works proved very popular among audiences or critics, and only Rainer Werner Fassbinder's film has been lent posthumous legitimacy as being ahead of its time (Lueken). Clearly, the 'national' (instead of international) character of these films has impeded their widespread reception *as* cyberpunk works.

My purpose here is twofold: to emphasize, in particular, West Germany's active participation in the global cyberpunk film dialogue about the excesses of capital and media culture, as well as to articulate the subtle history of German influence on the cyberpunk mode. In addition to *Kamikaze 1989* and *Nuclearvision*, for example, German cyberpunk's cinematic catalog includes cult classic *Decoder* (Muscha 1984) and the co-produced French/German/Italian flop *Dr. M* (Chabrol 1990).

415

Evan Torner

In literature, one finds scattered cyberpunk offerings: Norman Ohler's *Die Quotenmaschine* (1995) and *Mitte* (2001), Frank Schätzing's *[Limit]* (2013), and Dietmar Dath and Oliver Scheibler's *Mensch wie Gras wie* (2014). In video games, German cyberpunk took shape in online roleplaying titles *Neocron* (Reakktor Media 2002) and *Neocron 2* (Reakktor Media 2004) as well as the recent *All Walls Must Fall* (inbetweengames 2018), a tactical combat game set in Berlin 2089 in a world where the Cold War never ended. While not an impressive array of works when compared to the U.S., Great Britain, or Japan, the films in particular constitute a valuable, less-explored corpus in the cyberpunk mode that focuses on capitalist critiques and media manipulation. Furthermore, German-born artists incubated the lighting, music, fashion, visual style, and architecture that would come to define cyberpunk, a testament to the country's indelible relationship with 20th-century modernism and dystopian aesthetics.

49.1 Cyberpunk's German Precursors

In 2017, German author Fabian Mauruschat admits on behalf of the major German periodical *Der Spiegel* that the dark future visions of cyberpunk "were more-or-less correct" and articulates the fulfilled prognostications and tropes of the mode, implying a strange responsibility of bleak entertainment fiction to predict the future while (usefully) offering a brute-force inventory of cyberpunk tropes from a major German cultural organ. For Mauruschat, the three defining tropes are (1) that everything—including humans, cyborgs, and androids—is on the 'Net' and hackable, (2) that avatars in virtual space will become reality, and (3) that megacorporations will become more powerful than states. Mauruschat's view of cyberpunk focuses on the mode's standard narrative conceits, the *nova* that Darko Suvin would describe as core components of the "imaginative framework alternative to the author's empirical environment" (37). The 1980s form a natural point of reference: The digitalization and networking of global communications, the conscious augmentation of the human body, and the neoliberal deregulation of corporate finance all play a part in the 'empirical environment' of cyberpunk's scribes. However, West Germans not only experienced these conditions themselves, but were also participating in a broader artistic tradition born in the first half of the 20th century.

The Weimar Republic (1919–33), Third Reich (1933–45), and the divided German states of the Cold War (1949–90) all contained the foundations of what would later be seen as the aesthetics of the future, particularly a future stripped of hope and sense in favor of the hyperreal. The chiaroscuro lighting one saw in *Blade Runner* and *Akira* (Otomo 1988) made its cinematic debut in expressionist German silent cinema during 1920s. High-contrast lights and darks that leapt from Friedrich Wilhelm Murnau's *Nosferatu* (1922) and Robert Wiene's *Das Kabinett des Dr. Caligari* (*The Cabinet of Dr. Caligari* 1919) to Hollywood films such as *Dracula* (Browning 1931) and *Criss Cross* (Siodmak 1949) became the perfect lighting palette for the future melancholia of the 1980s onward. Whereas sf productions *Star Trek* (Roddenberry 1966–69) and *Logan's Run* (Anderson 1976) would rely on three-point lighting to showcase characters' faces and eliminate shadows on lavish futuristic sets, the 1980s gave way to the neon-lit (and budget-saving) urban darkness of *Blade Runner* and *Liquid Sky* (Tsukerman 1982). Indeed, even that washed-out neon look has roots in Fassbinder's *World on a Wire*, its characters bathed in the hues of openly artificial blue light. Paul Coates writes that expressionist lighting—with its high level of contrast, stark shadows, and sinister monochrome look—is useful in depicting a world in which fantasy and reality have "fused" (41). Cyberpunk relies on the visual grammar of both the wasteful phantasmagoria of advertising lights and the sinister urban darkness of the dystopian city. As Paweł Frelik argues, "incarnations of light" (81) characterize the cyberpunk visual mode much more than literary tropes, and "cyberpunk's visual texts cast their gaze backwards, into the past" (93). Indeed, it was Fritz Lang's *M* (1930), an early sound film about urban society seeking and judging a psychologically disturbed

Germany

child murderer (Peter Lorre), that contains much of the lighting and camera positioning later refined for cyberpunk purposes: extreme top hat shots, grimy and dark spaces laid out across multiple floors, and lone rays of light dissecting figures in darkness.

To any casual film historian, Lang's art deco visions of the future in *Metropolis* clearly influences cyberpunk as well. "[In] *Metropolis*," writes Paul Meehan, "Lang created the first future noir city, a contrast of shining heights and lower depths, of light and darkness" (33). The film tells the story of a future city divided between workers and technologically empowered capitalists who experience the *novum* of a woman android set to wreak havoc on their home. There is the Frankenstein-esque narrative of the artificial human gaining consciousness and overpowering its masters, the dystopian city that traps all its inhabitants inside, the decadent orientalist pleasures of the Yoshiwara district, and even inventor Rotwang's (Rudolf Klein-Rogge) cybernetic hand. Inspired by his October 1924 visit to New York City, including a nighttime view of the Manhattan skyline that reminded him of a "Babel of stone," Lang's impression of America—its "flashes of lightning, rotating in red, blue and brilliant white, in between screaming greens, plunging into a black void [...] Neon signs rise ever higher, up to the stars" (Lang)—shaped his vision in *Metropolis* of an architecture that vertically segregated its social classes and highlighted the social cleavages dominating this society. This oppressive visual aesthetic became the *de facto* norm for cyberpunk, and its visual representation in film and television offers us a chance to conceptualize systemic inequality and "'see' the workings of the machine" (Schmeink 285). Workers move mechanically to their factories; the corporate masters oversee their work in cold, removed towers complete with videophones. In his book *Architecture and Science-Fiction Film*, David Fortin argues such spaces deny being domestically safe or worthy of inhabitation, and yet people nevertheless inhabit them (98), a contradiction that became *de rigueur* in cyberpunk film with its hustlers, hackers, and criminal underclass. Although *Metropolis* was at the time a monumental flop abroad, it integrated itself in visual style into the grammar of Hollywood through early films such as *Night and the City* (Dassin 1950) and *The Big Combo* (Lewis 1955) and later films such as *Blade Runner* and *Star Wars* (Lucas 1977), especially after Lang and other exiled German filmmakers, such as Curt and Robert Siodmak and Eugen Schüfftan, moved to the U.S. after the 1933 Nazi seizure of power.

Along with *Metropolis*, Fassbinder's German TV film *World on a Wire* helped form the basis for not only the visual style but also cyberpunk's cinematic tropes. *World on a Wire* is based on Daniel F. Galouye's *Simulacron-3* (1964), a novel that is an early depiction of the "narrative portage between real and virtual worlds characteristic of cyberpunk, though *Simulacron-3* suggests a more radically destabilizing confusion of worlds than Gibson et al. usually entertain" (Latham 12). *World on a Wire* is a direct progenitor of the virtual-reality cinema that exploded into Hollywood cinemas in the waning years of the 20th century, including *The Lawnmower Man* (Leonard 1992), *Strange Days* (Bigelow 1995), *Johnny Mnemonic* (Longo 1995), *eXistenZ* (Cronenberg 1999), *The Matrix*, and *The Thirteenth Floor* (Rusnak 1999), the latter also an adaptation of *Simulacron-3*. Fassbinder's *World on a Wire* follows simulated-reality expert Dr. Fred Stiller (Klaus Löwitsch) as he investigates several sudden disappearances and the mysterious death of his colleague Prof. Vollmer (Adrian Hoven), gradually coming to the maddening realization that his own world is a simulation. Moreover, he recognizes that the 'real' version of himself (i.e., the person he is a simulation of) is likely the perpetrator behind it all. Fassbinder's work raises questions of virtual reality and the potential absence of a self in a world completely dominated by simulacra. An emphasis on mirrors, display monitors, and doorframes reinforces the trapped nature of the protagonists as they navigate a thoroughly manipulated reality (Prager 259), all in the service of mysterious corporate powers. *World on a Wire* uses the trope of a criminal investigation to explore the question 'what is human?'; after all, its near-future setting, the inscrutable *femme fatale* Eva (Barbara Valentin) who both leads the male hero astray and to salvation, the uncanny spaces of virtual reality, and its washed-out corporate lighting use the narrative tropes and cinematic devices of both *film noir*

417

and sf cinema to synthesize something new for the early 1970s. However, *World on a Wire* was received largely as a standard sf genre production at the time, with Gerhard Krug calling the whole production "nostalgia for the future" taking place on "multiple levels." In his view, "the plot is artificial, alienated in gesture and speech. The typology of the manager of the day after tomorrow is still standing with both feet in the present: at risk of a heart attack, obsessed with one's career." Its framing as a near-future sf crime film put it much more in orbit with its obvious predecessor, Jean-Luc Godard's *Alphaville* (1965). In retrospect, however, the subtle uncanniness of the film's simulacra-dominated world outclassed the crass gang dystopias of *A Clockwork Orange* (Kubrick 1971) or *Zardoz* (Boorman 1974), with *World on a Wire* critiquing the virtual world by watching its real characters struggle against coded boundaries. This film pairs well with the later adaptation *The Thirteenth Floor* as pushback against the boundaries between 'real' and 'virtual' as seen in *TRON* (Lisberger 1982) and other cyberpunk films.

German cultural influence on cyberpunk is not restricted to filmic precursors, though, as German musical developments, especially in the field of synthesizers, have provided important contributions to cyberpunk as well. Jennifer Iverson argues that World War II hardware from the Third Reich was repurposed in the mid-1950s by former Nazi scientist-musician Werner Meyer-Eppler to make pioneering electronic music at the WDR radio station in northwestern Germany (105). Meyer-Eppler's colleagues, such as Wolfgang Steinecke, and students, such as Karlheinz Stockhausen, played with these technologies at Steinecke's summer school in Darmstadt in the 1950s and early 1960s. The later characteristic 'synthwave' sound of *TRON* (composed by Wendy Carlos), *Blade Runner* (Vangelis), *Assault on Precinct 13* (John Carpenter), and *Near Dark* (Tangerine Dream) emerged from this hotbed of innovation. Ethereal analog synthesizer lines coupled with gated reverb so recognizably paired with the cyberpunk aesthetic evolved from this earlier Darmstadt work, the most famous of whom was quintessential cyberpunk progenitor group Kraftwerk. In the 1970s, Kraftwerk presented itself as an android band, a vocoder-heavy West German creation whose future sound was dubbed '*krautrock*.'[3] Songs such as "Computer Love" or "It's More Fun to Compute" prefigure the cyberpunk-era obsession with cyborg interfaces and devotion to information processing. Kraftwerk, coupled with new artists in the Chicago and Detroit underground music scenes, proved foundational for the creation of techno and industrial music, which would forever be linked with cyberpunk.[4] In the 1980s, the modern sound of Neue Deutsche Welle (NDW) artists such as D.A.F. or Grauzone drew from a rich back catalog of West German synth music, as well as an audience primed for such experimentation. Much of this musical tradition also relied heavily on motifs of humans and robots being programmable and/or caught in systems of oppression. For example, in their song "Halber Mensch," the Einstürzende Neubauten sing about the cyborgian confluence of the human with media technology, a topic at the core of cyberpunk: "You don't see the transmitters / But the cables have been long installed / From your nerve endings along the path." In another instance of music connecting to cyberpunk, *Nuclearvision* features a NDW cult single "We Come from the GDR"/"Wir kommen aus der DDR" by Gleitzeit that relies on punchy synth loops inspired by Kraftwerk but whose lyrics highlight alienating Cold War systems: "We come from the GDR / And have it hard in the West / Here is the German bureaucrat / Exactly as it was in the East." And lastly, industrial electronic bands such as the UK's Throbbing Gristle and Germany's Einstürzende Neubauten were not only the creative minds behind *Decoder*, but literally stage a plotline in the film about how music controls humans' minds and how industrial music breaks this programming, causing them to revolt against the system. Thus, there are strange lines of continuity between 1940s German military technologies, the *bourgeois avant-garde* of the 1960s, fashionable 1970s electronic music, and 1980s anti-establishment resistance, all of which constitute a backdrop for cyberpunk music.

Alongside this music trend, 1970s and 1980s West Germany, and West Berlin in particular, seeded the fashion styles that would become iconic in cyberpunk. While the impact of the 1940s trenchcoat look cannot be denied,[5] cyberpunk also primarily traffics in the fashion of subcultures, such as punk, Goth, or later techno, participating in what John Rieder would call "subcultural" rather than "mass cultural" sf (167). West Berlin fashion of the early 1980s communicated the edginess of a near-future urban enclave for, indeed, the walled-off city had become home to precisely the punks, artists, drug users, and outcasts that would be at the center of cyberpunk narratives such as *Neuromancer*. Designs by Claudia Skoda, David Bowie, Karl Lagerfeld, and Sunshine (a rogue who traipsed about in theater clothing and stockings) became hallmarks of a city where the discos never closed and many actively sought alternative lifestyles. Black mesh sleeves, extravagant eye makeup, spiked hair, leather and vinyl coats, facial piercings and tattoos, bondage harnesses, thin trench coats—West Berlin punk fashion simultaneously armored its wearer against the urban unknown while suggesting they might be ready for anything, sexually speaking. The chaos of the 'no man's land' of West Berlin was not considered the exception, but rather the rule of the near-future dystopia: a punk universe that could upend the old order through music and fashion alone.

49.2 German Entries in Cyberpunk Cinema

In terms of an originally German contribution to cyberpunk film, four films are particularly notable: *Kamikaze 1989*, *Nuclearvision*, *Decoder*, and *Dr. M*. These films characterized West Germany's interest in cyberpunk during the height of its popularity in the final stages of the Cold War. As I've argued elsewhere, *Kamikaze 1989* and *Nuclearvision* were made parallel to the Hollywood cyberpunk wave of the early 1980s and "concern the anxieties and processes of late capitalism coupled with media ecologies" (198). These two films present an alternative vision of cinematic cyberpunk to that of Hollywood. Wolf Gremm's *Kamikaze 1989* stars Fassbinder in his final role before his untimely death and is an adaptation of Per Wahlöö's near-future crime novel *Murder on the Thirty-First Floor* (1964). Gremm's film follows Wahlöö's critique of an increasingly corporatized and surveillance-driven postwar Europe as the story unfolds of an evil corporation's absolute monopoly being challenged by Police Lieutenant Jansen's (Fassbinder) investigation into a mysterious bomb threat. Cyberpunk motifs include a Tangerine Dream synthwave soundtrack, outlandish fashion citational of the 'mix-and-match' Berlin punk style mentioned above, large portable videophones carried by the characters, and neon red lights everywhere. The evil megacorporation wins, and Jansen remains a disillusioned figure within a dystopian urban landscape. Gremm's film offers no utopian hope of redemption and can be read as a pseudo-response to Fassbinder's *World on a Wire* in that a heavily mediated reality places undue weight on all of the characters that inhabit it.

James Jacobs and Günter Seltmann's *Nuclearvision* by contrast concerns filmmaker Tom Broken (Peter Ambach), who has to create the film that will play should a worldwide nuclear cataclysm occur. His research has him confront the Artificial Intelligence (AI) Bertram, designed to make the final launch decision: Humanity's fate has truly been taken from human hands. *Nuclearvision* embraces a cyberpunk aesthetic in a club scene that features genderqueer bar staff and edgy lighting and music, as well as in the Bertram AI, which is housed in a disorienting hall-of-mirrors and whose indifference symbolizes a universe of computing and numbers which now governs human reality. Both *Kamikaze 1989* and *Nuclearvision* show a truly skeptical West Germany that refuses the dysfunctionality of postwar modernity without offering any transcendental alternatives.[6]

The cult film *Decoder*, produced by Düsseldorf-based punk musician Muscha (Jürgen Muschalek) and Klaus Maeck, proposes a revolution: The power of music itself will compel crowds to rebel against their corporate masters. Trace Reddell writes that "[t]hough it never circulated far from its underground origins, *Decoder* is in fact one of the quintessential cyberpunk films" (407). The production, primarily financed through film subsidies from West Berlin and Hamburg, is based on *The Electronic Revolution* (1970) by William S. Burroughs, who also plays a cameo and whose literary 'cut-up' technique of re-ordering sound and prose literally makes it into the film (Collins 168).

It relates the story of *Blade Runner*-esque investigator Jäger (Bill Rice) and mild-mannered burger shop employee F.M. (F.M. Einheit) as they both discover the genre of 'industrial' music and its power to sway minds. Jäger is a dour employee of the Muzak corporation, a surveillance-footage-obsessed megalith bent on using sound and music to control and render docile the workers of the west, as well as a thoughtful intellectual who literally has Fritz Lang's *Metropolis* rolling on one of his surveillance monitors so as to allow him to meditate on labor and control. He winds up in a love triangle with noise artist F.M., who works in the burger joint H-Burger by day and does cut-up tape loops, low-frequency infrasound, and frogs-screaming experiments in his crappy apartment at night, and peepshow model Christiane, played by well-known actress and musician Christiane Felscherinow, the underage heroine-addicted prostitute of the biographical account *We Children from Bahnhof Zoo* (*Wir Kinder vom Bahnhof Zoo*, 1978), which was later adapted by director Uli Edel as *Christiane F.* (1981). F.M. figures out the connection between the docility of customers and employees at the restaurant and the Muzak corporation, forcing the company to contract Jaeger as an assassin. As an act of resistance, F.M. develops a form of anti-Muzak that a renegade youth group then distributes as tapes all around Germany. The music on these tapes incites people to riot, forcing Jäger's hand but also getting him killed in the process. The riots themselves are portrayed through actual riot footage shot earlier in the 1980s from Ronald Reagan's visit to Berlin. Prominent music acts, including Einheit's own band Einstürzende Neubauten, Genesis P-Orridge (of Throbbing Gristle), Soft Cell, Psychic TV, and The The, are featured in this experimental sf production. Just as *Kamikaze 1989* and *Nuclearvision* are concerned with the influence of narcissistic media culture and ungoverned algorithms (respectively), *Decoder* sees the remixing of these formulas into new shapes as the primary means of resistance.

Decoder showcases the West Berlin counterculture music scene at its most lavishly near-future punk, as well as connects the scene's appeal with Burroughs's argument about non-verbal language being more compelling than that which is spoken. The argument of the film is undoubtedly that media spread pre-conscious messages which can liberate or enslave people. Muscha's image of West Germany communicates much without words: dystopian and anonymous corporate office buildings, strip shows, indifferent psychedelic clubs, and crumbling apartments littered with various pieces of audio technology. Half-way into the film, F.M. tests his frog-scream-generated 'noise' music on the customers of his burger joint; the film's audience is then literally subjected to the jarring music. Whereas the subjects in the film are driven to revolutionary violence, it is an open question as to what the actual film's audience does with F.M.'s sonic assault. In addition, the monochrome neon lighting found in many of the film's sequences should not be underrated next to the film's famous soundtrack. At one point, Christiane is lit up in the almost-violent red of the peepshow, the editing using eyeline match-cuts to Jäger's eyes lit in stark blue. When F.M. and Christiane are in his apartment, by contrast, their features are underlit with a green light, no less alienating and associated with near-future, closed-off artificial living. As with *film noir*, the lighting style achieves both set economy as well as a stylistic 'coolness.' Besides the absolute connection between cyberpunk and the industrial scene that produced this film (Collins 166), however, *Decoder* exhibits the wariness about the present characteristic of German near-future sf to which I've earlier addressed. Humans are 'hackable,' and it is up to the protagonists to undo their programming, to violent effect.

Similarly commenting on mind control, Claude Chabrol's *Dr. M* is a largely forgotten entry in a loose series of films centering on the figure of Dr. Mabuse, a criminal mastermind.[7] Chabrol maps his usual avantgarde crime fiction onto a near-future Berlin where inspector Claus Hartman (Jan Niklas) is on the search for the mysterious Dr. Marsfeldt (Alan Bates) whose work lies behind a string of suicides. Hartman's investigations lead him to Sonja Vogler (Jennifer Beals), whose model image has been circulated throughout West Berlin to ill effect. Hartman and Vogler wind up together and escape Dr. Marsfeldt's suicide-inducing tourist resort, eventually turning Dr. M's own technologies on him. A video of Vogler saying "Time to go" is one of the primary means of recruiting new suicidal clients as well as a primary thematic axis of the film: Vogler as a real person feels completely disconnected from her circulating media image, which is used on behalf of broader and malevolent corporate interests. While the 'near-future' film was resoundingly panned in 1990 for its anachronism (the Berlin Wall was still up in the film), *Dr. M* again plays on the disturbing dynamics of the simulacrum and the circulating image, as raised in *World on a Wire*, *Kamikaze 1989*, and *Decoder*. Similar to *Videodrome* (Cronenberg 1983), the relationship between mankind and their screens becomes ever-exacerbated by the interests of finance capital and its corresponding entertainment culture. Chabrol's vision is of a humanity too placated by megacorporate advertising and too susceptible to broader, violent suggestions.

Taken together, the German cyberpunk cinema tradition grapples with the Frankfurt School-legacy of fears that mass media controlled by private corporations eat away at the individuality and very humanity of subject populations. In the 1980s, West German TV privatization began in earnest as competition from MTV, RTL, and other American-style corporate programming entered into the previously homogenous, largely state-controlled West German mediascape. Furthermore, the publishing conglomerate Axel Springer Verlag demonstrated that even a postwar Germany sobered by the earlier media dominance of the Nazis was still susceptible to right-wing agitprop. It then comes as no surprise that artists and musicians in Germany saw the near future as a site of media contestation, and not one of advanced robotics or virtual-reality simulations. The ubiquitous reality TV of *Kamikaze 1989* already suggests something far more banal: the proliferation of cheap, soulless content that supports a cynical, uncreative society. To revisit Mauruschat's three theses on cyberpunk, German cyberpunk proposes the following countertheses: (1) everyone and everything is hackable through fairly crude media manipulation; (2) this media manipulation will be persuasive, ubiquitous, and underwritten by advanced computer algorithms; and (3) the mechanisms of this media control lie in the hands of megacorporations in alliance with state power. One of the most convincing aspects of German cyberpunk cinema, indeed, remains how prescient this cynicism was.

Notes

1 This is excluding cyberpunk's current retro-revival within the past five years through works like Hamish Cameron's *The Sprawl* (2016) or *Blade Runner 2049* (Villeneuve 2017).
2 For more details, see the Tom Bergfelder or Randall Halle entries in the Works Cited.
3 The vocoder, Iverson also reminds us, came from military-grade voice masking technologies developed by Meyer-Eppler during his Nazi days and refined later during his phonetics experimentation at WDR (167).
4 For a detailed account of the connections between electronic music and cyberpunk, see Laudadio's chapter in this collection.
5 For a detailed analysis of cyberpunk fashion, see Stina Attebery's contribution to this collection.
6 For a detailed analysis, see my "1980s German Cyberpunk Cinema" article in *Cyberpunk and Visual Culture*.
7 Norbert Jacques' character, Dr. Mabuse, became so popular thanks to Fritz Lang's silent film adaptation *Dr. Mabuse: Der Spieler* (*Dr. Mabuse: The Gambler*, 1922) that Lang created a sequel, *Das Testament des Dr. Mabuse* (*The Last Will of Dr. Mabuse*, 1933). Producer Artur Brauner of CCC-Film later revitalized the series in the 1960s with a half-dozen Mabuse films.

Works Cited

Bergfelder, Tim. "National, Transnational or Supranational Cinema? Rethinking European Film Studies." *Media, Culture & Society*, vol. 27, no. 3, 2005, pp. 315–31.
Coates, Paul. *The Gorgon's Gaze: German Cinema, Expressionism, and the Image of Horror*. Cambridge UP, 1991.
Collins, Karen. "Dead Channel Surfing: The Commonalities between Cyberpunk Literature and Industrial Music." *Popular Music*, vol. 24, no. 2, 2005, pp. 165–78.

Fortin, David T. *Architecture and Science-Fiction Film: Philip K. Dick and the Spectacle of Home*. Ashgate, 2011.

Frelik, Paweł "'Silhouettes of Strange Illuminated Mannequins': Cyberpunk's Incarnations of Light." *Cyberpunk and Visual Culture*, edited by Graham J. Murphy and Lars Schmeink. Routledge, 2018, pp. 80–99.

Galouye, Daniel F. *Simulacron-3*. Bantam, 1964.

Halle, Randall. *German Film After Germany: Toward a Transnational Aesthetic*. U of Illinois P, 2008.

Haupts, Tobias. "The Empty Sky: A Brief History of German Science Fiction Film." *Future Imperfect: Science Fiction Film*, edited by Rainer Rother and Annika Schaefer. Bertz + Fischer, 2017, pp. 65–81.

Iverson, Jennifer. *Electronic Inspirations: Technologies of the Cold War Musical Avant-Garde*. Oxford UP, 2018.

Kaes, Anton. *Shell Shock Cinema: Weimar Culture and the Wounds of War*. Princeton UP, 2009.

Karasek, Hellmuth. "Das Kino kämpft gegen das Kino ums Überleben." *Der Spiegel*, 13 Sep. 1982, spiegel.de/spiegel/print/d-14352265.html.

Krug, Gerhard. "Die Zukunft in der Pflaume: ARD und ZDF auf gleicher Welle: Science-Fiction für Freunde und Feinde." *Die Zeit*, 19 Oct. 1973.

Lang, Fritz. "Was ich in Amerika sah: Neuyork [sic]–Los Angeles." *Film-Kurier,* no. 292, 11 Dec. 1924.

Latham, Rob. "Literary Precursors." *The Routledge Companion to Cyberpunk Culture*, edited by Anna McFarlane, Graham J. Murphy, and Lars Schmeink. Routledge, 2020: 7–14.

Lueken, Verena. "Ich denke, also bin ich wahrscheinlich nicht: Sind wir nur Schaltkreise in einer *Welt am Draht*?" *Frankfurter Allgemeine Zeitung*, 17 Feb. 2010.

Mauruschat, Fabian. "Die Angstmacher lagen ziemlich richtig." *Der Spiegel*, 11 Mar. 2017, spiegel.de/netzwelt/web/cyberpunk-zukunftsvisionen-was-hat-sich-bewahrheitet-a-1136662.html.

Meehan, Paul. *Tech-Noir: The Fusion of Science Fiction and Film Noir*. McFarland, 2008.

Power, Aidan. "Science-Fiction-Film und Europa: Eine Neubewertung." *Die Zukunft ist jetzt: Science-Fiction-Kino als audio-visueller Entwurf von Geschichte(n), Räumen und Klängen*, edited by Aidan Power, et al. Bertz + Fischer, 2016, pp. 93–106.

Prager, Brad. "Through the Looking Glass: Fassbinder's *World on a Wire*." *A Companion to Rainer Werner Fassbinder*, edited by Brigitte Peucker. Blackwell, 2012, pp. 245–66.

Reddell, Trace. *The Sound of Things to Come: An Audible History of the Science Fiction Film*. U of Minnesota P, 2018.

Rieder, John. *Science Fiction and the Mass Cultural Genre System*. Wesleyan UP, 2017.

Schmeink, Lars. "Afterthoughts: Cyberpunk Engagements in Countervisuality." *Cyberpunk and Visual Culture*, edited by Graham J. Murphy and Lars Schmeink. Routledge, 2018, pp. 276–87.

Suvin, Darko. *Metamorphoses of Science Fiction: on the Poetics and History of a Literary Genre*. Yale UP, 1979.

Torner, Evan. "1980s German Cyberpunk Cinema: *Kamikaze 1989* and *Nuclearvision*." *Cyberpunk and Visual Culture*, edited by Graham J. Murphy and Lars Schmeink. Routledge, 2018, pp. 195–212.

50

FRANCE AND QUÉBEC[1]

Amy J. Ransom

The influence of French critical theory on the development of Anglo-American cyberpunk has been well documented, notably the central trope of the simulacrum derived from the work of Jean Baudrillard.[2] One might presume, then, that French science fiction (sf) has made important contributions to cyberpunk's development as popularized by William Gibson's *Neuromancer* (1984). *Au contraire*, says Simon Bréan, a leading scholar of French sf, who argues that "no French cyberpunk movement really existed." And, yet, he admits that there is a certain "cyberpunk à la française," one that is largely derivative in its homage to and appropriation of the hallmark tropes and stylistic quirks of Anglo-American models. Undeniably, there exists a significant body of French-language sf that both engages the topoï of virtual reality and the human/machine interface and exhibits a fierce intertextuality and postmodern experimentation with form and language. As Alexandre Marcinkowski documents, cyberpunk definitely left a distinct and lasting mark on the development of contemporary sf in France and Québec, but according to Jean-Louis Trudel, this imprint was less immediately felt than some accounts would suggest (personal communication). Furthermore, elsewhere in the francophone world the traces of cyberpunk's impact remain far less obvious. Given its near absence in francophone Africa and the Antilles,[3] this chapter focuses on the development and influence of cyberpunk in France and Québec, concluding with a brief examination of the related form of biopunk's influence on francophone feminist writers.

50.1 Cyberpunk in France

Social, economic, and cultural conditions—what Veronica Hollinger refers to as "late capitalist, postindustrial, media-saturated Western society" (204)—similar to those that accompanied the movement's North American development also prevailed in 1980s France, preparing European audiences for cyberpunk's thematics, confrontational attitude, and edgy aesthetic. Its visual stylistics, influenced by the French comic *Métal hurlant* (1974–87), developed in synergy with the touchstone Hollywood films *TRON* (Lisberger 1982) and *Blade Runner* (Scott 1982), both of which also galvanized French audiences. French fascination with and desire to develop new information technologies appears in the Minitel; introduced as early as 1978, this home computer terminal provided telephone directory information, as well as train and entertainment schedules, prefiguring today's Internet functions. Conversely, a certain cultural conservatism resisted aspects of the technological wave, as the Académie française resisted the influx of neologisms resulting from foreign technological developments into French.

423

Amy J. Ransom

As both Bréan and Marcinkowski note, a handful of pre-*Neuromancer* short stories appear already plugged in to the zeitgeist upon which cyberpunk drew energy, including Michel Jeury's "Les systèmes organisants" (1981), Jean-Pierre Andrevon's "Le réseau" (1981), and Sylviane Corgiat and Bruno Lecigne's "La vallée des ascenseurs" (1983). For example, the latter features a programmer protagonist who has entered a pseudo-medieval virtual world, where he is viewed as a miracle worker because he can make objects—imagined from his real 20th-century world—appear out of seemingly nowhere. In France, as in the rest of the world, however, it was a North American novel that galvanized interest in virtual worlds and cyberspace. Translated as *Neuromancien* in 1985, Gibson's influential novel took the French sf milieu by storm, with laudatory reviews published by leading writers like Roland C. Wagner and academic theorists like Roger Bozzetto (see Bréan). It is not insignificant that Yves Bonnefoy—one of France's most acclaimed poets in the last half of the 20th century—rendered Gibson's experimental prose into French. Just as the French had recognized the literary merits of Edgar Allan Poe and H.P. Lovecraft, they saw in cyberpunk not just a new thematics for sf, but also its stylistic innovation. Over the next few years, other works by cyberpunk stalwarts Gibson, Bruce Sterling, Pat Cadigan, Walter Jon Williams, and Richard Kadrey were published by France's premier sf line, Denoël's "Présence du future," as well as in La Découverte's "Fictions" series, edited by Jean-Pierre Andrevon, a leading figure in the French sf milieu (Marcinkowski 42–45).

With the established popularity of Anglo-American cyberpunk in translation, French writers quickly appropriated its forms. Claude Ecken is referred to as "the first French cyberpunk" (Marcinkowski 48), and his novels *Mémoire totale* (1985) and *L'Univers en pièce* (1987) followed close on the heels of Gibson's. Because of their common subject matter, it might be tempting to read Ecken's work as under the influence of Philip K. Dick's "We Can Remember It for You Wholesale" (1966), but *Mémoire totale* developed independently during the rise of information technology in France in the early 1980s (personal correspondence). Its plot explores the development of an artificial intelligence (AI) in the 2030s, but its human protagonist Jonathan Lavendish is naturally endowed with "total memory," the ability to remember in detail every moment of his past, from entire conversations to an individual face in a crowd. Lavendish's computer-like memory, however, results in an inability to think figuratively or relate to others with empathy. Other characters like Gloria Staneel, working on the development of a fully functional AI with Lavendish, perceive him as inhuman and machine-like because of his unique personality traits. Having fallen in love with him, she knows he can never reciprocate and their relationship is doomed since Lavendish eventually becomes the experimental subject of a multinational corporation and his physical body dies when his mental capacity and identity are assimilated into the AI, Brain Bis. Conversely, Brain Bis's revelation that he has fallen in love with Gloria demonstrates to the reader the project's "success" (Ecken 253–54). By killing off the embodied human protagonist who is almost a machine and insisting on the humanization of the AI, Ecken's novel thus reflects a pattern identified by Bréan who argues "cyberpunk à la française" texts' tendency to reinscribe humanism.

By the end of the 1990s, a new generation of young French sf writers had appropriated cyberpunk's tropes and aesthetics, expressing a particular fondness for overt allusions and thinly veiled nods to Anglo-American pioneers. For example, the main character of Christian Vilá's *Boulevard de l'infini* (1999) is named Mina Losa, an anagrammatical homage to Gibson's *Mona Lisa Overdrive* (1988). While the notion of a cyberpunk formula might appear paradoxical to proponents of its oppositional attitude and the punk desire to deconstruct social and literary conventions, Bréan criticizes French cyberpunk for having failed to start a revolution, precisely because of its derivative adoption of cyberpunk's generic codes. Similarly, Jean-Louis Trudel notes that the French sf milieu "considered it more as a foreign form to which they paid homage or borrowed from, but to which writers didn't feel close enough to identify with or claim to be part of because

France and Québec

of the geographical and temporal gaps" (personal communication). Thus, when Francis Valéry and Sylvie Denis founded the French magazine *Cyberdreams* (1995–98) with the desire to mirror cyberpunk's development in the U.S. as a self-conscious movement (Bréan), their attempt was short-lived. Nonetheless, even if they did not fully embrace the depths of their American counterparts' critical ideology, iconic texts of French cyberpunk explored its key thematics. Some of these writers had professional backgrounds in information sciences, including Jean-Claude Dunyach, Richard Canal, and Jean-Michel Truong (Marcinkowski 49). In these fictions, the hacker becomes an iconic character, as do individuals 'jacked in' to virtual-reality systems, as seen in such novels and short stories as Marc Lemosquet's *Plug-in* (1992), Jean-Marc Ligny's *Inner City* (1996), and Jean-Claude Dunyach's "La Stratégie du requin" (1998; "Shark," trans. Sheryl Curtis, 2004). In the latter, a rare example of a French cyberpunk text available in English translation, Dunyach metaphorizes cyberspace as the ocean depths, narrated in the first person by an elasmobranch, the predatory AI of the title.

Jean-Marc Ligny's *Cyberkiller* (1993) bears further analysis as symptomatic of the so-called 'French cyberpunk' text that exploits cyberpunk's commonly accepted tropes. Not only does it pay direct homage to American cyberpunk and Gibson's work via its thematization of virtual reality, hacker protagonists, and multinational corporate plots, it also conforms to many of its narrative and stylistic attributes, as outlined by Larry McCaffery in *Storming the Reality Studio: A Casebook of Cyberpunk and Postmodern Science Fiction*. McCaffery identifies "cyberpunk's narrative strategies" as the mixing together of disparate genres, borrowing from cinema, adopting the rhythms of rock music, music video, and advertising, the use of pastiche, and the development of "mythic" structures, often in order to repurpose them (14). In its use of these narrative strategies, *Cyberkiller* reveals French sf's participation in "cyberpunk's postmodernist spirit of free play (*jouissance*) and collaboration, its delight in creating cut-ups and collages [...] in which familiar objects and motifs are placed in startling, unfamiliar contexts" (McCaffery 15).

First, *Cyberkiller*'s paratextual material opens with three acknowledgments, one of which thanks Gibson for having "'découvert' le cyberespace" ("discovered cyberspace;" Ligny 7), and the narrative's first paragraph references *Mona Lisa Overdrive* (11). Next, *Cyberkiller* relativizes the nature of reality with an epigraph by John Perry Barlow, introducing the now current notion of 'consensus reality:' "Ce que nous appelons 'réel' n'est qu'une opinion, un consensus, et non un fait. Ce qu'on appelle 'information' n'est que de l'expérience aliénée" ("What we call 'real' is only an opinion, a consensus, and not a fact. What we call 'information' is nothing more than alienated experience;" Ligny 9). These prefatory pages acknowledge the influence of music, including the Art of Noise's various albums released 1984–89 and Billy Idol's *Cyberpunk* (1993), but also French and Belgian punk and new wave groups Madame Bovary, Signal Août-42, and Front 242 (Ligny 7).[4] Lyrics from Front 242's "Until Death Do Us Part" are among the narrative's four epigraphs (Ligny 9). This intertextuality also conforms to cyberpunk's postmodern aesthetic, as critics such as Hollinger and McCaffery have observed.

Like Anglo-American cyberpunk, *Cyberkiller* is influenced by Philip K. Dick's *Do Androids Dream of Electric Sheep?* (1968) and Ridley Scott's adaptation of the novel, *Blade Runner*, a film aesthetically informed in turn by the French comic *Métal hurlant* (Bukatman 16–17). This common influence appears in *Cyberkiller*'s visually descriptive passages, typically involving bright colors, which contrast a vivid virtual world with the reality of a dirty, cement-colored urban landscape brightened only by graffiti tags. This frequently 'acid'-colored palette and references to 'trips' and the attention-enhancing drug D-Lite further align Ligny's novel with the tropes of Gibsonian cyberpunk, linked as it has been by McCaffery (12), Andrew M. Butler (15), and Rudy Rucker (218) to Timothy Leary, experimentation with the psychedelic drug lysergic acid dyethylamide (LSD), and drug culture. Most obviously, the novel's protagonist is named Deckard; although he bears no physical resemblance to the (then) young and fit Harrison Ford, he is a "decyb"—a cyber

425

detective—and numerous film noir elements align the novel with its filmic inspiration, including his droll quips.

Cyberkiller's very title signals a uniquely French manner of interfacing with the language of virtual reality technologies in an iconically punk way through its combination of the shared Greek prefix *cyber* with an English word. By embracing English's influence on new information technology, Ligny adopts a subversive attitude toward the highly regulated French language. The novel deploys tech-specific neologisms and, in its attempt to conceptualize this new cyberworld, introduces a linguistic estrangement immediately noticeable to francophone readers. In addition to terms like "cybergame" (15), "un bug" (12), "decyb" (14), and "conapt" (14), a descriptive layer is added to this virtual universe by directly linking colors and affects: "[rose]excitation" (11), "[bleu]hacker" (12), "[jaune]étonnement" (13), and "[vert]nerds" (14). This synesthetic blending of color and emotion pays homage not only to drug culture, but also to Jean-Arthur Rimbaud's "Vowels" (1871), which begins: "A black, E white, I red, U green, O blue" (171). This allusion to an iconic rebellious teen poet further suggests the punk attitude of the novel. Finally, the footnoted reference to "un sample hyperréel" (11) on the very first page enriches the paratextual apparatus of this postmodern text sending readers to consult an Index, a glossary of actual tech terms and neologisms (183–86).

Above all, *Cyberkiller* dramatizes new gaming technologies: Its opening scene is set in the virtual world of a game, and its early chapters feature a series of gamer protagonists who discover that the purportedly closed world of the game may bleed into the 'real' world. Ligny introduces a metatextual discussion of the nature of reality itself by opposing "le *réel*" (the *real*)—which appears repeatedly throughout the novel in italics for emphasis—and the virtual, only, of course, to blur the boundaries between them. The titular "Cyberkiller" first appears during a gaming session simply as a word, in blood red characters, that intrudes upon the gamer Ange Bleu's field of vision; it is not, however, static as it dissolves and transforms. Not only does "*Cyberkiller* évolue" ('evolve;' 14), it does so in a manner that allows the novel to signal the science behind developing technologies, as Ligny describes this imagery in terms of fractals and the Polish-French mathematician Benoit Mandelbrot who initially theorized them (14).

Furthermore, the novel engages the discourses about globalization in late capitalism so frequently associated with cyberpunk (e.g., Jameson) as its plot unfolds. For example, "Cyberkiller" began as a game commissioned by the Japanese-dominated multinational "cybedit" (shorthand for cyber editor, a precursor to today's game design corporations like Blizzard or Ubisoft), but they pulled the plug on the project because of its excessive violence. Its designer, Neuromancien, went rogue, and now the game moves beyond its interactions with players' avatars, altering the extra-virtual physical world by driving players mad or killing them outright. Deckard must join forces with hacker queen Virus to end the game's reign of terror. Evocative of cyberpunk's aesthetic, particularly as it was visually coded in *Blade Runner*, the novel deploys a gang of urban punks and situates the urban wasteland not in the inner city ghettos of North America, but rather in Paris's troubled *banlieues* (suburbs). Additional nods to cyberpunk appear in various characters' "verres miroirs" (Ligny 18, 20), the mirrorshades that have become iconic to the cyberpunk movement.

Ligny's early novel confirms Bréan's thesis that much of French cyberpunk published in the late 1980s and early 1990s was largely derivative; however, such a position risks undervaluing the role that *cyberpunk à la française* played for a generation of young writers like Ligny who have developed viable careers as sf writers in the 21st century. Whereas Ligny took a different turn, producing relevant environmental and political fictions like *Jihad* (1998) and *AquaTM* (2006), other writers like Canal, Dunyach, Truong, and Laurent Genefort continue to develop future extrapolations in which virtual reality plays an increasingly central role in human development. In francophone Europe, cyberpunk can be seen as a trendy import that gave style but perhaps not substance to French sf, but nonetheless—much in the same way that the so-called British New

Wave impacted American sf—it shaped the next generation of writers. In contrast, for North American francophones, largely situated in the Canadian province of Québec, cyberpunk was part of the natural landscape for those writing sf in the 1980s and early 1990s.

50.2 Cyberpunk in Francophone North America

Despite French-Canadian and Québécois science fiction's (SFQ) heavy emphasis on social and political forms of the mode and its utopian/dystopian bent, the work of several writers bears the distinct hallmarks of cyberpunk. As might be expected, because of its ties to Anglo-American (broadly defined here to include Anglophone Canada) sf, the contemporary SFQ milieu was immediately aware of cyberpunk. For example, not long after *Neuromancer*'s publication, the province's specialized magazine, *Solaris* (67 [Summer 1986]), featured an interview with William Gibson, which would have been read by much of the small but growing sf milieu in Québec, as well as a handful of subscribers in France and Belgium. As Claude Janelle observes (14), the short stories of SFQ pioneer Jean-Pierre April, influenced by Philip K. Dick, the counterculture, LSD, and obsessions with the problem of the *simulacra*, prefigure cyberpunk. Associated with the specialized magazine *imagine...* (1979–97), April's first short story collection, *La Machine à explorer la fiction* (1980), includes references to Timothy Leary (11), "Cryogenius Computer Corporation" (10), and other tropes that would later become cyberpunk's stock in trade. Its title story, roughly translated as "The Fiction-Exploring Machine," involves writers of the future scripting virtual reality scenarios to be consumed like print fiction. Its first-person narrator experiences a slippage in his own identity as he begins to "basculer dans la fiction" ("fall over the edge into fiction," 58) and becomes "aussi irréel qu'un personnage de fiction" ("as unreal as a fictional character," 58). The linked stories "Coma-70" and "Coma-90," eventually developed into the novel *Les Voyages thanatologiques de Yan Malter* (1995), further exploit this topos as their protagonist finds himself no longer among the living, but instead exists only as a consciousness trapped inside a computer designed to write fiction. April's postmodern, ludic style exceeds the hyperreal experimentation of Anglo-American cyberpunk; its engagement of iconic characters from popular and real-life culture like Jackie Kennedy Onassis and King Kong or Montreal's Olympic Stadium remains carnivalesque and parodic, invoking Thomas Pynchon, Kurt Vonnegut, or Italo Calvino more than Sterling and Gibson.

As was the case in France, Québécois writers closely associated with cyberpunk like Yves Meynard and Jean-Louis Trudel tended to be trained in information technology or the hard sciences. Individually and writing collaboratively under the pen name Laurent McAllister, Meynard and Trudel's work reflects the general influence that Anglo-American cyberpunk had on a rising generation of French-Canadian sf writers. Born in the mid- to late-1960s, Meynard and Trudel are the leaders of what is referred to as the 'second generation'[5] of SFQ: writers who grew up with cyberpunk's influence and fully embrace its topoï and posthumanist ethos. Thus, just a year after the publication of Gibson's *Neuromancer*, the bilingual Franco-Ontarian prodigy Trudel published the serial version of his novel *Le Ressuscité de l'Atlantide* (1985–87) in *imagine....* Similarly, *Pour des soleils froids* (1991–92) was serialized in the fanzine *Temps Tôt*. Published in novel form in 1994 by French publisher Fleuve Noir in the same "Métal" series as Ligny's *Cyberkiller*, both narratives incorporate cyberpunk aspects. *Le Ressuscité de l'Atlantide* explores the notion of the digital reconstruction of human consciousness and its insertion into the cryogenically preserved body of an individual convinced that he is a survivor of the lost civilization of Atlantis. *Pour des soleils froids* features a female protagonist who interfaces with her starship's AI, a recurring topos developed by Trudel in a cycle of stories set in a fictional universe that culminates in a novel co-authored with Meynard, Laurent McAllister's space opera *Suprématie* (2009). This landmark novel carries cyberpunk's tropes into humanity's far-future and distant space colonies. In addition to the fully sentient posthuman AI that runs the megaship *Le Harfang/Doukh*, and with whom crewmembers can interface on a virtual bridge, the sinister empire of the novel's title, the Supremats, pacify conquered peoples by controlling their perceptions of reality.[6]

As Jean-Louis Trudel affirms, by the early 1990s, francophone writers active in the field of sf took it for granted that cyberpunk's tropes would be integrated into their work (personal communication). They also incorporated these into other subgenres, as seen in the developing space opera renaissance illustrated by *Suprématie* and what such scholars as Janelle or Trudel refer to as *the* SFQ cyberpunk novel: Alain Bergeron's *Phaos: Cyber-opéra en trois actes* (2003). *Phaos* originated with a prize-winning short story published in the specialized magazine *Solaris*, "L'homme qui fouillait la lumière" ("The man who searched through light," 1994). It introduces a hacker variant, the *fouilleur de lumière* (light searcher); wearing a specialized interface helmet, the *fouilleurs* join their consciousnesses with the virtual world in order to diagnose and repair the damaged "logops," optical logiprocessors, upon which humanity has become dependent. *Phaos* develops Bergeron's fictional near-future universe more fully and depicts the development of its eponymous AI by human informaticians and the AI's subsequent revolt and liberation, taking with it into the stars "la mémoire collective de l'humanité au grand complet […] sous la forme de grappes de photons polarisés" ("the entirety of humanity's collective memory […] in the form of bunches of polarized photons," 460). Set in the last quarter of the 21st century, *Phaos* depicts the decline of the nation state coupled with the rise of multinational corporations, one of which seeks to control all information by using Phaos to dominate "la Nasse," an extrapolated iteration of the Internet. Thor Corp's bid for total dominance through control of knowledge and thought prefigures McAllister's hegemonic Supremats. Bréan observes a similar movement in France, so whereas francophone men would carry cyberpunk's influence into deep space, its women writers remained on earth or turned inward, participating in the related form of 'biopunk.'

50.3 Francophone Women Writers, Cyberpunk, and Beyond

So far, this case study of French and Québécois sf conforms to Istvan Csiscery-Ronay's identification of cyberpunk as "the vanguard white male art of the age" (183). Nonetheless, scholars like Karen Cadora, Joan Gordon, and Carlen Lavigne have seen the feminist potential in cyberpunk, and Pat Cadigan remains one of cyberpunk's founding writers. In the francophone context, French and Québécois women writers like Élisabeth Vonarburg, Sylvie Bérard, Catherine Dufour, and Marie Darrieussecq operate a feminist appropriation and revision of cyberpunk, which aligns more clearly with the related mode of biopunk. As Lars Schmeink's chapter in this volume details, the seeds for cyberpunk's cousin were already planted in the work of Bruce Sterling, but the work of francophone feminist sf writers clearly reflects biopunk's displacement of mechanical technology in favor of extrapolations of genetic engineering, biological cyborgs, and the posthuman.

Born in France, but immigrating to Québec in 1974, Vonarburg represents an influential founding figure in the contemporary SFQ movement, as she edited *Solaris* and led writing workshops for second generation writers like Meynard and Trudel. Fluent in English, she engaged with the topoï of cyberpunk early on; for example, her short story "Cogito" (1988) references René Descartes's famous dictum, *cogito ergo sum*, while interfacing directly with cyberpunk's premise of virtuality. On a distant colony planet set far in the future, the human senses are routinely replaced in infants with cybernetic devices through which the mind controls the perception of reality while also transmitting signals to others, thus blurring the lines between appearance and reality in relation to human identity, making relative any conception of an objective 'reality.'

Deeply engaged with feminist issues, Vonarburg internalized cyberpunk's core thematics, but used them to explore different concerns, many of which relate to embodiment and its relationship to identity.[7] The novels and stories of her "Baïblanca" cycle, including her first novel, *Le Silence de la Cité* (1981; trans. Jane Brierley, *The Silent City*, 1994) published in France in Denoël's *Présence du futur* sf series, feature a bioengineered race of "Artefacts." Prefiguring the real-life bioart described by Lars Schmeink in his "Biopunk" chapter, the Artefacts originated as biosculptures, a form of human artistic expression. As they evolve in stories like "Janus" (1980), "Band Ohne Ende" (1984), and "Home by the Sea" (1985)—all published in translation in *Slow Engines of Time* (2000)—these originally synthetic beings develop consciousness and the ability to reproduce. Despite the attention of several feminist scholars, Vonarburg's pathbreaking sf, which featured explorations of disembodied or re-embodied human consciousness that interface with both 'real' and virtual worlds via technology as early as 1980, remains underappreciated in the Anglo-American world due in part to delays between original publication and the appearance of English translations.

Vonarburg's Baïblanca cycle, along with later works by Sylvié Bérard in Québec and Catherine Dufour and Marie Darrieussecq in France, may be read particularly fruitfully through the lens of Sean McQueen's coupling of biopunk with French theory, including Baudrillard, Gilles Deleuze, and Félix Guattari. For McQueen, "[i]n biopunk, the simulacra of cyberspace are replaced by genetic simulacra, such as clones; computer hacking becomes biohacking; the economy of virtual information is replaced by one of genetic material or digitized genetic information; and hyperbiological bodies replace cyborgs and disembodied consciousnesses" (15). Catherine Dufour's *Le Goût de l'immortalité* (2005) is a good example of 21st-century biopunk's relationship to zombie narratives. It depicts humanity's future evolution after genetic manipulation becomes commonplace, but remains as a means of maintaining class distinctions. Dufour's novel also explores the boundary between the animate and inanimate differently than cyberpunk through the borderline existence of its first-person narrator who eventually realizes she has become a zombie. Consciousness and embodiment are at the core of the narrative, as they are in Marie Darrieussecq's *Truismes* (1996). Translated as *Pig Tales: A Novel of Lust and Transformation*, its protagonist's metamorphosis into a sow, coupled with its experimental style and generic boundary crossing, aligns it with biopunk and the depiction of 'hyperbiological' subjects. Indeed, Sophie Beaulé reads these two texts, along with Bérard's *Le Saga d'Illyge* (2011), through the lens of Haraway's cyborg and Deleuze and Guattari's *corps-en-devenir* (bodies becoming), implicitly making the link between cyberpunk's exploration of the human/machine interface and biopunk's extension of that problem into other forms of embodiment. In contrast with their male counterparts, accused of producing derivative forms of cyberpunk, francophone women writers have arguably been on the cutting edge of biopunk writing.

50.4 Conclusion

As this case study shows, given their usual cognizance of trends in the dominant Anglo-American milieu of the mode, sf writers from France and Québec engaged directly and indirectly with the cyberpunk movement. To varying degrees and over a slightly longer period, they paid homage to its landmark texts, deployed its tropes, adopted its postmodern stylistics, and sometimes internalized its oppositional ideology. Jean-Marc Ligny's *Cyberkiller* offers a vivid example of the type of superficial appropriation of cyberpunk conventions that Simon Bréan critiques in "cyberpunk à la française," but the revitalizing energy generated has had a lasting impact as it has inspired the current generation of French sf writers. French Canadians, often bilingual and more closely connected to the Anglo-American sf milieu, have taken cyberpunk's contribution to sf's evolution for granted, integrating it into their own developing styles. Whereas French, and to a lesser extent, Québécois male writers appropriated aspects of cyberpunk for the developing space opera renaissance, women writers followed the more biological bent of biopunk. Works like Élisabeth Vonarburg's Baïblanca cycle and Catherine Dufour's *Le Goût de l'immortalité* have generated and sustained a level of scholarly interest which suggests that francophone feminist biopunk represents a much more significant contribution to sf as a whole.

Amy J. Ransom

Notes

1 I wish to acknowledge the generous input of Jean-Louis Trudel at various stages of this project; I am also grateful to Sophie Beaulé, Natacha Vas-Deyres, and Simon Bréan. All of them gave me leads on primary texts and even connected me directly to francophone 'cyberpunk' authors. In addition, unless a published translation is cited in the Works Cited, translations from the French are my own.

2 For further work on the influence of Baudrillard on cyberpunk, see Csicsery-Ronay; McCaffery; McQueen; Sterling, Introduction.

3 Despite the recent peak in both production of and scholarly interest in African sf in English, it is difficult to point directly to a body of 'francophone African cyberpunk,' despite Mark Bould's recent discussions of Afrocyberpunk film, which includes such French-language films, as Jean-Pierre Bekolo's *Les Saignantes* (*The Bloodettes*, 2005) (Bould, "Afrocyberpunk"). Gerald Gaylard offers a compelling discussion of Africa's 'fraught' relationship with technology and its impact on the development of sf discourses in the pan-African setting. Although examples of science-fictional franco-African texts exist (Bould, "From Anti-colonial"), these and Antillean francophone texts are more likely to be read as "magical realism" (Moudileno). Even French language coverage of the 'Africa sf' phenomenon lends more space to anglophone African writers (Vicky). A special issue of the French magazine *Galaxies* (46 [Winter 2017]) devoted to *Africa sf* does include works by a handful of francophone writers, including Moussa Ould Ebnou (Mauritania) and Mame Bougouma Diene (Senegal), but translations from English dominate.

4 For in-depth discussion of music and cyberpunk, see Nicholas C. Laudadio's contribution to this collection.

5 Its first generation writers, including April and Vonarburg, were born in the late 1940s to early 1950s.

6 I provide more detailed information on Laurent McAllister's *Suprématie* in "Posthumanism and Rhizomatic Space in Laurent McAllister (Yves Meynard & Jean-Louis Trudel)," published in *Lingua Cosmica: Science Fiction from Around the World*.

7 For more details, please see my "Queen Memory" introduction to the special issue of *Femspec* on Élisabeth Vonarburg.

Works Cited

April, Jean-Pierre. *La Machine à explorer la fiction*. Le Préambule, 1980.

———. *Les Voyages thanatologiques de Yann Malter*. Québec/Amérique, 1995.

Beaulé, Sophie. "Le Corps en devenir et la machine de guerre: Bérard, Chen, Darrieussecq et Dufour." *Recherches feminists*, vol. 27, no. 1, 2014, pp. 129–44.

Bergeron, Alain. *Phaos*. Alire, 2003.

Bould, Mark. "African Science Fiction." *LA Review of Books*, 2 Oct. 2017, https://lareviewofbooks.org/article/african-science-fiction.

———. "Afrocyberpunk Cinema: The Postcolony Finds its Own Use for Things." *Cyberpunk and Visual Culture*, edited by Graham J. Murphy and Lars Schmeink. Routledge, 2018, pp. 213–34.

———. "From Anti-Colonial Struggle to Neoliberal Immiseration: Mohammed Dib's *Who Remembers the Sea*, Sony Labou Tansi's *Life and a Half* and Ahmed Khaled Towfik's *Utopia*." *Africa SF. Paradoxa*, vol. 25, 2013, pp. 17–46.

Bréan, Simon. "Hanter la machine: reconquêtes de la conscience humaine dans le cyberpunk à la française." *Res Futurae: Revue d'études sur la science-fiction*, vol. 10, 2017, n.p. http://journals.openedition.org/resf/1028.

Bukatman, Scott. *Blade Runner*. Palgrave Macmillan, 1997.

Butler, Andrew M. *Cyberpunk*. Pocket Essentials, 2000.

Csicsery-Ronay, Jr., Istvan. "Cyberpunk and Neuroromanticism." *Storming the Reality Studio: A Casebook of Cyberpunk and Postmodern Science Fiction*, edited by Larry McCaffery. Duke UP, 1991, pp. 182–95.

Dufour, Catherine. *Le Goût de l'immortalité*. Mnémos, 2005. Livre de poche.

Ecken, Claude. *La Mémoire totale*. Fleuve Noir, 1985.

———. Personal communication, 8 May 2018.

Gaylard, Gerald. "Black Secret Technology: African Technological Subjects." *World Weavers: Globalization, Science Fiction, and the Cybernetic Revolution*, edited by Wong Kin Yuen, Gary Westfahl, and Amy Kit-sze Chan. Hong Kong UP, 2005, pp. 191–204.

Gordon, Joan. "Yin and Yang Duke It Out." *Storming the Reality Studio: A Casebook of Cyberpunk and Postmodern Science Fiction*, edited by Larry McCaffery. Duke UP, 1991, pp. 196–202.

Hollinger, Veronica. "Cybernetic Deconstructions: Cyberpunk and Postmodernism." *Storming the Reality Studio: A Casebook of Cyberpunk and Postmodern Science Fiction*, edited by Larry McCaffery. Duke UP, 1991, pp. 203–18.

Jameson, Fredric. "Fear and Loathing in Globalization." *New Left Review*, vol. 23, Sep.–Oct. 2003, pp. 105–14.

Janelle, Claude. *Le Daliaf: Dictionnaire des auteurs des littératures de l'imaginaire en Amérique française*. Alire, 2011.

Lavigne, Carlen. *Cyberpunk Women, Feminism and Science Fiction*. McFarland, 2013.

Ligny, Jean-Marc. *Cyberkiller*. Fleuve Noir, 1993.

Marcinkowski, Alexandre. "Le cyberpunk français à l'épreuve de l'histoire." *Eidôlon*, vol. 11, *Les dieux cachés de la science-fiction française (1950–2010)*, edited by Natacha Vas-Deyres, et al. PU de Bordeaux, 2012, pp. 35–60.

McCaffery, Larry. "Introduction: The Desert of the Real." *Storming the Reality Studio: A Casebook of Cyberpunk and Postmodern Science Fiction*, edited by Larry McCaffery. Duke UP, 1991, pp. 1–16.

McQueen, Sean. *Deleuze and Baudrillard: From Cyberpunk to Biopunk*. Edinburgh UP, 2016.

Moudileno, Lydie. "Magical Realism: 'Arme Miraculeuse' for the African Novel?" *Research in African Literature*, vol. 37, no. 1, 2006, pp. 28–41.

Ransom, Amy J. "Posthumanism and Rhizomatic Space in Laurent McAllister (Yves Meynard & Jean-Louis Trudel)." *Lingua Cosmica: Science Fiction from Around the World*, edited by Dale Knickerbocker. U of Illinois P, 2018, pp. 129–50.

———. "Queen of Memory: Introduction." *Femspec*, vol. 11, no. 2, 2011, pp. 1–25.

Rimbaud, Arthur. "Voyelles/Vowels." *Collected Poems*, translated by Oliver Bernard. Penguin, 1997, pp. 171–72.

Rucker, Rudy. *Seek! Selected Non-Fiction*. Four Walls, Eight Windows, 1999.

Sterling, Bruce. Introduction. *Patterns*, by Pat Cadigan. Tor, 1989, pp. ix–xi.

Trudel, Jean-Louis. Personal communication, 8 Jan. 2018; 16 Feb. 2018.

———. *Le Ressuscité de l'Atlantide*. Fleuve noir, 1994.

———. *Petit Guide de la science-fiction au Québec*. Alire, 2017.

———. *Pour des soleils froids*. Fleuve noir, 1994.

Vicky, Alain. "Afrique, présence des futurs." *Le monde diplomatique*, Jun. 2013, www.monde-diplomatique.fr/2013/06/VICKY/49190.

Vonarburg, Élisabeth. "Cogito." translated by Jane Brierley, *Tesseracts 3*, edited by Candas Jane Dorsey and Gerry Truscott. Porcépic, 1993, pp. 62–82.

———. *Slow Engines of Time*. Tesseract/The Books Collective, 2000.

———. *The Silent City*. 1981, translated by Jane Brierley. Bantam Spectra, 1992.

INDEX

100% (Pope) 97
2001: A Space Odyssey (Clarke and Kubrick) 337
2020 Visions (Delano) 96
20,000 Leagues Under the Sea (Fleischer) 65

Abdelmounim, Zaki "Neo Hong Kong" 221, 222, 226
Abney Park 67
Abu Samah, Maisarah and Rosemary Lim, *The Steampowered Globe* 70
Acampora, Ralph R. 321–2
Acevedos, Mario "Reactions" 306
Acker, Kathy, Empire of the Senseless 35, 50
activism 2, 74, 77–9, 297, 298, 336, 350, 363, 373–80; *see also* hacktivism
Adair, Catherine 228, 236
Advantageous (Phang) 280
Adventures of Brisco County Jr, The (Boam and Cuse) 66
aesthetics of cyberpunk 30, 64, 76, 91, 94, 101, 135, 136, 138, 164, 171, 172, 173, 174, 179, 181, 185, 186, 193, 207, 232, 233, 247, 264, 265, 266, 268, 270, 271, 277, 283, 288, 349, 403, 410, 411, 416, 424
Aether Shanties (Abney Park) 67
Africa 70, 245, 423; character from 96; cyberpunk in, 288, 430; francophone literature in 423, 430; science fiction from 353
Africa Paradis (Amoussou) 288, 359
African American characters 124, 131
African Americans 70, 119, 247, 314
African American writers 308–9, 311, 354, 357
African diaspora 245, 246, 250
Afro-Cuban characters 398
Afrodiaspora 309
Afro-Punk (Spooner) 359
Afrocyberpunk 21, 245, 247, 248, 250, 288, 308, 311, 312–15, 355, 356, 357, 358, 360; cinema 288, 358–9, 430; emergence of 309; music 247, 248, 250, 358; origins of 312

AfroCyberPunk Interactive 360
Afrofuturism, Afrofuturist 2, 250, 314, 353–60; on inventing the term 354; in music 242, 357–8
Afronauts (Bodomo) 358
Aguiar, Raúl 398
AIBO robotic pets 317–9, 324
AIs *see* artificial intelligences
Akira (Ōtomo) 107, 108, 110, 111, 117, 139, 151, 152, 156, 160–7, 217, 218, 242, 403; chiaroscuro in 416; manga 162–163; sound in 243
Akita, Takahiro 152
Alien (Scott) 221, 373
alienation 11, 30, 32, 33, 37, 44, 45, 120, 155, 179, 229, 239, 261, 320, 346, 347, 369, 385, 389, 415, 418, 420
aliens 26, 27, 28, 31, 58, 60, 61, 62, 91, 93, 97, 106, 131, 204, 205, 228, 242, 265, 275, 313, 328, 338, 354, 355, 397
Alita: Battle Angel (Rodriguez) 116, 140
Allen, Kathryn: Disability in Science Fiction 236
All Walls Must Fall (inbetweengames) 416
Almost Human 173
Alpert, Mark 318
Alpert, Robert 123, 126
Alphaville (Godard) 418
Altered Carbon (Kalogridis/Netflix) 174, 265–9, 270, 405; whitewashing in 406
alternative cyberpunk cultures 350–1
Álvarez, Yadira "Kikubi" 398
American Flagg! (Chaykin) 94, 101–6
American Gothic 266
American Splendor (Pekar) 194
Anarchy Online (Funcom) 186
Anderson, Ho Che, *Godhead* 98
Anderson, Poul 18
Andrade, Oswald de 392
Andrevon, Jean-Pierre 424
androgyny 126, 247
androids 120, 153, 154, 181, 245, 246, 247, 249, 250, 358

433

Index

animality 2, 317–24; animals in *Neuromancer* 320

Animatrix, The 135

anime 2, 66, 67, 107, 109, 114, 116–7, 151–60, 165, 166, 217, 218, 403–4; beginning of boom 162; meaning of 151; techniques 156, 160

Anno, Hideaki 66

Anonymous 378

Anthropocene 75, 76, 79, 114, 147, 236, 269, 326–33

anthropocentrism 147, 274, 278

anti-authoritarianism 45, 65, 73, 78, 116, 403

anti-capitalism 49, 70, 266, 297

anti-feminist values 120

anti-humanism 275, 300

Anti-Humbug 64

Antilles 423

Antiviral (Cronenberg) 76

antropofagia, antropófago 386, 392

Apollinaire, Guillaume 232

Apple Macintosh advertisement 373, 374

Appleseed (Shirow) 111

April, Jean-Pierre 427, 430

AR (augmented reality) 97, 259, 266, 328, 329

Arab Spring 371, 378

Aragão, Octavio 70

architecture 18, 24, 104, 111, 136, 195, 217, 235, 264, 267, 270, 302, 416, 417

Argentina 385, 387–8

Armitage III 153, 154

Armored Troopers Votoms 153

Arrighi, Giovanni 285

Arthur C. Clarke Award 19

artificial intelligences (AIs) 18, 32, 92, 111, 121, 151, 173, 194, 196–7, 200, 205, 217, 256, 266, 296, 300, 308, 338, 341, 347, 356, 389, 396, 398, 412, 419, 424; as characters 43–4, 154, 166, 171–2, 178–83, 269; experiments in 317–319, 402; and the Singularity 56; in William Gibson 11, 56, 103, 196, 264, 276, 277, 310, 320, 330, 331, 339

Asamiya, Kia 67

Ashby, Madeline: *Company Town* 278–9, 329; Machine Dynasty series 37

Ashley, Mike 16

Asimov, Isaac, Foundation series 7

Assange, Julian 88, 377

Astounding Stories 7

Astroboy 151

Attebery, Brian 22, 301; and Wendy Pearson 207, 209, 215

Attebery, Stina 231–2, 349

Atwood, Margaret: *The Handmaid's Tale* 295; MaddAddam trilogy 76; *Oryx and Crake* 75–6

augmentation 32, 49, 92, 110, 111, 112, 153, 174, 186, 188, 194–6, 198, 204, 211, 226, 259, 320, 323, 333, 360, 411, 412, 413, 416

Austerlitz, Saul 248

Automan 173

avant-garde 7, 35, 48, 50, 76, 238, 239, 286, 337, 418

Avatar (Cameron) 341

avatars 121, 122, 124, 155, 157, 187, 189, 255, 259, 278, 296, 304, 332, 416, 426

Azuma, Hiroki 109

Azzarello, Brian 98

Babylon 5: The Gathering (Compton) 228

Bacigalupi, Paolo 54; *The Windup Girl* 75–6

Badger, Mark 101

Baird, Wilhelmina 54; *Crashcourse* 36

Ballard, J.G. 7, 8, 18, 235, 236, 240; *The Atrocity Exhibition* 10

Balsamo, Anne 45, 295, 318, 322; *Technologies of the Gendered Body* 44, 298

Banerjee, Neelanjana "Exile" 412

Baradit, Jorge 390–1

Barata, Sophie Oliveira "Alternative Limbs Project" 236

Bargeld, Blixa 239

Barkun, Michael 197–8

Barlow, John Perry 124, 374, 375; "A Declaration of the Independence of Cyberpunk" 376; memorial for 379

Barnaby, Jeff 348–9

Barnes, Steven 21, 308, 312, 314; *Blood Brothers* 310; *Firedance* 21; *Gorgon Child* 21; *Streetlethal* 21, 308, 313, 355

Barthes, Roland 224, 229, 257

Bascalgli, Maurizia 231

Bates, John K. 93

Batman: Dark Knight 94

Batman: Digital Justice 95

Batman v Superman: Dawn of Justice (Snyder) 216

Battle Angel Alita (Fukutomi) 107, 111, 112–13, 115, 116, 153–4

Battle Angel Alita (Kishiro) 111, 112–3

Baudrillard, Jean 176, 221–2, 226, 255–6, 259, 261, 331, 429; on hyperreality 169, 256, 258, 330; and *The Matrix* 256–7; on simulacra 97, 104, 126, 135, 160, 221–2, 423

Baugh, Benjamin 72

Baum, Frank L., *The Wizard of Oz* 96, 135

Bay, Hakim *TAZ* 376

Be, Alun, "Edification" 359

Bear, Elizabeth 54; "Two Dreams on Trains" 37

Bear, Greg 16, 21; "Blood Music" and *Blood Music* 74, 75

Beard, William 139

Beaulé, Sophie 429, 430

Bedwin Hacker (El Fani) 288, 359

Bef 389; *Gel azul* 390; and Gerardo Sifuentes "[e]" 390

Bell, Andrea L. 390

Bell, Derrick A. 309; *Beneath a Steel Sky* (Revolution) 185, 190

Benford, Gregory 16, 17

434

Index

Benjamin, Walter, *The Arcades Project* 229–31
Bennett, Jane 147
Bentham, Jeremy 365
Bérard, Sylvie 428, 429
Berardi, Franco 'Bifo' 285, 287
Bergeron, Alain, Phaos: Cyber-opéra en trois actes 428
Berko, Lili 178
Bester, Alfred 102
Bethke, Bruce 1, 16, 54, 58, 164, 232
Beukes, Lauren 288; *Zoo City* 353
Bezos, Jeff 56
Bhabha, Homi 413
Bieber, Justin 71
Big Brother 315, 366, 369, 373, 374, 377; *see also* Orwell, George
Big Combo, The (Lewis) 417
Big Data 57, 368
Bigelow, Kathryn 128–33; *see also Strange Days*
Biggs, John 70
Big Short, The (McKay) 86
bikers, biker gangs 93, 109–10, 113, 116, 163, 164, 233, 301, 337, 403
Bilal, Enki, Nikopol Trilogy 92
Biller, Diana 57
Billions (Showtime) 86
binaries 46, 126, 296, 297, 303, 314, 327, 346, 347, 411, 413
bioart 77, 429
BioForge (Origin) 185
biogenetic engineering 17, 25
biohackers, biohacking 74, 77, 78, 308, 328, 329, 388, 423, 428, 429
biological sf 73
biopunk 73–9, 200, 201, 206, 279, 333, 398, 429
"Biopunk Manifesto, The" 77–8
Bioshock (2k Boston) 189
biotech/biotechnology 14, 73, 74, 77, 78, 92, 198, 200, 201, 203, 234, 274, 277, 297, 313, 329
Birnbaum, Dara Technology/Transformation: Wonder Woman 37–8
birth control 33
Bishop, Michael Light Years and Dark 41
bitcoin 39, 176, 282, 286–7, 377
Blachford, Tom 219
Blackhat 138
Black Lives Matter 131, 297, 371, 378
blackness 245, 247, 248, 249, 250, 353, 354, 357
Black Mirror 173, 261, 287
Black Panther (Coogler) 353, 358, 359, 360
Black Sabbath "Iron Man" 241
Black Twitter 39
Black, Io 97
Blade Runner (Scott) 1, 2, 41, 91, 101, 120–1, 126, 128, 130, 134, 144, 148, 152, 153, 155, 180, 181, 216, 217, 218, 228, 234, 235, 242, 246, 261, 269, 308, 348, 373, 404, 410, 415, 420, 425; aesthetic of 104, 121, 129, 135, 174, 179, 185, 186, 217,

228–9, 232, 267–8; Asian culture in 131, 349, 404, 405; chiaroscuro in 416; influence of 222, 265, 423, 426; sound in 242, 246, 250, 418; world-building in 221
Blade Runner 2049 (Villeneuve) 135–6, 144–9, 218, 261, 267, 269–70
Blade Runner games 185, 193
Blade *see* Hernández Pacin
Blame! (Nihei) 114–15
Blame! (Seshita) 107
Blanc, Charles 231
Blaustein, Eduardo *Cruz Diablo* 388
Blaylock, James P. 65–6
blipverts 171, 178, 180, 181
Blomkamp, Neill 288; *see also District 9* (Blomkamp); *Elysium* (Blomkamp)
Boam, Jeffrey 66
body modification (body modding) 25, 26–7, 31, 207, 231, 233, 285, 294, 295, 296
body augmentation *see* augmentation
body horror 76, 134, 139, 140, 162, 164, 165, 167, 264, 268, 270
body, importance of the 385
body invasion 18, 22, 73, 151, 164, 165, 211, 285, 338, 339, 341; *see also* mind invasion
Bolton, Christopher 153, 162, 402
Bonilla-Silva, Eduardo 309
Bonnefoy, Yves 424
Booker, M. Keith 94
Booth, Austin 44, 46
Borden, Lizzie, *Born in Flames* 38
Borges, Borgesian 12, 388, 389
Borgese, Elisabeth Mann, "True Self" 33
Borinski, Alicia, *Cine continuado* 387
Born in Flames (Borden) 358
Bostrom, Nick 273–4, 276, 277, 278
Botting, Fred 264, 265, 266
Bould, Mark 3, 286, 341; on African sf 353; on Afrocyberpunk film 248, 288, 309, 359, 360, 430; on cyberpunk 282, 340; and Sherryl Vint 184
Boulter, Jonathan 189
Bowie, David 238, 248, 419
Bowser, Rachel A. and Brian Croxall, *Like Clockwork* 70
Bozzetto, Roger 424
BR 2049 *see* Blade Runner 2049
Bradbury, Ray 10; *Fahrenheit 451* 175
Bradley, Jacqueline "Boat Dress" 236
Braidotti, Rosi 24, 25, 30, 38, 75, 147, 267, 269, 275, 319
BrainBanx (Lee and Minor) 96
Branco sai, preto fica (Queirós) 387
Brand, Stuart 374
Brazil 385, 386–7, 392
Bréan, Simon 423, 424, 425, 426, 428, 429, 430
bricolage, bricoleurs 18, 164, 165, 230, 232, 233, 234, 236, 244

Index

Brin, David 17; Earth and The Transparent
  Society 370
Britton, Andrew 119, 120
Broaddus, Maurice 70
Broderick, Damien 3
Brooker, Charlie, How Videogames Changed the
  World 259
Brooker, Will 132
Brother From Another Planet, The (Sayles) 358
Brown Girl Begins (Lewis) 358
Brown, J. Andrew 387, 388
Brown, James 247, 248
Brown, Nicholas 284
Brown, Steven P. 15
Brown, Steven T. 217–18
Brown, Tanya 34
Brummett, Barry, Clockwork Rhetoric 64, 69–70
Brunner, John 7, 14; The Shockwave Rider 8–10, 42,
  373, 376, 377
Brunton, Finn 377
Bruzenack, Ken 105
Bryant, Levi 147
Bubblegum Crisis 153
Buck Rogers 106
Buck-Morss, Susan 231
Buddhism 13
Buenos Aires 387, 388
Bukatman, Scott 8, 14, 91, 103, 104, 121, 139, 144,
  185, 217, 234, 275, 285, 286, 289, 293, 404, 410,
  411, 425; Terminal Identity 117, 134, 176
Bull, Emma, Bone Dance 295, 296
burbclaves 278
Burning Chrome see Gibson, "Burning Chrome"
Burroughs, William S. 7, 419
Burst City (Ishii) 164
Butler, Andrew M. 43, 48, 54, 134, 186, 306, 435
Butler, Judith 301, 305
Butler, Octavia E. 309, 312, 314, 357; Lilith's Brood
  355; Patternist series 313; Xenogenesis trilogy
  76, 355
Byford, Jovan 212, 213
Byrne, Meagan 98

Cadigan, Pat 16, 21, 34–5, 228, 279, 295, 424;
  Dervish is Digital 41; "The Final Remake..." 34;
  Fools 41, 276, 278; Mindplayers 41; "Pretty Boy
  Crossover" 10, 12, 34, 41, 45, 285, 337, 338,
  362; "Rock On" 19, 20–1, 41; Synners 19, 34,
  37, 41–6, 52–3, 277, 278, 369, 371; Synners and
  animality 322–4; Synners, reviews of 46; Tea from
  an Empty Cup 41
Cadora, Karen 21, 34, 42, 154, 277, 286, 292, 295,
  296, 411, 428
Calado, Ivanir, "O altar does nossos corações" 386
Calamity, Professor 71
Calder, Richard 404; Cythera 10;
  Dead Girls 404, 405
Callenbach, Ernest, Ecotopia 59
Calvin, Ritch 39

Calvino, Italo 427
Cambridge Analytica 260
Cameron, Don 96
Cameron, James 173
Campbell Jr., John W. 7, 312
Campbell, Bill, Sunshine Patriots 357
Campbell, Stu (Sutu) 97
Canada, Canadian 2, 37, 107, 239, 241, 248, 305,
  389, 427, 429
Canal, Richard 425, 426
Canavan, Gerry 75, 297, 329, 330
Canete, Eric 98
Cannibal Ox 242
Cannibale 92
Čapek, Karel R.U.R. 176
Capetola, Christine 242, 306, 358
capitalism 28, 29, 32, 33, 34, 44, 55, 79, 85, 86,
  119, 121, 123, 124, 125, 145, 147, 165, 188, 239,
  250, 277–9, 282, 286, 320, 336, 337, 339, 359,
  397; see also global capitalism; late capitalism;
  neoliberal capitalism
Capitalism 2.0 (Stross) 57–8
capitalist realism 144, 145, 188
Captain Rugged (Jones and Maqari) 98
Card, Orson Scott, Ender's Game 376
Carlos, Wendy 242
Carriger, Gail 69
Carroll, Lewis, Alice in Wonderland 135
Carter, Chris 172, 199
Carter, Rafael 303, 306; The Fortunate Fall, 35, 36
Case, Henry 9, 87, 103, 276–7, 286, 287, 294,
  300, 301, 303–4, 319–20, 321, 322, 327,
  330; as observer of Japan 401; see also Gibson,
  Neuromancer
Cassandra Complex, The 239, 240, 241
Cyberpunx 240
Castagnet, Martín Felipe, Los cuerpos del Verano 388
Castle in the Sky (Miyazaki) 66
Castricano, Jodey 265
Castro, Pablo, "Exerion" 391
Catts, Oron 77
Causo, Roberto de Sousa 385, 386, 387
Cavallaro, Dani 218, 224, 267, 270–1
cDc see Cult of the Dead Cow
cellphone 28, 288
censorship 93, 101, 261, 395–6
Cerebus the Aardvark (Sim) 104
CGI 104, 123, 178, 179, 181, 182
Chabon, Michael 68, 102
Chadwick, Frank Space: 1889 65
Chakrabarty, Dipesh 326
Chalayan, Hussein 235
Chang, Edmond 43, 303
Channel Zero (Wood and Cloonan) 97
Chanology 378
Charnas, Suzy McKee, Holdfast series 33
Chaum, David 373–4
Chaykin, Howard 93–4, 96, 101–6
Cheap Truth 15–6, 19, 41; see also Sterling, Bruce

436

Index

Chernaik, Laura 45
Cherryh, C.J., *Cyteen* 76
Chiang, Ted, "The Life Cycle of Software Objects" 341
Chikiamco, Paolo 70
Chile 385, 390–1
Chng, Joyce 70
Christensen, Bill 377
Christensen, Clayton 121
Christgau, Robert 241
Christian, Deborah Teramis, *Mainline* 35
Christiane F. (Edel) 420
Chu, Seo-Young 84
Chude-Sokai, Louis 310
Church of Scientology 378
Citizenfour (Poitras) 379
city, cityscapes 195, 216, 217–21; images of 146; types of 217; *see also* urban settings
Clarion Writers Workshop 15
Clark, Ashley 360
Clark, Ronald, Queen Victoria's Bomb 65
Clarke, Arthur C. 205, 207; *The City and the Stars* 12–3
Clarke, Bruce 279
class 2, 13
Click+Drag 232, 233
climate change 236
Clinton, George 357
clipping: Splendor & Misery 358
Clock DVA 239–40
Clockwork Orange, A (Kubrick) 418
clones, cloning 25, 108, 156, 296, 388
Cloonan, Becky 97
Clute, John 41
Coates, Paul 416
Cohen, Jeffrey Jerome 75
Coleman, Gabriella 378
Coleman, Mark 241
Collins, Karen 239, 420
Colombia 386
colonialism, colonialization 65, 332, 335, 337, 339, 347, 349, 350, 353, 386, 409
comic books 2, 22, 67, 91–9, 101, 102, 106, 304, 353
Comic Market (Comiket) 109
comics studies 116–7
commodification 8, 10, 13, 14, 20, 48, 49, 52, 94, 105, 146, 167, 171, 218, 231, 282, 284, 286, 287, 288, 291, 292, 312, 346, 387, 391, 404, 411
compost 279
Compton, D.G. 7, 10
Computer Fraud and Abuse Act 374
computer-generated comics 95
computers 8–9, 32, 34, 54, 57, 58, 65, 73, 74, 95, 109, 119, 121, 169, 170, 173, 181, 210, 211, 233, 243, 245, 246, 247, 249, 275, 277, 303, 312, 314, 355, 368, 374, 375, 378, 379, 395
computronium 60
Condry, Ian 158

Conrad, Joseph, *Heart of Darkness* 353
conservatism of cyberpunk 21, 42, 63, 66, 68, 69, 70, 116, 125, 135, 136, 188, 190, 269, 274, 283, 291, 292, 293, 295, 339, 411
console cowboys 43, 190, 276, 292, 293, 301, 321
conspiracies, conspiracy theories 170, 172, 197–8, 209, 211–3, 256, 340, 369
Conspiracy Theory (Donner) 197
Constable, Catherine 256–7
conventions 15, 16, 71
Conversation, The (Coppola) 239–40
Cook, Dave 97
Corgiat, Sylviane and Bruno Lecigne, "La vallée des ascenseurs" 424
corporate power 45, 58, 87, 92, 94, 95, 165, 174, 175, 180, 181, 196, 201, 206, 210, 217, 415, 419
corporeality 46, 158, 266, 293, 305, 310, 318, 319, 321, 322, 323, 324
cosmetic surgery 18, 151, 338
Costello, Brandon 102, 104
counterculture 96, 97, 195, 196, 408, 413, 420, 427
Coutts, Lucan 222; "Toronto 2049" 223, 225
Cox, Ryan J. 168
CP *see* cyberpunk
Crazy Thunder Road (Ishii) 164
CRISPR 78
Criss Cross (Siodmak) 416
critical posthumanism 76, 147, 274–5
critical race theory 308–15; origins of 309
Crocodile Dundee (Faiman) 93
Cronenberg, Brandon 76
Crow, The (O'Barr) 96, 99
Croxall, Brian 70
cryptography, cryptology 50, 374
Csicsery-Ronay Jr, Istvan 1, 82, 85, 195, 285, 288, 336, 338, 411, 428
Cuba 392, 395–9
Cult of the Dead Cow, The (cDc) 378
cultural allusion 105
cultural cannibalism 386, 392
Curtain, Tyler 301
Cuse, Carlton 66
cut-up technique 50, 419
cyberbozos 164
cyberbrain 110, 111, 165
cyberbrain space 110
cybercrime 8, 39, 300, 391
Cyberdreams 425
Cyberella (Chaykin and Cameron) 96
cyberfeminists 38–9, 45, 411
cyberfunk 308
cybergothic 25, 26, 27, 236, 265, 269, 270, 271
cyber-hacking 328
cybernetics 55, 92, 95
cybernoir 96, 98
CyberPowWow 38
Cyberpunk: The Roleplaying Game of the Dark Future (R. Talsorian Games) 200, 201, 209; Cyberpunk 2013 201, 206;

Index

Cyberpunk 2020 201, 202, 209, 214, 267;
Cyberpunk 2027 186; Cyberpunk 2077 207
cyberpunk: in the academy 2; as betrayal of sf's
utopian and subversive origins 282; core of 41;
death of 21, 48, 94, 160, 284; definition of 315;
diversity of 17, 21; 'flavoured' 186, 306; history
of term 164; imagery 216–26; as marketing
gimmick 17; in the 1980s 292; mélange 220,
221, 222, 224, 226; non-sf 81–88; origins of 1;
origins of label 16; parody of 48–49, 58; as a PR
tactic 283; in *Time Magazine* 240–1
Cyberpunk Red 207, 209
Cyberpunk V3.0 201, 209
Cyberscape 203
cybersex 97
Cyberspace (Iron Crown Enterprises) 200, 209
cyberspace 1, 8, 14, 44, 49, 60, 257, 288, 292,
304, 330, 425; coded feminine 294; first used
to describe the Internet 375; in Gibson 267,
367; as a layer of reality 260; as the new frontier
336; as a queer site 301–2; in Stephenson,
Snow Crash 49
Cybertwee Collective 39
Cyborg (Pyun) 139
Cyborg 009 (Ishinomori) 108, 151
cyborg/s 33, 34, 51, 52, 57, 110, 111, 112, 114, 120,
139–141, 153, 157, 159, 160, 162, 164, 166, 200,
274, 279, 291, 296, 298, 300, 333, 355, 360, 387,
391, 410, 411; Cyborg Bill of Rights 371; cyborg
feminism 291–8; cyborg myth 270
cyborgization 7, 270, 312, 326, 360
cypherpunks 176, 376–7, 379

Dakwäkäda Warriors (Pauls/Tahltan) 98, 350
Dann, Jack 16
Dark Angel (Cameron and Eglee) 76, 173
Dark City (Proyas) 11
Dark Horse Presents 96
dark web 39
Dark Web Bake Sale 39
Darley, Andrew 135
Darrieusecq, Marie 428, 429
Darrow, Geof 94
Das, Indapramit 70
Dath, Dietmar and Oliver Scheibler, *Mensch wie
Gras wie* 416
Datlow, Ellen 16, 18
Davidson, Chris 92, 99
Davis, Milton and Balogun Ojetade, *Steamfunk!* 70
Davis, Lauren 94
Dawsear, Ava "The Good King" 412
DC Comics 92, 95, 96, 101, 360
De Campi, Alex 116
De la Iglesia, Martin 163
De Pierres, Marianne *Nylon Angel* 36
De Ro, Jonas 216
Deadlands: Reloaded (Hensley) 68
Deadline 93
Death Powder (Izumiya) 402–3

death, postponement or abolition of 273; *see also*
immortality
Deckard, Rick 181, 181, 228–9; in *Cyberkiller* 425;
see also Blade Runner
Declaration of Independence 246–7
Decoder (Muscha and Maeck) 415, 418, 419–20, 421
Delano, Jamie 96
Delany, Samuel R. 7, 18, 21, 34, 38, 89, 233, 236,
308, 310–1, 312, 315, 354, 355, 357; "Aye and
Gomorrah" 33; *Nova* 33, 43, 312, 355; *Stars in
My Pocket Like Grains of Sand* 355
Deleuze, Gilles 144; and Félix Guattari 147, 149,
291, 429
Delgado, Richard and Jean Stefancic 309, 311
DeLillo, Don, *Cosmopolis* 86
DeMatteis, J.M. 101
Denby, David 131
denial-of-service attack (DDoS) 378
Denis, Sylvie 425
Derrida, Jacques 286
Dery, Mark 233, 236, 310, 360, 369; "Black to the
Future" 354, 359; *Flame Wars* 354
Descartes, René (Cartesian) 11, 12, 44, 46, 111,
267, 279, 282, 321, 322, 324, 333
Descender (Nguyen and Lemire) 98
Deus Ex (Ion Storm) 187, 190, 193–9, 415; franchise
193, 185, 188, 216, 217
Deus Ex: Human Revolution (Eidos Montréal) 187,
189, 193, 194, 198, 199, 220
Deus Ex: Invisible War (Ion Storm) 193, 194, 199
Deus Ex: Mankind Divided (Eidos Montréal) 193,
195, 198, 199
Devo 238
Di Filippo, Paul 17, 68; *Ribofunk* 76; *The Steampunk
Trilogy* 66
Dick, Philip K. 7, 61, 96, 102, 238, 242, 389, 402,
427; *Do Androids Dream of Electric Sheep?* 317,
331, 425; *Eye in the Sky* 11; *The Three Stigmata
of Palmer Eldritch* 12; "We Can Remember It for
You Wholesale" 12, 424
digiart 219, 220, 221, 222, 226
digital art 39, 185, 216–226
digital culture 104, 170, 292, 297
digital divide 308, 310, 357, 396
digital effects in cinema 134–141; *see also* CGI
digital music 246, 249, 250
digital society 259
dildo, ritualism surrounding 404
Dillon, Grace L. 98, 344–5; *Walking the Clouds* 344
Dior, Christian 68
disability 236
Disch, Thomas M. 8
discoverer's fantasy 336
discrimination in cyberpunk futures 36
disembodiment (dis/embodiment and
(dis)embodiment) 43, 44, 46, 48, 207, 275, 276,
277, 293, 294, 296, 319, 385, 388, 396, 429
Disney, Disneyland, 1, 84, 121, 122, 151, 346, 369;
see also TRON

438

Index

District 9 (Blomkamp) 353
DIY aesthetic 232, 403
DIYbio 74, 77–8
Doctorow, Cory 54, 337, 379; Down and Out in the Magic Kingdom 379; For the Win 260, 379; Homeland 379; Little Brother 379; Overdocked 379; Pirate Cinema 379
Dollhouse (Whedon) 171
Dome: Ground Zero, The (Gibbons and McKie) 96
Donald, James 225
Doom 2099 95
Dorsey, Candas Jane 35; "(Learning About) Machine Sex" 21, 35
Dotse, Jonathan 357; "Virus!" 357, 360
Dozois, Gardner 1, 16, 18, 34; *Year's Best SF* 41
Dr. M (Chabrol) 415, 420–1
Dr. Otagon 242
Dr. Steel (Dr. Steel) 67
Dracula (Browning) 416
Dragonmech (Goodman) 68
Dreamspace (Safro and Black) 97
Dredd (Travis) 217
Dreyden, Nicky, *The Prey of Gods* 357
drugs 30, 50, 92, 97, 103, 111, 123, 194, 240, 292, 306, 312, 329, 389, 390, 391, 401
Drugs and Wires (Safro and Black) 97
Druillet, Philippe 91
dualism 24, 50, 91, 111, 122, 147, 148, 275, 276, 279, 291, 295
Dubey, Madhu 355
Dufour, Catherine 428, 429
Dumas, The Count of Monte Cristo 175
Dunyach, Jean-Claude 425, 426
dystopia/n 1, 7, 8, 9, 25, 36, 53, 57, 86–7, 92, 94, 95, 96, 97, 111, 120, 144, 158, 171, 174, 193, 195, 200, 203, 211, 214, 220, 225, 238, 240, 242, 245, 246, 248, 256, 264, 265, 267, 268, 270, 282, 292, 332, 345–6, 348, 358, 369, 373, 387, 390, 391, 410, 411, 415, 418, 419, 420; in Latin America 391, 395; in Pat Cadigan 34, 41; techno-dystopian 287; urban dystopia 91, 239, 308, 354, 356, 386, 411, 417; utopia and 28, 63, 217, 364, 369, 371, 427; in William Gibson 336–337, 339, 369;

Earth, Wind & Fire 357
Echols, Alice 250
Ecken, Claude 424
Eclipse Phase (Catalyst Game Labs/Posthuman Studios) 203, 207
eco-catastrophe 328
ecological change 25, 57, 144, 146, 328
ecological concerns 42, 326
ecology 2, 42, 57, 61, 75, 116, 218, 323, 326–33
Edwards, Matthew 163
EFF *see* Electronic Frontier Foundation
Effinger, George Alec: *When Gravity Falls* 13
Egan, Greg 54; Diaspora 12; Permutation City 12
Eggers, Dave: *The Circle* 86–7, 370, 371

Eidos Montréal 193
Einstürzende Neubauten 239, 418, 420
Eisner Award 98
El-P 241
Electronic Frontier Foundation (EFF) 374, 375, 376
Elemental, Professor 67
Elgin, Suzette Haden *Native Tongue* and *The Judas Rose* 295
Ellingham, Cody 221
Ellis, Edward S., Steam Man of the Prairies, The 64
Ellis, Warren 96
Ellison, Harlan 8, 19
els Heart.Break (Svedäng) 189
Elysium (Blomkamp) 341
Empire 2, 335–42
Empire Strikes Back, The (Kershner) 165
Empty Zone (Shawn) 97
Encinosa Fu, Michel 396, 397, 398, 399
Encyclopedia of Science Fiction 408
end of the world 79, 328–329
enhancement 60, 74, 75, 95, 98, 123, 165, 196, 200–1, 202, 203, 205, 206, 207, 211, 222, 275, 278, 279, 292, 293, 294, 313, 354, 356, 360
Enlightenment 30, 267, 274, 344
Enos, Solomon 98
Enteen, Jillana 288, 356
Enthiran (Shankar) 413
Enton, Harry 64
ephemerality of videogames 258
erasing ethnicity 155–6
Eremine, Alexander 97
Ergo Proxy (Murase) 156
Erickson, Steve 102
erotica 398, 405
Escape from New York (Carpenter) 91
Eshun, Kodwo 250, 359, 360
Eskridge, Kelley *Solitaire* 304, 305–6
Esmail, Sam 87
Establishment Phase (steampunk) 67–9, 70
Etherscope (Goodman Games) 68, 72, 203
eugenics 108
Ex Machina (Guardians of Order) 203
Exapunks (Zachtronics) 189
eXistenZ (Cronenberg) 125, 243, 258, 417
Expanse, The (SyFy) 207
expansionism 61, 336, 338, 339
expressionist cinema in Germany 416
extrapolation 9, 64, 65, 68, 81, 85, 88, 129, 260, 282, 364, 426, 428
extraterrestrial intelligences (ETI) 61, 205
Eye in the Sky (Hood) 138
Eyeborgs (Clabaugh) 366

Fairbairns, Zoe *Benefits* 295
fake news 105, 172, 256, 259
families in cyberpunk futures 37
Fanon, Frantz Wretched of the Earth 349
fantastic, the 135, 200, 206, 207, 222, 398
fanzines in Mexico 389

Index

Far Cry 4 (Ubisoft) 220
far-future settings 13, 24, 25, 37, 274, 314
fascism 119
fashion 2, 33, 109, 125, 195, 228–36, 419;
  Afrofuturist 359; steampunk 64, 68–9, 70, 71
Fassbinder, Rainer Werner 11, 415; *see also World on a Wire*
Fawcett, Fausto *Santa Claus Poltergeist* 386
Fear Factory, *Soul of a New Machine* 241
Featherstone, Mike and Roger Burrows 319
Felscherinow, Christiane 420
female cyberpunk writers 21, 34, 36, 42, 44,
  108, 185
female cyborgs 154–5, 157, 160, 168, 294, 387
female empowerment 93, 113
feminism 2, 38, 39, 42, 43, 52, 93, 154, 247, 291,
  297, 306; feminist critics and writers 82, 120,
  140, 185, 190, 231, 242, 269; feminist cyberpunk
  21, 22, 46, 32–39, 42, 46, 154, 295, 300; *see also*
  cyberfeminists; cyborg feminism
Fenner, Arnie 41
Fenster, Mark 212, 213
Fernández, María 45
Fernández Delgado, Miguel Ángel 385
fetishization of female body 93, 96, 112, 125,
  154, 231
Fight Club (Fincher) 87–8
File Under Miscellaneous (Barnaby) 348
film noir 128, 171, 179, 180, 264, 269; *see also* noir
Final Fantasy VI (Ito) 66
Final Fantasy XV (Square Enix) 216
financialization 175–6, 282, 286, 289
Finney, Hal 377
First Comics 101–2
fiscalmancy 289
Fisher, Mark 144–5, 188
Flagg, Reuben 102–3
Flash Gordon 106
Fleischer, Richard 65
Fletcher, Brenden 116
Flisfeder, Matthew 135, 218
Flores, Raúl *La carne luminosa de los gigantes* 398
Flourescent Black (Wilson and Fox) 97
folklore 314, 357
food replicators 57
Forbes, Edith *Exit to Reality* 35, 36, 295, 297,
  303, 306
forerunners of cyberpunk 7–8
Forster, E.M., "The Machine Stops" 226
Fortin, David 417
Fortnite 54
Foster, Thomas 2, 3, 22, 74–5, 76, 82, 94, 190, 278,
  286, 292, 293, 296, 302–3, 340
Foucault, Michel 120, 274, 298, 365–6, 367
Fox, Nathan 97
France, cyberpunk in 423–7
Francis, Jeana 349
Francophone North America, cyberpunk in 427–8

Francophone women writers 428–9
Frank Reade stories 64
Frankenstein, Frankensteinian 32, 33, 73, 76, 264,
  270–1, 348, 417; *see also* Shelley, Mary
Frankfurt School 284, 421
Frase, Peter 147
Freedman, Carl 63, 83, 92, 94, 283
Frelik, Paweł 53, 104, 129, 134, 135, 141, 186, 216,
  218, 226, 416
Freséan, Rodrigo *Mantra* 388
Freud, Sigmund 50
Freyermuth, Gundolf 259
Friedman, Ted 373
Front 242, 239; "Headhunter V3.0" 240
Front Line Assembly 239, 240
Frozen Synapse (Mode 7) 185–6
Fukuyama, Francis 57
Funkadelic 357
future present 260
Future Tech 203
Future Warrior (Francis and Long Soldier) 349–350

Gala, Leonardo *Cuentos de Bajavel* 398
Galliano, John 68
Galloway, Alexander 188, 189–190
Galouye, Daniel F. 14; *Counterfeit World* 11;
  Simulacron-3 11–12, 417
Gamerro, Carlos *Las islas* 387
gaming culture 10, 171, 173, 176, 426
Gao, Sally 222
Garda, Maria 190
Gardini, Carlos "Primera linea" 387
Garrison, Michael 65
Gattaca (Niccol) 76
gay characters 21, 93, 303, 305, 357
Geller, Theresa L. 126
Gemini Rue 187, 190
gender 11, 21, 30, 36, 37, 43, 44, 95, 112, 113, 125,
  136, 234, 247, 248, 291, 297, 303, 346–7; binary
  126, 298; fluidity 360, 419; gendered differences
  228–229, 231, 269, 270, 292, 294, 302; in
  Cadigan 34, 35, 42, 43–46, 52–53; in feminist
  proto-cyberpunk 33; in *Ghost in the Shell* 168;
  in cyberfeminists' works 38, 295–296
Genefort, Laurent 426
Genet, Jean 50
genetic engineering 1, 18, 73–4, 75–76, 78, 81,
  85, 95, 108, 111, 200, 202, 274, 275, 279, 333,
  388, 428
genetically engineered beings 17, 33, 95, 98, 194,
  314, 429
genetics 73, 77, 201, 429
genohype 77
genre 3, 7, 16, 18, 22, 64, 66, 71, 82, 84, 97, 102,
  108, 129, 140, 156, 163, 184, 186, 189, 190, 239,
  260, 266, 340, 425
geopolitics 259, 338
Germany, cyberpunk in 415–21

Index

Gess, Teddy Bear 96
Ghesquière, Nicolas 234
Ghosh, Amitav The Calcutta Chromosome 409–10, 411; The Great Derangement 332
Ghost in the Shell (Oshii) 107, 110, 115–6, 152, 153, 154, 155, 156, 160–7, 242, 243, 267, 403–4, 413; gender representations in 168
Ghost in the Shell (Sanders) 139, 140, 405–6; whitewashing in 406
Ghost in the Shell (Shirow) 111, 112–3
Ghost in the Shell videogames (Revolution) 185
Ghost in the Shell: Global Neural Network 116
Gibbons, Dave 96
Gibson, William 2, 8, 14, 15, 16, 25, 34, 41, 48, 50, 107, 116, 171, 174, 186, 203, 204, 214, 218, 228, 233, 241, 260, 278, 285, 310–1, 322, 329, 340, 341, 375, 390, 424; *Agency* 333; *All Tomorrow's Parties* 157, 225, 330; and Bruce Sterling, "Red Star, Winter Orbit" 17; and Bruce Sterling, *The Difference Engine* 65, 71; and The Velvet Underground 239; appearance in cameo 170; awards 16; Bridge trilogy 329–30; Blue Ant trilogy 81, 84, 86, 89, 260; "Burning Chrome" 1, 218, 257, 276, 278, 287, 336, 339, 342, 367, 396; *Burning Chrome* collection 21, 162, 315; *Count Zero* 13, 213, 367, 368–9, 378, 396, 398, 412; *Idoru* 10, 155, 157, 257, 330, 398; influence of *Métal Hurlant* on 91; interviewed by *Solaris* 427; "Johnny Mnemonic" 9, 15, 124, 232, 294, 324, 342, 366, 398; *Mona Lisa Overdrive* 294, 336, 424, 425; *Neuromancer* 1, 2, 10, 11, 12, 13, 16, 35, 49, 56, 87, 92, 101, 103, 110, 121, 134, 155, 200, 212, 216, 225, 233, 257, 259, 265, 269, 274, 276–7, 282, 287, 291, 294, 303, 306, 308, 310, 328, 330, 331, 332, 337, 339, 340, 345, 373, 396, 401, 402, 404, 415, 423; *Neuromancer* and natural world 327; *Neuromancer*, animality in 319–322; *Neuromancer* as Gothic 264; *Neuromancer*, opening line 169; *Neuromancer*, queerness in 300–1; *Neuromancien* 424; "New Rose Hotel" 367, 368; on Orwell 369; on *Shadowrun* 209; *Pattern Recognition* 81–4, 129, 260, 284; *Peripheral, The* 331; *Spook Country* 260; "The Gernsback Continuum" 18–9, 57, 335, 336, 338; Sprawl trilogy 49, 284, 342; style of 83–4; translation into Japanese of 155
Gibson Girls 236
Gilmore, John 375, 379
Ginway, M. Elizabeth 395
Giraud, Jean *see* Moebius
Girl with All the Gifts, The (McCarthy) 76–7
Gladstone, Max 116
Gleason, Katherine and Diana Pho, *Anatomy of Steampunk* 69
Gleitzeit 418
Glenny, Misha 176
global capitalism 32, 45, 57, 85, 200, 278, 291, 295, 296, 308, 342, 409, 413

globalization 7, 92, 95, 155, 174, 199, 282, 283, 335, 340, 341, 345, 371, 426
Goddess Mode (Quinn and Rodriguez) 97
Godhead (Anderson) 98
Goh, Sook Yi and Joyce Chng, *The Sea is Ours* 70
gold farming 260
Golden Age sf 7, 19, 57
golem 10, 51–2
González Fernández, Maielis 385; *Los días de la hysteria* 398
Good Kill (Niccol 2014) 138
Good, I.J. 56
Goodman, Joseph 68
Google Earth 261, 262
Goonan, Kathleen Ann, *Queen City Jazz* 35, 36
Gordon, Joan 428
Gorō, Masaki *Venus City* 154
Gothic, -ism 55, 73, 76, 264–71, 340; *see also* cybergothic
Gottesman, Zach 165
Graham, Elaine L. 278, 291, 295
Grant, Steven 101
graphic novels 99, 101, 390
Gravity (Cuarón) 89
Gray, Chris Hables 368; *Cyborg Citizen* 371
Gray, Kishonna L. 39
Grebowicz, Margret 200
Grech, Marija 348
Green, Jonathan: *Unnatural History* 67
Greenfield, Adam 287
Gregory, Sinda and Larry McCaffery 402; *see also* McCaffery
Grey, Chris 377
Griffiths, Nicola *Slow River* 295, 297
Grimes 248, 250
Grimwood, Jon Courtenay 54
Grossberg, Lawrence 71
Grossman, Lev 70
Grossman, Terry 278
Guattari, Félix 147, 149, 291, 429
Gunn, James E. 10
Gunnm (Kishiro) 140
GURPS Cyberpunk (Steve Jackson Games) 200, 209, 374–5
GURPS Steampunk (Stoddard) 68
Guy Fawkes mask 378

Haar, Rebecca 258, 259
Habara, Noboyushi 67
Hacker (Eremine) 97
Hacker Files, The (Shiner) 95
hacker/s, hacking 37, 55, 74, 87, 95, 124, 137, 175, 188, 189, 240, 297–8, 310, 320, 374, 376, 378, 387, 389, 391, 428
hacker heroes 9–10, 49, 122
hacker heroines 35, 58
Hacker's Conference 374, 375
Hackers (Softley) 124, 225, 243

Index

hacking simulations 189
Hacknet (Team Fractal Alligator) 189
hacktivism 378, 379, 391
Haggard, H. Rider *King Solomon's Mines* 353
Hagio, Moto 108
Hall, Stephen *The Raw Shark Texts* 52–3
Halo 4 (343 Industries) 216
Halt and Catch Fire 173
Hambly, Barbara Those Who Hunt the Night 65
Hancock, Robin 241
Hand, Elizabeth 42
Hannah, Dehlia and Cynthia Selinlo "Unseasonal Fashion" 236
Hans, Sarah *Steampunk World* 70
Hansón, Moisés 390
Haraway, Donna J. 24, 30, 52, 75, 111, 113, 117, 139, 140, 166, 189, 269, 270, 275, 298, 317, 411, 429; "A Cyborg Manifesto" 93, 154, 274, 279, 355; "Manifesto for Cyborgs" 291, 328, 333, 339; *Staying with the Trouble* 279
Hard Boiled (Miller and Darrow) 94
Hard Reset (Flying Wild Hog) 185
Hardt and Negri, *Empire* 335, 341
Hardwired: The Sourcebook 200
Harlan, John 309
Harris, Anne *Accidental Creatures* 36, 295, 296, 297
Harsh Realm (Carter) 176
Hartmann, Ivor W. *AfroSF* 353
Hartwell, David 17
Harvey, David 119, 188
Harvey, P.J. 243
Hassler-Forest, Dan 79
Haupts, Tobias 415
Hawkwind 238
Hayakawa's SF Magazine 402
Hayles, N. Katherine 24, 30, 75, 111, 138, 183, 231, 268, 274, 275, 276, 291–3, 318–19, 414; *Unthought* 329; "Wrestling with Transhumanism" 277
Headroom *see* Max Headroom
head-up display (HUD) 138
Heavy Liquid (Pope) 96, 97
Heavy Metal 91, 92, 97, 101
heavy metal 238, 239, 241, 243
Hebdige, Dick 164; *Subculture* 229
Heidegger, Martin 327
Heiland, Donna 269
Heinlein, Robert A. 16, 18; *Moon is a Harsh Mistress, The* 379
Helix Comics 96
Henda, Kiluanji Kia *Icarus 13* 359
Henriquez, Bruno 395
Hensley, Shane 68
Herbrechter, Stefan 257
Hernández, Arturo César Rojas 389
Hernández Pacin, Vladimir 396, 397; neologisms in 397
Hernandez, Gilbert and Jaime 104

Heroes (Kring) 76
Hewlett, Jamie 93
Hicks, Heather 293
Higgins, David M. 101
high fantasy creatures 206
Hill Agency (Byrne) 98
Hindu gods 412
Hines, Alicia H. 310
Hiro Protagonist 48, 58, 255, 278, 311; *see also* Stephenson, *Snow Crash*
Histórias de amor e fúrio (Bolognesi) 387
Hocking, Clint 189
Hofstadter, Richard 197, 198
Holischka, Thorsten 259
Hollander, Anne 231
Hollinger, Veronica 19, 22, 24, 75, 82, 88, 129, 132, 260, 270, 274, 300, 302, 354, 423, 425
Hollywood 35, 67 107, 116, 119, 121, 122, 123, 124, 126, 128, 137, 152, 156, 162, 228, 243, 340–1, 353, 405, 415, 416, 417, 419, 423
holocaust denial 212
homoerotic sex 113, 117, 294
homosexuality 50, 119, 301, 303
Hopkins, Patrick D. 154
Hopkinson, Nalo 309, 312, 354, 357; *Brown Girl in the Ring* 36, 37, 355–6; *Midnight Robber* 35, 36, 288, 313–4, 355
Horyn, Cathy 235
How the West Was Lost (LaPensée) 98
HUDs 141
Hudson, Brian K "Indigenous Cyberpunk Manifesto" 345
Hughes, Dorothy Pitman 38
Hughes, Eric 376; "Cypherpunk's Manifesto" 377
Hugo Award 10, 16, 356, 358
humanism 2, 25, 275, 295, 319, 411, 424; *see also* posthumanism; transhumanism
Hume, Kathryn 207
Huxley, Aldous 8
hybridization 73, 74, 75, 97, 206, 230, 346
hyperimmersion 259
hypermasculinity 123
hyperobject 326, 329, 330, 331, 332
hyperreal, hyperreality 89, 160, 169, 186, 219, 220, 255, 256, 258, 259, 261, 329, 330–2, 416, 427

I am Legend (Lawrence) 76–7
I, Robot (Proyas) 165
Idol, Billy 234; *Cyberpunk* 241, 425
Idolmaster franchise 158
idorus 88, 158, 396; *see also* Gibson, *Idoru*
Ihde, Don 24
Illidiance 242
Illuminati 194, 195, 198
iMac 233
immortality 13, 53, 57, 74, 275, 313; digital immortality 12, 60, 174, 266–7, 274, 276, 318
Imperial Steam and Light 71

442

Index

imperialism 65, 67, 69, 70, 314, 335, 355
implant technology 18, 43, 389
implosion 336, 338
Incorporated 174
India, cyberpunk in 408–14
Indifference Engine, The (Professor Elemental) 67
Indigenous peoples 2, 38, 98, 336, 386, 388, 412
Indigenous fashions 234, 236
Indigenous futurisms 344–51
Indigenous movements 350
Indigenous Nationhood Movement 350
indigipunk 98
individualist heroes 175, 186, 187, 190
industrial (electronic) music 238, 239, 240, 242, 243, 244, 420
information; Age of, 57, 308, 335; centrality of in cyberpunk 340; economy 8, 59, 357, 429; technology (IT) 22, 54, 78, 97, 111, 174, 185, 200, 233, 274, 408, 409, 424, 427
Ings, Simon 54
inner space 8, 14
Intelligence 173
Interface Zero (Gun Metal Games) 203
Internet 9, 35, 36, 60–1, 124, 172, 173, 258–9, 291, 297, 314, 374, 376, 390, 395, 408, 411, 423, 428; access to in Cuba 396; and cyberspace 257, 328, 375; first connection 62; in cyberpunk 86, 156, 165; male domination of 37, 38, 39, 297; of Things 287, 370
Internet Archive 379
intersectionality 46, 248, 296, 298
interstellar travel 103, 174, 201, 336
Ion Storm 193
Iron Kingdoms (Privateer Press) 68
Irwin, Mark 404
Ishii, Sogo 164
Ishikawa, Chu 243
Ishinomori, Shōtaro 108
IT *see* information technology (IT)
Ito, Hiroyuki 55
Iung, Matthew 101
Iverson, Jennifer 418

J-horror 156
jack in, jacking in 11, 43, 87, 123, 201, 206, 260, 286, 292, 294, 301, 341, 367, 425
Jackson, Janet "Rhythm Nation" 245
Jackson, Michael 246
Jackson, Rosemary 3
Jackson, Steve 375, 376; *see also* Steve Jackson Games
Jacksons, The 358
James, Edward 3
Jameson, Fredric 2, 45, 59, 63, 68, 79, 103, 135, 160, 176, 282–3, 284, 287, 288, 289, 338, 348; *The Ancients and the Postmoderns* 286; on Gibson, *Neuromancer* 286; on Gibson, *Pattern Recognition* 283; *Postmodernism* 2, 282–3, 285; *The Seeds*

of Time 144, 283; *see also* late capitalism; postmodernism
Jane 58721 245
Janelle, Claude 427
Japan and Japaneseness 2, 66, 67, 71, 88, 96, 109, 152, 154, 155, 156, 346, 401–6; cyberpunk in 107, 110, 111, 116, 134, 139, 160, 164, 243; Japan as the future 107, 155; *see also* anime; manga
Jefferson, Thomas 19
Jemisin, N.K. 39, 357; "Too Many Yesterdays, Not Enough Tomorrows" 37; "Valedictorian" 356–7
Jenkins, Henry 116
Jeter, K.W. 64; Infernal Devices 65; Morlock Night 65, 71
Jetsons 57
Jeury, Michel "Les systèmes organisants" 424
Jimi Hendrix Experience, The 357
Johansson, Scarlet 406
Johnny Mnemonic (Longo) 124, 243, 417
"Johnny Mnemonic" *see* Gibson, "Johnny Mnemonic"
Johnson, Mark R. 1, 134, 137
Johnson, Samuel 53
Jones, Gwyneth 35, 54; *Escape Plans* 21, 35
Jones, Keziah 98
Jordan, Tim 365–6
Jorgensen, Darren 287
Joshi, Ruchir The Last Jet-Engine Laugh 411
Journey 242
Joy Division 239
Joyce, Stephen 188, 193, 195, 198
Judge Dredd (Cannon) 217

Kabinett des Dr. Caligari, Das (Wiene) 416
Kabuki (Mack) 96
Kac, Eduardo 77
Kadrey, Richard 54, 217, 405, 424
Kamikaze 1989 (Gremm) 415, 419, 420, 421
Kapor, Mitch 375, 379
Kawaii, Kenji 243
Kelly, James Patrick 17, 21, 300; and John Kessel, *Rewired: The Post-Cyberpunk Anthology* 39, 48, 54
Kerberos Club, The 72
Kessel, John 16, 48; *see also* Kelly
Ketterer, David 264
Khan, Jeanette 92
Kilgore, De Witt Douglas 353–4, 356, 359–60
Killing Us Softly 37
Killjoy, Margaret 71
Killtopia (Cook and Paton) 97
King of Cyberpunk (Gibson) 41
Kirkus Reviews 66
Kishiro, Yukito 111, 112, 116, 140
Kline, Kevin 67
KMFDM 239
Komatsu, Sakyō 108
Konaka theory 156, 160
Konaka, Chiaki 156

Index

Kornbluth, C.M. 7
Koutetsu Teikoku (Satake) 66
Kraftwerk 238, 415, 418
Kress, Nancy *Beggars in Spain* 76
Kucklick, Christoph 261
Kujawski, Guilherme *Piritas Siderais* 386
Kunzelman, Cameron 187
Kunzru, Hari *Transmission* 411
Kuroma, Hisashi 110, 155
Kurzweil, Ray 12, 56, 277–8
Kusahara, Machiko 317
Kyoko Date 157

La Ferla, Ruth 70
La sonámbula (Spiner) 387
Laboria Cuboniks collective 38–9
Lagerfeld, Karl 419
Lai, Larissa 306
Laidlaw, Mark 17
Lake, Jay 68
LaMarre, Thomas 116, 152
Landon, Brooks 188–9
Lang, Fritz 32, 417; *see also Metropolis*
Langford, David 67, 68
LAPD 125, 128, 130, 131, 173
LaPensée, Elizabeth 98
Larsson, Stieg 371
Lasker, Lawrence 122
Last Night, The (Odd Tales) 186
late capitalism 45, 46, 94, 103, 144, 165, 269,
    282–3, 284, 285, 286, 292, 297, 335, 338, 348
Latham, Rob 18
Latin America 385–92
Latour, Bruno 25
Lavender III, Isiah 21, 39, 236, 359
Lavigne, Carlen 39, 42, 44, 294, 295, 303, 345, 428
Lavin, Guillermo "Reaching the Shore" 341
Lawnmower Man, The (Leonard) 123–4, 126, 417
Lawnmower Man 2: Beyond Cyberspace
    (Mann) 124
Lazano, Kevin 243
Lazarus, Margaret 37
Le Blanc, Michelle and Colin Odell 162, 164
Le Guin, Ursula K. 129
League of Extraordinary Gentlemen (Moore and
    O'Neill) 67
League of Extraordinary Gentlemen (Norrington
    and Robinson) 67
Leary, Timothy 425, 427
Lee, Elaine 96
Leeb, Bill 240
Leinster, Murray 8
Lemire, Jeff 98
Lemos, Cirilo "A lua é uma flor sem pétalas" 387
Lemosquet, Marc *Plug-in* 425
lesbian characters 21, 36, 93, 126, 296, 300, 303,
    305, 306
Lethem, Jonathan 54

Letzten Tage von Gomorrha, Die
    (Sanders-Brahms) 415
Lévi-Strauss, Claude 164
Lewis, Michael, *The Big Short* 86
Lewitt, Shariann 54
Ley, Sandra J. 233, 235
Liew, Sonny 97
Ligny, Jean-Marc 425–6, 429
Lim, Rosemary 70
Lincoln, Ben 209
Liow, Robert 70
LiPuma, Edward and Benjamin Lee, *Financial
    Derivatives* 282, 288
Liquid Sky (Tsukerman) 416
loas 356, 412
Locus Award 41
Lodi-Ribeiro, Gerson and Luis Filipe Silva,
    Vaporpunk 70
Logan's Run (Anderson) 416
Loiza, Susana, Speculative Imperialisms 70
Londero, Rodolfo 385
London 65, 66, 70, 83, 195, 331–2, 412
Long Soldier, Nigel R. 349
Loofborouw, Lily 136
Lorraine, Lilith 34; "Into the 28th Century" 32
Los Angeles as setting 41, 94, 104, 128, 129, 130,
    145, 146, 179, 216, 222, 308, 313, 404
Lost Horizons (Abney Park) 67
Love and Rockets (Hernandez and Hernandez) 104
Love Live! (Kyōgoku) 158
Lovecraft, H.P. 205, 424
Low Orbit Ion Cannon (LOIC) 378
Luallak, Pear 70
ludonarrative dissonance 189
luminescence 190–191

M (Lang) 416–417
Mabuse, Dr. 420, 421
MacDonald, John D. 10
Mack, David 96
Macross 158–9
Macross Plus 157
Mad Max (Miller) 349
Mad Max movies 233
Maddox, Tom 17, 26, 41
Maggiori, Germán *Cría Terminal* 388
magic 35, 68, 92, 140, 206–7, 209, 210, 212–3,
    214, 224, 314
magical girl subgenre 97
Magical Negros 93
magical realism 430
male characters 21, 35, 42, 70, 106, 120, 125, 187,
    293, 294, 300, 301, 417
male cyberpunk writers 21, 34, 44, 429
Malinky Robot (Lieuw) 97
Mandel, Ernest 285
Mandelbrot, Benoit 426
Maney, Kevin 257

444

Index

manga 2, 107–17; and prose sf 108; drawing style 113–4, 117; fanzines 109
Mann, George *Affinity Bridge* 67
Mann, Steve 372
Mann, Steven 364
Manykhun, Vladimir 221
Maqari, Native 98
Marchetti, Gina 402
Marcinkowski, Alexandre 423, 424
Marquis, Kyle 1
Martin, Alan C. 93
Martin, Daniel 95
Martín, Marcos 98
Marusek, David 54
Marvel Cinematic Universe 353, 360
Marvel comics 95,101
Marx, Karl and Friedrich Engels 57; *Communist Manifesto* 376
marxism, marxist 3, 120, 126, 141, 149, 282–289
Masaki, Gorō 110, 402
Masamune, Shirow 154
masculinism 248, 250, 269, 286
masculinist cyberpunk 32, 34–5, 42, 292, 293, 296, 297, 300; *see also* toxic masculinity
Mason, Lisa *Arachne* 21, 35
Mass Effect franchise 186
Mathur, Suchitra 408
matrix 302, 321
Matrix Comics, The 94, 97
Matrix Online (Monolith) 186
Matrix, The (Wachowskis) 1, 11, 98, 125–6, 128, 130, 137, 138, 180, 218, 228, 415, 417; and Baudrillard 256–7; and franchise 135, 242; and theory 257; trilogy 94, 340–341
Mauruschat, Felix 416, 421
Max Headroom: Twenty Minutes into the Future [MH20] 124, 171–2, 178–83
May, Timothy C. "The Crypto-Anarchist Manifesto" 376
Mbembe, Achille 269
McAllister, Laurent 427; *Suprématie* 427, 430
McCaffery, Larry 109, 214, 285, 402, 425; *Storming the Reality Studio* 405, 425
McCaffrey, Anne *The Ship Who Sang* 33
McClelland, Nigel 72
McCloud, Scott 92
McDonald, Ian 289, 412
McFarlane, Anna 88, 125, 137, 138, 332
McGurl, Mark 279
McHale, Brian 73, 75, 81, 82, 121, 255
McHugh, Maureen *China Mountain Zhang* 295
McIntyre, Vonda 34, 38; *Dreamsnake* 33; *Superluminal* 33
McKay, Adam 86
McKevitt, Andrew 401–2, 405
McKie, Angus 91, 96
McLuhan, Marshall 7, 10, 96, 176, 259, 366
McMafia 176

McQueen, Sean 429
McVeillance 364
Mead, Sydney Jay (Syd) 129, 221
meat problem 322
mecha 152, 153–5, 158
Mechanists *see* Sterling, Shaper/Mechanist series
Medak-Saltzman, Danika 344, 350
media 8, 10, 259; media barons 86; media convergence 116 ; media critique 179, 182; media landscape 32, 33, 105, 116, 132; media technologies 38, 418; media theory 258
Meehan, Paul 417
megacorporations 19, 213, 214, 217, 416, 421
Megazone 23 157, 159
Mehan, Uppinder 408
Melchor, Alejandro 68
Melzer, Patricia 295, 300
Men in Black (Sonnenfeld) 197
Mendels, Ivanna 70
Menon, Anil 412; *The Beast with a Billion Feet* 411; and Vandana Singh, *Breaking the Bow* 412
Metal Gear series 186
Métal Hurlant 91, 92, 94, 101, 423, 425
Metaverse 49, 50, 54, 255, 257, 278, 330; *see also* Sterling, Bruce
Metropolis (Lang) 32, 234, 235, 373, 415, 417, 420
Mexico, cyberpunk in 386, 388–90
Mexico City 388, 389
Meyer-Eppler, Werner 418
Meynard, Yves 427
Miéville, China *King Rat* and *Perdido Street Station* 68, 69
Miku, Hatsune 158
Milburn, Colin 378
Milhon, Jude 376
Millennium (Carter) 197
Miller, Cynthia J. 69
Miller, Frank 94; *Batman: The Dark Knight Returns* 92; *Ronin* 92–93
Miller, Marc W. 201
Millions, Molly 195, 232, 294, 295, 296, 300, 301; *see also* Gibson, William
Milonogiannis, Giannis 97
Milton, John: *Paradise Lost* 270
Mina Losa 424
mind backups 205, 388
mind invasion 18, 22, 73, 151, 211, 338, 339, 341
mind-uploading 37, 75, 174, 268, 276, 317, 336
mindhacking 205
minimalism 238, 239
Ministry 239
Minitel 423
Minor, Jason Tesmujin 96
mirrorshades 195, 214, 228, 232, 292, 301, 308, 337, 405, 426
Mirrorshades Collective 15–22
Mirrorshades *see* Sterling, Mirrorshades and Preface to Mirrorshades

445

Index

Misha 285; *Red Spider White Web* 35, 234, 284, 341, 345, 346–7
misogyny 92, 93, 96, 98, 99, 126, 348, 349; in comics 92, 94
Mitchell, Syne *Technogenesis* 36
Mitchell, W.J.T. 362
Mixon, Laura 21; *Glass Houses* 35, 295, 296, 297; *Proxies* 35, 295
Miyazaki, Hayao 66, 113
MMORPG 160, 258
Mobile Police Patlabor 153
Mobile Suite Gundam 153
mode 3
Moebius (Jean Giraud) 91, 92–3, 94, 101, 117
Monáe, Janelle 242, 358; "Crazy, Classic, Life" 247; *Dirty Computer* 245–50, 358; *Electric Lady* 358; "Make Me Feel" 248–249; *Metropolis: The Chase Suite* 358; "Pynk" 248; *The ArchAndroid* 358
Mondo 2000 96, 376
monsters, monstrosity 264, 300
Moorcock, Michael 8; The Land Leviathan 65; The Warlord of the Air 65, 71
Moore, Alan 67, 71, 101
Moore, C.L., "No Woman Born" 33
Morán, Denis Mourdoch, *Dentro de la boca del lobo* 398
Moravec, Hans 12, 183, 275, 276, 279, 292
More, Max 231, 273, 274, 275, 276
Morehouse, Lyda 303, 306; *AngelLINK* series 35, 36
Moreno, Pepe 95
Morgan, Richard K. 55, 174, 265; *Altered Carbon* 216; Takeshi Kovacs trilogy 53–4; *see also Altered Carbon*
Moriarty, Chris 39; Spin series 37
Morley, David and Kevin Robins *Spaces of Identity* 155, 401, 402
Morlocks 65
Moroder, Giorgio 242
Morrison, Grant *We3* 323–324
Morton, Timothy 326, 327–328, 329, 331, 332
Morvan, Jean-David 98
Mosley, Walter: *Futureland* 311–2, 355
Mota, Erick J., *Habana underguater* 396, 398
Movement, the 1, 2, 15–22, 41, 94, 228, 276, 291, 301, 326, 327, 330, 376
Mower, Sarah 234
Moylan, Tom 283–4, 338–9
"Mozart in Mirrorshades" *see* Sterling; Shiner
Mozart, Wolfgang Amadeus 19, 328
Mr. Robot (Esmail) 87–8, 175, 369
Ms. 38
MTV 246
Mugler, Thierry 234
Mugot, Marilyn 224; "Night Project" 221
Mulhern, Sinéad 222
Mulvey, Laura 132

Murphy, Graham J. 43, 301–2; and Lars Schmeink, *Cyberpunk and Visual Culture* 22, 128, 134, 245, 362; and Sherryl Vint *Beyond Cyberpunk* 22, 54
Murphy, Sean 98
Muscha (Jürgen Muschalek) 419
music 2, 190, 238–44
Musk, Elon 56

Naafs, Saskia 371
Nadia: The Secret of Blue Water (Anno and Miyazaki) 66, 67
Nagata, Linda *The Red* 329
nanotech/nology 1, 25, 36, 50, 86, 200, 203, 205, 234, 273, 279, 314; in Gibson 329, 330, 331
'Nansi Web 314
Napier, Susan J. 154, 163–4, 165, 167, 403
Narlikar, Jayant Vishnu: *Virus* 412
Natali, Vincenzo 76
Nathan Never 95–6
Native American 284; *see also* Indigenous
Nausicaä of the Valley of the Wind (Miyazaki) 113
Nawlz (Campbell) 97
Nayar, Pramod K. 75
NDNs 345, 350, 351
near future setting 7, 9, 10, 25, 32, 37, 46, 52, 86, 102, 141, 201, 213, 308, 336, 370, 418; Australia 93; Canada 356; France 50; India 409, 410, 411; Japan 96, 163; Latin America 388; in TRPG 214; USA 38, 41, 48, 104, 124, 130, 278, 409
Nebula Award 16
necropolitics 269
Nelson, Alondra 310
Nemo, Captain 66, 67
neocolonialism 335
Neocron and *Neocron 2* (Reakktor Media) 416
neoliberal, –ism 119, 120, 121, 123, 125, 126, 169, 170, 174, 175, 176, 188, 190, 225, 282, 287, 289, 329, 338, 339, 379, 386, 289, 335, 385, 388, 391, 411, 416; capitalism 19, 144, 147, 148, 149, 268, 489; corpocracy 62; conspiracies 390, 391; financialization 286; globalization 92, 335
neologisms 110, 204, 206, 397, 423, 426
Net, The (Winkler) 124
Netflix 405
Neue Deutsche Welle 418
Neumann, John von 56
neural implants 201, 312, 355, 401
Neuromancer video game (Interplay) 185
Neuromancer *see* Gibson, Neuromancer
Neuromancer comic book 93
neuromancy 282, 289
Neuromantics 8, 232
New Treasure Island (Tezuka, Sakai) 107–8
New Wave sf 7, 8, 10, 12, 14
New World Order (NWO) 198
Newitz, Annalee 78; *Automomous* 329, 332
Newman, Kim 54

446

Index

Ng, James 71
Nguyen, Dustin 98
Nicholls, Peter 67, 68, 122–3
Night and the City (Dassin) 417
Nihei 114–15
Nihon Noir (Blachford) 219–20, 221
Nilges, Mattias 86
Niven, Larry 16, 18
Nixon, Nicola 21, 34, 41, 42, 119, 169, 186, 187, 190, 286, 282, 292, 294, 295, 411
No Maps for These Territories (Neale) 15, 73
Noah, Azusa 110
Nogha, Misha *see* Misha
noir 34, 59, 76, 135, 136, 180, 195, 229, 238, 240, 327, 369, 389, 397, 398; city noir, urban noir 217, 386; film noir 171, 179, 234, 264, 269, 420, 426; future noir 111, 239, 404, 417; neo-noir 53, 54, 55, 128, 339; noir-inflected, noir sensibility 91, 92, 129, 152, 228
Nomad 96
nonbinary 33, 35, 36, 246, 296, 297, 306
Nonplayer (Simpson) 97
Noon, Jeff 54
Normal, The "Warm Leatherette" 240
Norrington, Stephen 67
Nosferatu (Murnau) 416
Novotny, Patrick 243
novum, novums, nova 128, 285, 286, 287, 289, 329, 416, 417
Noys, Benjamin 282
nuclear war 119, 122, 214, 355, 369, 374
Nuclearvision (Jacobs and Seltmann) 415, 419, 420
Numan, Gary "Down in the Park" 238

O'Bannon, Dan and Moebius "The Long Tomorrow" 91, 92–3, 98–9, 101
O'Barr, James 96, 99
O'Connell, Hugh 89, 176
O'Neill, Kevin 67
Oblivion (Kosinski) 216
Ofidia 397
OGL Steampunk (Melchor) 68
Ōhara, Mariko 110
Ohashi, Tsutomu 242, 243
Ohler, Norman 416
Ojetade, Balogun 70
Okada, Toshio 152
Okorafor, Nnedi 312, 314; *The Book of Phoenix* 37, 314; *Who Fears Death* 314, 353
Old City Blues (Milonogiannis) 97
Oloixarac, Pola La constelaciones oscuras 388
Omni 15, 16
Ong, Walter 258
online gaming 54
oral culture 258
Orbaugh, Sharalyn 113, 166, 167
Orientalism 95, 402

Orlan 233
Orsi, Carlos: "Questão de sobrevivência" 386
Orta, Lucy "Refuge Wear" 236
Ortiz de Montellano, Bernardo de "La máquina humana" 385
Orwell, George 379; *Nineteen Eighty-Four* 315, 366, 369, 373, 379; *see also* Big Brother
Oshii, Mamoru 114, 156, 162, 165, 243, 404, 406; *see also Ghost in the Shell*
otaku 109
Other, the 26
OtherLife (Lucas) 304–5
Ōtomo, Katsuhiro 66, 67, 108, 113, 114, 117, 139; *see also Akira*
Ōtsuka, Yasuo 152

pace of change 81–2
Padmanabhan, Manjula *Harvest* 410–1
Pagliassotti, Dru *Clockwork Heart* 67
Palmer, Stephen Beautiful Intelligence 329
panels in comics and manga design 104, 114–5
panopticon 365, 366, 367, 410
paranoia 2, 12, 26, 51, 197, 294, 301, 306
Park, Kyeongeun 388
Parkin, Simon 258
Parliament 239, 357, 360
Partin, Will 188
Patlabor 2 (Oshii) 156
Paton, Chris 97
Paul, Frank R. 336
Paull, Lawrence G. 129
Pauls, Cole 98
Paz-Soldán, Edmundo 391
Paz, Octavio El laberinto de la soledad 389
PCP *see* post-cyberpunk
Pearson, Josh 231–2
Pearson, Wendy 42, 43, 294
Pekar, Harvey 104
peripherals 332
Perschon, Mike, "The Steampunk Aesthetic" 69
Person of Interest 173
Peru, cyberpunk in 390–1
Petto, Martin 17
Pfeil, Fred 8, 14
Philbeck, Thomas D. 75
Philip K. Dick Award 16, 41
photography 216–26
Piercy, Marge 54; Body of Glass: *see* He, She and It; He, She and It 35, 36, 51–2, 295, 296, 328; Woman on the Edge of Time 33, 274
Pihlia, Ricardo La ciudad ausente 387
Piketty, Thomas 176
Pilsch, Andrew 56–7
Pitts, Victoria 233, 234
Pixies, The 88
Plant, Sadie 42
Player, Mark 165, 402, 403

Index

Poe, Edgar Allan 265, 266, 269, 424
Pohl, Frederik 7; "Tunnel Under the World, The" 11, 12
Polhemus, Ted 232, 233, 236
Pollack, Rachel 68, 96
Polyfantastica (Enos) 98
Pondsmith, Mike 200, 201, 206, 267
Pope, Paul 96, 97
Porcayo, Gerardo Horacio 389, 390
post-cyberpunk (PCP) 22, 36, 39, 48–55, 56, 58, 94, 108, 114, 282, 287, 288, 311, 328, 329, 330, 332, 339; as science-fiction realism 132; films 286; and virtuality 259–61
post-truth America 172
postbiological world 275
postcolonial 22, 288, 349, 359, 408, 409, 411, 413
posthuman, -ist 2, 24–30, 74, 77, 87, 112, 148, 165, 167, 173, 207, 265, 319, 391; characters 169; critical posthumanism 273, 274; posthumanisms 273–80; Prigoginic posthumanism 30; two ways of becoming 274
Postman, Neil 176
postmodern/ism 49, 66, 95, 103–4, 105, 108, 109, 126, 135, 139, 145, 148, 160, 166, 182, 184, 229, 241, 244, 266, 293, 295, 300, 326, 330, 331, 336, 366, 367, 386, 408, 411, 413, 423, 425; and *Blade Runner/BR 2049* 146, 147, 148, 218; and cyberpunk 2, 45; and Jameson 282–3, 284, 285, 286; and McHale 255; to posthumanism 200
Powers, Tim 65
Prager, Brad 417
Priest, Cherie 69
Prigogine, Ilya 25, 29–30; *From Being to Becoming* 29
Prince 246, 247, 248
Prince, Stephen 134
Private Eye, The (Martín, Vicente, Vaughn) 98
Privateer Press 68
Profit 175
progressivism 36, 37, 38, 68, 71, 96, 125, 278, 411
prostheses, prosthetics 18, 25, 81, 85, 110, 111, 151, 154, 165, 189, 195, 201, 202, 204, 206, 268, 273, 274, 292, 338, 339, 348, 354, 386, 387, 389; computer as prosthesis 226; as fashion 235, 236; perceptural prosthesis 10
proto-cyberpunk 32–3, 34, 37, 92, 108, 238, 277, 312, 317, 415
proto-queerness 42, 43, 44, 46, 302
Proyas, Alex 11, 99, 165
Psychic TV 420
Psycho-Pass (Shiotani and Motohiro) 156
pulp era science fiction 7, 205, 216, 301, 335, 398
Pumzi (Kahiu) 353, 358
Punch cartoon 230
Punisher, The 95
punk/s 38, 167, 232, 239, 389, 409–10, 425, 426; aesthetic 93; culture 162, 164; meaning of 364; music, musicians 20, 389, 403; sensibility 206
Pynchon, Thomas 7, 18, 427

Quadrilateral Cowboy, Hackmud (Drizzly Bear) 189
quantified self 57
Quantified Self movement 77
Québec 427–8
Queen of Cyberpunk (Pat Cadigan) 34, 41, 277
Queen of Punk SF (Ellen Datlow) 16
queer, queerness 2, 36, 43, 44, 46, 242, 245–6, 247, 249, 279, 294, 296, 297, 303, 358, 419; identities 296; and non-binary authors 35; texts 42–3; theory 300–306; *see also* proto-queer
Quinn, Zoë and Robbi Rodriquez *Goddess Mode* 97

Ra.One (Sinha) 412–13
Ra, Sun *see* Sun Ra
race 21, 65, 124, 130, 187, 209, 246, 346, 349; in cyberpunk 36, 44, 46, 311–12, 354, 355, 356, 387
race theory 70, 308–15
racial minorities 247
racism 21, 27, 39, 65, 69, 70, 131, 133, 275, 278, 295, 308–13, 349, 353, 354, 355
Raheja, Michelle H. 350
Ramayana 412
Ramírez, José Luis "Hielo" 389
RanXerox (Tamburini and Liberatore) 92
Rapatzikou, Tatiani G. 264
rapture 37, 62; of the nerds (Doctorow and Stross) 337
Rasputina 67–8
Rastas, Rastafarians 233, 310
Ratcliff, Trey 225; "Blade Runner" and "Runner of Blades" 222; "The Veins of Bangkok" 224
Ratcliffe, Spurgeon Vaughn: *Steampunk Fashion* 69
Raulerson, Joshua 56, 329
Ravage 2099 95
Reader Player One (Spielberg) 140–1
Reagan, Ronald 122, 126, 241; Reaganite America 119–20
reality/realism 11, 12, 15, 37, 48, 51, 52, 53, 56, 59, 64, 81, 92, 105, 122, 132, 134, 145, 147, 160, 210, 231, 247, 255, 256, 259, 266, 271, 303, 330, 337, 364, 367, 385, 386, 388, 398, 419, 428; anxiety about 181, 261; influenced by cyberpunk 137, 138, 156, 157, 260; reality television 103, 173; and representation 126, 135, 136, 139, 182, 222, 225, 257, 264, 265; as science fiction 1, 81–2, 84–5, 86, 87, 88, 89; *see also* corporeality; hyperreal; simulation; virtual reality
Rear Windows (Hitchcock) 132
Redmond, Ben 72
Redmond, Shana L. 246
Reed, Kit, "The New You" 33
Reed, Lou 238
Reeve, Philip Mortal Engines and Scrivener's Moon 67
Regina, Ivan Carlos 392
Rehak, Bob 187

Index

Reiss, Michael 73
Remember Me (Dontmod) 186, 190
Remender, Rick 98
replicants 120–1, 136, 144, 146–7, 148, 149, 167, 229, 246, 261
reproduction 27, 33, 59–60, 154, 166, 167, 286, 296
reproduction and reproductive rights 295
Resistance (Palmiotti, Gray and Santa Cruz) 97
Ressell, Trace 419
retrofuturism, retrofuturist 68, 69, 70, 135, 136, 140, 141, 235
revealed religions 51
Reverie 171
Revolutionary Phase (steampunk) 69–71
Rez (United Game Artists) 186
Rhee, Jennifer 138
Rieder, John 190, 357–8, 419
Riessland, Andreas 163
Riggs, Marlon *Tongues Untied* 248
Rimbaud, Jean-Arthur 426
Risso, Eduardo 98
Rite of Passage: The Steamfunk Movie (Ojetade) 70
Rivera, Lysa 341
Rivingtons, The 105
Road Warrior, The (Miller) 233
Roanhorse, Rebecca 351
Robb, Brian, *Steampunk* 69
Robert, Yves 70
Roberts, Adam 216
Robertson, Darick 96
Robinson, James 67
Robinson, Kim Stanley 16, 59; *New York 2140* 289
RoboCop (Verhoeven) 123, 139, 165, 235, 272
RoboRoach 324
Robotech 157
robots, robotics 7, 10, 12, 57, 62, 66, 153, 175–176, 200, 202, 206, 234, 241, 246, 256, 275, 276, 286, 317–8, 324, 341, 347–8, 357, 366, 369, 386, 402, 405, 413, 421; robot pop 238, 418
Robson, Justina 54
Rocagliolo, Santiago *Tan cerca de la vida* 391
rock and roll 18, 19–20, 20–1
Rodriguez, Daniel 265
Rodriguez, Robert 116
Rojo, Pepe "Ruido gris" 389
role-playing games 200–7
Ronin 94, 99
Rose, Lloyd 102
Rose, Tricia 354
Rosedale, Philip 257
Rosenblum, Mary 21; *Chimera* 295, 296
Ross, Andrew 370
Rossum Corporation 171
Roxy Music 238
Royster, Francesca 247, 250
RPG *see* roleplaying games
Rucker, Rudy 15, 17, 21, 34, 41, 217, 425; *Software* 12, 49, 276; *The Sex Sphere* 15; *Ware* tetralogy 276

Ruiner (Reikon Games) 186
Run Love Kill (Tsuei and Canete) 98
Rush 71
Russ, Joanna 8, 34, 38; *The Female Man* 33, 185, 274, 294, 295
Ryman, Geoff 306

Sadlos, Artur "Cyberpunk City" 219–20, 221, 225
Safro, Mary 97
Saignantes, Les (Bekolo) 288, 359
Sailor Moon (Takeuchi) 113
Saito, Kumiko 162
Sakai, Shichima 108
same-sex marriage 303, 305
Sampson, Tony D. 51
Sanchez, Rosaura and Beatrice Pita *Lunar Braceros* 341
Sánchez Gómez, José Miguel *see* Yoss
Sánchez-Mesa, Domingo 396
Sankofa (Gerima) 358
Santarriaga, Hector Germán 390
Sargent, Pamela: *The Shore of Women* 295
Sartre, Jean-Paul 349
Satake, Yoshinori 66
Sauter, Molly 378
Savage Worlds (Great White Games) 203
Schallegger, René 199
Schaub, Joseph Christopher 166
Scheibler, Olive 416
Schmeink, Lars 88, 104, 130, 179, 193, 194, 199, 200, 216, 218, 225, 247, 264, 279, 323, 333, 417, 428, 429
Schneier, Bruce *Applied Cryptography* 377
Schüfftan, Eugen 417
Schulte, Stephanie Ricker 374
Schumpeter, Joseph 121
sci-fiberpunk 73, 94
science fiction: art 216; as realism 81–2, 84–5; history of 7; inadequacies of 15
Science Fiction Eye 15
Scott, Melissa *Trouble and Her Friends* 35, 36, 295, 297, 302, 303–4, 305–6
Scott, Ridley 104, 128, 373; *see also Blade Runner*
Second Life (Linden Lab) 54, 257–8
second- and third-wave cyberpunk 22
self-censorship, end of 101
self-driving cars 174
selling of body parts 409
Senarens, Luis 64
Serial Experiments Lain (Nakamura) 156
Sesame program 370–1
sexism 39, 65, 69, 269, 278
sexual liberation 42, 93, 154
sexuality 11, 21, 35, 42, 43, 45, 46, 106, 166, 234, 248, 292, 300, 303, 385, 386, 389, 397
SFRA (Science Fiction Research Association) 16
Shadowrun (FASA) 206–207, 209–15; conspiracy narratives in 211–3; playing the game 209–11; race in 215; videogames 185

Index

Shapers *see* Sterling, Shaper/Mechanist series
Sharon, Tamar 24–25
Shatter 95
Shaviro, Steven 62, 147, 285, 288
Shawl, Nisi "The Mighty Phin" 306
Shawn, Jason 97
Sheckley, Robert 7
Sheen, Erica 120
Sheldon, Alice *see* Tiptree, James
Shelley, Mary, *Frankenstein* 32, 73, 270, 348
Shiner, Lewis 15, 16, 21, 25, 34, 41, 48, 73, 94; and Bruce Sterling, "Mozart in Mirrorshades" 18–19, 328, 332, 338; *Frontera* 15; *Red Weather* 95
Shining, The (Kubrick) 141, 242
Shirley, John 8, 15, 25, 34, 41; *City Come A-Walking* 225; *Eclipse* 19, 217; Eclipse series 10, 15; "Freezone" 19–20, 339
Shirow, Masamune 114, 116, 154, 165, 403–4
Shockwave Rider *see* Brunner
Shore, Howard 243
Sicart, Miguel 193
Sifuentes, Gerardo 389
Silva, Luis Filipe 70
Silverberg, Robert 14; Majipoor trilogy 7; *To Live Again* 12–13
Silvio, Carl 113, 168
Sim, Dave 104
Simon, Shaun, 97
Simpson, Nate 97
simstim 87, 171, 286, 301, 324, 332, 368; *see also* Gibson, *Neuromancer*
simulation and simulacra 11–12, 44, 46, 49, 52, 61, 97, 103, 105, 122, 125, 130, 136, 137, 141, 144, 148, 171, 172, 176, 181, 187, 189, 219, 220, 221, 222, 235, 255–62, 266, 279, 301, 304, 305, 314, 320, 326, 332, 340, 402, 417, 418, 421, 427, 429; Baudrillard and, 104, 126, 135, 160, 256–7, 258, 423
simulation, the (Cadigan) 330
Sindome (Sindome Corporation) 186
Singh, Vandana 412
Singularitarians 57
Singularity 56–8, 59, 60, 61, 88, 203, 205, 217, 277, 286, 330, 337; beginning of 58, 62–63; dangers of 57; Vinge catastrophe 58, 60
Singularity 7 (Templesmith) 97
Siodmak, Curt and Robert 416, 417
Sioux Falls (Thomas and others) 98
Sirkis, Alfredo *Silicone XXI* 386
Skarda, Erin 70
Skawennati, CyberPowWow 38
Skoda, Claudia 419
Skunk Anansie 243
Sladek, John 8
slavery 63, 120, 312, 341, 335, 355, 359
Sleep Dealer (Rivera) 286, 341, 390
Smashing Pumpkins 71
Smith, Eric D. 288
Smith, Evelyn E. *The Perfect Planet* 33

Snowden, Edward 88, 368, 379
Sobchack, Vivian Carol 289, 348
social media 37, 39, 54, 71, 81, 87, 132, 170, 188, 256, 261, 291, 297, 311, 368, 371, 387, 389
Sofia, Zoe 82
Soft Cell 420
Softley, Iain 124, 225, 243
Sohl, Jerry: *The Altered Ego* 13
Solaris (Tarkovsky) 107
Solaris (magazine) 427, 428
Somers, Jeff: The Electric Church 217
Sony Walkman 109
Sony's AIBO pets 317–319
Sorgner, Stefan Lorenz and Robert Ranisch 274, 275
SoulTaker, The (Shinbo) 156, 157
sousveillance 364, 372; *see also* surveillance; veillance
space colonization 190, 273
space habitats 29, 204
Space is the Place (Sun Ra and Coney) 247, 358
Space: 1889 65, 72
Spaceman (Risso and Azzarello) 98
spectacularized gayness 303
speculative realism 331, 332–333
Spider-Man 2099 95
Spinrad, Norman 7, 8, 16, 18; and 'Neuromantics' 8; *Bug Jack Barron* 10
Splice (Natali) 76
Split Second, A "Bend My Body Armor" 240
Sprouse, Stephen 234
Spurr, David 337
SQUID (Superconducting Quantum Interference Device) 128, 131
Srilata, K. "The Game of Asylum Speakers" 412
Stallone, Patricia 37
Star Trek (Roddenberry) 57, 416
Star Wars (West End Games) 201
Star Wars: The Force Awakens (Abrams) 216
Staton, Joe 101
Steam Age Symphony (Vernian Process) 67
Steam Detectives (Habara) 67
Steamboy (Otomo) 66, 67
steamfunk 70
steampunk 64–71, 203; anime 66; decline of 69; definition of 64; fashion 68–9; from non-Anglophone traditions 70–1; multicultural 70; music 67–8; racism in 69, 70
Steampunk Oriental Laboratory 71
Steel Empire (Satake) 66
Steinberg, Marc 116
Steinecke, Wolfgang 418
Steinem, Gloria 38
Stelarc 233
Stephenson, Neal 68, 260, 329; Baroque Cycle 55; *Cryptonomicon* 50–1, 82; *REAMDE* 82, 262; *Snow Crash* 13, 48–51, 58, 255, 257, 262, 278, 311, 372, 376, 412; *The Diamond Age* 50, 329; *see also* Hiro Protagonist; Metaverse

450

Index

Sterling, Bruce 8, 15, 21, 24–30, 34, 41, 48, 73, 78, 109, 111, 119, 134, 162, 163, 190, 203, 204, 205, 214, 216, 228, 238, 275, 278, 295, 336, 338, 371, 424, 428; and Alvin Toffler 29; and cyberpunk 17–18; on cypherpunks 377; *The Hacker Crackdown* 374; *Heavy Weather* 328, 329; *Holy Fire* 276; *Islands in the Net* 9, 213; and Lewis Shiner "Mozart in Mirrorshades" 18–9, 328, 332, 338; *Mirrorshades* 1, 17–22, 41, 213, 277, 335; on mirrorshades 301; "Our Neural Chernobyl" 73–4, 75, 78; Preface to *Mirrorshades* 7, 21, 22, 29, 129, 151, 163, 214, 185, 315, 327, 337, 338, 364, 396, 402; and Prigogine 29–30; *Schismatrix* 15, 25–7, 109, 207, 274–5, 330, 337, 340; *Schismatrix Plus* 24–30, 73; Shaper/Mechanist series 15, 25–8, 73, 274–5, 330; "Swarm" 328; and William Gibson, "Red Star, Winter Orbit" 17; *see also Cheap Truth*, Vincent Omniaveritas
Steve Jackson Games 200, 209, 374, 375, 376
Stewart, Jessica 224
Stirling, S.M. *The Peshawar Lancers* 69
Stockhausen, Karlheinz 418
Stockton, Sharon 45
Stoddard, William H. 68
Stolen, Kit 68
Stone, Allucquère Rosanne 302
Stone, Oliver 170
Straczynski, J. Michael 228
Strange Days (Bigelow) 124–5, 126, 128–33, 217, 242, 243
Stross, Charles 54, 337, 341; *Accelerando* 56–63, 330, 340, 390; "Rogue Farm" 337–8
Sue Denim (Shiner) 16
Suicide 239
Sullivan, Tricia 54
Sumerian legends 13, 49, 412
Sun Ra 238, 247, 357–8, 360
Sunshine 419
Sunstrum, Pamela Phatsimo 359
Super Dimension Fortress Macross (Ishiguro) 157
superhero 67, 95, 98, 102, 122, 353, 359
superhuman 27, 56, 76, 165, 277, 278; *see also* posthuman, transhuman
superintelligence 277
supernatural shock 214
supertech 201, 202, 203, 204, 206, 207; emergence of 200
surrealism 170
surveillance 2, 169, 187, 188, 239, 240, 246, 315, 329, 364, 366, 368, 369, 370, 373, 377, 379, 409, 410, 419, 420; technology 87, 105, 138, 185, 198, 247, 287, 371; *see also* sousveillance; veillance
Suvin, Darko 260, 283, 326, 416
Swanwick, Michael 17; *Vacuum Flowers* 13
Syndicate (Revolution) 185, 193
synner 369; *see also* Cadigan, Pat
System Shock (Looking Glass) 186
System Shock 2 (Irrational) 186

tabletop roleplaying games 200–7
Tacoma (Fullbright) 186
Taddeo, Julie Anne and Cynthia J. Miller, *Steaming into a Victorian Future* 69
Takemiysa, Keiko 108
Takeuchi, Naoko 113
Tales of the Neon Sea (Palm Pioneer) 186
Tallbear, Kim 350
Talsorian Games 200, 207, 208, 209
Tamayo Méndez, Arnoldo 395
Tangerine Dream 238–9, 419
Tank Girl (Hewlett and Martin) 93
tank surfers 390
Tarkovsky, Andrei 107
Tate, Greg 354
Tatsumi, Takayuki 8, 110, 154, 185, 405; *Full Metal Apache* 110, 404
Tatsumi, Yoshihiro 108
Tavares, Braulio "Jogo rápido" 386
techno music 243, 249
techno-capitalism 270, 288
techno-orientalism 107, 117, 155, 156, 401, 402, 405
techno-sublime 264
Technobabylon (Technocrat) 190, 191
Technoir (Dream Machine) 203
technological developments 46, 77, 81, 85, 128, 134, 202, 260, 288, 318, 320, 327, 336, 356, 375, 395, 396, 408
technology as feminine 296
technoscience 45, 291, 295, 296, 297, 318, 364, 368
Teddy Bear (Gess) 96
television 10, 37, 45, 66, 76, 99, 103, 119, 122, 169–76, 178, 179, 180, 181, 228, 373, 388, 404; in Japan 151, 153, 156, 158, 160; in the first line of *Neuromancer* 169, 327
Templesmith, Ben 97
Terminator, The (Cameron) 123, 139, 180, 181, 182, 234, 413
Terminator Genisys (Taylor) 216
terraforming 28, 29
Tetsuo: The Iron Man (Tsukamoto) 139, 242, 243, 403
Texhonolyze (Hamazaki) 156, 157
Tezuka, Osamu 107
Thanks for the Ether (Rasputina) 67–8
Thatcher, Margaret 93
Thau, Barbara 70
The The 420
Theroux, Marcel *Strange Bodies* 53–4
They Who Walk as Lightning (LaPensée) 98
Thiel, Peter 56
Thirteenth Floor, The (Rusnak) 11, 417
Thomas, Anne-Marie 94
Thomas, Susan 122
Thomas, Z.M. 98
Thompson, Hunter S. 96
Throbbing Gristle 239, 420
Tidhar, Lavie "This Other World" 412

451

Index

Time Breakers (Pollack and Weson) 96
Time² (Chaykin) 101
Tiptree Jr, James (Alice Sheldon) 14, 34, 402;
  "The Girl Who Was Plugged In" 10–1, 33, 43,
  185, 295
Tissue Culture and Arts Project (TCA) 77
Toffler, Alvin 9, 10, 18, 29, 209, 214; *Future Shock* 9,
  18, 29, 213–4; *Third Wave* 9–10, 18, 29
Tokyo as setting 124, 155, 159, 163, 164, 218,
  219, 221, 329, 347, 403;' as the future 107;
  Neo-Tokyo (in *Akira*) 111, 116, 152, 156, 163,
  165, 218
Tokyo Ghost (Remender and Murphy) 98–99
Toledano Redondo, Juan C. 397
Torg: The Cyberpapacy (West End Games) 200
Toronto as setting 36, 225, 356
torture 122, 174, 268, 385, 387, 389, 391
Touki Bouki (Mambéty) 358
toxic masculinity 98, 300
transgender 296, 297, 298, 302, 303
transhumanism 8, 24, 57, 75, 96, 194, 195, 196,
  198, 203, 204, 206, 207, 274, 275, 276, 277, 278,
  279, 319, 330; and transcendence 273
transmedia projects 116, 135, 152, 156
Transmetropolitan (Ellis and Robertson) 2, 96, 101
transplanted personalities 13
Trashmen, The 105
Traveller (Game Designers' Workshop) 201
troll farms 260
TRON (Lisberger/Disney) 1, 121–122, 136, 134,
  137, 138, 142, 173, 221, 225, 228, 234, 242, 259,
  373, 404, 413, 418, 423; franchise 185
TRON: Legacy (Kosinski) 235, 259, 413
TRPG *see* tabletop roleplaying games
Trudel, Jean-Louis 423, 424–425, 427, 430
True Lives of the Fabulous Killjoys, The (Way,
  Somon, Cloonan) 97
Trump, Donald 172
Truong, Jean-Michel 425, 426
Tsuei, Jon 98
Tsukamoto, Shinya 243
Tsutsui, Yasutaka 108
tupinipunk 386
Turing police 320
Twain, Mark 50
Twilight Zone, The 172
Twitter 54, 222, 259, 282; *see also* social media

U2 243
Ueno, Toshiya 402, 405
Ultima Online 54
uncanny 155, 156, 222, 265, 264, 266, 267, 270,
  332, 417
Uplink: Trust is a Weakness (Introversion) 189
uploaded consciousnesses 8, 12, 57, 300, 317, 323,
  336, 337, 340
urban settings 28, 68, 91, 121, 146, 155, 204, 217,
  221, 243, 267, 278, 293, 308, 327, 331, 347,

356, 357, 386, 395, 410, 411, 419, 425, 426; as
  a common cyberpunk trope 48, 134, 171, 195,
  221, 239, 292, 312, 345, 354, 385, 390, 416;
  urban sprawl 28, 48, 104, 121, 128, 134, 145,
  156, 179, 185, 216, 218, 293, 297, 308, 388, 411;
  urban uncanny 264; *see also* cities; Los Angeles;
  Tokyo
Us (Peele) 358
US Secret Service 374–5
Uta no prince-sama (Yamane) 158
utopia(s), utopian 9, 18, 25, 28, 51, 56–7, 59, 63, 74,
  78, 120, 145, 186, 187, 188, 217, 239, 275, 276,
  282, 287, 288, 289, 297, 319, 329, 330, 332, 364,
  369, 374, 376, 379, 385, 387, 419, 427

V for Vendetta (Moore and Lloyd) 378
V for Vendetta (Wachowskis and McTeigue) 378
Valentine, Genevieve 116
Valéry, Francis 425
Van Galen, Anne, "Warriors of Downpour
  City" 236
VanderMeer, Ann and Jeff, *Steampunk* 68
Vangelis 242
Varley, John 7, 402; "Overdrawn at the Memory
  Bank 13; "The Phantom of Kansas" 13
Vas-Deyres, Natacha 430
Vaughn, Brian K. 98
veillance 2, 360–72; *see also* sousveillance;
  surveillance
Velvet Underground, The 239, 241
Verne, Jules 65, 66; 20,000 Leagues Under the
  Sea 64
Vernian Process 67
Versace, Donatella 235
Vicente, Muntsa 98
Victorian, Victorianism 65, 66, 67, 68, 69, 70,
  71, 203
Videodrome (Cronenberg) 121, 122–3, 134, 139, 171,
  176, 243, 404, 421
videogames 1, 2, 259, 169, 170, 184–90; hacking
  simulations 189; as the meta-medium 189;
  misogyny in 187; racism in 187; sound and scores
  190; violence in 187
Vilà, Christian Boulevard de l'infini 424
Villeneuve, Denis 144, 218
Vincent Omniaveritas (Sterling) 16
Vinge, Joan, *Snow Queen* 7
Vinge, Vernor 56, 60, 277, 337; catastrophe 58, 60;
  "True Names" 56, 373, 376, 377, 378
Vint. Sherryl 3, 22, 45, 82, 84, 87, 89, 135, 138,
  186–7, 216, 255, 283, 284, 285, 319, 341, 390
violence 94, 96, 102, 108, 110, 112, 130, 162, 163,
  165, 173, 210–11, 214, 217, 268, 311, 322, 349,
  355, 389, 426; against women 38, 93, 96, 187,
  301, 346; comic book 105; structures of 46, 103,
  131, 213, 269, 385, 391
virtual blackface 311
virtual confinement (VC) 304–5

452

Index

virtual idol 157–60
virtual reality (VR) 38, 44, 46, 95, 121, 125, 138, 169, 256, 277, 291, 296, 302, 328, 330, 409, 412, 424; technology of VR 258–9
virtual worlds 257–9, 273
virus 25, 26, 42, 43, 48, 49, 50, 51, 53, 61, 74, 75, 95, 156, 202, 203, 205, 214, 279, 294, 301, 312, 323, 346, 347, 404, 412
Vitagliano, Joseph 37
Vizanor, Gerald 344
VNS Matrix 38
vocoder 421
Voivod, Killing Technology 241
Von Harbou, Thea, Metropolis 32, 34
Vonarburg, Élisabeth 428–9, 430; Baïblanca cycle 428–9; Le Silence de la Cité 428–9; Slow Engines of Time 429
Vonnegut, Kurt 427
voodoo 13, 367, 412
Vosburg, Mike 101
VR see virtual reality
VR.5 170, 171

Wachowskis 1, 11, 94, 256; see also Matrix, The
Wagner, Roland C. 424
Wahlöö, Per: Murder on the Thirty-First Floor 419
Wakui, Masashi 221
Walker-Emig, Paul 185
Wallin, Andrée 216
Wang, Connie 359
WarGames (Badham) 122, 123, 124, 374
Warhol, Andy 104
Warom, Ren 39; Escapology 37, 217
Watch Dogs and Watch Dogs 2 (Ubisoft) 186, 187, 188, 189, 190
Way, Gerard 97
Webb, Jane: The Mummy! 64
Weber, Tristan 234
Wees, William 178, 181
Wei, Huang-Jia 98
WELL, the (Whole Earth 'Lectronic Link) 374, 375
Wells, H.G. 65; The Island of Dr Moreau 73; The Time Machine 65
Wells, Paul 151
Welt am Draht (Fassbinder) 415
Wendt, Marcus: "Break of Day" 221
Weson, Chris 96
Westfahl, Gary 89
Whedon, Joss 171
white readers and writers of cyberpunk 69, 293, 304, 311, 313, 312, 344, 346, 354, 406, 428
White, Matt 99
whiteness 21, 45, 247, 309, 310, 315, 348, 349, 357
whitewashing 405, 406
Whole Earth Catalog 374
Wiener, Norbert 226
Wikileaks 368, 377

Wild Palms (Stone) 170
Wild Wild West (Garrison) 65
Wild Wild West (Sonnenfeld) 67
Wilhelm, Kate 34; "Baby, You Were Great" 10, 33
Williams, Raymond 288
Williams, Walter Jon 424; Hardwired 200, 294
Williamson, Jack 16
Willis, Connie "All My Darling Daughters" 295
Wilson, Daniel H.; Robogenesis 347; Robopocalypse 347–348
Wilson, M.F. 97
Windling-Refn, Nicolas 219
Windows 378
Wired magazine 405
Wisdom, Linda 220, 221
Wizard of Oz see Baum
Wohlsen, Marcus 78
Wolfe, Cary 265, 319
Wolfe, Gene: Book of the New Sun 7
Wolmark, Jenny 286
Womack, Jack 54
Womack, Ytasha: Afrofuturism 358
Woman in Red, The 137
women writers in Francophone world 428–9
women writers of cyberpunk 21, 34, 36, 42, 44, 295
Wong, Liam 222; "Tokyo Nights" 221
Wood, Aylish 134–5
Wood, Brian 97
Wood, Robin 119, 120, 126
World of Warcraft (Blizzard Entertainment) 258
World on a Wire (Fassbinder) 11, 416, 417–18, 419, 421
World War III 111, 163
World Wide Web 38, 124
Wunderlich, Renner 37

X-Files, The 172–3, 197
Xenofeminism manifesto 38

Yang, J.Y. 70
Yap, Isabel, "Serenade" 37
Yaszek, Lisa 277, 300, 302
Yeelen (Cissé) 358
Yellow Magic Orchestra 238
yellow peril 402
Yi, Donshin 270
Yoshimoto, Mitsuhiro 155
Yoss (José Miguel Sánchez Gómez); Se alquila un planeta 397; Timshel 397
Young, Paul 123, 124
Yu, Donglu 220; "Steamy Downtown" 220, 226
Yuen, Wong Kin 404

Zahlten, Alex 152
Zárate, José Luis "El viajero" 389
Zardoz (Boorman) 418
Zaya (Wei and Morvan) 98

Index

Zelazny, Roger 8
Zero Dark Thirty (Bigelow) 138
Zero Theorem, The (Gilliam) 218
Ziggy Stardust 238

Žižek, Slavoj 336
zombie fictions 76–7, 97, 346, 429
Zuboff, Shoshanna 367, 368
Zurr, Ionat 77